"Huff is one of the best writers we have at contemporary fantasy, particularly with a supernatural twist, and her characters are almost always the kind we remember later." —*Science Fiction Chronicle*

"A wild romp, full of dark humor, a delightfully twisted version of the usual haunted house story." —*Locus*

"This inventive adventure combines fantasy, horror, and mystery, making a unique stew of unexplainable events, detective work, and things spotted out of the corner of one's eye." —*VOYA*

"Plot-driven, at a pace worthy of NASCAR, and the characters are well-drawn and compelling. Huff also takes aim with a freshly sharpened stake, skewering conventions with finesse and style. Huff's novel amply demonstrates that genre fiction doesn't have to be junk-food fiction." —*The Globe and Mail*

"[Huff's] delightfully light touch lends a sense of timeliness to this effortlessly told fantasy mystery." —*Library Journal*

"Fans of *Buffy* and *The X-Files* will cheer the latest exploits of Tony Foster, wizard-in-training, in the third novel of Huff's contemporary fantasy series. This spin-off from Huff's popular Blood series stands alone as an entertaining supernatural adventure with plenty of sex, violence and sarcastic humor." —*Publishers Weekly*

"Start it on Friday night so you can read it straight through to the finish." —*SFRevu*

"I'm going to want to read this one again, just for the pleasure of Huff's trademark dialogue, her character interactions, her cutting wit and her clever, if black, humor." —*Fantasy & Science Fiction*

THE COMPLETE SMOKE TRILOGY

SMOKE AND SHADOWS

SMOKE AND MIRRORS

SMOKE AND ASHES

TANYA HUFF

DAW BOOKS, INC.

DONALD A. WOLLHEIM, FOUNDER

1745 Broadway, New York, NY 10019

ELIZABETH R. WOLLHEIM

SHEILA E. GILBERT

PUBLISHERS

www.dawbooks.com

INTRODUCTION

(Smoke 'em if You've Got 'em)

A long time ago—after dinosaurs roamed the earth but before Clippy the Paper-clip went to its eternal rest—I wrote a series of five books known colloquially as "The Blood Noun Books" (mostly because Clive Barker had already used The Books of Blood). These books were about Vicki Nelson, an ex-police officer turned private investigator; Mike Celluci, a police officer turned in circles by an expanding view of the way things work; Henry Fitzroy, the bastard son of Henry VIII turned vampire some 430 years previously; and, to a lesser extent, Tony Foster.

Tony was a street kid; the ex-cop's informer, the current cop's problem, and the vampire's lover. Thrown into the weird and not particularly wonderful world of the supernatural, Tony thrived. When Henry Fitzroy moved from Toronto to Vancouver at the end of *Blood Pact*, Tony went with him.

These books, *Smoke and Shadows*, *Smoke and Mirrors*, and *Smoke and Ashes*, are Tony's story. And a little bit Henry's story, because he's a bit posses-sive. But mostly Tony's.

Tony's made a life for himself in Vancouver. He went to film school, he got his own apartment, he fell in love with old black and white movies, and he got a job as a production assistant for CB Productions, currently responsible for *Darkest Night*, the highest rated vampire detective series in syndication.

Bit of background: I have a degree in Radio and Television Arts from Ryer-son Polytechnic. (It's a university now, it was a Polytechnic when I was there.) This means that twenty-one years later, when I started *Smoke and Shadows*, I might have had only the vaguest idea of how Canadian television worked, but I knew what questions to ask when a friend gave me the chance to spend a few days on the set of *Nero Wolfe*. CB Productions owes a lot to the ex–box factory turned sound-stage used by A&E's *Nero Wolfe*.

Sidebar: In 2007, Kaleidoscope Entertainment made the Blood Noun books into the 22 episode TV show *Blood Ties*. We shot in Maple Ridge, BC, which is sort of a suburb of Vancouver. While we were shooting, I was impressed by how much of the details around the making of a television show I got right (pats self on back). I chose to keep Tony from *Blood Ties* because having his own books, the books you're holding in a convenient omnibus edition, meant he could possibly have a TV series of his own in the future. This future has not yet come, but I live in hope . . .

Tony's story becomes complicated when it turns out that the special effects wizard at CB Productions is actually a wizard. And something chased her from her world to this one.

And when haunted house movies turn out to be more traumatic in real life than on film, but messing with a tight shooting schedule is more traumatic still.

And when a demon decides to return to this world through his eternal handmaiden, who's currently doing stunt work in Vancouver.

These books were supposed to be lighter than the Blood Books and for the most part, they are. There's more opportunity for humor in television production than in police work. Tony's a lot less angry than Vicki. Vancouver's a lot more laid back than Toronto. That said, there's still a significant body count and *Smoke and Mirrors* teeters perilously close to the horror side of urban fantasy. Perilously close to horror with witty repartee, mind you, but still perilously close to horror.

Someday, I might get around to writing the novella where Tony and Lee end up in 1890's Vancouver. Someday. But for now, this is all there is. I hope you enjoy it.

Tanya Huff
February 2019

SMOKE AND SHADOWS:
For Karen Lahey, because until I met her
I never made the connection that "people" write books.
(Where I thought they came from, I have no idea.)
Essentially, Karen's responsible for my being a writer
so if you've enjoyed any of my books, you should thank her.
Thank you, Karen.

I'd like to thank Blanche McDermaid and the cast and crew of
A&E's *Nero Wolfe Mysteries*, who graciously allowed me
to hang about the set. I'd especially like to thank Matt and
PJ, the PAs, who were more than patient with two solid days
of stupid questions. Anything I got right, I owe to them.
Mistakes are all my own.

SMOKE AND MIRRORS:
For Judith and Dave
who opened the door
and then gently shoved
me through it.

SMOKE AND ASHES:
For Violette and Paul,
who rebuild our house, look after our cats,
and are even attempting to teach me how to
dress. Definitely above and beyond!

Smoke and Shadows

∽ ONE

Leaning forward, brushing red-gold hair back off his face, he locked eyes with the cowering young woman and smiled, teeth too white within the sardonic curve of his mouth.

"There's no need to be frightened," he told her, his voice holding menace and comfort equally mixed. "You have my word that nothing will happen to you; unless—and I did warn you about this—unless you've been holding out on me, Melissa."

A full lower lip trembled as her fingers clutched the edge of the park bench. "I swear I've told you everything I know!"

"I hope so." He leaned just a little closer, his smile broadening as she trembled. "I truly hope so."

"Cut! Mason, the girl's name isn't Melissa. It's Catherine."

Mason Reed, star of *Darkest Night,* straightened as the director moved out from behind his pair of monitors. "Catherine?"

"That's right."

"Why does it matter, Peter? She'll be dead by the end of the episode."

Safely out of Mason's line of sight, the actress rolled her eyes.

"It matters because everyone else is calling her Catherine," Peter told him calmly, wondering, and not for the first time that morning, what the hell was taking the tech guys so long to come up with believable CGI actors. Or, conversely, what was taking the genetics guys so long to breed the ego out of the ones they had. Years of practice kept either thought from showing. "It matters because Raymond Dark called her Catherine the last time he spoke to her. And it matters because that's her name; if we start calling her by a different name, the audience will get confused. Let's do it one more time and then we'll rig for close-ups."

"What was wrong with the last take?" Mason demanded, fiddling with his left fang. "*I* liked the last take."

"Sorge didn't like the shadows."

"They changed?"

"Apparently. He said they made you look *livide*."

Mason turned toward the director of photography, who was deep in conversation with the gaffer and ignoring him completely. His expression suggested he was less than impressed with being ignored. "Livid?"

"Not livid, *livide*," Peter told him, tone and expression completely nonconfrontational. They had no time to deal with one of Mason's detours into ego. "It's French. Translates more or less as ghastly."

"I'm playing a vampire, for Christ's sake! I'm supposed to look ghastly."

"You're supposed to look undead and sexy. That's not the same thing." Flashing their star a reassuring smile, Peter returned to the director's chair. "Come on, Mason, you know what the ladies like."

The pause while he considered it could have been scripted. Right on cue: "Yes, I do. Don't I?"

As the visibly soothed actor returned to his place on the park bench, Peter sent a prayer of thanks to whatever gods were listening, settled back behind his monitors, and yelled, "Tony!"

A young man standing just off the edge of the set, ear jack and harried expression marking him as one of the crew, jerked as the sound of his name cut through the ambient noise. He stepped around a five gallon jug of stage blood and hurried over, picking his way carefully through the hydra snarl of cables covering the floor.

"We're not going to need Lee until after lunch." Peter tore the wrapper from a granola bar with enough force that the bar itself jerked out of his hands, bounced off his thigh, and was heading for the floor when Tony caught it. "Thank you. Is he here yet?"

"Not yet."

"Fucking great." An emphatic first bite. "Have someone in the office call his cell and find out where the hell he is."

"Do they tell him that you won't need him until after lunch?"

"They remind him that according to the call sheets, his ass was supposed to be in makeup by 11:00 . . . Tina, was what's-her-name wearing that color nail polish in scene sixteen? She looks like her fingertips have been dipped in blood."

The script supervisor glanced up from lining her pages. "Yes." Looking past Peter's shoulder, she indicated that Tony should get going. "I think dipped in blood is what they were trying for."

Shooting Tina a grateful smile—it wasn't always easy to tell when Peter's abrupt subject changes were, in fact, a dismissal—Tony headed for the office. A muffled shriek from the actress playing Catherine stopped him at the edge of the park.

It seemed that Mason was getting playful. Testing out his teeth.

As the gaffer's crew adjusted two of the lights, shadows danced against the back wall of the set, looking in their own regard, if not ghastly, then strange. Forming shapes that refused to be defined, they moved in weirdly sinuous patterns, their edges overlapping in ways normal shadows did not.

But this is television, Tony reminded himself as he left the park, cut across Raymond Dark's office, and hurried past the huge mahogany coffin on his way to the production office. *There's nothing normal about it.*

The studio where CB Productions shot *Darkest Night* had been a box warehouse in its previous incarnation and much of it still looked the part. Chester Bane, creator and executive producer of *Darkest Night,* as well as half a dozen other even less successful straight to syndication series, had gone on record as saying that he refused to spend money the viewer wouldn't see on the screen. His comments off the record had been more along the line of, "I'm not spending another cent until I start seeing some return on my fucking investment!" Since CB had only one actual volume and that volume had been known to send the sound mixer running for his board to slap the levels down, *off the record* essentially meant that no reporter was taking notes within a two-kilometer radius.

Leaving the sound stage, Tony pushed his way through racks of clothing— the wardrobe department's solution to a ten-by-sixteen office and no storage space. Given the perpetual shortage of room, he was always fascinated to note that many of the costumes hanging along both sides of the hall were costumes that had never been used on the show. Granted, he covered enough second unit work that he wasn't on the set all the time, but he somehow doubted he'd have forgotten the blue taffeta ball gown, extra large, with size twelve stiletto-heeled shoes dyed to match. Assorted World War II uniforms had been used for a flashback sequence two episodes ago, but he had no idea when or if they'd ever needed half a dozen private school uniforms. And he couldn't help but wonder about the gorilla suit.

Maybe a few shows down the road they were going after a whole new demographic.

He'd been with the series as a production assistant since the beginning— thirteen of twenty-two episodes in the can and word was they were about to be picked up for a second season. There was no shortage of television work in the Vancouver area—half the shows that filled the US networks were shot there— and there'd certainly been more high profile production companies hiring, but *Darkest Night* had piqued his curiosity and once hired he found himself unable to leave. Even though, as he'd told Henry, some days it was like watching a train wreck.

"They don't know shit about vampires," he'd complained after his first day on the job.

Henry had smiled—his teeth too white within the cupid's bow of his mouth—and said, *"Good."*

Henry Fitzroy, writer of moderately successful romance novels, had taken Tony Foster, a nineteen-year-old street kid into his home, his bed, his heart. Had moved him from Toronto to Vancouver. Had bullied him into finishing high school, had provided stability and encouragement while he worked in a video store by day and attended courses at the Vancouver Film School by night.

And although Henry Fitzroy, bastard son of Henry VIII, once Duke of Richmond and Somerset, had, in the end, allowed Tony to leave and live the life his protection had made possible, he'd refused to cut all ties—insisting they remain friends. Tony hadn't been sure that would work—the whole Prince of Man thing made Henry frighteningly possessive of those he considered his—but however unequal the relationship they'd had, it turned out that the friendship they'd built out of it was solid.

Henry Fitzroy, vampire, Nightwalker, four hundred and fifty odd years a member of the bloodsucking undead, wavered between being amused and appalled about *Darkest Night.*

"They seem to know less about detectives than they do about vampires."

"Yeah, well, it's straight to syndication . . ."

Tony'd learned early on that no one wanted to hear the opinion of a production assistant so, after a few aborted attempts, he surrendered to the inevitable clichés and set about making himself indispensable.

Which was the other reason he stayed with CB Productions. Chester Bane was notorious for hiring the minimum crew the unions would allow and, as a result, his PAs ended up doing a wide variety of less than typical jobs. This resulted in turn in a higher than usual turnover of PAs but Tony figured he'd learned more about the business in thirteen shows than he'd have learned in thirteen seasons elsewhere. Granted, some of it he'd have rather not learned, but after spending his teens on the streets—not to mention unmentionable experiences with demons, mummies, zombies, and ghosts—he had a higher tolerance for the unpleasant than skinny blondes out of West Vancouver by way of UBC who apparently thought themselves too good to empty vomit out of Raymond Dark's file cabinet. He hoped she was very happy being the TAD at the honey wagon on *Smallville* location shoots.

The dressing rooms were just past makeup, which was just past the bathrooms. Tony figured he'd check them first in case Lee'd arrived while he was on the set. As he passed the women's washroom, he reattached a corner of the frayed sign covering the top half of the door and made a mental note to remind the art department they needed a new one. The sign should have read, "DON'T FLUSH WHILE RED LIGHT IS ON—CAMERAS ARE ROLLING" but had been adapted to read, "DON'T FUCK WHILE RED LIGHT IS ON." Fucking was not actually a problem, but air in the pipes made them bang while flushing and the sound mixer had threatened to strangle the next person who ruined her levels.

He stuck his head into makeup, covering all the bases.

"Lee?" Thumb stroking the graying line of his thin mustache, Everett blinked myopically at Tony from behind his glasses. "I haven't seen him, but I'm almost positive I heard him out in the office. Don't quote me on that, though."

Someday, when he had the time, Tony was going to find out just when Everett had been misquoted and about what.

Lee's dressing room was empty, shadows fleeing as Tony flicked on the lights. He frowned past his reflection in the mirror. Were the shadows pooling in the corners? Lingering past the time the overhead lights should have banished them? But when he turned . . . nothing. Lee's wardrobe for the day had been laid out on the end of the couch, his Gameboy left on the chipped garage sale coffee table, two cushions tossed on the floor . . . but nothing looked out of place. Any strangeness could be explained by a bulb missing from the track lighting.

Chatter over his radio suggested the camera crew had gotten involved in the lighting debate and that the problem of shadows marring Raymond Dark's youthful yet patrician features was unlikely to be resolved any time soon.

Four phones were ringing as he opened the door to the production office, the usual chaos cranked up a notch by their current lack of an office PA. He'd been sent out for coffee a week ago and no one had seen him since; his resignation had been written succinctly on a Starbucks napkin and stuffed through the mail slot late one night.

". . . understand why it might be a problem, but we really need that street permit. Uh-huh." Rachel Chou, the office manager, beckoned him toward her desk. "Tell you what; I'll let you talk to our locations guy. No, we totally understand where you're coming from here. Hang on." She hit hold and held the receiver out toward Tony. "Just listen to her, that's all she really wants and I don't have the time. If she asks you if it has to be that street at that time, say yes. You're very sorry but you can't change anything. I doubt she'll let you get a word in edgewise, but if she does, be charming."

Tony stared at the receiver as though he were likely to get a virulent disease from it. "Why can't she call Matt?"

"She tried. She can't get through."

They used the services of a freelance location finder—who no one could ever find.

"Amy . . ."

"Is busy."

Across the office, Rachel's assistant flipped him the finger and continued convincing someone to do something they clearly weren't happy about.

He sighed and wrapped his fingers around the warm plastic—as far as he could tell, the office phones never got a chance to cool down. "Who is it?"

"Rajeet Singh at the permit office." Rachel had a second receiver halfway to her ear. "Just let her talk," she told him again, reached across to hit the hold button on his phone, and snapped, "CB Productions."

Tony moved as far away as the cord allowed, and turned his back. "Ms. Singh? How can I help you?"

"It's about that night shoot you've got lined up on Lakefield Drive . . ." Everything after that disappeared into the argument coming through the jack in his left ear and the ambient noise in the office. Resting one cheek on the edge of Rachel's desk, Tony did as instructed and let her talk.

From where he was sitting, he could see the front doors, nearly blocked by a stack of cardboard boxes, the door leading to the bull pen—the cramped hole that the show's three staff writers called their own, although not in CB's hearing—and CB's office.

If he turned a little, he could see Mason's office and through the open door, Mason's personal assistant, Jennifer. Snide remarks about just what exactly her job entailed had ended the day she'd pushed past a terrified security guard and strong-armed a pair of Mason's more rabid fans off the set and back into their 1983 Dodge Dart. She rode with the Dykes on Bikes during Pride Parade and someday Tony promised himself he'd find the guts to ask her about her tattoos.

Next to Mason, the art department—one room, one person, and a sideline in erotic greeting cards everyone pretended they didn't know about. Then finance, the kitchen, and the door leading to post production. Somewhere amid the half dozen cubbyholes crammed with equipment, Zev Sero, CB's music director, had an office but Tony hadn't yet been able to find it.

Behind him and to the right, the costuming department. Directly behind him, the stairs leading to the basement and special effects. Given CB's way of making a nickel scream, Tony had been amazed to discover that the FX was done in house. He was more amazed when he found out Arra Pelindrake was a middle-aged woman who'd been with CB—through bad television and worse—for the last seven years. Safer not to think of the possible reasons why.

". . . so does it have to be that street at that time?"

He glanced over at Rachel who appeared to be attacking a pile of order forms with a black magic marker. "Uh, yes."

"Fine. But I'm doing you guys a significant favor here and I want it remembered on election day."

"Election day . . . ?"

"Municipal elections. City council. *Don't* forget to vote. I'll send your permit over this afternoon."

"Thank you." But he was thanking a dial tone. He handed Rachel the receiver in time for her to answer another line and turned to see Amy's shadow come out of Mason's office.

Or not.

His own shadow elongated and contracted again as he walked across the office and by the time he reached Amy's side, he'd almost convinced himself that he'd merely seen Amy's do the same thing. Almost. Except Amy had been standing, essentially motionless, beside her desk.

"You okay?" she asked, sitting down and reaching for her mouse.

"Yeah. Fine." Her shadow reached for the mouse's shadow. Nothing overtly strange about that. "Just having an FX moment."

"Whatever. What do you want?"

"Lee's not here yet and he was supposed to be in makeup at eleven."

"Do I look like his baby-sitter?"

"Peter wants you to call him."

"Yeah? When? In my copious amounts of . . ." She snatched up the ringing phone. "CB Productions, please hold . . . spare time?"

"Yeah."

"Fine." She reached for the rolodex. So did her shadow. "What are you looking at? I got a boob hanging out or something?"

"Why would I be looking at that?"

"Good point." Glancing past his shoulder, she grinned. "Hey, Zev. Tony's not looking at my boobs."

"Uh . . . good?"

Tony turned in time to catch the flush of red on Zev's cheeks above the short black beard and smiled in sympathy. On her good days, Amy went about two postal codes beyond blunt.

The music director returned his smile, hands shoved into the front pockets of his jeans as though he suddenly didn't know what to do with them. "You're off set? I mean, I know you're off set," he continued before Tony could answer. "You're here. I just . . . Why?"

"Peter sent me out to have someone call Lee. He's not here yet."

"He is. I, uh, saw him from Barb's office."

Barb Dixon was the entire finance department.

"What were you doing in there with Madame Number-cruncher?" Amy asked.

Zev shrugged. "She gets swamped at the end of the month. Sometimes I help her out; I'm good with numbers."

"Yeah?" Tony'd been leaning out around the boxes, watching for Lee to come in the door, but that got his attention. "I totally suck at math and I'm trying to come up with a budget. I've got to buy a car—the commute's fucking killing me. Maybe you can help *me* out sometime."

"Sure." Zev's cheeks darkened again and yanking a hand from his pocket, he ran it back through his hair.

"You . . . uh . . ."

"I know." He replaced his yarmulke and headed for the door to post production. "You know where I am, just give me a call."

At least that's what Tony thought he'd said. The words had run together into one long, embarrassed sound. Fortunately, months on the ear jack had made him pretty skilled at working out the inaudible. "Hey, Zev?"

The music director paused, one foot over the threshold.

"That piece behind Mason at the window last ep? With all the strings? It really rocked."

"Thank you." His shadow slipped through the closing door at the last minute. *I'm losing my mind.*

"He likes you."

"What?" Caught up in concerns about his own sanity, it took Tony a moment to figure out what Amy was talking about. "Who? Zev?"

"Duh. He's a nice guy. Oh, but wait, why would you notice a nice guy who likes you when there's . . ." She paused and smirked.

"What?" Tony demanded as the pause lengthened.

Behind him, the front door opened and a familiar velvet voice said, "Man, you would not believe the traffic out there! I almost had to take the bike up on the fucking sidewalk at one point."

Answering Amy's sarcastic kissy face with a single finger, Tony turned.

Lee Nicholas, aka James Taylor Grant, Raymond Dark's junior partner and the vampire detective's eyes and ears in the light, was six foot one with short dark hair, green eyes, chiseled cheekbones and the kind of body that owed as much to lucky genetics as his personal trainer. Although the show kept him in preppy casual, he was currently wearing a black leather jacket, faded jeans, black leather chaps, motorcycle boots . . . When he unzipped the jacket to expose a tight black T-shirt, Tony felt his mouth go dry.

"Hey, Lee, how many cows were killed for that outfit?"

"Not a one." He grinned down at Amy, showing perfect teeth and a dimple one of the more poetic online fan sites had described as wicked. "They all lived long, fulfilled bovine lives and died happily of old age. How many migrant workers did you exploit for all that cotton?"

"I picked every blossom with my own lily white . . . CB Productions, can I help you? Left you on hold?" Mouthing *Oops*, she waved both Tony and Lee away from her desk.

"So, you're off the set." He handed Tony his helmet in full knowledge that it would be taken and carried for him. "Has Peter finished up early?"

"No. Uh, late. That is, he's going to be finishing late and he wanted me to tell you that you wouldn't be needed on the set until after, you know, lunch." Tony smiled weakly, fully realizing how he sounded. He'd been taking care of himself, one way or another, since he was fourteen. He'd seen things that redefined the word terrifying. He'd fought against the darkness—not metaphorically, *literally* fought against the darkness. Well, helped . . . He was twenty-four years old for Christ's sake! And yet he couldn't talk to Lee Nicholas without coming across like a babbling idiot. Idiot being a particularly apt description since the actor was straight with a well-documented weakness for the kind of blondes he couldn't take home to Mother.

Lee's mother was a very nice woman. She'd been to the studio a couple of times.

Tony suddenly realized that Lee was waiting for him to reply to something he'd totally missed hearing. "What?"

"I said, thank you for carrying my helmet. I'll see you on set."

"Right. Yeah. Uh, you're welcome." And the dressing room door closed, the scuffed paint less than a centimeter from his nose.

Tony had no memory of leaving the production office.

He walked back to the sound stage; his shadow lingered outside Lee's door.

"Hey, Tony, you up for some second unit work tonight?"

Marshmallow strawberry halfway to his mouth, Tony turned to see Amy approaching the craft services table waving a set of sides—the night's schedule reduced to pocket size. "Out on Lakefield?"

"That's the one. Arra's going to blow the beemer. You'll pick up a little overtime and get to watch a symbol of bourgeois excess take a hit. Hard to beat."

"Bourgeois excess?" He snorted and chewed. "Who talks like that?"

"Obviously, me. And if you're going to give me a hard time, I'll call in another PA to do it."

Tony waited. Picked a marshmallow banana out of the bowl.

"Okay, Pam asked for you and CB wouldn't let me call in even if she hadn't. Happy?" She shoved the cut sheets up against his chest. "Trucks are there at eleven, shoot by midnight, gone by one and if you believe that, I've got some waterfront land going cheap."

* * *

"He led his city through the darkest night toward the dawn."

Heart slamming against his ribs, Tony jumped forward and spun around, managing to accomplish both movements more or less simultaneously and still stay on his feet. He scowled at the shadowy figure just barely visible at the edge of the streetlight's circle, knowing that every nuance of his expression could be clearly seen. "Fuck, Henry! You just don't sneak up on a guy and purr bad cutlines into his ear!"

"Sorry." Henry stepped into the light, red-gold hair gleaming, full lips curved up into a smile.

Tony knew that smile. It was the one that went along with *It's fun to be a vampire!* Which was not only a much better cutline than the one plastered all over the *Darkest Night* promo package, it was indicative of an almost playful mood—playful as it referred to an undead creature of the night. "Where did you park?"

"Don't worry; I'm well out of the way."

"Cops give you any hassle?"

The smile changed slightly and Henry shoved his hands into the pockets of his oiled-canvas trenchcoat. "Do they ever?"

Tony glanced down the road to where a pair of constables from the Burnaby RCMP detachment stood beside their cruiser. "You didn't, you know, vamp them?"

"Do I ever?"

"Sometimes."

"Not this time."

"Good. Because they're already a little jumpy." He nodded toward the trucks and, when Henry fell into step beside him, wet dry lips and added, "Everyone's a little jumpy."

"Why?"

"I don't know. Night shoot, moderately dangerous stunt, an explosion . . . pick one."

"You don't believe it's any of those reasons."

Tony glanced over at Henry. "You asking?"

"Not really, no."

Before he could continue, Tony waved a cautioning hand and continued the movement down to pull his walkie-talkie from the holster on his belt. "Yeah, Pam?" One finger pushed his ear jack in a little deeper. "Okay, I'm on it. I've got to go see when Daniel's due out of makeup," he told Henry as he reholstered. "You okay here?"

Henry looked pointedly around. "I think I'll be safe enough."

"Just . . ."

"Stay out of the way. I know." Henry's smile changed yet again as he watched Tony hurry off toward the most distant of the studio's three trailers. In spite of the eyebrow piercing, he looked, for lack of a better word, competent. Like he knew exactly what he was doing. It was what Henry came to night shoots to see—Tony living the life he'd chosen and living it well. It made letting him go a little easier.

Not that he had actually *let go.*

Letting go was not something Henry did well. Or, if truth be told, at all.

But within this small piece of the night, they could both pretend that he was nothing more than the friend he appeared to be.

Pretend.

He made his living writing the kind of books that allowed women—and the occasional man—to pretend for 400-odd pages that they lived a life of romance and adventure, but this, these images captured and manipulated and then spoon-fed to the masses as art, this was pretense without imagination. He'd never had to actually blow up a BMW in order for his readers to imagine a car accident.

Television caused imagination to atrophy.

His upper lip pulled back off his teeth as he watched the director laying out the angles of the explosion for the camera operator.

Television substituted for culture.

The feel of watching eyes turned him to face a middle-aged woman standing beside the craft services table, a coffee clutched between both hands, her gaze locked on his face, her expression asking, *What are you?*

Henry pulled his masks back into place and only then, only when he presented a face that spoke of no danger at all, did he turn away. The woman had been curious, not afraid, and would easily convince herself that she'd been asking *who are you?* not *what.* No harm had been done, but he'd have to be more careful. Tony was right. *Everyone* was a little jumpy tonight.

His nostrils flared as he tested the air. He could smell nothing except . . .

"Hey, Henry!"

. . . a chemical fire retardant.

"This is Daniel. He's our stunt coordinator and he'll be crashing the car tonight."

Henry took the callused hand offered and found himself studying a man not significantly taller than his own five six. Given that Tony was five ten, the stunt coordinator could be no more than five eight. Not exactly what Henry had expected.

"Daniel also does all the stunt work for Mason and for Lee," Tony continued. "They almost never get blown up together."

"I'm pretty much the entire department," Daniel admitted, grinning as he brushed a bit of tangled wig back off his face. "We can't afford to blow them up together. Tony says you're a writer. Television?"

"Novels."

"No shit? My wife used to write porn, but with all the free stuff out on the web these days there's no money in it so she switched back to writing ad copy. Now, if you'll both excuse me, I've got to go make sure I'll survive tonight's pyrotechnics." He sketched a salute and trotted across the road to a parked BMW.

"Seems like a nice guy," Henry said quietly.

"He is."

"There's free porn on the web?"

Tony snorted, his elbow impacting lightly with Henry's side. "Stop it."

"So what's going to happen?"

"Daniel, playing the part of a car thief . . ."

Eyes narrowed, Henry stared across the road. "Whose head is being devoured by a distant relative of Cthulhu."

"Apparently that's what happens when you soak dreadlocks in fire retardant."

"And the size?"

"The wig's glued to a helmet."

"You're kidding me?"

"Yeah, that's what our hairdresser said." Tony's shrug suggested the hairdresser had been significantly more vocal. "Anyway, he's going to drive the beemer along this stretch of road until he swerves to miss an apparition of evil . . ."

"A what?"

"I don't think the writers have decided what it actually is yet, but don't worry, the guys in post always come through."

"I'm actually more concerned that this vampire detective of yours drives a BMW."

"Well, he won't after tonight, so that's okay. So Daniel swerves to miss this apparition and the car flips, rolls, and bang!"

"Cars don't blow up that easily." Henry's pale hand sketched a protest on the night as Daniel slid behind the wheel.

"Explosions make better television."

"It makes no logical sense."

"Now, you're getting it." Tony's face went blank for a moment, then he bent and picked up the fire extinguisher he'd set at his feet. "Looks like we're ready to go."

"And you're . . ."

"Not actually doing anything while we're shooting since we've got Mounties blocking the road, so I'm part of the safety crew. And as long as you're not planning on telling the union . . ."

"I'm not talking to your union as much as I used to."

He could feel Tony staring at him but he kept his gaze on the car.

"You're in a weird mood tonight. Is it . . . ?"

Henry shook his head, cutting off the question. He didn't know what it was. He wasn't entirely certain it was anything at all.

Jumpy.

Everyone was jumpy.

The car backed up.

A young woman called scene and take, then smacked the top down on a piece of blackboard in front of the closer of the two cameras. About fifteen people, including Tony, yelled, "Rolling," for no reason Henry could immediately determine, since the director's voice had carried clearly over the entire location.

The car began to speed up.

When they finished with it in editing, it would look as though it was racing down Lakefield Drive. Considering that Daniel was driving toward a certain crash, it was moving fast enough.

A squeal of brakes just before the outside tires swerved onto the ramp.

Grip tightening on the fire extinguisher, Tony braced for an impact even though he knew there was nothing there.

Nothing there.

Except . . .

Darkness lingered on the other side of the ramp.

An asinine observation given that it was the middle of the night and the darkness had nowhere else to go. Except . . . it seemed darker. Like the night had thickened just in that spot.

I must've inhaled more accelerant than I thought.

Up.

The darkness seemed to be half in the car, although logically, if the darkness existed at all, the car should have been halfway through it.

Over.

The impact of steel against asphalt as the car hit and rolled was always louder than expected. Tony jerked and winced as glass shattered and the BMW finally skidded to a stop on its roof.

Flame.

"Keep rolling!" That was Pam's voice. "Arra, what the hell's going on?"

There shouldn't be flames, not yet.

Daniel wasn't out of the car.

Couldn't get out of the car, Tony realized as he started to run.

He felt more than saw Henry speed by him and by the time he arrived by the driver's side door, the crumpled metal was screaming a surrender as the door opened. Dropping down to one knee, he allowed Daniel to grab onto his shoulder and, backing up, dragged him from the car and out through the billowing smoke.

The rest of the safety crew arrived as the stunt co-coordinator gained his feet, free hand waving away any additional help. He stared at the car for a long moment, brow furrowed under the masking dreadlocks then he visibly shook it off. "Goddamned fucking door jammed! Everyone back off and let it blow."

"Daniel . . ."

"Don't worry about it, Tony. I'm fine." Guiding the younger man away from the car, he raised his voice, "I said, let it blow!"

The explosion was, as all Arra's explosions were, perfect. A lot of flash, not much smoke, the car outlined within the fire.

For a heartbeat, the shadows held their ground against the flames. A heartbeat later, they fled.

And a heartbeat beyond that, Tony glanced away from the wreck to find Henry beside him, smelling of accelerant. "He was muttering about something touching him. Something cold."

"Daniel?"

The vampire nodded.

"Something touched him before you got there?"

Henry glanced down at his hands. "I didn't touch him. He didn't even know *I* was there."

The light from the fire painted the night orange and gold as far back as the director's monitors. It looked as though Daniel, helmet in his hands, sweat plastering his short hair to his head, was telling Pam what happened. Leaving Henry staring at the burning car, Tony headed for the craft services table— well within eavesdropping range.

". . . hardly see the end of the ramp, then I could hardly see at all. I thought it might be some kind of weird fog except it came with me when I rolled."

"I didn't see anything."

"I didn't exactly *see* anything either," Daniel pointed out acerbically. "That's kind of my point."

Tony waited for him to mention the touch. He didn't. "It was probably just the fumes from the fire retardant affecting my eyes."

"Probably."

It sounded like a pact. An agreed-upon explanation.

Because what else could it have been?

As Daniel moved away, Arra came into view behind Pam's shoulder. She looked terrified.

Not for Daniel.

Not about the part of the stunt that had nearly gone wrong.

Given her expression, Tony'd be willing to bet serious money that she'd forgotten both Daniel and the stunt.

Tony found himself quietly murmuring, "Apparition of evil," as Pam finally yelled "Cut!" and Daniel's crew moved in with the fire extinguishers.

⎯⎯ TWO

"Tony?"

He glanced up from his sides to find a sprite-like figure with enormous blue eyes attempting to both stare at him and simultaneously watch everything going on inside the soundstage.

"Hi, I'm Veronica. I'm the new office PA. I just started. Amy sent me to tell you . . . Oh, my God, that's Lee Nicholas, isn't it? He's my . . . I mean he's just so . . ."

And the sprite devolved into yet another new hire too starstruck to last—although Tony had to agree with the sentiment. Lee was sitting on the edge of Raymond Dark's desk, one foot on the floor, one foot swinging, khaki Dockers pulled tight across both thighs as he waited to do his reaction shots. Tony had been doing his best not to look. He'd discovered early on that he could watch Lee or he could do his job, but he couldn't do both.

Taking a deep, strengthening breath, he turned his back on the set. "Amy sent you to tell me . . . ?"

"What?" Veronica's already wide eyes widened further as though they could encompass both the vision that was Lee Nicholas and the more mundane view of the person she was actually supposed to be dealing with. Tony could have told her it wouldn't work, but he doubted she'd listen. "Oh. Right. Mr. Bane wants to see you in his office . . ."

Peter's voice cut her off. "Let's go right away, please! Can I have a bell!"

As the bell rang out, Tony took hold of Veronica's arm, his fingers nearly encircling her tiny bicep, and tugged her gently away from the set. "Mr. Bane wants to see me in his office . . . ?" he murmured.

"About last . . ."

"Quiet, please!"

All color blanched from Veronica's cheeks and Tony had to fight a snicker, as he and half a dozen others echoed the first half of Peter's injunction, their voices bouncing around the soundstage. First day on the job, he'd been afraid to breathe after the bell and had stood frozen like a particularly geeky statue until one of the sound crew had come up behind him and knocked his knees out.

Maintaining his grip, he tugged her across the terrace, as the assistant director yelled, "Let's settle, people!"

Two sets away from the action and still moving, he said, "Mr. Bane wants to see me about?"

"Last . . ."

"Rolling!"

". . . night."

Tony laid a finger against his mouth as the second assistant camera called the slate.

"Scene eight, take four."

Veronica jumped at the crack.

"Mark!"

And she jumped again as Peter snapped, "Action!"

Even the muttering in Tony's ear jack stopped. They were far enough from the actual set to allow quiet movement, so he continued pulling her across the concrete floor, past the back walls scribbled over with cryptic construction notes to the line of small dressing rooms for the auxiliary cast.

Most production companies with similar space limitations used a second location trailer parked close to an outside door. Chester Bane refused to pay for the power necessary to keep one running and had the construction crew throw up a row of cubbyholes against the back wall. Each unpainted "dressing room" was six by six, with a padded bench across the back, a full-length mirror, a row of hooks, and a shelf. The whole thing looked not unlike the "private rooms" in some of the sleazier bathhouses. The only thing missing: a dented condom dispenser.

Gesturing for Veronica to remain quiet, Tony scratched lightly on the door marked with *Catherine* scrawled across a strip of duct tape.

The door opened.

Darkness spilled out.

Tony leaped back and, heart pounding, found himself pinned under the questioning eyes of two confused women.

Catherine's shadow stretched from her feet to his.

Dredging up a smile, he flashed a fifteen minute sign, nodded as she did, and watched as she closed her shadow back in with her. Wondering if he should say something. Do something.

About what?

Shadows?

I've got to start getting more sleep. He waved Veronica in front of him, pulled her back as she nearly stepped on the edge of a new hardwood floor—where the hardwood was paint and the actual floor was plywood. The art director, faking slightly salacious Delft tiles by the fireplace, turned and flashed him an emphatic thumbs-up.

Life had been a variation on that theme all morning.

By the time he'd hit the craft services truck at seven, the genny op had been embellishing the story of him pulling Daniel from the burning car for almost an hour. No one had made a huge fuss—well, no one except Everett although that was pretty much a given regardless—but most of the crew had taken a moment to say something.

"Jaysus, Tony, you couldn't of let the bugger fry? I'm after owing him fifty bucks."

Under other circumstances he wouldn't have minded being the center of attention, but he hadn't actually done much. Since he couldn't explain that Henry had yanked the car door open, all he could do was hope that something else provided a new focus for people with long stretches of too much time on their hands—and provide it sooner rather than later.

Just as they reached the exit, the red light went off and as he waved Veronica through, the voices started up in his ear again.

". . . redress, reload, redo . . . let's go, people, we haven't got all day."

Unhooking his radio's microphone from the neck of his T-shirt, he waited for a break in the tumbling current of voices. "Adam, it's Tony. CB wants to see me, but I gave Catherine her heads-up on the way. Over."

His head murmured *soon* at him.

Soon?

"Yeah, great." The first assistant director turned his head from the microphone and carried on a low-voiced conversation as Tony followed Veronica along the hall, envying the way she could move through the costumes without actually touching them. She was what? Ninety pounds soaking wet? *"Listen, Tony, while you're passing, tell Everett that Lee's got that cowlick thing happening again and we need him in here."*

"Roger, that." He holstered and peeled off into makeup to deliver his message, emerging to find Veronica waiting for him practically quivering.

"Amy said Mr. Bane wanted to see you right away!"

Tony frowned and shook his head. What was her damage? He'd been moving toward the office since she'd given him the message. "You're going to give yourself an ulcer if you don't calm down."

Wide eyes widened impossibly further. "It's my first day!"

"And all I'm saying is that you need to pace yourself."

As they emerged out into the pandemonium of the office, Amy stood, leaned out around Rachel, and beckoned them over to her desk without pausing her conversation. ". . . that's right, two hundred gallons of #556. Well, it might be battleship gray on your side of the border but ours are more a morning-after green. Yeah, great. Thanks. New supplier in Seattle," she said, hanging up. "Charlie knew someone who'd cut us a deal."

"Who's . . . ?" Veronica began.

"One of the construction crew." Her gaze switching to Tony, she added, "Hail the conquering hero! So, for an encore, do you think you could save Canadian television?"

"No."

"Way to stop and consider it. Fine. Veronica, you've got dry cleaning to pick up. Here's the slips." Amy shoved a sheaf of pink paper into the new PA's hand and closed her fingers around it. "And if Mr. Palimpter tries to make you pay, remind him that we're on monthly billing and if he wants to know where his payment is for last the two months, tell him you're just the messenger and he's not to shoot you."

"Is he likely to?"

"Probably not."

"Doesn't the dry cleaner deliver?" Tony asked, abandoning an attempt to read what looked like a legal document upside down.

Amy snorted. "Not for about two months now, funny thing. Oh, and while you're out grab two grande Caffe Americanos, a tall cinnamon-spiced mochaccino, and three tall, bold of the day unless they're Sulawesi, then get two of them and one decaf. Don't panic, I wrote it down." She snatched a ripped corner of paper clipped to a twenty up off her desk. "I had to print kind of small, but you should be able to read it."

"Unless they're Sulwhat's?"

"Sulawesi. Go! And smile, you're in show business! So . . ." As Veronica ran for the door, she sat back down and flipped a strand of fuchsia hair back off her face. ". . . Zev's still in with Mr. Bane, which gives you time to tell me all about last night."

Tony shrugged. "What's to tell? I'm just not as used to this stuff as Daniel's guys, so I panicked first." Four years with Henry had taught him the most believable way to lie usually involved the truth. "You think it's safe sending her for coffee? Isn't that how you lost the last one?" Deflecting attention he'd always been good at.

"Trial by fire. If she can handle Starbucks at lunchtime, she can handle . . . CB Productions, can I help you? One moment please." Jabbing at the hold button, she leaned across her desk and yelled, "Barb, line three!"

A faint, "Thanks, sweetie," drifted out of the accounting office.

"Intercom busted again?"

"Still. Too bad it wasn't Lee in the car. You could have given him mouth to mouth."

"It was a car crash; he wasn't drowning."

Amy looked arch. "So?"

Before Tony could think of a suitable reply, the boss' door opened and Zev emerged carrying a stack of CDs.

"Well?" Amy asked.

"He wants Wagner."

"Under the stunt? Isn't that a little . . . Wagnerian?"

Zev grinned. "Actually, yes." Spotting Tony, he flushed and nodded toward the office. "CB says you can go right in."

The static in Tony's radio seemed to be making patterns that were almost words.

"Tony?"

He flicked at his ear jack and shot Zev half a reassuring smile as he started toward the open door. "It's nothing."

"If you're sure . . ."

"Oh, yeah." No. Maybe.

To give CB credit, he'd spent no more cash on his office than he had on anyone else's. The vertical blinds had come with the building, the rug that covered the industrial tile floor was the same cheap knockoff they used in Raymond Dark's study, and the furniture had been jazzed up by the set builders to look less like Wal-Mart and more like Ethan Allan. The tropical fish tank and the three surviving fish had been used as a prop in episode two.

Not that it mattered because at six six and close to three hundred pounds, Chester Bane dominated any room he was in.

As Tony stepped onto the rug, he lifted his head slowly.

Like a lion at feeding time . . .

If lions had significantly receding hairlines and noses that had been broken more than once while playing pro football.

"Tony Foster?"

"Yes, sir."

Lying flat on the desk, the huge hands covered a good portion of the available space. "You're the set PA?"

"Yes." Tony found himself staring at the manicured fingernails and had to force himself to look away. They'd met three or four times since he'd started working for *Darkest Night*—Tony couldn't decide if CB really had forgotten him or was just trying to screw with his head. If the latter, it was working.

"You did good work last night."

"Thank you."

"A man who thinks quickly and can get the job done can go far in this business. Are you planning on going far, Tony Foster?"

"Yes, sir."

"Think quickly and get the job done." The dark eyes narrowed slightly under scant brows. "And keep your tongue between your teeth; that's the trick."

A warning? Or was he being paranoid? *If I haven't said anything yet, I'm not likely to start talking now* seemed like an impolitic response. Tony settled for another, "Yes, sir."

"Good." One finger began to tap a slow rhythm against the desk.

Was he being dismissed?

"So. Get back to work."

Apparently.

"Yes, sir." Resisting the urge to back from the room, Tony turned and left; walking as fast as he could without making it seem like he was running away.

He stepped back into the production office as Arra emerged from the kitchen, a pale green mug cupped between both hands. Their eyes met.

And the voice in his ear breathed a name he didn't quite catch.

What the . . . ? Flicking a finger against his ear jack, Tony bent to adjust the volume on his radio, wondering where the hell the barely audible voice was coming from. He had to be picking up bleed-through from someone else's frequency.

When he looked up again, Arra was gone.

"TONY? WHERE THE HELL IS CATHERINE?"

With Adam's unmistakable bellow echoing inside his skull, he cranked the volume back down. "I'm on my way back to the set, I'll get her."

Amy glanced up from the photocopier as he passed her desk. "What did the boss want?"

"Are you planning on going far, Tony Foster?"

"Honestly?" He shrugged. "I'm not really sure."

Mason Reed, in full Raymond Dark, was standing just inside the soundstage door. He jumped as he saw Tony, turned the movement into an overly flamboyant gesture, and snapped, "The girl is not on the set."

"Adam told me. I'm going to get her now."

"I was looking for her."

Tony had no intention of arguing with him although it was obvious he'd been having a quick smoke—the gesture hadn't waved off all the evidence. Legally, he couldn't smoke on the soundstage, but the whole crew knew he did it whenever he had a break but not enough time to return to his dressing room. Stars didn't stand outside in the rain with the rest of the addicted.

Used to skirting Mason's ego for the sake of the shooting schedule, they ignored him for the most part, accepted his lame excuses at face value, and bitched about it behind his back.

Mason, who seemed to think no one knew, maintained a carefully crafted public image of an athletic nonsmoker making sure he was photographed on all the right ski hills and bike trails.

Actors, Tony snorted silently, as he walked back toward the auxiliary dressing rooms. *It's all "fool the eye. Don't look at the man behind the curtain."*

He rapped against the plywood door, knuckles impacting the strip of duct tape at about the middle of the sign reading *Catherine.*

No answer.

About to call out, he discovered he had no idea of what her actual name was. If he thought of her at all, she was just Catherine—her actual identity wiped out by the bit part she was playing. Unexpectedly bothered by this, he pulled the day's side from his pocket and stepped back into the light—nearly stepping on Mason who'd apparently followed him. "Sorry."

The actor's lip curled. "Why don't you just open the door?"

"Well, she could be . . ."

"Could be?" His tone was mocking and Tony realized with some dismay that the young actress was about to pay the price for Mason almost having been caught with a cancer stick on the soundstage. "I don't care what she could be; she *should* be on the set right now and I have no intention of waiting any longer." He curled his fingers around the cheap aluminum doorknob, twisted, twisted harder, and yanked.

With a rush of cool air, shadow spilled out onto the soundstage, pooling on the concrete, running into the cracks and dips in the floor.

A body followed.

She'd been pressed up against the door, her right arm tucked across the small of her back, her fingers clamped around the doorknob. They retained their hold as she fell backward. She dangled for a moment, then cheap nails pulled out of the chipboard and with a shriek of metal against wood, the door came off its hinges.

A small bounce as the back of her head impacted with concrete.

Enough of a bounce to rearrange her features into the *nobody's home* expression of death.

Enough to wipe away the expression the body had worn on its way to the floor.

Terror.

She looked as though she'd been scared to death.

Mason scowled down at his errant guest star. "Catherine? Get up!"

"She's dead." Tony shoved the sides back in his pocket and unhooked his microphone.

"What? Don't be ridiculous; she doesn't die until tomorrow afternoon."

"And her name was Nikki Waugh." It was the name he'd almost heard out in the office. He'd realized it the moment he'd read it on the cast list.

"Was?" Mason sounded like he was about to fall apart, like his hindbrain knew what the more civilized bits refused to acknowledge, so Tony let it go. Reality would bite him in the ass soon enough.

At least Nikki's shadow seemed to be staying where it belonged.

"You seem remarkably calm about this, Mr. Foster."

RCMP Constable Elson said *Mr. Foster* the way Hugo Weaving said *Mr. Anderson* in *The Matrix*. Maybe it was subconscious, but Tony was willing to bet it was on purpose—a guy in a uniform with delusions of grandeur. He shrugged. "I spent a few years living on the streets in Toronto. I've seen dead bodies. Four or five poor fucks freeze every winter." No point in mentioning the baby soul-sucked by a dead Egyptian wizard.

"Living on the streets? You got a record?"

He didn't think they were legally allowed to ask him that, but they'd find out as soon as they ran him so what the hell. "Small stuff. You want to talk to someone in Toronto about it, call Detective-Sergeant Michael Celluci at violent crimes. We go back."

"Violent crimes isn't small stuff, Mr. Foster."

"I just said he knew me, Officer, not that he'd booked me."

"You being smart with us?"

There were a hundred answers to that. Unfortunately, most of them were *not* smart, so Tony settled for a sincere but not too sincere, "No."

The constable opened his mouth again, but his partner cut him off. "Let's just go over this one last time, shall we? Ms. Waugh was late coming onto the set. You went to get her, followed by Mr. Reed. He pulled open the door. Ms. Waugh fell out, still holding the handle. The door pulled off and she hit the floor. You told Adam Paelous, the first assistant director, who told Peter Hudson, the director, who called 911. Correct?"

"Yeah, that's right."

"And you didn't call because . . ."

"No one carries their phone on the soundstage."

Constable Danvers flipped her occurrence book closed and tapped the cover with the end of her pen. "I think that's everything, then." As Tony started to stand, she raised a hand. "Wait; one more thing."

He sighed and sat.

She leaned forward slightly, elbows braced on the edge of the ancient table the office staff had secured for their kitchen and said, "So, is Mason Reed always so full of himself? Because he's nothing like Raymond Dark."

Tony stared at her, hoping his reaction didn't show on his face. He'd never actually thought of cops as people who watched bad syndicated television and were just as into the whole celebrity thing as everyone else. Which, he supposed, was fairly stupid of him—a uniform and a gun didn't necessarily come with taste and cops, more than most, could use a few hours of escape into the tube.

Two guys in front of the camera, forty behind, and everyone wanted to know about the actors.

The short answer to Constable Danvers' question was: Yes.

Longer version: Most of the time, he's an egotistical pain in the ass.

The answer from someone who intended to go far in this business: "You know actors." He shrugged. "They're always acting."

"So we can take his observation that he knew instantly Ms. Waugh was dead with a grain of salt?" Elson growled with an impatient look at his partner. It seemed that Constable Elson was not a *Darkest Night* fan.

Tony shrugged again. "Don't know enough about him. I guess he could of known." He'd certainly recovered from his initial shock fast enough.

"You knew."

"I figured. Like I said, I seen . . . I've seen dead bodies before." Twenty minutes with the cops and street rhythms were creeping back into his voice. *Jesus, good thing Henry's not here.*

"At the risk of going all Professor Higgins on you, people judge you the moment they hear you speak. If you want to be taken seriously by the people in power, you use the words and inflections they use." Henry had stopped pacing and turned to stare down at Tony sprawled on the couch. *"Do you understand?"*

"Sure. 'Cept I don't know who this Higgins dude is."

A third RCMP constable stuck his head into the kitchen. "Body's bagged. Coroner's moving out." His gaze flicked down to Tony and back up to his fellow officers. "You done?"

"We're done." Elson stood, Danvers a second behind him. "If we need anything else, Mr. Foster, we'll be in touch."

"Sure." He stayed where he was until they'd cleared the kitchen, then he went to the door to watch them cross the office. He'd missed the first part of their conversation, but the end of it rose clearly over the chaos.

". . . and I got to talk to that Lee Nicholas guy you like."

"Bastard. Did you check for the nipple ring?"

"Why the hell would I do that?"

" 'Cause I've got twenty bucks riding on it."

And the door closed behind them.

Tony supposed it was mildly reassuring that certain members of the RCMP were as shallow as the world at large. Added benefit—should the need arise, he knew how to get on the good side of Constable Danvers. Provided that twenty bucks was pro nipple ring.

Amy mouthed *Get your ass over here!* at him and he obediently crossed to stand in front of her desk. There was half a grande Caffe Americano tucked between her monitor and the phone, so he assumed Veronica, although nowhere in sight, had made it back from the wilds of downtown Burnaby.

"That's great, thank you." She hung up, looked for a moment like she was going to take his hand, and settled instead for lacing silver-tipped fingers together. "You okay?"

Interesting question. "Why wouldn't I be?" he asked, honestly curious.

"Duh, I don't know. Maybe because you found a corpse?"

Oh, yeah. He shrugged. "Compared to the corpses we usually get around here, it was pretty anticlimactic."

"What do you mean, anticlimactic?"

"No chew marks, no demon slime, no attempting to shove twenty feet of intestines made of condoms stuffed with spaghetti sauce back into the body . . ."

"Eww." Amy tossed a crumpled piece of paper at his head. "This was real, fuckwad!"

"Yeah. It was." But, sadly, still anticlimactic.

A moment of silence.

Amy rubbed her forehead, smudging ink across pale skin. "I never even talked to her, you know? I feel like I should have."

"Why?"

"I don't know."

There was nothing Tony could say to that, although he sort of understood.

"Anyway . . ." More rubbing and the ink smudge moved down one side of her nose. ". . . Adam came in while you were with the cops and he wanted me to tell you that Peter's going to shoot reaction shots this afternoon. Lee first. Mason's all . . ." She sketched a remarkably sarcastic set of air quotes. ". . . 'I'm too stressed to work,' but he hates to think Lee's getting attention he's not getting so . . ." She shrugged. "Peter's hoping Liz'll have found a close enough match for Nikki by tomorrow that he can pick up today's schedule."

"We're not ditching the ep?"

"Can't afford to." Tone and cadence added *the show must go on* as clearly as if she'd spoken the cliché out loud. "Besides, Catherine's only in two more scenes and she dies horribly in one of them."

Tony pulled out his sides and flipped through to the script. "Today's pages were all about her exposition in the office. That's going to need a good match."

"So she'll be distraught. With enough runny mascara no one'll ever notice as long as the hair and clothes match."

"The original Catherine's still *in* the clothes."

"Oh, yeah." Amy looked intrigued by the macabre thought. "Bet you CB has them back by tomorrow."

Skin crawling, Tony shook his head. "No bet. But will the new Catherine be willing to wear them?"

"Hello? We went to Liz."

Liz Terr's agency wasn't called Starving Actors R Us, but it should have been.

"Good po . . . What are you looking at?"

"You've got an audience."

Tony turned in time to see one of the writers jerk back behind the shelter of their workroom door.

"He was staring at you like you're suddenly a resource."

"For what?"

"Dead bodies. Police interaction. How should I know?"

"Those guys need to get a life."

"If they had a life, would they be working here, fleshing out the boss' holy writ? Giving form and function to the dark thoughts of Chester Bane?"

Glancing over at the open door to CB's office, Tony wondered at the risk Amy had just taken. Rumor had it that CB didn't care what was said about his size, his temper, or his fish, but the very short leash he allowed the writing staff was never to be acknowledged. Impossible to blame disaster on the writers if it was. "Are *you* okay?"

"I'm fine. CB Productions, please hold." She rested the phone against her cheek and sighed. "It's just . . . one minute she was alive and then she wasn't; you know?"

"Yeah." Although Tony had a terrible feeling it hadn't happened that quickly. "You'd better get back to work before this whole place falls apart."

"You, too."

He turned his radio back on as he crossed the office, but all he could hear was the kind of quiet chatter that said nothing had started happening yet. Hand outstretched to open the door that led to the halls of costumes and ultimately the soundstage, he paused, his attention caught by his shadow. The banks of flickering fluorescent lights lit him up in such a way that it looked as though he was going one way and his shadow was going another, gray and barely visible fingers stretching out across scuffed paint to turn the handle of the basement door.

The basement.

Where the FX workrooms were.

Where Arra Pelindrake was. She'd been on location last night and he'd seen her today just before he found Nikki's body. He'd been looking right at her when that voice had murmured Nikki's name in his ear jack.

Maybe his shadow knew something he didn't.

*   *   *

The big room at the bottom of the basement stairs was remarkably well lit. Between the fluorescent lights and the scattered fill lights, the illumination was essentially constant. Floor, walls, and ceiling had been painted a pale gray. Doors were set flush and the various tools of Arra's trade were arranged neatly on gray metal shelves in such a way that they . . .

. . . that they threw no shadows.

One hand still on the banister, Tony glanced down at the floor, twisted and looked over his right shoulder, examined the nearest walls. *No* shadows. He had the strangest feeling that if he turned around, he'd see his shadow waiting for him at the top of the stairs, unable to come any farther.

After a moment's reflection, he decided not to look.

Arra's desk was in the far left corner of the room. He couldn't see her behind the bank of multiple monitors, but he could hear the shuff-click of her mouse.

What was he doing down here again?

He couldn't remember even speaking to Arra during all the months he'd been with CB Productions. Even when called in to do second unit work, he did his job and she did hers and long conversations over the state of the industry or what gunpowder makes the prettiest boom never happened. Was he actually going to walk up to her and say, *"I think you know what's going on."*

Considering he was halfway across the room and still moving, it certainly seemed as though he was going to say *something*.

She didn't acknowledge him in any way as he came around the monitors although she had to know he was there. Right hand on her mouse, left hand on the keyboard, her eyes remained locked on the half-dozen screens of various sizes and resolutions—every one of them showing a different game of solitaire. Two were the original game, two spider solitaire single suit, one spider double suit and one the highest level, all four suits.

She lost that one as he watched.

Dragging her mouse hand up through short gray hair, Arra sighed without turning. "I've been expecting you."

Not good. In Tony's experience, when slightly scary people said they were expecting you, things were about to go south in a big freakin' way.

"You have seen things," she continued, quickly placing three cards. "You are not certain what you have seen, but neither are you willing to disregard the evidence of your own eyes merely because it does not fit with a contemporary worldview. This leads me to believe that you have seen things on other occasions."

And worse. It was *always* bad news when people started talking without using contractions. Since she seemed to be waiting for a reply, Tony pointed toward the far left monitor, an old VGA with a distinct flicker. "You can move that black jack."

"I know. I'm just not sure I want to." Kicking away from the desk, she swung her chair around and stared up at him. "So, Tony Foster, tell me what you've seen."

She knows my name!

And closely following that thought, *Of course she knows your name, you idiot, you work together. Sort of. More or less. In a way.*

He could still walk away. Shrug and lie and leave. Not get mixed up in whatever the hell was going on. If he answered her question, which wasn't so much a question as an expectation of an answer, he'd pass the point of no return. Putting it into words would make the whole thing real.

Screw it. It can't get any more real for Nikki Waugh!

"I've seen shadows acting like shadows don't. Don't act," he added when Arra's brows rose. He'd never noticed before that her eyes and her hair were the exact same shade of gray. "And that's not all. I've heard a voice on my radio."

"Isn't that what it's for?"

"Yeah and that'd be funnier if someone wasn't dead."

"You're right. I apologize." She looked down at the front of her *Darkest Night* sweatshirt and brushed a bit of imaginary fluff off Raymond Dark's profile.

Tony waited. He knew how to wait.

Eventually, she looked up again. "Why have you come to me?"

"Because you've seen things, too."

"I saw your friend last night. On location. He walks in shadow."

"Different shadows."

"True."

"You know what's happening."

"I have my suspicions, yes."

"You know what killed Nikki."

"If you believe this, why not go to the police?"

One moment the baby was alive and the next moment it was dead.

"Some things, the cops can't deal with." Before she could speak again, he held up one hand. "Look, this dialogue is heavier than even the guys upstairs would write; can we just cut to the chase and leave this crap to those who get paid to say it?"

Arra blinked, snorted, and grinned. "Why not."

"Good." He wiped damp palms on the front of his thighs. "What the hell is going on around here?"

"Do you have time for a story?"

"*Tony!*" He jerked as Adam's voice jabbed into his left ear with all the finesse of an ice pick. "*Where the hell are you? The cops left fifteen minutes ago!*"

Apparently not. "I'm sorry. I have to go."

"Wait. Give me your radio." When he hesitated, she frowned. "I don't care what he wants you for. This is more important."

He unholstered the unit and passed it over, carefully stepping back out of her personal space.

Arra looked distastefully at the ear jack and left it lying on her shoulder as she raised the microphone to her mouth. "Peter, it's Arra. I've stolen your PA for a while."

The director's voice sounded tinny but unimpressed. *"What for?"*

"Do you care?"

"No. Fine. Whatever. I've only got a show to shoot here. Do you want a kidney, too?"

"No, thank you. Tony will do."

As she handed the radio back to him, he realized two things. He shouldn't have been able to hear Peter's reply—not from a meter and a half away—and she hadn't changed the frequency. She shouldn't have been able to reach Peter on that frequency.

"So, it seems you have time for a story after all."

It seemed he did.

∽ THREE

"It's a fairly long story." Arra nodded toward an old wooden chair nearly buried under a stack of paper—mostly technical diagrams and the mathematical notations necessary for pyrotechnics. "You'd better sit down."

The time it took him to clear the chair gave her a bit of a breathing space, a chance to collect her thoughts.

Tony Foster had seen the shadows. More importantly, he had *seen* her.

He wanted to know what he had seen.

Fair enough.

Curiosity had been the driving force behind the rise—and fall—of innumerable civilizations. It prodded creation and destruction equally. And once let off the leash, there was no catching it again until it was satiated. This left Arra only one option.

Well, actually, two options; although the odds of her taking the second were so infinitesimally small she felt it could safely be ignored.

As he settled himself, she leaned back, crossed her legs, and steepled her fingers. When those pale blue eyes—eyes with the rare ability to see the world as it was without the usual filters of disbelief and denial—fastened on her face, she began. "I came to this world from another seven years ago."

Fingers stopped worrying at a faded patch of denim. "From another world?"

"Yes." She waited, but he only indicated she should continue, his expression suggesting he'd merely asked for clarification in case he'd misheard. "My people were about to lose a war they had been fighting for many years. The enemy was at the gate and the gate had fallen and hope was dead. As it happened, hope had been *dying* for days—the last battalions of the army had been destroyed and nothing remained of our defenses save terrified men and women fighting individual losing battles against the shadows. I stood on the city wall, I watched the darkness advance, and I realized it was over. Certain I was about to die, I retreated to my workroom. It would only be a matter of moments before the enemy found me. In desperation, I tried something believed impossible. I tried to open a gate between my world and . . . and any world. My order had long insisted that the number of worlds were as infinite as the possibilities, but all previous attempts to break the barriers between them had failed.

"I don't know why I succeeded that day. Perhaps because failure would not result in a scholar's footnote but rather a shallow grave. That kind of certainty tends to give one . . ." She could still feel the panic clawing at her; still taste the bile in the back of her throat. A drop of sweat rolled down her side, pebbling a line of flesh as she fought to keep her voice from trembling. ". . . encouragement. Perhaps I succeeded because for the first time a world—this world—was close enough to reach. I don't know. I'll probably never know. The gate opened up into an empty cardboard box factory just as Chester Bane was investigating its potential as a home for his production company."

"So CB knows about . . . ?" A disapproving flick of pale fingers served to indicate the general situation.

"Not all of it. He hasn't seen the shadows."

"Why haven't you told him?"

Easy to hear the subtext—*Why haven't you told him so he could've done something?*

"There's nothing CB can do." This was the absolute truth. If not all of it.

The boy seemed to consider that for a moment, brows drawn in, a fold of his lower lip caught up between his teeth, then: "So, in this other world, you were a scientist?"

"A what?" Arra hurriedly revisited everything she'd just said and snorted. "No, in this other world, I was a wizard." She waited, but the comment about robes and pointy hats and Harry Potter never came. Upon reflection, hardly surprising. She very much doubted that Tony's friend the Nightwalker slept in a crypt on a layer of his native earth. Their relationship—whatever it was and she was certainly in no position to judge—would have dealt speedily with cliché or it wouldn't have lasted long enough to develop the bonds so obvious between them. "Our enemy was also a wizard. Naturally powerful, he had . . . It's difficult to describe exactly what he had and what he did without indulging in excessively purple description."

"Yeah, well, too late." From the sudden flush, it was obvious the comment had slipped out accidentally. Arra decided to ignore it—and not only because she had a strong suspicion it was accurate. The story was difficult to tell without falling into the cadences of home.

"Wizards, like most people, are neither good nor evil, they merely are. This wizard, the enemy wizard, made a conscious decision in his search for ever more power to turn to the darkness and, in return for that power, accept its mantle."

"The mantle of darkness?"

"Yes. It sounds like the title of a bad fantasy novel, doesn't it?"

A sudden grin. "I didn't want to say . . ."

"He had a name once, but he came to be called the Shadowlord."

The grin disappeared. "He's found the gate and he's followed you through."

Arra blinked. *That* was unexpected. "Has anyone ever accused you of leaping to unwarranted conclusions?"

"Unwarranted?" Tony's eyes narrowed and Arra found herself surprised by the intensity of his emotion. She had expected astonishment, wonder, even, in spite of all he'd seen, disbelief. Perhaps fear when he finally realized what her story meant. But rage? No. She'd forgotten that anger was the first response of the young; the gods knew she'd seen the evidence of that often enough in the past. His left hand raised, one finger flicked up into the air. "You opened a gate from another world where . . ." A second finger. ". . . you were fighting an evil wizard called the Shadowlord and, hey . . ." A third and final finger. ". . . the shadows around here are suddenly Twilight Zoned!" All three fingers folded into a fist. Not threatening, but definitely challenging. "I'm right, aren't I?"

Was there any point in denying it? Maintaining a carefully neutral expression—her emotional responses were hers alone—she picked up a pad of drawing paper and pencil. "Not entirely, no. He hasn't *found* the gate. It only remained open for a brief time after I arrived. He's used the research I left behind to reopen it. And the Shadowlord himself hasn't dared to cross over. He's merely sent shadows—minions—through the gate to see what he might find on the other side."

"Merely? There's no merely!" Anger pulled him up off the chair. "Nikki Waugh is dead!"

"And there's nothing you can do about it. Rage will not return the dead to life." The pencil moved over the center of the page with enough pressure to indent the lines into the paper. "Neither will sorrow." The lead broke and Arra laid the pencil down, exerting all her will to keep her hand from shaking. When she finally looked up, it was to see Tony staring down at her. "Neither will guilt," she continued as though there'd been no pencil, no pause. "Trust me that I know this, Tony Foster."

"All right. Fine. You know." He whirled around, walked three steps away, whirled again, and walked two steps back, hands opening and closing by his sides. "What are you going to do to stop it from happening again?"

Ah, yes, the sixty-four thousand dollar question, unadjusted for inflation. "There's nothing I can do."

"Why the fuck not? You're a *wizard!*"

He said the word like it was an answer. Or a weapon. Stretching out an arm, she scooped a square art eraser up out of the clutter in her desk drawer. "Weren't you listening? We lost. The Shadowlord cannot be defeated. Now he has tasted this world. The next shadow he sends will have more purpose." The pattern she'd been doodling began to disappear. "It will find a host and use that host to gather specific information."

"A host? What does that mean?"

"Exactly what it sounds like. The shadows are his spies, his advance scouts. They're simple creations at first, but he uses the information they bring him to make each successive sending more complex. Nikki Waugh's death will allow him to tailor a very complex shadow indeed."

Tony's brow furrowed. "He can make a shadow that can take over a person?"

"Yes."

"A person here?"

"Yes. Here is where the gate is and these shadows—unlike the simpler versions—can't travel far."

"Close the gate permanently."

"Research seems to indicate that the gate can only be manipulated from the originating world."

"Research seems to indicate?" he repeated incredulously.

Fair enough, that *had* sounded a bit pompous. "It was one of the few things my order discovered that they were certain of," she clarified.

"All right. Fine. If you can't close the gate, then stop the shadow!"

Arra sighed. She lifted her head, met his gaze squarely, and, although it would weaken what she hoped to accomplish here, lied. "I can't."

"You can't?"

"The Shadowlord was not affected by anything we threw at him." And back to the truth. Such a small lie, like a single dropped stitch, could hopefully be ignored. Not that hope was something she had in great supply of late. The important thing was that all of Tony Foster's questions be answered. That his curiosity be satisfied.

"I have to do something."

"I'm getting that impression." The pencil lines were gone and nothing remained on the paper but a little pile of eraser leavings, dark with lifted graphite.

"I'm *going* to do something!" Pivoting on one rubber heel, he stomped back toward the stairs—young, defiant, and dead sooner rather than later if he interfered.

At least that was the reason she gave herself as she carefully lifted the sketch pad toward her mouth. And paused.

There was always the chance that his friend, the Nightwalker, would notice her work. Although it was coming to an end, she liked the life she'd built for herself here in this new world and the last thing she wanted was to be noticed by those who lived in Mystery.

Well, actually not the *last* thing she wanted . . .

One step from the top of the basement stairs, as his hand reached out for the door handle, Arra murmured, "Forget," and blew the top sheet of paper clean.

Tony stood by the basement door and realized he felt a lot better about things. The questions that had been gnawing at him seemed to have lost their teeth. Nikki Waugh was still dead and that truly sucked, but there was nothing he could do to bring her back so maybe, just maybe, he should let her go.

"Hey!"

He let Amy's beckoning finger pull him across the office.

"What were you doing downstairs?"

"Downstairs?"

She rolled her eyes. "In the basement. The dungeon. The wizard's workshop."

"Wizard?" Something waved from the edge of memory; gone when he tried to work out exactly what it was.

"Duh. CB's own special effects wizard. Arra. Short old broad who blows things up." Artificially dark brows drew in. "You okay?"

"Yeah. Sure. I'm . . ."

The shrill demand of the phone cut him off. "Don't go anywhere," Amy ordered as she lifted the receiver. "We're not done. CB Productions." Her voice dropped nearly an octave. "Where the hell are you? It *does* matter, Gerald, because you were supposed to deliver that replacement coffin pillow today!"

Shaking his head, Tony propped a hip on her desk. Welcome to the macabre world of vampire television.

"Hey, Tony!"

He jumped as Adam's voice blared from his ear jack and bounced around his skull a couple of times. Cheeks flushed—he hadn't overreacted like that since his first week on the job—he reached for his radio muttering, "The volume control on this thing is totally fucked," just in case Amy or anyone else in the office had seen. Then, dropping his mouth to the microphone: "Go ahead, Adam."

"If Lee's up to it, we're ready for him on the set."

Tony glanced at his watch. Nikki's body had been out of the building for just over an hour. An hour? That seemed . . .

"Tony! Thumb out of your ass, man!"

"Yeah. Sorry. Uh, what if Lee's not up to it?"

The 1AD snorted. *"Peter says you're to get him up to it but I'm not touching that. Just do what you can to get him back out here. Losing a day won't bring Nikki back."*

"The show must go on?"

"Yeah, like I haven't heard that a hundred times in the last hour. Hustle up, we're burning money."

Death came, death went, and it was amazing how fast everything got back to normal. He waved a hand in front of Amy's face and pointed toward the exit.

She nodded. "No, we don't need it immediately, but that's not the point . . ."

Shadow following, Tony headed for the dressing rooms.

For all his bulk, Chester Bane knew how to remain unnoticed. If being Chester Bane meant bluster, then a lack of bluster meant a lack of Chester Bane. He stood silently just inside his open door and watched the door leading out of the production office swing closed.

Tony Foster had been in the basement.

The one good thing about finding a dead body was that the rest of the day, no matter how mired in suckage, could only get better. That was the theory anyway, but by quitting time, Tony figured no one could prove it by him. He had to talk to someone about this.

Someone.

Yeah. Right. There was only one person he *could* talk to about this.

Although he hadn't lived at the condo for almost eighteen months, he still had his keys. He'd tried to give them back, to cut the final tie but Henry, his eyes dark, had refused to take them.

"Many people have keys to their friends' apartments."

"Well, yeah, but you're . . ."

"Your friend. Whatever else I may have been, whatever else I am, I will always be your friend."

"That's uh . . ."

"Yeah, I know. Way over the top."

The place was a little neater without him, but nothing else had changed since he'd left. "Henry?"

"Bedroom."

Henry slept in the smallest of the three bedrooms, the easiest one to close off with painted plywood and heavy curtains against the day. He wasn't there now, so Tony continued down the hall. Henry *slept* in the smallest bedroom but he kept his clothes in the walk-in closet attached to the master suite. For a dead guy, Henry Fitzroy had a lot of clothes.

He paused in the doorway and watched the vampire preen in front of the mirror. Popular culture had gotten a few minor details wrong. Vampires had reflections and, if Henry was any indication, they spent a significant slice of eternity checking them out. "The pants are great, but strawberry blonds can't wear that shade of red. The shirt doesn't work."

"You're sure?"

"Trust me. I'm gay."

"You have a gold ring through your eyebrow."

"And it clashes with nothing."

"You're wearing plaid flannel."

"I'm getting in touch with my inner lesbian." Tony pointed toward the discarded clothing on the bed. "Try the blue."

Henry stripped off the shirt, yanked a cream-colored sweater off the pile, and dragged it over his head.

"Or not." Grinning, Tony backed away from the door so Henry could leave. Feeling better than he had in hours, he fell into step beside the shorter man. Feeling grounded. Which said something about the entertainment industry, when he turned to a vampire for grounding. Or maybe it just said something about him.

"You sounded upset when you called."

And the ground disappeared again. Once the show had stopped going on, once he was on his way home from the studio, he hadn't been able to stop thinking about what had happened. He'd found himself thumbing in Henry's number before he came to a conscious decision to pull out his phone.

"Someone died at work today."

Henry paused at the end of the hall, turning to look at him. "The stuntman?"

What stuntman? It took Tony a moment to remember that Henry had been at the second unit shoot. "Daniel? No, those guys are hard to kill; knock them down and they just bounce back. Daniel's fine. It was the victim of the week. On the show," he added hurriedly as Henry's eyes widened. "There's always a body; I mean there has to be, right? The show's about a vampire detective. But this was a real body." He swallowed, although his mouth had gone so dry it didn't help. "I sort of found it."

"Sort of?"

"Mason Reed was with me. He yanked open her dressing room door and she fell out." One hand dragged back through his hair. "Dead."

Cool fingers on his elbow, Henry steered him over to the green leather sofa and gently pushed him into a sitting position before dropping down next to him. "You okay?"

"Yeah . . ."

"But you don't think you should be."

"It's not that she's dead. That's bad, but it's not what's got me so . . . I don't know, freaked, I guess." Resting his forearms on his thighs, hands dangling, Tony laced and unlaced his fingers, not really seeing the patterns they made. Trying not to see Nikki's face. "Just for a moment, before her head hit the floor, she looked terrified. You've seen a lot of bodies, Henry. Why would she look terrified? Never mind, don't answer that. Obviously something frightened her. But she was alone in the dressing room. I mean, of course she was alone; those things are so small most actors can barely fit their egos in with them, but she was alone . . ."

"I've left a lot of people alone in locked rooms."

"Well, it wasn't you, so you're saying . . ." Twisting around, he raised a hand as Henry opened his mouth to reply. "Oh, don't give me that fucking 'more things in heaven and Earth' quote. You're saying it was something like you. Something not of this world . . ." Not of this world. Not *this* world. Fuck! He almost had it.

"Tony?"

"I feel like I've put down the last bit of toast and now I can't find it. I know I haven't eaten it, but it's gone and that unfinished feeling is driving me bugfuck!" Unable to remain still, he leaped to his feet and walked over to the window. He laid one hand against the glass and stared out at the lights of Vancouver. "She shouldn't be dead."

"People die, Tony. They die for a lot of reasons. Sometimes, it seems like they die for no reason at all."

The glass began to warm under his palm. "And I should just accept that?"

"Just accept death? I think you're asking the wrong person."

"I think I'm asking the only person I have a hope in hell of getting an actual answer from." When he turned, Henry was less than an arm's length away. He hadn't heard him move. "I don't need more platitudes, Henry."

"All right. What do you need?"

"I need . . . I need . . . Damnit!" He tried to turn again, but an unbreakable grip on his shoulder held him in place.

"What do you need, Tony?"

He fought for a moment against relinquishing control then surrendered and sank into the dark, familiar gaze. "I need to remember."

"Remember what?"

Impossible not to answer. His mouth moved. He wondered what he was going to say. "Remember what I've forgotten."

The dark eyes crinkled at the corners as Henry smiled. "Well, that's a place to start."

In a business where twelve-hour days were the norm and seventeen not unheard of, Chester Bane often stayed late at the office. His third wife had divorced him because of it. He'd enjoyed her company, but he'd preferred to walk around the soundstage, around the world he'd created, without the distraction of actors and crew. Over the years, security and cleaning staff both had learned to avoid him.

Tonight, fish fed, he walked across the dark production office and stood outside the basement door. His set PA had been down in the basement the day after he'd distinguished himself at a second unit shoot.

The day after something had gone wrong at a second unit shoot.

The day a young actress had died, the body found by that same set PA.

Individually, the first was unusual, the second unexpected, and the third a tragedy. Together, they added up to something. CB didn't believe in coincidence.

In the seven years since buying the old box factory, he'd seldom gone down to the basement. He could have. Nothing stopped him. He just hadn't. Arra Pelindrake provided him with inexpensive special effects and he in turn provided her with a way to exist in this new world. They never spoke of how the air had torn above his head and she had dropped through the rent stinking of blood and smoke. They never spoke of flames that didn't burn and squibs that used no gunpowder. They never spoke of what she did or how she did it as long as his shows came in on budget. In under budget; even better.

That was the sum total of their relationship.

He neither knew nor cared if she spoke of him outside the studio although he expected she did. Everyone bitched about their boss.

He was unable to speak of her. His choice. He wasn't fool enough to believe that he'd never want to share so unbelievable a story and rather than lose her—and what she could do for him—he'd asked her to ensure his mouth stayed shut. He remembered everything and could put the necessary spin on her activities vis-à-vis the outside world but he was incapable of discussing what she was or where she'd come from.

At the time, it had seemed like the smart thing to do in order to protect his investment. All of a sudden, he wasn't so sure.

His hand closed around the door handle.

Something was going on. Something attempting to make an end run around his control.

The stairs made no noise as he descended into the gray on gray of the lower level. He noted models and masks as he crossed to the desk, adding them to the mental inventory he kept of his possessions. Although the computer had been powered down, the ready lights on both monitors and speakers glowed green. He barely resisted turning them off. Wasted power meant wasted money.

There were modern fetishes scattered all over the desk. Little plastic Teletubbies. An octopus with only six arms. A red cloth frog exuding cinnamon and dust about equally mixed.

He had no idea what he was looking for and suddenly felt ridiculous.

A startled squeak from the stairs spun him around and he glared silently at the cleaning lady standing frozen in place about a third of the way down. The CB in CB Productions stood for Chester Bane and he had every right to be where he was. When it became clear she was not going to move without his permission, he beckoned her forward and, as she stepped off the last tread, he growled, "Do your job and go."

Arms folded, he watched her scuttle across to the desk and scoop up the garbage pail. As she tipped it up into the green plastic bag she carried, he frowned.

"Hold it!"

She froze again; a tiny statue in a green duster.

He scooped half a dozen sheets of paper out of the trash one-handed. "These are not garbage. The writing staff can use the backs for notes."

She nodded although it was clear she had no idea what she was agreeing with.

"Carry on."

For her age, she moved remarkably quickly back up the stairs. CB followed considerably more slowly, the knees that ended his football career protesting painfully as they hauled his weight back up to the first floor. He flicked off the basement lights, recrossed the production office, and paused at the door to the bull pen. No. He'd give the paper to the writers in the morning. They'd likely need it explained.

Back in his own office he tossed the papers on the desk.

Paused.

Picked up the top sheet. Thick, slightly rough. Drawing paper. Blank on both sides. Wasteful. Perhaps it was time to have a word with . . .

Flicking on the desk lamp, he aimed the circle of light directly at the sheet of paper. Faint gray lines ghosted across the page. There. And then gone. Although under the caress of a fingertip, the imprint of a pattern remained.

Something was *definitely* going on.

"It's no use." Henry sat back in his chair, allowing Tony to look away and break the contact between them. "There's definitely something blocking the memories."

"Shock?"

"Perhaps. I've seen shock block memories in the past and for all your experience with the . . . unusual, you've never had the corpse of a friend drop at your feet before."

Tony sighed. "She wasn't exactly a friend."

"And you feel guilty about that now she's dead?"

"No. Maybe." He picked at the faded patch of denim on one thigh. "I don't know. Henry, what is it if it *isn't* shock?"

"I have no idea."

"Educated guess?"

Prince of Darkness safely tucked away, Henry smiled and stood, dragging his chair back to its usual place at the dining room table. "You must believe I had an interesting education, Tony."

"Well, yeah. Interesting experiences anyway."

"True enough. But, in this instance, none of them seem to apply."

Tony didn't entirely believe that, but since he had nothing to back up an accusation except that Henry was spending just a little too much time fiddling with the chair, he dropped his gaze to his watch before his face gave the whole thing away. The numbers took a moment to sink in, but when they did he stood. "Oh, crap. It's almost 3:00. No wonder I'm feeling so punchy. I've got to get going."

"Why not stay here?"

"Why *not*?"

Henry ignored him. "There's an extra bed and a change of clothes and we're not a lot farther from Burnaby than your apartment. What time do you have to be at work tomorrow?"

"Uh . . . unit call's at 9:30."

"An early enough call given that it's nearly 3:00."

What he could see of Henry's expression showed nothing more than an almost neutral concern. They were long over and he'd ended it. They were friends. Friends had the keys to friends' apartments. Friends offered crash space. "I guess it wouldn't hurt to stay."

"Good."

"Will you be . . ." Funny how a distance of eighteen months suddenly made what had once been a perfectly normal question sound like horror movie dialogue. ". . . going out to Hunt?"

"No." One hand rose to tug at the edge of the cream-colored sweater. "It's too late."

Suddenly the earlier indecision over which shirt to wear made sense. Tony felt his cheeks flush. Knew Henry was aware of the sudden rush of blood and that only made it worse. "You were on your way out."

"Yes."

"You were going to feed."

A graceful nod in acknowledgment. "I'll call her tomorrow and explain."

"I'm sorry . . ."

"Weighing a new acquaintance against the needs of an old friend was no choice at all, Tony."

"I'm not your responsibility."

One red-gold eyebrow rose. "I know."

"I feel bad about you not feeding."

"I can wait until tomorrow night."

You don't have to. He could feel the words waiting to be said and was fairly certain Henry could as well. And if not, he *knew* Henry could hear his pulse pounding. Trouble was, he couldn't think of a way to say them that wouldn't make him sound like a desperate heroine in a bad romance novel. Not that he read bad romance novels or anything. It was just something that he thought a desperate heroine would say because it had been eighteen months, for fuck's sake, and Henry saw him now as a person, an individual, and surely that meant they could—all right, *he* could—act like an adult and not fall back into need at the feel of teeth through skin.

The moment lengthened, stretched, and passed.

Henry smiled. "Good night, Tony."

"Yeah . . ."

"It's a great piece of music, Zev, pretty damned near perfect, but you know CB won't pay much for it."

"Not a problem. It's a local band; they're desperate for publicity, and I can get the rights for little more than a screen credit." The music director glanced up and smiled as Tony came across the office. By the time he reached Amy's desk, Zev's smile had slipped slightly. "Are you all right? You look . . . tired."

"Just didn't get much sleep last night. All I have to do is hang on until lunch, then I can catch some zees on the couch in Raymond Dark's office."

"Catch some zees?" Amy snorted. She slid the headphones off and passed them back to Zev. "Do people actually say that?"

He shrugged. "Apparently."

Before Tony could get up enough energy to wave a finger at the two of them, the door to CB's office opened and Barb emerged looking pale.

"Your turn, babe," the company's financial officer muttered to Zev as she passed the desk. "Word of warning, if you want him to spend money, he's in a mood. Play this wrong and you'll end up humming the score yourself."

Amy raised a hand as Barb disappeared into her office. "I can help. I used to play the kazoo!"

"Everyone used to play the kazoo."

"In a marching band?"

"Okay, that's different."

"Sero!"

The three of them winced in unison.

"Our master's voice," Amy whispered dramatically. "Good luck. Vaya con dios."

"*Tracht gut vet zein gut.*"

"What does that mean?"

"Think good and it will be good."

"SERO!"

"Yeah, you just keep thinkin', Butch. In this particular situation, I'd push the *free* in free band." Amy watched Zev until the door closed behind him then turned her attention to Tony. "He's right. You look like crap. Hot date?"

He sighed. "Weight of the world. Wasn't your hair pink yesterday?"

"Fuchsia. And that was then. What do you want?"

"Tina sent me in to see if they . . ." A nod toward the closed bull pen door. ". . . have spit out something like the final rewrite of next week's script."

"You're in luck." She lifted a file folder off the stack of assorted papers on the floor beside her desk and handed it over. "Hot off the press. I'd have sent it in with Veronica, but she's dropping off a deposit for our next location shoot at the city manager's office. And then getting coffee."

"What's wrong with the pot in the kitchen?"

"The writers emptied it again. What do you mean, 'weight of the world'?"

"Things on my mind."

"Like?"

"I don't remember."

"You need more B vitamins."

"I need . . ." He stopped, ran a hand up through his hair, and exhaled explosively. "I need to get back on set."

Her eyes narrowed. "Before something happens."

"What?"

"That's the part you didn't say. Before something happens. What's going to happen?"

"Answer the phone."

"It's not . . ." The ring cut her off. "How did you . . . ?"

Tony shrugged, turned, and headed out of the office, the familiar "CB Productions" sounding behind him. A no brainer on the phone ringing since it rang every thirty seconds eight to ten hours a day.

Before something happens.

He had no fucking idea what Amy was talking about. All that dye was obviously affecting higher brain functions.

The red light went off as he passed the women's washroom and the sound of flushing followed him out onto the soundstage. The living room set for the whatever-the-hell-they-decided-to-call-it estate looked incredible even though it was the same old furniture from Raymond Dark's living room, jazzed up with a couple of cushions, a blue-and-yellow sheet, and some duct tape. One of the electricians was already sound asleep on the couch. Had Peter called lunch? Tony checked his watch, the movement dumping papers out of the file and all over the floor.

"Son of a fucking bitch."

It had just been that kind of a day. Nothing had gone right from the moment he'd woken up in Henry's condo. Between the whole déjà vu of that and the forgotten toast problem with his memory, he hadn't been able to concentrate on anything. Fortunately, they were killing Catherine this morning and once Nikki's replacement had been safely delivered to the set, he didn't have a lot to do.

Dropping to his knees, he started gathering up the papers.

One of them had slid almost to the edge of the fake hardwood floor. He stretched out his hand and froze as a line of shadow crossed the piece of paper and was gone. His heart started beating again as he realized the sleeping electrician's boot had moved for a moment into the light. Boot shadow. That was all.

Given the variety of lights in play, the soundstage was filled with unexpected shadows.

Tony had no idea why the thought made him feel like running.

From the corner of one eye, he caught sight of another shadow moving past him, moving out toward the offices. He whirled around too fast for balance and nearly fell. The shadow was attached to a sound tech. Probably heading in to jiggle the toilet handle.

This is insane.

His fingers closed around the last piece of paper and he refused to turn as a second shadow slipped along the concrete heading for the door. A darker shadow. Its edges more defined.

Hurrying to catch up as the door whispered closed.

A quiet click as it latched.

There, and he hadn't looked.

Clutching the file, he stood, took half a dozen steps toward the set, and realized he'd only heard one set of footsteps go by. The sound tech.

The second shadow had been moving in total silence.

Something . . .

Peter's voice jerked him away from the thought. "That's it for now, people. Lunch!"

Thank God. He really needed to get some more sleep.

∼ FOUR

The body lay crumpled against the side of the building, a smear of blood against the bricks tracing its trajectory toward the ground. Shadows hid most of the details, but an outstretched arm placed one pale hand, like a crumpled flower, out into a spill of light.

"An inch more to your left."

The hand moved.

Tina consulted the photograph she'd taken before lunch, cocked her head to check the body from another angle, and finally straightened out of her crouch. "That's got it."

"Good." Adam took the picture from her as she passed and shoved it into the continuity file on his clipboard. "Let's freshen up the blood and I want a warm body in there to check Lee's light levels. Mouse . . ."

The camera operator looked down from his rig. "What?"

"You're six one, right?"

"Six two. And I'm twice his size horizontally. And I'm working."

"Fine. Dalal, hit Lee's marks beside the body."

Looking like he was wishing he'd stayed at his worktable, the prop man shook his head. "I'm five eleven."

"So think tall. You're not doing anything, get over there. Tony! Go get Lee!"

As Dalal reluctantly crossed the set, Tony headed off the soundstage. Technically, the part of the warm body should have been played by a stand-in, and whether or not they had one on set was generally a fairly good indication of the company's current financial standing. Given the hurry-up-and-wait nature of shooting television, there were always people standing around with nothing to do until someone else did their job. Given the people CB tended to hire, no one was likely to report him for screwing with union rules. Those who might didn't last long.

So far, Tony had managed to stay on the move and out from under the lights. The thought of being in front of the camera, even without the camera actually being on, made him sweat.

"Lee?" He took a deep breath, reminded himself that geeky was not a good look, and rapped on the dressing room door. "They're ready for you."

The door opened almost before he moved his hand away. Frowning, Lee peered out at him as though he wasn't entirely certain he understood what he was seeing. "For me?"

"Yeah. Scene 22B." The room behind the actor seemed unusually dark. "You discover the body."

"The body?"

"Catherine's body." With the wig and the blood—and according to bar talk, *Darkest Night* used more blood than any other program currently shooting in the Vancouver area—fans of the show would never know it wasn't Nikki.

Stepping back, Tony indicated that Lee should precede him down the hall. He'd learned early on that expecting actors to follow was like expecting cats to follow and after the whole "quickie in the broom closet" incident with Mason and the previous wardrobe assistant, he never let them out of his sight. When Lee continued to merely stand and stare, he stepped forward again, suddenly concerned. "Hey, are you all right?"

"I'm fine."

Tony wasn't so sure. "You look . . ."

"I'm fine." Lee gave himself a little shake and slowly moved out into the hall. It seemed that rather a lot of the shadows moved with him. The dressing room visibly lightened as he left.

And that's just wrong. Tony stood where he was for a moment, eyes narrowed. *Not to mention, well, wrong!* He'd have asked himself if he were imagining things except that he had no idea what he thought he might be imagining. Finally, when it became obvious that nothing was out of place, he hurried after Lee, careful not to step on the actor's shadow.

"Oh, for Christ's sake, it's one goddamned line and I've already said it seventeen fucking times!"

The crew suddenly became very busy, looking anywhere but at Lee and Peter.

"It's not about your performance, Lee," the director said calmly, "it's a technical glitch. There's a shadow . . ."

"So get rid of it!"

"That's what we've been trying to do." Peter's genial voice picked up an edge. "We've been trying to do it all afternoon." As one, they turned toward the lighting crew clustered around the director of photography, who continued describing his latest concept in an exasperated mix of English and French.

Although over the course of the afternoon the lighting layout had practically been rebuilt, the shadow continued to reappear in take after take. Scene 22B, take one: it had covered Lee entirely as he'd leaned forward and flipped over the body. Scene 22B, take seventeen: it was a dark bar across his eyes.

Watching from the sidelines, Tony found himself wondering where the shadow was going. And then wondering when he'd started thinking in cheap horror clichés. Actually, he knew the answer to the second question: right after he'd met Henry.

"Get rid of it in post!" Lee snapped. "And why is it so fucking cold in here?" Usually someone who took the inevitable technical delays of television in stride, his temper had frayed a little more with every take. Hartley Skenski, the boom operator, had tried to make book on whether or not he'd stomp off the set before they were finished, but no one had taken him up on it.

"We'll do it just once more. I promise," Peter added as Lee's lip curled. "If it's still there, I'll let the guys in post deal with it." He opened his mouth and closed it again, clearly deciding to leave the temperature question unanswered.

Green eyes glittered during a long pause. "One more."

While another five hundred milliliters of blood were applied to the latex gash in the actress' throat, Lee dropped back onto one knee.

Tony moved quietly around behind the video village and checked out the monitor showing the close-up of the actor's face. The bar of shadow was still in place. He stepped hurriedly out of the DP's way and winced as Sorge began to swear.

The shadow quivered.

And disappeared.

The torrent of French profanity stopped between one word and the next. "Go now."

Peter dropped into his chair and jammed on his headphones. "Quiet!"

No need for anyone to repeat. The soundstage was so quiet, Tony reminded himself to breathe as he crossed his fingers.

"Roll cameras! Slate!"

"Scene 22B, take 18!"

Lee didn't wait for *action*. Reaching down, he grabbed the corpse's shoulder, flipped her over onto her back, and snarled, "Well, it looks like Raymond's secret is safe."

"Cut! Print."

"It looked good," Sorge murmured.

"It sounded like shit," Peter snapped. "But we can fix that in post. Tina, I want the sound from take one."

"Sound from one, got it." As she noted it on her lined script, everyone else turned to watch Lee stomp off the set.

Peter pulled off his headphones as the corpse sat up and rubbed her shoulder. The crew moved about their usual post-print routine strangely subdued, as though they weren't entirely certain how to react. "I don't need a second prima donna around here," the director sighed as the distant sound of a slamming door marked Lee's passage from the soundstage.

"Maybe he's still upset about the body. The *real* body," Tony elaborated as everyone now turned to look at him. "You know . . ." He added a shrug to the explanation. ". . . Nikki."

After a long moment, during which Tony mentally rewrote his résumé, Peter sighed again and gestured wearily in Lee's wake. "Go make sure he's all right."

"I told CB we should have taken at least one day off," he added as Tony hurried away.

Sorge snorted, the sound remarkably French. "And CB said the show must go on?"

"No, he told me to get the fuck out of his office."

Lee's dressing room door was open when Tony reached it. He paused, wiped sweaty hands against his thighs, and leaned forward just enough to see inside. Still in costume, Lee stood in the center of the room, slowly turning in place. It looked almost as though he was seeing the room for the first time.

"Uh, Lee?"

He continued turning until he faced the door, then stopped and frowned.

Tony had no idea why he was suddenly thinking of Arnold Schwarzenegger in *The Terminator*. "Are you okay?"

"Yes."

And the *Terminator* thing fell into place. Lee was staring just slightly beyond him, like he was accessing an internal filing system. "Can I, uh, get you anything?"

Focus snapped onto his face and a long finger beckoned Tony forward. "Come in and close the door."

"The door?"

He'd never seen Lee smile like that before. It was almost . . . mocking. "Yes. The door. Come into the room and close it behind you."

Unable to think of a reason why he shouldn't, and not sure he wanted to, Tony did as he was told.

"Turn off your radio."

"But . . ."

"Do it. I don't want to be interrupted."

While you're doing what? Tony wondered as his left hand dropped to the holster on his belt. But Peter had sent him. He was supposed to be here.

"I want you to tell me things." The actor's voice stroked over him like wet velvet. "In return, I will give you what you desire." The requisite vampire-show leather coat slipped off broad shoulders and hit the floor. The burgundy shirt followed a heartbeat later.

Half a dozen heartbeats actually, given how quickly Tony's heart had started beating. The total weirdness of the situation helped him keep a partial lid on his physical reaction although he was definitely reacting. A dead man would react to a half-naked Lee Nicholas and—given a specific dead man— Tony knew *that* for a fact.

As Lee reached for him, he astounded himself by stepping back.

This was rapidly becoming everything he'd ever dreamed of and a bad soap opera scenario pretty much simultaneously.

No! Another step and his shoulder blades were against the door. This was wrong! It was . . .

It was . . .

He slammed his head back against the door, almost had it, and swore as the memory slipped away.

CB stared down at the sheet of drawing paper on his desk. The lines pressed into the surface had gone gray again, just for an instant. He frowned. He didn't like mysteries and he had already wasted far too much time on this one.

Still frowning, he opened his desk drawer and pulled out a pencil.

Palm flat against the cool skin of Lee's chest, Tony struggled to ignore the little voice in his head trying to convince him to shut the fuck up and enjoy the ride. "Lee, this is, uh . . ."

"What you want. I give you what you want; you give me what I want. There are other ways I could gain the information, but since you're here . . ." His voice trailed off as his hand connected with Tony's crotch.

"No, you don't WANT to be doing THIS . . . Fuck! Stop DOING that!"

"No."

"Look, I don't want to hurt you." The words emerged kind of jumbled together, but he managed to sound like he meant the threat.

Again, a smile that didn't look like it belonged on Lee's face. "Try."

Damn. Four years on the streets, four years with Henry; he could take care of himself if he had to. A little more difficult when he really didn't want to hurt the guy feeling him up, but still . . . Tony tensed, and froze. There was something wrong with Lee's shadow. There was something wrong with shadows in general.

"... *nothing remained of our defenses save terrified men and women fighting individual losing battles against the shadows.*"

CB worked carefully, methodically, quickly; stroking a line of graphite along the imprinted pattern.

"*The Shadowlord cannot be defeated. Now he has tasted this world. The next shadow he sends will have more purpose.*"

Tony jerked back against the door, partially because of the sudden rush of memory. Partially because of what Lee was doing. Wondering how a guy got selected for sainthood, he twisted away and gasped, "You're a minion of the Shadowlord!"

Which sounded so incredibly stupid, he regretted the words the moment they left his mouth.

Lee stared at him for a long moment, blinked once, and started to laugh. "I'm a what?"

Oh, crap. Now he was going to have to repeat it because there really wasn't any variation on this particular theme. "You're a minion of the Shadowlord."

"That's what I thought you said." Scooping his shirt up off the floor, Lee shrugged into it, still chuckling. "You know, you're a very weird guy."

Tony merely pointed.

Lee's shadow appeared to be investigating a pile of shadow magazines.

It was a cheesy effect on screen and unexpectedly terrifying in real life.

The actor sighed, reached out, and slapped Tony lightly on one cheek. "Who's going to believe you? You're nobody. I'm a star."

Tony cleared his throat. "You're a costar."

The second slap was considerably harder and almost seemed to have more of Lee in it than shadow. "Fuck you."

"You're not leaving this room."

"Is this supposed to be where I strike a dramatic pose and tell you that you can't stop me?" Lee leaned closer, his position a parody of his earlier seduction. "Guess what? You can't."

And he couldn't.

The shadow dropped the magazine and swept across the room, holding him against the wall. Tony couldn't move, he couldn't speak, and most importantly, he couldn't breathe. It was like being trapped under a pliable sheet of cold charcoal-gray rubber that covered him from head to foot like a second skin, curving to fit up each nostril and into his mouth. Obscenely intimate.

As the door closed behind the thing controlling Lee's body, the shadow flexed, flopped away from him, and slipped through the final millimeter of open space.

Bent over, sucking his lungs full of stale, makeup redolent, slightly moldy, but glorious air, Tony spent a moment or two concentrating on breathing before straightening and staggering toward the door.

He had to stop Lee before he left the building.

He should never have let him leave the dressing room.

He should never have gone *into* the dressing room.

I should have figured something was up when the straight guy started coming on to me.

And hard on the heels of that thought, came a second.

If that thing's in Lee's head, then Lee knows how I . . . what I . . . want.

And a third.

This just keeps getting better . . .

Completely redrawn, the pattern appeared to be a random squiggle. A pointless collection of curves. Nothing had happened when the final line had been retraced. The pencil set aside, a hand laid flat on each side of the paper, CB stared down at the nondesign and wondered exactly what he thought *would* happen.

How could he recognize the answers when he didn't know the questions?

"CB?" Rachel's voice over the intercom broke into his fruitless speculation. "Mark Asquith from the network is here."

He swept the paper into the trash. "Send him in."

Tony pounded out into the middle of the production office and realized his quarry was nowhere in sight. Had he guessed wrong? Had the thing gone through the soundstage instead? He took the half-dozen extra steps to Amy's desk. "Have you seen Lee?"

"Yeah. He's gone."

"What do you mean gone?"

"I mean, gone. As in not here." She snorted derisively. "As in was an ass to Zev and strutted out. As in Elvis has left the building. As in . . ."

"I get it." Gone. But maybe not too far gone. "He didn't take his helmet."

Amy shrugged. " 'Cause he didn't go for a ride on his motorcycle. He walked out the front door and grabbed the network guy's cab."

"Oh that's just fucking great." That thing had Lee's wallet, Lee's credit cards; if it got to the airport, it could go anywhere in the world.

"You got a message for him from Peter?" Amy picked up the phone before he could answer. "No problem. I'll just call his cell."

"That's not . . ." He frowned. "Do you hear a phone ringing?"

She glanced down at the flashing light and back up at Tony as the office line rang again. "Duh."

"No, in the distance." He turned slowly, trying to make it out. "It's in the dressing room." The sound could have been coming from any one of half a dozen small rooms behind the thin interior walls, but Lee's phone had been in the charger on the coffee table. "He didn't take it with him."

"An actor without a phone." Heavily penciled eyebrows rose dramatically. "Isn't that against some kind of . . ."

"Amy!" Rachel's bellow cut her off. "Would you answer that damned thing, I'm on another line!"

As the familiar "CB Productions" sounded behind him, Tony ran for the basement stairs. Arra. The wizard. She'd know how to stop him. It. How to stop the shadow and get Lee back.

Except that Arra wasn't in the basement.

Tony stared at the empty chair, at the bank of monitors, and fought a sudden urge to smash something. The bitch had screwed with his memories. Made him forget. Made him forget the shadows, and the Shadowlord, and the danger they were all in.

He'd told her he was going to do something and she'd stopped him.

Maybe even stopped him from protecting Lee.

Heart pounding, he took the stairs back up to the production office three at a time, slamming the door behind him hard enough to pull curious glances from the surrounding smaller offices. Even Zev reemerged from post, a set of headphones slung around his neck like a stethoscope.

"If you'll excuse me a moment." As his visitor nodded a confused assent, CB surged to his feet and walked over to his open door. He considered himself to be a lenient employer, but petty displays of unnecessary noise were among the few things he refused to put up with. If it was one of the writers overreacting to script changes again, he would not be pleased.

He reached the doorway in time to see Tony Foster race across the production office.

"Where's Arra?"

Amy slammed a staple through a set of sides and frowned up at him. "What?"

"Arra!"

"I'm not deaf, dipwad. She's with Daniel, checking out cliffs for a new car-blows-up-in-midair-releases-a-fire-demon-into-the-world shot."

"Where?"

"Somewhere along the coast, I guess. She said she was heading home after; that just because we're running obscenely late, there was no point in her hauling ass all the way back out here." The frown became more questioning than accusatory. "Why?"

Tony shook his head. "Where does she live?"

"I'd have to look it up."

"A co-op on Nelson," Zev put in unexpectedly, crossing to the desk. "Downtown Vancouver, across from the Coast Plaza Hotel. What's the problem?"

Already turning, Tony paused. *An evil wizard is about to come through a gate between worlds and kick ass.* No. Not a good idea. That just wasn't the kind of news that most people took well. "Let's just say it's none of your business." It came out sharper than he'd intended and he regretted the sudden hurt on the music director's face, but he didn't have time to regret it for long. He had to find Lee.

"Man, you're two for two on assholes today," he heard Amy murmur as he ran for the door.

Returning to his desk, CB bent down and plucked the piece of drawing paper out of the trash. He slipped it under the edge of his desk blotter and settled back into the large leather chair, smiling across at his network visitor. "You were saying?"

He needed wheels. Riding transit, no matter how environmentally sound, was just not going to cut it. Fortunately, he knew where there were wheels to be had.

Lee's helmet was in the dressing room. So was his biker jacket. He'd left wearing his costume; gone out into the world as James Taylor Grant. And the only good thing about that was, given their latest numbers, the odds were high no one would recognize him.

Bike keys were in the jacket pocket.

One hand gripping the smooth leather, Tony had a sudden flashback to the feel of smooth skin.

It wasn't really Lee, he reminded himself, shrugging into the jacket. *It doesn't count.*

He hadn't been on a bike in years and never one so powerful. As he guided the big machine into the city, Tony prayed that the cops were busy busting more deserving heads. If he got pulled over, he was totally screwed.

He'd never had a license.

But he had to get to Arra and this was the fastest way. He had to force her to help him. Help him find Lee. Help him free Lee. Then they'd talk about the whole forgetting thing.

Except . . .

She could just make him forget again.

She was a wizard.

And she blew things up for a living.

He was just a PA for a third rate production company. How could he stop her?

Roaring past a late '70s pickup, he squinted into the red and gold of a brilliant sunset over the distant towers of the downtown core and smiled.

Tony's message had been short and to the point. *"I've remembered. I need you to meet me at the Coast Plaza Hotel or she'll make me forget again."*

So Henry had canceled his plans for the second night in a row. Just like Tony had known he would. He couldn't quite decide if he was pleased that the young man not only needed his help but acknowledged his right to give it or if he was annoyed at being so predictable it was unnecessary to even *ask* for his help, secure in the knowledge that he wouldn't refuse. A bit of both, he decided as he parked the car.

And there was, of course, the curiosity factor. What had Tony forgotten? Who had made him forget and how had she done it?

After four hundred and fifty years, the unexpected was almost as great a motivation as concern for a friend or plain possessiveness. Impossible to separate the latter two anyway.

He spotted Tony pacing in front of the hotel, caught his eye, waved, and walked over to him.

Tony had phoned the moment he'd parked the bike behind the wizard's building. Specifically, the moment his hands had stopped shaking enough for him to actually hit the right numbers. Adrenaline had started letting him down about the time he reached the city and the last bit of the ride in rush hour traffic had been less than fun. Waiting for Henry to arrive, he'd worked through his reaction and emerged ready to be freaked about wizards and shadows and Lee once again. "Hey. Thanks for coming."

"You knew I would; in spite of how remarkably cryptic you were."

"Sorry. I didn't have time for *War and Peace*." He turned and started across the wide sidewalk toward the road.

Assuming he was to follow, his concern deepening toward worry as tension rolled off the younger man like smoke, Henry caught up at the edge of the asphalt.

Traffic held them in place.

"There's an evil wizard sending shadow minions through from another world." Tony tried to sound matter-of-fact about it, hoping his tone of voice would make the whole thing more believable. Unfortunately, he had a bad feeling that his matter-of-fact sounded more like about-to-totally-lose-it. "One of the shadows has taken over Lee. From the show. Lee plays, um . . . he plays . . ." Oh, just fucking great, now he couldn't remember *that*.

"I know who he plays," Henry said gently.

"Right. We need to find him and free him." He slipped into a break after a parade of SUVs and hurried across to the center line. Henry's hand on his arm kept him from moving on although he continued to shift his weight back and forth from foot to foot as traffic roared by inches away both in front of and behind them. "Arra, the woman who does special effects for the show, she's a wizard from the same world as the shadows. I'd seen some stuff and I told her and she told me what was going on, and then she made me forget."

Henry maintained his grip as they crossed the final lane. Just in case.

"Anyway, this is where she lives." Tony nodded up at the six-story, peach-colored building. "I checked the mailboxes before you got here; she's on the fourth floor in one of the front apartments. I have to make her tell me how to save Lee, and I need you to stop her from making me forget again."

"All right."

For the first time since Henry'd arrived, Tony was still. Pale eyes locked on Henry's face, he murmured, "You believe me? Just like that?"

"Why wouldn't I?"

"Wizards, shadow minions . . ."

"Vampires, werewolves, demons, mummies, ghosts." Henry smiled reassuringly. "And besides, why would you lie about something like that?"

"I guess." He shrugged, more because he needed to move than because he needed to add a physical emphasis to his words. "I mean, it's just that between Lee and the memories and the motorcycle . . ."

"I understand." Well, not about the motorcycle, but under the circumstances, it seemed unimportant. Henry frowned at the building. It had gone up during the '80s real estate boom and was definitely not traditional architecture. Personally, he found the multiple angles aesthetically unpleasant but had to admit he was probably biased about the number of additional windows the design allowed. Large sunny apartments were not to his taste. "Are you sure she's home?"

"Someone's home. The lights are on and I saw a shadow moving behind the blind. A real shadow. Not the invading kind."

"Are you sure she hasn't seen you?"

"Please." This time the shrug was pure disdain. "From her angle I'm just another guy, and there's no shortage of *guys* around this neighborhood. The gym on the second floor of the hotel is one of the best cruising spots in the city. She's not going to expect us; she thinks I'm still completely fucking clueless."

"Good. I imagine that a wizard on her own ground with a chance to prepare a welcome can be very, very dangerous."

"You imagine?"

"This is my first wizard, too, Tony. They're not something you run into every day."

"But you can handle her, right?"

"I don't know."

"She knows you walk in shadow. I didn't tell her; she saw you at the night shoot and she just knew."

"Probably because she's a wizard."

"You think?"

"Best that one of us does." Tony rolled his eyes and, Henry was pleased to see, looked as though the verbal sparring had helped him regain control of his emotions. For Tony's sake then, he was glad he'd managed to keep the edge from his voice. If this wizard had seen him at the night shoot, seen him with Tony, knew what he was, and still used her power on one of his . . . he'd do what Tony needed him to but the whole slightly ludicrous situation had just become personal.

They slipped into the building as one of the tenants left, a tan Chihuahua cradled in the crook of his arm. The tenant took one look at Henry's face and higher brain functions dealing with self-preservation in the twenty-first century kicked in, assuring him he had not seen what he thought he'd seen. That he had, in fact, seen nothing at all. The dog curled her lip and, in spite of the relative size differences, informed the invading predator he could just get the hell out of her building.

"I just don't get the whole gay men and Chihuahua thing," Tony muttered as they headed for the elevators. The shrill, indignant yapping could still be heard fading into the distance.

"How do you know he was gay?"

"You means *besides* the Chihuahua?"

Three elderly women watched them pass from the safety of the laundry room. Before they could decide whether or not to raise the alarm, the elevator door closed and made the decision for them.

Tony jabbed at the button for the fourth floor, then bounced heel to toe as they slowly rose. "The stairs would be quicker."

"I doubt it."

"It's just Lee's out there, with that thing in him . . ."

"You saw this happen?"

"Yeah. I've been seeing lots of weird shit with shadows, Henry. That's what Arra made me forget. But she said the next shadow would take over someone in the studio to get information about this world and I saw it take over Lee."

"And that made you remember?"

"Maybe. No. I don't know. I just did."

Hard to keep his lips down over his teeth. "Well, we'll speak to her about that, too."

"She's going to help him!"

"Yes. She will."

"What are you smelling?" Henry's nostrils had flared.

"Besides you? Cleansers."

Tony jerked as the elevator chimed and barely managed to stop himself from forcing his fingers between the doors and yanking them open faster. The moment the opening was large enough, he slipped through and raced down the hall, his Doc Martens thudding against the carpet. Although he'd neither seen nor heard him move, Henry was beside him when he reached Arra's door.

"Now what?"

Henry reached past him and knocked.

"Yeah, okay, I suppose that'll work."

He waited, thought he heard movement, and had raised his hand to knock again when Henry's fingers closed around his wrist.

"She heard it the first time. She's standing just inside the door." The words didn't so much get louder as more definite, more penetrating, as though they were being thrust through the painted wood. "I can hear her heart beating. It sped up the moment she saw us and it's beating so quickly now that I have a strong suspicion she knows exactly why we've come. And she knows that if she doesn't open the door, I will break it down, and even if there's an alarm or she's called for help, she'll be dead before security even knows there's a problem."

Tony punctuated the threat by punching the air. He only just barely resisted the urge to sneer, *I've got a vampire by my side and I'm not afraid to use him!*

The door opened.

"Do I have to invite you in, Nightwalker?"

"No."

Arra nodded and stepped back out of the way. "There was always a risk you'd realize his memories had been tampered with."

"*He's* right here!" Tony snapped, pushing into the apartment. "And Henry's not here because you screwed with my memories. Not *only* because you screwed with my memories," he amended as her brows rose. "There's a piece of shadow in Lee Nicholas!"

"What?"

He turned to face her, his hands curled into fists. "You heard me. There's a piece of shadow in Lee Nicholas! It came through and it took him over just like you said it would."

"Are you sure?"

"Yeah, I'm sure. I saw it happen!"

"So you're sure." The sound of the door closing was almost the sound of a door slamming. "What do you want me to do about it?"

"Fix it!"

"I can't."

This time, Tony heard the lie. "You can."

She stared at him for a long moment, then brushed a bit of cat hair off her sleeve. "All right, then; I won't. And at the risk of sounding childish, you can't make me."

"I got that covered. I can't make you, but Henry . . ."

"Can what?" she asked wearily, walking into the living room and dropping onto the end of the couch. "You can kill me, Nightwalker, but you can't force me to have anything to do with the shadows."

Henry swept his gaze slowly around the apartment. Arra had turned out to be the middle-aged woman with the coffee who'd seen behind the masks that night on the street. He wasn't exactly surprised. He could smell two cats in the bedroom, judged by their heart rate that they were asleep. "All right."

"All right what?" she snapped.

"As I'm sure you're aware, my kind are very territorial. Tony is mine."

About to protest, Tony bit back the words. This was, after all, why he'd wanted Henry with him. To lean on the wizard. To act as metaphysical muscle. The whole *Tony is mine* thing was just a lever. At least he hoped it was because they'd settled that when he left.

"You put your mark on him and I can't have that." He was at her side between one heartbeat and the next. Tony was almost used to the way Henry could move when he had to; Arra had no frame of reference and she paled.

"If you kill me, I can't help you with the shadow."

"You've already said you won't help."

Her nostrils flared. "You could try and convince me." His hands cupped her head in an almost loverlike fashion. "I don't want to."

Tony couldn't see Henry's face, but he could see the sudden realization on Arra's that this was Death standing in her apartment. Not an abstract death sometime in the future, but a flesh and blood and immediate death. Even knowing that Henry would no more follow through on this particular threat than he would feed on fear, Tony's skin crawled.

Lee had been out in the city, ridden by shadow, for over two hours. They didn't have time to be subtle.

"All right! I'll do what I can."

Death lingered.

"Henry."

Henry turned slowly, the Hunger still very close to the surface. He hadn't fed the night before and having allowed so much of the Hunter to rise, he would have to feed tonight. He fought for focus as Tony stepped forward, understanding in his eyes, and murmured, "The moment Lee's free of shadow." No need to be more specific, his blood spoke for him.

"Why wait? Go now. Eat, drink . . . or rather just drink and be merry." Arra looked from the Nightwalker to Tony and sagged back against the cushions in defeat. "Or not. Just a suggestion."

⤳ FIVE

"So, Tony . . ." Arra settled back into the couch cushions and crossed her legs, her posture suggesting that while Henry may have shaken her confidence he had by no means destroyed it. ". . . just what is it you and your friend . . ." Her eyes flickered left to where Henry stood; the motion involuntary. ". . . expect me to do?"

Tony couldn't believe she was asking. "Find Lee and get that thing out of him!"

"You know, you're really overreacting," she sighed.

"I'm overreacting?" He wanted to grab her and shake her until she admitted that Lee was in danger. Until she agreed to do something about it. "There's a dark wizard from another world sending shadows through some kind of gate to gather information. Yesterday, one of those shadows killed someone, and today one of them took over Lee Nicholas and sent him off into the city acting way out of character. And I'm *over*reacting?"

"Well, I'd have to say you're underreacting about the wizard, but given your friends . . ." Another corner-of-the-eye glance at Henry ". . . that's hardly surprising. You're *over*reacting . . ." She matched his emphasis. ". . . about Mr. Nicholas. You don't need to go looking for him—and I certainly don't—because the shadow will return to the gate approximately twelve hours after it came through."

"What?" Tony froze in place and stared down at her, searching for another lie. "It'll bring Lee back to the gate and just leave him?"

"Essentially."

"So all we need do is make our way to the soundstage and wait?" Henry asked.

Arra nodded. "Be there at 11:15, it's as simple as that. Research also indicated . . ." She glanced over at Tony, who curled his lip. ". . . that the mirror image of the gate equations would also work. On this world, that means there's the potential for a gate every twelve hours. The Shadowlord will want to retrieve his spy and the information it carries as quickly as possible—he won't wait until tomorrow."

"Wait a minute!" Tony took two quick steps closer to the couch. "What the hell does 'essentially' mean?"

"It means that it's unlikely to be as simple as Ms. Pelindrake is indicating. It never is," Henry continued when Tony spun around to face him. He returned his attention to the wizard. "Is it?"

She shrugged. "It could be. The gate will open, the shadow will leave; any complications will be completely separate from that."

"Lee?" When she didn't answer immediately, Tony knew he was right. "Any complications will involve Lee, won't they?"

"It's possible he may have been damaged by the shadow's possession."

"Possible?"

"Some are; some aren't. Those who are . . ." She looked inward, toward memory, and obviously didn't like what she saw. "Some of them shake it off, some are damaged beyond repair; it depends on the individual and there's no way of knowing until the shadow's gone."

"So what do we do?" Tony demanded.

"To prevent the damage? Once the shadow is in control, there's nothing you can do. After . . ." Another inward look, then she shook herself free of the past. "There was a potion we had some success with in the early days, but the ingredients are a world away."

"Can you substitute?"

An emphatic snort made her opinion of Henry's question clear. "And what would you suggest I substitute for glinderan root, Nightwalker?"

"That would depend on what its properties were."

"You're serious?" When his expression made it obvious that he was, she snorted. "What do you care? Lee Nicholas isn't yours."

"No, but Tony is and Tony cares."

"So you're here, threatening me, because your ex-boyfriend . . ." She jerked her head in Tony's direction. His lip curled. ". . . has a crush on an actor?"

"I'm here, threatening you, because an evil wizard is attempting to gain a foothold in this world, my world. And the fact that I can make so ludicrous sounding a statement with a straight face should give you some indication of how serious I am." Henry's eyes darkened as he allowed the Hunger to rise, capturing the wizard's gaze and holding it. "I will not sit by and allow that to happen and neither will you."

When he finally released her, Arra shivered. "Fine. If you put it like that, I guess I don't have much choice."

"Astute of you to notice."

"Thank you." She heaved herself up off the couch, pushing past Tony without really acknowledging him, and walked into the dining room alcove where two computers were set up on a long table. Both screens showed partially completed spider solitaire games. "I'm blocked here by the queen of spades." Arra waved toward the laptop. "Caution and an older woman. Now that you two have arrived, it's easy enough to interpret the problem as my refusal to become involved." She reached down and closed off the game. "Not really relevant now that my choices have narrowed a bit. This one, though . . ." The big seventeen inch monitor showed a game with almost all the cards in play. ". . . here I'm blocked by red twos. Hearts for love, diamonds for outside influences, twos for those unable to make a decision." She turned that game off as well. "Signs are hazy; ask again later."

"You use computer games for divination?" Henry sounded fascinated by the concept.

"Why not? Three or four games puts me into a trance state anyway. I might as well make use of it." Dropping into a chair, she reached for her mouse. "I'll find an herbal encyclopedia on-line, then you two will have to go out and do some shopping."

"Lee . . ." Tony began.

"Will return to the soundstage in . . ." Arra glanced at the lower right corner of the screen. ". . . a little more than four hours."

"Yeah, but right now he's out in the city controlled by shadow and acting weird! You're a wizard; can't you do a locator spell or something?"

"I could or I could create a potion that will hopefully keep him from spending the rest of his life eating soft foods while wearing an adult diaper. I can't do both. Your choice."

He looked at Henry who was clearly waiting for him to make the decision. *Oh, that's just fucking great; one minute I'm his and the next minute I'm in charge.* That whole on and off again, "I'm over four hundred and fifty years old and a prince and a vampire so I know best," possessive attitude had been one of the main reasons he'd walked. There were times, and this was one of them, when he just wanted to punch Henry Fitzroy right in the fangs. *Not that I'm ever going to. And right now, I need to stop reacting and start thinking.*

They didn't know where Lee was now.

They knew where he was going to be in four hours.

They *didn't* know what condition he'd be in when the shadow left.

"Fine. Make the stupid potion."

Wonderful. He sounded like he was twelve and a petulant twelve at that.

Fortunately, Lee was an actor; acting weird was part of the off duty persona and, in an area overpopulated by actors, most people had stopped noticing.

*   *   *

"Alright, I got the stuff." Tony kicked the apartment door closed behind him, causing both of the wizard's cats to glare up at him like he was some kind of big, scary door-slamming army. "Can we get started now?"

"Elecampane will the spirits sustain," Arra muttered, taking the bag. "At least according to www.teagar-dens.com. And the vodka?"

He handed over the bottle. "What's this for?"

"Screwdrivers." She walked past Henry and into the kitchen. "After you two leave, I'm going to need a drink." As they crowded into the tiny space after her, she glanced up at them and shook her head. "No sense of humor, either of you." Cracking the seal, she poured the vodka into a Pyrex pot. "The alcohol will lower his inhibitions and open him up to the possibilities inherent in the potion." She dumped in four tablespoons of the powdered elecampane root then: "Lemon balm to dispel melancholy. Bay leaves to protect the user from witchcraft—used sparingly because of narcotic properties which may, however, also come in handy. Interesting that even the worst stews in the world always have a bay leaf tossed in. Maybe we're supposed to hallucinate better-tasting food. Catnip used to treat hysteria and boredom." She tossed a handful on the floor where the black and white cat and the orange and white cat began drooling all over it. "And a little valerian because, well—why not; your herbalists call it a heal-all and we can use the insurance."

Tony leaned toward the pot and then back again, nose wrinkling. "It stinks."

"It always does."

"It doesn't look like wizardry either. It looks like . . ."

"Like something my mother used to do," Henry finished. "Ignoring the vodka, of course."

"Oh, don't ignore the vodka." Arra tipped the bottle back and took a drink.

"I get the feeling you're not taking this seriously," Tony snarled.

She nodded toward Henry. "Ask him if I'm not taking this seriously."

"You're taking *him* seriously, but the whole shadow thing . . ."

"Is something I've been through before and if I was taking it as seriously as you think I should be, I'd be sitting in the closet with a blanket over my head unable to function. I watched a good green land destroyed and the people right along with it. So, to put it in a way you might understand, to put it, in fact, in the vernacular of this world, if you don't think I'm taking this seriously, you can kiss my wrinkled ass!"

The rhythmic thrum of two cats purring, the buzz from the fluorescent light over the sink, the shuff of clothes rearranging as Tony shifted his weight—but mostly silence. He felt he should apologize, had a strong suspicion Henry was waiting for him to apologize, but he wasn't going to do it. He wasn't sorry—he was right. Arra had messed with his memory, let Lee be taken over by shadow, and, in spite of knowing that the evil wizard was spying on them, had no intention of doing anything but playing computer games. If he hadn't gotten his memories back, if he hadn't brought Henry with him, she'd still be *sitting* on her wrinkled ass.

And the silence continued.

Henry could wait, predator patient, for as long as he had to. Apparently, so could Arra.

Tony squared his shoulders, lifted his chin, and said softly, "You'd think, having seen one world conquered, that you'd be working a little harder to keep the same thing from happening here."

The wizard turned from the stove and stared at him for a long moment. Stared until Tony began to run over recent memories just to make sure they were still there. "I said destroyed, not conquered," she pointed out at last.

He shrugged. "Same thing, aren't they?"

"Not always." Her brows drew in and he felt like he did when Henry turned that kind of intensity on him. Like she was looking inside his skin. "In this case, yes." Still frowning, she bent and picked a clean jam jar out of the recycling container beside the fridge. "Find the lid for me."

What did your last slave die of? He'd have asked the question out loud except that he was half afraid she'd have an answer. The lid had slipped down to the bottom of the bin, under a dozen or so washed and crushed cat food tins. Tony brushed it off against his jeans as Arra laid a strainer over the top of the jar and decanted the hot, greenish-brown vodka into it. When she held out her hand, he placed the lid in it, asking, "Shouldn't that cool down a bit before you close it?"

"Expert on potions, are we?"

"No, but . . ."

"Then be quiet, I'm concentrating." Cupping the jam jar in both hands, she took a deep breath and, exhaling, sang a string of words that seemed to be made up mostly of vowels held together with a couple of L's. Henry stepped back. The cats roused themselves from their catnip stupor and raced for the bedroom. The liquid began to glow. Placing the jar carefully on the counter, she took her hands away. Multiple lines of tiny lights swirled through the potion.

Okay, *that* looked like wizardry.

From the glance she shot him, Tony was momentarily afraid he'd actually spoken.

"You'd better hurry if you want to get to the soundstage on time," she said, moving over to the sink and running cold water over her hands. "Get that down him before the last light goes out and he should be fine."

"Should?"

"You won't know until you try. He might be fine without it. He might not be fine with it."

"Oh, that's helpful."

"Maybe. Maybe not. You have my number; you can let me know how it turns out."

"I thought you were coming with us."

"No. I made the potion. I'm done."

Catching sight of Henry's expression, Tony remembered that the vampire almost always had his own agenda. "The shadow within Lee Nicholas cannot be allowed to take the information it carries back to its master."

"What kind of information is an actor going to pick up?" Arra snorted, drying her hands on a blue-checked dishcloth. "Apple martinis are in. Nicotine is a memory aid, not a poison that'll take years off your life. And if you can't manage a vacant expression 24/7, botox will take care of those embarrassing facial lines."

As much as Tony hated to admit it, at least where Lee was concerned . . . "She's got a point, Henry. You don't have to come either," he added as Henry's attention switched over to him. "I appreciate your help, I really do, but you've got me what I need; I'll take care of Lee, then meet you at the condo."

"The condo?"

"Yeah, you know. I don't want you to think I've forgotten about . . . uh . . ." He tapped the inside of his left wrist with the first two fingers of his right hand.

Arra rolled her eyes. "He . . ." She nodded toward Tony. ". . . hasn't forgotten the offer he made you . . ." An identical nod in Henry's direction. ". . . earlier. You feed. He bleeds. As long as I'm not on the menu, feel free to discuss it. I'm not squeamish."

"No, you're terrified." Henry was using his Prince of Man voice, as commanding of attention as his Prince of Darkness although in a different way. Slightly different. Death wasn't quite so imminent. "You hide it well, but I saw it on your face two nights ago when the stunt went wrong, and I can smell it on you now. It clings like the smoke from a crematorium."

Nice image. Tony leaned a little forward and sniffed.

They both ignored him.

"We're all going out to the soundstage," Henry continued, "because any information that shadow takes back is too much. We have no defenses here against wizardry and, unless we want to see this land destroyed, he can't know that. Evil is never content with what it has. It has to keep moving, keep acquiring. That shadow must be stopped before the Shadowlord is convinced we're ripe for conquering."

"Too late." Her smile held no humor. "Not the first shadow, remember?"

"But one of the first. Perhaps it took time for us to muster our defenses; he can still be convinced."

"We're not defenseless," Tony broke in. He jabbed a finger toward Arra. "She can defend us."

"She is the cat's mother."

"What?"

Arra draped the cloth over the oven door handle, carefully spreading it flat. "Just something my gran used to say. If you know a person's name, use it."

"Fine. *You* can defend us." Another jab for emphasis. "If you destroy the shadow, he'll know we're not helpless."

"If I destroy that shadow, he'll send more." Her lip curled as she straightened and turned. Under lowered brows, her pale eyes were hard. "Do you think we didn't destroy them the last time? That we sat around with our thumbs up our collective asses? We fought back. And we lost."

Tony could hear that loss in her voice. The anger. The pain. The screaming.

"Then close the gate. You opened it originally," Henry reminded her. "Surely you can close it."

"I've been over this with him." She jerked her head at Tony, who muttered, "He is the cat's father." Wizard and vampire ignored him. "I can't affect the gate from this side. Only from the world of origin."

"Then, when it opens, go through it and *affect* it."

"If I go through it, I die, Nightwalker, and we've agreed—you and I—that I'm not yet ready to die."

"So basically," Tony said as Henry considered that last bit of information, "what you're saying is, now that he knows about us, about this world, we have no hope."

The smile she turned on him was so bleak it closed around his chest and squeezed. "Now, you've got it. Still, look at the bright side." Lifting the jam jar off the counter, she placed it in his hands. "You might get Lee back in one piece." A quick glance at the clock on the microwave. "If you hurry."

She followed them to the door, all but pushing them from the apartment.

Once in the hall, Tony headed straight for the elevator but Henry paused, turned, and said, "The spell you put on Tony, the one that took away his memory?"

"Yes," she answered warily, unsure of where the question was.

"It only lasted one night. I'm just wondering if maybe it failed because you didn't want it to last."

"You think I wanted to be threatened in my own home?"

"I think that, deep down, you wanted other people to know what was going on."

Her brows rose. "So you're a psychiatrist now? You have no idea what I want, Nightwalker!"

And the door slammed shut.

Tony parked Lee's motorcycle in its usual spot, pulled off the helmet, and stared at the cinder-block building that housed CB Productions. It was dark, deserted looking, but since the greater portion of it was windowless, that was hardly surprising. The exterior security lights around the office windows made it hard to tell for certain if anyone remained in the building.

At only 10:50, it was highly likely that the geeks in post were still at their consoles and entirely possible that at least some of the writing staff were hanging around the bull pen—although Tony wasn't entirely clear about what the latter might be doing at that hour besides drinking CB's coffee.

Chester Bane, the man himself, might be a problem. Rumor had it that he wandered the sets at night, in the dark.

"Blocking out new shows?" Tony asked.

The writer shook her head, bloodshot eyes flicking from side to side. "His last divorce really wiped him out; we think he lives in Raymond Dark's apartment."

"There's no bed. Raymond sleeps in a coffin."

"Your point?"

Not entirely believable, considering the source, but CB on set, for whatever reason, would be a problem.

One they'd have no choice but to deal with, Tony acknowledged as Henry parked his BMW in Mason Reed's reserved spot. Still, if worse came to worst, Henry could always do the vampire mind whammy on him.

"There's a door in the back," he said quietly as Henry came up beside him holding the jar of potion in both hands. "It's got one of those electronic security locks on it, but I know the code." Catching sight of Henry's expression, his face illuminated by the light coming off the liquid, Tony smiled tightly. "No, I'm *not* supposed to have the code, but I watched the key grip open up one morning and it kind of stuck in my head."

"Useful."

"Yeah. That's what I thought at the time."

Tony steered clear of the shadows as they hurried toward the back of the building. He told himself that skulking through them would scream "people up to no good" should a cop car or the private security hired by the industrial park happen to pass by. Two guys walking to the back door, well, that was obviously two guys who were there for legitimate reasons. That's what he told himself, and it was an accurate enough observation. But it *wasn't* why he was staying out of the shadows.

"Don't codes get changed on occasion, to prevent this very thing?" Henry asked as they reached the door.

Tony flipped up the cover on the keypad. "Yes."

"And if they have?"

"Then we're screwed. Unless you can climb up onto the roof, go down a ventilation shaft, and open the door from the inside."

Henry looked at his watch. "In less than twenty minutes? I'd rather not."

"Then I guess it's a good thing they haven't changed the code." He pulled the door open, slowly and carefully, and only far enough for them to slip inside.

"Does Lee Nicholas know the code?"

Frowning, Tony paused, the door almost shut. "I doubt it."

"Then you'd better leave it unlocked. He's going to have to get into the building and it would be better for all concerned if he did it quietly."

Arra hadn't been entirely certain where the gate would open.

"It was a big empty room when I arrived and I wasn't in the best condition. It was closer to the offices than the back wall, but that's all I can remember. I suggest you wait until Lee arrives and follow him. The shadow will know exactly where the gate is."

"Who knows what gates lurk within the heart of CB Productions. The sha . . ." Tony broke off as both Arra and Henry turned to stare. "You were thinking it, too," he grumbled.

The jar of potion shed enough light for Tony to find an alcove that would hold them both, giving them a clear line of sight to the door and along the closest thing to a central aisle the soundstage had. Once inside, pressed shoulder to shoulder, Henry tucked the jar in under his coat.

The darkness was nearly absolute, the dim red of the exit sign barely enough for Tony to orient himself. "He'd better make some noise," he murmured, "or we'll never see him arrive."

"I will."

"Oh . . . yeah." The darkness was nearly absolute to *human* eyes.

Tony tried not to fidget, but he'd never been much good at waiting. "Henry? Are you still going to try and stop that shadow?"

It took so long for the vampire to answer, Tony began to think he hadn't been heard. Which was stupid because Henry could hear his heart beating. Although, at the moment, it wasn't so much beating as pounding.

"Yes."

"How?"

"I don't know. The wizard may be right; now that the Shadowlord has found this world we have no chance, no hope, but I choose to think differently."

"Because no one messes with what's yours?"

He could feel Henry's smile in the darkness. Knew how it would look, sharp and cold like a knife.

"Something like that."

A sudden line of gray below the exit sign warned them that the door was opening. For barely an instant, a body stood silhouetted against the night, then an arm reached in and around to the right. Way up above the heavy steel grids where the grips hung the heavy kliegs, banks of low-level fluorescents came on.

It made sense. Shadows needed light to survive.

Tony shrank back into the alcove as Lee hurried by. He looked like he had when he left that afternoon and that was a good thing. Probably. It meant the shadow was still there, but it also meant it had done no visible damage. He let Henry slip out first, knowing the vampire could stay close without being spotted—standard operating procedure for Raymond Dark and *his* sidekick. When Lee and Henry disappeared around one of the walls defining Raymond Dark's office, he followed, eventually catching up to Henry by the video village on the edge of the new living room set.

Lee stood near the couch, looking up toward the ceiling and trembling.

There was—although had Tony not known what he knew, it would have been easy enough to convince himself he wasn't seeing it—an arc of shadow rising up above the actor's head.

"The shadow's separating," Henry murmured, mouth close to Tony's ear. "But it seems to be taking some time."

"Yeah, it took some time getting in. Henry!" He'd set the potion on the seat of Peter's canvas chair and was walking across the set. "Where are you going?"

Henry stopped an arm's length from Lee and leaned forward, nostrils flaring. The possessed actor didn't move, didn't twitch, didn't acknowledge his presence in any way. "The separation seems to be keeping all senses occupied."

"It wasn't like that going in. Except . . ." Tony frowned, remembering. "Except that going in took most of the afternoon."

Henry glanced up. "If the gate's about to open, it doesn't have that kind of time. Nor, when leaving, does it need to fit itself into a complex template."

"Yeah, whatever." Tony glanced up as well. He swept his gaze across and back, up and down, over and out but couldn't see anything resembling a gate. He *could* see . . . "Henry. What destroys shadow?"

"Light."

He pointed.

"Arra's people would have tried something like that."

"Maybe." His lips pulled off his teeth in a pseudo smile, a smile he'd learned from Henry as it happened. "But they didn't have one of those babies." Not really caring if Henry thought it would work, he ran for the light board.

Sorge, the gaffer, and the key grip had completed a rough setup for the next day's shoot. The script called for a meeting in this living room on a bright, sunny afternoon. Bright sunny afternoons in the middle of box warehouses required a lot of light. Most shows would use a couple of 10-K lamps, but at some point CB had acquired a high intensity 6,000 watt carbon arc lamp—speculation among the crew was that he'd won a bet—and the gaffer liked to use it for high contrast between daylight shots and the creature-of-the-night lighting they usually used. The actors hated it since it cranked up the temperature on the set. Lee had been heard to say, "To hell with Raymond Dark, *I'm* about to burst into fucking flames." But it had been a major contributor to the "look" of *Darkest Night*.

Critics were split on whether or not that was a good thing.

As it was far too powerful for the enclosed space, the gaffer had rigged it with its own dimmer; planning on starting low and then cranking it up until Sorge stopped him. His hands sweating so badly that he left damp prints on the plastic, Tony spun the dimmer around as far to the left as he could then hooked one finger behind the switch.

Turning, he could see only the outside wall of the living room. Crap. "Henry, let me know the instant the shadow's out of Lee."

"I'm not sure . . ."

"I am. And you'd better get under cover."

"That had occurred to me."

It wasn't sunlight, but Henry's eyes were sensitive and . . . "What was that?" It felt as though his fillings were vibrating loose.

"I can't see anything, but I suspect it's the gate opening."

"The shadow?"

"Not quite free. Almost."

Needing to act or scream, Tony started counting the pulse pounding in his temples. *One-two. Three-four. Five-six. Seven . . .*

"Now!"

He didn't so much flip the switch as bring it along with him when Henry's voice jerked him forward.

Without fill lamps to soften its edges, the light slammed through the set like a battering ram. Even behind the beam, Tony's eyes watered.

Then the soundstage plunged into total darkness.

For a moment, Tony was afraid he'd gone blind. A moment later he realized it was only a tripped breaker and began stumbling back toward the set. Once he cleared the wall—not hard to find after slamming face first into it—the light from Arra's potion guided him to the two men in the center of the fake hardwood floor.

"Get his shoulders up," Henry instructed as Tony dropped to his knees. "We've got to get this down him."

Tony slipped an arm behind leather-clad shoulders and lifted. Lee was heavier than he thought he should be, as though some of the shadow lingered, weighing him down. *Don't be such a dumb ass. He's a big guy, that's all.* He looked like hell, but that was probably the fault of the light source. Tony didn't need Everett to tell him that green and glowing complimented no one's complexion. Case in point: pouring the potion down Lee's throat, Henry looked demonic.

"Did it work? Did it destroy the shadow?"

"I don't know." Continuing to pour, the vampire managed a shallow shrug. "I wasn't looking into the light."

"Oh. Right."

"It was a good idea, though, something Vicki might have tried."

"Yeah?" Tony felt his ears grow hot and shifted his grip on Lee's shoulders to hide his pleasure. From the first time she'd hauled his fourteen-year-old ass in off the streets, Vicki Nelson had been his hero, a cop who honestly wanted to serve and protect, a friend when he needed one, his entry into Henry's life. He wasn't sure she knew about that first part, the hero bit. He wasn't sure he wanted anyone to know.

Lee coughed and tried to shove the jar away, jerking Tony's wandering attention back to the matter at hand. The jar was about half full. "Does he have to drink it all? I mean, that's one fuck of a lot of vodka."

"Arra was nonspecific, but I think we should try to get as much as possible into him." Henry's thumb stroked Lee's throat, coaxing him to swallow. "Good thing he's semiconscious or we'd have a fight on our hands. Vodka has no real flavor and this sort of herbal mix traditionally tastes as foul as it smells."

"He's getting a little more active!" Which was interesting considering the amount of alcohol they were pouring into him. "You don't think he's going to hurl, do you?"

"Hurl what?"

"Puke."

"Let's hope not."

It was taking all of Tony's strength just to hold the actor in place. A line of sparkling liquid ran down his chin, the tiny lights dancing over a hint of dark stubble. He spent a moment wondering what they were going to do in about thirty seconds when the last of the liquid disappeared, taking the light with it—Henry would have to find the panel—then a leather clad elbow caught him hard in the ribs.

"Perhaps we'd better change places."

"Good idea," Tony gasped. "Let the guy with super vampire strength take the . . . Henry?" He twisted around, following the line of Henry's narrowed gaze, to see a circle of light sweep the set behind him. From behind the light came the deep bellow of a familiar voice.

"What's going on in here?"

Chester Bane.

Wonder-fucking-ful. The rent-a-cop he might have been able to bullshit. *Looks like it's vampire whammy ti . . .* Strong fingers grabbed his arm, hauled him to his feet, and threw him into the only available hiding place—the triangle of space between the couch and the far wall.

"But Lee . . ." He protested against Henry's ear as the vampire landed beside him.

"We've done all we can for him."

"What if the potion didn't work?"

"The potion was all we had."

"But CB . . ."

"Needs Lee Nicholas, doesn't need you."

Unpleasant, but true. Production assistant was an entry level position and a lot of people were banging on the door to get in. Lee, on the other hand, had a vocal and growing fan base. As much as Tony hated abandoning him, he'd hate to be fired a lot more.

Jamming his shoulder and head under the back edge of the couch, he reached out and lifted the front edge of the slipcover a centimeter off the floor in time to see the circle of light return to illuminate the figure lying in the center of the floor.

Although not entirely certain of what he *had* expected to see, finding Lee Nicholas flat on his back was not it. When the power had suddenly gone off throughout the building, CB had spent long moments finding his flashlight then—followed by the anguished screams of a writer whose creative genius had swept her right past the concept of saving her prose—he'd made his way to the soundstage.

Security had joined him by the women's washroom and left him again when the sound of voices had drawn him away from his search for the panel.

"Mr. Nicholas."

The actor moaned and drew one knee up.

He closed the distance between them and glared down at the sprawled body. Drunk, definitely. Hopefully, only drunk. Before he could speak, the beam from a 6,000 watt carbon arc lamp burned the words away.

And left a few new ones as the soundstage plunged into darkness again.

"Go to the light board, Mr. Khouri! Turn the largest dimmer all the way to the right, then try the main breaker again!"

The security guard's disembodied voice drifted down out of the darkness. "Yes, sir, CB."

By the time the dancing blobs of color had cleared from his vision, Lee Nicholas was sitting up in his own personal spotlight, rubbing his eyes.

"Oh, man, my head!" He peered beyond the flashlight beam. "CB? Is that you?"

"It is."

"What are you doing here?" A tentative swing from left to right of a precariously balanced head. "Forget that, what am *I* doing here?"

"I was about to ask you the same thing."

"I just . . . that is, I don't . . ." Brows drew in. "I have no idea."

As the younger man rose unsteadily to his feet, Chester Bane's eyes narrowed. "You're in costume."

"I'm in what?" From the panicked look on his face, it was clear he was not expecting to see the conservative clothing of James Taylor Grant, vampire associate. Embarrassment quickly followed relief. "I'm shonny . . . shoory . . . sorry, CB."

"Good." It was a reaction that would have piqued the producer's curiosity at any other time but not right now. "Change. Then come to my office; we'll talk."

"Yeah. Sure. Talk."

He swept the flashlight beam around the set, then fell into step beside the actor—fully aware of how intimidating his size had to be. "It must have been some party."

"I don't remember a party." Lee staggered, fell against CB's large and unyielding surface, and hurriedly hauled himself erect.

"I expect tomorrow's tabloids will tell us everything we need to know."

"Oh, God."

"Prayer is always an option."

The dribble of liquid running down Lee Nicholas' chin had held a line of moving sparkles. One by one, the tiny lights had dimmed and disappeared. CB had a strong suspicion the tabloids would have even less of a handle on the truth than usual.

ᕲ SIX

Tony waited for the Translink bus to pull away and then, squinting a little in the early morning sunshine, stared diagonally across the intersection at the studio. It looked like it had on a hundred previous mornings—or at least like it had on the thirty of those hundred mornings when it hadn't been raining.

There were no mystical messages indicating that he'd fried the shadow, discouraged the Shadowlord, and stopped an invasion. There were no declarations of surrender. No proffered treaties. Not even a simple, "You win. I quit."

He glanced down at his watch. 7:20. He had about four hours to wait before the gate was scheduled to reopen. Four hours before he found out if the gate was even going to reopen.

And if it did?

What then?

He took another look at the studio. Nothing about it gave any indication of what might or might not happen in only four short hours.

Which was too bad, really, because if it had looked different, if physical evidence of either the gate or the Shadowlord had marked the building, he'd be able to take what he knew to the proper authorities. It was the twenty-first century after all; surely *someone* had plans for dealing with an off-world invasion. Someone, that is, besides people who ran web sites called theyarecoming. com or prob_me.org and who clearly had way too much free time. He made a mental note to scrub that prob_me.org cookie or he'd be getting porn spam for the rest of his life.

Unfortunately, the only evidence he had supporting an invasion was an invisible gate that made his teeth hurt, a wizard who'd deny everything, and an actor who hadn't remembered being possessed—although one of the tabloids did have a slightly blurry, page 17 shot of him coming out of the main branch of the public library, which would certainly strengthen the possession story. Not much in the way of support. Fox Mulder couldn't have made a case out of it.

The light changed and Tony headed across the street, absently rubbing his right thumb across the nearly healed puncture in his left wrist. Spending two nights in a row at Henry's condo hadn't been smart. And that was the problem. He wasn't smart around Henry, he was . . . dependent. Sure, running to Henry for help the moment things got weird made a kind of sense—friends with specialized knowledge and all that—but allowing it to go further, supporting that whole vampire *everyone I make a connection with is mine* attitude—his wrist throbbed—what had he been thinking? Other body parts made a couple of suggestions. He ignored them.

There was no chance of leaving Henry out of things now; if the gate reopened, he'd have to be told. But the next time . . .

Oh, yeah, Tony snorted, stepping up on the curb. *Because this sort of thing is likely to happen again.*

And anyway, since Arra seemed pretty damned sure they wouldn't survive this time, speculation seemed a bit moot.

Arra.

Tony'd called from Henry's to fill her in and ended up leaving a message on her machine. He knew she was standing beside the phone, listening, and refusing to become further involved. Too bad. If that gate reopened, he wasn't going to give her a choice.

He wondered if blackmail would work. *You help stop the Shadowlord and I won't tell everyone what you really are.*

Yeah, that'd work. Tony snorted again. If it came down to his word against Arra's, his story against Arra's, well, he'd put money on people believing the part that didn't involve wizards and dark shadow invasions.

Maybe he'd try guilt. *Never mind, you've been through enough. You just stay home with your cats while the rest of us die.* He had to try something because without Arra, it was up to him, and unless it turned out that a 6,000 watt carbon arc lamp was all it took, the world was fucking doomed.

As he retraced last night's steps to the back door, he glanced over at Lee's bike. Given the amount of vodka they'd poured into him, he'd probably taken a cab home. Lee had told CB he didn't remember anything and that was good. Tony knew his memory of what had happened in the dressing room was going to make it hard enough to face Lee—the last thing he needed added in was Lee's reaction. In his experience, a straight guy with a morning-after memory of copping a feel off a gay guy was more likely to blame the gay guy and get freaked and angry than think, *Oops, my hand must've slipped.* It was just human nature and Tony was usually fine with that, but it wasn't something he wanted to find out about Lee.

For the first time since he'd started working on *Darkest Night*, he wasn't looking forward to seeing the actor on set.

The problem was, the whole dark wizard, gate, shadow, invasion thing was just a little too big to really get a hold of.

The thing with Lee; *that* he had a hold of just fine.

Oh, that's just fucking great. Like I don't have enough going on without mental innuendo.

As usual, most of the early crew stood gathered around the craft services truck nursing coffees and muffins. Carpenters talking with electricians, talking with drivers, talking with the props guy, talking with camera operators; the craft services truck was the studio's Switzerland. Neutral ground. By unspoken agreement, arguments were left on the soundstage and a certain level of good manners was carefully maintained—people who regularly worked a seventeen-hour day were willing to do what it took to help facilitate the smooth delivery of carbs and caffeine.

Tony grabbed a coffee and headed inside to pick up his sides. He'd gone chasing off after Lee in such a hurry yesterday afternoon that he hadn't . . .

"Mr. Foster. A word."

Wondering what he'd done, Tony crossed over to where Peter was standing with Sorge and the gaffer by the light board. As he closed the distance, he told himself that the positioning had to be coincidence. Unless he'd dusted for fingerprints, there was no way the director could tell he'd been at the board the night before.

Eyebrows raised high enough that they seemed to be following his receding hairline back up over his skull, Peter held out a set of sides. "I believe these are yours."

He'd gone chasing off after Lee in such a hurry yesterday afternoon, Tony's brain reminded him.

Chasing off after Lee before Peter had called a wrap.

Without even considering what he was doing, he'd just left work.

Crap.

"I can explain."

"Good."

"Remember how you sent me in to check on Lee? To see if he was all right because he was acting so strangely on the set? Well, he just left, in one hell of a hurry, and so I went after him because I didn't know if he was all right." He flashed the smile he'd perfected on Toronto street corners staring up at uniformed cops and had kept around to grease his way through slightly more legal problems with authority. "See?"

"You ran out after Lee because I told you to go check on him?"

"Yes."

"You were so worried about him, you forgot you were still wearing your radio. Remembered to turn it off, but forgot you were wearing it."

Tony glanced down at the holster riding his hip. "Yeah. I was worried."

"And how was he?"

Controlled by a minion of the Shadowlord.

Flat on his ass under a gate leading to another world.

Sloshing with vodka . . .

None of the above.

"I . . . uh, I never actually caught up to him."

"So you're saying you left early and still didn't do what I asked you to?"

"Uh, yeah. Sorry."

Peter stared at him for a long moment, then snorted softly. "You just used up all your saved-the-stuntman goodwill, Tony. Next time you run off like that, you can return the radio and keep on going."

"Right. Sorry."

"Tell Alan Wu I need him on set to run over his blocking the moment he's done then hit the office and see if those dialogue changes are ready. And," he raised his voice, "I'd like to get started on time for a change, people! Why aren't those cameras set?"

As Tony hurried for the exit, he heard the soundstage begin to rev up behind him. And the good news, he still had a job. And the bad news, that job was still at ground zero for a Shadowlord invasion.

Unless it wasn't.

Seven fifty-one.

Three and a half hours.

He hated waiting.

Alan Wu, who played Detective Emanuel Chan, *Darkest Night's* recurring police presence, guaranteed at least one day's work a week, was still in the chair when Tony reached the makeup room.

"Look at this hair, Tony." Everett waved a thick strand of black hair in Tony's general direction without much regard for the head it was attached to. "Don't quote me on this, but is this not beautiful hair?"

"It's the same hair he had last week, Everett." Tony grinned as he moved around so Alan could see him in the mirror. Everett's fascination with Alan's hair and the crew's awareness of it left the actor alternately flattered and embarrassed. "As soon as you're done here, Peter would like to see you on set so that he . . ."

". . . can run over my blocking. Same old. Same old."

Detective Chan liked to move when he talked, his constant motion in direct and deliberate contrast to Raymond Dark's brooding stillness. It made his scenes harder to shoot, as a stationary actor was easier for both light and sound but, since CB himself had been responsible for that bit of character development, no one argued too loudly against it; they just scheduled extra time and counted on Alan to hit his marks.

Fortunately, twenty years in the business made Alan the closest thing to a sure bet on the set.

The late Catherine's less-than-loving mom and dad were in the other two chairs being worked on by Everett's assistant—who worked part-time for CB Productions and part-time at a local funeral parlor. She'd told Tony once that thanks to *Six Feet Under,* people saw her second job as the more exotic. "But for me—you know, corpses, actors—meat's meat. At least the dead dudes don't complain that natural beige foundation makes them look fat."

Lee was in the same scene, but he wasn't due on set until 8:30. Two hours and forty-five minutes before the gate. Tony paused outside his dressing room door, imagined he could hear the rustle of fabric, actually could hear muffled profanity, raised his hand to knock, changed his mind, and ran.

Terrified he'd hear Lee's door open before he was out of sight.

Jesus. What are you afraid of? He's a guy; it's not like he's going to want to talk about it.

He hit the production office just as Amy, hair and fingernails a matching burgundy, was shrugging out of her jacket. Crossing toward her, he lifted a hand in greeting. "Hey."

"Hey yourself, Kemosabe. You still work here?"

It appeared that yesterday's early departure was common knowledge. Great. The last thing he needed was a reputation as a slacker. Well, maybe not the last thing; he supposed he needed homicidal shadows less, but still . . . "All has been forgiven," he told her, pushing the staple remover around her desk with the tip of one finger, "but apparently I'm going to have to rescue another stuntman before I do it again."

Amy glanced around the office. "Don't see anyone in need of rescue."

"Too bad. Did you know that clock is two hours off?"

She turned to look and snorted. "We reset it to Hawaiian time."

"That's not . . ."

"Did you come in here to criticize, or are you actually hanging around for a reason?"

"I need today's dialogue changes."

The changes weren't on Amy's desk. Just to be on the safe side, she quickly checked Rachel's desk, the top of both filing cabinets, and the gray metal shelving unit.

Together, they turned toward the bull pen.

"I went in last time," Amy told him, crossing her arms over her UBC sweatshirt.

"I'm the *set* PA," he reminded her. "The bull pen's way outside my job description."

"You want to get anywhere in this business, Tony, you have to show initiative."

"I'd rather wrestle Richard Simmons."

"You wish."

"Hey, guys, what's up?"

Together, they turned toward the office PA.

Veronica's eyes widened at the sight of their smiles and she took a step back. "What?"

"I need you to pick up some dialogue changes from the writers for this morning's shoot," Amy told her while Tony tried to keep the word "sucker" from showing on his face in any way.

She looked a little confused but nodded. "Sure, no problem."

They watched her stride purposefully into the bull pen and exit considerably faster a few moments later clutching four sheets of paper to her chest.

"What is that smell?"

"No one knows." Amy pried the pages from Veronica's white-knuckled fingers and headed for the photocopier. "What're we up to? Blue?"

Tony checked his sides for the latest script revision color. "Yeah, blue."

"Why blue?" Veronica asked.

Tony shrugged. "Because the camera breakdowns are on green."

"That's not a reason for blue."

Amy patted her on the shoulder as she handed Tony the photocopies. "One of the first things you've got to learn in this business, kid, is that a lot of stuff happens just because."

"But why do . . . ?"

"Because."

"Yes, but . . ."

"Just because." Dropping into her chair, Amy reached for the ringing phone. "And while we're on the topic, can you try and find another ream of blue paper in that stack of office supplies in the kitchen. CB Productions. How can I help?"

When Veronica continued to look confused, Tony turned her toward the kitchen and gave her a little shove. He'd taken two steps toward the soundstage when the front doors opened and Zev came in, one hand beating time to the rhythm in his headphones. Tony waited until he was sure the musical director could see him, then he smiled and waved.

Zev's return salutation was distinctly frosty and he continued straight through to post without stopping to talk.

By the time Tony had turned to ask Amy what was up, she already had her hand over the mouthpiece of the phone.

"Because you were a shit to him yesterday."

"You could at least wait until I asked."

"Time is money, buckaroo. Go apologize."

He waved the dialogue changes in answer as she turned her attention back to the phone and headed for the soundstage. Apologize? A suggestion that proved Amy didn't understand guys. Guys didn't apologize; the other guy, the guy not being apologized to, got even. *Fucking great. If Lee thinks what happened yesterday was my fault, I'm going to have to pull CB himself out of a burning car if I want to keep my . . .*

"Shit. Sorry." He sidestepped the body heading for the makeup room, realized who it was an instant later, and kept walking. Maybe a little faster. Places to go. Things to do. Dialogue changes to deliver.

"Hey, Tony!"

Crap.

Half hidden behind a not very convincing fake bearskin hat, he turned and tried to look as though he wasn't remembering the feel of bare skin under his hands. "Yeah?"

"Yesterday, after I left, Brenda says you took off on my bike."

And crap again. The wardrobe department's windows looked out into the parking lot and Brenda had been trying to get into Lee's pants in more than a professional way for months. Over half the crew believed she already had.

Not surprisingly, Lee sounded pretty pissed off.

"Uh, yeah. Don't you remember?" Because if Lee'd gotten his memory back overnight, Tony needed to know now.

"Remember what?"

Good. Anger turning to suspicion and uneasiness. Well, not exactly *good* but definitely better than it could be. Tony dredged up a smile and proceeded to lie through his teeth. He'd been told more than once it was one of his most marketable skills. "You told me to take it to your condo for you, but you never showed and I couldn't get into the garage so I brought it back here."

"I told you to take it to my condo?"

"Yeah."

"Why?"

Tony shrugged and flipped a bit of off-color fur back and forth. "Beats the hell out of me. You said you had a killer headache, asked if I could ride, I said I could and . . ." He shrugged again and played the only hand he had. "That must've been one hell of a headache if you can't remember. You okay?"

"Uh . . ." Lee's brow furrowed and Tony flinched to see the flash of panic in his eyes. Sure, anyone might panic at losing so large a chunk of time, but for an actor to suddenly feel he couldn't rely on his memory . . . After a long moment, Lee decided to grab the line Tony'd thrown him. "It was a killer headache, totally killer—still not entirely gone, I'm afraid. Listen, thanks, man."

"No problem." He waved the blue sheets again, like cerulean semaphore for *I've got to haul ass*, and hauled ass for the soundstage. *And the Oscar goes to* . . . Except this was television not movies and syndicated television besides but an Oscar caliber performance regardless. He just wished he didn't feel like such a shit.

I should tell him. I should tell him that it has nothing to do with him. That the shadow minions of a dark wizard took over his body and that's why he can't remember. Tony snorted as he shoved through the last of the costumes. *Oh, yeah, I'm sure it'd comfort him to think that while he was losing his memory, I was losing my mind.*

Better the comfort of a lie than the absurdity of the truth.

And ain't that a proverb for the millennium.

At the monitors, he handed Peter the changes. The director glanced over them then passed all but two sets to Tina. Those two sets, he passed back to

Tony. "Give these to Mum and Dad. Tell them I need them out here in . . . Sorge!"

The DP glanced up from sketching Alan's path across the living room in the air with long sweeping movements of both arms.

"How long?"

"*Vingt.*" Unaware he was standing directly under an interdimensional gate, Sorge shrugged. "*Vingt-cinq.*"

"Make it twenty." Peter turned his attention back to Tony. "Tell them I need them out here in twenty minutes. Suggest that they actually know the new lines."

"Really?" That last bit sounded suspect.

"Be diplomatic."

"Uh, sure." Apparently not.

"And get them back here on time."

"Right."

He could be diplomatic. He checked his watch against the time code running across the bottom of the tech monitor and headed back toward the dressing rooms. Odds were good they were both out of makeup by now and anyway, the dressing rooms were on the way.

Memory making his heart pound, just for that moment envying Lee's memory loss, Tony reminded himself that *that* shadow was gone. That the shadow following it had been destroyed. *He'd* destroyed it.

The door to Catherine's—Nikki's—dressing room remained off its hinges and Mom and Dad—he didn't bother checking their actual names; if the morning went well, they'd be gone by lunch—were in the two farthest away. Fortunately, both doors were open. *Fortunately*, because Tony was suddenly afraid that if he had to knock, he wouldn't be able to. Dad was reading the paper. Mom had her laptop out.

Their shadows were muted and gray.

He cleared his throat and held up the pages. "Dialogue changes, guys. The director needs you on the set in twenty minutes with the changes down."

"In twenty minutes?" Mom looked appalled.

Tony glanced at the top page. "I think most of the changes are Alan's. Detective Chan's. He usually gets the exposition and that's what the writers keep changing, so it's probably changed a couple of your reactions." He smiled reassuringly as they took the pages. "Nothing big."

"I mean, I know my lines."

The newspaper was abruptly folded down. "Are you implying I don't?"

"I wasn't talking about you. Jesus, Frank. Get over yourself." She flipped through the pages and frowned, the makeup on her forehead creasing. "We're doing all four pages today?"

"Hopefully, we're doing all four pages by 11:00," he told her, glancing at his sides. Her name was Laura. He couldn't know one and not the other, it just didn't seem fair. "Then three more before lunch and we're doing seven this afternoon—touch wood." Reaching out, he pressed a finger against a two by four. "We're a bit behind."

Both actors turned to look at the far dressing room.

"Because of . . . her?" Frank asked.

"Nikki Waugh."

"Right." He stepped far enough away from the dressing rooms to get a better look. "That's where it happened, isn't it?"

Shadow spilled out onto the soundstage, pooling on the concrete, running into the cracks and dips in the floor.

"Yes."

"She didn't die of anything catching, did she?"

A small bounce as the back of her head impacted with concrete.

"No. Nothing catching."

"I heard she was all twisted up." Laura moved out to stand beside her temporary matrimonial partner. "Heart attack, my ass."

"I heard it was drugs."

Tony checked his watch. Fifteen minutes until he had to get them to the set. No way he could take fifteen minutes of lurid speculation. Not when he knew. Hell, not even if he hadn't known. "Excuse me. I have an errand I have to run; I'll be back for you."

"Don't worry about it, Tommy . . ."

"Tony."

"Of course." Laura cocked her head toward the sound of Sorge's voice, his unmistakable hybrid of French and English loud enough to echo against the distant ceiling. "I think we can find our way."

"It's all part of the service." He found a smile from somewhere and managed to keep it in place as he hurried for the exit. Behind him, Mom and Dad—Laura and Frank—settled down for a good gossip, script changes forgotten in their need to visit rumor and innuendo.

Nothing like human nature to make incoming Shadowlords look good. Keeping an eye out for Lee, he pushed his way back through the costumes, out into the production office, and down to the basement when Amy's back was turned.

He didn't want to go down to the basement.

There was no reason for him to go down to the basement.

If he needed to talk to Arra, it would be a lot more efficient if he just called her and had her come up to the soundstage.

Tony stopped about halfway down the stairs. He turned, raised his foot to start back up again, and stopped.

He *did* want to go down to the basement.

And he had a damned good reason for going.

Two steps farther down and he began to feel slightly nauseous.

Who knew what chemicals she was using down there. Half of them would probably blow up if looked at the wrong way and the other half were likely toxic. Better he just go back upstairs and call her.

He was three steps up before he stopped himself.

Bite me, old woman!

Four steps from the bottom, the hair lifting off the back of his neck, sweat running down his sides, he said a silent, *Screw it!* and jumped.

He felt better the moment he landed.

Wiping his palms against his jeans, he came out from behind a set of shelves and face-to-face with a rotting corpse standing and swaying in the middle of the room.

Sagging gray flesh had ripped open under its own weight and well-fed maggots squirmed out of the rents. A hand with bones protruding through three fingertips reached out for him while white rheumy eyes tried to focus on his face. Dark, withered lips parted and a voice said, "It takes a lot to discourage you, doesn't it? All right, fine. As long as you're here, you can tell me if the maggots are too much."

"Th . . . th . . . th . . ." It felt as though all connections between his mouth and his brain had been severed.

"The maggots, Tony. Are they over the top? I think they give a corpse a nice lived-in look, but they're not for everyone."

"Arra?"

The corpse sighed and was suddenly the much shorter, older wizard—the maggots nowhere in sight. "It's just a glamour," she said, checking her fingertips. "Raymond Dark'll be stopping the villain du jour from raising the dead in a couple of weeks and I need to work out the details. It's not as easy as it looks maintaining three separate glamours over moving actors. Good thing CB's too cheap to hire more than three corpses. So . . ." An eyebrow rose. ". . . what can I do for you?"

"That was . . ." He waved a hand. "Fuck. I mean . . ."

"Thank you. Always nice to have an appreciative audience. I take it Mr. Nicholas is functional this morning?"

"Uh, yeah."

"Good." She waited, then folded her arms and sighed again. "Since you managed to get down here in spite of wards set to prevent that very thing, I assume you want something. What?"

"Right." Tony glanced down at his watch. Seven minutes before he had to get Laura and Frank to the set. "The gate. We're shooting right under it."

"So?"

"I don't think we'll be done by 11:15."

"I repeat, so?"

"You have to be there. You should be there. Just in case."

"As I believe I mentioned last night, there's no just in case."

"But I . . ."

"Yes. I got your message. You used a really bright light on the shadow leaving Mr. Nicholas and you think you destroyed it, but you're not one hundred percent positive." She folded her arms. Tony had read somewhere that people folded their arms as a protective gesture. Arra didn't so much look like she was protecting herself as putting up battlements, raising the moat bridge, and hanging out *No Trespassing* signs. "The shadow could have returned unaffected," she continued, "and therefore the shadows that would have been sent today will still be sent. It could have been injured but not destroyed, in which case shadows will come through to find and remove the threat. It could have been destroyed and so nothing went back through the gate at all, in which case shadows will come through to find out why.

"The Shadowlord will continue to send his shadows through. You might as well just live your life while you can because there's nothing you can do about it."

"Hey, I have access to a 6,000 watt carbon arc lamp!"

"*If* the lamp destroyed the shadow, can you shine it on the gate every time it opens?"

"No, but you can . . ."

"I can what?"

"I don't know!" Everything he knew about wizards came from the movies and none of it was particularly helpful. "You could help!"

"I helped last night and unless my memory is faulty, which it isn't, I told you that I'm not going after the shadows. As you might say, been there, done that, got the scars." Her arms still crossed, her right hand gripped her left sleeve with white-knuckled force.

"You fought before!"

"Older and wiser now. Didn't you have somewhere you need to be?"

He looked at his watch. Shit! "This isn't over." Arra shrugged—although a certain twist to her mouth made the motion look more fatalistic than nonchalant. "That's what I keep telling you."

"All right, let's get Mom's reaction shots." Finding himself at the end of his tether, Peter yanked off his headphones and tossed them back to Tina before walking out onto the set. "Lee, if you don't mind . . . ?"

Cracking open a bottle of water, Lee indicated that he didn't.

There were stars, Mason Reed among them, who saw no reason they should have to reread their lines so that the cameras could catch the reactions of the secondary characters. On more than one occasion, Tony, as the least essential member of the crew, had found himself holding a script and trying not to sound like a complete idiot while reading Raymond Dark's dialogue. Given Raymond Dark's dialogue, that wasn't exactly a job for an amateur.

Unless Lee had another commitment, he always stayed. Tony felt this gave his scenes a depth that Mason's didn't have and that it could be at least part of the reason for the amount of fan mail Lee had started to receive—although he didn't kid himself that the larger reason involved the eyes, the smile, and the ass. It had taken *him* a couple of months to actually notice Lee's acting ability and he was a trained professional.

Under normal circumstances, Tony was all in favor of Lee's presence on the set. Today, he'd have been happier had Lee been out of the building. Hell, out of the country. If Arra was right and the next opening of the gate would release more shadows into the world, Lee needed to be as far from the gate as possible—not standing underneath it chatting to the boom operator while Peter went over the reactions he wanted with Laura.

If Arra was wrong . . . well, Tony would still have been happier with Lee anywhere but unavoidably in sight. He couldn't stop thinking about what had happened between them—between him and Lee's body at any rate—and it was distracting.

"TONY!"

He jerked his head toward the microphone so quickly he nearly gave himself whiplash. "Yeah, Adam?"

"Find Everett and get him out here. Frank's comb over needs to be touched up before his shots."

And faintly from the background. *"It's not a comb over!"*

Everett was in makeup with Mason Reed in the chair. Startled, Tony checked his sides. "Uh, Mr. Reed, you're not . . ."

"Promo shots," the actor snapped. "For *The Georgia Straight*. Yet another article about my personal life—rich and single in Canada's hippest city." His sigh was deep enough to waft a cotton ball off the counter. "They should be concentrating on my art; I don't know why they're so fascinated by what I do in my minimal amount of spare time."

They're not fascinated, they're inundated—you won't shut up about it. Flashing Mason the "sorry I'm interrupting but I'm carrying a message from someone much more important than me" smile he'd perfected after three days on the job, Tony turned to the other man, currently wiping lotion off his fingers. "Everett, you're needed on set."

"He's not finished with me."

"It's not a problem, Mason. We need a moment for that bronz . . . moisturizer," Everett corrected quickly as Mason glared at him, "to set."

"*Georgia Straight* interview my ass," the makeup artist muttered a moment later as they made their way back to the soundstage. "They've never shot him in anything but black and white. I'm betting he has a hot date with one of his parasailing, snowboarding bimbos. Hard bodies young enough to be your daughter are seldom impressed by vampire pallor. Don't quote me on that, though."

Tony winced. "Harsh."

"I call them as I see them, kid. And I knew Frank's combover wouldn't be up to the overacting he was going to put it through. What happened to subtlety?" he demanded as they waited at the soundstage door for the red light to go off.

"It's a show about a vampire detective," Tony reminded him, opening the door and motioning him through. "Subtle isn't exactly the selling point."

". . . which is when the police arrived."

"Keep rolling," Peter called as Laura allowed her shocked expression to fade. "Let's try it again with more sorrow less indignation. Lee . . ."

"Unfortunately, Mr. and Mrs. Mackay, that was when Raymond Dark found your daughter. It was too late for him to do anything, too late for anyone to do anything, which is when the midget basketball team arrived."

"Keep rolling. Do it again. A little *less* sorrow this time although the tear was terrific if you can work up another one. Lee, stop trying to make her laugh. We've got nine pages to get through today and you know how CB feels about overtime."

Laura smiled across the set. "That's all right Peter; I don't find midget basketball funny."

"Yak herders? Operatic mutes? The Vancouver Canucks?" Lee grinned at the older woman. "You've got to be able to laugh at the Canucks or you'll die of a broken heart."

"That's a fiver for the hockey jar, Lee." The hockey jar was a direct result of differing opinions during the previous season's playoffs; differing opinions that had resulted in a black eye, two broken fingers, and an assault with a blueberry muffin. "And line . . ."

"Unfortunately, Mr. and Mrs. Mackay . . ."

As he delivered the line once again, Lee seemed fine. He was a little hyper, but his energy levels were always high while the camera was rolling. Had Tony not been specifically looking for the effects of yesterday's adventure, he would have missed the pinched looked around the actor's eyes or the way his usual fluid gestures had picked up a slight staccato movement—like a physical stutter. It could have been a lot worse—he'd expected it to be a lot worse—and it could, in fact, be nothing more than a perfectly normal reaction to being force-fed half a bottle of warm, catnip-flavored vodka.

The shadow appeared to have caused no actual damage.

Tony glanced at his watch. 11:10.

That shadow appeared to have caused no actual damage. And as much as he wanted to believe it was over, lessons learned from a thousand movies and a hundred television shows were telling him it couldn't possibly be that easy.

A thousand movies, a hundred television shows, and one real downer of a wizard.

Arra had every intention of staying away from the set—from the set, from the gate, from the whole inevitable disaster. At 11:11, according to the clock on the tech monitor, she was standing behind the video village wondering just what, exactly, she thought she was doing.

Gathering information?

Yes. That sounded safe enough.

She needed information in order to plan, in order to survive, which meant that vested self-interest had brought her out of her workshop—not curiosity nor, heaven forbid, an inexplicable desire to become involved. Once was enough. More than.

The big carbon arc lamp was on, maintaining ambient light for the close-ups. It was throwing an uncomfortable amount of heat, and was clearly the reason her T-shirt was now sticking to a line of sweat dribbling down her spine. As long as it stayed on, she couldn't see a shadow making it through.

Peter sat back and pushed his headphones down around his neck. "That's got it."

And the light shut off.

Cue dramatic irony.

"No!"

As all eyes turned toward him, Tony suddenly realized he'd spoken aloud. Yelled actually.

Peter leaned around the edge of the monitor to fix him with an interrogative gaze. "Problem, Mr. Foster?"

Mister? He was so screwed. He could feel the vibration beginning, the gate opening. What difference did it make if he looked like an ass? He had to say something! Arra! Arra was there. Behind Peter. She'd back him up. *Right. Who the fuck am I kidding.* "Sorry. I uh . . . thought I saw one of the lights shift."

Everyone looked up. Everyone but him.

He looked at Arra. Who was looking up. But *not* at the lights.

Her face had paled and she was panting; even from ten feet away, he could see her chest rise and fall. He could almost see the terror oozing off her like . . . like the maggots oozing out of the corpse. *Oh, yeah, I really needed that image.*

The vibrations grew stronger.

"Can anyone else feel that?"

Together, Tony and Arra stared at Lee.

"Feel what?" Laura asked cautiously.

Frowning, the actor rubbed his jaw. "It's like there's a . . . I don't know, like a bee trapped in my head."

Tony would have said dentist's drill, but bee was close enough. No one else seemed to be noticing. *Because of the shadow in him?* he mouthed at Arra.

She shrugged—he had no idea if the gesture was an answer or because she couldn't lip-read.

"All right people, if we give it some gas, we can get Dad's reactions in the can before lunch. B-camera, you ready?"

"Good to go, Boss."

"Lee?"

A shadow brushed across Lee's face. He stiffened and screamed.

⟳ SEVEN

Tony jumped forward as Lee's knees began to buckle and managed to slide an arm under his head just before bone impacted with concrete.

A small bounce as the back of her head impacted with concrete.

He'd reacted as much for his own benefit as Lee's; he didn't think he could bear hearing that particular sound again. A line of cold air brushed feather light against his cheek, and he turned his head in time to see a shadow pour off his shoulder. And another slide across the floor.

When Lee screamed again, Tony turned back toward him so quickly he courted whiplash, saw a tendril of shadow pool in the hollow of the actor's throat, saw it dribble down to join the shadow cast by solid flesh, saw it separate and disappear behind the camera mount.

"What the hell is going on?"

"Shadows."

Arra's whisper pulled Tony's gaze past Peter to where the wizard stood, visibly trembling.

"Shadows?" The director looked as well, and when no answer was forthcoming, directed his next question out at the floor. "What the hell does that mean?"

Multiple shoulders lifted and fell.

No one else had seen them. Or, possibly, no one else was willing to admit that such a thing could exist. It was a defense mechanism Tony'd seen a hundred times. Henry and his kind survived because of it. And Henry'd made it pretty much impossible for him to use it.

He pulled a word from the air. "Seizure?"

Someone dropped down at Lee's other side. A hand moved his arm away gently and placed a pad of fabric between concrete and skull. Tony looked up to see Laura on her knees, her sweater off and her fingers against the pulse point in Lee's throat.

"I don't know about a seizure," she said briskly, "but his heart's racing, his temperature is up, and there's a certain rigidity in his muscles that I don't like." The silence that followed held so many questions, she looked up and frowned. "I've been a nurse for twenty years. You can't honestly think I can make a living doing the occasional character role on Canadian television?"

The murmur of agreement from cast and crew held distinct overtones of relief; *someone* knew what they were doing.

"We're heavily syndicated in the American market," Peter muttered under his breath.

"Not my point." Laura sat back on her sensible heels as Lee opened his eyes.

The clear jade green looked murky. Flawed. *Or I could be overreacting just a bit*, Tony admitted, his own heart working in quick time.

"Lee, are you back with us? How are you feeling?"

His eyes locked on Laura's face with a desperate need to know. "Is it over?"

"It seems to be."

Question and answer held no subject in common, but Tony was just as glad he hadn't had to answer the question actually asked. No. It wasn't over. Including the original shadow that had set Lee off, he'd counted four, but with his focus so narrowed, he couldn't swear there hadn't been a dozen more.

Adam stood at Lee's feet, pencil tapping against the edge of his clipboard, eyes narrowed as though he was working out the logistics in his head. "Should we call a doctor?"

Suddenly aware he was flat on the floor and the center of attention—and *not* the kind of attention actors required—Lee struggled to sit up. "I'm fine."

Tony inched back, aware he had no right to be inside the other man's personal space but unwilling to surrender his position entirely.

"Screaming and collapsing doesn't generally indicate fine," Laura told him, helping him sit up. Her tone was so matter-of-fact it cut the ground out from under rising panic.

Drawing in a deep breath, Lee managed a wobbly smile. "That was then, this is now."

"Can you tell me what happened?"

The smile wobbled a little more. "No. I was cold then . . ."

"He should see a doctor."

"Hey, I'm good." He sounded fine. But then three weeks ago he'd sounded like a fifteenth-century Italian nobleman by way of a Canadian screenwriter, so Tony wasn't putting much stock in the pronouncement.

Neither was Laura. "Something caused that reaction. It would be wise to see a doctor."

He stood as Lee did, fairly certain the other man had no idea whose shoulder he was using and, considering their interaction over the past two days, just as happy. The last thing he wanted was to be tied in Lee's mind to personal disaster. Although given the whole memory-loss, screaming-and-falling-over thing, it might already be too late.

Lee glanced around at his audience. "We're behind already."

Heads nodded. Someone had died and the show had gone on. Falling over and screaming was fairly far down the list in comparison.

"We'll be further behind if this continues," Laura pointed out reasonably. "It could be something serious. It might be nothing. But you should know."

Heads nodded again. The same heads.

Hands spread, Lee smiled; the wobbles under control, the only indication that anything had happened a certain tightness around his eyes. He was a better actor than most people gave him credit for. "I'm fine."

"Obviously, you're not." The deep voice pulled everyone's attention around. CB, who never came out on the soundstage while they were shooting, stood at the edge of the set. It looked significantly smaller than it had. He waited until the murmurs of surprise died down—waited with an attitude that clearly said they'd better die down damned fast—and then continued. "You are too valuable to me and to this show to allow what might be a potentially serious situation to continue. Do you have a doctor in the area, Mr. Nicholas?"

"No, I . . ."

"Then you will see mine. I will take you myself. Now."

"But the scene . . ."

"Reaction shots can be done without you."

Tony wondered how CB knew they were on reaction shots. Direct video feed to his office? Psychic powers? Lucky guess?

"Mr. Wu . . ."

Alan jumped at the sound of his name.

". . . can read your lines to Ms. Harding and Mr. Polintripolous. Mr. Polintripolous can read your lines to Ms. Harding and Mr. Wu. While I appreciate your willingness to do the job, at this exact moment I would rather you tend to your health. Mr. Foster."

Tony's turn to jump.

"Accompany Mr. Nicholas to his dressing room and then, once he has washed up and changed into his own clothing, to my office." As Lee began to protest, he raised a hand. "If whatever happened just now happens again, I want someone near enough to you to help."

So much for not being associated in Lee's mind with personal disaster.

A lesser man would have extended his scene by sweeping those assembled with an imperious glare; CB merely turned on one heel and left, his force of personality such that Tony almost expected to see the swirl of an Imperial cape and hear the studded sandals of his Praetorian guard slap against the floor.

No one moved until they heard the door to the soundstage close.

"All right, people, let's reset for Laura's reactions. Alan, you're reading Lee's lines."

As Peter moved back behind the monitors, Adam gently took hold of Lee's shoulder and shoved him toward the exit. "You'd better go; he's waiting."

"I don't need to see a doctor." He sounded annoyed. It wasn't quite enough to cover the fear.

"CB thinks you do, so . . ." Adam shrugged. "What can it hurt? It's probably nothing."

"Probably," Lee repeated, but from the look on his face he was thinking of some of the things it *probably* wasn't.

Tony wanted to tell him that it was none of those. It wasn't MS, it wasn't ADSS; it wasn't any of a dozen neurological disorders that would destroy his career then finally take his life. Unfortunately, it was something worse. Worse numerically anyhow, since an invasion by the Shadowlord would also destroy his career and take his life—along with countless other lives.

"Tony."

About to fall into step beside the actor, he glanced over at Adam.

"The moment Lee's in CB's office, you head right back."

He felt his cheeks flush. "Sure." Skip out early once and never hear the end of it.

Lee was half a dozen steps in front of him now, the set of his shoulders announcing that he neither needed nor wanted company. Too bad. As Tony hurried to catch up, he checked out the spot where Arra had been standing and wasn't surprised to find her gone. He hadn't actually expected her to stay around and do something useful. Something wizardy.

The red light came on seconds after they closed the door.

The show going on.

Stepping into the cleared area in front of the washroom, for the first time walking side by side, a shadow skittered across their path. They jerked back. Lee caught a kind of moan in his throat and held it there.

"Just this coat," Tony said, grabbing a fistful of fabric and yanking the coat still. "It sort of moved out in front of the light."

Lee had shoved his way through the costumes with enough force to set the racks swaying and, in turn, the costumes. He looked at the coat, then turned just far enough to stare at Tony; kept staring long enough so Tony was sure he was going to demand an explanation.

"You know what's happening around here, Foster. Spill it."

Or perhaps a little more twenty-first Century. *"What the hell is up with these shadows?"*

Lee's eyes narrowed. Then, without a word, he stomped the last three meters to his dressing room, entered, and slammed the door.

"Yeah." Tony leaned on the scuffed drywall between Lee's dressing room and makeup. "I'll just wait out here."

"... go through thousands of bottles of water every week and so crushing them before they go into the recycling bin is crucial or they're just not going to fit." Amy speared a piece of spiral pasta and frowned into its pattern. "Not to mention that whole wind catching them when they're dumped and bouncing them over hell's half acre thing." Looking up, her frown deepened. "Tony? Are you even listening to me?"

He tore his gaze away from a patch of shadow climbing the soundstage wall. "Yeah. Crushing plastic water bottles. I heard you. Amy, can I tell you something a little ... weird?"

"About Lee?"

Lee was the principal topic of a hundred lunch discussions. "Sort of."

"Good thing Mason wasn't on the set," she snorted, picking through her chicken fettuccini. "He hates it when Lee gets more attention than he does." The office staff had their own kitchen and their own caterer, but every one of them believed that the food on the soundstage was better. When the show was shooting on set, they ran a lottery to see who'd get to eat with the cast and crew. Amy won fairly often and when the inevitable protests arose, she reminded her coworkers that eventually someone would complain and the odds were good she'd be the one catching the shit. So far, no one had. Since there was always enough food for a dozen extra people and Mason usually ate in his dressing room, it was unlikely anyone ever would. She looked up, caught sight of Tony's face, and stilled. "This is serious." When he nodded, she put down her fork. "Go ahead."

Where to start? "There's a gate to another world, like a metaphysical gate, in the soundstage."

When he paused, unsure, she nodded. "Go on."

"Shadows come through it controlled by an evil wizard they call Shadowlord."

"He controls the gate or the shadows?"

"Both."

"And the shadows call him Shadowlord?"

"No. The people of that world." He slipped his hands under the table and wiped sweaty palms against his thighs. This was going better than he'd hoped. "The other world."

"Right."

"These shadows are like his spies and they're coming through to find out about this world so that he can invade and conquer it."

"Why?"

"Why what?"

"Why invade and conquer? What's his motivation?"

"I don't know; invading and conquering, I guess. What difference does it make?"

"You have to know his motivation, Tony."

"It doesn't matter!" As heads turned he lowered his voice. "The point is; these shadows can kill, have already killed, and now there's at least four more."

"So how do you stop them?"

"I don't know."

"You need a hero."

"Tell me about it. Although I'm not sure a hero would solve the problem. Arra's a wizard . . ."

"So she's working on this, too?"

"Not really. She doesn't want to get involved. I think she's afraid."

"Of what, bad writing?" Amy snorted. "Because if she is, she's working on the wrong show."

"Of the Shadowlord!"

"Well, he doesn't sound very scary. But let me take a look at the script; you never know."

"Script?"

"Yeah, for your show about the Shadowlord." Her brows drew in as she reached for her butter tart. "Or was it an episode of *this* show? You weren't exactly clear on that."

"It's not a script! It's . . ." About to say it was real, Tony paused, looked, really looked into Amy's face, and realized he'd never convince her. She had nothing to anchor this kind of a situation on. She'd never faced the possibility of a demon's name written in blood across her city, never seen an ancient Egyptian wizard kill with a glance, never felt sharp teeth bite through the skin of her wrist, never heard the soft sounds of her lover feeding. Well, maybe the latter, but . . . never mind. The point was; if he tried to convince her, she'd think he was either yanking her chain or losing his mind. "It's not a script," he repeated. "It's just an idea." He shoved back his chair and stood. "I need to go talk to Arra."

"Can I have your Nanaimo bar?"

He found a smile from somewhere, probably the same place Lee'd found his earlier. "Sure."

"Work on the hero. The whole thing falls apart without one."

The magic on the basement stairs tried once again to turn him back. Tony gritted his teeth and ignored it. It wasn't real. Or it wasn't any more real than anything thing else she did for *Darkest Night*. It was all smoke and mirrors. Or maybe smoke and shadows . . .

Arra was at her desk, back toward him as he crossed the shadowless room. All but one of her monitors showed solitaire games. On the final monitor she seemed to be combining a graphics program with data entry. Equations scrolled up around a complex spiral made up of strange symbols rather than a solid line. As Tony closed the final distance, the last equation reached the center and disappeared. Arra right clicked her mouse and the spiral flared . . . he had no idea what color that was although watering eyes insisted purple came closest. The light lasted for less than a second, then vanished, and the monitor screen was blank.

About to ask her what she was doing, Tony suddenly realized he didn't have to.

"You're going to gate out. That was a computer mock-up of a new gate!"

"A computer mock-up of a metaphysical construct?" Arra spun around to face him, eyes rolling. "You know that's impossible, right?"

"There are more or less sentient shadows falling through a hole in the air and killing people!" He was shouting. He didn't care. The situation certainly called for shouting and he had no idea how he'd resisted to this point. "I think you'll find that the bar for impossible has been set pretty damned high!"

"Don't you mean low?"

"I have no fucking idea!"

"You tried to tell someone, didn't you?"

"What?"

She jerked her head back toward the solitaire games. "Sixes blocked on all of them. A romantic idea of responsibility and justice; you tried to warn people, to raise the alarm." Her tone softened slightly as she met his eyes again. "The trouble is no one will believe you. You're talking about things that ninety-nine percent of the people of this world refuse to see."

"Yeah. I get that." He'd dialed down the volume, but the anger was still very much there. "They'd believe you."

"Me?"

"You could make them believe you. You could prove that it's real."

"How? With magic? I should show them walking corpses or turn a sofa into a flock of geese? Tony, I do that every day and all they see is a special effect. They've seen wizards fly and petrify their friends and strike down their enemies from across the room. They *know* it's a trick. Nothing I can do will convince the ninety and nine otherwise."

"Fine! What about the one percent?"

"Well . . ." Arra sighed and spread her hands. ". . . that would be you."

"You can't make this whole thing my responsibility!"

"I'm not."

She sounded so calm and matter-of-fact, it drove the volume right back up again. He wanted to wrap his hands around her throat and shake her until she took him seriously; until she agreed to help; until she destroyed the shadows—unfortunately, he could only shout. "You can't just fucking run away from this!"

"Yes, I can."

"But it's *your* fault! You opened the gate to this world! You gave him a way to get here!" A small voice in the back of Tony's head seemed to be suggesting that pissing off a wizard was less than smart. Tony ignored it. "If you run, eventually he'll find that gate, too, and he'll think, 'oh, good idea, another world to conquer' and you'll have to run again. And again. You're thinking of no one but yourself!"

Her lip curled. "And who do you suggest I take through the gate with me? Who chooses who lives and who dies? Do I take you and leave the rest?"

"That's not what I fucking meant! How many worlds are you going to leave in ruins behind you?"

"Do you think I wanted it to turn out this way?" She surged up out of the chair with enough force to slam it back against the desk and shake the monitors.

"I think you don't care that it has."

"Caring means *nothing*!" Loud enough to echo, the word circled around them for a moment. When it faded, she took a deep breath and continued, back in control. "It didn't then, it won't now. It won't ever! If I could have saved my world, I would have! If I could save this world, I would. But I couldn't and I can't, and if all I can save is myself, then I'm not going to sit around here and die! Tell the world if you want to. Give a news conference. Maybe someone in that one percent is a person in power and, convinced, will face the Shadowlord with soldiers and weapons. It still won't matter. It didn't and it won't. He can't be stopped. And if you need to hear it, I'm sorry. But that doesn't matter either. He's barely begun and the end is already in the can. You can't stop it."

"I have to try."

Her snort spoke volumes. "If you go down fighting, you're just as dead as if you lived out your final days happily ignoring the inevitable. I can make you forget again."

"And that worked so well last time," he sneered. "In fact, now that I think of it, your previous work was not exactly inspiring. We don't even know if your potion did anything but drop Lee drunk on his ass. You said that sometimes the shadows have no effect. This could have been one of those times. So you know what? I'm going to take out those four new shadows my . . ."

"Seven."

"What?"

"I counted seven shadows."

"Fine. Whatever. Seven. I'll take them out myself." He spun on his heel, the rubber screaming against the floor, and headed for the stairs. "I don't need you."

"Good. Because I have no intention of watching another world die."

Anger carried him to the top of the stairs, then, hand on the latch, he paused. And turned. He couldn't see the desk, couldn't tell if Arra was still standing where he'd left her but, to borrow a phrase he'd heard too damned many times in the last few minutes, it didn't matter. She could hear him. "What about your cats?"

"What?"

"Your cats. They'll die, too."

"Grow up, Tony. They're cats."

"And you took responsibility for their lives."

As he closed the basement door behind him, he thought he heard her say, "What's two more?" but the words were so quiet and weighted with sorrow, he couldn't be sure.

"Tony, what the hell are you doing?"

It wasn't quite a scream. The complicated patterns of light and darkness that came with television lighting had been scraping at his nerves. Shadows that were nothing more than patches of blocked light kept moving, changing shape, and disappearing. Crawling out from under the worktable, Tony switched off the beam of the strongest flashlight he'd been able to find and twisted around until he could stare up at Adam. "I thought I saw . . ." A quick glance to either side, an obvious check for eavesdroppers, and a lowering of his voice. ". . . a rat."

"Jesus."

"Yeah, well I thought that while I wasn't needed for other stuff, I should have a look and see if I could find droppings and shit."

"Droppings are shit."

"Right."

The 1AD waited a moment then sighed. "And?"

"And what?"

"And did you find any?"

"Not yet, but this place has a billion nooks and crannies."

"Yeah, it's a regular English muffin."

"What?"

"Nothing. Forget it. And keep looking. The last thing we need is to be part of *another* remake of *Willard*."

Official sanction—of a sort—didn't help. By the end of the afternoon, he'd found a dozen pens, a radio, three scripts for two different shows, a rather disturbing number of condom wrappers, and some rodent droppings, but no minions of the Shadowlord.

Seven shadows.

Twenty to thirty people on the soundstage. But not him, or Lee, or Arra. And why not Lee? Because he'd already been taken over and therefore pumped dry of all relevant information? Why not; that theory made as much sense as any of this did. So say, twenty-five minimum. Unless . . . was that why Arra was leaving? Because she was controlled by shadow? Possible, but not likely. After yesterday's adventure in Lee's dressing room, he was about 99% certain that he'd be able to spot the shadow-controlled; so, no easy excuses for the wizard. She was leaving because she was a . . .

"Tony."

Still not quite a scream but getting closer.

Peter frowned. "Are you all right?"

Any one of the twenty-five could have been taken over by shadow. Peter's looked to be attached to his heels, but they were sneaky. Tricky. "Just a little jumpy."

"Well, don't be. I get enough over-emoting from the actors." His smile suggested a shared joke. Tony tried to respond and didn't quite manage. "Anyway, good job on the rat thing. Those little bastards can do more damage than a touring fan club. Which reminds me; there'll be one through on Monday. One of Mason's, I think. So, on your way out, tell someone in the office to order some poison."

"For the fans?"

"Don't tempt me."

"Not poison. The rats eat poison, then they die in the walls or under a piece of equipment and the whole place stinks more than it usually does. We need traps. And not the sticky traps either because then you've just got a scared, pissed-off rat with his feet stuck to a giant roach motel, I mean it's got to be embarrassing for them. We need the kind of traps that . . ." Amy brought the side of her right hand down on the palm of her left.

Tony jumped.

"Are you all right? Because you're looking a little spooked."

"Rat traps. You know, things dying," he continued when she frowned. Amy had been in the soundstage for lunch. He leaned around her desk trying to get a look at her shadow.

"What the hell are you doing?"

"I just . . . nothing. I thought I saw something fall. Off your desk."

Eyes rolled between dark green lashes. "It had better not be the damned highlighter again. I spend half my life crawling around after it." Holding a fall of cranberry hair back with one hand, she shoved her chair out from the desk and bent down. Her shadow went with her.

Not Amy, then.

Not unless this lot was cleverer than yesterday's and were lying low until they got away from the people who might identify them. The person. Him. How was he supposed to follow twenty-five people. *No, stupid, you don't need to. You just need to be back here at 11:15 tonight to take them out. One zap of the lamp. A bright idea that'll shed a little light on the matter. Ha! Take that, Shadowlord. We laugh at your darkness!*

"Yo! Earth to Tony! Is there like a laser site aimed at my forehead or something? Because you've been staring at that same spot for a truly uncomfortable amount of time."

"What?" He blinked and focused on Amy's face. "Sorry. I was thinking."

"It looked painful."

"You'd be surprised." *Oh, man, I'm going to need gallons of that potion.*

"What about?"

He dragged his focus back into the production office and away from the thought of trying to get half a liter of warm, green, sparkly vodka down the throats of seven semiconscious people. Next thing to impossible even with Henry's help. "What was I thinking about?"

Amy snorted. "Duh. Are you dehydrated or something because . . ." She spun her chair around and glared at Veronica, seated at the office's third desk, receiver under her ear and an expression of near panic on her pale face. "Are you going to get that?"

The office PA's eyes widened and "near panic" inched closer to losing the word "near." "I'm already talking to three people, well one person and two on hold, and Barbara wanted me to go through last week's files to find an invoice from Everett and Ruth wants the phone bills entered and filed and . . ."

"Never mind." She turned back to her desk, mouthed *wuss* at Tony, and picked up the phone. "CB Productions . . ."

Allowing the familiar sound to wash over him, Tony turned away from the desk just as Zev emerged from post. Zev! Zev hadn't been on the soundstage in days. There was no way he could be a minion. Although he *was* clearly a little confused by the way Tony was smiling at him, considering how things had been left between them earlier.

Time to fix that. Tony needed to be with someone he knew wasn't possessed and work a little of the twitchy out. Get himself grounded so he could plan. Fill at least some of the time between now and 11:15. Amy would be likely to ask him about his "script" and besides it was Friday night. She probably had a date. Arra—well, he'd had a bellyful of her for one day and he still had to approach her about the potion. Given the cooperation he'd got from her this afternoon, he was definitely going to need Henry for that and Henry wouldn't be awake for another three hours. But Zev! Zev was . . . starting to look just a little nervous.

Ratcheting down the smile, Tony crossed to where the music director was standing. *Hang on. Maybe he has a date, it being Friday night and all.* A little late to worry about that now. "Hey. Sorry I was such an ass yesterday. Can I make it up to you?"

"By not being an ass?"

"Well, yeah. That, too, but I was thinking maybe we could go out for coffee or a beer or you know, something."

Zev's brows rose—arched innuendo.

"No, not that kind of something. I mean, I just thought . . ." He sputtered to a halt and was relieved to see Zev smile.

"Coffee or a beer would be fine. When?"

"Now. Well, as soon as I finish up, which should be no more than half an hour. With Lee gone, we're stopping early."

Zev glanced down at his watch. "I've got to be parked by sunset so that might be cutting it a little close."

"Sunset's not for *three* hours," Tony pointed out then added, as Zev's brows rose again. "They list it in the paper. I just happened to remember." After all those years with Henry, he couldn't stop remembering—no need to mention that.

"Friday night traffic can be a problem, even heading into the city, but I guess half an hour won't make that much difference. It had better be coffee, though. There's a place that carries kosher about four blocks from my apartment; it'd make it a little easier for me if you don't mind."

"I don't mind."

They agreed to meet back in the office and as Zev disappeared back into post, Tony turned to see Amy giving him two thumbs up. Fucking great. Now everyone would assume he and Zev were out on a date. And, except for in Amy's tiny little mind, it wasn't a date. He liked Zev and all, but the music director just wasn't . . .

. . . Lee Nicholas.

God. I really am an ass.

The clientele in the coffee shop/bakery was mostly the same Gen-X group that hung around in coffee shops all over the city; the main difference being that most of the men wore yarmulkes and the bakery sold hamantaschen, the triangular Purim cookies.

"Oh, man, I love these things," Tony enthused as the counter staff put two on a paper plate.

"So do a lot of people," Zev sighed as he moved his tray toward the cash register. "That's why they bake them all year now."

"Is that a problem?"

He shrugged and smiled a little sheepishly. "No, I just think it makes them less . . ."

"Special?"

"Yeah."

"Just part of the whole strawberries in February thing. I have a friend who thinks the world went to hell when we started being able to get strawberries in February," he elaborated as Zev looked confused. "He says we've lost touch with the circle of life."

"I'll pass on the singing warthogs if it's all the same to you."

"Okay, I'm paraphrasing a bit. He doesn't actually quote Disney." Although the thought of Henry facing off against the Mouse was pretty funny. Reaching for his wallet with one hand, he grabbed Zev's arm with the other. "I'll get it. I asked."

"I made you come all the way to South Granville, I'll get it."

"You drove and I'm a lot closer to home than I was."

"I make considerably more than you do."

"Okay." Grinning broadly, Tony stepped back and motioned him forward. "That's convincing."

Although they'd said very little during the drive into the city and had barely spoken during the short walk after parking the car, the silence when they sat down was suddenly weighted. Watching Zev take a swallow of coffee, Tony tried to come up with something they could talk about besides work. Talking about work would just remind him of shadows. Seven shadows. Seven shadows possessing. Seven shadows spying . . .

"Tony?"

"Sorry." He took a bite of apricot hamantasch, chewed, swallowed, and said, "So, what do you do when you're not working?"

It was a good thing they *weren't* dating. He sounded like a major spaz.

"Um . . . you know. The usual stuff. Laundry. Television. Scrabble."

"What?"

His cheeks slightly flushed, Zev stared into his mug. "I play competitive Scrabble."

"Really? I mean, I don't doubt you or anything," Tony hastened to add, "it's just that's so cool. I had a cheap Scrabble CD-ROM I got attached to a box of cereal and the computer kicked my ass, even at the idiot level. And you play competitively?"

"Yes."

"Wow."

"Sometimes I play in Hebrew."

"Now, you're bragging."

"A little."

They shared a smile and all of a sudden it wasn't so hard to find things to talk about.

Zev was an ardent Libertarian, slightly unusual in Socialist-leaning British Columbia. Tony, who'd picked up most of his political beliefs from the bastard son of Henry VIII, had to admit that a number of Zev's points made a lot of sense. Someday, when he thought life was getting dull, he'd mention them to Henry. Fortunately, before Zev could wonder just what he was smiling about, a fan of the show spotted their production jackets, enthused for a few minutes, and reminded Tony that he'd wanted to ask a question about the *Darkest Night* theme.

"That creepy bit under the title; what instrument is that?"

"The piece under the title is all voice. A trio, two women, one man—Leslie, Ingrid, and Joey are their names—I think, it's been a while—but they go by FKO."

"Okay, I get the KO; that's Knockout, but what's the F stand for."

Grinning, Zev raised both hands. "I didn't want to ask."

Eventually, they segued into a discussion of the Olympic highway extension up to Whistler—an obligatory topic when two or more Vancouverites got together.

Away from work, CB Productions' musical director let loose a sardonic sense of humor and was actually a pretty funny guy. And it *wasn't* a date or anything, but Tony was having a good time. Starting to relax. No longer jumping at shadows. Much.

"Is that the time?" Zev shoved his chair out from the table and stood. "I've got to get going."

Tony checked his watch as he got to his feet. 7:25. A little more than half an hour until sunset. Still plenty of time to get Henry and have him convince Arra to prepare more sparkly green vodka.

"I hadn't realized it was so late," Zev continued as he hooked the strap of his laptop case up over one shoulder. "I'm sorry, but I can't drive you home."

"It's okay, I didn't expect you to."

"Do you even know how to get home from here?"

Smiling, Tony fell into step beside him as he headed for the door. "There's a transit stop about ten meters up Oak, Zev. I think I can manage."

"Up Oak along Broadway . . ."

"I've got it."

"It's raining . . ."

"It's Vancouver."

"Good point." Another awkward silence. "I'll, uh, see you at work on Monday."

"Sure." Unless the world ended over the weekend; and a 6,000 watt carbon arc lamp aside, Tony wasn't ruling that out. They stood in the rain for a moment, then Zev shrugged, waved, and headed west along Fifty-first.

There was one other person in the transit shelter, a big guy staring at the city map Plexiglas-ed into one wall. Shifting his backpack onto one shoulder, Tony projected the *I'm not worth bothering vibe* he'd perfected living on the street as he dug around in his backpack for his phone. Past time to call Henry.

Then the big guy looked up.

"Mouse? Jeez, I didn't recognize you."

The cameraman blinked at him, headlights from a passing car throwing shadows across his face.

Except that when the car was gone, the shadows remained.

Crap.

Minion of the Shadowlord front and center.

Big minion.

Really wishing he'd gotten that whole hero thing worked out, Tony stepped back until his shoulders hit Plexiglas and back was no longer an option.

∽ EIGHT

The leading edge of the shadow army was less than a day's march away. Standing on the city walls, mirror raised to catch the late afternoon light, Arra could see past the pockets of battle, past the men and women struggling to defeat an enemy their superior in both strength and numbers, past the black tents well warded against magical attack, and into the swath of destruction that stretched back to the border.

Crops had been burned in the field and the ground salted. She could see the remains of livestock slaughtered and devoured by the invaders. After his victory, the Shadowlord would feed those who abased themselves before him; those who forgot pride and honor and crawled on their bellies to his feet.

Every building still standing after the front line passed by had been put to the torch. When winter came, only the abject would survive.

Above the camps of the captured were stakes that held the bodies of those who had tried to escape, those who had tried to stand up to the random cruelty of their guards, those who hadn't quite given up hope. Some of the bodies were moving, but they were still bodies for all that. The living were prisoners now, slaves when the conquest was complete.

Arra looked away from her mirror and out at the empty landscape between the city and the army. She could see shadows lying where shadows should not be. Moving in ways shadows did not move. The vanguard of the Shadowlord—his eyes and ears.

Magic kept them from the city—hers and the two remaining members of her order. Three. All that was left. Four had died in battle, unable to stand against dark magics fueled by a seemingly endless supply of pain and blood. Two had been killed when they returned to the city controlled by shadow—but not before the shadows had used their power to do great damage. The eldest had died finishing the wards that protected the walls, wards fraying under the constant onslaught of power, wards that would fail, by her calculations, just about the same time the invading army reached the gates.

The last three wizards would walk out together to face the Shadowlord.

In spite of all they had done, in spite of all they had made ready, in spite of all they hoped, their linked power would not be enough.

Arra had looked into the crystal. She knew how this would end.

They would die, then the wards would fail, the gates would fall, and the city, filled to overflowing with those who had thought it a refuge, would be destroyed.

She turned, the heavy rubber soles of her sneakers squealing against the dressed stone. The city stretched out before her now, both the large icons like Stanley Park, Lions Gate Bridge, and Science World as well as the smaller, more personal ones like the Sun-Yat-Sen Garden, The Boathouse, and Café Bergman. All these would fall to shadow, the people into slavery.

No more walking down to the coffee shop on the corner for the *Saturday Globe and Mail* and a double mocha latte.

She looked deep into the cardboard cup she held between both hands and breathed in the steam rising off the foam, enjoying for maybe the last time the scent of . . .

. . . tuna?

That wasn't right. The cup filled with shadow. She fought to draw in breath against the weight on her chest. A point of pain on her chin. And then another . . .

Arra opened her eyes to find Zazu perched on her sternum, one paw half raised, the claws still extended. Freeing her hand from the tangle of the afghan, she rubbed between the black ears.

"We asked for help from those countries we traded with across the sea. And do you know what they said?"

Zazu blinked amber eyes.

"They said, 'This is no concern of ours. *We* are not under attack.'" Arra sighed and waved on the lights. She hated falling asleep on the couch. Sinking into the overstuffed cushions eventually folded her spine into serpentine shapes and the less than comfortable position always brought on dreams. Memories. "Those who conquer for the sake of conquering," she continued, lifting the cat off of her chest and onto the coffee table, "will not let so small a thing as an ocean stand in their way. Do you think the Shadowlord is a concern of theirs now or does he search through the gate for an easier conquest?"

Zazu's answer concerned an empty food dish. Whitby, always the less vocal of the two, knocked a stack of CDs off the table.

"You're right." She grabbed the back curve of the couch, and hauled herself into a sitting position. "This is no concern of yours."

Standing, she watched both cats run for the kitchen and sighed. "Yet."

Tony should never have brought them into this.

Henry had been to Tony's newest apartment, the compromise apartment halfway between downtown Vancouver and Burnaby, only once officially—the week Tony had moved in. Twice if he counted the time he'd caught Tony's scent at a club, followed it out to an alley, then later followed Tony home—wanting to ask just what the hell the younger man thought he was doing but unable to find a way that wouldn't make it seem as though he'd been stalking him like some clichéd horror movie creature of the night. He'd sat in his car, in the rain, watching a shadow move behind curtained windows and reminding himself that Tony was not his responsibility. That he hadn't been for some time. That it was possible to have a friend—to be a friend—and not control the relationship. He wasn't certain which aspect he was trying to convince: vampire or prince. Or if, in this instance, there was any difference between the two.

It was raining again on this, his third, visit, although he was there for a better reason. Tony should have called right after sunset to let him know what had happened at the studio when the gate had opened. What fallout, if any, had there been from their adventure last night. What reaction, if any, from the Shadowlord at the loss of his minion.

Tony hadn't called. Not right after sunset. Not since.

Perhaps he was busy.

The television industry worked obscene hours. It didn't seem to make any difference to the end product, most of which seemed created for hormonally challenged adolescents, but he knew that twelve or thirteen-hour days were the standard. Tony could easily still be at work although it was unlikely that he'd consider a bad forty-three minute syndicated program more important than the possible end of life as he knew it.

Perhaps he was in trouble.

It was possible that the Shadowlord had reacted aggressively and that Tony had borne the brunt of whatever had come through the gate.

Neither possibility could be confirmed by breaking into Tony's apartment, but it was a place to start. And, as it was almost exactly halfway between his condo and the studio, it only made sense to check it first. The answering machine had picked up when he'd called; the recorded voice no answer at all. But then, if CB Productions *had* fallen under the thrall of a dark wizard, it was unlikely anyone would be manning the phones.

Henry'd also called the wizard—who worked with Tony, who'd theoretically also been there when the gate had opened at 11:15 AM. If she was home, she'd invoked the modern magic of call screening.

Tony's building, a three-story brick cube built like a thousand others in the late seventies, had no security. The door leading into the stairwell from the small vestibule holding the mailboxes had been locked while open so that the steel tongue slammed against the frame preventing it from closing. Handy if the residents had friends coming over. Not so handy if they had anything worth stealing. Given the condition of the halls, Henry suspected the latter was unlikely.

The building superintendent was in apartment six. Moments after he answered the door to Henry's knock, Henry was in Tony's apartment and the superintendent had forgotten he'd ever moved away from his recliner.

Tony's sofa bed was unmade, his breakfast dishes still in the sink, and the clothes he'd worn yesterday in a pile on the bathroom floor. The fridge held mostly packets of condiments from various fast food establishments as well as eight eggs, a loaf of bread, a half-empty jar of peanut butter, and a bottle of generic cola. It took Henry a few minutes to find the television remote—although upon reflection the top of the toilet tank was an almost logical place. Disk one of the extended *Two Towers* was in the DVD player and last week's episode of *Federation,* the new *Star Trek* series, was in the ancient VCR. Tony'd mentioned he was saving for a TiVo, but apparently he hadn't managed it yet.

Henry tossed the remote back onto the tangle of blankets. He was no farther ahead than he had been. Although Tony's scent permeated the apartment, he clearly hadn't been there for some hours. He'd gone to work. He hadn't returned.

There were only two possible scenarios. He was still working. He'd been taken by the Shadowlord. Either way, he was still at the studio.

About to open the door, Henry paused. He could feel a life in the hallway; he'd wait until the way was clear. If Tony was all right, if it turned out he was only working late, the fewer people who saw him here the better. Less embarrassing for them both.

Then the life paused outside the door.

And knocked.

Lee Nicholas' familiar face filled the peephole. The distortion made it difficult to read his expression.

As Henry understood it, Tony and the actor were barely considered co-workers given their respective positions on *Darkest Night.* While they might be friendly, they were certainly not friends, and no matter how much Tony might want it to be otherwise, it was highly unlikely that anything more than friendship would ever develop between them.

So, what was Lee Nicholas doing at Tony's door on a Friday night?

Henry smiled. He opened the door, the Hunger held carefully in check. There was always the chance that the actor was controlled by shadow once again and he had no intention of giving away more than he had to.

"Yes?"

The flash of a photogenic smile. "I was looking for Tony Foster." He was nervous. He hid it well, but Henry could smell it. That, and expensive cologne, was all he could smell—there was no taint of another world.

"Tony's not home from work yet."

"That's strange." One hand swept up through dark hair. "I heard they quit early today."

"Early?" Not good.

"Yeah."

"How early?"

"About . . ." The green eyes narrowed slightly as he looked past Henry's shoulder. "Who are you?"

And Henry realized that he'd never bothered to turn on the apartment lights. About to explain that he was on his way out, he watched Lee's gaze track back to the damp patches on the shoulders of his trench coat and decided the truth would serve better than a lie. "I'm looking for him, too." He held up his own key ring. "I have a key." Well, most of the truth.

"Oh." And a visible jump to the wrong conclusion. "Right."

"Did you want to leave a message?"

"What? No, that's okay. I, uh . . . I have to . . . um . . . I left my *date* waiting in the car. I'll see Tony at the studio on Monday."

Interesting emphasis; although the *date* in the car meant this next part had to be quick. He allowed the Hunger to rise to the border of terrifying where coercion waited then caught Lee's gaze with his and held it. "What do you remember of your time under the control of shadow?"

"I don't know what you're talking about!"

Not a lie. Tempted to turn the question to a command, Henry reluctantly acknowledged that the hallway of an apartment building where neither of them lived, with a *date* waiting, with no idea of how the actor would react to the memories, was probably not the best place. So he settled for, "What did you want to speak to Tony about?"

"He was there, this morning, when I . . ." Terror surfaced from the depths of the green. Terror Henry wasn't evoking. ". . . collapsed. I just wanted to know if he . . . If there was anything . . ." Hands rose to waist level, opening and closing as though trying to hang on to the thought. "I just . . ."

This was a man perilously close to the edge. Half tempted to push him over to see where he'd land, Henry allowed his better nature to rule and backed the Hunger down, releasing the actor's eyes. "I'll tell him you stopped by."

"No, that's . . . yeah, sure." Barely holding it together, he turned away then turned back again, dark brows drawn in. "Do I know you? I mean, have we met before?"

Interesting. As far as Henry could remember, they'd never actually met before last night. "Perhaps you've seen me with Tony."

"Yeah. Sure. That must be it." Squared shoulders and a crisp nod, but Henry could see the tremors mortal eyes would miss.

He waited in the hall until he heard the door to the building clang not-quite-closed then hurried down to the landing to look out the window. Shoulders hunched against the rain, Lee Nicholas trotted across the street to where a busty blonde waited in his classic Mercedes. As he got into the car, he said something to make the blonde laugh, his body language suggesting that nothing worse than bad hair had happened to him in the last forty-eight hours.

The man was definitely a better actor than most people gave him credit for.

Tony was with him when he collapsed. Something had happened when the gate reopened. What? And where was Tony?

On cue, his cell phone rang.

"Tony? Where the hell have you been?"

"Close but no cigar, Nightwalker. I assume he's not with you?"

"No."

"He's not answering his phone."

Henry glanced up the stairs toward the apartment before he realized which phone the wizard was referring to. "He can't turn it on in the studio."

"He's not at the studio. They finished early today."

"Sometimes he forgets to turn it on when he leaves." He was grasping at straws and he knew it.

"Seven shadows came through the gate this morning, Nightwalker. Seven. He would have called and told you about that were he able. And then the two of you would have appeared at my door demanding more of my time. More of the potion."

Were he able. "Yes."

"Where are you?"

"At Tony's apartment."

"I assume there's no sign of him?"

"None."

"Wait there. I'll make a couple of calls and get right back to you."

"I had thought, wizard, that you were unwilling to become involved in this fight."

"Did I say anything about fighting?"

He stood there holding his silent phone and admitted that, no, she hadn't. Enough for now that she was willing to help find Tony—who, it seemed, had, one way or another, been taken by shadow.

"You see me."

"Jesus, Mouse, you're a big guy." Tony tried for a sardonic snort and didn't quite make it. "How could I miss you?"

The cameraman's callused hand closed around the back of Tony's neck. "You see me," he repeated. "The voice of the light did not see me. But you see me."

"Yeah, well, seeing a little too much of you right now." Mouse's face loomed so close over his that Tony could see every broken capillary, every enlarged pore, and he was getting a really good look at the scar from where Mouse's ex-wife had jabbed a nail file through his nose. He placed both hands flat against the barrellike chest and shoved. It worked about as well as he'd expected it to. "You want to back off a bit?"

"No. You and I are going to have a . . ." He fell silent, eyes squinted nearly shut as a set of high beams swept through the bus shelter.

Out of the direct line of light, Tony could see the police car approaching. Could see it slowing down. *Yes! Let's hear it for law and order. Little guy's getting manhandled by big guy, and the police . . .*

Mouse's mouth closing over his cut off the thought. And pretty much every other thought besides: *What is it with shadows in straight boys coming on to me?*

By the time Mouse lifted his head, the police car was gone.

Just fucking great, Tony thought, wiping his mouth on his sleeve. *We couldn't be in Toronto, where the cops'll bust your ass for PDAs. Oh, no, we have to be in fucking officially-tolerant-of-alternative-lifestyles Vancouver.*

"Don't do that again," he snarled.

"Or you'll what?"

"Tell Mouse's old lady."

A flash of fear. Either Mouse was in there listening or the shadows took on more than the physical form of the bodies they wore. Tony had a feeling that was important, but he didn't have time to work out why as Mouse's hand tightened to the point of pain and he was propelled out of the bus shelter and into the rain. "Hey! Where are we going?"

"Somewhere . . . quiet."

That didn't sound good. Tony went along without struggling, being no threat, no problem, giving Mouse no reason to think he might make a run for it. When they stopped beside Mouse's 1963 cherry-red, Mustang convertible, when Mouse—or rather the thing in Mouse's body—started digging for his keys, Tony dropped straight down to his knees, spun around, surged back up onto his feet, took two running steps away, and crashed face first into the wet sidewalk. His teeth went into the edge of his lip and his mouth filled with blood. He spat and twisted around. Within the circle of the light from the streetlamp, Mouse's shadow tangled with his.

The shadows in the bodies controlled the shadows of the bodies—he should have remembered that—and those shadows could mess with the shadows of people—like him—who weren't being controlled. And that made so little real world sense it sounded like one of the less than brilliant ideas the bull pen horked up after a night of generic beer and cheese pizza.

Mouse smiled broadly enough for a pair of gold crowns to glitter. "Get in the car."

Tony spat again. He was through making it easy. "Make me."

One huge hand grabbed the waistband of his jeans, the other both straps of his backpack. A moment later he was in the passenger seat. He spared half a thought for the total shit-fit Mouse was going to have when he was back in control of his body and saw his upholstery and then tried to fling himself out the door.

Mouse's shadow flowed up and over his face.

Oh, crap . . .

Clawing at it didn't work. It gave under his fingers and then seeped back into the gouges. He already knew he couldn't breathe through it . . .

*　　*　　*

Phone cradled between ear and shoulder, Arra tossed another handful of lemon balm into the vodka. "You might want to write this down, Nightwalker. He's at the Four Corners Bakery and Coffee Shop on Oak by Fifty-first—in South Granville. It's right by Schara Tzedeck, the Orthodox synagogue."

"You did a locator spell."

"No, I called Amy, his friend from work." A sniff of the steam and a bit more elecampane root. "She overheard Tony and Zev talking as they were heading for the parking lot."

"Tony and Zev?"

"Uh-huh." She pushed Zazu away from the stove with the side of her foot and wondered if she shouldn't have waited until the last minute to add the catnip.

"He had a *date?*"

"He's young, he's single, and it's Friday night." Arra grinned as the Nightwalker sputtered. "Jealous?"

"No. I am *not* jealous! I am . . ." The pause lasted long enough for her to get the cap off the jar of bay leaves. ". . . *appalled.* How can he consider dating, knowing what he knows about the Shadowlord."

"Knowing what he knows, he's wise to enjoy himself while he can." She could feel the grin slipping away. "I'll have potion enough for seven ready before the gate opens again."

He started to say something, but she shrugged the phone down into her hand and hit the disconnect. If he wanted to find Tony and if the two of them wanted to shine bright lights on the Shadowlord's spies, that was their business. Eventually, one of two things would happen; they'd realize they were whistling into the wind or they'd die fighting.

Since they'd already forced her involvement, she'd continue to make sure the taken had a chance to recover. Having done it once, balking at doing it again seemed foolish. And it put her in no more danger than any other person on this world.

This world.

Just another place she couldn't save.

There were people in the building who'd take the cats when she left.

"I saw you this morning."

"Yeah? So?" Tony had pressed himself back as far into the bucket seat as he could, trying and failing to get away from Mouse's shadow as it pooled in his lap like a big, black . . . really creepy thing! It moved continually, like liquid but not, and in a futile attempt to get out from under its cool weight, his balls had climbed up so high they were practically sitting on his shoulder.

"You ran to Lee's side."

"Because he fell!"

"No." Mouse glanced over at him and then turned his attention back to Friday night traffic on the Granville Bridge. "You moved before he fell. You know something."

"I don't know anything! I just did what anyone would do."

"No one did."

"Did what?"

"What you did."

Tony rolled his eyes. Mouse had always been one of those guys who saw no point in using five words if three would almost do the job. "I was already there, so no one else had to do anything, did they?"

The cameraman/minion of the Shadowlord shrugged; a minimalist move of one burly shoulder that was all Mouse. As was the two-wheeled turn onto Hastings Street and the speed he was using to maneuver the Mustang around lesser vehicles. Tony thought the driver of a dark green Chevy Impala flipped them off as they passed, but they went by too quickly for him to be sure. *Oh, sure, if he drove like this across the border in the US, some guy with a Bud tucked in his crotch'd get so pissed off he'd haul out the shotgun and pop a few off, which would get the cops into the act and we'd end up on the next episode of FOX TV's* High Speed Chases *heading for a dramatic finish where minion-guy here rolls the Mustang and I get rescued!*

Unfortunately, they were in Canada and the worst that could happen would be having the license plate recorded by the occupants of a police car who weren't allowed to participate in a high speed chase lest someone get hurt. There were times, and this was one of them, when that whole peace, order, and good government thing totally sucked.

And if Mouse allowed himself to be pulled over? A massive fine, six points off his license, and no chance in hell any cop would believe Tony's story. Amy hadn't believed him and Amy was his friend. Of course, years of experience with cops meant he'd have no trouble coming up with the kind of commentary that'd get his ass hauled out of the car. Police brutality, use it wisely. Then Henry'd come bail him out and he'd be safe. His moment of hope faded when he realized Mouse—or rather the minion riding in Mouse—would never allow himself to be pulled over.

A sudden lane change—closer to a lateral movement than should have been possible in a thirty-year-old Ford—nearly threw the shadow off Tony's lap. Without thinking, he caught it and scooped it back into place. It sloshed a bit and then settled, cool and weighted, against him.

His hand felt . . . soiled. He scrubbed it against the side of the seat.

"Stop that."

"But . . ."

"Now."

No mistaking the threat in Mouse's low growl, but it almost wasn't enough. Tony'd never wanted his hands clean quite so badly. And, once, way back, he'd held vomit. Someone else's vomit. Sitting there, suddenly terrified, he understood why people took wire brushes to their own skin.

A little surprised that a kosher bakery hadn't closed for the Sabbath—although there was no actual reason *all* the staff had to be Orthodox or even Jewish for that matter—Henry picked up Tony's scent on the door. He wasn't inside, he wasn't anywhere in sight, and it was still almost raining in that ubiquitous West Coast more-than-a-mist not-quite-actual-drops way. It wouldn't be easy to track him.

On the bright side, in this neighborhood at this time on a Friday, there weren't a lot of people on the street.

Maybe he'd gone home with Zev.

And if he has . . . The growl sounded low in his throat before Henry could prevent it. An elderly man sitting at one of the bakery's small tables glanced up and, feeling a little foolish, Henry turned back toward the street. He should just call the wizard for Zev's address. The music director was a nice guy, attractive, smart—Tony could do worse. Perhaps a little of Arra's end-of-the-world pessimism had rubbed off and Tony was taking advantage of an opportunity to do what any young man would do in the same circumstances. Perhaps he'd decided to celebrate their victory over the shadow that had possessed Lee Nicholas. Perhaps whatever had happened with Lee Nicholas at the studio that morning had driven him into the arms of another.

Henry shook his head to clear that last thought. *Perhaps I've been writing romances for far too long.*

There were any number of valid reasons Tony hadn't called him.

But the wizard's phrase "were he able" kept sounding over and over again in Henry's head.

If Tony hadn't gone home with Zev, he'd have taken the bus north up Oak. A three-meter walk to the transit shelter would settle it once and for all. If Tony's scent wasn't in the shelter, he'd call the wizard for Zev's address. If it was . . .

It was.

The damp air had kept the scent from dissipating. Scent of Tony. Scent of fear. Scent of another world.

Seven shadows had come through that morning.

One of them seemed to have been studying the city map on the side of the shelter.

A mix of the two—one dragged by the other against the outside wall.

Away from the shelter, the rain had washed most of the Tony scent away but had had little effect on the other. Even the weather seemed to be avoiding it. It was easy enough to follow, though.

Henry snarled as the Hunger surged up at the scent of blood; faint, diffused, but unmistakable. Unmistakably Tony's.

On the sidewalk, caught in cracked concrete.

Again at the edge of the road, a drop against the side of the curb barely above the water running past in the gutter.

The obvious explanation: Tony had been flung, injured, into a car. The shadow-held had followed.

And the car had then been driven away.

He could be anywhere.

They were heading for the studio. There was no other reason for them to be in Burnaby. Well, actually, according to the Burnaby Chamber of Commerce there were any number of reasons, but in this specific instance Tony had a feeling that only the studio and its gate to another world was actually relevant. "I won't tell you anything."

Mouse merely swung out around an SUV, muttered, "Fucking Albertans," and kept driving.

"I don't *know* anything!"

"You see me."

"Total fluke, I swear. I had a few years there where I did a lot of drugs. Probably melted the 'I don't see you' parts of my brain." He was babbling. He knew it, but he couldn't seem to stop the flow of words spilling out of his mouth. "I've seen a lot of things, you know. Things you wouldn't believe. That's probably why I see you. That's all."

Racing the end of an amber light, Mouse turned his head, eyes narrowed. "What have you seen?"

Shit.

"Nothing like you!"

The shadow pooled in Tony's lap began to slosh slowly back and forth, its movement independent of the movement of the car.

"Like what?"

A truck roared by in the other direction, horn blaring.

"Like watch the fucking road, man!" Heart slamming against his ribs, half convinced that the puddle in his lap was significantly warmer than it had been, Tony fought to bring his breathing under control as Mouse calmly swerved back into the eastbound lane. What would happen to the shadow if its host was jam under an eighteen wheeler? *And since I'll be jam along-side him, do I really want to know?*

*   *   *

Arra had no intention of getting into the Nightwalker's car. She'd bring the two thermoses of potion down to the curb, pass them over, and wish him godspeed. Pick a god. If Tony had been taken by one of the shadow-held—Well, it was a shame, but it wasn't her concern.

"But it's your fault! You opened the gate to this world! You gave him a way to get here!"

"I did not." She shrugged into a bright yellow raincoat and pulled her umbrella out of the painted milk can by the door. "All right, technically, I opened the gate, but it closed behind me. I went through it and it closed, and that's where my part in this ended."

Zazu rubbed up against her ankles and she pushed her away from the door. "Don't even think about it." A thermos tucked neatly into each of the huge yellow pockets. "I'll be back in . . ." Whitby raced down the hall chasing invisible invaders. Fur up, tail to one side, he slid to an undignified heap under the coffee table. Arra sighed. "Well, I'll be back."

"You're thinking of no one but yourself!"

Locking the door to her apartment, she headed for the elevator, ignoring with the ease of long practice the voice shouting accusations in her head.

"Caring means nothing!"

Her own voice had taken up the litany. That was new.

"If you're expecting me to argue that, think again," she muttered as the elevator doors opened.

Julian Rogers, her neighbor from across the hall, shifted his chihuahua to his other arm and sniffed disdainfully as he pushed past her. "Talking to yourself again, Arra?"

"I find it's the only way to have an intelligent conversation around here. And your dog is fat," she added with the doors safely closed.

The Nightwalker's car pulled up to the curb seconds after she arrived. If he'd taken a little longer, given her more time to think . . . but he hadn't, and when he reached across the front seat and opened the passenger door, she folded her umbrella, shook it once, and climbed in. She wouldn't waste either her time or her strength fighting the Shadowlord, but if the Nightwalker intended to rescue Tony, she had information that might help.

Might.

Might not.

Of course the whole thing would be moot if she died in a fiery car crash before she even got her seat belt done up. Thrown left and then right as the Nightwalker roared back onto the street and then around the corner onto Denman. The thermoses were making it impossible to do up her seat belt, so she pulled them out and set them at her feet—under her feet after a particularly angular lane change cracked one against her ankle.

"What makes you think the shadow-held is taking Tony to the studio?" she asked, finally managing to buckle up.

"He's being taken somewhere and the only somewhere these things have is the gate."

"That's logical enough, I suppose."

"You suppose? If you have a better idea . . ."

"No. And watch the road!" As he turned his gaze back to traffic, Arra tugged at a plastic fold in her lap. "I won't face it. I won't get that close to the shadow-held. Not again."

"Then why are you here?"

"We used to say, in my world, in my order, that knowledge is power."

"We say that here as well."

"Duh."

A muscle jumped in the Nightwalker's jaw. "You have knowledge I can use."

She shrugged, the plastic over her shoulders crinkling. "I have knowledge; whether or not you can use it, that's up to you. What I know is theory, extrapolated from past experience and the little I've observed since this . . . invasion began. The first shadows were scouts with no independence. It was as though the Shadowlord swept dark sponges through the gate and then squeezed out what they'd picked up. A second-generation scout followed us away from the studio on that location shoot and then returned with us. Then he sent through a shadow specifically seeking to know if there were lives here he could use . . . and Nikki Waugh died. He examined her life and decided that, yes, these were lives he could control."

"How do you know what he decided?"

"The people here are very like my people were—a little more technologically advanced but otherwise not so different." The streetlights divided the night into flickering shadow. Arra stared at the dashboard. "And that was what he decided the last time; when his shadow brought him one of *our* lives. Now, he sends spies to gather information to ease his conquest. The shadow in Lee Nicholas was what we called a rider, designed to live his life for a time and then return to be—reusing the sponge analogy—squeezed dry. On my world, the first riders stayed no more than a couple of hours. Then days. The last two we destroyed had been within their hosts for just over a week, making over those hosts into dark shadows of themselves."

Two members of her order died screaming, darkness pouring from them.

Arra shook herself free of the memory. "If one of the shadow-held has grabbed Tony . . ."

"One has." The two words were a low growl.

"... then they're showing a greater degree of independence than he granted them in the past."

"He's had some years to work on refining them. In the time since you left, he could have created a whole new kind of shadow with, as you say, a greater degree of independence."

"So you're saying my information is out of date? Useless to you?"

Eyes locked on the road, he ignored her question. "I think he's sent these shadows through to discover what destroyed the shadow that was in Lee Nicholas. I think he sent them through looking for the light."

"It was a carbon arc lamp . . ."

"The metaphorical light."

The metaphorical light? Arra repeated silently. Then asked aloud, "And what makes you think that?"

"I've done some detective work in the past . . ."

"A vampire detective? Well, that's . . . original."

The steering wheel creaked under the Nightwalker's tightened grip. Probably not wise to poke at him—all right, definitely not wise—but impossible to resist. "The . . . shadow-held as you call it, grabbed Tony less than two blocks away from the largest, oldest Orthodox synagogue in Vancouver."

"And you think?"

"That Tony was coincidence. He was grabbed because he was there and knew the shadow for what it was. That the other six shadows are checking out churches and mosques. This world has no wizards, but it *has* light."

Temples fell, bodies seeking sanctuary were crushed under burning rubble.

"Not the kind that will help."

He glanced over at her, his eyes dark. "It causes you pain."

"What does?" she asked suspiciously.

"Talking about the shadows."

"Yeah. Well . . ." Arra grabbed for the dashboard as he accelerated through the end of an amber light and the beginning of a red. Horns blasted out a protest from two different directions. ". . . it's a welcome distraction from your driving!"

It was Mouse and it wasn't Mouse, Tony decided by the time they reached the industrial park. The shadows were a separate personality—it had referred to itself as *me* so it had to be self-aware—but obviously they used parts of the personalities of their hosts. *Unless that other world comes with muscle cars and Vin Diesel wanna-bes.* Tony closed his eyes as the Mustang slithered between two trucks and opened them again as they turned into the studio parking lot.

Unfortunately, symbolism—not to mention the whole minion-of-an-evil-wizard thing—suggested the shadows used the darker parts of their hosts. These days, Mouse was a quiet guy who worked hard and seldom partied, but Tony'd heard some stories about Mouse's past, stories that came with interesting scars, stories that always finished with, "You should see the other guy."

He really didn't want to be the other guy.

He didn't think he'd be strong enough not to spill his guts. He wrapped a hand around his stomach, just above the line of shadow. He'd talk. He'd tell them how much he'd seen since the beginning. He'd tell them how he destroyed the shadow as it left Lee.

Lee . . .

Had it been the shadow or the darker parts of Lee putting the moves on him? And this was *so* not the time to be thinking about that.

✒ NINE

Way past time to change that code, Tony thought muzzily as Mouse worked the keypad one-handed. The shadow covered his mouth and lapped at the edge of his nose, sending the occasional tendril up into his nostrils—playfully or threateningly, Tony wasn't sure. His stomach heaved, but puking wasn't an option with his mouth already full.

The moment the car had stopped, he'd thrown open the door and flung himself out into the parking lot, mouth open to scream for help. They'd crossed the too-macho-to-scream line way back on Oak Street. Cool weight around his ankles had slammed him to the ground. The double pain of gravel cutting into his palms had been lost in the feel of shadow wrapping around him and cutting off all sound by slithering into his mouth.

Mouse had taken the time to lock the car, then had hauled him onto his feet and half carried, half walked him to the studio's back door. Struggling had resulted in the remaining airflow being cut off until he calmed. One short visit to suffocation land had been enough to convince Tony that struggling was a very bad idea.

The door opened. A large hand between his shoulder blades shoved him into the dark soundstage. Stumbling forward, he missed the sound of the door closing behind him, but as he found his balance, he clearly heard the snap of the lock reengaging. It was the first sound in a while to drown out the pounding of his heart. So much for rescue.

Tony strained to see as Mouse dragged him off to the left, moving unerringly around bits of set and equipment, the ambient light from the exit signs and various scattered power indicators obviously enough for him to maneuver. Unlike Lee last night, he didn't bother turning on the overhead lights. Hang on . . .

Shadows required a minimum amount of light for . . . well, definition was probably the closest word. A shadow without definition would be fuzzy. Fuzzy meant a weaker shadow, right? Not the shadow in Mouse but Mouse's shadow. The shadow actually holding him.

He took a tentative breath through his mouth.

Found he could breathe.

Ripping free of Mouse's loose grip on the back of his neck, Tony ran for the far end of the soundstage and the door to the production offices. *It can't be much after 9:00. 9:30 tops. Maybe quarter to ten. Ow! Son of a bitch!* He stumbled around whatever he'd run into—a light pole from the crash as it hit the floor—bounced off a wall, got his bearings, and lengthened his stride. No way the geeks in post were gone so early. It wasn't like they had somewhere to go on a Friday night. All he had to do was get to the . . .

The rounded edge of Raymond Dark's leather wing chair caught him across the stomach. Gasping for breath, he fell forward, rolled across the seat on his shoulders, and hit the floor. He was still fighting to untangle his feet from the coffee table when the lights came on. Definitely a good news/bad news situation. He could see—he kicked himself free and scrambled to his feet—but the moment Mouse caught up to him, he'd be . . .

The fake Persian rug spread over the concrete floor did nothing to cushion the impact. He rolled sideways, slammed up against Mouse's legs, and was hauled to his feet.

"You done?"

The knee in the crotch took the big man completely by surprise. More than willing to fight dirty—the definition of someone who fought fair against a guy twice his size was *loser*—Tony put everything he had in it and hit the ground running. Fingers closed around a handful of his jacket. He squirmed free.

And then he was back on the floor, the rug grinding into his cheek, a massive knee grinding into the center of his back.

Oh, yeah, I'm done.

No more messing around with shadows, Mouse had taken that last blow personally. Not much point in defending himself either although Tony did what he could. When Mouse finally hauled him back onto his feet—*Third time lucky, big guy?*—he dangled. Heels dragging, he watched the ceiling go by as Mouse hauled him out of the office, across a concrete corridor, and into the empty space that had been the living room set. Monday morning it was due to be set up as a Victorian dining room for a dinner party flashback.

He couldn't quite keep his head from bouncing as he hit the floor. Once the bells had stopped ringing, he realized he was in the exact spot, and pretty much the exact position, Lee had been in last night. Under other circumstances, he'd have appreciated that more.

The gate wouldn't open for hours—hour . . . a while . . . he'd kind of lost track of time—so what the hell were they doing here? Mouse couldn't take him home and whale on him, not without having to do some explaining to the old lady, but surely there were better places for the kind of question and answer session about to happen. Unless ET's shadow was about to call home.

Humor hurt.

So did a number of other things.

Tony didn't think his ribs were broken. *Broken* ribs would have hurt a lot more when Mouse squatted beside him, grabbed the front of his T-shirt, and yanked him into a sitting position. He was working on passive resistance now. And apologies to Mr. Gandhi, but it didn't seem to be any more successful than the active kind.

About the only part of him unpummeled was his face; it seemed black eyes and broken noses would be making up the big finale. Looking at the bright side, at least he had a head start on passing out.

As he sagged forward, he caught sight of Mouse's shadow flowing up over his feet. So they were going back to suffocation land. *Been there, done that. Hurts less. Yay.*

Except Mouse's shadow was also stretched out behind him; across the floor, up the side of a chair, behaving its two-dimensional self.

Two shadows?

Seven shadows had come through the gate.

Oh, fuck.

"I'm not getting out of the car, Nightwalker." Arra locked both hands around the shoulder strap of the seat belt. "If I get too close, the shadow-held will know me."

"Then why . . ." When she turned to face him, Henry realized there was no point in finishing the question. He knew terror when he saw it, knew what it could do, how it could hold a person. The wizard's reasons for accompanying him this far were moot—she wasn't going any farther. "Fine. How do I fight it?"

Her grip relaxed slightly and he wondered if she'd honestly thought she'd be strong enough to prevent him from dragging her out of the car had that been his decision. "I'd use the same light you used last night."

"Will that work while the shadow's still in a host?"

"I doubt it." Her gaze turned inward for a moment; when she focused on him again, her expression was bleak. "Kill the host and the shadow will leave."

"Kill the host?"

"Don't even try to tell me you have a problem with that, Nightwalker."

"And you have never killed to survive?"

"Yes, but . . ."

"Killed for power?"

"Not the innocent."

"And who declared them guilty?"

Another night, questions from another wizard. The similarity was . . . ultimately unimportant.

"I don't kill the innocent."

This wizard shrugged. "Suit yourself, Nightwalker. But it's the only way."

The other wizard had also called him Nightwalker; used it as this one did, as a definition. He turned into the production company's parking lot. "Call me Henry."

"It doesn't matter what I call you, I know what you . . . Mouse."

"What?"

She nodded toward the red Mustang as Henry pulled into the parking place beside it. "That's Mouse Gilbert's car. He's one of the cameramen. He's big. Strong. If he's shadow-held, you might have a little trouble."

Henry stopped the car, slammed it into neutral, and turned off the engine. "No. I won't."

He was at the back door before the sound of the engine died.

And then back at the car again.

Arra jumped as his face appeared outside her window, a pale oval suspended in the night. A pale *pissed* oval. She rolled down the window.

"It's locked. Do you know the code?"

"Why would I?" she snorted. "I never go in through the soundstage; I have a key for the front door . . . oh. Right."

The front door lock was stiff. After a moment wasted, Henry reamed the key around hard enough to twist half of it off in the hole—fortunately, *after* the tumblers had turned. He slipped inside, leaving the ruined key where it was.

There were people in the small offices to both his right and his left. Two right, three left; five hearts beating out an espresso rhythm. They were noted in a heartbeat of his own and ignored. He moved on. Farther in.

The doors on the far wall were labeled, black letters on sheets of white office paper, the contrast so great that in spite of the darkness even mortal eyes would have been able to read them. WARDROBE. POST. SPECIAL EFFECTS. KEEP THIS DOOR CLOSED.

Henry opened the last door and found himself pushing through racks of clothing. He couldn't hear Tony. He should have been able to hear Tony. If Tony's heart was still beating. If it wasn't, a second death became a lot more likely. Easy enough to race along scent trails to another door and another sign: DO NOT ENTER WHEN RED LIGHT IS ON.

The soundstage.

Soundproof.

As he pushed open the door, the terrified pounding of Tony's heart rushed out to fill all available spaces. Snarling, Henry ran toward the source, following it unerringly through the maze of walls and cables and equipment. There was light, but he didn't need it. Tony's terror acted as both guide and goad.

He found Tony on the floor under the gate, half-sitting, cradled in a parody of affection against the body of a large man. His heels drumming on the floor, Tony clawed at both meaty arms wrapped around his chest.

Henry came one running step closer.

And saw the band of shadow across Tony's eyes.

Two steps.

The shadow disappeared.

Three steps.

Tony stopped struggling. His heart slowed between one beat and the next to just below normal speed.

The man—Mouse—let go. Head cocked to one side, Tony folded his legs and sat cross-legged on the concrete. Then he looked up and met Henry's eyes.

"I see you, Nightwalker."

Henry snarled to a stop inches from Tony's folded legs.

"Just so you know, I'm not going to let you stop this," the thing that wasn't Tony added as Mouse rose slowly to his feet.

In his own time, Henry had not been tall. In this century, he was short. Mouse—the thing that was Mouse—towered over him.

"You have no power over us, Nightwalker."

Henry glanced down at Tony, back up at Mouse, smiled and swung, not particularly caring about the crack of bone. From the look of him, the cameraman had probably been in hundreds of fights. This one ended before he had a chance to join in. His head snapped back, his eyes rolled up until only the whites showed, and he crumpled to the concrete.

His shadow hit the concrete with him and no metaphysical shadows appeared. It seemed that an unconscious body produced an inoperative shadow. That was definitely something to remember.

"He'll be pissed when he wakes up." The Tony-thing sounded almost cheerful as he stood. "Even think of slamming me like that and before I go, I'll fry the kid's wetware."

Henry forced his fists back down by his side and growled, "Get out of him!"

"No problem. The moment the gate opens, I'm gone. I know what he knows and he knows what the boss wants to know."

"He doesn't know anything."

"And I'd believe that, too, except I'm in his head and you aren't, dude."

"Dude?"

"Hey, that's in here."

Perhaps, but it wasn't a designation Tony would ever use for him. The impersonation was off by just a few degrees. Something else to remember.

"And so's the info on what destroyed the earlier minion," he continued. "Not as much about this world's tech as the boss'll want, but the other stuff he knows, that'll so make up for it. This guy . . ." An exaggerated tap to one temple. ". . . knows where that pesky wizard ended up. Who'd have thought she'd be stupid enough to stay so close to the gate?" The thing rolled Tony's eyes. "Wizards, eh? Too stupid to keep running, too fucking freaked to save the world. Boss'll be overjoyed to have found her after all this time. Unfinished business, you know how it is."

Henry let the words wash over him as he circled around, looking for an opening. Although an opening to what, he wasn't certain. Tony's body turned with him, pivoting around on one heel.

"You're making me dizzy. I'm going to hurl hamantaschen." It glanced down at Tony's watch. "10:02. A little more than an hour. What are we going to do with ourselves, Henry? You hungry?" Familiar fingers pulled the collar of the T-shirt down off Tony's throat, exposing bruises rising along the ridge of his collarbone.

The sight of blood pooling under Tony's skin, the knowledge of exactly what had to have been done to mark him so, pushed Henry back to the edge. He stopped circling. His lips pulled back off his teeth. He let the Hunger rise. Scavengers would not have what was his until he was done with it.

"Tony. Is. Mine."

"I recognize your power, Nightwalker." Tony's cadences were gone. "But you cannot move me from this body until I am ready to leave."

The thing's words were drowned out under the song of Tony's blood.

He felt a warm weight wrap around his legs and he ignored it. All that mattered was the life he had claimed, not once but countless times. "Mine."

"Not right now, dude."

"MINE!"

Sudden recognition flared behind the shadows in Tony's eyes. Followed by a fear so primal all else fled before it. His heart began to pound. Faster. Faster.

Then his eyes rolled back and he doubled forward, retching.

Shadow poured from his mouth and nose, pooled on the concrete, moved toward Henry. He retained barely enough hold on self to realize this was not something he could fight and in the face of it, the Hunger began to fade. One step back. Two. He had no idea how to control the light they'd used the night before or even if it was still in place. Tony, who knew, was on his knees, arms wrapped around his body like he was trying to hold disparate pieces of flesh together.

Arra pulled the front door open, paused, and looked down at the broken lock. Maybe she should just stay here and fix it. Maybe she should have just stayed in the car. Actually, no *maybe* about it . . .

She stepped into the office.

What the hell am I doing?

The thermoses were comforting weights in her pocket. Their contents would be useless as long as the shadow remained in Mouse, but they were a clear indication of what her role was in this . . . this ridiculous attempt to save a world already lost.

She glanced toward CB's office and almost wished he was there. Almost wanted to walk through his door, walk past the fish tank, almost wanted to stand in front of his desk and confess all. Fortunately, he was in Whistler with two of his kids from his first marriage. She had no idea what they were doing in Whistler at this time of the year, but whatever it was, it was keeping her from making an ass of herself in front of the one person in this world likely to ask the right questions.

The costumes rustled as she passed as though they whispered among themselves; a choir boy's cassock asking a slightly shiny tux what was happening.

Good question.

It was curiosity; that was all, the same thing that had prodded her out of the basement and up onto the soundstage in time for the morning opening of the gate. Wizards were like cats. Curious. Sometimes, it got them killed.

Not me. I know when to run.

She pushed open the door and heard retching. In the silence of the soundstage, it could have been coming from anywhere.

Yeah, right. Who am I kidding . . .

Tony was on his knees under the inactive gate, looking like crap, the last bit of shadow dribbling from his nose. Mouse was stretched out behind him. Maybe dead. Fully separate now from its last host, the shadow slithered across the floor toward Henry.

He was fast. It was faster.

Did it know what he was? Would it be able to control him? From the look of things, it was going to have a damned good try at it. If it succeeded, a shadow-held Nightwalker would be able to destroy this small resistance.

As darkness swarmed up Henry's body, Arra reacted. The questions and the commentary shut off and her hands rose. She'd cast the incantation countless times in the last futile attempt, it wasn't one she was ever likely to forget.

The shadow froze, twisted in on itself, and vanished with a soft *sputz*.

Moving quickly, before the questions had a chance to start up again, she jogged across the empty set to Mouse's side, the rubber soles of her sneakers squealing against the floor. She dropped to her knees, and, grabbing two handfuls of his jacket, heaved him over onto his back. As his head bounced once against the floor, his eyes opened.

"You!"

"Me," she agreed and drove her hand wrist-deep into his chest. Only the element of surprise gave the maneuver any chance at all, and for a moment she was afraid surprise wouldn't be enough. Then her searching fingers closed. Leaning back on her heels, she hauled the shadow clear, flinging it free and destroying it in the same movement.

If asked, she'd have had to say that final *sputz* was one of the most satisfying sounds she'd heard in the last seven years.

Except that no one was asking.

When she turned, it was to see Henry crouched in front of Tony, one pale hand extended. To her surprise, Tony flinched back from his touch.

"Not yours," he said hoarsely. "My own!"

The Nightwalker nodded. "I know."

And then they both pretended to believe it.

Holding in the hurt, Tony remembered. Lee hadn't remembered—maybe because the shadow had left him, not been puked out—but Tony did. Remembered how it felt to be trapped in the back of his own head, able to feel his body, to know it was his, but to have no control over it. He felt it move, heard it speak, and could do nothing to prevent either. It threw him back to his worst times on the street, when he was young and new and too stupid to run. He couldn't win if he fought and screaming made no difference because no one would hear him. He'd learned to hide, to just let things happen.

Maybe that was why he remembered; because he'd been there before.

Christ, he hurt. Ribs, back, arms, legs, brain . . .

When Henry stood, he almost laughed. Henry standing. Him on his knees. That final "MINE!" still sounded with every beat of his heart and resounded at every pulse point. The barely healed bite on his wrist throbbed.

It didn't help that Henry's Prince of Darkness face was essentially the same face he wore for everyday. Nothing changed; no bumpy foreheads, no road map of veins, just a thin veneer of civilization over a primal Hunger. A Hunger that seduced even as it devoured.

"*MINE.*"

The seduction frightened Tony more than the Hunger. Even shadow-held, he'd responded. Death had called in its marker and his answer had been to evict the current possessor, acknowledging the earlier claim. He was alive because Henry wanted him alive. He'd die when Henry decided it was time. Sure, that applied to pretty much everyone who shared a vampire's territory, but he *knew* it. Personally. Hell, Biblically. He bit his lip to keep from laughing. If he started, he doubted he'd be able to stop.

Henry would never let him go.

As unpleasant as the implications were, bottom line, it had saved him.

Right on cue, Henry held out a hand.

Tony forced himself not to flinch back again.

"Tony?"

He understood the question Henry was asking. Were they okay? He supposed it depended on the definition of okay. Henry's mask was back in place so, honestly, had anything changed? Same mask as he'd been wearing, covering the same power. And the shadow was gone. And it wasn't like that whole possessive thing should be a surprise. *And fuck, Tony, stop fucking thinking so goddamned much!*

It all came down to trust, really, and if he trusted Henry enough to let him open a vein and drink, then he might as well keep trusting him to not abuse the power that gave him.

Not to abuse it much, anyway.

Unwrapping his right arm from around his stomach, he gripped Henry's cold fingers and allowed the vampire to pull him to his feet. "We're cool." He turned to Arra before Henry could respond. Further conversation on the topic was way more than he wanted to face. "How's Mouse?"

She looked up, liquid continuing to dribble from a thermos cap down between Mouse's lips. "Well, I'm no doctor, but I think his jaw's broken."

"Broken?"

"Interesting purple knot coming up on one side, too." Her lip curled slightly. "You don't know your own strength, Nightwalker."

Tony had no need to turn to know that Henry's lip had curled in answer.

"Yes," he said. "I do."

Arra's gaze flickered between the two men, settled on Tony, and she made a speculative noise that could have referred to anything. Setting the plastic cap on the broad shelf of Mouse's chest, she reached down into her pocket and pulled out a second thermos. "Here, get some of this down you."

She tossed it in a slow, underhanded lob, but Tony couldn't seem to get his arms to move away from his body. An inch from impact, Henry bent and scooped it from the air.

"You'd make a hell of a shortstop."

Henry grinned as he placed the thermos in Tony's hands. "Only for night games."

"Well, yeah." As long as they could play the denial game, they were maintaining a version of same old/same old. Same old/same old was doable. He looked dubiously at the thermos. "Is this . . . ?"

Arra snorted. "Yes."

"I'm fine."

"Drink some anyway."

"But I was only a minion for like a really short time and . . ." A sudden memory of being trapped and helpless, of being used. He came back to himself as Henry wrapped his fingers securely around slick curves of orange plastic. He didn't think he reacted, but Henry backed away.

Giving him space. And a thermos top filled with magic potion. It smelled exactly like he remembered.

It tasted pretty much like it smelled, like a cocktail for alcoholic cats. He'd had worse but not recently and he was out of practice.

"It doesn't do any good coming back up your nose," Arra snapped as he choked and coughed. "You have to swallow it."

He flipped her off with his free hand—at this point he honestly didn't give a crap about being rude—and took another mouthful. It didn't taste any better, but after the fourth mouthful the vodka started numbing things out. A little. "How much . . . ?"

"Drain the cup."

"All of it?"

"Isn't that what drain means?"

"Give me a break," he muttered, wondering if the tip of his nose was supposed to be tingling. "I've had a rough night."

"And it's not over."

"Fucking great."

Hands shoved in the pockets of his coat, Henry took a step closer to the wizard. "So, you're involved now."

"I'm . . ."

"The shadow in Tony said you were unfinished business. That his master would be thrilled to know where you were after all this time. And the one in . . ." His gesture took in the fallen cameraman. ". . . knew you."

"Would be thrilled," Arra repeated, screwing the cap back onto the thermos and sitting back on her heels. "*Knew* me, past tense. Both shadows have been destroyed, so no information's going back through the gate. No one's going to be thrilled on my account."

"But it seemed to know you'd be here."

"Well, of course, it knew. As Tony pointed out," she added wearily, "I'm the one who opened the original gate. The son of bitch found this world by using my research."

"It said you were unfinished business."

She shrugged. "Who likes loose ends?"

"Your hand was in his chest."

The non sequitur seemed to throw her for a moment, then she snorted. "You saw that, did you?"

As far as Tony could see, Mouse's chest looked pretty much like it had all night. Okay, the horizontal part was new, but other than that, big and plaid pretty much covered it. "You had your hand in his chest?"

"I had the essence of my hand in the essence of his chest. I reached into the place where the shadows have substance and we don't."

"How . . . ?"

"Clean living." Raincoat crinkling, she got slowly to her feet, her opinion of the question clear.

"Look, magic might be the obvious answer where you come from, but it isn't here." Tony swallowed the last of the potion and belched. A spray of tiny green sparkles danced in front of his face. "Not usually, anyhow." The world tilted slightly sideways. "I think I need to sit down." The floor seemed like the best option. It was close and he'd already proved that he could hit it. His legs folded. Another belch. More tiny sparkles.

"Is it the shadow?" Henry's face swam in and out of focus.

Tony stretched out a finger and poked him in the cheek. "The objects in your mirror may be closer than they appear."

"What?"

"I'm guessing it's the eight ounces of warm vodka." He poked him again. "I'm fine."

Henry straightened. All he could do at this point was believe him. "Will there be others tonight?" he asked the wizard.

"Other shadows returning?" She glanced toward the ceiling and although Henry heard her heart speed up, there was no outward manifestation of her fear. "Could be, but I doubt it. These seem to be the extended wear version, good for a few days. And if you're right and they've been sent purposefully to look for the . . ." She sketched a set of air quotes. ". . . light, then they'll stay as long as they can."

"What was the waiting one waiting for?" When both wizard and vampire turned to look down at him, Tony waved. "There was one in Mouse and one waiting here by the gate."

Arra frowned. "I'd guess it was guarding the gate—the gate was open when you destroyed the shadow last night. The Shadowlord probably felt it die and wanted to make sure that wouldn't happen again."

Tony's eyes widened as sudden realization dawned. His mouth opened and closed a couple of times and then he said, "I killed . . ."

"No, you didn't." Arra cut him off. "They're pieces of the Shadowlord, of the evil he has become. They have no life, no sense of self, until they imprint with a host. You destroyed a tool. A weapon. A thing, not a person."

"Oh." He rubbed his fingertips along the painted floor. "That's okay, then."

Pulling Henry to one side, Arra leaned close to his ear and murmured, "Look, you stay here with him and deal with whatever shows up, and I'll take Mouse to a hospital. He smells like a vodka-catnip cocktail and he's clearly been fighting, so there shouldn't be any questions I can't deal with."

"Given your ability to banish the shadows; shouldn't you be the one who stays?"

"First, I'm obviously not the one who hit him. They might not believe that so easily of you. Second, you haul that light stand around and you can banish them just as easily. You already have. Third, there's no point in chancing me so close to the gate. If the Shadowlord knows I'm here . . ."

About to ask *He'll what?* Henry changed his mind at her expression. Or rather her lack of expression; in all his long life, he'd never seen anyone so desperate to hide her true feelings. There would be a time of reckoning between them but not now, not with innocents needing their attention. "You can drive?"

"I can ride the heart of the whirlwind secured in place with a rope braided from the dreams of trees."

"That's not what I asked."

She rolled her eyes. "How hard can it be?" A raised hand cut off Henry's reply. "Kidding. Of course I can drive. I live in downtown Vancouver and I work in Burnaby—only the young have the kind of stamina commuting by transit requires." A glance down at Tony and then over to Mouse. "Carry him out to the car for me, Henry, time's wasting."

Still on the floor, Tony watched Henry follow Arra out of the soundstage, Mouse's large body cradled ludicrously against his. *He says he's coming back,* he reminded himself. *Don't get rid of a vampire that easily.*

Don't get rid of a vampire at all.

His head felt like the city was doing road repairs across his cerebral cortex. Jackhammers, hot tar, the whole nine yards. As far as he could tell, it was the potion's only effect. Even the alcohol seemed to be wearing off. If he poked at the right place, he remembered how it felt as the shadow shoved him to the back of his own mind . . .

Not going there.

A deep breath and he got to his feet, just as glad he was doing it out from under Henry's watchful gaze. He couldn't have really indulged in the wincing and the groaning with Henry there.

He was unlocking the wheels of the carbon arc's stand when Henry returned. "This thing's worth a fortune," he said, motioning Henry around to the other side. "The security around here sucks."

"That thought had crossed my mind, not the price of the lamp but definitely the sucking."

Tony pointed and Henry rolled the heavy lamp back where it had been on the edge of the set.

"When you were asking Arra . . ." He stopped and started again. "Do you think the Shadowlord is looking for Arra, specifically?"

"I don't know. If he knew he was opening the same gate she did, he had to know she'd be here somewhere. But I got the impression he didn't expect her to stay around the gate."

"Maybe you should ask her why she did?"

Red-gold brows rose. "Me?"

"Why not you?"

"I don't think she likes me much."

"Vampire, remember?" He dragged the sleeve of his jacket across the glass lens. "You could make her like you."

"You know it doesn't work like that."

Tony discarded half a dozen responses. Some of them were even true. Finally, he sighed and nodded. "Yeah. I know." Bending to resecure the brakes, he had to catch himself on a cross brace, sucking in air through his teeth.

Henry didn't say anything until he straightened.

"You're hurt."

"It's just bruises."

"There's blood."

Right. Tony picked at the bits of gravel embedded in his other hand. "I'll heal."

I always have.

When he looked up, he knew that Henry'd heard the subtext. Another night, he might have said something. Tonight, he was allowing the illusion of boundaries.

The lighting crew had merely moved the lamp out of the way without unhooking it from the board. Since this wasn't going to end tonight, since another night they might not be so lucky, he studied the setup, noting where everything was plugged in.

Which reminded him . . .

"Henry, when the gate opens, you should go stand by the circuit board. It blew last night, remember?"

"Yes."

An interesting tone to that single syllable. Tony sighed and turned, not quite meeting dark eyes. "What?"

"You seem very calm." The long pause echoed with a shouted *MINE*. "All things considered."

"Hey, have I ever done the hysteria thing? I mean baby-eating ancient Egyptian wizards and ghosts screaming for vengeance aside?"

After a heartbeat, Henry smiled. "No, you haven't."

"Well, then." He folded his arms, trying to move as though muscles weren't shrieking at him, carefully missing what bruises he could. "I was thinking—we have to wait until the gate opens and the shadow separates before the light works, right?"

"Yes."

"So the Shadowlord'll still be able to sense that his guys are continuing to die on his doorstep."

Henry glanced up toward the ceiling. "Yes."

"What do you think he'll do?"

"I think," Henry said slowly, "at some point, he'll send something through that can't be killed by light. Something physical."

"You sound upsettingly happy about that."

The mask slipped. "If it has flesh and blood, I can deal with it."

Tony's blood agreed.

⤳ TEN

Saturday morning found Tony standing in the fourth floor hall outside Arra's apartment. She opened the door before he knocked. Standing there, one hand raised, he had a strong suspicion he looked like he'd just seen Siegfried and/or Roy get up close and magical with a white tiger. Arra's expression confirmed it.

Shaking her head, she stepped back out of the way. "It's a front apartment, Tony. I was removing Zazu from the dieffenbachia and saw you coming up the walk. Even Raymond Dark—hampered as he is by writers with but a single brain cell between them—could have figured that one out. Wipe your feet and hang your jacket to drip over the mat."

He did as he was told, then followed her into the kitchen, nearly tripping over the orange and white cat.

"That's Whitby. Ignore him, he's eaten."

"Does that mean don't feed him or don't worry, he won't go for my throat?"

"Bit of both." The wizard studied him for a long moment while he pretended he was paying attention to the cat. "You look like shit," she said at last. Turning, she took a big blue mug from the cupboard and filled it from an opaque thermal carafe. "This should help."

"What is it?" His tongue was still fuzzy from the aftereffects of the potion and his sense of smell was dicey at best. The frozen spring roll he'd heated up for breakfast had smelled strongly of acrylic paint—which, granted, might have been the spring roll since it was a month or two past its best-before date.

"It's coffee; organic, free-traded Mexican, picked by barefoot, sloe-eyed virgins."

"Really?"

"I couldn't swear to the virgins. There's cream in the fridge and sugar in that bunny bowl on the counter." She shoved Whitby out of the way with the side of her foot and headed out of the kitchen.

Tony hurriedly splashed some cream in his coffee—wondered briefly about a bloody plate of liver a little too *interestingly* arranged to be food—and followed. He found the wizard at her computers, both screens showing games of spider solitaire.

"Mouse is fine," she told him, laying a jack of hearts on its queen. "Where fine means he has a broken jaw and an extraordinarily pissed-off wife. I told the hospital I found him wandering around disoriented and he passed out once I got him into the car." She shuffled two columns, finished the run of hearts, and moved to the other game as the cards flipped down to the bottom of the screen. "They bought it." Eight of clubs on a nine of spades, six of diamonds on the seven of spades, and the eight of clubs moved again to the proper nine now uncovered. "How are you?"

His lip hurt, both palms were scabby, his torso was coloring up nicely, but he wasn't pissing blood so, all good. "I'm fine."

"All right. What happened at the gate?"

"Nothing."

"Where nothing means . . . ?"

Tony forced his attention away from the hypnotic movement of the cards. "Nothing . . ."

"It's about to open."

Tony glanced over at Henry and wished he hadn't. The vampire's eyes were dark and his lips were pulled back off his teeth. Nothing he hadn't seen a hundred times before, but tonight the knowledge of his place in the Hunter/ hunted scheme of things was just a little too close to the surface. Then he started to feel the buzz and Henry became of secondary importance.

As the vibrations grew stronger, he had a pretty good idea why Lee had reacted the way he had.

The last gate opening had been no more annoying than having a wasp caught in his skull. The potential for disaster was there, sure, but the actuality was pretty much all sound and fury. Tonight it was like having teeth drilled just as the Novocaine was wearing off. Not screaming pain, not yet, but every muscle tensed against the rising vibrations, anticipating the moment when the soft tissue would be hit.

"There's no one here. None of the other shadow-held have returned," Henry clarified as Tony stared at him blankly.

"So what do we do?"

"Stop anything that comes through from the other side."

"And did anything?"

"No." Tony took a long swallow of coffee. "The gate stayed open for a couple of minutes and then it closed."

"A couple of minutes?"

"Or less. Or more. When you're thinking about evil wizards and brain-sucking shadows, you don't really have a grip on time passing."

"Next time check your watch. The interval might be important later."

"What do you care? I thought you weren't helping."

"And yet you keep showing up at my door."

He wasn't sure that twice merited "keep showing up." Setting his backpack on the floor, he sat down and almost instantly had a black and white cat on his lap.

"That's Zazu." Brows drawn into a deep vee over her nose, Arra didn't look happy. Tony slowly moved both hands away from the cat. "She doesn't ever do that."

"Do what?"

"Sit on strangers."

"She's not exactly . . . OW . . . sitting."

"She's just making your lap more comfortable."

The cat's claws went once more through denim and into skin. "For who?" Tony yelped.

Arra's expression suggested the question was too stupid to answer. She went back to her games and Tony tried to hold perfectly still. God only knew what the cat would stick a claw into if she thought she was in danger of falling.

"I could feel it more this time," he said after a moment when no further blood loss seemed imminent. "The gate, I mean."

"It's because you were shadow-held."

"Yeah, I figured. But it was more of a shadow-grab than a hold. I mean, shouldn't there be a time limit on *held*?"

Hand poised over the laptop's touch pad, Arra turned to face him, brows up. "Does humor help?"

He risked a shrug. Zazu rolled over on her back in the crease between his tightly clamped legs, all four feet in the air, her stomach a blaze of white. The fur looked soft. He tentatively reached out a finger.

"I wouldn't."

And he snatched the finger back. The cat looked disappointed.

Arra snorted and turned back to the games. "So, as much as I'm thrilled to have the company, why are you here?"

"I brought back the thermoses." About to bend over and open his backpack, he caught sight of the expression on Zazu's face and reconsidered. "We didn't use any more of the potion, but I wasn't sure how long it would last. You know; the sparkly part of it."

"The potion part will last indefinitely but I will need to reactivate it before it'll do any good magically." She turned up a king, moved queen to ace over, and waited while the line collapsed. "Now why are you really here?"

"The potion . . ."

"See that?"

He leaned forward. "The game?"

"Stalled on that seven. I had no way of knowing what was under the king, but it was my only option." Swiveling her chair around, she lifted a limp Zazu off his lap. "Look beyond the obvious. Examine the truth behind your motives. Buy low, sell high."

"What?"

She sighed as the cat leaped back onto Tony's lap. "Why are you really here?"

"I was thinking . . ." He paused, waiting for a smart-ass remark that didn't come. ". . . the construction crews are going to be in today building new sets. I might be able to hang around, but I'm not going to be able to move the lamp back into place and I sure as hell won't be able to turn it on."

"Your point?"

His point seemed obvious but she was going to make him say it. "You have to be there."

"No. I won't go near the gate while it's open."

"You don't have to. You don't even have to leave the basement. You're my cover story—just send me upstairs with a light meter or something to take some readings."

"The carpenters will still be working . . ."

"Yeah." He snorted. "Like it's hard to get them to take a break."

"They'll still be there, though. If one of the shadow-held does show up, how will you explain it?"

Greatly daring, he stroked the top of the cat's head. "I have no idea. Which is why I think we need to get the addresses of everyone who was on set yesterday. We need to find where the rest of the shadows are and take them out before they get back to the soundstage."

"Take them out?"

He mimed shoving his hand in someone's chest. Zazu stretched out one paw and embedded the claws in his leg.

Ignoring his whimpers, Arra snorted. "So this whole 'I'm your cover story' on the soundstage is just a . . . cover story? You want *me* to take the shadows out."

"Two part plan!" Tony protested. "First the soundstage because we don't have time to get them all before the gate opens, and then we go after whoever doesn't show up away from the gate."

"Fine. You still haven't told me how you'll explain the shadow-held to the carpenters then."

"I thought you . . ."

"What part of I'm not getting involved in this do you not understand?"

"I'm not asking you to do any more than you've already done." Even to his own ears that sounded sulky. "Look, we're trying to stop an invasion and save the world without a lot of options, so we need to make the Shadowlord wonder a bit. Confuse him. Throw him off-balance. Not, why are my shadows being destroyed at the gate but why aren't they coming back to the gate at all? Maybe that'll convince him there's something here he doesn't want to tangle with."

Arra set up a new game on the laptop. "Have you spoken to the vampire about this?"

"Yeah. Sort of . . ."

"Tony . . ."

"I'm fine."

"I don't doubt it, but I'd appreciate it if you could move just a little faster; I've got to feed."

Still struggling with his seat belt, Tony froze. *I can't.*

Something of the thought must have shown on his face because Henry sighed. "Not on you. I don't think that would be safe for either of us tonight."

"Good call." The buckle jammed. Working the release with one hand, he yanked on the strap with the other. It didn't help. In fact . . . "Uh, Henry. I think I've really fucked this up."

Cool fingers shoved his out of the way. "It's stuck."

"No shit."

Henry glanced up at him, his eyes darkening, the mask slipping. Vampires didn't screw around with seat belts. The strap separated from the buckle. Vampires ripped their victims free.

Adrenaline lent Tony's bruised body speed and he all but threw himself out onto the sidewalk. Then, in an attempt to reclaim a little dignity, he braced himself between the door and the roof and leaned back into the car. "I was thinking that maybe we should try dealing with these things before they get back to the studio."

"Fine." The dashboard lights painted eerie highlights in Henry's eyes which were . . .

Oh, fuck. And the worst of it was; Tony wanted to climb back into the car. To offer his wrist or his throat. To offer his life. No. That wasn't the worst. It was much worse that Henry knew it, too. Leaping back, he slammed the door closed and muttered, "Why don't I just leave a message on your machine," at the BMW's ass end as it disappeared down the street.

"Yes, I'd say that fits the definition of *sort of.* His kind are not unknown on my world; I'm amazed you've managed to retain as much self-determination as you have. A man cannot serve two masters after all."

Tony's lip curled. "That's not how it is."

"And I believe you where thousands of others wouldn't." Arra closed down the laptop and stood. "Let's go."

"Go?" The cat on his lap showed no indication that it planned to move any time soon.

"Studio, gate, shadows . . ." The wizard sighed as he continued to sit awkwardly in place, not daring to stand. "Just dump her on the floor, she won't break."

Figuring he had enough mayhem in his life at the moment, Tony tucked his hands in Zazu's armpits—front leg pits?—and carefully lifted her down to the floor. She snorted, sounding remarkably like Arra, sat down, and licked her butt. Never having spent much time with cats, Tony'd never realized they were so good at making their opinions known. "I thought I didn't understand about you not getting involved?"

"What?"

"You *said* you weren't going to get involved." He stepped carefully around Whitby who was now winding between his feet, determined to be punted across the apartment.

"I'm still not going near the gate when it's open, but I suppose I can bullshit you past a few carpenters."

"What changed your mind?"

She paused, yellow raincoat up over one arm, and stared for a long moment at a framed *Darkest Night* promotion poster. "The cats like you," she said at last.

"Arra!"

She jabbed at the elevator call button a couple more times as though hoping it would realize she was in a hurry and arrive.

"Arra!"

"I don't think he's going to go away," Tony murmured.

Smiling tightly, she turned. "Julian."

He shifted the Chihuahua in the crook of his left arm and, eyes narrowed suspiciously, stared around her at Tony. "It's your turn to dust and vacuum the party room."

"I don't even live here," Tony protested.

"Not you. Her."

Except he was still staring at Tony—who'd have found it creepy had his creep level not risen over the last few days. It was, however, becoming more than a little annoying.

"The party room's done."

That snapped an equally suspicious gaze back to Arra. "It wasn't *done* a moment ago."

"Well, it's *done* now. And look, here's our elevator." Her hand closing tightly around Tony's arm just above the elbow, she propelled him inside, following right on his heels.

"Ow!"

"Sorry." Arra turned and waved jauntily at Julian through the last six inches of open space.

Shoving his foot back into his shoe, Tony waited until the door was fully closed before asking if the wizard had magicked the room clean. He hadn't seen any incantations or a wand or even an ambiguous gesture but then, what did he know about wizards?

She leaned against the back wall and folded her arms. "No. I lied."

"You lied?" Wizards lied. All things considered, it was something to remember.

"Prevaricated, even. Julian's an ac-tor, you know. He got up my nose before he became president of the co-op board; now he's unbearable."

Even on such short acquaintance, Tony could see where *unbearable* might be a justified definition. "And his dog is fat."

"Tell me about it."

"What if we shot flamethrowers through the gate?"

Arra finished merging her mid-'80s hatchback with traffic and glanced over at her passenger. "Flamethrowers?"

"Yeah. We just sit under the gate and when it opens . . ." He mimed shooting toward the ceiling. ". . . whoosh."

"Where would we get flamethrowers?"

Tony shrugged, shuffling his feet into a more comfortable position among the discarded coffee cups that littered the floor. "Same place we get them for the show; the weapons warehouse."

"They aren't . . ." Her voice trailed off and Arra scowled out at the road, her frown deepening slightly at each slap of the windshield wipers.

When she didn't say anything more for about five kilometers, Tony figured that was it. The suggestion of flamethrowers had clearly brought up some bad memories. Beginning to doze off—even with all the lights on, it hadn't been a particularly restful night—he jerked awake as she started talking again.

"I think he'd take it as a challenge. He's never been stopped, so at this point he has to believe he never can be."

"We've stopped some of his shadows."

"Minor players. They are to his power as UPN is to network TV. He wouldn't for a moment assume that because you've defeated them you could defeat him." She snorted. "Evil wizards who style themselves the Shadowlord and go on to conquer vast amounts of territory seldom have a problem with self-esteem."

"Do you think he's conquered your whole world?"

"He's headed for this one; does it matter?"

"I guess not."

Another three kilometers passed. Tony wondered what was happening during the silences. Finally, she shrugged. "It's only been seven years; I doubt it."

"Then why is he coming here?"

He was looking at her when she turned toward him, but it wouldn't have mattered if he hadn't been; the force of her expression would have dragged his head around. Pain and anger and other emotions less easily defined chased themselves across her face.

"You're right," he told her soothingly. "It doesn't matter why he's coming here, only that he is. Now, could you do me a favor and get your eyes back on the road!"

As the old analog clock on Arra's workshop wall ticked around toward 11:00, Tony moved restlessly from shelf to shelf picking up and putting down the heads and hands and other accumulated body parts. "I thought your special effects were all, you know . . ." He waggled his fingers in the air.

"Piano playing?"

"Magic."

"Some of them are. Most of them are a combination. A glamour works better than an illusion and a glamour has to be cast on something. Even computer-generated effects work better with some kind of reference point. Sometimes it's manipulating pixels, sometimes it's squibs and corn syrup, and sometimes it's magic."

He manipulated the snarl on a stuffed badger and frowned; he'd been with the show since the first episode and he couldn't remember them ever needing badgers. There'd been an episode with wolves once and an inadvertent raccoon on a night shoot but never badgers. It smelled funny, too—although that might have been the jar of rubber eyeballs propping it up. "It never looks this fake on the screen."

"It's television, Tony. You've been in the business long enough to know that nothing is what is seems, it's all smoke and mirrors."

"It *was* all smoke and mirrors," he muttered, walking over to her desk. "Now it's smoke and shadows."

"Very profound if a little obvious." As he stopped behind her, Arra placed a six of diamonds on a seven of clubs. Four of the monitors showed games in progress.

"Don't you ever get tired of that?"

She shrugged. "When it happens, I switch to a mah-jongg for a while."

"Don't you ever work?"

A snarl cut off her response and he whirled around to see the badger charge toward him—the force of its leap having knocked over the jar of eyeballs, which hit the floor and shattered. Dodging away from tooth and claw, Tony's foot came down on something round that popped wetly. When he glanced at the floor, an eyeball rolled to face him, pupil dilating in the midst of familiar blue. Then he felt claws catch the back of his jeans . . .

"Yes."

Badger and jar were back on the shelf. He supposed they'd never actually left it. Heart pounding, he clutched at the back of Arra's chair. "Yes, what?"

"Yes, on occasion, I work."

"Right." Straightening, he forced his voice back down to its usual register. "That wasn't funny."

"It wasn't supposed to be." She spun her chair around to face him, her expression serious. "If you're going to fight the Shadowlord, you'll have to know what's real."

"You took me by surprise."

"And he won't be e-mailing you his intentions. Your ability to see has cost him the element of surprise. It is your greatest weapon." Gray brows drew in. "It's pretty much your only weapon," she added thoughtfully.

"Great."

"Probably not." Reaching into her desk drawer, she pulled out a light meter and tossed it to him. "Here, gird yourself with this and get going or you'll miss the gate."

"Right." He bent and pulled a set of sides out of his backpack. "These are from yesterday. They'll have most of the names we need, you'll just have to pull the addresses out of the files."

Arra snorted as her fingers closed around the papers. "Who put you in charge?"

Tony's snort answered hers. "You did."

"Any particular reason she can't keep her knees together until we go to lunch?"

"She didn't give me one, Les." Tony rolled the carbon lamp into position and picked up the coil of cable. "She just said she wants it done now."

The head carpenter scratched at an armpit and sighed. "Whatever. You going to be long enough for me to do a little research?"

"I doubt it." He flipped the cover off the light board. "How's the dissertation going?"

"Not good. 'Pastoral Imagery in Late Eighteenth Century Amateur Poetics' just isn't enthralling me like it used to."

"Hard to imagine."

"Yeah. And the thought of teaching freshman English gives me hives."

"You could always commit to a career in show business."

Les snorted. "At the rates CB pays, it's not a career, it's a job. So, Sorge know you're using the board?"

"I have no idea." Tony checked that the big lamp was the only thing plugged in, then stepped away, casting a critical eye over his work. With only one connection to get right there were limits on how badly he could screw it up. On the other hand, if he did screw up, he'd not only blow all the power to the building and destroy a very expensive piece of equipment he shouldn't be touching, not to mention an equally expensive light—resulting in him being unemployed at the very least—but also grant the Shadowlord unopposed use of the gate. *So, no pressure.* Without a clear line of sight, he squatted to peer under the loops of cable to check that the board was plugged into the grid and that this particular junction was live. When he straightened, Les was still standing there, clearly waiting for him to expand on his answer. "Look, if Sorge has a problem, he can talk to Arra. I'm just doing what I'm told; it's safer that way."

"You getting paid for this?"

"No." 11:07. Eight minutes, give or take, until the gate opened. *Les, go the fuck away!* "Just a little free on-the-job training. You know, learning the business."

Les rolled his eyes. "Because some day you want to be a director."

That pulled Tony's gaze up off his watch. "How did you know that?" He didn't think he'd ever mentioned it.

"Jesus, Tony, I'm hardly psychic; everyone from the meat on up wants to be a director. I got three guys in my crew working on scripts as a means to that end. Although one of them isn't looking past being a writer, God knows why."

"Says the guy working on 'Pastoral Imagery in Late Eighteenth Century Amateur Poetics.'"

"Yeah, well . . ."

Les' voice got lost amid the rising vibrations in Tony's head. A dribble of sweat ran cold down his side. As his muscles began to tense, he reached out and, with his hand poised over the switch, paused. If something happened and Les saw it, there'd be another voice to cry warning. Enough voices and people would have to listen!

But if something happened and he didn't stop it, what then?

Could he risk another Nikki, another death, on the off chance that Les would see what a vampire, a wizard, and he had seen? No. *And why me?* he demanded as the vibrations pushed past the point of pain. He flipped the switch, blasting the half demolished set with light. *I'm nothing special. I'm nothing supernatural. And I'm no fucking hero.*

"Ah, Tony?" Les' grip on his arm dragged his attention out of his head. "Didn't Arra want you to take readings?"

Right. The flaw in the plan. In order to take any kind of believable reading, he'd have to get a lot closer to the gate. A lot closer to the source of vibrations ripping great jagged holes in his brain.

Memo to self; next time come up with a less painful cover story.

Unsure if he was holding the light meter believably, and not really caring, Tony followed the cable to the back of the lamp, took a deep breath and, with his eyes squinted nearly shut, stepped forward.

Step out into the light.

Hang on, isn't that what they say to dead guys?

Oh, yeah, just what he needed; portents of doom from inside his own head.

Either the light levels were making his eyes water or his eyeballs had burst and the fluid was now dribbling down his cheeks. Either option seemed equally possible. His vision had gone not so much blurry as fizzy.

Tony thumbed the control to capture and hold the reading, turned, and realized he was directly under the gate. Not at the board, not crouched by Lee's side—directly under the gate. Every hair on his body lifted—not a pleasant feeling—and, unable to stop himself, he looked up. Light. And barely visible through the light, the ceiling. Beyond that, or beside it—there weren't really words to describe how the gate both was and wasn't there—distance. And at the end of that distance, something waiting . . . trying to see . . . trying to decide. Something cold. Calculating. Terrifying.

Then the lamp shut off and a heartbeat later the gate closed.

"Are you trying to blind yourself?" Les' voice boomed out somewhere behind him. "Even pointed up at the ceiling this big bastard's putting out enough lumen to do some damage."

Tony swiped at the moisture on one cheek, realized his eyeballs were intact, saw that Les was waiting for him to say . . . something. "Uh, I got the reading."

"Good on you. Now put this fucking thing back where it belongs and get the hell off my set. I got work to do." The tone of voice suggested a deeper concern than the words.

"Right. Sorry."

"Dumb ass."

As Les called his crew back to the job, Tony rolled the lamp back along the path of its cable. With his stomach tying itself in knots, he quickly separated it from the board, secured the wires, and made sure everything was exactly the way he'd found it. Somehow, he managed to keep his hands from shaking too badly.

Outside of his conscious control, his shadow flickered around the edges.

Arra was just hanging up the phone as Tony walked down the stairs into the basement. She turned as he tossed the light meter onto her desk, looking him up and down. Her brows drew in as she completed the inspection. "You okay?"

He wondered what he looked like. Wondered if she could see the fear that had his guts in knots and stuck his shirt to the sweat on his back. "I'm fine."

"Uh-huh."

It sounded like she didn't believe him. Tough. He was fine. "No one showed up. Nothing came through. He's sitting up there considering things."

"He?"

"The Shadowlord."

Her frown deepened. "You felt that?"

"Not the sitting." Dragging the second chair out into the middle of the room, out where the arrangement of the overhead fluorescents banished shadow, he dropped onto it. "But the considering, yeah." He'd never seen anyone's eyebrows actually touch before. "What?"

"You felt the considering."

"Yeah. I guess." The noise she made was in no way reassuring. "What?"

"Nothing."

"Something!" he snapped.

"I'm just impressed by your sensitivity."

She sounded sincere and even if she wasn't, he suspected he didn't want to know the actual answer. Slouching deeper in the chair, he shoved both hands in the pockets of his jeans. "Yeah, well, I'm gay."

"So I've heard." Twisting around, she plucked a piece of paper off her desk. "I made a few calls while you were gone."

"On the phone?"

"There's an alternative I haven't discovered in the last seven years?"

"I just wondered why you don't do a locator spell or something."

"Because if I locate them using wizardry and we don't stop them and they get back through the gate . . ."

"He'll know you're here," Tony interjected into the pause. "Does it matter? There's only one of you here and you said that back in the day he wiped out the rest of your order." Her expression didn't change, but her cheeks paled and Tony realized he might have put his foot in it. "I mean, it's not like he's going to be afraid of you being here."

The presence he'd felt on the other side of the gate caused fear, it didn't feel it.

After a long moment, when it was quite obvious that Arra was seeing neither him nor the basement workroom, she sighed, blinked, and focused. "No. He won't be." She held the piece of paper out toward him. "The names underlined in red are the possibles."

Okay. If that's how she wanted to play it. Tony was just as glad to move on; a little more sitting around wallowing in the terror and he might start joining Arra's chant of *this is it; we're all going to die.* Good thing she'd gone into television because she sucked as a motivational speaker.

Thirteen names on the much longer list were underlined. He tried not to see significance in the number. "What about Alan Wu?" The actor's name wasn't only underlined, it had been circled.

Arra shrugged. "His wife says he didn't come home last night."

"There could be a hundred reasons for that."

"He was on the soundstage, on the set, practically under the gate and his wife gave me the impression that this was very unusual behavior."

"Yeah, Alan's pretty dependable." He stood, folded the paper in quarters, and shoved it in his pocket. "So let's go get him back." Two steps toward the stairs, he paused, and turned to see Arra sitting where he'd left her. "Are you coming?"

"You do realize that in the long run it won't matter. The moment the actual invasion begins . . ."

". . . you're out of here. I know, you've said." Over and over and over. "But if you go home now, Julian's just going to ride your ass about cleaning the party room."

She looked startled, then, to Tony's surprise, she smiled. "True enough. So we find them one shadow at a time and we make sure that one doesn't get back to the gate."

We. She'd used it twice. Tony figured he'd better not point that out. "It's a big city."

"But they're searching for the light."

"Henry told me his theory."

She shrugged and stood. "It seems sound." Opening the middle drawer on her desk, she pulled out the Greater Vancouver Yellow Pages. Turning, she jerked her head to one side, indicating that Tony should move out of the center of the room. The instant he was clear, she heaved the massive book up into the air and shouted two words that seemed made up mostly of consonants.

In the midst of a shower of pale ash, a single box ad fluttered down to the floor.

Tony grinned. "Cool."

The Royal Oak Community Church was a large, fake Tudor building on Royal Oak just down from Watling Street. The multiple additions gave it a comfortable, welcoming appearance only slightly offset by the disturbing presence of a pair of trees so severely pruned they looked like giant gumdrops on sticks.

Tony leaned forward and peered through the streaks of rain on the windshield. "You figure he's inside?"

"That would be where they keep the light."

"Yeah, but they don't usually keep the doors unlocked."

"That wouldn't stop a shadow."

"No, but it would stop the guy they're riding. Unless these things come with break and enter already downloaded."

Arra pulled in behind a battered station wagon and turned off the car. "I expect Alan Wu called the minister and asked for a meeting."

"It can do that?"

"It knows everything Alan knows. I imagine Alan knows how to use a phone."

Since that level of sarcasm seldom required an answer, Tony got out of the car. The sky was still overcast and threatening although the rain had stopped. He waited until the wizard joined him—not entirely positive she was going to until she was standing beside him—then started up the three steps to the concrete walk. "Everything Alan knows?" he asked after a moment.

"That's right."

"So, that'd include pages and pages of really crappy dialogue."

"Probably."

"You know, it'd almost serve the Shadowlord right if we let this one back through."

"No, it wouldn't."

"That was a joke," he pointed out, glancing over at Arra's profile.

"It wasn't funny."

Okay.

The front door of the church was locked. The side door was open. Even though it was just past noon, so little sun shone through the many windows that the lights were on. A lone figure stood at the front of the sanctuary staring up at the altar. Even at this distance there was no mistaking Alan Wu's great hair. Or the fact that his shadow was facing in another direction entirely.

Arra closed her hand around Tony's arm and when he turned toward her, she laid a finger against her lips.

Momentarily distracted by the depths to which the wizard chewed her nails, he jumped when she pinched him. Since he hadn't planned on bellowing a challenge as he charged forward, he nodded, rubbed his arm, and together they started up the aisle. Twenty feet. Fifteen. Ten . . .

Alan Wu's body turned. His eyes widened. "You!"

Then they widened further as the shadow surged free in one long whiplike motion, clearly trying to escape.

No. Not escape. Attack. It was heading straight for . . .

He dove into a pew as Arra lifted her hands and shouted out the incantation. This time, the third time he'd heard them, the words almost made sense. Might have made sense had they not been immediately followed by a scream from Alan Wu. Tony lifted his head over the barricade of polished wood just in time to see the actor hit the floor in convulsions.

Scrambling back out into the aisle, he raced forward, dropped to his knees, and ripped off his backpack. He had one hand inside, fumbling for a thermos, when Alan's back arched, his shoulders and heels the only body parts touching the floor. Then he collapsed, apparently boneless.

"Fuck!"

Throwing the backpack to one side, Tony pressed his fingers into the cold and clammy skin of Alan Wu's throat searching for a pulse.

"What is going on here?"

No pulse.

"I said . . ."

"I heard you!" Tony glanced up at the astonished minister as he started CPR. "Call 911!"

"Tony Foster." RCMP Constable Elson stepped out of the path of the paramedics as they wheeled Alan Wu out of the church, but his gaze never left Tony's face. "Another body and here you are again. It's a small world, isn't it?"

Tony nodded. He wasn't going to argue the point, not when explanations were going to be . . . complicated. Two deaths connected with *Darkest Night* and he'd found both bodies; a guy didn't have to be on the crew of *DaVinci's Inquest* to know that wasn't good.

Interesting to note that not only was Arra nowhere in sight, her car was gone.

Yeah, well, she's good at running, isn't she.

More interesting to realize that he had no idea if the shadow had been destroyed or if it had found another ride.

Where *interesting* had a number of meanings, each darker than the last.

⤳ ELEVEN

"All right, let's go over it one more time. Just to be sure."

Tony fought the urge to roll his eyes and nearly lost. A messy desk away from a cop who clearly didn't much like him was not the time for street kid attitude to reemerge. Squaring his shoulders, he took a deep breath—hoped it sounded like impatience and not the start of a practiced speech—and stared down into his empty coffee cup. "I was driving along Royal Oak with a friend . . ."

"Arra Pelindrake. The special effects . . ." Constable Elson checked his notes. ". . . supervisor at CB Productions."

"Yeah." And now possibly the shadow-held wizard. Tony wet his lips and tried not to think about that. "Like I said, I was doing a little on-the-job training with her; learning a different bit of the business. She was working on this new thing and she says she thinks better when she drives, so she was driving. I was just along for the ride. Anyway, I saw Alan Wu go into the church and I remembered I needed to tell him that he hadn't filled out the ACTRA sheet on Friday . . ." A safe lie because Alan never remembered to do his paperwork. ". . . so I got Arra to stop and I went into the church and he fell over. I couldn't find a pulse. I started CPR. You guys showed up. Well . . ." He picked up the cardboard cup and turned it around in his hand. ". . . the paramedics showed up first."

"And Arra Pelindrake is where?"

Looking the RCMP officer in the eye, Tony shrugged. "I have no idea. I guess she kept driving after she let me out."

"What is it about her that makes you nervous?"

"What?"

Constable Elson's eyes narrowed, but he didn't repeat the question.

Oh, crap. He's not as dumb as he looks. Unfortunately, *I'm afraid she might be a minion of the Shadowlord* wouldn't go over well.

"The Shadowlord? Is this some kind of a gang thing?"

"No, it's an evil wizard setting up to invade thing."

"Funny guy, eh? You know what we do to funny guys around here?"

Make them listen to bad tough cop dialogue. Make them piss in a cup. Make them miss the next gate so that a shadow gets back through with the information needed to destroy the world.

And Constable Elson was still waiting for an answer.

Tony shrugged again. "She blows stuff up. And there was this thing with maggots . . ." The shudder was legit. Yeah, not very butch of him, but so what.

"So you being there in the church when Alan Wu dropped dead, that was coincidence? Bad luck on your part?"

"Worse luck for Alan."

"I guess it was. Bad luck for Nikki Waugh, too."

"Yeah, well, if I am killing them, I wish you'd find out how because I'd really like it to stop!" He rubbed a hand over his mouth, gave some serious thought to puking—just, well, because—and looked up to find Constable Elson watching him, wearing what was almost a sympathetic expression. Or the closest he'd come to it all afternoon.

"No one's accusing you of killing anyone."

"I know. It's just I was there and you were there and . . . fuck it." He sagged back in the chair, confused by the outburst. It was either spontaneous method acting or he was more screwed up about all the shit going down than he thought. "Any chance of another coffee?"

"No."

So much for that growing camaraderie. "Are you almost done with me?"

"Why? Do you have someplace to go?" Pale blue eyes flicked over to Tony's backpack sitting open on a corner of the desk. "That's right. The party you were bringing your vodka-catnip cocktails to."

He could have said no when they asked if they could go through his backpack. He could have. But he wasn't that stupid. "Hey, there's nothing illegal about vodka or catnip!"

"Are you two still on about that disgusting combination?" Constable

Danvers asked, coming back into the squad room. "And it *is* illegal to carry open containers of alcohol."

"They were closed." Fortunately, not sparkling. *Wouldn't that have been fun to explain.*

"Unsealed containers," she amended, tossing the backpack into his lap and propping one thigh in its place on the scuffed wood. "Contents did wonders for our drains. I called your friend in Toronto, Detective-Sergeant Celluci—just as an unofficial character reference."

This time, he let his eyes roll. "Yeah? He must've been thrilled."

"Not really."

"Let me guess. You mentioned the name Tony Foster and he said, 'What's the little fuck got himself into now?'"

She grinned. "Word for word. Then he expressed some concern and allowed that you were a good kid . . ."

"Christ, I'm twenty-four."

One shoulder lifted and fell as the grin broadened. "Kid's a relative term. Then he said you should call and that Vicki wanted him to ask if you've forgotten how to use a phone."

Elson snorted. "Vicki is?"

His vampire. "His partner."

"On the force?" Danvers asked, looking interested.

"She was, but she had to quit. Long story."

"Skip it," Elson growled.

Tony wondered if they were playing good cop/bad cop or if Constable Elson really suspected something was going on. The last thing he needed was to be on the wrong side of a cop playing a hunch. Hell, at this place and this time it was the last thing the world needed. But if a hunch had already done the priming, maybe he could tell him what was going on. Get some reinforcements with weapons. Back in the day, if he'd gone to Vicki with this, she'd have . . . assumed he was shooting up again and hustled his ass off to detox.

Never mind.

"So, where are you going now?"

"Now?" Confused, he glanced from constable to constable.

"Looks like you were just in the wrong place at the wrong time."

"Twice," Elson interjected.

His partner ignored him. "We've got your statement. You're free to go."

"Okay." He stood, swung his backpack over one shoulder, found himself caught by two pairs of eyes, and realized that last question was still hanging there, waiting for an answer. "I guess I'll go back to the studio, see if Arra's there." *See if she's still Arra. And if not, well, I'll probably die.*

Fucking great. I think I'm getting used to the possibility.

"She's not answering her phone."

Good news or bad? He had no idea. "Then I guess I'll go home."

Elson's lip curled. "Not to your party?"

"Not at 3:20 in the afternoon, no." It had been a long day. Tony figured he was entitled to the attitude. Fine upstanding members of the community would be screaming for their lawyers by now. Only people who had history with the cops played nice.

Both RCMP officers knew it, too.

"Thank you for your cooperation, Mr. Foster. If we need you, we'll be in touch."

"Yeah. Well, you're welcome."

He was almost at the door when Elson growled, "Don't leave town."

"Oh, for Christ's sake, Jack, get off his case. He's a witness—not a suspect."

Since Constable Danvers seemed to have his defense well in hand, Tony just kept walking. Out the door. Into the hall. It was weird that squad rooms all smelled the same. Past the front desk. He ignored the speculative stares. Tried not to care that another three cops could pick him out of a lineup. Out the front doors.

It was raining again.

Nikki Waugh was dead. Alan Wu was dead. Arra was . . . who the fuck knew.

He was in way, way over his head.

Man, this place had better be on a fucking bus route.

Arra wasn't at the studio. She wasn't at her condo. She wasn't in either of the two churches he'd gone to just because he had to go somewhere.

The sunset over English Bay was a brilliant display of reds and oranges that made it look as though sea and sky were on fire. With any luck, it wasn't an omen.

Although, given the way his luck had been running . . .

Bouncing the keys to Henry's condo in the palm of one hand, he admitted he didn't have a hope in hell of finding her without help.

"It's like she's totally disappeared!"

Henry nodded thoughtfully. "She's good at running."

"Yeah, I thought that, too, except that if the shadow took her, she's not running—she's investigating. Checking out the light. Or not." Unable to remain still, Tony paced back and forth in front of the wall of windows in Henry's living room. "Maybe she'd just hang around out of sight, waiting to go back through the gate. The one that was in me, it said that the important news was that she was alive, so a shadow in her, well, it's going to want to get that information back to the boss. Right? So all we have to do is destroy the shadow in her just like we destroyed Lee's shadow."

"I doubt it will be that easy. Obviously, these things can protect themselves and with the wizard's knowledge it'll be able to set up protections we won't be able to break."

"So we get there early and when she arrives, we sneak up behind her and hit her over the head." He punched his right fist into his left palm.

"And then we're stuck with an unconscious wizard and no way to remove the shadow in order to destroy it—the shadow can't separate from an unconscious host or the one in Mouse would have gone for me last night."

Last night. Tony slid past the memory. "Fine, then while she's unconscious, we tie her up and we gag her. When she wakes up, we stick her under the gate, let it suck the shadow out, and then we hit it with the light."

"Again, I doubt it will be that easy."

"That sounds *easy* to you?" He turned and laid his forehead against the cool glass and wondered if the lights across False Creek looked like the campfires of an advancing army. Probably not; too much neon. "She'd better have been grabbed by that shadow. She ditched me, man. Just tossed me to the cops."

"Perhaps she thought you'd do better on your own and she didn't want to cramp your style."

Tony snorted, his breath misting the window. "Yeah. *Perhaps* you were right when you said she was good at running."

"*Perhaps* I was right?"

He pivoted his head around just far enough to grin at Henry. Realized he was doing it when it pulled on the swollen edge of his lip. Stopped. Watched Henry's expression change. He'd walked in and started talking—about finding Alan Wu, about the cops, about Arra. Until now, there hadn't been a big enough opening for an awkward silence to slip through. *Oh, fuck; here it comes.*

"Tony, about last night . . ."

"Hey, you were hungry, I understand. You had to feed. No big."

"What?" Realization dawned before Tony had to explain. "No, not when we parted. Earlier, when . . ."

"When you called and I came running? Like I said; no big. I've found my happy place with it, Henry. I'm living with it, just like I have been since we met. And you know what else? I'm bored with it. You own my ass—it's old news. I have a life because you allow it? Well, thanks. Let's move on. We don't need to keep revisiting the . . ." He sketched the most sarcastic set of air quotes he could manage, knowing full well that Henry could hear the pounding of his heart. ". . . underpinnings of our . . ." And a second set, air quotes Amy would have been proud to display. ". . . relationship. This isn't one of your romance novels, this is real life and no one talks about this kind of thing in real life. Okay?"

Now *he* could hear the pounding of his heart—mostly because it was the only noise in the room.

Finally, after what felt like a year or two, Henry sighed. "Never underestimate the North American male's capacity for denial."

Tony's lip curled. "Bite me."

Red-gold brows rose.

One of the two dozen or so tiny lights in the chandelier over the dining room table flickered. The refrigerator compressor kicked on, the noise spilling out of the kitchen. A gust of wind off False Creek blew rain against the window, the drops hitting the glass in a sudden staccato rhythm.

Henry snorted.

Snickered.

Started to laugh.

Tony blinked, stared, and actually felt his jaw drop. Had he ever seen Henry totally lose it like that? The vampire had collapsed back into the couch cushions. Was, in fact, bouncing himself against the padded green leather, eyes closed, arms wrapped around his stomach. Just as he started to calm, the hazel eyes opened, he looked up at Tony, and lost it again.

"Hey, it wasn't that funny!"

Henry managed a fairly coherent, "Bite me?"

And then again, maybe it was.

It took a while before they stopped setting each other off. His ribs were aching as they walked together to the elevator.

"You have no idea how worried I was that you would . . ."

He bumped his shoulder against Henry's. "Hate you?"

"At the very least."

"Nah, we're good." Motioning Henry in first, Tony stepped over the threshold and hit the button for the lobby. "Although I am feeling a rousing chorus of 'You and Me Against the World' coming on."

"You're twenty-four; how do you even know that song?"

"The woman who runs the craft services truck is a big Helen Reddy fan. Plays the greatest hits tape over and over and over."

Henry winced. "I'm fairly sure the Geneva Convention doesn't cover evil wizards; if you could get your hands on it, we could toss it through the gate."

"And that really bad cover of 'Big Yellow Taxi.'"

"And polyester bell-bottoms. I went through the seventies once and I don't think I should have to do it again. Platform shoes, big clunky gold chains, hair spray . . ."

Leaning against the elevator wall, Tony listened to Henry listing the flotsam and jetsam of modern life he could do without and felt something he thought he'd lost. Hope. And annoyance. Because now he couldn't get that damned song out of his head.

"Has Arra ever said that the gates are one way only?"

Tony ran back over every conversation he'd had with the wizard and shook his head.

"Then it seems to me that a shadow controlling her could take more than mere information back."

That was a possibility he hadn't considered. "You think it'll take her? I mean, physically?"

"It depends on how independent these shadows are. If they're operating on very narrow parameters, like say . . ." Henry's voice dropped into a doom and gloom octave. ". . . find the light that is capable of destroying the others, then . . ." His voice lifted back into normal ranges on the last word. ". . . no. But if they've been given more autonomy and since they obviously know their master wants the wizard that got away, then I think it's something we need to consider."

"Yeah, that's . . ."

"That's what?" Henry asked after the pause lengthened to the point where prodding seemed necessary.

"I was just thinking of something Amy asked me. About . . . Turn left! Now!"

Henry deftly slid between an SUV and an approaching classic VW Beetle and turned left onto Dunsmuir Street.

"That was Tina's van. She's the script supervisor. She was on set when the shadows came through, and if she's heading this way, then she could be heading toward Holy Rosary Cathedral."

"That's a lot of qualifiers. Are you sure it was her van?"

"Yeah, we all chipped in and got her vanity plates for Christmas. There!"

"OURSTAR?"

"Because everything in that place revolves around her," Tony explained as Henry tucked his BMW in behind the van. "Cast, crew—if there's a problem, Tina deals with it. If Peter thinks Dalal—that's the prop guy—isn't taking what he wants seriously, he complains to Tina who talks to him. If Dalal thinks Peter's being unreasonable because he never said *how* he wanted the potted plant wrapped . . ."

"Not a random example?"

"Like I'd make that kind of thing up . . . Anyway, Dalal will whiffle to Tina in turn and she'll work the whole thing out without damaging any delicate egos in the process."

"The prop guy has a delicate ego?"

"It's show business, Henry. It's all about ego."

"Good thing you're immune."

"Isn't it. She's parking."

"Good for her." As in any major city, finding parking in downtown Vancouver depended as much on luck as anything. Henry drove another block past the van—slowing to get a good look at Tina as he passed—before he found an empty spot almost at the cathedral.

"I'm not sure this spot's legal," Tony pointed out as he parked. "In fact, given that we're under a no parking sign, I'm pretty sure it's not."

"We won't be here long. I'll go back and meet her, find out if she's shadow-held." He tossed Tony the keys. "Here. Move the car if there's a problem."

"Right. Hey, what are you going to do if there is shadow?" The car door slammed and he was sitting alone in the front seat. "Never mind."

Over short distances, Henry could move too fast to be seen if he had to. Tina was barely three meters from the van when he caught up to her, slipping into a triangle of darkness made by the corner of a building, before she was aware of his presence. Caution was called for. The world through the gate knew his kind and he had no doubt that he would, like the wizard, be returned to the Shadowlord as a prize were he to be taken.

And that would be the good news.

The damage a shadow could do while in control of his body didn't bear thinking about.

As Tina passed him—her stride purposeful, her gaze fixed on the middle distance—he sifted the night air for an otherworldly taint. She was flesh and blood and as much in control of herself as anyone in this day and age.

Flesh and blood. He felt his lips draw up off his teeth. The Hunger flared. It was always harder to put the genie back in the box. "Tina."

She turned at the sound of her name, curiosity taking care of the very little choice Henry's voice had left her. "Yes? Hello?"

Stepping out into the circle of illumination cast by the streetlight, he smiled and caught her gaze with his. "Just a moment of your time."

When he stretched out his hand, she frowned slightly, not fighting the compulsion but very nearly questioning it. When he called her name a second time, she cocked her head, considered, then smiled and laid her fingers across his palm.

Two steps back and they were both shielded by the darkness. He lifted the hand he held to his mouth, turned it, and touched his lips to the soft skin of her wrist. Her eyes, still locked on his, widened then, as she sighed, half closed. For a change, the emotional component of feeding was more on his side than hers. A chance to stroke the Hunger—a gentle acknowledgment that left it easier to control.

To the casual observer they were now more than just friends. Anyone looking closer would refuse to see what was actually happening.

"Fuck, Henry; you fed off her?"

Half into the driver's seat, Henry paused. "How . . . ?"

"It's all over your face."

Startled, he leaned toward the rearview mirror.

"Not blood," Tony snorted. "It's this whole preternatural calm thing you've got going just after you feed."

"Preternatural?"

"Don't change the subject. You fed off Tina."

"There was no shadow." He held out his hand for the keys.

"So very much not the point," Tony told him, dropping them on his palm.

"It was, in one way, for her own protection."

"Against what? High blood pressure?"

"Against the shadow."

Tony waited for the rest of the explanation as Henry started the car and put it in gear.

"You were able to disgorge the shadow when I called on the link we share," Henry continued calmly, pulling into traffic. "While I can't protect the whole city, it is possible that should it come to it, Tina will be able to do the same."

"Disgorge the shadow?"

"Yes."

"After one quick snack? Don't you think highly of yourself."

"Tony . . ."

He slouched as far as the seat belt allowed, picking at one of the scabs on his palm. "And she's old enough to be my mother!"

Although not a good judge of human aging—it went by too fast as far as he was concerned—Henry guessed the script supervisor was in her mid to late fifties. "I'm significantly older than that."

"Yeah, but you don't look it. You and Tina, well, there's this whole creepy *Harold and Maude* thing going on."

"Who?"

"*Harold and Maude*. A Hal Ashby movie from 1971. Bud Cort and Ruth Gordon; it was brilliant, a cult classic, and you need to watch more movies without subtitles but again, not the point." Tony ran his less scabby hand back through his hair and sighed. "You don't just do that whole crunch, munch, thanks a bunch thing with people like Tina."

"She won't remember it."

"Good."

Henry turned onto Hastings and sped up to make the next light. "You were about to make an observation, back before we spotted the van?"

"Was I? Well, it's totally gone now."

"Let's hope it wasn't important."

"Yeah, let's."

There were half a dozen cars in the studio parking lot when Henry turned off Boundary Road; Arra's hatchback conspicuously not among them.

Henry parked where he had the night before, hoping that passing security would consider it to be his spot and not question his presence. He'd long ago learned that life was simpler if it was arranged in his favor rather than adjusted after the fact. "Do you know who these cars belong to?"

"No." Tony popped his seat belt and opened the car door. "I think the old Impala belongs to one of the writers."

"I used to have a car just like that," Henry noted as they started for the back of the building.

"Well, you know what they say, there's a dark green Chevy Impala in everyone's past."

"Who says that?"

"Them."

"And who are they?"

Tony snorted softly as he stopped in front of the keypad. "The same guys who say you don't put the bite on women old enough to be my mother."

"You don't think that attitude's a little ageist?" Henry asked, leaning against the wall.

"No." The lock released and Tony carefully pulled the door open. "I think . . ." He stiffened as Henry raised a quieting hand and decided not to get pissed off about it when he saw the vampire's eyes were fixed on the line of black that was the soundstage. Henry'd put on his hunting face. There was something in there. Someone . . .

One of the shadow-held or one of the crew?

The lights were off.

It could be one of the crew sleeping it off before heading home after a few too many drinks at the bar down the road.

Or it could be security patrolling on the other side of the soundstage, flashlight beam blocked by the permanent sets. Okay, probably not that. According to one of the writers, if CB wasn't in the building, the rent-a-cop spent most of his time in the office kitchen working on his screenplay.

It *could* be one of the shadow-held. Lee had turned on the lights, but Mouse hadn't. If it wanted the body it wore to remain unseen, then darkness was better—better for hiding even if it meant it lost the ability to use its cast shadow as a weapon. It wouldn't need a weapon if it wasn't seen.

Maybe it had other weapons. Maybe it had a gun. *Maybe I've been watching too much American television.*

Hang on: it could be *all* of the remaining shadow-held. Unless there were rules he didn't know, nothing said they had to show up one at a time.

A quick glance down at his watch. 10:43.

Half an hour early for the gate.

He stepped back as Henry stepped forward. No point in speculating, when all he had to do was ask. "How many?" he whispered.

"I hear a single heartbeat."

"Arra?"

"I don't know."

"Shadow-held?"

A flash of teeth. "I'll let you know. Give me thirty seconds."

"And then?"

"Make your way to the gate and start setting up the big light."

"In the dark?"

"Use the flashlight. Remember that the darkness handicaps them. They can't use the shadows the body casts in the dark."

"Duh, Henry. My intel, remember?"

Henry's brow creased in annoyance. "Then why did you ask?" he demanded and slipped into the soundstage.

The darkness in the soundstage was not absolute, but then in this day and age, darkness seldom was. Exit lights and LEDs on equipment left running gave Henry illumination enough to see by. Not clearly, but sufficiently.

The taint of the otherworld seeping through twice a day prevented him from scenting and identifying the life he could hear, and the reek of fresh paint permeating the soundstage like a mist didn't help. No matter. The heart rate told him his quarry was awake and humans seldom sat awake in darkness. Shadow-held, then. Waiting for the gate.

He slipped around a false wall and paused, close enough now to scent his quarry as female. The wizard? Still too many other, stronger scents masking subtleties.

It was standing just under the gate, wrapped in the ubiquitous plastic raincoat.

". . . twenty-eight Raymond Dark, twenty-nine Raymond Dark, thirty." Tony dried damp palms against his thighs and squared his shoulders. "Ready or not, here I come." He hoped a thirty-second lead was enough time for Henry to take care of things—not that it mattered if it wasn't. The big lamp had to be in place and ready to go when the gate opened.

He thumbed on the flashlight, pointed it at the floor, and headed for the light board.

Not the wizard. A girl, Tony's age. She had the raincoat shoved back and her hands deep in the front pockets of a pair of bib overalls. As Henry stopped at the edge of the open set—she was standing where they needed her to be, he had no need to go any farther—she shifted her weight back and forth from one red high-top to the other. Impatience, not anticipation. She couldn't know he was . . .

When the lights came on, the last thing Henry saw before being flung to the floor was her smile.

Lights?

Tony blinked toward the spill of lights from the dining room set.

Why would Henry turn on the lights?

Answer: Henry wouldn't.

He started to run.

Henry struggled against the shadow that wrapped around him from wrist to cheekbones; his arms held to his sides, his mouth and nose covered. It bulged but held.

When the girl squatted beside him, the shadow squirmed off his ears.

"We left a guard on the gate," she said conversationally. "It wasn't here, so someone had to have destroyed it. If someone knew how to do that, then that same someone knew way, way too much and would likely be back. Hello, someone. I was waiting for you. You should've checked for traps." Her smile broadened as she held up the remote switch she'd used to turn on the lights. "You'll be unconscious soon, and then you'll be dead."

Not soon. Definitely not before the gate opened. Although Henry needed to breathe, the air in his lungs would last him long enough. He could hear cables hitting the floor, the lamp's wheeled platform moving. All he had to do was lie here, listen to the shadow-held gloat, and wait for the gate to open. The shadow would attempt to leave, Tony would hit it with the light, and he'd be released. A slightly less dignified scenario, granted, but it would get the job done. And a good thing, too, since the tensile strength of the shadow meant he wouldn't be doing the superman-breaking-his-bonds thing any time soon.

Her smile slipped and her eyes narrowed. "You're different."

He fought to keep the Hunger from showing, but it was still too close to the surface. Tina had helped but not enough.

"Nightwalker." One finger flipped a strand of his hair back and forth. "This one doesn't believe in you, but I wouldn't be too upset about that since she doesn't believe in me either. It's all metaphors and symbolism in here." The plastic raincoat crinkled as she leaned forward, one hand going to the floor beside his head to keep from overbalancing. "What's it like in there, I wonder? I imagine you've got a better grip on what's real. Shall we find out? Besides, it's always smartest to take over the strong. Makes it harder for the weak to stop you."

From the corner of one eye, Henry noticed a patch of darkness under the huge rectory table. Dark enough? Only one way to find out. Rolling seemed to be his only option.

"Oh, no, you . . ."

He was under the table before she finished her protest. He felt the binding ease—apparently it was *just* dark enough—and he ripped his way free; aware he was snarling as he got to his feet but not really caring.

Her lip curled in answer. "A creature of darkness fighting for the light? That's not how it works where I come from."

"It's how it works here."

She flashed him a cheeky smile and turned to run; *Chase me, chase me!* so strongly implied she might as well have shouted it aloud. Henry held the hunter in check, dodged the cast shadow she was attempting to distract him from, and stood in front of her before she could turn again. "Apparently my kind move slower where you come from."

She stiffened in his grip, her eyes staring at nothing as the shadow within her began to rip free.

Vibration in blood and bone announced the opening of the gate.

"Henry! Close your eyes!"

Even through closed lids the world turned a brilliant white. Tears streaming down his cheeks, Henry threw the girl forward, dropped to his knees and buried his face in his arms.

After a long moment, the light turned off.

"It's okay. You can look up now." Figuring Henry could take care of himself, Tony ran across the set toward Kate Anderson's crumpled body. She was Mouse's focus puller and that was the only thing Tony knew about her. Muttering, "Not again!" over and over like a mantra against a worst-case scenario, he dropped to his knees, rolled her onto her back, and felt for a heartbeat. Lost it in the screaming pain still vibrating his skull. Found it again.

"She's alive."

"Yeah." Tugging the raincoat back into place, he looked up at Henry. "Why did you throw her?"

"I hoped that being right under the gate would activate the shadow's primary function—to return home with information—and keep it from re-membering that it was heading for me. Seems to have . . ."

"Not real. Not real. Not real!" One hand clamped around Tony's arm, the other grabbed for the collar of his shirt. Kate's pupils had contracted down to black pinpricks and her eyes were opened painfully wide. "Not real!"

"Sorry." Tony wasn't sure why he was apologizing; it just seemed the thing to do. Then he remembered. "Henry, we don't have any potion, the cops dumped it. We didn't even stop to buy vodka!" Dropping his ass to the floor, he dragged her up onto his lap. "You're going to have to vamp her!"

Kate's heels began to drum as Henry dropped down by her other side. "To what?"

"You know, touch the primal terror. Convince her you're real and that'll help her deal with the rest!"

His mouth slightly open, Henry stared at him, his expression caught half-way between astonishment and amazement. "And if she can't deal with me?" he asked after a long moment.

"Jesus, Henry, she's twenty-three years old and you're . . . you. Just crank up the sex appeal!"

Shaking his head, Henry took hold of the girl's jaw. "Do you have any idea of what you're talking about?"

"Hell, no! I'm making it up as I go along. Do you have a better idea?" he asked as Henry stared down into Kate's face. "Or *any* other idea?"

"No."

"Then what can we lose? Damn it, Henry, there's already two people dead!"

Henry looked up at him then, his eyes dark, and, after a moment, he said, "What's her name?"

"Kate." Tony grunted as a plastic clad elbow drove into one of the bruises Mouse had pounded into him.

"Catherine?"

"Could be."

"Kate, then." Henry bent his head toward hers and called her name.

Tony stiffened. Literally stiffened. He knew the whole Prince of Darkness thing was going to affect him, no way it couldn't, not after last night, but this he hadn't expected. His whole body longed to answer the call. Blood was rush-ing south fast enough to leave him light-headed and he had an erection he could pound nails with pressed up against Kate's back. *Deal. You're the one who told him to crank up the sex appeal.*

The good news was, it seemed to be working on Kate, too. She'd trans-ferred her grip from his collar to Henry's and stopped thrashing.

And thank God for that. Friction, even friction of the spine-encased-in-raincoat variety was not helping.

Teeth gritted, he fought to maintain his hold as Henry's voice caressed them both. It didn't seem to matter that it wasn't meant for him. Kate gasped as teeth met through the skin of her wrist. Tony gasped with her. She moved languidly on his lap. He closed his eyes and barely kept from . . .

. . . didn't quite keep from . . .

Then she was a limp weight against him and cool fingers touched his cheek.

"Tony? Are you all right?"

"Fine. Just a little sticky." He opened his eyes to see Henry, only Henry, staring into his face. The relief would have left him limp had that not already been taken care of. "You're not all carried away?"

"I've fed twice tonight. The Hunger is replete."

"I thought too much blood got it going."

"I didn't take too much. Hardly any from young Kate."

"Is she?"

"She's asleep."

"Doesn't like to cuddle, then."

Henry paused, about to lift Kate into his arms. "What?"

"Never mind." Tony adjusted his jeans as her weight went off him, saw Henry's nostrils flare and silently dared him to comment. "I've got to put the lamp back. Why don't you put her in the car and see if she's got her address written in her raincoat or something."

"Or something," Henry agreed. He straightened, Kate's head lolling against his shoulder. "You know, eventually we're going to miss one. Or they'll get smarter and all hit the gate at once."

"Yeah, I thought of that," Tony said as he got to his feet. Then he frowned. "They could get smarter?"

"The longer they ride their hosts, the more information they absorb."

"Oh, that's just fucking great."

They walked together to the lamp.

"On the bright side," Henry murmured as he turned toward the exit, "that's three down and only four to go."

Tony bent and began coiling cable. "Unless one's in Arra, in which case we're just generally screwed."

"So much for the bright side."

"Yeah." He sighed as Henry began walking and said softly as he heard the door open, knowing Henry would hear him even at that distance. "I'm thinking there's got to be a better way."

Arra watched the Nightwalker leave with the girl, watched Tony clear away all signs that anyone had been in the soundstage after hours. Although the pull of the gate had been nearly overwhelming, she'd needed to be there as they dealt with the shadow, keeping just enough of her consciousness present to see and hear and not enough to alert the vampire.

It wasn't enough to know what they did, she had to know how.

And, knowing, what should she do with that knowledge?

⟿ TWELVE

At first he thought he was in the east end. The buildings on both sides of the street were long abandoned, their dark windows staring down at him accusingly. There were no people, no traffic. The only sign of life was a small flock of pigeons strutting about the nearest intersection searching for food in the cracks between slabs of buckled asphalt.

Tony walked slowly down the center of the street, flanked on either side by the burned-out remains of cars and trucks and minivans. A glance into one of the cars gave him a pretty good idea of where the people had gone.

Then he nearly tripped over a charred a-frame advertising Italian ice cream and he realized he wasn't in the east end at all. He was on Robson Street. The abandoned buildings had once been rows of trendy boutiques and high-priced restaurants. He stepped from the street into Robson Square to find the trees dead and a body facedown in the six inches of dirty water filling the skating rink.

He was walking through the establishing shot of every post-apocalyptic move ever made. Could it get any more clichéd?

Behind him, a sign creaked ominously in the breeze and the light began to fade.

Apparently, it could.

Then the hair rose on the back of his neck. Off the back of his neck? Well, it was standing, like it knew something he didn't and he didn't like that feeling at all.

There was something behind him.

Of course there was.

Screw it. He'd just keep walking and not give in to it. He wouldn't turn, he wouldn't look, he wouldn't play the game. Two steps, three—on four he felt himself begin to pivot. He hadn't intended to turn, but he wasn't driving anymore.

Oh, crap.

He'd just become a passenger in his own body.

Been there. Done that. Didn't want to do it again.

Robson became Boundary and the thing in his body walked him through the front door of the studio. Amy came toward him, asking him a question through lips the exact same fuchsia as her hair. He could see her lips move, but he couldn't hear her. He couldn't hear anything but the pounding of his own heart. And the hard/soft melon-on-concrete crack of her head hitting the floor as he shoved her out of his way.

Lee and Mouse were waiting on the soundstage under the gate. They moved in on either side of him and his world dissolved into hands and mouths and flesh that felt like clammy rubber and wouldn't let him breathe. When the gate opened, they separated and it drew them up one at a time; first Lee, then Mouse, then him. Through light, through pain, into a room with blackboards covered in patterns that might have been words that might have been illustrations, that might have been mathematical notation; it was impossible to tell because two of the three boards had a body crucified against them and the third had clearly been prepared for a body of its own.

Their eyes were open and their expressions suggested they'd been alive for a very long time after they'd been nailed to the walls.

There was a man—he *knew* there was a man, was as certain of it as he'd ever been of anything in his life—but he could only see a formless shadow stretching out dark and horrible along the floor. He felt his body move toward it, as unable to stop itself as he was to stop it. His heart raced. If he touched the shadow, he'd be absorbed the way Lee and Mouse had been absorbed. He'd lose the self he'd found. Become nothing more than a part of the darkness. He couldn't let that happen. Not again.

But the compulsion was everything.

Greater than terror.

Greater than the need to be.

Darkness.

The room through different eyes. An instant of being himself *and* someone else. An instant of cold cruelty. Arrogance. Impatience. Why was such a simple task taking so long?

And a voice. A loud, obnoxious, unignorable voice. "It's 8:30 on a beautiful Sunday morning and you're listening to CFUN and another forty-five minutes of commercial free music. Let's start things off with a little Av . . ."

Tony was out of bed, across the room, and slapping off the radio before he was truly awake—a total aversion to so-called soft rock and Amy's suggestion of putting the radio where he couldn't reach it from the bed were the only things he'd ever found guaranteed to get him up. Eyes squinted nearly shut, he wondered for a moment why it was so bright in the apartment and then remembered that for the second night in a row, he'd gone to sleep with all the lights on.

Not that it had helped much.

His skin prickled under a fine sheen of sweat as the terror returned and a glimpse of his shadow lying on the grubby carpet drove him two stumbling steps back into the wall.

"A dream. It was just a dream." And fuck but his subconscious was anything but subtle. He swallowed, suddenly felt trapped in the enclosed space of the apartment, and staggered around the pull-out couch to the window where he threw back the curtains and squinted up at an overcast sky. It was threatening rain.

And that was normal enough that he managed to get his breathing under control.

A walk to the bathroom to empty his bladder helped and by the time he'd flushed and washed his hands, he walked to the refrigerator feeling almost normal. Well, as normal as he ever felt first thing in the morning.

Opening the fridge, he leaned in, grabbed the bomb bottle of cola off the top shelf, and twisted off the cap. A quick taste determined it was flat but not totally undrinkable. Besides, neither the caffeine nor the sugar was in the bubbles.

Bottle tipped back, feeling more human with every swallow, Tony closed the fridge door and screamed. Unfortunately, that resulted in rather a lot of flat cola going back up his nose. Once he'd finished with the coughing and the choking, he stared across the room with various liquids dripping from every facial orifice.

Arra was still sitting on his only chair.

Suddenly remembering he was naked, he rather belatedly moved the bottle in front of his crotch. "What the fuck are you doing here?"

She stared at him blankly and he realized she was wearing the exact same clothing she'd had on the day before. Not good. Not good at all.

"I don't know."

It took him a moment to figure out that she was answering his question. "You don't know why you're here?" he asked, shuffling forward until he could squat down and grab a pair of jeans off the floor.

"I don't know why I didn't just keep going."

"Right." Personal modesty had already gone to hell so Tony set the bottle on the counter and shrugged into his jeans, turning around to tuck himself inside. A careful closure—because getting caught in the zipper would make the morning even more special—and he felt a little better prepared to face his uninvited guest. "So . . ." He faced her again with studied nonchalance. "Am I talking to the wizard or the shadow operating the wizard?"

That elicited a bleak smile. "If I was shadow-held, would I tell you?"

"Yeah, well, so far, the shadows . . ." The edge of the counter pressed into his back and his right hand closed around the handle of the silverware drawer. He was pretty sure not *everything* in it was plastic. ". . . big on the bwahaha."

"On the what?"

"They gloat."

"Ah. Yes, they do. They didn't used to." She closed her eyes for a moment. When she opened them again, her expression was strangely familiar. "They used to stay hidden, doing as much damage as they could for as long as they remained undiscovered."

"Maybe that was because they knew they had something to stay hidden from."

"Maybe."

"And it's been all television people this time; big egos to deal with."

"True."

Releasing the drawer handle, he took two steps forward. He'd known almost immediately that Mouse was shadow-held—one look at his face and he'd seen it wasn't the cameraman at the controls. He didn't like to look at Arra's face because he'd realized why her expression seemed familiar. The last time Tony'd seen it, the body it belonged to had been spiked to a blackboard. Bodies, actually. "Arra, what happened yesterday in the church?"

"I destroyed the shadow."

"Good." Another step.

"But Alan Wu was dead and I could do nothing more."

"So you ditched me."

"I knew there would be authorities to deal with and this is your world."

"You're living in it. On it."

Plastic crinkled as she shrugged. "My history only goes back seven years."

"So you were afraid the cops would find out you've got no past?"

"No past *here*."

"Okay." Sounded reasonable, but reasonable didn't explain why she'd disappeared, why she was still wearing yesterday's clothes, and why she was in his apartment. "What else happened?"

The snort was a pale imitation of her usual explosive exhalation. "What makes you think something else happened?"

"I don't think you've been home."

"Adults don't stay out all night on this world?"

Tony sighed. "Who fed your cats?"

Her eyes widened and the nailed-to-a-blackboard expression was replaced by the dawning realization that the world hadn't actually ended—even though it might be better for some concerned if it had. "Oh, shit."

He grabbed her arm as she tried to rush by him. "Wait. I'm coming with you."

Her car had been parked a couple of blocks away. After he'd thrown on some clothes, they'd all but run to it. Arra'd burned rubber out of the parking spot before Tony'd barely got his door closed.

Finally buckled in, he sank down in the seat and wondered where he should begin.

"How did you get into my apartment?" The door had been locked, the chain still on when they left.

"I'm a wizard. I have powers."

Well, duh. "You teleported?"

"I got a demon to carry me through . . . GREEN!" The light obediently changed. ". . . the Netherhells and emerge in your apartment."

Fucking great. He'd done the demon thing. It was how he'd met Henry— ripped up by said demon and in desperate need of blood. "Seriously?"

"No. I suppose you could call it teleporting. The senior among us could move ourselves from point to point over short distances. It's what made us start thinking about other worlds."

"Why?"

"We had to be moving through something, didn't we?"

"I guess." He closed his eyes as she inserted the hatchback into a space maybe an inch larger than the car. When he opened them again—after the g-forces had returned to normal—he noticed something on the dash. "Is it magic that keeps this car going without gas?"

"What?" Her gaze dipped to follow his line of sight. "No. The gauge is broken, so I fill up based on mi . . . Get out of the damned way! I am in no mood to take prisoners!"

Silently urging the SUV in front of them to give it some gas, Tony frowned. "You were a senior?"

The pause lasted long enough he knew the answer had to be important. Or the SUV was about to be moved over a short distance.

"I was."

He breathed a sigh of relief when the sport vehicle turned. "Like Dumbledore or Gandalf?"

"Less hairy."

His frown deepened. Arra wasn't young, but he wouldn't have said she was old. Kind of in that in-between who-the-hell-can-tell age. If he'd had to guess, he'd have looked at the gray and the lines around her eyes and mouth and said mid-fifties but mostly because it seemed like a safe number—after a certain age it was always safer to guess low. But no matter what she looked like, Arra wasn't human. Not from this world at all and who knew how they aged where she came from. *And* she was a wizard—they probably aged differently. "Were you *the* senior? The head wizard?"

Both of her fists came down on the steering wheel. "These lanes are wide enough for transports and you're in a fucking GEO! Pick a lane and stay in it!"

The Geo swerved to the right so abruptly it looked as though a giant hand had come down and shoved it to one side. Tony couldn't be absolutely sure one hadn't.

"No."

"No?" One hand clutched at the dash, the other at the side of his seat, his fingers almost a joint deep in the cheap vinyl, and he was still being flung about within the loose confines of the seat belt.

"No, I wasn't *the* senior."

Her emphasis was slightly different than his. Almost bitter. Had she thought she should be? Tony added that new question to the bottom of the list and returned to the top. "Why were you in my apartment?"

"Honestly, I'm not sure. You and your Nightwalker are the only people on this world who know me and the sun was up . . ."

What there was of an answer sounded like truth, so he let it go. "Where did you go yesterday?"

Her sigh was deep enough to lightly mist the inside of the windshield. "Whistler. I had a foolish idea of finding CB and telling him everything."

Again an interesting emphasis. Everything? He had a suspicion Arra's everything included a few somethings he didn't yet know about, but before he could ask, she continued.

"I saw him with his daughters and I realized that a man who has no idea he's being played by an eight year old and an eleven year old couldn't help me."

"Harsh."

"Perhaps. There's always the chance I just chickened out at the last minute and ran."

Given her history, Tony found the latter more likely. "Uh, you know that if the police stop you, you'll be a lot later getting home."

"The police don't see this car."

"Damn."

"I move from world to world and this is what impresses you?"

"*This,* I understand. And . . ." Another light changed after only a moment of red. ". . . I was also impressed by the maggots."

The corner of her mouth he could see twisted up into a close approximation of a smile. "Fair enough. What happened to the girl?"

"What girl?"

"Kate."

"You know about Kate?"

"I was there. I saw. I needed to see." Her tone lengthened the list of questions even further—although the new ones hadn't quite acquired actual words.

"Henry took her home." At least he assumed Henry took her home. He'd been dropped off first and although Kate was sprawled across pristine upholstery in the back seat of the BMW still totally out of it, she was smiling. He'd reminded himself he trusted Henry, had stripped and fallen into bed. Sleep hadn't been long in coming and he really wished he hadn't thought about sleeping. Images from the dream played out like a slide show in his head.

Arra's voice disrupted the show. "You found a way without me."

"It's easier with you."

"Not always."

Okay. Enough was enough. "Stop doing that!"

"Doing what?"

"Adding another layer. Talking to you is like opening one of those nested doll things. You open one and there's another. I get that you're thinking things through, working out old shit—really I do get that—but every time you open your mouth, you're saying six or seven things besides the stuff you're saying out loud, but you're leaving me to figure out what those things are! How come I have to be the hero *and* figure all this shit out?" Whoa. Where had that come from? He didn't even feel better having said it.

"Maybe I should just drive."

"Yeah. Maybe you should."

Arra screeched into her parking place at the co-op, turned off the car, tossed Tony her keys, and disappeared. Damp air rushed in through the open window to fill the empty space.

He swallowed as his ears popped. "Guess I'm taking the scenic route."

It took him a while to lock up the car and figure out which key went where. By the time he got to the apartment, Whitby had his head buried in a bowl of food, but Zazu was nowhere in sight. Dropping his backpack by the door, Tony followed Arra's voice into the living room to find her with her butt in the air and *her* head nearly under the couch. Wincing, he looked away.

"Look, I said I was sorry. What more do you want?" The wizard was sounding increasingly desperate with every word.

"Is everything okay?"

"She's making me pay."

"Pay?"

"For abandoning her." Shuffling backward on her knees, Arra straightened. "No one does guilt like a cat."

"And you were only gone one night."

From the way Arra narrowed her eyes she'd picked up the subtext. *Just think of how she'll feel if you abandon her for good.* But all she said was, "Grab that catnip lizard out of the basket. It's her favorite toy."

Tony grabbed the stuffed animal that looked the most like a lizard and tossed it across the room.

"This isn't a lizard, it's a platypus!"

Say what? "Who the hell makes catnip platypuses?"

"Platy*pi*. I get them at a local craft fair." She ducked back under the couch. "Zazu, sweetie, see what I've got for you."

"It's almost quarter to ten. We don't have time for this."

Arra shuffled backward again. "Don't tell me, tell her."

Tony snagged the platypus out of the air as she tossed it back to him. As Arra stood and headed for the kitchen, he suddenly realized she expected him to coax the cat out from under the couch. "I don't know anything about cats!"

"Good. Maybe a fresh approach will work."

He thought about refusing, decided there was no percentage in it, and took up the position. Zazu glared at him from what was clearly just out of reach. Wait a minute. Just out of Arra's reach . . . He wasn't tall but he had a good four inches on her.

Grabbing the cat by a foreleg he started to slide her across the hardwood floor and nearly lost his hand at the wrist.

Ow! God damn it! Bad idea!

Except that it seemed to have worked. Whether she was satisfied now that she'd drawn blood or whether she was so mortally insulted she wasn't staying under the couch for another moment, Tony couldn't tell—nor, he supposed, did it matter. Point was, as he nursed his injuries, Zazu swaggered toward the kitchen, tail in the air.

Tony followed with a little less swagger, sucking his wrist.

"That Nightwalker of yours teaching you bad habits?"

"What? Oh." A final lick and he let his arm fall to his side. "No. And he's not mine."

She tested the temperature of the alcohol in the pot and began adding herbs. "Does he come when you call?"

"Well, yeah, but . . ."

"That's more than you can say about cats and most people would tell you that these two are mine."

"Most people?"

"Some people know better. Pass me the bay leaves."

As he handed them over, Tony wondered just how disturbed he should be about finding the smell of warm vodka and catnip comforting. A sharp pain in his right calf drew his attention down to an imperious black and white face. "What!"

Arra snickered and, stirring with her right hand, tossed him the paper bag of catnip with her left. "Try this. Why so jumpy when I showed up at your place this morning?" she continued as he tossed a handful of the dried leaves on the kitchen floor.

"Why was I so jumpy?" He stared at her in disbelief. "I don't know, maybe because I'm in the middle of breakfast and this wizard who might have been taken over by shadow—based on the whole ditching and disappearing thing—suddenly appears in my apartment! Not to mention being caught with my dick waving around."

"Ah, I see."

At first he thought she was laughing at him, but what he could see of her expression looked serious.

"Still have my thermoses?"

"In my backpack."

"Get them."

If anyone had *reason* to be jumpy . . . He set the pair of thermoses on the counter by the stove. "You know, I've got to say, this morning, even after I knew you weren't shadow-held, I was concerned about you."

"Why?"

"You looked bummed."

"Bummed?" The first soup ladle of potion splashed into the first thermos with a hollow sound. "I suppose that's as good a word as any." The sound grew higher pitched and less hollow as the thermos filled. "The shadow from Alan Wu touched me before I destroyed it. Only for an instant, but in that instant I knew what the shadow knew." She set the first thermos to one side and began filling the second. "It is one thing to extrapolate the probable fate of your home; it's another entirely to see it."

"I'm sorry."

"About what?"

He shrugged, made uncomfortable by the question. "I'm not sure. It's a Canadian thing."

Her snort sounded more like the Arra he'd started to know. Setting down the ladle, she wrapped her hand around each thermos in turn, singing out the vowels she'd used to make the first potion sparkle. After the whole beam-me-up-Scotty, now-you-see-me-now-you-don't it seemed unnecessarily . . . twee. She snorted again when he mentioned it.

"All magic involves the manipulation of energy. Lesser magics like this are, as you say, unnecessarily twee because lesser wizards need their cue cards to get the desired result. Doing it their way is, therefore, easier."

Tony didn't see the "therefore." "So what's the cost?"

"Cost?" She paused, the second lid half tightened.

"Yeah, there's *always* a cost."

"You're really a very remarkable young man."

Pointing out that flattery didn't answer the question seemed rude, so he waited. He was still waiting when she screwed the cup back on over the lid and passed the first thermos back to him. He was good at waiting. By the time the second thermos was ready, Arra'd realized that.

She sighed. "The more energy manipulated, the more it takes of the wizard's personal strength."

Tony nodded. That sounded reasonable. As he tucked the potion into his backpack, he decided not to make the obvious "you're so strong" declaration. In the last twenty-four hours, Arra had destroyed a shadow, driven to Whistler and back, snuck onto the soundstage to watch him and Henry deal with the gate, spent the night away from home wrestling with personal demons—probably not literally, but he wasn't ruling it out—popped into Tony's apartment, shielded her speeding car from the cops, popped into her own apartment, and zapped two liters of potion. Energy manipulation levels: high. Wizard's personal strength . . .

"Give me a minute to change."

"Change?"

"Clothes." She tossed the word over her shoulder on the way to the bedroom, adding, just before she closed the door behind her: "You won't make it out to the studio by 11:15 unless I drive, and I reek."

She was right. Not about the reeking—not by guy standards anyway, although he had no idea how women her age defined reek—but about the driving. Sunday transit schedules sucked as far as hitting the burbs in a hurry.

So, wizard's personal strength: energizer bunny levels.

In fact, ever since he'd reminded her about the cats it had been like he'd pulled a plug and the momentum of that initial "oh, my God" was keeping her moving. The faster she moved, the more she did, the less she had to deal with the crap the shadow had called up when it touched her.

Memo to self. Prepare for the crash and burn.

And hope it didn't happen at 80K.

Or at 120K, for that matter . . .

Both hands white-knuckled around the shoulder strap, Tony couldn't decide whether he preferred eyes open or eyes closed. Eyes open, he could see his imminent death in a fiery car crash approaching and prepare. Eyes closed, he could pretend he wasn't in a hatchback whipping diagonally through westbound traffic and occasionally, when things were tight, into the oncoming lane.

He liked taunting death as much as the next guy, but since the next guy was a middle-aged and possibly old wizard from another world and there were still four shadows unaccounted for, all bets were off. She was worse than Henry and Mouse combined.

"So do you always drive like this?"

"Scared?"

"No."

"Lying?"

Like he'd tell her. "No."

"Good. To answer your question, almost never. But we're in a hurry."

There were high spots of color on her cheeks—technically cheek since he could only see one. On the bright side: at this speed they'd be there soon. On the other side, the less bright side: any idiot knew that the more energy burned, the faster it ran out.

He had to distract her or at least slow her down. "The other reason I was so jumpy . . ."

"Jumpy?"

"When you played pop goes the weasel . . ."

"Wizard."

"Whatever. . . . in my apartment was that I'd just had a dream."

The eyebrow he could see, waggled.

"Not that kind of a dream. A bad dream. I dreamed that the shadow was back in control and it took me through the gate."

"To Oz?"

"To a room. It looked like a schoolroom or maybe a lab. There were books and blackboards with, I don't know, equations covering . . ." When Arra hit the brakes, he realized distraction was relative. He tightened his grip as the car fishtailed across the wet asphalt and into a Timmy's parking lot.

When the squealing stopped—and he was 99% sure the squealing had come from the tires—and the only sound was the rain on the roof and the swish/click of the windshield wipers, Arra turned to face him and said, "Were there more than equations on the blackboards?"

Their eyes were open and their expressions suggested they'd been alive for a very long time after they'd been nailed to the walls.

"Yeah."

"People?" The steering wheel creaked under her hands.

Tony nodded.

She closed her eyes for a moment and when she opened them again, he knew he wouldn't have to describe what he'd seen. She'd seen it, too. "You weren't dreaming. Those were images the shadow left behind. While it controlled you, you touched its memory."

"I touched?"

"Yes. It explains why the shadow-stain is stronger on you than the others."

Shadow-stain. Fucking great. *Excuse me while I go home and soak my soul in cold water.* And then he realized . . . "So that . . . what I saw, it was real?"

"Yes."

"Who were they?"

"The last two members of my order who stood to face the Shadowlord."

"I'm sorry."

"Why? You didn't do anything."

"That was . . ." He sighed and sank back against the seat. "Forget it."

A light touch on his arm drew his attention back to the other side of the car. "*I'm* sorry."

"Hey." He shrugged. "They were your friends."

"Yes." A simple acknowledgment carrying an emotional payload that filled the car like smoke.

Because he couldn't look at her and because he had to do *something,* he checked his watch. Crap. 10:40. He'd just wanted to distract her, slow her down, not bring her back to a complete stop. "Arra, we have to get going or we won't get to the gate in time."

"Right." She fumbled the car into reverse and nearly backed over an elderly man carrying three medium coffees on a cardboard tray.

"Did you want me to drive?"

"Don't be ridiculous."

A skateboarder flipped her the finger as she cut him off.

"I'm just saying . . ."

"Well, don't!"

They got to the studio at 11:02, only to find that the code on the soundstage keypad had been changed. Three sets of wrong numbers would set off the alarms. Tony remembered with one number to go and snatched his hand away from the pad. Alarms would bring police and with his luck Constable Elson would ride back into his life. "Can you do something about this?"

"No."

"Can you pop inside and open it?" He knew the answer before she opened her mouth. Reaction had finally kicked in and her cheeks had turned an alarming shade of gray. "Are you all right?"

"I'll manage."

"This thing's been the same since I got here." The pad was off limits so he kicked the concrete foundation blocks. "Why are they fucking changing it now?"

"They had to change the front door lock. It probably reminded them about the back."

"Fucking great. Hang on; you have a key for the . . . *old* front door lock. Never mind." 11:07. This was going to be close. Actually, if he didn't come up with something, it wasn't going to be at all. "The carpenter's door!"

"The what?"

"The big door they use for deliveries of lumber and building crap. Three of them smoke and they won't want to keep locking and unlocking the door every time they want a butt." He started to run and stopped when he realized Arra wasn't beside him.

"Keep going," she snapped. "I don't sprint!"

"You'll catch up?"

"If you don't move your ass, I'll run you over."

Kicking up gravel, Tony raced around the corner and up the west side of the building. As long as she didn't ditch him again . . .

The carpenter's door looked like a corrugated section of the wall. Because the tracks were hidden and the latch had been painted with the same dark brown antirust paint as the door, it was hard to find without knowing where to look. Deliberately so.

And it looked like it weighed a fucking ton.

Fortunately, it was already open about an inch. Tony hooked his fingers around the edge and threw all his weight against it. It flew open so fast it dropped him on his ass, the big door sliding soundlessly along its tracks until his dangling weight stopped it.

Plus ten for maintenance. Minus several thousand for not warning a guy!

He scrambled to his feet, stepped over the lower track, and left the door open for Arra as he ran toward the gate. At least two hammers were pounding out a staccato rhythm back behind the permanent sets that made up Raymond Dark's office, but the dining room was finished and deserted. His back teeth beginning to vibrate and his hands sweating so heavily he could barely maintain his grip, he yanked the big lamp into position, threw a cable out of the box, and bent to make the connection.

"And what the hell do you think you are playing at?"

Shit! Sorge—no mistaking the DP's accent. *He's probably here to work out the lighting for tomorrow morning.* Unfortunately, knowing that was no help at all.

"I am waiting."

Teeth gritted in an effort to keep his skull from blowing apart, Tony finished making the connection and straightened. The gate was about to open. All he had to do was turn the lamp on; he could lie about what he was playing at just as easily with the gate blocked. Easier. More easily? Bottom line, he could concentrate on the lie if he knew the shadows—incoming, outgoing, pogo-ing—had been stopped. But Sorge was between him and the lighting board and it didn't look as if he was going to move.

Tackle him?

And get fired; losing access to the gate and any chance to stop the Shadowlord.

Reason with him?

Given how pissed off he looked, that seemed even less likely to succeed.

The sudden brilliant light took them both by surprise.

"Tony's doing some work for me, Sorge." Arra released the switch and came out from behind the light board. "I need a number of readings off this lamp." She tossed Tony the light meter. "Go."

He trotted toward the set, allowing Sorge's protests and Arra's answering argument to wash over him. In another couple of minutes, it wouldn't matter. The gate would close and Arra could even let the DP think he'd won. In the meantime, Tony maintained the charade, holding what looking like a light meter but felt like a battery from one of the radios up in the light. He was as far from the actual opening as he could get and still make it look real but it wasn't far enough to escape the feeling of being examined.

Yeah, and me wearing a big fucking shadow-stain.

Then the gate closed and the lamp switched off a heartbeat later.

"Oh, don't be so Gallic!" Arra snapped. "Your lamp is fine and I have all the readings I need. Tony!"

"Yeah." He tossed her back the alleged light meter.

She nearly fumbled the catch and just for an instant it looked like a battery.

Sorge frowned and Tony prepared to assure him that he hadn't seen what he'd thought he'd seen.

"You are not well?"

Okay, *that* he had seen.

"I'm just a little tired."

"You look like shit. You should not be here. Go home."

Blunt, but accurate.

Apparently Arra thought so, too. "I think I will." Rummaging in the pocket of her raincoat, she pulled out her car keys. "Tony, you're driving."

"Sure." He ignored Sorge's dramatically raised eyebrow and obvious assumption—*Hello, gay! And she's old enough to be my grandmother so eww*—and fell into step beside the wizard. Her fingers closed around his arm. He bent it up and a step later was holding about half her weight. As soon as they were far enough away so they wouldn't be overheard, he bent toward her and murmured, "Are you okay?"

"Maintaining that glamour took about all I had left."

Tony paused as she staggered and walked on a little more slowly.

"It's been too long since I've been what I am. Too long since I shaped a world's energy to my personal use. I shouldn't have wasted all that power this morning."

He shrugged, carefully so as not to dislodge her. "Everyone has shouldn'ts. You drag them around with you, they just weigh you down."

They were at the back door. She patted his arm as she released him. "You're a good kid."

"I'm twenty-four."

Her turn to shrug. "I'm a hundred and thirty-seven."

"No shit?"

"If you're asking about my bowel movements, that's none of your damned business." She reached up and tore a taped piece of paper off the wall. "Here, you'll need this tonight."

It was the new code numbers for the lock.

"You know, I was thinking . . ."

Arra snorted. "Well, it's a start."

" . . . if one of the shadow-held showed up to use the gate, they wouldn't be able to get in. You know—new code . . ." He waved the paper and shoved it in his back pocket. "New front door lock. And if they didn't know about the carpenter's door . . ." *Fuck.* "Except it was open."

"I closed it behind me."

"Okay, then. They couldn't get in, so they could still be out in the parking lot." He threw open the door. The sun had come out, puddles sparkled, and a pair of pigeons stared up at him with vapid avian indifference. "Or not."

"Or they could be returning to their car," Arra allowed. "You'd better run and check. I'll follow as fast as I can."

"Yeah, but . . ."

"I'll be fine. I'll be better if I can kick shadow ass."

"But you look . . ."

"Go!"

So he went. The pigeons took flight, their shadows trailing earthbound behind them.

There were half a dozen vehicles in the parking lot and an unshaven man in damp, rumpled clothes about to get into one of them.

"Hartley!"

The boom operator didn't even look up. Fortunately, the car locks seemed to be giving him a little trouble.

"Hartley! Wait up, man. I got to tell you about the really weird thing that just happened inside!"

That got his attention. He glanced up just as the locks thunked down. "Weird thing?"

All the hair lifted off the back of Tony's neck. *Oh, yeah, definitely shadow-held.* He jogged to a stop beside the car, let his backpack slide off his shoulder, and forced a smile. "Buzzy shit and then it got dark and then there was music. Bad eighties power rock." He dropped the pack by the back tire, played a couple of air guitar riffs and decided, as Hartley's eyes narrowed, that maybe the music was a bit over the top.

"You see me."

Or maybe it wasn't the music at all.

"Of course I see you. Duh. You're standing right there."

Actually, he didn't blame shadow-Hartley for growling and grabbing. That line hadn't worked the first time and this time, even he didn't believe it. This time, however, he was ready for the grab. As Hartley's fingers closed around his jacket, he threw himself backward. They hit the ground together and Tony rolled the older man to the bottom.

"You cannot hold me."

He tightened his grip on skinny wrists. "Bet?"

The shadow began to separate.

"Arra!" She had to be in the parking lot by now, but he couldn't see her. The car was in the way.

The shadow was now a distinct shape, rising up out of Hartley toward him. If he let go, it would suck back in and make a break for it. If he didn't . . .

If I bash his head against the ground, could I knock him out? Unlikely. And he'd have to let go to do it.

"Arra!"

Six inches. Four. He wasn't . . . He couldn't . . . If it touched him . . . Releasing his grip, he scrabbled backward on his hands and knees, down the length of Hartley's legs until he slammed up against the open car door.

Only a short strand of darkness connected the shadow to the boom operator.

It surged against that last restraint. Snapped it. Slid along Hartley's prone body. Flowed down over his legs. Connected Hartley's shadow to Tony's as Tony flung himself up and into the car.

As Tony crawled as fast as he could across the bench seat, reaching for the handle on the passenger side, he could feel it still moving along his shadow, using it as a safe path through the midday sun. Then cold air caressed his ankle and he bit back a scream. They could move faster than this. They could move faster than Henry. It was toying with him.

Arra could taste blood in the back of her mouth as she forced herself over the last few meters to the car. What the hell had she been thinking this morning? Right. She hadn't been thinking. She'd been reacting. She'd been stupid. Careless.

She tripped over a groaning body, glanced down to see the boom operator as she slammed against the trunk of the car, and saw the shadow slip off his lower legs. No time to recover. One hand bracing herself against the warm metal, she sucked air in and breathed out the incantation. Sucked in air. Breathed out incantation. Her pulse was pounding so hard in her temples she couldn't even hear her own voice, but it didn't matter. She could say this particular incantation in her sleep. Had.

Sucked in air. Staggered forward. Finished incantation.

Dropped to her knees, looked up to see Tony staring down at her from the front seat of the car. She blinked and managed to focus. Recoiled a little as the taint rolled over her strong and dark. Relaxed as that was all she felt.

"Arra?"

"I'm fine. You?"

"Fine."

He looked terrified, but considering the alternative, that was close enough to fine. She dropped to her knees beside Hartley's writhing body as Tony got out of the car, and worked a thermos out of the backpack. "You need to get some of this down him."

When he reached for the thermos, she clutched it close and glared. "Get your own, this one's mine."

The vodka helped.

"Get as much of it into him as you can, then get him into his car and get the bottle out of the glove compartment and put it in his lap."

"How do you know he has a bottle in the glove compartment?"

She took another long comforting drink and shrugged, the warm car against the back almost making up for the gravel digging into her butt. "People talk. Next person out will find him, assume he went on a bender, and deal."

"I never knew."

"The one thing alcoholics excel at is hiding; hiding what they are, what they do, what it's doing to them."

"But right now he's okay?"

About to snap out something rude, Arra took a closer look at Tony's face and reconsidered. He honestly cared. "Probably." It was the closest to reassurance she could manage, but it seemed to be enough. She watched as Tony handed the last cup of potion to Hartley and let him drink it himself, watched him help the boom operator into the front seat, watched him lean in, and saw him emerge a moment later with a set of car keys that he dropped and kicked under the car. She winced as he slammed the door. Everything had gone a little fuzzy and she was beginning to get remarkably cold.

The vodka was good, though.

Tony's shadow stopped about a quarter inch from her leg. She looked up to see Tony looking down at her.

"We should go."

She snorted as he took her thermos and screwed the cap back on, his shadow waiting impassively for him to finish. "I should have gone a long time ago."

Arra wasn't exactly a dead weight as Tony helped her into the passenger seat of her car, but she wasn't light either. Not muscular, but solid. Heavier than she looked. He thought about making a "weight of the world" crack, but the smell of vodka combined with the distinctly lighter thermos decided him against it.

Besides, if anyone was holding the weight of the world, it was him.

Like she keeps saying . . . He fastened her seat belt, closed the door, and walked around to the driver's side. *. . . . it's not even her world.*

If not those exact words, something like that.

As he pulled out of the parking lot, she unscrewed the thermos and took another drink. He thought about protesting, but figured the alcohol was more legal in her than in an unsealed container—just in case.

Traffic was light heading back into the city. He could feel her watching him, but he kept his eyes on the road. Still, the watching reminded him of something.

"Arra? You said you were there last night, watching in the soundstage, because you needed to know. What did you need to know?"

He started to think she'd fallen asleep by the time she answered. "I needed to know if you'd fight without me."

"Oh."

He fought the urge to speed up as another car pulled out to pass and then slowed to let it back into the lane. *Easy enough to fight without you,* he said silently. *You're not fighting!* Then he frowned and remembered how she'd looked at the back door, and how she'd made it to the parking lot and, running on empty, had still vanquished the shadow.

Maybe there was more than one fight going on.

⟿ THIRTEEN

Laid out fully clothed on her bed under a fuzzy blanket stamped with a Hilton Hotel imprint, Arra muttered an incoherent protest and immediately went to sleep. Both cats made wide circles around Tony, then leaped up onto the bed and settled on either side of the wizard, matching glares and lashing tails making it quite clear they thought he had no business being there.

Which, he supposed, he didn't.

On the other hand, he had a strong feeling he had to stay hidden. Remembering the feeling of being watched as he stood under the gate, he could only hope that the whole shadow-stained thing wasn't equivalent to a big neon sign—*In case of invasion break this guy.* And there were still three shadows on the loose. Arra's apartment felt safe.

His stomach growled.

Ears saddled, Zazu growled an answer.

Because he didn't feel right about raiding Arra's fridge, he slipped her keys into his pocket and headed out looking for food. The hall was empty. He moved quickly and quietly toward the elevator. The general paranoia might be undefined, but *this*, this was specific. The last person he wanted to explain himself to was Julian-from-across-the-hall as he had a strong suspicion that Julian would consider three visits grounds for assigning chores.

The elevator gave him a few bad moments, the word "weak" repeating itself over and over in his head. *Weak? Trapped, I could understand.* He squinted around the tiny, brightly lit space made even more claustrophobic by all the highly polished surfaces. Still, given the way *eau de disinfectant* seemed to be replacing a good part of the oxygen, maybe weak wasn't that surprising.

Crossing the co-op's lobby gave him no problems.

He paused on the threshold, strangely unwilling to step outside.

Three mountain bikers rode by closely followed by a skateboarder and two preteens on in-line skates. It was the kind of early spring day that made Vancouverites, who conveniently forgot the 250 days of rain a year, unbearably smug about their weather—winds off the ocean had blown away clouds and pollutants and the sun shone brilliantly down through a crystal clear sky. Micas in the concrete sparkled and the city gleamed.

No shadows, at least none that weren't the result of a solid object blocking the sun, and no Shadowlord. *There's nothing out there waiting for me except lunch.*

Heart pounding, he took a fast step, almost a hop, over the threshold.

Nothing happened, but the feeling of being watched remained.

Fine. He'd grab food and he'd head right back to Arra's apartment. Sighing at his interior drama queen, he glanced back at his shadow, still lying predominantly in the co-op lobby, and muttered, "Come on, then!"

All things considered, he was relieved when it followed.

A thousand voices cried, "Save us! Save us! You are our only hope!" Hands clutched at her, desperate fingers shredding clothing and the skin beneath it. She was drowning in their need. They were pulling her under. How could she save them when she couldn't save herself *from* them?

The cats were still on Arra's bed when he returned and they stayed there while he ate, watched some golf—the one thing on television he was sure wouldn't wake the wizard—and worked his way through five days of the *Vancouver Sun*. He didn't usually read newspapers; he just didn't have the time and from the pristine folds, he guessed Arra's time had been a bit short lately, too. *Wouldn't want to cut into all that spider solitaire . . .*

It seemed to be business as usual in the lower mainland.

While he hadn't been expecting to see SHADOWS STALK CITY in banner headlines, it was weird to think he was one of only three people who knew of the danger and if he told anyone what he knew, told them that two people were dead because of shadows slipping through from another world, they wouldn't believe him. Not without having seen the things he'd seen. Done the things he'd done. Known the people he knew.

Eyes rolling, Tony tossed the last paper aside. Right. The people he knew . . .

A vampire, a wizard, and a production assistant go into a bar . . .

Fortunately, a snort from the bedroom saved him from having to come up with a punch line.

Cats winding around her feet, Arra stumbled out into the living room, glowered at him for a long moment from under lowered brows, and finally snapped, "Make coffee!" before turning on one heel, going back into the bedroom, and slamming the door.

Tony did as he was told.

"There's three shadows left and we have seven hours until the gate reopens. You've been very lucky so far, but there's nothing to say all three of them won't show up together and I can think of any number of ways that they can stop you."

So could Tony.

"Finding them and stopping them individually before they get to the gate was a smart plan. Is still a smart plan. We need to pursue it."

"Are you strong enough?" There were still dark circles under her eyes and the skin on the backs of her hands looked thin and translucent.

"In spite of the morning's evidence, I know how to marshal my power." Sitting at the tiny kitchen table, Arra held out her mug. "I will find them, I will destroy the shadow, and you will do everything else," she announced as Tony refilled it.

"Uh . . . You'll need to make more potion."

"Fine! *And* I'll make more potion." She nodded toward the living room. "Bring me my Yellow Pages. But first put a bagel in the toaster oven."

Apparently *everything else* meant everything else.

One of the shadows was at Richmond Nanak Sar Gursikh Temple on West-minster Highway.

Holding the phone book entry in one hand, Arra sifted through the ashes with the other and sighed. "We need to find another phone book."

"No shit."

"No time to waste," the wizard added pointedly.

Which was when Tony realized *he* had to find another phone book.

"There should be one up in the party room. Sixth floor."

Even better. "You want me to steal the Yellow Pages out of your co-op's party room so that you can destroy them?"

"So that I can use them to discover the location of a shadow-held." She dusted the ash off her fingers. "A shadow-held that might be held by *the* shadow-spy that takes the information back through the gate that convinces the Shadowlord to invade and destroy your world. Yes."

"Yeah. All right. Perspective; I get it." Wondering when they'd started calling them shadow-spies—*Like shadows alone aren't enough?*—he headed for the door, dancing sideways as Zazu hissed at him.

"What did you do to my cat?"

It had to be the attempted drag out from under the couch. Clearly, Zazu was holding a grudge. "Nothing."

He heard Arra snort as the door closed behind him. She was the wizard; if she wanted to know, she could ask the cat. Stepping out of Arra's apartment didn't seem to have the same emotional effect as it had earlier. He felt . . .

Tony frowned. Actually, the feeling of safety had vanished about the time Arra woke up, and he'd felt antsy ever since. Doing her wizardship's bidding had masked it, but now that he had nothing to occupy his mind, it was hard to ignore. The empty hall felt crowded with indefinable dangers and during the short walk to the elevator, he kept spinning around, certain someone or something was walking behind him, treading on his shadow.

There was never anything there *but* his shadow, clinging to his heels as if it, too, was sensitive to whatever the hell was going on. The elevator was just as distressing as it had been earlier. Squinting, Tony pressed the button for the sixth floor and hoped the shadow-stain wasn't somehow making him sensitive to light.

Or Henry . . .

"That Nightwalker of yours teaching you bad habits?"

Henry had been feeding from him off and on for the last five years. More off than on lately, but still . . . Were there cumulative effects? He ran his tongue over his teeth. They didn't feel any sharper. Mythically—and Tony'd made a point of checking out the myths way back when—it didn't work that way, but Henry'd always insisted that the myths were flawed. Insisted without specifying exactly what the flaws were.

Was he changing?

Oh, get the fuck over yourself, he snarled silently as the elevator doors opened. *There isn't enough shit going on, you have to come up with new crap?*

At just past five on a sunny Sunday afternoon, the party room was empty. He could hear two people talking out on the deck, but a row of trees in pots blocked the view through the window and the phone books were stacked in a pale bookcase by the door—the perfect setup to grab and go without being seen. Yellow Pages for Vancouver and the lower mainland in hand, Tony wasted a moment checking out the room. About 99% certain Arra still hadn't cleaned it, he figured someone else must have because it looked spotless. Blue—carpet, walls, upholstery—but spotless.

If anything, he was feeling even more freaky riding down in the elevator. Maybe it was guilt although, given his life prior to Henry, he somehow doubted it. Lifting a set of Yellow Pages would easily be among the least of his crimes.

Massive tome tucked under one arm in an effort to be as inconspicuous as possible, he stepped out through the elevator's opening door and into a barrage of sound.

"Hush, Moira! Quiet, girl!"

Although still safely tethered in Julian's arms, the Chihuahua was making it perfectly clear that if Tony wanted to get any farther into the hall, he'd have to pass her. Ears ringing, Tony gave some serious thought to doggie-flavored chalupas and stepped sideways.

Julian stepped with him, the dog continuing to yap hysterically. "You're that friend of Arra's."

"Yeah. So?"

"So tell her that common room isn't going to clean itself!"

"Sure." Tony suspected that if Arra wanted it to, the common room wouldn't only clean itself, it'd take itself out for dinner and a movie.

"And tell her . . ." He pushed his voice through Moira's continuing protest. ". . . that I *will* bring this up with the Borg!"

The Borg? That put a whole new slant on co-op management.

"And I guarantee the board will have something to say to her!"

Oh. The board. Not nearly as interesting. Holding the phone book like he had every right to it, Tony put his back to the wall and managed to slide past. Twisting in Julian's arms, Moira's eyes never left him although the high-pitched barking was mercifully replaced by a low growl, the vibration causing her substantial jowls to quiver. It seemed she had better phone book sense than her owner.

Julian's high forehead started to crease.

Or maybe not.

He clearly knew something was wrong and it would only be a matter of moments before he figured out what. Time for a major distraction.

"You're an actor, aren't you? I can tell by the way you use your voice." Smiling insincerely, Tony cranked the bullshit up to full power. Two syllable ac-tors were the most susceptible to unsubstantiated hope. "I work out at CB Productions, in Burnaby—we do *Darkest Night*, the highest rated syndicated vampire detective show in North America—and we're always looking for new faces. You know, people who haven't already cropped up in every show shooting out here? You should stop by sometime. Talk to Peter—he does most of the casting."

"I'm theater mostly . . . Moira, quiet!"

"Sure, but there's no harm in making some solid cash to help support the arts, right?" His reaching fingers touched Arra's door. Just another few inches . . .

"Well, I was critically acclaimed for my Mustardseed at Vanier Park last year when Bard in the Park did—Moira, shut up!—*Midsummer Night's Dream*."

"Great. Experience." Three fingers hooked around the doorknob. "Peter loves Shakespeare. Hope to see you out there!" He was inside before Julian could reply, a final volley of yipping sounding through the door.

"What was that all about?" Arra called from the kitchen.

"Moira objected to me stealing the phone book."

"Fortunately, Moira's small enough to punt down the hall, but how did you keep Julian from calling the police?"

"He never noticed. He had his dick in a knot about you blowing off the party room and then I . . ." Tony flushed as Arra turned from stirring the potion and raised a speculative brow. "Nothing like that. I just told him he should stop by the studio sometime and talk to Peter, him being an ac-tor and all."

"Oh, Peter's going to love that."

"Two people are dead. If these shadows get back through the gate, more people will die." The phone book slammed down on the counter. "Besides, you keep saying the Shadowlord can't be stopped. With any luck, we'll be ass-deep in Armageddon before he gets there."

She looked at him strangely for a long moment.

"What?"

"Nothing."

It was obviously something, but Tony didn't bother pushing. Arra's explanations never actually explained anything and he had enough unanswered questions already on his plate.

The second shadow was at the South Delta Baptist Church.

"They're widening their search."

"Yeah." Tony stared at the scrap of yellow paper. "Where the hell is Tsawassen?"

"About half an hour south of the city, very nearly at the US border. Now, we'll need one more phone book."

"No." He shook his head, addresses laid out on the table. "This first one, the temple? It's in Richmond. That's south of the city. Then this one is farther south. What's to say that when you did this first one that's where the shadow *was* and now it's here, at this one? It moved while I was finding the book."

"It doesn't work that way."

"Yeah, but . . ."

"That's not the way the spell works. I ask where I can find the shadow and this . . . these . . . are the answers."

"I get that; but time has passed. So, logically . . ."

Arra snorted. "And how long have *you* been doing this?"

"What?"

"Because I've been doing it for a while now and I know what the hell I'm talking about." She handed him the pair of thermoses. "Put these away and let's go."

But he noticed she didn't ask again for a third phone book.

Children raced around the small groups of adults standing outside the Nanak Sar Gursikh Temple—something family oriented had obviously just finished. Tony parked carefully, then reached over and shook Arra awake.

"The Light of Yeramathia!"

"Okay."

She blinked up at him, the edges of her eyes pink and swollen. "What did I say?"

He told her, then asked what it meant.

Arra snorted as she straightened and unbuckled her seat belt. "It means nothing. It was hope that became a lie."

Since this was about as clear as her explanations usually got, Tony merely shrugged and stepped out onto the sidewalk looking for someone he knew. Someone who'd been on Arra's short list of the potential shadow-held. He looked for Dalal first, figuring that since the prop man was Sikh, this would logically be one of the places where he'd look for the light.

Yeah, like logic has anything to do with my world . . .

Barking drew his attention to the temple parking lot where an elderly man, who was definitely not Sikh and had probably just been out for an early evening walk, was attempting to control his dog. Breeds didn't mean a lot to Tony; dogs came either large enough to avoid or small enough to ignore and this was one of the former. And then he noticed who the dog was barking at.

Ben Ward, one of the lighting crew.

Also not Sikh and looking like he hadn't been home in nearly forty-eight hours.

"Arra?"

"I see him. Let's go."

He glanced over at her. "Let's go? You make it sound like we're in an episode of *Law and Order: Magic and Mayhem.*"

"Don't laugh." She started across the grass. "They pitched it."

Actually, Tony wasn't laughing. "What exactly are we about to do?"

"I get close enough to haul the shadow out of him, then I destroy it."

"That's what *you're* about to do."

"While you make with the potion and come up with a plausible story."

"Story?"

"For the three dozen or so witnesses."

"Right."

It looked like Ben had been heading across the parking lot away from the temple when he'd crossed paths with the dog. He was staring at it like he'd never seen one before. Maybe he hadn't. For all Tony knew, Arra's world didn't have dogs. Or, he amended, remembering his dream, dogs just hadn't been a part of the shadow's short life.

Too much to hope for, that even distracted by the dog, Ben wouldn't see them approach. They were still more than ten feet away when he turned, stared at Tony in confusion, then at Arra in fear. "You!"

Tony half expected to see the shadow surge out of him like it had out of Alan Wu but shadow-Ben smiled, winked, and ran toward an extended family piling kids into a minivan. He careened through them like an out of control billiard ball. A child screamed. Men and women yelled in two languages. Strong fingers grabbed the stranger and threw him away from the van.

Leaping out at the end of her leash, the dog kept barking.

Ben hit the ground and stayed there.

"It's left him!" Arra announced, panting a little as they quickened their pace.

"And gone where?"

In answer, one of the preteen boys raced away from his family and charged into a clump of older kids. More shouting. And a moment later, another body on the ground. The remaining teenagers scattered.

Men and older boys were running toward the parking lot.

Tony stopped at the edge of the asphalt. "Is that kid . . . ?"

"Dead?" Fingers closed around his arm as Arra leaned on him, catching her breath. "No, but if that shadow keeps moving through this crowd, I guarantee it's going to hit someone who can't handle it."

"Like Alan?"

"Exactly like."

"Where is it now?"

"I don't know!"

Someone did.

Twisting free, Tony sprinted toward the old man with the dog, tripped over the leash, and ripped it free of a tiring grip.

The dog took off across the parking lot.

"Shania!"

"I'll get her!" Tony leaped to his feet and followed, ignoring the deserved string of expletives flung after him. *Sorry about your dog, mister. Trying to save the world here!*

It seemed the shadow was still in one of the teenage boys. Great. They'd had a chance of pulling this off as long as it was in Ben, but the Sikh community was very protective of their own and Tony could only see this ending badly.

Still barking wildly, the dog slammed into a running teenager, flinging the boy into the outstretched arms of a middle-aged woman. She screamed as he sank into her embrace. He jerked, then stiffened and slid bonelessly to the ground.

Shania sailed over the boy and landed on the woman, making contact with all four paws. Ringed fingers stopped snapping teeth an inch from flesh.

This time Tony saw the shadow move.

Shania yelped once. Woman and dog collapsed together to the ground.

Tony got to the dog before the first boot could impact with her ribs. He took the blow on his thigh, gathered the trembling body up in both arms and rolled away yelling, "You don't understand; she wasn't attacking. This dog's a hero! We're from the health department," he continued, not giving anyone else a chance to talk. "The first man who fell was contaminated by some stupid kid with a new designer drug. It's a dust that works on contact with skin, he passed it on to that boy who passed it on to that boy." He jerked his head toward the two teenagers, now standing and being fussed over by family. "Who passed it on to this woman. The dog could smell it. This dog has kept everyone else from being contaminated."

"You're touching the dog!" But the voice held as much confusion as anger and Tony realized they actually had a chance of pulling this off. Witnesses were still too spread out for mob mentality to have taken over.

"I'm immune to the drug, that's why we were sent."

In the face of the inexplicable, people looked for explanations, something to make sense of what hadn't made sense. The explanation didn't have to make sense; it only had to sound like it did.

"And you're from the health department?"

"We are." Tony relaxed slightly as Arra pushed through the crowd holding up what looked like official documentation.

"Get out of my way," she snapped, "and let me make sure it ends at this dog."

"We should call 911," someone muttered.

They should, Tony agreed silently, but given cultural politics they probably wouldn't. *Lucky break for our side.*

Dropping heavily to her knees, Arra pressed a hand against the dog's heaving ribs. Only Tony saw that the hand had slipped through fur and flesh and emerged holding a writhing shadow. Murmuring the incantation under her breath, she forced her hands together as the shadow struggled to survive, finally squashing it into nothing.

Shania whined, wriggled, and bit Tony on the hand. Hard. As he jerked back, she squirmed free and ran into the arms of her owner.

"Good," Arra announced in a tone that brooked no argument. "The dog has neutralized the drug. Ought to get a medal. Now then, move aside and let me look at this woman. Thermos!"

It took Tony a moment to realize the last word had been directed at him and then he shrugged out of his backpack and pulled a thermos free.

"Eww." A girl in the crowd wrinkled her nose. "It smells like that stuff in the back of Uncle Virn's garden."

"Be quiet, Kira."

"No," another voice said thoughtfully. "It does."

"Catnip is a medicinal relaxant," Tony said with as much authority as he could muster. "Let's get those others over here, we'll need to have the . . . m looked at, too." He'd been about to identify Arra as a nurse and changed his mind at the last minute. With his luck there'd be a nurse in the group and he didn't want them suddenly thinking they should get involved.

Arra helped her middle-aged patient sit up. "How are you feeling?"

"What happened?"

The wizard rocked back on her heels, and nodded toward the surrounding people. "Explain it to her." She started for the teenagers as half a dozen voices began half a dozen different versions of the story. The younger teenager was protesting he was fine, the other, to Tony's critical eye, seemed to be milking his collapse for all it was worth.

Snagging Tony's arm as he tried to follow, she muttered, "I'll deal with the kids, you get as much out of the other thermos into Ben as you can, then get him into the car. If we give them time to think, we're . . ."

"Screwed?"

"Well put."

Fortunately, Ben wasn't much bigger than Tony, and they were essentially being ignored. By the time he had the electrician in the car, Arra was crossing the lawn toward him. "Final words," she murmured as she slid into the passenger seat.

"Thank you for your cooperation. If you have any questions, call health services." About to remind them that the dog was a hero, he noticed the dog and her owner were nowhere around and decided not to bring it up. *Out of sight, out of mind,* he told the world silently as he started the car. *Do* not *let any of this come back on Shania.* Shifting out of park, he pulled into traffic and headed away from the temple faster than could strictly be considered safe. But *safe,* experience had taught him, was a relative term. "Where are we going now?"

Arra waved the second piece of the Yellow Pages at him.

"With Ben?"

"We don't have time to take him home. We'll do it after."

"Man, the wife's going to kill me!" Ben slurred from the backseat.

"Let's hope not," Arra snapped. "Go to sleep."

There was a muffled thud as Ben's head hit the rear window.

"Health services?"

Tony shrugged as he slowed for a yellow light. "It worked."

"Yes. It did."

Safely stopped he turned to look at her. She was frowning speculatively. "What?"

"Nothing."

"The trick is to keep talking so no one has time to ask questions and then, you know, you show up with the paperwork. Official documents carry a lot of weight. The whole Canadian peace, order, and good government thing."

"I'm sure. But there will be questions."

"Not our problem, now they'll call health services."

"And they are—specifically?"

"Good question. You okay? I mean you did some power stuff there."

"Very little. I'm fine." She sounded tired, but he wasn't going to argue.

Tony didn't know how it worked on the wizard's world, but on this one *I'm fine* meant any injuries short of decapitation weren't to be discussed. "You?"

"I got bit," he said as the light changed.

"No surprise. It wasn't a fun experience for poor Shania. Or the shadow. It must have thought the dog was a perfect host; four legs against two, we'd never catch it. But the dog didn't have quite enough sense of self to sustain it."

"I was going to ask."

"I know."

"And," he added, his leg throbbing as he remembered, "I got kicked."

"Why?"

"They were aiming at the dog. Where are we going again?"

"Tsawassen. Near the border."

"Right." He headed up the ramp off Westminster and onto 99 South. "So the people are going to be okay? I mean, the shadow wasn't in any of them for very long."

"The one boy may not recover."

"What?" Tony fought the car back onto pavement as his jerk toward the wizard put the right wheels on the shoulder.

"The second boy, the older boy, was twisted—his pattern wasn't compatible. I doubt the potion will be enough."

"Can't you do something?"

"Like what?"

His fingers tightened around the steering wheel. "I don't know; untwist him."

"No."

"Fuck."

"This isn't all bright lights and vodka, Tony." He would have protested he knew that, but the memories weighing down her voice kept him silent. "Stopping the Shadowlord is about stopping death and destruction. Only two dead and one injured; we've been very lucky so far."

He supposed that was hard to argue with. They were twelve kilometers down the highway before he tried. "If we'd waited for Ben to come to the gate, this never would have happened."

"But if he'd gotten through the gate, if he'd given the Shadowlord the information he needs to invade, it would start happening with a soul-destroying frequency." After a long moment she sighed and said, "All the easy answers get lost in the shadows."

They reached the South Delta Baptist Church at 8:10. Tony parked in the nearly empty lot, twisted around, and dragged his backpack out from between Ben's legs. "It's past sunset," he told the wizard, nodding west to where the sky had turned a thousand shades of orange and yellow and pink. "I need to call Henry."

"The Nightwalker cannot help us now."

Oh, great. Serious lackage of contractions. What's up her nose? The larger part of the drive south had been accomplished while listening to *The Best of Queen, Vol. 1* because it was the only tape in the car. Arra's eyes had been closed, so Tony'd assumed she'd been napping. Maybe she had. Given her history, the odds were good she hadn't been dreaming about Mel Gibson.

"Henry's helped in the past," Tony pointed out, punching in the number one-handed. "And he'll be helping later, so if it's all the same to you, I think I'll keep him in . . . Henry!" Henry could do both Prince of Darkness and Prince of Man over the phone, but tonight he sounded like neither. *Talk about locking the garage after the car's been stolen . . .* After making arrangements to meet at Arra's at 9:30, Tony hung up to find the wizard staring out the window at the collection of red brick buildings.

"That's a large facility," she said before he could speak. "It won't be easy finding the shadow."

"We'll split up . . ."

"Oh, yes, that always works so well." Her hands closed around her seat belt strap though she made no move to release it. "It won't always be so easy."

"Easy?" He waved the dog bite, now purple and swollen, in front of her. "*And* I've been grabbed, pummeled, kicked, shadowed . . ." Words seemed less than capable of describing what had happened with Henry, so he skipped it. "Two people are dead, one's twisted, Mouse has a broken jaw, Lee thinks he's going bugfuck, we have an enchanted electrician in the backseat, I've been living most of the last few days in a state of high terror, and you say it's been easy?"

"Yes. So far, it's been easy." She turned to face him. "Even on you. Realize that it's going to get a lot worse. The longer the shadow remains in a body, the more of the host's characteristics it absorbs—it stops acting and starts becoming. Humanity didn't become the dominant species on this world by playing nice. The shadow in Alan Wu chose to attack. His shadow . . ." She jerked her head toward the backseat. ". . . chose to run." Her voice roughened. "There are other more terrible options."

Tony stared at her for a long moment then pulled out the thermos holding the lesser amount of potion. "Drink?"

"Why the hell not." There was just enough remaining to fill the cup. She drained it in one long swallow. Tony's eyes watered in sympathy.

"Feeling better?"

"No. Now I've got to piss."

*   *   *

Too early for air-conditioning, too warm for heat, the air inside the church still had a filtered feel in the back of Tony's throat. It smelled of cleansers—although not as overwhelmingly as Arra's co-op—and faintly of aftershave and perfume. "I don't like leaving Ben in the car."

"He won't wake up until I tell him to."

"So remember to save enough power to play alarm clock."

"I know what I'm doing, Tony."

"I'm just saying . . ."

"I know what you're saying. Stop it."

He shrugged and stepped away from the women's washroom. Right inside the west doors, it hadn't been hard to find. "I'll wait here."

"Fine." One hand against the wall, Arra disappeared from view.

It was obvious she still hadn't recovered from her reckless use of power. No, not reckless, Tony amended, leaning against the wall. Thoughtless. As in, she didn't think about it. Her reaction to being touched by the shadow had been essentially hysterical. Run and react; no thought for the consequences. And physical exhaustion often led to emotional exhaustion—thus the doom and gloom announcement in the car.

It all made sense.

They were winning. They had to be winning.

He tensed as voices sounded in the distance, but they headed in another direction and he relaxed again. And then he frowned. Was Arra taking longer than she should? Definitely longer than a guy would. How long did women take? He couldn't shake the feeling that she might have done a bunk and climbed out the window. Be halfway to Seattle and a new identity by now.

With a glance around the hall to make sure he wasn't observed, he pushed the door open a crack and heard, "You!" followed by a familiar string of nonsense syllables, and a soft *sputz*.

"Arra?"

"Better get in here with that potion."

He took two steps farther in to the washroom and peered around a cinderblock corner. Women's washrooms definitely smelled better than men's. Arra was at a line of stainless steel sinks washing her hands. Lying stretched out on the floor was one of the girls from the catering company.

"Shadow-held?"

Arra snorted. "Not anymore."

"We forgot about the caterers when we made the list." Dropping to the floor, he lifted her head up against his leg. "They must've been setting up for lunch."

"Lunch." Red-rimmed eyes snapped open. "Do we always have to have lasagna? I am so tired of making lasagna!"

"Hey, it's okay." The potion sparkled as it dribbled between her lips.

She swallowed, looked up at him and said, "Three kinds of cookies are quite enough. There's cake." Another half a dozen small swallows. "Fifteen hundred bottles of water a month."

"That's a lot of water."

Her brows drew in as she finished the last of the potion in the cup. "Who the hell are you?"

Before Tony could tell her, Arra muttered, "Sleep." And her eyes closed.

"Why did you do that?"

"Easier than explanations. Also . . ." Stepping away from the sink, she indicated that Tony should pick up the snoring young woman. ". . . easier transport."

"So, easier?" He swung the girl up into his arms. Grunted, shifted her weight, and headed for the bathroom door. "I thought you said it was going to get terrible?"

Arra snorted, as she retrieved the backpack. "I've only been on this world for seven years, but even I know that if a young man gets caught carrying an unconscious young woman from the ladies' room in a Baptist church, terrible will be an understatement."

She had a point.

"What's with the 'you'?"

Arra twisted around from checking on their two passengers and frowned toward Tony. "The what?"

"Every time a shadow sees you, it says 'You!' in exactly the same way."

She shrugged. "The shadows are all cast by a single source; this makes their reactions less than original."

"Makes sense."

"Thank you."

Ouch. Sarcasm that cut. "In the dream I had, the shadow didn't want to go back to the Shadowlord; it didn't want to lose its sense of self."

"So?"

His turn to shrug; his shadow, dark against the pale upholstery, shrugged with him. "So maybe we can reason with them."

"Reason with them?" She sounded surprised.

No, he decided, pulling out to pass a line of Sunday drivers heading home to the city, *surprised* wasn't quite enough. Astonished.

"They're still evil, Tony, even if they're only bits of evil. And you don't reason with evil!"

"Granted. But you can, you know, reform it. During the war on your world, didn't anyone ever try to . . . ?"

"No!"

"Why . . ."

"Because that's not the way it works!"

Rolling his eyes, he tried again. Old people often had trouble with new ideas. "But . . ."

"If you want to meet your Nightwalker at 9:30, you'd best concentrate more on driving and less on suggesting perversions!"

She had a point although *perversions* seemed a little harsh. "It's just . . ."

"When I said concentrate less, I meant not at all!"

Right.

"Arra, you don't have to go with us tonight. We've got the potion; Henry and I can handle things at the studio. There's only the one shadow left."

Eyes locked on the spider solitaire game, Arra grunted something that might have been *good*. Or *sure*. Or *get stuffed*, were "get stuffed" only a single syllable long.

"You can move that black jack."

From her tea cozy position on the dining room table, Zazu hissed at him. "Or not."

The wizard's concentration on the game—games, since she was running one on each computer—was a little disturbing.

They'd dropped Ben and the caterer off two blocks from Ben's condo since neither of them knew anything about the girl and she was carrying no ID. Arra had woken them and then they'd driven off before they were noticed.

"*Oh, crap. Their cars. We left their cars behind; no way they got that far south walking.*"

"*It's a minor point.*"

"*Not to them, it won't be.*"

"*They have a forty-eight-hour hole in their memories. I think it will be.*"

Put like that, Tony'd admitted she had a point.

She'd been pretty quiet the rest of the way to the co-op, and had said next to nothing while she made a new batch of potion. Too busy eating the burger and fries he'd picked up to worry about the silence, Tony hadn't really noticed something was wrong until she'd capped the second thermos and headed straight for her computers.

And essentially disappeared.

Scratch a little disturbing. It was definitely freaking him out.

He swung his backpack up onto one shoulder, taking what comfort he could from the familiar feel of the thermoses smacking him in the kidneys just above one of the bruises Mouse had left him. "I'll just meet Henry out front."

This time, not even a grunt. One game ended. She started a new game immediately.

"I'll see you tomorrow morning at work."

"Tony."

He paused and turned to face her again.

"Remember that the gate works both ways. You have to stop the shadows returning to him, but you also have to make sure nothing worse comes through."

All of a sudden the lines of electronic playing cards took on a new menace. "Is that what you're looking for? Something worse?"

"I don't know."

"Something worse," Tony muttered moving the lamp into place. "Way to be specific."

"Let it go."

"How?"

Henry wisely decided not to answer. "The gate's about to open."

They were alone in the soundstage. The gate opened and closed and they were still alone. Wherever—whoever—the last shadow was, it wasn't going home. Not yet. Tony had no idea what the hell he was going to do tomorrow morning. *Not going to be as simple as turning on a light,* he acknowledged, his hands shaking as he rolled up the cable.

"Are you all right?"

"Sure. Fine." He'd never felt the pull of the gate so strongly. Had actually found himself stepping toward it, his body practically vibrating with need. New call, familiar feeling. Only a white-knuckled grip on the sound board had held him in place. Not moving—not answering—hurt.

"This shadow-taint of yours; did the wizard mention how we can remove it?"

"No, because that would require a lack of ambiguity." Cables stowed, he straightened. "Just takes time, I guess."

In the dim glow of the emergency light, he saw Henry frown. "It seems stronger than it was."

"Seems stronger or *is* stronger."

The vampire shrugged.

"Okay, then, let's not worry about it." Plastering on a fake smile, Tony added *shadow-taint getting stronger* to his list of things to worry about. Right under *something worse* and *more terrible options.*

He briefly considered adding *finds dark comforting* to the list but comforting wasn't quite the right word. Walking back to the rear doors, he felt hidden, safe, and hyperconscious of the man walking at his side—but then Henry'd been on his list for a few days now.

The circle of light on the back wall announced trouble of a different sort. Crap. Security.

They hadn't been seen yet, but they were seconds away from discovery.

Grabbing Henry's arm, Tony threw him against the wall, hooked a leg between his, and locked their bodies together at mouth, chest, and groin—realizing too late that Henry might not understand the game.

Fortunately, Henry seemed willing to play regardless.

"Hey! You there! Break it up!"

Pulling away, Tony turned, faked surprise at the sight of the rent-a-cop, and murmured, "Wait here, babe." As red-gold brows flicked up, he turned and stepped forward, launching into a low-voiced and urgent "This is who I am and I'm trying to impress this guy with the whole working-in-television thing."

The security guard rolled his eyes but allowed that he understood a guy doing what a guy had to do to get laid. "Just don't fucking do it here!"

"We're on our way out."

"Good." He'd clearly already dismissed them and was anxious to move on. He had a script waiting, after all. "Lock up behind you."

Henry said nothing until the door was closed and locked, then he smiled, his teeth too white in the darkness. "Very clever."

"Thanks." Tony just barely managed to resist the urge to wipe his mouth. He'd kissed Henry a thousand times, but this was the first time he'd tasted blood. Kate's blood, Tina's blood, his blood . . . older blood.

He knew it was all in his head.

It was nothing but . . . shadow-stuff.

The shadows had surrounded her, a ring of darkness she couldn't break. Trapped. No escape. If she banished one, the others would attack. She drew herself up to her full height and began to gather power, determined to make them pay as high a cost as possible for their victory.

As they moved closer, she could hear their voices in her head.

Help us.

Don't let him destroy us.

Help us.

We want to live.

Help us.

We need you.

"So I'm to be responsible for your lives as well?"

In answer, faces began to flicker around the circle. Lee. Mouse. Kate. Ben. Tony . . .

. . . Kiril, Sarn—eyes bulging, tongues protruding as they were nailed to the boards—Haryain, heavy white brows raised above his glasses.

"What's your damage?" he asked in another's voice. "You knew the job was dangerous when you took it."

"This . . ." She waved a hand around the circle, the shadows bending toward the gesture. ". . . isn't my job. I won't let it be my job."

Haryain snorted. "Who says you get a choice?"

Arra jerked awake. Squinting up at the pair of monitors, she reached for her mouse with one hand while wiping away drool with the other. There was always a choice.

There was always another gate.

∽ FOURTEEN

"So how'd the date go?"

"Date?"

"With Zev? Friday night? I was going to call you, but I had a busy weekend." Amy laid a salacious emphasis on *busy* and waggled her eyebrows in Tony's general direction.

"Barry?"

She punched his shoulder. "Brian! Dipwad. Now tell." Setting her extra-grande mochaccino on the corner of her desk, she dropped into the chair and grinned up at him. "Mama wants all the gory details. Make this Monday morning worth her while."

"I had hamantaschen."

Heavily kohled eyes widened. "Kinky!"

"Cookies."

"You had cookies? What are you, twelve?"

Tony shrugged. So much had happened since Friday night he'd almost forgotten about his non-date with the musical director. "We went out for coffee."

"*I* was drinking coffee at twelve," Amy told him with a pointed slurp from her cup. "That was it?"

"And we talked."

"Jesus fucking Christ. I always thought gay men were supposed to be getting more than the rest of us. Don't you guys have a quota to keep up or something?"

He felt himself smiling for the first time in what seemed like days. "Not since the eighties."

"The eighties?" She smirked as she reached for the phone. "I guess *you* were doing more than coffee at twelve. CB Productions, how can I help you?"

Maybe it was Amy's "the world wouldn't dare fuck with me attitude," maybe it was her electric-green hair, maybe it was the familiar sound of her answering the phone—whatever it was, he felt energized, anticipatory. Like he'd been waiting for something big, something amazing, and that wait was almost over. The fear and doubt that had haunted his dreams and his ride to work were gone.

"Tony!"

And they're back. He turned in time to see Arra emerge from CB's office. She still looked like crap, full sets of luggage under both eyes and her hair sticking up in uncombed gray spikes—exhaustion creating the same hairstyle Amy had probably needed a liter of gel to achieve. Obviously, a good night's sleep hadn't been in the cards.

Given that she'd probably spent most of the night trying to define the future by way of spider solitaire, that could have been an amusing observation. Except that it wasn't.

She took him by the arm, her fingers hot through the sleeve of his jean jacket, and walked him toward the basement door. "I spoke to CB . . ."

"So he knows?"

"Knows what?"

Fully aware that Amy could listen to half a dozen conversations simultaneously, Tony dropped his voice to a low murmur. He'd deal with her opinions on him keeping secrets from her later. "Everything. You said you were going to tell him everything."

"Oh. Right. No. I told him I need you to work that big carbon arc lamp for me this morning; that I'm working on that ghost effect he wants for later in the season and I need more light levels. He'll clear it with Peter and Sorge."

"I don't . . ." He didn't want to go anywhere near the gate. He didn't want to be within a hundred kilometers of it when it opened. And it didn't matter. There wasn't anyone else. "Sure. Whatever."

Arra's grip tightened for a heartbeat, as though she'd known what he'd been thinking. "I did a search for the last shadow this morning. It's in the studio."

"Who?"

"I don't know and it doesn't matter. Be careful. It'll know the others have been destroyed and it'll be desperate to get back through the gate."

"What about stuff coming this way?"

"I doubt it. Not yet. The Shadowlord hates to move without information; it's his strength and, to a certain extent, his weakness. He likes to be sure. Worry once this last shadow is destroyed—although by destroying some of them away from the gate, we may delay his reaction."

"Swell. That gives us time to prepare."

"There's nothing to prepare!"

"Yeah." He sighed. "I knew that." When she released him and reached for the basement door, it was his turn to take hold of her. "Arra, I was wondering, why do they need to bring the people back to the gate? I mean, one of them followed us out to that location shot last week so obviously the shadows move around fine on their own."

"No, remember I told you that the more specific a shadow is, the more constrained its movement? And these latest shadows are really mobile only before they've taken a host," she continued when he nodded. "After they've experienced physical definition, their mobility is pretty much limited to moving a short distance to another host."

"But they can survive on their own, right?"

Tony saw a muscle in her jaw jump as she clenched her teeth. "You cannot reform them!"

"That's not what I meant." Not entirely. "I just thought that it might be more . . . I don't know, intelligent if they bailed on the host after they got the information. I mean lurking shadows are a lot harder to spot than people acting like they're disappearing and acting like night of the living pod people."

Her eyes narrowed and she stared at him for a long moment. She'd been doing that a lot lately and it was beginning to get seriously disturbing.

"Don't give them ideas," she snapped at last, shook off his hand, and headed down to her workshop.

For the seven years she'd been his entire special effects department, Arra had made no close attachments among the crew. She'd interacted as much as necessary to perform her job but no more. Now, it seemed, in less than a week she'd made a friend. Or acquired an accomplice. Chester Bane wasn't sure which, but given everything else that had been going on, the timing was interesting.

Standing just inside his office, he watched Arra head downstairs and, after a long moment spent staring at the closed door, he saw Tony Foster disappear in the direction of the soundstage.

It, whatever it was, had something to do with light levels.

There was nothing he hated more than being lied to, so before he asked questions, he liked to make sure he could identify the answers.

About to return to his desk, he paused as the outer door opened and the two RCMP officers who'd investigated Nikki Waugh's unfortunate death walked into the office. He watched as Rachel hurried to meet them and stepped forward as she turned in his direction.

"Mr. Bane, these officers would like a word with you."

"Of course." He indicated they should precede him into his office. The man, Constable Elson, moved like he was hunting and close to his quarry. The woman, Constable Danvers, rolled her eyes before she followed her partner. There was disagreement between them, then. Not on the larger issues, perhaps, but she was definitely indulging him on the smaller.

Interesting.

"Alan Wu is dead."

About to lower himself into his desk chair, he paused and turned, staring at the two officers. After a moment, Constable Danvers added, "He died Saturday afternoon."

"I'm sorry to hear that." And he was. In a profession with more than its fair share of insecure nut jobs and delusional divas, Alan Wu had been dependable. He sat, indicated that the police officers should sit, and he waited.

Constable Elson made an obvious and obviously unnecessary show of checking his notes. "Alan Wu is the second of your employees to die in less than a week."

Less than a week. *Now, it seemed, in less than a week she'd made a friend.*

"Alan Wu was not my employee. He was an actor who I regularly employed."

"Tony Foster was with him when he died. He told us he'd been driving around with another of your employees, an Arra Pelindrake. They do both work for you?"

"They do."

"Good. And that's not all."

He locked his gaze on the younger man's face. "Go on."

It got more interesting by the moment.

One of his cameramen had been dumped in emergency at Burnaby General with a broken jaw. No record of who left him there. An electrician and one of the caterers both reported missing by their spouses, gone for forty-eight hours only to turn up Sunday night with no memories and their cars missing.

"I flagged anything that mentioned your company and pulled this together from a number of sources."

"You've been busy."

"I got curious. I don't much believe in coincidence, Mr. Bane. A number of very different roads all seem to lead right back here, and that tells me that there's something going on."

No doubt.

"Tony!"

Tina's voice froze him in place. Tina was the last person he wanted to deal with this morning. He'd already seen Kate standing by the camera smiling at nothing, right thumb rubbing over her left wrist. Praying that he'd never looked quite so dopey, he'd tugged his jacket cuff halfway over his hand and taken the scenic route around to the coffee maker.

"*Just so you know,*" Henry announced as they drove along Adanac Street toward Kate's apartment. "*I didn't like doing that.*"

"*Doing what?*"

"*Cranking up the sex appeal.*" He repeated Tony's phrase like it left a bad taste in his mouth. "*The moment you bring sex into it like that, it becomes too much like I'm forcing myself on an unwilling victim.*"

Tony snorted as he twisted around to check on Kate sleeping in the backseat. "*News flash, Henry; sex is always a part of it.*"

"*Not so overtly. Not under those circumstances.*" He paused, as though realizing the circumstances weren't usual. "*Not on my part.*"

"*What's not on your part?*"

"*When sex isn't actually occurring, I am not always thinking of sex when I feed.*"

Since they were both well aware of what the other person was thinking of, neither mentioned it.

"*So you weren't thinking of sex when you fed on Tina?*"

"*No.*"

"*Good.*"

"*Which is not to say that under other circumstances . . .*"

"*I didn't need to hear that.*"

And now, looking at Tina approach, all he could think of was her and Henry humping like naked monkeys. The visuals were seriously disturbing.

"Tony, don't forget that the *Darkest Night* fan club will be showing up in about half an hour. They'll watch us shoot, Lee and Mason will pose for a couple of pictures, and then they'll . . ."

Be taken over by shadows from another world.

". . . have some lunch. Tony, are you listening to me?"

"Yeah. Sorry." He forced himself to concentrate.

"After lunch, give them each one of the old scripts and get them the hell out of here before we start . . ." She paused, eyes narrowed. "Is there something on my face?"

"What?"

"You're staring at me."

I know how Henry looks when he's come from feeding on you . . .

"Sorry." His life was just too weird.

"Stop apologizing and pay attention. You know how Peter feels about fans in the studio, so this has to go smoothly or we're all in for an unpleasant afternoon."

"Uh, Arra needs me to do some stuff for her this morning."

"I heard. Just don't leave the fan club unattended. I can't think of anything worse than another fan getting locked in Mason's coffin."

Unfortunately, Tony could.

Three of the games had been stopped by fours. *Fixed opinions will hinder your process.* What was she missing? What was she fixating on? On the other screen, two black jacks prevented her from making the last move that would finish the game.

"This is ridiculous!" Arra shoved her chair out from the desk hard enough to roll her halfway across the workshop. "I might as well try to divine the future from a bowl of instant oatmeal."

Her stomach growled. Desperately trying to discover the source of her unease—although unease was far too mild a word for the feelings of doom filling her head like toxic smoke—she'd skipped breakfast. It was possible that hunger was distracting her just enough to keep her from making sense of the cards.

Possible. But not likely.

She'd been able to cast auguries right until the end, unheeding of the destruction raining down around her. She'd seen the fate of the city and of the wizards. She'd known there was nothing she could do to stop it.

Nothing.

But here and now they hadn't reached *nothing*—although they would.

Here and now, she needed to identify just what was going wrong.

If memory served, the Rice-Krispie square she'd grabbed from the craft services table last week should still be in her desk drawer. It wasn't exactly food, but it was as close as she could get without going upstairs.

Slowly chewing the first bite—slowly because the square had solidified into a substance that defied speed, Arra cleared all screens but one. Maybe if she concentrated on a single game . . .

Two black jacks.

And again.

Sucking the last bit of marshmallow off a corner of the plastic wrap, she scowled down at the clock on the corner of the screen. 11:02 A.M. The gate would open soon and the last shadow would make a move for home. The light would destroy it. It knew it was the last on this world, but would *he* know as he . . .

Plastic hanging limply from a corner of her mouth, Arra stared at the monitor.

Two black jacks.

There were two shadows left on this world.

Not one.

Two.

Somehow, one of them had escaped her spell. Exactly how wasn't import-ant right now; she had to warn Tony.

But the gate was about to open.

If both shadows were there . . .

If he needed help stopping them . . .

If she went to the gate . . .

But if she didn't . . .

Using power with the gate open would be like sending up a flare.

A hundred thousand voices cried out for her to save them. Clutched at her. Dragged her down under the weight of their need. *The Shadowlord comes; you are our last and only hope.*

Tony fought without her. When he reached for her, it was to ask her to fight at his side, not to fight for him. He stubbornly held to hope even as she de-nied it.

Pushing her chair away from the desk, she spun it around and scanned the workshop shelves. There had to be something . . . Yes! One of the baseball bats they'd blown up in Raymond Dark's hands during the batting cage scene in episode three. The hands had, of course, been Daniel's and the ad lib about switching to aluminum, Lee's—although Mason had claimed it the second time they'd shot Lee pulling the bloody shard of wood from Raymond Dark's shoulder. With CB complaining about the expense, she'd bought six bats, practiced on three, blew two for the camera, and tucked the last one away figuring that sooner or later she'd find a use for it.

Stopping the shadow-held from reaching the gate would also stop the shadow.

With half his attention on the time, half worrying at the hundred and one things likely to go wrong as he attempted to stop a shadow from returning to another world while surrounded by people who wouldn't believe that's what he was doing if it came with a director's commentary, and trying to keep sev-enteen members of the *Darkest Night* fan club out of trouble, Tony was feeling a little overwhelmed.

And the thought of Arra sitting safely in her basement while he was up here saving the world was pissing him off. *She doesn't need to go near the fuck-ing gate*, he growled silently as he counted the fans. *She could just take a mo-ment and turn this lot into . . .*

One short.

Three guesses where the runaway had gotten to and the first two didn't count.

"Excuse me, but this set's off limits."

The fan froze, one leg hooked over the side of the coffin. "I was just . . ."

"Yeah. I know." Tony jerked his head toward the high-pitched squeals coming from the other side of the soundstage. "I think Mason just appeared."

He got out of the way barely in time to avoid being run over.

Emerging out beside the monitors, he could only assume from the sounds of adoration that Mason was on the other side of the group of hysterically bobbing and weaving bodies.

"Great. Just great." Headphones down around his neck, Peter sounded ready to chew scenery. "I am never going to get him onto the set now."

"Sorry."

The director snorted. "You think you could have prevented that? You are suffering from serious delusions of grandeur, Mr. Foster. You should know by now that nothing comes between Mason and his adoring fans. Particularly when they're carrying cameras." Eyes narrowed as he watched the ebb and flow of the crowd. "At least if he's out where we can see him, we have a chance of avoiding lawsuits."

"Do you want me to tell him you're ready to shoot?"

"He knows. That's why he finally emerged from his dressing room. One of the reasons. And obviously not the most important. You try to remove him from that little love fest there, and he'll treat the world to a scene where you're cast as the villain and he's just trying to give a little back to the people who make the show possible. Forgetting, of course, that there won't be a show if we don't get it shot."

"Could we do my reaction shots first?"

Both Tony and the director turned.

"Lee, I didn't see you there."

Lee smiled. "It seemed safer to stay out of the way."

Tony opened his mouth to ask him how he felt and then closed it again. Not his place. It wasn't like they were . . . friends.

"Sorge?"

The DP glanced up.

"Lee's reaction shots; do we need to relight?"

"I don't think so . . ."

As the DP headed out onto the office set, Peter nodded toward the sides sticking out of Tony's pocket. "You can read him Mason's lines."

From elation to depression in less than a second. Probably a new record. "I can't."

"You *can't?*"

He couldn't look at Lee while he explained. "I have to do that thing for Arra."

"Now?"

The feel of the gate powering up was making his eyeballs twitch. He glanced down at his watch. "Three minutes. She, uh, she says timing is everything in special effects."

"Fine. Whatever. Go. Lee, get out there. Adam . . ."

The 1AD broke off a conversation with a boom operator Tony'd never seen before. Seemed like Hartley hadn't made it in this morning.

". . . make sure that lot shuts up when I call quiet."

Trying not to look like he was walking into pain, Tony made his way to the lamp.

Behind him, Peter called, "Quiet please!"

Adam's voice rose over the continuing fannish babble, "If you lot keep quiet until I give the word, Mason'll pose for pictures with you when we're done."

The babble switched off.

"Rolling!"

Grabbing the rack at the last moment, Constable Elson remained on his feet as he finished his accidental dance with a tattered antediluvian ball gown. "This looks like a fire code violation to me," he muttered, untangling the distressed gray taffeta from around his legs.

"I assure you, Constable, it is not."

"There's not a lot of room in this hall." He stepped back, got poked in the ass by the hilt of a cheap replica cavalry sword, jumped forward, and very nearly tangled with the taffeta again.

"There is, however slight, a clear passageway and the fire marshal has given his approval." The fire marshal also had a teenage son looking forward to a career in television, but CB saw no point in mentioning that. "The soundstage door is just ahead."

It was, in fact, a mere dozen paces ahead, although impossible to see until the last corner had been rounded and a rack of white hazmat suits passed. He'd picked the suits up cheap from another show's going out of business sale and instructed the writers to make use of them. Their ideas to date had been less than stellar but he knew that eventually one of them would dream up something the show could use—after all, if an infinite number of monkeys could write Hamlet . . .

His hand was actually on the door when the bell rang and the red light went on.

"Why are we stopping?"

"Cameras are rolling," he said, inclining his head toward Constable Danvers. "We'll have to wait."

"How long?"

He shrugged. "Until the director feels he has what he needs."

"Jack . . ." She turned to her partner, who shook his head.

"No. I want a look around that soundstage and I want another word with Mr. Foster."

"We could come back."

Elson folded his arms. "We're here."

He translated the female constable's expression to read: *You wouldn't have half as big a bee up your butt if this wasn't television.* She was probably right. Television, invited into homes 24/7 remained a mystery; to add mystery on top of that would be more than such a man could resist. Although the odds of him actually discovering anything were slim; he wouldn't be waiting to enter the soundstage if CB believed otherwise.

Running feet, pounding between the costumes, pulled all three of them back around the way they'd come.

Baseball bat held across her body, Arra stumbled to a halt by the hazmat suits and stared at the red light beside the door. Damn! Had CB been on his own, she'd have taken her chances with a line of bullshit and charged right on in. But with strangers standing there . . .

Put them to sleep; you can call it a gas leak!

"Problem, Arra?"

Now would be the time . . .

Time.

11:16.

Too late anyway. Tony was on his own. She lowered the bat. "No. No problem."

"Arra Pelindrake?" The blond man stepped forward. "I'm Constable Jack Elson, RCMP. As long as we're all waiting here, I'd like to ask you a few questions."

Beyond the constable, CB's expression said much the same thing.

The lamp was in place, a light blanket arranged behind it to prevent any possible leakage into the set in use. All Tony had to do was hit the switch on the lamp itself—the gaffer had plugged him into the board and told him in no uncertain terms that if he came near it, he'd get a light stand up the ass.

Oh, yeah. Things were going well.

He'd seen a PBS special once—or maybe it was a horror movie, details were fuzzy—about this guy who attacked people with vibrations until their eyeballs melted. That was pretty much exactly how he felt. Like his eyeballs were melting.

Definitely time to turn on the last best hope for humankind. *And the part of the hero will be played by a carbon arc lamp.*

As his hand moved toward the switch, his shadow surged up his legs.

He had time to jerk back futilely before darkness slammed into his head and he was no longer in control.

"I did a search for the last shadow this morning, it's in the studio."

Fuck. Fuck. Fuck. It's in me! Except it hadn't been in him, it had been hiding in his shadow. *How long . . . ?*

And then the gate was open and he was walking—being walked—out underneath it.

Déjà vu all over again.

The shadow hadn't taken over so much as pushed him aside. He was in his own mind, he just wasn't there alone. Henry could have pulled him free with a cocked finger, but Henry wasn't here. Arra wasn't here. Just him.

And shadow.

"Hey. If you go back, you'll die. You know that. You don't have to die!"

No response. And time was running out. Tony could feel the attention of the man on the other side of the gate. Could feel the pull. Could feel the shadow beginning to separate.

So he reached out and grabbed it. Not physically, of course. Physically, he was still standing like a total doofus in the middle of the set.

He wrapped his mind around the *concept* of shadow.

Contact.

Everyone has dark memories they can't purge. Memories that creep out of mental corners on sleepless nights, perch on the edge of consciousness, and gnaw. Lucky people remembered things they read in newspapers or saw on television; cruelties that didn't involve them personally but still cut deep. People who lived without the security of freedom or justice had darker memories, memories that often fit neatly into the inflamed map of physical scars. Tony had once seen an ancient Egyptian wizard devour the life of a baby while the baby's parents walked on, unaware their child was dead.

The shadows were pieces of the Shadowlord. Dark memories. Memories of a world where those parents would thank the gods that their baby was safely dead.

The shadow had known what he knew from the moment it had entered his body. Now he knew what the shadow knew. It was like seeing a private slide show of atrocities against the front of his skull.

Had Tony been in control of his mouth, he would have screamed.

Then a cruel intelligence on the other side of the gate called the shadow home and the slide show stopped.

Somehow, Tony managed to hang on.

"You don't have to go!" He fed it the memory of being absorbed, of becoming nothing once again. Of losing self.

And if I stay.

It sounded like Hartley, the boom operator, had Hartley been able to list "enjoys inflicting torment" as one of his hobbies. It also sounded remarkably like the voice in Tony's head.

"*That was you. The bright lights in the elevator were freaking you out!*"

Yes.

He was losing the tug-of-war. He could feel the shadow slipping away.

If I stay, will you give me your body?

Its tone went beyond innuendo. Tony shuddered, unable to control his body's visceral response and lost a little more of his grip. Strangely, the rush of blood away from his brain helped clear his mind. If a lack of information was all that was keeping the Shadowlord from attacking . . . He couldn't . . . He had to. Arra could deal with whatever that made him and Henry could call him back from wherever he'd gone and another little bit of shadow slipped free while he tried to work out the consequences. "Yes!"

Too late.

As the shadow roared free and his world became pain, he realized it had been taunting him, that however much it feared the loss of self, it *had* to rejoin the whole. It had just been indulging itself before it went home—offering a glimpse at hope, then snatching it away again.

Tony regained consciousness to see a familiar face bending over him. Green eyes were concerned and a warm hand had a comforting grip on his shoulder.

"Tony?"

He clutched at Lee's voice as dark memories threatened to overwhelm him. Lee being there when he woke up was a bit of a dream come true and he was damned well going to hang onto it. "What . . . ?"

A slightly confused but comforting smile. "You tell me. You yelled and when Adam came over to tell you to shut up, you were on the floor." He glanced around and the smile faded. "I was on this floor . . ."

Tony struggled to sit up, wondering, if the 1AD had come to check on him, where the hell he'd gone. *Through the gate? No. The* shadow *went through the gate.*

Oh. Fuck.

As his head cleared the floor, his stomach rebelled and just barely managing to turn away from the actor, he lost what remained of his breakfast and half a dozen strawberry marshmallows all over the fake hardwood floor. Oh, yeah, this was how he dreamed of waking up with Lee . . .

"Eww. Is that real vomit?"

Tony didn't recognize the voice, figured it had to be one of the fans, and briefly considered crawling over and puking on her shoes. In comparison to how he now felt, melting eyeballs had been a good feeling. Coughing out what had to be a piece of his spleen, he managed to gasp, "Arra."

"You want Arra?"

From the sound of it, Lee had moved away, but he was still closer than anyone else in his extended audience. In between heaves that achieved nothing more than a thin stream of greenish-yellow bile, Tony managed a nod.

"He was doing some work for her."

Peter's voice. And running footsteps. More than one set.

"Tony!"

"Arra, don't kneel down there!" Peter's voice again. "He's been . . . Never mind. It looks like you missed it."

He felt a hand on his shoulder and . . . something. It settled his stomach, but more importantly it pushed the darkness back to where he could . . . not ignore it but exist with it. Darker than what he was used to existing with, but he'd manage. Not like he had a choice.

Dropping over onto his back, he looked up into the wizard's eyes and felt tears rise in his own. *So much for what's left of my macho image.*

"It's all right, Tony . . ."

"It isn't." He couldn't cope with platitudes, not from her. "He knows."

"I think . . ." CB dropped his voice to a level most of his employees wouldn't have recognized as his, "it might be best if you speak with Mr. Foster another time."

Constable Elson snorted. "Trust me, Mr. Bane. I'm not put off by puke. I've questioned suspects covered in it."

"Have you? And Mr. Foster is a suspect in . . . ?"

"He's not a suspect," Constable Danvers interjected smoothly before her partner could answer. "We just want to speak to him, which . . ." Her voice sharpened as she directed it at the other officer. ". . . we can do later."

CB inclined his head toward her. "Thank you, Constable. It seems that Mr. Nicholas was among the first on the scene. Would you care to speak with him?"

"No, thank you," Elson began. "That's not . . ."

"Yes." Danvers flushed slightly as both men turned to stare at her. Given her skin color it was difficult to tell for sure, but he was fairly certain she was blushing. "I mean, we're here. Let's get something out of the trip."

"Like what?"

"Mr. Nicholas was second on the scene."

"And?"

"It wouldn't hurt to get a statement." Her tone suggested that she'd been promised some one-on-one time with a very attractive actor and she wasn't leaving until she got it. Elson heard the subtext, opened his mouth to protest, and finally shrugged.

He beckoned the actor over. "Mr. Nicholas, if you could give Constable Danvers and her partner your full cooperation." He locked eyes with the younger man, making sure he understood he was to dazzle them with celebrity and get them the hell out of the building.

"Tony . . ."

"Will be fine."

"Peter?"

"I'll speak with Peter. I'll let him know you're doing me a favor." Nothing as crass as emphasis on the second sentence. Mr. Nicholas knew very well for whom he was doing a favor and the director had undoubtedly heard the entire conversation.

When the actor bestowed a brilliant smile on the female constable and she visibly melted, CB nodded once to the now oblivious officers and walked across the set to where his director stood watching Arra help Tony Foster to his feet. The police were no longer his concern. The one would have her full attention on the actor and the other would have his full attention on making sure she did nothing he considered embarrassing. After Mr. Nicholas turned his considerable charm on Constable Elson, they'd leave—if not convinced that they'd gotten what they came for, at least quite sure that their concerns had been taken seriously.

Mr. Nicholas was a much better actor than most people gave him credit for being.

He was destined for so much more than one small, straight to syndication genre program where he played second to a man with half the ability.

Fortunately, CB Productions had him tied up in a contract Daniel Webster wouldn't have been able to break.

"Arra, why don't you take Mr. Foster down to your workshop? He'll be out of the way down there until he's feeling better."

He kept his face carefully blank as her eyes narrowed. "Yes, thank you, CB. I think I will."

"Peter."

The director started, looking from the producer to the two people slowly leaving the set and back to CB.

"I believe it's time everyone went back to work."

"Right." The big man knew what was going on; Peter could see it in his face. He could also see that he wasn't going to get an explanation. Whatever. He just wanted things to stop screwing up long enough for him to get this episode in the can.

"This is not, after all, the first time someone has been sick in the sound-stage."

Peter sighed. "True enough." Raymond Dark's filing cabinet was still a little whiff under the lights.

"Can you manage without him?"

"What, without Tony? Jesus, CB, he's just the production assistant. I think I can struggle on. Adam!" The director's voice echoed off the ceiling. "Where the hell has Mason got himself off to?"

No one seemed to know.

"Well, find him, for Christ's sake. And count the fan club, a couple of them were minors! And get someone over here to clean up this puke."

Confident that things were now back as they should be, at least on the surface—essentially business as usual for television—CB turned . . . and stopped as the director called his name.

"Yes?"

"Tony and Arra."

"Yes?"

"Is there something going on with them? You know . . ." He waggled a hand. ". . . going on?"

Chester Bane favored the director with a long, level stare. "I wouldn't like to guess."

In point of fact, he very much disliked guessing. He liked to know.

He intended to know.

∽ FIFTEEN

"It was . . . It was in my . . ."

"Shhhh, not yet."

Tony leaned heavily on Arra's arm as she walked him down the basement stairs and sighed in relief as they stepped out onto the workshop floor, realizing the significance of the observation he'd made the first time he came down here. There were no shadows.

He stumbled toward a chair, dropped onto it, and didn't have the strength to protest when Arra grabbed a folded space blanket from a shelf and wrapped it around him. The security of something between him and the world actually felt pretty good.

"Now tell me," the wizard commanded as she sat.

So he did.

"It was hiding in your *shadow*?" She frowned. "That explains the deepening of the shadow-taint, but they've never . . . This is new behavior for them."

Tony considered shrugging, decided his head might lose its precarious balance if he tried, and snorted instead. "They were in Hartley for just over twenty-four hours. You said that no one knows how to hide like an alcoholic. I guess they learned a few tricks."

"No . . . I banished the shadow holding Hartley."

"It slipped through the pauses in your banishing spell. You were breathing kind of heavy so it wasn't one long string of syllables like usual."

Her frown deepened. "It told you that or are you guessing?"

"I touched it. Remember, I told you." Unsure of what might be useful *wizardly* information, he'd told her everything.

"Did I tell you what a stupid thing that was for you to have done?"

"You kind of choked when I got to it the first time. So . . ." He was about to ask: *What now?* What happened now that the Shadowlord had the information he was waiting for? And then he realized he didn't really want to know. Not yet. He could use a few more minutes of ignorant bliss. ". . . so what's your story?"

No doubt Arra heard his original question in the pause. Less than no doubt that she didn't want to deal with the answer either. "The moment I realized there was more than one shadow remaining, I headed for the soundstage but was prevented from entering by the presence of CB and the two officers."

"And the shooting light," Tony muttered, wrapping the space blanket more tightly around him.

"The light alone wouldn't have stopped me—it's a social contract, not an impenetrable barrier—but barging in past witnesses would have required explanations I couldn't give. Not when two of those witnesses were police officers whose suspicions were already aroused. While we waited, they interrogated me about what we were doing together on Saturday, but I don't think they believed what I told them."

"May/December fag-hag romance?"

"What?"

"Never mind. What did you tell them?"

"Exactly what you told them. That you were spending your time off learning another aspect of the business, expanding your skill set, and keeping yourself employable."

"And they didn't believe that?"

"She seemed fine with it. He seemed reluctant."

"Why didn't you . . . ?" He snaked a hand out from under the blanket and used it to wiggle his nose. As Arra stared at him blankly, he sighed. "You never watched *Bewitched*? No," he realized, "how could you? You pretty much just got here. Why didn't you do magic? Make them believe what you wanted or forget you were there as you made a run for the soundstage?"

"The gate was opening. To use power so close to the open gate . . ."

"He would have known you were here. Well, he sure as shit knows now." And things fell into place with a nearly audible click. "He was never looking for another world to conquer, he was looking for you." Tony knew he was right. Knew it because of the way the color left the wizard's face, leaving her looking old and gray. Knew it because of the way she turned and walked to her desk and sank down into her chair as though her legs would no longer hold her weight. "You're the one that got away."

"He killed everyone else in my order." For the first time since he'd known her, Arra sounded old.

"And he wants to complete the set." A flash of bodies nailed to a blackboard and Tony thanked God that his stomach was empty. Not everyone had died quickly and before these two were finally allowed an end to pain, they'd probably told the Shadowlord everything he wanted to know.

"They didn't know what variables I'd used to open the gate," Arra said, as though she'd been reading his mind. "They couldn't tell him where I was. He must have had to keep opening gates at random until he got lucky."

"Why didn't you keep moving? Open another gate and another until you crapped up the trail so badly he'd never find you?"

"Opening a gate requires precise calculations and a sure knowledge of how the energy flow of the world works. It took me a little over five years before I thought I might be able to do it and . . ."

"By then you had a life. Cats."

"The cats have nothing to do with this."

"If you gate away, he'll kill them because they were yours. He'll torture and kill everyone who might have known you just like he did before—just in case one of them might know where you've gone."

She stared at him as though she'd never seen him before. "How . . . ?"

"The shadows are shadows of him. When I grabbed this one, I knew what it knew. It didn't know much, but it was pretty clear on that. He's obsessed with finding you."

"He likes to finish what he starts. Vindictive bastard."

That wasn't quite . . . Searching for the right memory, Tony ended up back at the bodies on the blackboard and shied away. He couldn't go there again. Not right now. Enough of the depths; they were dark and dangerous, and he needed a few minutes in the light and safety of the shallows. "Hey, shouldn't I be having my vodka-catnip cooler?"

"It's not necessary; I poured power into you directly. The potion is essentially a battery, holding the power for transport."

"Okay." From the little Arra had explained about the workings of wizardry, that made sense. "I could still use a drink."

"I expect your backpack is up by the lamp."

"Right." Crap. "So what was the baseball bat for?"

"I was wondering that myself." CB's voice flowed down the stairs and filled all the spaces not otherwise occupied with a mix of anger and impatience. Arra started and watched through narrowed eyes as he followed his voice into the workshop. Grateful he wasn't between them, Tony decided it might be best if he remained a spectator in this conversation.

"You came through my wards." When CB looked blank, she sighed, her frown deepening. "My protections. They were meant to keep out the people I don't want down here."

"What you want is irrelevant; this is *my* building. My studio. What I want . . ." He stalked out into the center of the workshop and the space seemed suddenly much smaller. ". . . is information. You may begin with the baseball bat." The bat was dangling from his left hand and from the businesslike way he was holding it, Tony realized he was half inclined to use it.

"Uh . . . CB . . ."

"Not a word, Mr. Foster. I'll deal with you in a moment."

Great.

"It's all right, Tony. It's about time CB knew what was going on. It is happening in *his* studio, after all." Sighing deeply, apparently unable to look the big man in the eye, Arra picked up a pencil and doodled on a scrap of paper as she talked. "I had the bat because I suspected Tony was going to be attacked by a . . ." Explanation and pencil paused. ". . . by another member of the crew."

"Why?"

To Tony's surprise, Arra spilled the whole story. From the shadow glimpsed at the location shoot, right down to what Tony had just told her. She'd didn't give up Henry's secret identity as a creature of the night but laid out the details of everything else. CB's expression never changed. Tony had to give him credit for not interrupting unless, as was likely, he was too stunned to interrupt. Tony'd been a part of the story from the beginning and even he found it hard to believe.

When Arra finally stopped talking, he nodded slowly. "So it appears Constable Elson's instincts are correct. There is something going on at my studio."

"The police," Arra snorted, "are less than useless in a case like this."

"Very probably. Why was I not kept informed from the beginning?"

"You were there when I fell through the gate. You would have realized much, much earlier than Tony here that the Shadowlord wasn't planning an invasion—no matter how much I personally wanted to believe that. You'd have realized he was looking for me." She lifted her head then and met his gaze.

"Given the destruction he's capable of, I wasn't entirely convinced you wouldn't just toss me back up through the gate."

"It is a solution that occurred to me as you were speaking."

It hadn't occurred to Tony. But then CB hadn't seen the blackboard.

"So. Mr. Foster here has survived two encounters with the shadows; why, then, did they kill Nikki Waugh?"

Arra sighed and ran a hand back through her hair, standing it up in gray spikes. "That was a different kind of shadow; primitive and sent here to gather the information that would allow the Shadowlord to create the more complex shadows that interacted with Tony and the others. The information was Nikki Waugh's life."

"He sent it to kill?"

"Essentially, yes."

"He needed that information—the information that killed Nikki Waugh—in order to continue his search for you?"

"Apparently."

"So your presence here is responsible for . . ."

"For everything. Yes." Arra slumped down in her chair, her tailbone barely on the edge of the seat. "Trust me, I've added Nikki to the li . . . Damn it!" She picked up the piece of paper she'd been doodling on. "I've just scribbled over an invoice for blasting caps."

"Leave it," CB commanded as she reached for an art eraser.

"Not likely. These have to be filed with the local police and they're already not fond of me."

"Us," Tony reminded her as bits of graphite-covered rubber began to pile up on the paper. *Déjà vu all over again . . .* Although he couldn't quite hold on to just what exactly was evoking the feeling. "So now what?"

CB turned his head just enough to catch Tony's gaze and hold it. Before the shadows and the realization that Henry was holding a lien on his life, Tony would have been—had been—pretty near shitting himself in this kind of situation. Things change. Times change. He didn't look away though; no point in being rude. *Particularly to your six-foot-six employer who's not only already pissed off but happens to still be holding a baseball bat.*

"Now," CB growled, "we close that gate. I will not have my studio destroyed or my people murdered because they got in the way of a dark wizard's vendetta."

"The gate can't be closed from this side," Arra pointed out wearily.

He pivoted his entire upper body to face her directly. "Then it must be closed from the *other* side."

"Sorry." Lifting the invoice, she blew the eraser rubble to the floor.

And Tony remembered.

As Chester Bane forgot.

"Ah, you brought me my bat." Arra slipped the invoice into a hanging file. "Thank you."

"Yes, I . . ." He stared at the bat. Blinked once and frowned. "There was something . . ."

"Arra!"

"Be quiet, Tony."

No. He was not going to be quiet. There was no fucking way he was going to let her just blithely go around erasing chunks of people's lives. Taking the easy way out. Refusing to deal. Except, he couldn't speak. Couldn't make a sound. Couldn't even snap his fingers. Couldn't be anything but quiet.

"Tony." CB frowned. "I was wondering how Mr. Foster was."

Gagged. That's how I am. Fucking cow. He glared at the wizard. *Yeah, and I'd trade you in a heartbeat for three magic beans! Hell, I'd trade you for lima beans!*

"He's still a bit under the weather. I'm beginning to think there's a bug going around. You'd better check into it before we get a visit from the Public Heath Nurse. You know how the media's always looking for the next medical crisis."

"That's not . . ."

"Constable Elson has a bee up his butt about the studio already and he saw Tony was sick. If he speaks to the wrong person . . ." Her voice didn't so much trail off as collapse under the weighted innuendo it carried.

CB's forehead creased. "Constable Elson had best watch himself," he growled. Shoving the bat onto the shelf, he headed up the stairs. "The constable isn't the only one who can *speak* to people."

"Have fun."

His response was wordless but explicit.

As the door closed, Arra slumped. "All right, Tony. Tell me. Tell me that I've crossed a line. That I'm abusing my power; making arrogant and unilateral decisions. That ability doesn't give me the right to run the lives of others. That small abuses lead to larger ones, and that all power corrupts and that I'm already on the slippery slope to the decision the Shadowlord made—that my desires are the only ones that matter. That just because I can, is reason enough."

Shrugging free of the blanket, he stood, too angry to remain still. "I was going to say you can't goddamned well rip out chunks of people's lives, but that's good, too."

"I know how CB thinks. He would have solved the problem in the simplest way possible by dragging out that old chestnut about the good of the many outweighing the good of the one—regardless of whether or not the one agrees with the sentiment—and tossed me back through the gate."

"You're a wizard! You don't have to let him toss you anywhere!"

A sardonic eyebrow lifted. "I didn't."

"Don't let him doesn't mean my way or the highway! It means you bring him around to your way of thinking!"

"How do you suggest I convince him?"

He had no idea, but he knew one thing for certain. "Not by running away. Again! You didn't even try!"

"Because trying makes it so? Do your best and happy endings are inevitable?" Her lip curled. "You're living in a fantasy world."

"Hello!" Tony jabbed a finger toward her. "Wizard!" Held up his hand to show her the small scars on his wrist. "Vampire!" A larger gesture to take in the entire studio. "Television! Fantasy's seeming pretty damned real to me right about now. You're just too goddamned scared!"

"You would be, too, if you knew what I know!"

"So what don't I know?"

She was on her feet now, facing him, her hands curled into fists by her sides. "The Shadowlord destroyed my *entire* order!"

"Yeah? Well, he didn't get the last two until after you buggered off on them!"

It probably wasn't a lightning bolt because a lightning bolt would have killed him. It was probably just the biggest static shock in history. It slammed into Tony's chest and threw him backward against a set of shelves. They rocked, but held and he slid down them to the floor, pain sizzling along each individual nerve ending. Tony had no idea there were so many of them. He could have stood not knowing.

"Get out!"

Blinking away afterimages, he dragged himself to his feet. Besides pain, he was feeling remarkably calm. "I think we've pretty much established that the Shadowlord will kill us looking for you." He held up a hand as Arra raised her palm toward him again. "I'm going." Half a dozen steps down from the door, most of his weight on the banister, he turned. "This is your mess. Take some responsibility and clean it up."

"Responsibility!" She spat the word back at him.

"Maybe you've heard of it; it's the flip side of power."

Her angle was bad and she missed him with the second shot.

Zev was standing just inside the production office, balancing a pile of CDs in one hand and dangling a set of small computer speakers from the other. He looked up as Tony came out of the basement, his nose wrinkling at the distinct smell of char cut off by the closing door. "What's burning?"

"Rome." Tony touched a fingertip to his eyebrow piercing. The skin felt puffy and the slightest pressure hurt like hell—not surprising, he supposed; gold was a good conductor. "And I was just speaking to Nero."

"Ah." The musical director frowned. "Did you and Arra have a fight?"

"A disagreement."

"Ah, again. I never knew you were that interested in special effects. You didn't mention it on Friday."

"Slipped my mind. We, uh . . ." he began, just as Zev said, "If we, uh . . ."

A moment's silence.

"Go ahead." A simultaneous polite injunction which, after another moment's silence, degenerated into two thirds of a Three Stooges routine as the stack of CDs started to slide. Zev shifted his grip, Tony reached out a hand to help, and the spark was clearly visible even under the fluorescent lights.

The clatter of the CD cases hitting the floor almost drowned out Zev's reaction.

"Bloody HELL!"

Almost.

"Man, Zev, I'm sorry." Tony dropped to his knees and began gathering up the spilled music. "It's that thing that Arra and I were working on. I guess it got me all charged up."

"You guess?" Clutching his right hand with his left, Zev sucked air through his teeth. "What did she have you doing down there; rubbing cats with glass rods?"

"What?"

"High school physics experiment. Never mind." He worked his fingers and, satisfied they were still functional, reached down to take back the stack of CDs. "I guess if it got you on your knees, I can suffer the pain." As Tony grinned in surprise, his eyes widened. "I said that out loud?"

Tony nodded.

The skin between the top edge of his beard and the bottom edge of his glasses flushed red. "Great. I'll just . . ." Speakers banging against his legs, he backed up. "Look, I've got a ton of . . . um." Somehow, although Tony wasn't sure how, he got the door to post open with his elbow. "Later." And vanished.

"Do we have to have another conversation about Zev being a nice guy?" Amy demanded from her desk.

"I didn't do anything!" Tony protested as he stood.

"Please. I could see the sparkage from here."

"There's nothing going on. He's a friend!"

"No, literally, I could see the sparkage." She spread her hands, miming explosions. "What's Arra been doing to you?"

Frowning hurt. "Nothing I shouldn't have expected."

"Well. Aren't we obscu . . . CB Productions, how may I help you?" Her expression clearly stated they weren't done.

They were as far as Tony was concerned. He'd have been gone, except that every step brushed a tiny buzz off the carpet and he had a horrible vision of what would have happened to some very expensive equipment if he touched it in this state. He had to bleed the residual juice off.

Metal. He needed metal but not something he'd destroy. An old dented filing cabinet just outside the door to the bull pen caught his eye. That should do. A quick laying on of hands and with any luck he and the filing cabinet would survive the experience.

Standing with his back to the cabinet, hoping it looked as though he was waiting for Amy to finish giving directions back to the studio from Centennial Pier; he reached back and touched the metal with both hands. *Go on, take it all. Someone around here must know CPR.*

The hollow boom wasn't entirely unexpected, although the volume was impressive.

Dropping the phone to her shoulder, Amy glared past him to the bull pen. "What the hell are they up to now?"

"Beats me." Tony shrugged. His palms were sizzling, but he didn't seem to have done himself any damage. "You know; *writers*. Listen, Amy, I've got to get back to work." About to step away, he paused. "Who's out at Centennial Pier?"

"Kemel, the new office PA."

"What happened to Veronica?"

"She quit."

"And why's the new guy out at the pier?"

"Rachel got a call from the location scout and sent him out with the digital to get some pictures of North Vancouver Cemetery."

Tony ran over the geography in his head. "Which is nowhere near Centennial Pier."

"He's lost."

"No shit."

"We'll talk about you and Zev later."

"Right." *Or we'll all die by smoke and shadows. Can't think of which I'm looking forward to more.*

He'd never noticed how many shadows filled the hall to the soundstage. No wonder he'd felt safe walking it earlier; his hitchhiker had felt safe. When he realized he was trying to outrun his shadow, he forced himself to slow down.

"Hey, Tony!" Everett's door was open and Lee was in the chair having his cowlick dealt with yet again. "You okay?"

He'd just been nearly electrocuted by a wizard who seemed more than willing to deal with a disaster she'd set in motion by running away. Everyone in the immediate area was about to become painfully dead and he was the last best and only line of defense. Well, him and Henry. And two thermoses still full of vodka-catnip cocktails.

Green eyes narrowed and Tony wondered just how much of that had shown on his face.

"I'm fine."

"Henry, I told you, I'm fine."

"She attacked you."

Subtext: *She attacked something of mine.*

Tony rolled his eyes. *Jesus, Henry, get an afterlife.* "I provoked her. I said some stuff that really pissed her off."

"But you said it in order that she reconsider her position."

"Bonus if she does it, but no." As he remembered it, he'd been so angry, he'd been hitting out at the only thing available. "I said it pretty much just to piss her off."

"Because you have a death wish?"

He elbowed the vampire lightly in the side. "Duh. I'm here, aren't I?" He didn't want to be there. He wanted to be safe at home, safely oblivious, eating nachos in bed and watching one of Lee's old movies. He wanted his biggest concern to be about his pointless attraction to a straight boy. He didn't want to be in charge of saving, if not the world, the immediate area and anyone who might have ever had anything to do with Arra Pelindrake. No one seemed to care what he wanted. "What time is it?"

They were standing so close, he felt Henry lift his arm to check his watch. Standing in the soundstage with just the emergency lights on, he couldn't even see his wrist, but Henry had an advantage in the dark. "It's just turned 11:00."

"Do you hear anything? I mean anyone? Here."

"Only you. Your heart is racing."

No shit. "Just revving up for the fight."

"Of course."

They had the lamp, and the leftover potion, and a baseball bat picked up on the way home from work, and a certain small amount of experience in kicking metaphysical ass. They didn't have a wizard—she wasn't answering her phone or her buzzer—but they were as ready as they'd ever be. If that last shadow made a break for home, they'd stop it and if the Shadowlord sent new minions through the gate, solid minions, impervious to the light, they'd be facing . . .

Crap.

They knew they'd be facing a vampire. They knew what he knew. "They'll come through prepared. Ready to take you out."

"I am not so easy to kill."

Prince of Darkness voice. *Yeah, that'll impress them.* "But you *can* be killed."

"Not easily."

"But . . ."

"You'll have my back."

"Right." Like that made it better. Tony shifted the bat to his other hand and wiped his sweaty palm against his jeans. "You know, this morning Arra was all ready to rush in and take her bat to the shadow-held. I wonder how she would have explained it, you know, after, while she was standing over the body. I mean, you can't call smacking a coworker with a Louisville Slugger a special effect."

"She probably didn't even consider that." He could hear the smile in Henry's observation. "She thought you were in danger and she rushed in."

"Using up her entire stock of helping out." Tony, on the other hand, wasn't smiling.

"Did she tell you she wasn't going to stand against the Shadowlord?"

"Well, yeah. Right from the start she said she wouldn't face him."

"And in the beginning she said she wouldn't help, but she has."

"As long as it was at no risk to her; she's always planned to run."

He felt Henry shrug. "Plans change."

"I can't believe you're defending her. She's not here, is she?"

"No. She's not here."

"A minute ago you were all pissed off because she'd attacked me."

"The two things are unconnected."

Tony opened his mouth and closed it again, sputtering slightly as the dozen or so things he could say to that got tangled on the way out. When it seemed as though he'd been listening to nothing but his own ragged breathing for half an hour he muttered, "What time is it now?"

"11:17."

"Is that all?" And then he realized. "No gate."

"Apparently not. I suspect our enemy has things to prepare."

That sounded reasonable. Not in the least comforting, or encouraging, but reasonable. "Why face you when he can come through in the morning when you're out of it."

"Why, indeed."

"He can come through in the morning when it's just me." And as long as they were speculating . . . Tony lined up another couple of points as Henry moved the lamp back by the light board and rolled the cables. "He's got to have learned that it's harder for us to stop them when we're shooting. All those people hanging around trying to create a television show really screws with the hero's ability to defend against dark wizards invading from another reality."

Henry's smile flashed white in the dim light. "A television hero would manage."

"Fucking television hero's got fifty people behind the camera making him look good. I'm going to get fired. You know that, right?"

"It's not a given."

"Yeah, it is." They fell into step, heading for the rear door. "Even if we save the world, I'm going to lose my job, lose my apartment, and end up turning tricks in Gastown. All of a sudden, I'm feeling a lot more sympathy toward season six Buffy."

"Is that supposed to mean something?"

"Twenty-first century, Henry; try to keep up."

At 9:30, Tony had vetoed the idea of breaking into the wizard's apartment.

"Look, if she doesn't want to come, you can't force her."

"You can't force her," Henry had corrected. *"I can."*

"And can you force her to fight when she gets there?"

"You'd be surprised how many people fight when cornered."

"Yeah, like rats. She's cornered now." Frowning, Tony'd rubbed at his chest. *"If we go in there, and if she's home, she'll fight us. If she wins, there's no one to block the gate."*

"Alone stood brave Horatius, but constant still in mind; thrice thirty thousand foes before and the broad flood behind."

"What?"

"'Horatius at the Bridge.' Lord Macaulay."

"Fuck that. Just drive, would you."

So Henry had pulled away from the wizard's co-op wondering what had happened to change Tony's attitude toward her from acceptance to sullen resentment. Immortal patience was a godsend as bit by bit the events of the morning emerged. As he pulled into the studio parking lot, he'd learned about the new circular bruise in the center of Tony's chest, purple and angry amidst the not-yet-faded leftovers of the earlier beating.

With the gate unopened and battle delayed, he'd dropped Tony at his apartment and waited outside, out of sight, until he'd heard his heartbeat—too familiar to him to mistake—slow in the cadences of sleep. Henry could see from the street that all the lights were on and he'd snarled, frustrated by a battle that dealt in terror and left him nothing to fight.

At 2:15, after a quick drive into downtown Vancouver, he followed another of the co-op's members into Arra's building.

If the wizard had warded her door, she hadn't warded it against brute strength. With the sleeves of his sweater pulled down to mask fingerprints, one hand on the door handle and the other up by the dead bolt, Henry gave a short, sharp push. The sound of steel flanges punching out of the wooden frame sounded like a gun going off, but he was in the apartment with the door closed behind him before any of the wizard's neighbors had roused. From the hall, there would be no sign of forced entry.

The wizard was not in the apartment; he couldn't feel her life. He searched every room regardless. Who could say what a wizard's abilities encompassed?

The laptop was gone from the dining room table. In its place a stamped envelope addressed to Anthony Foster. On the envelope a Post-It Note that read, *Vera, please drop this in the mail after feeding the cats.*

Henry set the note aside and carefully ran his thumbnail under the seal of the envelope. The cheap glue parted with a minimum of protest.

A steady regard turned him toward the living room. Both cats sat on the sofa and stared disdainfully at him. Dogs always insisted on playing pack politics with his kind. Cats were smarter.

"I need to know what she's told him."

Zazu snorted.

"If you expect me to believe that you've never made a morally ambiguous choice, think again. Cats are all about morally ambiguous."

Whitby yawned.

He'd half expected the letter to be handwritten in flowing black script on thick linen paper, instead it was Times New Roman, 12pt, on 20lb white bond. There was no salutation or signature.

I saw him win. As he advanced on the city, I cast the crystals and I saw he would win. I cast again, and again, and every time the Shadowlord was victorious. I tried to convince Kiril and Sarn to leave with me, but they refused. They refused to understand that there was nothing they could do—that they could not win. Fight for us, the people of the city screamed. Die for us. They walked out to their deaths and I opened the gate.

Even after seven years, my sight is not so clear in this world, but every time I look, I see him win. What point in trying when loss is foreseen—although I no more expect to convince you of this than I could convince Kiril and Sarn.

I can only hope that on some new world this will change.

Now you know what I know.

For what it's worth, I'm sorry.

"It's not worth much," Henry snarled, folding the letter back along its original lines. Then he stood for a long moment with his hand above the phone.

Tony, it's Henry. Don't go into work tomorrow.

Don't be among the first to die.

Wait until sunset when I am there to fight beside you.

Their tie was strong enough that even at a distance he could make it a command, not a request.

But he'd neither asked nor commanded it in the car as they drove away from the studio, both of them well aware of what the morning could bring.

As much as Henry wanted to, he would not take Tony's choice from him. He stepped away from the phone, hand dropping to his side. "The choices we make, make us," he told the cats.

Zazu snorted. Whitby yawned.

Arra's letter to Tony back in its envelope, back on the table, Henry slipped out into the night.

∽ SIXTEEN

The carpenters had been called in at 6:00, Peter and Sorge together having decided that the location they'd intended to use for the streets-of-London-circa-1870 flashback was unsuitable owing to half a dozen junkies who flat out refused to move. A set, therefore, had to be built. By the time Tony arrived at 7:30, the scream of saws and the pounding of hammers could be heard all the way out to the craft services truck.

As he came in through the open back doors, Charlie Harris, one of the painters, handed him a paint roller duct-taped to a broomstick and pointed him at five meters of plywood wall saying, "Get a layer of the medium gray down. I want to start airbrushing the stone on by 9:00."

"Yeah, but . . ."

"We've got time constraints here, bucko, and Peter said to use anyone who wasn't either directly in front of or directly behind a camera."

"Bucko?"

Hazel eyes blinked myopically at him through paint-flecked glasses. "You're the production assistant, right? You got something more important to do?"

More important? Still a little thrown by *bucko*, Tony glanced toward the set under the gate and realized with horror that the nervous bray of laughter still echoing around the soundstage had come from him. "I've got to save the world at 11:15," he announced. Well, why not? At least when the shit hit the fan, one guy might know enough to duck.

"Christ, you've got hours yet, you'll be long done by . . . Hey! Shit for brains! I told you to paint those doors matte black, not gloss!"

As Charlie hurried off, Tony looked down at the roller and stepped up to the paint tray. It wasn't like he had anything to prepare. The world's last line of defense pretty much consisted of him declaiming, "You shall not pass," and everyone knew how well that had worked out the *last* time. Oh, sure, eventually, it was happily ever after and all that, but first there was the whole falling through fire and dying thing. *And if I die, I don't come back.*

If I die . . .

Die . . .

"Hey, Foster! You want to get some of that paint on the wall instead of the floor?"

Paint dribbled off the roller to puddle by his foot. Wet, it didn't look much like medium gray. It looked like liquid shadow.

"Foster!"

"Right. Sorry."

Painting left him far too much time to think. Thoughts of the gate, thoughts of what might come through the gate, thoughts of what he might do to stop it, thoughts of whether Arra might or might not have screwed off and left him alone—*mights* and *maybes* and *what ifs* chased themselves around in his head, but he couldn't get a grip on any of them. By the time he covered the last bit of plywood, he was so frustrated at the complete and total lack of substance that he was starting to look forward to the possibility of the Shadowlord's army charging through the gate after Arra with swords drawn. One thing about an army, it made it easy to convince people that something was going on.

Drop an army through the gate and at least I won't be facing it alone.

Alone.

Fucking great. He knew that *almost* voice. There was still a shadow here on the soundstage! Whirling around, Tony tried to get a good look at his own shadow as it danced with his heels over the concrete floor.

"Foster, what the hell are you doing?" Charlie glared at him over an armload of Styrofoam capstones. "If you're done, get out of my way."

"I'm, uh . . ." Did his shadow look darker? Occupied?

"You're, uh, nothing. Haul ass over to the workshop and bring the box of sticks for this glue gun."

"I have to . . . I mean, there's someone . . ."

The capstones hit the floor; sticky hands closed around Tony's shoulders and turned him away from the wall. "Workshop. Glue sticks. Now. And, Foster, if you're having a nervous breakdown, I suggest you raise your caffeine levels and get over yourself. Today's a bad day!"

Tell me about it. It wasn't in his shadow, he decided—the voice wasn't clear enough for that or maybe it wasn't enough in his head. Any kind of accurate description took a beating around this sort of shit. Relief mixed with apprehension as he hurried toward the workshop. If not in his shadow, where? Or, more specifically, who?

Peter and Lee were running through phone dialogue as he passed the office set, Lee sitting with one thigh propped on the edge of the desk in what had become one of James Grant's signature positions.

". . . is still good and evil is still evil and good people continue to do what they can to negate the effects of evil people. But it's your choice, Raymond; I won't make it for you. After all, you're the one with the centuries of experience." Moving the phone away from his ear, Lee shook his head. "Did that last bit sound as over-the-top listening to it as it did saying it?"

Peter shrugged. "You're talking to a vampire detective freaking out about a coven of aristocratic witches he's just discovered he didn't destroy back a hundred odd years ago; does it get more over-the-top than that?"

Tony walked on as the actor acknowledged the point.

"Three minute warning, people!"

Across the soundstage, other voices took up the cry and construction noises began to drop off. With no time to either stop shooting or stop building, the day would be a patchwork of both, carpenters and painters playing statue as the bell sounded, and bursting into antlike frenzy the second after "Cut."

Glue sticks in hand, Tony got back to the office in time to see the first take of the scene.

". . . won't make it for you. After all, you're the one with the centuries of experience."

"Cut!" As hammers and saws started up again, Peter stepped out from behind the monitor and walked as far onto the set as his headphones would allow. "Let's do it again, only this time, put the emphasis on *centuries* instead of *you're* and then put a little sharpness into the way you hang up."

"I'm mad at him?"

"You're not happy."

"Go from the top of the scene?"

"Not this time. Start in at 'morality hasn't changed.'" Heading back, the director caught sight of Tony and beckoned him in. "Where's your headset, Tony? Get it on and get to work."

"Charlie had me painting."

"London?"

He thought about it for a minute. It certainly hadn't looked like London, but this was television so who the hell knew? "I guess."

"You guess? Wonderful." Stepping behind the monitors, Peter moved out of Tony's line of sight. About to continue on his glue sticks delivery, Tony froze like a deer in the headlights as he realized that Lee had been watching him the entire time. Was, in fact, staring at him wearing the kind of speculative expression he'd been seeing on Arra of late.

Honesty, or something more visceral, forced Tony to admit the expression looked better on Lee.

But it did remind him that he couldn't put off the Arra problem any longer.

*   *   *

"...cowled robes, how hard is that? No, not bathrobes. Kind of a black caftan with hoods. Yes, they have to be black. Because it's an evil coven, for chrissakes, not a freakin' pajama party!" Amy hung up with a studied lack of emphasis and smiled tightly up at Tony. "That was Kemel. He's in town trying to pick up our rental of a dozen cowled robes. But they can't find them. And the six they *can* find are pink."

"Pink cowled robes?" Tony quickly ran through everything that had shot in Vancouver over the last couple of years and came up with zip. "Doesn't wardrobe usually make that kind of stuff?"

"Wardrobe is busy trying to make our one Victorian walking dress look like it's not the same dress we used back in episode four. And, yes, we could rent, buy, or make another one, but since we already have one, CB wouldn't approve the budget. Isn't it amazing what you can do with trim. Did you actually want something or are you just out here hanging around?"

"The door to Arra's workshop is locked." He'd spent a good five minutes rattling the knob; pushing, pulling and getting nowhere. It said something about the level of the cowl crisis that Amy hadn't noticed.

"No, it isn't."

"Yeah, it is."

"Can't be." She smiled smugly. "There's no lock on the door. Every now and then, it just jams and only Arra can get it open."

"Is she here?"

"Haven't seen her, so, no, I'd say she's not."

No real surprise. "Did she call in?"

"Do I care? Wait . . ." An uplifted emerald-tipped finger cut him off. ". . . let me answer that. If she wasn't bringing a dozen black robes in with her, then, no, I don't."

"Amy, this is important."

"Why?"

"I can't tell you." The big clock on the wall read 12:20. His stomach plummeted and then he remembered to glance down at his watch. 10:20. "You haven't fixed the clock yet."

"Gosh." Heavily kohled eyes opened emphatically wide. "You're right, I haven't. Get over it."

It'd be over soon enough; he had a little less than an hour to go.

Soon.

God damn it! He grabbed at his head, his fingers closing over a sticky smear of paint. *Stop fucking doing that!*

Amy frowned up at him, tapping the end of a pen against her lower lip. She might have looked concerned, she might have looked annoyed—Tony was too distracted by the shadow-voice to decide. "I didn't talk to Arra," she said at last. "Hang on and I'll see if Rachel did."

A scribbled note shoved under the office manager's nose brought no pause in her heated discussion with their ISP about a lack of cable internet hookup and a negative response.

"I guess she'll be in later." Amy's tone fell halfway between statement and question. Trouble was, Tony didn't have any answers.

Although he did have more questions. Would later be too late?

"Tony?"

"Yeah. Sorry." About to ask if CB was in, he changed his mind. What would be the point? Anything CB knew had been erased and even if he had time to start an explanation from scratch, Tony had no way to prove any of it. Murderous body-snatching shadows on the loose from another world—it still sounded like a bad pitch from the bull pen. "I've got to get back to work." Really wishing that Amy would stop staring at him, he spun around on one heel, took two steps, and slammed into a warm, yielding obstacle. CD cases clattered against the floor.

"Zev. Sorry, man. I've uh . . . I've got to go." A glance back over his shoulder. "If Arra calls, tell her . . ." What? Get her magical ass in here? "Fuck it. She knows. Don't even bother."

Amy watched Tony disappear through the door leading to the soundstage and shook her head.

"What was up with him?" Zev asked as he shoved aside a pile of uncollated scripts and stacked his retrieved CDs on the corner of her desk.

"I'm not sure, but I think you've been replaced in his affections by a fifty-five-year-old woman who blows things up."

"Well." After a long moment, the musical director sighed. "That definitely sucks."

The big carbon arc lamp was gone. It wasn't by the set. It wasn't by the lighting board.

Tony stared at the empty space as the first vibrations from the gate started the liquid in his eyeballs quivering. *Crap. Crap! CRAP!* Heart pounding in his throat, he raced to the racks where the extra kliegs were stored. It wasn't there either. Back to the edge of the gate, every hair on his body lifting.

"Three minute warning, people!"

Right. They were shooting in the office set. They were using the lamp.

They weren't using the lamp.

"Sorge said we were done with it, so CB rented it to that buddy of his who's doing that new sci-fi show over in Westminster. Charged him a freakin' arm and a leg, too. He took it out first thing this morning."

When I was painting . . .

The gaffer looked down at his arm and then up at Tony. "You want to let go of me now?"

"Yeah. Right. Sorry." It took him a moment to remember how his fingers worked.

"If Arra was still using it, she should've said something. Not that it would've made any difference if CB had a chance of making a buck off renting it. Good thing I didn't need it," he added, turning back to his board as Peter called for quiet on the set. "He'd have me using freakin' flashlights if it'd save him a few bucks."

"Rolling . . . slate . . . and action!"

Lee's voice talking of good and evil got lost in Tony's rising reaction to the gate.

Flashlights? Digging the heels of both hands into his temples, he staggered back to the dining room. Leaning against one of the vertical two-by-fours, he stared into the set. No one there. No one trying to send a shadow home. This was a good thing until he forced himself to consider why the last shadow wasn't heading home. Last minion left in this world could be staying to act as a welcoming committee. Welcoming what; now that was the question. Odds were good that flashlights wouldn't be enough to stop it and the baseball bat was in his bathroom leaning against the sink.

His nose was running.

A quick touch with the back of his hand.

No, his nose was *bleeding.*

Stupid vampire. Stupid sleeping all day. What the fuck good is that?

The actual opening of the gate felt as though the two halves of his brain were being ripped apart. Slowly.

A weapon. He needed a weapon.

And an aspirin, but that would have to wait.

Just outside the set, he found a metal stand and with shaking fingers unscrewed the upright. Four feet of aluminum, threaded on both ends—after all those years with Henry, he knew the kind of damage a simple stake could do.

Holding the pipe across his body, he stepped back into the set in time to see a man fall about four feet and land facedown on the dining room table.

The gate closed.

The man laid his palms flat against the wood and pushed himself into a sitting position.

Tony could hear hammering, swearing, wood dragging across concrete, and Sorge's distinct mix of French and English as he spoke to the key grip—with two separate crews working, there were easily thirty people in the soundstage and not one of them had seen anything out of the ordinary. No new allies. No one who wouldn't still demand to see proof of an insane-sounding story.

And all Tony's brain seemed capable of coming up with in the way of reaction was, *Your clothes, give them to me.* Which didn't work on a number of levels but mostly because the stranger was already dressed—black dress pants, black shoes, a gray silk shirt, and a black leather jacket. The shoes were a little off and the jacket not quite right, but all in all, it was a good casual business look.

Oh, for Christ's sake; quit being so fucking gay!

In his own defense, it was easy to look at the clothes. Harder, almost impossible to look at the man. Hair, eyes, mouth . . . Tony assumed they were there, but he couldn't seem to focus on them. Not that it really mattered. Lifting the pipe, he forced his right foot forward.

He'd barely completed the step when Mason Reed hurried across the set, both hands outstretched, his shadow trailing behind him like it would really rather be anywhere else.

Mason. Son of a bitch. The last shadow was in Mason. Tony'd forgotten the actor was in the studio that day. He'd been with Everett, not out on the soundstage; he hadn't been on the list of possibles.

In full *Raymond Dark* makeup and costume, he stopped at the edge of the table and helped the other man to his feet.

"Shouldn't you be kneeling?" Quietly curious.

"It is not done on this world, Mast . . ."

Something twisted. Mason whimpered and dropped to his knees.

"It is now." Tanned fingers lifted a strand of the actor's hair, turning it so the red-gold glimmered in the light. Tony could see Mason shudder and, as much as he'd never liked the other man, he wouldn't have wished this on him. He managed another step forward as the strand of hair was released and a bored voice murmured, "Get up, fool, before someone sees you and leaps to the wrong conclusion."

On *conclusion*, the stranger lifted his head.

His face came into focus. Eyes locked with Tony's.

The pipe clattered against the floor as it fell from suddenly nerveless fingers. Tony recognized the feeling of being studied like an insect under a magnifying glass. This was what . . . who . . . had been peering through the gate. He felt shadows stirring, wrapping around his soul. Found a word. "Shadowlord."

The pale gray eyes widened slightly. "You know me. How . . . interesting. I know you as well, Tony Foster. I hold a shadow of you." A glance down at the pipe. "Seems there's more substance to you than that, though."

Tony tried to flinch away as warm fingers pinched his chin, but his shadow rose up behind him and held him in place. Not the Shadowlord's minions. Or the Shadowlord's army. The Shadowlord. Here. Himself. Why would he do that? Why would he travel to another world just to take out Arra when he'd already fried her entire order?

"Able to question . . ." The grip on his chin tightened and his head was forced first one way then the other. ". . . but nothing else. As you are, you are no danger to me." The Shadowlord smiled. His teeth were very white and the smile, wreathed in shadow, was intended to be terrifying, but Tony had seen smiles wreathed in Darkness and the joy of the Hunt . . .

And maybe he shouldn't have made that thought so obvious.

The smile snapped off, no longer dangerously charming, merely dangerous. "Where is she, Tony?"

No reason to waste hero points—he suspected he was going to need all he could muster. "I don't know."

The hand not holding his chin reached out, grabbed his shadow, and pulled it forward. Pulled it through flesh. Screaming would have been nice, but the hand holding his shadow also held back his voice. *Holy fuck, that hurts!*

"You're not lying."

The release hurt almost as much as his shadow snapped back.

"But she hasn't run. Not yet. I can sense only one gate. Mine." An amused tone, at odds with the vicious grip. "It was foolish of her to have waited; the moment she tries to open a gate, I'll know exactly where she is and I'll be on her between a heartbeat and her dying breath. Ah, you didn't know that, did you? You didn't know she was trapped. You're wondering if she knows how loudly the gates call to those who use power. Probably not." The grip became almost a painful caress. "Last time she opened a gate, I was regrettably delayed. This time, there's no one to delay me. Oh, wait, I'm sorry. There's a boy and a Nightwalker. I tremble. I truly do. Tell me where the Nightwalker hides from the sun."

Why don't you already know? Why hadn't the shadow taken that information back through the gate? Granted, it hadn't been in his head for very long, but Arra had said they knew what he knew. Seems Arra was wrong about that. The resulting emotion was more *nah nah nah* than hope, but he found strength in it. "Never."

"And that would be the required cliché response. Do you think I'm giving you a choice?" His hand stretched again over Tony's shoulder. "So foolish."

"Master, this boy is nothing. A production assistant. He does what he is told."

A silver eyebrow lifted. "My point exactly."

"He is beneath your notice."

Yeah, Mason always hated it when someone else was getting all the attention. *You want him?* Tony thought above the rising tide of pain. *He's all yours.*

"Would someone mind telling me what the hell is going on over here?"

Released, Tony could still feel the indentation of the Shadowlord's fingers in his flesh. His knees threatened to buckle, but he gritted his teeth and managed to stay standing.

"And who," Peter continued, sweeping an annoyed gaze over the evil wizard, "is this?"

"You know me. Interesting."

Apparently, no one else *knew* him. Although Tony had no idea how they couldn't feel the power writhing around the Shadowlord like smoke.

"He's a friend of mine, Peter." Gone was the whining sycophant, back was the star of *Darkest Night*, a man who knew his friends would be welcomed for no other reason than that they were his friends and he was essential to the continued employment of a great many people. "He's just dropped by to watch me shoot."

"Right. Fine." Peter was clearly maintaining a fingernail grip on his temper. "Then he'll have a lot more to watch if you'd go over to the office so we can start scene seven. Lighting's set and we've been ready for you for a while now, Mason."

"Which is why Tony came and got him."

Peter shook his head, clearly a little confused about why Mason's friend was speaking to him, defending a member of his staff; his shadow seemed to be on its knees. "Well," he said at last. "Nice to see someone's doing their job."

The Shadowlord held out a hand. "Michael Swan."

A cursory handshake. "Right. Mason, if you would . . ." As he turned, sweeping Mason before him, he added to the soundstage at large, "Let's go, people; we've got another nine pages to get through today!"

"Your thoughts were filled with this . . . television. Shadows made of light. We have nothing similar. I find the whole concept fascinating." His hand closed gently over Tony's shoulder. Under his shirt, Tony's skin tried to crawl away from the touch. "I do hope Arra cowers for a while—just think of what I could do with something like this."

Evil television? Or was that redundant? He'd come to kill Arra himself because Tony's shadow memories had made television fascinating?

That was . . . unexpected.

As the Shadowlord released him, Tony had a strong suspicion that hysteria was one more touch away. He could feel it beating its fists against the inside of his skull. He watched the Shadowlord catch up with Mason. Felt the panic begin to ease with distance. Wanted nothing more than to run. And didn't.

And followed. He didn't bother hiding, or skulking, or trying to be anything less than obvious. What would be the point?

Lee had moved to the edge of the set and was standing with his eyes closed, holding a cup of coffee. His lips were moving, so Tony assumed he was running over lines. Mason passed him without acknowledgment, but the Shadowlord paused and glanced back at Tony, his expression clearly saying, *So, this is the one.*

Great. He hadn't given up Henry, but he'd given up Lee. Or at least his attraction to Lee. *Don't . . .* Don't *what*, he had no idea. *Just don't.*

And the Shadowlord moved on.

Tony released a breath he hadn't known he was holding just as the color drained from Lee's face and his eyes snapped open.

Oh, shit!

Spasm.

But the Shadowlord wasn't touching the actor. Wasn't even near him.

The coffee mug smashed against the floor, coffee spraying against the shadow that stretched from Lee's back to the Shadowlord's heels. It seemed to be driving serrated spikes into Lee's head.

God fucking damn it!

No lights handy.

What else defeated shadow?

Darkness weakened them.

Gray-on-gray patterns flickered across the floor as a camera rolled into position.

Patterns . . .

Half a dozen running steps took Tony to the edge of the set—the edge of the lights. His shadow fell over Lee's and the Shadowlord's, wiping out the definition of the attack, leaving nothing but a formless shape of darker gray on the concrete.

Lee's breath caught on the edge of a scream and then eased out of him in a wavering exhalation. Then Elaine from craft services was there with a roll of paper towels. And Carol, who was on the lighting crew. And Keisha, the set dresser. With Lee surrounded by concerned women and no place on the floor for new patterns, the Shadowlord's shadow now extended no farther from his heels than it should.

Tony moved one tentative step away; moved his shadow one tentative step away.

Lee seemed fine.

As Mason ran over his blocking with Peter and Sorge, the Shadowlord moved up to stare through the camera's viewfinder. He was Mason's friend;

no one would move him. No one wanted to set Mason off and lose an afternoon's work.

Tormenting Lee had obviously been nothing more than a way to yank Tony's chain. How long would the Shadowlord just hang around if Arra stayed hidden? How long before he started killing people to bring Arra out of hiding? And would Arra come if he did?

What would he do if she didn't?

Flush her out with destruction?

According to Arra, it took time to learn the energy of a new world. The longer they had to wait for the other shoe to drop, the more the Shadowlord learned, the more powerful he became. Although it seemed as though shadows were shadows—that power he had now.

Bottom line, he had to be stopped sooner rather than later.

Yeah, and now we've come to that amazing decision, we're no farther ahead than we were. There's a big fucking evil thing hanging around being a fanboy—I'm the only one who knows it and I can't do a thing about it. I can't even take out his minion.

Mason was settling into character although he kept shooting "look at me" glances toward his master.

"Tony?"

Heart in his throat, he spun around so quickly he almost fell over.

Lee backed up a step, both hands in the air. "Are you okay?"

"Me?"

"Your nose is bleeding."

Still? He touched his upper lip and stared down at sticky fingertips. "It's nothing."

Arms wrapped around his torso, Lee nodded. "Sure."

"Are you . . ." A wave back toward the damp spot on the concrete. ". . . okay?"

"Good question." The green eyes stared past Tony's shoulder. "There's some weird shit going on around here ever since Nikki Waugh died. The doctor thinks my little memory lapse was something they call Transient Global Amnesia. Except, according to the cops, I'm not the only one forgetting things and your nose was bleeding yesterday, too—same bat-time, same bat-channel. And if I didn't know Mason was straight, I'd say he was one short step from bending over for that friend of his."

Tony didn't bother turning to look. "You might want to stay away from Mason. And his friend."

"Lee." Adam leaned between them. "We're ready for you."

"I'll be right there."

The 1AD nodded and headed for the monitors.

"I'm about to shoot a scene with Mason." He almost seemed to be asking if he'd be safe.

"That's not Mason, though." Tony nodded toward the set. "That's Raymond Dark."

Lee looked confused for a moment then he smiled. "Right. I wonder if he's going to take his friend to his interview."

"Interview?"

"Yeah, he's on *Live at Five* tonight. Again."

"They're live . . ."

"That would explain the title of the show, yeah. They seem to think Mason's the only actor on the West Coast."

"Lee!"

As Adam beckoned, Lee nodded at Tony and walked onto the set. Any other time, Tony wouldn't have been able to look away as the actor shed Lee Nicholas and became James Grant. Today, the Shadowlord held his entire attention.

"I wonder if he's going to take his friend to his interview."

"They're live . . ."

"Shadows made of light . . . just think of what I could do with something like this."

And it seemed as though shadows were shadows—that power he had now.

Oh, fucking crap.

The Shadowlord wasn't *only* after Arra. It was also an invasion. And Tony'd handed him the weapon he needed to win it.

The production office was empty. Tony could hear Rachel and Amy and one of the writers in the kitchen arguing over who'd emptied the coffeemaker. Keeping his head down, he hurried toward the open door of CB's office. He had to find a way to break Arra's spell because Chester Bane was the only person Mason ever listened to. The only person with even half a hope in hell of keeping him—and by extension the Shadowlord—from that live interview.

He might even know where Arra was.

But he wasn't in his office.

There was an appointment book open on the desk. CB disapproved of electronic calendars, saying paper and ink never got wiped out by a thunderstorm. Tony'd never heard of anyone's PDA being wiped out by a thunderstorm, but he had no intention of ever pointing that out to CB. The book was open to the current date. CB'd had a breakfast meeting with one of the networks, but the rest of the day was clear. Therefore, he was somewhere in the building.

"Lots of help. It's a big fucking building!" Nothing on the desk suggested *where* in the building CB might be; if he was on the move, they could chase each other around all afterno . . .

Tony slid the appointment book to one side and stared down at the sheet of art paper tucked into the edge of the blotter. The pattern penciled on it looked incredibly familiar. A closer look showed that the pattern had been, in fact, redrawn—lines drawn hard enough to etch the paper erased then filled back in.

Lines erased.

But this wasn't the pattern Arra had used to erase CB's memory.

No.

"My memory."

She'd erased it; he remembered seeing her erase it. Even when he'd forgotten everything else, he'd remembered that. CB must have found the paper and filled the lines back in.

Coincidence? Tony's thoughts flicked back to the vodka-catnip cocktails still in his thermos. If CB was also a wizard, he was going to need a very stiff drink.

After erasing it, Arra had slipped the paper she'd drawn CB's pattern on into her desk.

So, logically, in order to return CB's memory . . .

Finally! Something was going right!

Except that the door to Arra's workshop was still locked. Jammed. Whatever. Point was, he couldn't get the damned thing open! *She's probably got a spell on it. That's why it only opens* . . . He braced one foot against the trim and pulled. . . . *for* . . . Again. Harder. . . . *her.*

Fuck!

The argument in the kitchen built to a crescendo. Any minute, the losing participant would stomp out and demand to know what he was doing. Or Zev would emerge from post. Or Adam would come looking for him.

I don't have time for this! Not only was the door rock solid without so much as a wobble on its hinges but the doorknob wasn't even turning. His hands dropped to his sides. *Completely, fucking hopeless!* Breathing deeply, he closed his eyes and banged his head lightly against the painted wood. *Please. Just. Open.*

The latch rattled against the latch plate.

Tony grabbed for the doorknob, twisted, and pulled.

The door swung open without even the expected ominous creak.

Arra really *had* drawn CB's pattern on an invoice for blasting caps, which made it just a little hard to retrace. If he got it wrong, would it just not work or would CB remember things that hadn't happened? He paused, pencil frozen on the paper. If he got it wrong, would he completely screw up CB's brain? Did he have a right to risk it? As far as he could remember a distant and not very pleasant childhood, he'd always sucked at coloring between the lines.

"Screw it." The pencil started moving again. "He redrew me."

And anyway, the alternative was the Shadowlord live at five.

"What the hell is going on?" Stomping down the stairs, CB's voice bludgeoned the silence out of his way. "We had an agreement, old woman, and if I find you've broken . . ." He caught sight of Tony and paused. His gaze flicked down to the sheet of paper, the pieces falling into place so quickly Tony practically heard the click as they lined up. "Ah . . ."

"Yeah."

"Where is she?"

"I have no idea. I was hoping you might know."

"Has she . . ." One huge hand sketched an unidentifiable pattern in the air. They so didn't have time for obscure. "Taken up Balinese dancing? What?"

"Opened another gate."

"Apparently not."

CB glanced down at his watch. "The original gate has opened. Did she go through it?"

"No."

"Are you certain?"

"Pretty much, yeah." Tony point-formed the events of the morning, stopping twice to remind CB that he wasn't finished and that roaring off to wring necks without all the information wouldn't help. "You've got to stop Mason from doing that interview," he concluded. "If the Shadowlord gets in front of a live camera, we're talking shadows of light going out into millions of homes!"

"Millions?" The big man snorted. "Their ratings are nowhere near millions, Mr. Foster. Thousands at best."

"Fine. Thousands. Thousands of shadows taking over people's lives."

"But these shadows won't be able to leave the television."

"Wanna bet? My shadow shouldn't be able to get me in a hammerlock, but it did. Mason's shouldn't be able to roll around like a whipped puppy, but it is. Shadows shouldn't have been able to kill Nikki Waugh or Alan Wu, but they did!" Suddenly unable to remain still, he paced the width of workshop and back as he talked, CB's head turning to follow his passing like he was the ball in a tennis game. Which was pretty much how he felt. "I got a feeling that convincing shadows to leave the box is going to be no big. Then we've got mi . . . thousands of shadow-held who'll hunt down Arra for that son of bitch, forcing her to fight them—or save them from doing stupid things like jumping off an overpass. Draining her power until she can't fight him and . . ." Tony ground his palms together.

"Then he goes home and it is over."

Breathing a little heavily, Tony stopped pacing and stared at the older man. "You don't believe that. Powerful men seek power. It's what they do; hell, it's what they are. There are places on this world without indoor plumbing that still have a television and he's fascinated by television. He's going to take the television road to power!"

"He is fascinated by television because the shadow he holds of you is fascinated by television."

"Fine. Whatever. My bad." Man, CB was big on placing blame. First Arra, now him. "Point is, he's not just going to go home. Arra isn't going to be the only casualty. And Arra, by the way, works for you and is therefore your responsibility—at least a little," he amended as CB scowled down at him. "And more importantly, you are the only one who can stop Mason."

"I arranged this interview."

Oh, for . . . "Un-arrange it! But replace it with something good so Mason doesn't suspect—something ego stroking that'll make them both happy. Because if Mason suspects, then the Shadowlord will suspect and he'll take you out. Right now, he's thinking this world is his oyster—whatever the hell shellfish has to do with anything—and we don't want him to un-mellow. He's a lot less dangerous when he thinks he's already won and . . ."

"You've made your point, Mr. Foster. I understand power politics and I have no desire to compete with those who do . . ." The pause dripped with distaste. ". . . magic. While I am confining Mason to the studio, what will you be doing?"

"Trying to find Arra. She's our only chance of defeating him."

"As I understand it, then, not much of a chance."

"Yeah, well, I'm not so sure. I think there's layers working here and I've almost figured what's . . . Damn!" Every time he tried to shove the last pieces into place, they slipped shadowlike from his grasp. "Look, when he got a bit of me, well, I got a bit of him—of the Shadowlord—you know, a bit, and so next to Arra, I know him better than anyone, anyone alive that is. And I know her. And, I'm outside their history, so I've got a whole new perspective on things. I just think he's putting too much effort into finding her if he's that certain she can't hurt him, so I've got to convince her that . . ."

"Mr. Foster?"

"Yeah?"

"Perhaps," CB said slowly, weighting each word, "until this is over, you should switch to decaf."

⌐ SEVENTEEN

It took him forever to get to downtown Vancouver, although Tony had to admit that saving the world by public transportation was a particularly Canadian way to do things. By the time he reached the Burrard Station, however, he was well into the "screw it, I'm buying a car" mindset. Or a bike. Something like Lee's. Except he hated getting wet and, most years, wet was the defining weather for the lower mainland. So, back to the car.

He didn't care what kind of a car.

He just needed something that wouldn't take so goddamned long to get him anywhere. *Hey! I'm trying to find a wizard and save the world here, so could you get the fuck OUT OF MY WAY!*

A trio of elderly Asian women shot a variety of worried glances at him and shuffled to one side, clearing his path from the station to the street. He thought about apologizing, had no idea what he'd be apologizing for since he was about ninety percent certain he hadn't actually said anything out loud, and flagged down a cab. To hell with the expense; maybe CB would kick in a few bucks.

There was a police car parked in front of Arra's building when he arrived. Tony threw some money at the cabbie and raced across the road, ignoring the horns and shouted curses. Mason drove a Porsche 911, a very fast car that he drove very fast, relying on his minor celebrity to get him out of tickets, and when that didn't work, relying on the studio to pay the fines. If Mason and the Shadowlord had left just after he had, they'd have easily gotten to Arra's before him.

Hell, if they'd waited half an hour, had lunch, and then drove Zev's aging sedan into the city, they'd have easily gotten to Arra before him.

If I'm alive at this time tomorrow, I'm buying a damned car.

It was good to have goals. It made the possibility of imminent death not so imminent.

Both doors to the lobby were propped open, allowing the police to come and go as they pleased. Tony moved quickly past the elevator to the stairs—in case of trouble, stairs came with a lot more options than a sealed box hanging off cables.

No surprise upon emerging on the fourth floor to see a small crowd of murmuring tenants staring at the bright yellow police tape stretched across the front of the wizard's apartment. Staying tight against the wall, he worked his way past the edges of the audience until he could peer through the open door.

Something—someone—had pushed the metal sockets holding the latch and the dead bolt right out of the frame. And done it without putting a mark on the door. *Fucking great. Evil wizard with super-strength.*

"Can I help you with something?"

Only one profession ever wrapped such a seemingly innocuous question in so much sarcasm. Tony looked up from the damage, got a firm grip on his increasing need for profanity, and asked, "Is there a body?"

On the other side of the tape, the official police glare deepened. "Who wants to know?"

"Tony Foster. I work with the woman who lives here."

"And yet you don't seem to be at work."

No body, then. Cops at a homicide didn't take the time to exchange smart-ass observations with people hanging around the crime scene. Particularly not at a crime scene that involved a metaphysical, inexplicable death. The sudden surge of relief was intense enough to nearly buckle Tony's knees. Which was when he realized two things: One, that there didn't necessarily need to *be* a body; there had to be a hundred different ways an evil wizard could get rid of a rival that didn't involve an inconvenient corpse. And two, the cop was still waiting for a response. Tony shrugged. "She didn't come in, she didn't call. The boss sent me down to make sure she was all right."

"Uh-huh. Can anyone here vouch for you?"

Anyone here? Tony turned toward the watching/listening crowd of Arra's neighbors and spotted a familiar face. "Julian can."

Julian was ready for his close-up. At the sound of his name he pushed forward, Moira cradled in one arm. "He's been here before, Officer, with Arra Pelindrake. They do, indeed, work together." A dramatic pause. "We have spoken together, he and I."

Oh, yeah. Tony thought as the cop rolled his eyes. *I bet that was some Mustardseed.*

"I don't know why Arra didn't inform her employer she was going away for a few days," Julian continued. "We all knew."

"Well, *I* don't know why *he* knew." The new speaker was short and kind of round with her graying blond hair cut in a bowl shape. "*I* knew because *I* was feeding her cats. I'm the one who discovered the break-in." She clutched at Tony's arm with a small plump hand. "I found it this morning when I went in to feed them."

"Are they all right?"

"Oh, yes. They're in *my* apartment now." The emphasis came with a distinct sneer in Julian's direction.

"Moira is allergic to cats."

Last night. Not the Shadowlord, then. And not Mason—so far being shadow-held hadn't come with super powers, and Mason's muscle was more show than substance. Which left—Henry.

He'd leave the question of *why* Henry had broken into Arra's apartment for after sunset and only hoped that their earlier visits had left enough fingerprints to screw up any kind of an investigation. Had Arra been here when the vampire arrived? Had Henry locked her away somewhere so she couldn't run? Probably not. If she'd been out and around, free to make up her own mind, there was at least a chance she'd have shown up at the gate this morning—Henry wouldn't take that chance away from him. He'd probably just been looking for her, searching her apartment for some idea of where she'd run off to.

"So you have no idea of where Ms. Pelindrake might be, or how to reach her?"

What? Oh, right, the cop. "Sorry, no." He'd hoped she was home, just hunkered down and not answering the phone. Failing that, he'd wanted to do the same thing Henry had—search the apartment for clues. He'd had no plan for actually getting into the apartment, but it seemed Henry'd taken care of that for him—if the police would just haul ass out of his way.

And right on cue . . .

"Right, we're done." Cop number two appeared behind his partner. "Television's there, TiVo's there, computer's there, seventy bucks in a dish on the coffee table—if it was a burglary, they were after something specific and small."

"No way of knowing until Ms. Pelindrake reappears." Turning his attention back to the crowd, he swept it with a patronizing expression although he'd probably intended said expression to be stern. Not the first cop Tony'd ever met who didn't know the difference. "The moment any of you hears from her, have her call the station. You all have the number."

Since Tony had no intention of having Arra call the station if found, the fact he didn't have the number was irrelevant. *Okay, or not.* As he didn't seem to have an option, he took the offered business card and stepped back out of the way as both constables ducked under the tape, pulling the apartment door closed behind them.

"There's a locksmith on the way," Julian informed them. "I'll personally see to it that no one crosses that tape."

"The tape? Right." Cop number two turned and pulled it off the door. "We're done here. Can't just leave this stuff lying around. People use it for the damnedest things."

Cop number one murmured something too low to be overheard and they laughed together in a manly way as they stepped into the elevator. By the time the doors shut behind them, Tony, Julian, Moira, and the woman with Arra's cats were alone in the hall.

Julian's lip curled. "Assholes."

"No argument from me," Tony muttered. Faggot comments had a distinct tone of their own. No need to hear the actual words. And while they were sharing this moment of solidarity . . . "Listen, Julian, there's a chance that Arra may have left something about where she was going in the calendar on her computer. We ought to have a look."

The "we" was almost enough.

"If I don't find her, she could lose her job."

Which was more or less the truth.

"No." The woman with Arra's cats shook her head. "*I* don't think that's a good idea."

And that settled it.

Julian shifted the Chihuahua to his other arm and pushed the door open. "I'm the president of the co-op board and *I* think we should do everything we can to help a neighbor keep her job."

"Well, when I was president . . ."

"You *were* the president, Vera. You aren't now."

Moira growled an agreement.

Tony ignored all three of them and headed toward the computers, moving slowly enough to give the place a thorough once over. No shadows where they shouldn't be. No inexplicable stains. The laptop was gone, but the desktop was exactly where he remembered it although he couldn't remember ever having seen one of Arra's computers without a game of spider solitaire running. And, as it turned out, he couldn't get into her documents without a password.

"*I* think the police should be doing this!"

His escort had caught up.

"The police can't crack her computer without a warrant. I know. I was on *DaVinci's Inquest.*"

"Years ago and you were a corpse!"

Tony tuned out the argument and typed in "ZazuWhitby."

When it worked, there was a gratifying intake of breath from Julian. "How did you know?"

"Those cats are the only things she cares about." Working the mouse with his right hand, he dragged his phone out of his pocket with his left and thumbed the speed dial. Still no answer from her cell. Pity. He'd had a sudden idea that involved telling her he was taking both cats to the Shadowlord. That'd get her thumb out of her ass PDQ.

Nothing on her calendar. It didn't look like she ever used her calendar.

She *was* using 100GB of a 120GB hard drive—although at least 30G of that seemed to be porn. *Didn't need to know that. It's like finding out your parents had sex.* Totally fucking creepy. Literally.

He double-clicked a bitmap file labeled Gate and an almost familiar pattern of swirls and equations appeared on the screen. It seemed to be the same pattern he'd glimpsed on her computer at the studio. It was definitely *not* the same pattern written on the blackboards on the other side of the gate, even given that part of it had been covered by . . .

"*I* don't think you should be looking at her private things."

"You're right." He closed it out, grateful to have the memory interrupted. No doubt she had a copy of the gate file on the laptop. Probably why she'd taken the laptop with her.

Her wallpaper was a sunset over water. *Yeah, great. Very helpful.* As far as Tony was concerned, all water looked the same.

"What are you doing?" Tucked in behind his left shoulder, Julian seemed to require a play-by-play.

"She obviously likes this picture, right?" He clicked through the control panel and into design to get the jpeg's name, then into Arra's photos. "I want to see if it's local." There were two dozen similar pictures of sunsets in the folder labeled Kitsalano Point.

"Kitsalano Point, it's that part of Kits Beach just west of the Maritime Museum, that part that pokes out into the bay."

Yeah, that would be why they call it a point. Couldn't be Sunset Beach, which was maybe six blocks away. It had to be across the fucking creek. Still, it was a place to start.

"Are you going to look for her there?"

"Thought I might."

"Do you want a drive?"

Okay that was unexpected. "I thought you had to wait for the locksmith. President and everything . . ."

Julian dropped his attention to the dog. "Right."

"Look, if you boys want to go off together, *I'll* stay and wait for the locksmith."

"No, that's okay, it's my responsibility." Shifting Moira to his other arm, he held out his hand. "Good luck, Tony. I hope you find her."

"Yeah. Me, too." For all his affectations, Julian's handshake was surprisingly firm. *Must've missed that one when he was filling in the stereotypes form.*

"Wait!" Vera grabbed at his arm. "Your name is Tony?"

"Yes . . ."

"Tony Foster?"

"Yes . . ."

"How silly of me." Her giggle suggested they should agree with the assessment. "I heard you tell the police your name, but it never sank in. If you're Tony Foster, Arra left you a letter. I found it when I went to feed the cats, but then this whole burglary put it out of my mind. It's in my apartment, I didn't, of course, have a chance to mail it. Is it short for Anthony?"

"Is what?"

"Tony. Is it short for Anthony?"

"Yes. It is. My letter?"

"Wait here." A pat on the place she'd grabbed. "I'll get it."

Back in the hall, the two men and the dog watched Vera scuttle off to her apartment.

"You're thinking of strangling her, aren't you?" Julian asked conversationally.

"Oh, yeah."

The letter was no help at all. It didn't tell him where she was. It didn't tell him what to do. It didn't offer anything but more excuses.

What point in trying when loss is foreseen . . .

Nice attitude, old woman.

"The point of trying is trying!"

"You have a fortune cookie back there?"

"What?" Tony stared at the back of the cabbie's head for a moment. "Uh, no. Just thinking out loud."

"Do or do not, there is no try!"

"What?"

"Yoda."

"Right." That would make him Luke Skywalker, Amy could be Princess Leia, Henry'd have to be Han Solo riding to the rescue at the last minute, the Shadowlord had that whole Darth Vader thing down although he was significantly better looking, and Arra could be the irresponsible old wizard who chicken shitted away from a fight without even considering that she was fucking taking it somewhere else and now that it had found her was bailing on the whole goddamned mess!

"Please do not drive your fingers through my upholstery."

"Sorry."

Less caffeine might have been a good idea.

Tony had the cab let him off at the corner of Ogden and Maple, which put him west of the museum and shortened his walk out to the point. He hoped like hell he didn't have to search the whole beach. It was a big damned beach and even given the crappy weather lately, it was still pretty busy. Not so crowded as it would be in high summer, when an oiled sun worshiper couldn't change position without flipping the whole row, but there were bodies on the sand, at least one volleyball game that he could see, and, if he listened carefully, he could hear the grunts of the body builders heading for hernias. Squinting into the sun, he could see heads bobbing in the choppy water like sea otters. Oh, wait. Those were sea otters.

He had sand in his shoes, the late afternoon light bouncing off the bay was making his eyes water even behind his sunglasses, and he was in a significantly bad mood by the time he was out on the point.

No Arra.

"God fucking damn it!" He dropped down cross-legged and stared west. Since he was here, maybe he should take a moment to think quietly. To try and put all the pieces together. Yanking his phone out of his pocket, he punched in the personal and very private number CB'd given him.

"Not even my ex-wives have this number. Do not abuse it."

"I won't. I swear."

"Profanity will not be necessary." Tony'd stared at him in confusion. *"That was a joke, Mr. Foster."*

CB answered on the second ring. "Where are you?" he demanded.

Tony swallowed, trying to force his heart down out of his throat. "How did you . . . ?"

"Call display."

Right. Idiot. "I'm at Kits Beach. On the point."

"Why?"

"Arra apparently liked it here."

"I see. And is she there?"

His mouth open to form the negative, Tony paused. Frowned. Changed his response for no reason he could have given except that he suddenly wasn't . . . *sure.* "I don't know yet. Is Mason . . . ?"

"Mason has been taken care of. I rescheduled the interview and arranged to shoot a new pitch piece to take down into the American markets."

"Mason would give his right nut to have the show picked up by a big station."

"Indeed. There's also a photographer coming in to take shots for magazine ads."

"You're doing magazine ads?" The studio had never been willing to spend the money on the glossies before.

"No."

It was amazing how much CB managed to cram into two letters. A negative. A warning of lines about to be crossed. Impatience that Tony had no answers yet. A willingness to take matters into his own hands if it came down to it.

It might.

Tony supposed he should be happy he wasn't about to die alone. Except that he really didn't want to die at all. And CB would likely end up shadowheld, not dead—lots more effective to take over the guys in charge. Unless . . . He chewed at his lower lip. Unless the personalities of the people in charge were strong enough to be a threat. *Fuck, I'd hate to be the shadow trying to hold Chester Bane.*

"Mr. Foster."

"Yeah. Sorry." Looked like he wasn't going to be dying alone after all.

"I suspect that many of the people here are no longer in my employ. When Mr. Swan . . ."

It took Tony a moment to remember who Mr. Swan was.

The Shadowlord held out a hand. "Michael Swan."

". . . wants to know something, the answers he gets are detailed. Fawning. When he makes a suggestion, it is followed."

Peter, Adam, Tina . . .

"Lee?"

"I don't know. As far as I can tell, he seems to be concerning himself mainly with the crew—Mason excepted, of course. He's fascinated with television, how it works, what it can do, and has every intention of going with Mason to the interview tomorrow."

"Then maybe you should have rescheduled it for a little further away!" Tony yelped, his voice shrill enough to garner a response from a passing gull.

"That would have made Mason very suspicious. We stop this tonight. Before he leaves the studio. Find Arra. Bring her here."

Only Chester Bane could cut a connection quite so definitively.

Find Arra. Bring her here.

"Oh, yeah, like that's the easy part," he muttered at the phone before slipping it back into his pocket.

Unwilling to leave—not sure why but trusting his instincts—Tony swept his gaze over the beach, north then south. If asked, he'd probably say he was waiting. Actually, since he didn't know anyone in the immediate area, if asked, he'd probably tell the nosy bastard to fuck off.

What was he waiting for?

"Who the hell knows."

The otters were gone and the water offered no immediate answers. He shimmied himself into a more comfortable position. Seemed like he was going to be here for a while. The sand was dry and warm and Tony scooped up a handful, pouring it slowly into his other palm; then back again, and again, the action mesmerizing. He'd never really watched the way sand moved before; all the tiny pieces falling . . .

. . . into . . .

. . . place.

Amy'd asked the right question. What's his motivation?

"Not conquest—not until I gave him that new and exciting tailor-made for a Shadowlord way to use television to reach the masses. No, if all he wanted was to conquer and destroy and enslave, he could have done that any time to any world the moment he worked out the gates and he hasn't." The shadow had been fairly clear on the whole searching thing. "He's been searching seven years for this particular world. For the wizard who got away."

A young gull, its feathers still mottled brown, stared at him curiously, decided the noise didn't involve eating, and moved on.

"And while he's definitely—as Arra pointed out—a vindictive bastard, he's not just tying up loose ends. He's put way too much effort into this for that. It took him seven years to piece together the bits of information she left behind. Getting what information he could from those last two . . ." Tony swallowed, seeing them again, seeing them like he saw them every time he closed his eyes. "A guy like that—a guy who can do something like that—doesn't put this kind of work into a project without a bigger payoff than dotting the i's and crossing the t's. He has a gradational scale of minions, for God's sake, he's very much the center of his own universe! For all this, he has to believe she's a danger to him."

Tony tossed aside the old handful of sand—it had lost that silky, sunwarmed feel—watched the pattern the wind made as it caught the grains, and scooped up a new one.

"He came himself. He didn't trust this to minions. You know something, Arra. Something that can hurt him. Big magic's complicated, it's all math and patterns and you have to write it down to work it out. Big magic like the gate. Big magic like whatever's written on a blackboard he hasn't erased for seven years."

The sand wasn't enough now. The pieces coming together were bigger. Tony tossed his second handful after the first, then started sifting stones out of the beach and piling them one on top of the other. "What did you call it that day in the car? The light of Your-a-manatu or something? You woke up and yelled it out like it was important. Like it was a eureka moment. You wizards, that order of yours, worked out something you thought could stop him. But you did that crystal ball thing and saw that it didn't work." A hand against his pocket. The letter crinkled. "You saw him win and you believed what you saw and you ran. The last two wizards weren't enough. Self-fulfilling prophecy."

The stone on top of the pile was about as big around as a twonie and maybe twice as thick.

"Just . . ."

The stone felt good in his hand.

". . . like . . ."

Tony drew back his arm.

". . . this . . ."

And threw the stone as hard as he could off to his left toward the water. Off the way the wind had been blowing the sand.

". . . TIME!"

"OW!" Rubbing her shoulder, a hummock of beach became a wizard who turned and glared at him. "I didn't decide to gate until after I cast the stones and saw him win countless times."

"I think that deep down you decided to bail when your eldest got flamed." He picked up another stone. "I think you'd been second to him for a whole lot of years, got used to thinking that he was the better wizard, the best even, and when he was taken out, it all came down on you. They wanted *you* to save them now and you cracked under the pressure. That's what I think."

Arra clutched at her laptop case so tightly her knuckles whitened. "You don't know what you're talking about!"

"Yeah?" The beach had gone quiet. Even the waves were whispering against the shore. Tony stood, walked across the sand, and dropped to one knee so his eyes and Arra's were level. "You know how I survived on the street for five years? I heard all the bits and pieces that everyone else heard, but *I* put them together. *I* figured out what they meant. You tell me one thing I've gotten wrong. One thing."

The silence continued.

Then a gull screamed and noise rushed back in to fill the spaces.

"It's the Light of *Yeramathia*!" Arra snapped. "Not Your-a-manatu."

"Fine." He sat down, yanked some room into his jeans, and crossed his legs. "One *other* thing."

"This time isn't at all like that time. This time there's only one wizard, not three. Or two."

Tony shrugged. "He thinks there's a chance you can beat him or he wouldn't have put this much work into finding you. Besides, new world—new rules."

"What are you talking about? He's evil; he doesn't follow rules!"

"Not those kind of rules." He had to believe she was being deliberately obtuse. "You told me it takes time to learn to manipulate the energy of a new world. You've had the time; you've had seven whole years that he hasn't. All he has are shadows."

"All he has?" Arra snorted.

"Yeah, and if we don't stop him by tomorrow evening, he'll control every-one who watches *Live at Five.*"

"What?"

The expression on her face was everything he could have hoped for. "It's a two-for-one deal—double your pleasure, double your fun. It's a search for you and it's a conquest. Hell, for all I know it could also be a dessert topping."

"Tony!"

"He'll probably do the people who produce *Live,* too, come to think of it—that'll give him access to their studio, the morning show, the noon show, the news, and a whole lot more people."

"Tony, what the hell are you talking about?"

"Television." He buried his fingers in the sand. "Shadows made of light. Your Shadowlord's going to use it to create enough shadow-held to find you, help destroy you, and then take over the world. Henry said it way back in your apartment: evil is never content with what it has. It has to keep moving, keep acquiring."

"He doesn't know anything about television!"

"He knows what I know. And he's a smart guy with access to everyone in the studio; he's figuring it out."

Her eyes widened. "He's in the studio? He's here?"

It was Tony's turn to stare for that long moment. Arra seemed to be doing her best to make him believe that she wouldn't be sitting here if she'd only known it had gotten that bad. Just another lie to make it easier to live with herself. With what she'd done. *Lie to yourself if you have to, but leave me out of it.* "Don't give me that crap. You had to have felt him come through the gate this morning. You couldn't have missed that kind of an energy . . ." There was a word. He couldn't think of it. ". . . thing. You had to have known he was here while you were moping around getting sand in your knickers." And drawing gate patterns with a stick, he realized suddenly. Reaching out in front of her, he rubbed them out with the side of his hand. "What you might *not* know is that the moment you open the gate, he'll know where you are and he'll be on you like a dirty shirt."

"And you know so much, Mr. Smart-ass!" She shook her head, looking old as the burst of anger faded. "As it happens, you're right; he'll know, but he won't be able to manipulate enough energy to jump here."

"He doesn't have to." Tony pointed at a gull's shadow skimming over the beach. "He controls shadows."

"Not the ones he hasn't touched."

The shadow of Tony's arm lying on the sand, waved. Tony stopped waving as Arra got the point. "He's touched me. A couple of times. Touched me;

touched my shadow. That's why he let me leave, knowing what I know about him. Because of what he knows about me. Why should he exert himself to find you when I will? Especially since *when* I find you, he has a weapon handy."

Arra's pale eyes narrowed as she stared at a darker patch of sand. "So you're a threat to me. I could remove that threat."

"I don't think he'll do anything until you try to gate," Tony told her hurriedly. This was the weak point in his presentation. She could take him out and open the gate and leave this world. Except that running was one thing. Killing a friend . . . ally . . . coworker, at the very least . . . first was something else again. He hoped. Apparently, the Shadowlord thought so. Or at least he thought Arra thought so because evidence suggested he was definitely the kind of guy who'd cheerfully skin a friend, ally, or coworker alive. "If you'd gone before I found you, you'd have probably been fine."

"You knew that and you came after me anyway?" she asked, lifting her gaze to Tony's face. The clear subtext in both tone and expression said, *I don't like being manipulated.*

"Actually, I just figured that out. Just now." He nodded toward his shadow. It had seemed so obvious when he saw it moving across the sand. "Like right now. Thirty seconds ago." When she seemed at least partially convinced, he added, "Why didn't you?"

"Why didn't I leave? I don't know."

"For the same reason you hung around the gate, knowing he'd find you eventually. Because you're basically a decent person and the guilt's been eating at you for seven years."

"Shut up."

The fabric covering her shoulder felt damp under his hand and he wondered how long she'd been sitting there. "You've got a second chance, the chance you've been waiting for. Hoping for. We can take him."

"We?"

"You and me and CB. And Henry." He nodded toward the west where the sun was still a good distance above the horizon. "Sunset's not until 8:00, but that'll give us time to prepare."

"And the Shadowlord will wait patiently while we marshal our forces against him?"

If the level of sarcasm was any indication, she was starting to perk up.

"He might think you have a chance, but he believes he can win." Tony flicked up a finger. "He thinks you believe the same thing and that's what gave him the TKO in round one." A second finger joined the first. "He's already told me I'm no threat to him." Finger three. "And besides, CB waved some shiny stuff in front of Mason that'll keep him on the soundstage until late. He needs

Mason to get on *Live at Five*." He folded the fingers into a fist and shook it out as Arra snorted derisively.

"He doesn't need Mason if he has CB."

"Would you try taking over CB if there was another option?"

"Valid point." She sighed and stared out over the water. "I love it here. It reminds me of home. The sky, the water, the smells, the sounds . . . I just look straight ahead and pretend that if I turn around I'll see the city walls and not half a dozen broiled bimbos courting melanoma. How did you find me?"

He told her about the picture on the computer.

"Very clever, but not what I meant. When you were sitting back there, behind me, how did you know I was here?" One palm patted the sand. "Right here."

"I don't know." Although he'd definitely known she was there when he threw the stone. "I just did."

"Uh-huh."

"Honestly. I have no idea." He made a mental note to get freaked about that later.

The same juvenile gull wandered past again, gave them a dirty look, and took to the air.

Arra watched him fly, her eyes squinted nearly shut.

"You should have sunglasses on."

"Because you know everything." She snorted explosively, then squared her shoulders and snapped. "Do you really think we can beat him or are you just throwing words at me in a desperate attempt to get me to help?"

Yes. "I think this time you're going to have to fight him regardless. You open a gate, he'll come through shadow and stop you."

"Or I could kill you to clear the shadow away and then gate safely."

"And he'll have won because you'll have become him. Like him. Evil."

She raised a hand as he searched for other synonyms. "Yeah, I get it."

"Good. Because if you have to face him, why not go in believing you'll win?"

Tony half expected her to say: *Because we won't.*

She surprised him.

"All right. I won't fight for you. But I'll fight beside you."

"All I'm asking."

"I know."

"It was all I was *ever* asking."

"I know. Now help me up. I've got to get my cats back from that idiot Vera before they convince her that they always have fresh salmon for dinner."

"And yet you were going to leave them with her when you bailed."

Her hand tightened almost painfully around his as he helped her to her feet. "Don't push it, boy."

"Sorry."

She tucked her arm into his as they walked toward the parking lot, graciously allowing him to support more and more of her weight as they traveled. Tony suspected she was making a point, but since he had no idea what that point was, he just braced himself and kept going. Maybe she was just making sure he wouldn't drop her. *Yeah, of the two of us, I'm the only one who's never run out on an entire world. I won't be the one doing the dropping.* Maybe she was just being a pain in the ass because she could.

The latter seemed more likely.

"I know something else about the Shadowlord," he said as the muscles in his arm started to protest. "Something you don't know."

"You have no idea what I know."

"He's gay."

"You're right, I didn't know that." Shifting her weight, she leaned far enough away to sneer up at him. "However, he's an evil wizard from another world; I doubt very much your gaydar applies."

"Never doubt the gaydar," Tony snorted as they stepped over the concrete divider and into the parking lot. "But that's not it. I told you, he's touched me. I mean, talk about queer eye on the straight guy—every time I come in contact with a straight boy that's being shadow-held, they go after my ass."

"Do they now?"

"They do."

"So that would be Lee and Mouse and Ben . . ."

"Technically Ben just winked at me, but yeah." He really didn't like the speculative sound she made as they reached the car. With any luck, it was about the car. Not that his luck had been great of late.

"Maybe it's not them. Maybe it's your ass." Arra leaned back, looked down, and made a small dismissive moue. "And then again, maybe not. Did you happen to mention that CB has his memory back?"

"I didn't, exactly, but he does."

A raised brow invited him to continue.

"I retraced the paper. Like he did for me." Might as well spread the reaction around.

"Did he now?"

"Yeah. He's kind of pissed."

"No doubt. How fortunate, then, that I'm probably going to my certain death."

↪ EIGHTEEN

"Uh, Arra, that's a new lock. Remember, I told you about the break-in."

"I'm not senile, boy." She paused and tossed a twisted grin at him over her shoulder. "At least you'd better hope I'm not, all things considered." The key turned smoothly and she pushed open the apartment door. "You put the supplies in the kitchen; I'm going to rescue my cats."

Wondering whether it was wise for her to waste energy on something that could be solved by a visit to Julian—and the next instant realizing that the thought of a visit to Julian was probably why she'd done it that way—Tony set the two bags of groceries and the single bag from the liquor store on the counter. By the time he heard the door open again, he had the frozen dinners in the oven and the coffeemaker on. A bottle of vodka in each hand, he watched both cats stalk down the hall, noses in the air and tails lashing from side to side.

"I thought they'd be glad to see you," he said as the wizard came into the kitchen.

Arra snorted. "You've never had cats, have you? Put those down; we'll eat first, then you can put the potion together while I try to remember just how the Light of Yeramathia goes."

"*Try* to remember?"

"Give me a break." She pulled the coffeepot out and shoved a mug under the drip. "It's been seven years, it was a joint effort originally, and it may have to be adapted for local conditions."

"Yeah, but . . ."

"But what?"

Good question. "Nothing." Wait. Something. "*I'm* to put the potion together?"

"That's right. Better make a double batch, we're probably going to have to pour it down the throats of the entire crew. Those that survive anyway."

"But . . ."

"Until the final . . ." A spark leaped off her fingertip. ". . . zap, it's nothing more than organic chemistry—no more complicated than putting together a decent salsa."

"I don't cook," he protested, shooting a wary glance at her fingers.

"You do now." She took a long swallow of coffee and peered at him over the edge of the mug. "I'm not doing this on my own; that was the deal."

"*I'll fight with you, not for you.*"

"Yeah, that was the deal, but . . ." Fuck, he wished people would stop staring at him. If he hesitated, if now she was willing to fight he even once suggested it was all up to her, she'd bail. Guilt or no guilt, she was still on the edge; he could see it in her eyes. "Okay, fine. I'll make the damned potion. What's the recipe?"

Arra shrugged and bent down to peer into the oven. "You know the ingredients, just use as much as seems right to you. How long until these things are ready? I'm starving."

Tony stared down into the pot of heated vodka and took a cautious sniff. Mostly, it smelled like catnip and since that's what this potion mostly smelled like when Arra made it, he supposed it smelled like it was supposed to. What kind of measurement was *as much as seems right to you* anyway?

"So much for wizardry being an exact science."

Arra had paused on her way out of the kitchen. *"It's not a science at all, kid, it's an art. It's like television—art and science blended."*

Knowing how big a part luck played in making good TV, comparing it to wizardry didn't exactly inspire confidence. As far as he was concerned, a world where Joss Whedon got canceled was exactly the kind of world where the Shadowlord could win.

The contents in the second pot weren't quite the same shade of green. He tossed in another bay leaf and a few more flakes of catnip, changed his mind and attempted to scoop them out again. Unsuccessfully. Sucking his fingers, he realized he should have used a spoon.

"I told her I didn't know what I was doing," he muttered down at Whitby.

Whitby stretched out a paw and languidly poked Tony in the ankle.

He sprinkled a few more flakes of catnip on the cat. Getting stoned seemed like a good idea to him, but since that wasn't an option, he'd have to mellow vicariously.

Someone knocked on the apartment door.

Tony checked his watch. Not quite 4:30—way too early for Henry and Julian had already been by. Twice. Which didn't, of course, rule out the fact that this could be Julian dropping by again.

He turned both pots down to simmer and hurried toward the door. Arra had made it quite clear after Julian's second visit that a third would result in the Shadowlord knowing exactly where she was because she'd open a gate to the world of annoying gits and return her unwelcome visitor to his own kind. And his little dog, too.

A second knock as Tony's fingers closed around the door handle convinced him to yank it open immediately. He very much doubted Arra *would* open a gate but, as the lock, the spark, and the incident with the litter box had proven, she could do smaller magics without attracting unwelcome attention.

"Look, Julian, you've got to sto . . ." Propelled by Keisha's fist, the final consonant exploded out of him along with all the air remaining in his lungs. Gasping for breath, he was able to offer little resistance as the set dresser shoved him up against the wall, his head impacting against the drywall with a distinct crunch.

"So here you are." Her forearm up against his throat, she leaned a little closer. Her dark eyes gleamed. "I was wondering who'd find you first."

Shadow-held.

Holy obvious observation, Batman.

"You don't have to do this."

"Do what? Kick your ass?"

As her knee came up, Tony brought his own leg up and around, hooking hers while simultaneously slamming her on the opposite side of her head with his elbow. Between the double blows she went down. He followed her to the floor, landing on her torso as hard as he dared.

Keisha grunted, reached between his legs, grabbed a handful of crotch, and squeezed.

Tony yowled. Rearing back, he clutched at her arm with both hands and tried to free himself from her grip. Free her grip from him. Stop the pain!

When his balls dragged away from his body with her fingers, he changed his plan of attack. Unless he could knock her out and take the shadow controlling her out of play, just hitting her wouldn't do any good. Catching her free hand around the wrist, he pinned it to the floor then, twisting his body as much as the pain allowed, began to tickle her exposed side.

The release hurt almost as much as the initial grab and he yowled again as blood flowed suddenly back into abused tissue. Bright side, he hardly felt the back of Keisha's fist drive the edge of his lower lip in over his teeth, reopening the cut he'd received during his earlier dance with Mouse. Her hips canted up between his thighs, throwing him forward, off-balance. Barely managing to keep from kissing the linoleum, his weight slammed down on his elbow.

"The master says we can't kill you," she growled, her teeth closing around his ear. "But we can hurt you."

If he yanked his head away, he'd lose a piece of his ear.

Jesus FUCK!

If he *didn't,* he'd lose a piece of his ear.

Tony could feel warm and wet running down his neck and he really hoped Keisha was drooling.

Something was making a strange half growling, half howling noise. He didn't think it was Keisha. He punched her in the stomach. She grunted and grabbed his wrist. Small bones ground together. The noise continued uninterrupted. Nope, not Keisha. Him?

"Keisha!"

A small eraser bounced off the set dresser's close-cropped hair and hit him on the cheek.

"Go to sleep!"

Her mouth separated from his ear with a wet slurp. Her left leg settled slowly toward the floor. Her hand fell from his wrist. Tony clamped his hand immediately on his ear.

"Stop being such a baby." Arra's voice sounded both muffled and annoyed. "It seems a little over the top after you had someone deliberately jab a hole through your eyebrow."

"Not the same thing," he muttered, checking his palm. Damp but not bloody. As Keisha sighed under him, he pushed himself carefully up onto his knees.

"Zazu, be quiet!"

The growling howl stopped.

Reaching behind him, Tony untangled a long leg from around his. The moment he was clear, he fell to one side, crawling away until he could brace his back against the wall, cradling all his injured bits close. "Is she . . . ?"

"She's fine," Arra told him as she stared down at the younger woman. "Physically anyway. Unless you did damage."

"I *took* damage." And as soon as he got the chance, he was heading for the bathroom to check things out. They still fucking hurt!

"The shadow-held aren't stronger than they were before, but they have no inhibitions. They have no fear of injury, so they hold nothing back."

He picked the eraser up off the floor. "So what was this for?"

"To get her attention."

"Right." And then he remembered. "You said she's physically fine. What isn't?"

"What isn't what?"

"Fine."

"Ah. Yes." Arra pressed her lips together into a thin line, all color leaching out. "It's like this," she began just as Tony thought she wasn't going to answer him. "Putting Keisha to sleep involved her energies only—it's undetectable at a distance. The shadow is still in there, confined. If I destroy it, the Shadowlord will know immediately where I am and I am not yet ready for him."

"You've destroyed shadows before."

"So it's true, then. Men really do think with those?" She nodded toward his crotch and he covered it instinctively. "Because you're not thinking now. The Shadowlord wasn't on this world, wasn't part of this world's energy flow before. She'll have to hold the shadow until we defeat him once and for all. And if we don't, well, she'll have worse problems than a few nightmares."

"A few nightmares?" Now he knew to look, he could see Keisha's eyes moving behind her closed lids.

"Constant nightmares."

Constant. Babies dying. Rotting. And he was the only one who could see it. Their parents kissed and hugged and played with the tiny corpses until bits started falling off. "You've got to wake her up."

Arra snorted. "And do what? Smack her on the head with a frying pan? You can't knock someone unconscious without doing damage, Tony. There's no such thing as a Vulcan neck pinch or any other tidy television solution. This is war—not everyone comes out . . ."

The only sound for a long time was Keisha's labored breathing.

". . . whole." Turning on one heel, Arra headed back to the dining room. "Put her on my bed. She won't wake up until I tell her to."

At 5:57, Carol from the lighting crew showed up.

"If another shadow-held shows up searching for me, you'll have to let them in. They're just as likely to grab one of my neighbors and gouge an eye or something out in front of the peephole in order to get a reaction. With my luck, they'd probably grab the wrong neighbor."

"Why don't you let them in? Open the door and nighty-night them?"

"Because they'll see me and he'll know where I am. He'll have something in them set to my power signature."

"Keisha . . ."

"Didn't see me. You distracted her."

"Yeah, and she sure as hell saw me!"

"Didn't you tell me that he doesn't care about you? Now go away and let me finish this. Try putting your brains on ice if they're still not working."

Tony sighed. Carol had a black belt in some kind of martial art. He hadn't been paying enough attention to the overheard conversation to know exactly which martial art but, bottom line, it didn't much matter since he had equivalent training in absolutely nothing. Plastering a fake smile on his face, he opened the door. "Hey. What's happening?"

"Don't play dumb," she snapped, pushing past him.

"All right." He grabbed her shoulder, spun her back around, and threw the contents of his mug in her face. The coffee wasn't exactly hot, but it distracted her just long enough for him to sweep her legs out from under her and send her crashing to the floor.

Really close contact kept her from landing any serious blows, but she still beat the crap out of him.

"What took you so long?" he gasped, not being at all careful of anything but aching ribs as he crawled off of Carol's sleeping body.

"Time is relative. There's one of those gel cold packs in the freezer. Maybe you'd better use it."

"You think?" His voice already sounded higher. The way things were going, by the end of the night only dogs would be able to hear him.

At 7:02, it was Elaine from craft services.

Keisha, Carol, and Elaine—the three women who'd run to comfort Lee. Wiping up his spills, holding his hand, offering comfort, and making it quite clear there was more being offered . . . Tony had to wonder if this was a message to him from the Shadowlord. If his nose was being rubbed in Lee's obvious unavailability.

A sudden chill ghosted down Tony's spine. Or was the message that Lee was at the studio with the Shadowlord, unprotected?

Elaine knocked again.

And, nice change, she went for his eyes not his balls.

"Put her on the bed with the others."

"Yeah, yeah," he muttered, patting the bleeding scratch on his cheek. "What did your last servant die of?"

Arra's eyes lost their focus for a moment. "One of my order killed him while shadow-held. She melted his bones and left him lying in a fleshy puddle in the great hall. Without structure enough to scream, he died gurgling."

Fighting the urge to vomit, Tony reached down and tucked his hands in Elaine's armpits. He had a vague memory of deliberately not asking that question earlier. Apparently, his instincts had temporarily deserted him. Smart instincts. If he didn't *have* to be around, he wouldn't be. "You suck as a motivational speaker. You know that, right?"

"You asked."

He laid Elaine out as comfortably as he could beside Carol and Keisha and stared down at them for a moment, hating to leave them trapped. Tormented. Keisha had cried out half a dozen times. Carol's head almost continually jerked from side to side on the pillow. Unfortunately, if even the glare of light in the elevator hadn't been enough to destroy his hitchhiker, there was no way anything in the entire co-op would affect, let alone destroy, these shadows. Well, nothing except Arra and she was saving herself for the final battle. At least, that was the benefit of the doubt explanation.

"I'm sorry," he told them, as Elaine began to tremble. "It's just . . ." Just what? He sighed. "It's just, I'm sorry."

Arra was packing up her laptop as he came out of the bedroom, "Have you worked it out, then?" he asked her, as she slid it into the case. "The light thing?"

"Yes, I have. I charged the potion while you were in with the girls; seal it up and let's get going."

"It's still early. Henry won't be awake for another forty minutes."

"You told him to meet us at the studio?"

"Well, yeah, but . . ."

"I won't be using any power during the drive. We'll be moving more slowly than usual."

That was the best news Tony'd had in days.

"And," Arra continued, swinging her laptop case over her shoulder, "the shadow-held will have a lot more trouble finding us if we're in a moving vehicle. Charging the potions may have created enough of an energy blip to alert him."

Made sense; they were anti-shadow potions and if *he* was the Shadowlord, he'd be watching for something like that. Tony sealed up the four thermoses—they'd bought two new ones with the groceries—and packed them quickly away in his backpack. Then he went for the elevator while Arra locked up and set wards.

"Think of a ward like a spiderweb made of energy," she'd explained earlier when he'd asked. *"Some webs warn the spider there's prey nearby, some capture it."*

"And you're the spider?"

She'd snorted impatiently. *"No, I'm the walrus. I thought I told you to put those on ice?"*

The elevator was taking its own sweet time arriving. A door opened. A familiar yap drove through his eardrums and straight into his brain.

"Julian . . ."

Tony spun around, ready to intervene, but the wizard was smiling almost benignly across the hall toward her neighbor. "Would you mind telling anyone you hear knocking on my door that I've gone to Victoria? With Tony." She gestured.

Julian and Moira leaned out of the doorway to look.

Tony waved.

"Victoria?"

"Yes. There's no point in them knocking and knocking and knocking and disturbing everyone on this floor, is there?"

"If you're not home, they can't get in," Julian pointed out archly. "You can't buzz them up."

Moira yapped agreement and Tony wondered how the Shadowlord felt about dogs.

"You and I both know there are ways around that. At the last board meeting you were trying to put more money into security."

"You weren't at the last board meeting."

"I read the minutes. Thank you for your assistance." The elevator announced its arrival. "We'll be going now."

Julian followed.

Eyes rolling, Arra shoved Tony inside, turned and hit the "close door" button. "Remember: Victoria with Tony," she said as Julian's and Moira's disapproving expressions disappeared.

"Do you think he'll do it?"

"He might."

"Why Victoria?"

"Why not? The farther the shadow-held are from the studio, from where he can call on them for help, the better."

"Will Julian be all right? I mean, will he be in any danger?" Tony corrected as Arra's lip curled.

"Hard to say. Depends on whether or not they think he knows more than he's saying. Do I have to keep repeating that this is war?"

"No."

"Do I have to make the observation about omelets and breaking eggs?"

"God, no!"

"Good. It's a stupid observation."

Traffic was heavy on Hastings until they cleared Chinatown, then it spread out and started moving a few kilometers above the limit. Tony drummed his fingers against his thigh and tried not to think of what they were heading toward.

War.

Broken eggs.

Around Clark Drive South, he frowned. "You were working that light thing out on a laptop."

"So?"

"So we could have been in a moving vehicle all afternoon. I drive, you work."

Arra nodded agreement. "Yes, I thought of that after Keisha arrived."

"And?"

"And then I realized I work best in a familiar environment."

Tony stared at the side of her face. "I had to beat up girls," he said at last.

"That's a bit sexist, don't you think?"

"No."

"And given the results, not entirely accurate. There're still *girls* at the studio," she added when he didn't respond.

"Your point?"

The brow he could see lifted into a distinctly sardonic arch.

"Never mind." He glanced at his watch. "I'd better call CB. Make sure the

Shadowlord's even still at the studio. Maybe he's convinced Mason to take him clubbing."

"I thought CB had arranged to have promo shots done?"

"Yeah. So?"

"So, it would take more than an extraordinarily powerful, evil wizard to keep Mason Reed from having his picture taken."

"Valid point." CB's cell phone rang half a dozen times before he answered. Worried that the boss might be standing where he could be overheard by the enemy, Tony started talking immediately. *Safest if he just has to answer yes or no.* "Hey, CB, it's Tony. Is he still there?"

"Yes, he is." A dark, smooth voice that caressed each word. Definitely *not* CB's voice. "And he's wondering what's taking you so long."

The line went dead.

Tony dropped his phone like it was contaminated. "He's got CB."

"The Shadowlord answered CB's phone?"

"Yeah."

"Tell me exactly what he said." She frowned as Tony told her. "He's posturing. Trying to frighten you. Rattle you."

"News flash. It worked." His palms left damp streaks on his jeans.

"Yes, but if he'd said nothing at all, you'd have kept talking. Probably said you were with me. Said we were on our way." Her voice trailed off and she drummed her fingers on the steering wheel. "This isn't like him," she announced three blocks later. "He could have gathered information, but he didn't—he played boogeyman instead. That's just not like him."

"How do you know?"

"I may not have stuck around for the big finish, but I was there for the rest of the war," she snapped. "I know him."

"Uh-uh, you *knew* him," Tony amended. "You knew him when he was conquering. He's conquered. He's been 'the conqueror' for seven years. He's not the same guy you faced. Seven years—fuck, *everyone* changes over that long a time."

"Your Nightwalker?"

Tony thought of Vicki Nelson's conquest of Vancouver and snickered, amused for the first time in . . . well, since girls started smacking him around anyway. "You have no idea."

"No. *You* have no idea." But it was a playground response and she sounded unsure and Tony figured that shaking up a few of her carved-in-stone opinions about the Shadowlord was probably a good thing.

Probably.

Maybe not.

When Arra turned onto Boundary Road, he closed his eyes for a moment, confronted the fear that had been chewing at him since the call, and said, "Do you think CB's dead?"

"No. He knows too much. He could be too useful. The Shadowlord can't have changed so much he'd throw away that kind of resource."

Which would have been more reassuring had she not so obviously been trying to reassure herself.

At 8:43 the parking lot was still surprisingly full. Zev's car was gone and so was Amy's—Tony thanked any gods that might be listening for small mercies—but Lee's bike was still there.

"They're shooting promo stuff," he murmured, realizing. "Lee had to stay."

"Any new shadows will be for control, not information, so he's probably shadow-held."

Again? Oh, that's just fucking great. The thought of Lee shadow-held came with the memory of Lee's hands on his body, scrambling his responses.

"He survived it the first time," Arra reminded him, misreading his silence.

"Yeah. That's not very comforting."

She shrugged and turned off the engine.

"What do we do now?"

"Right now? We wait for your Nightwalker. No point in going over the battle plan twice."

Seat belt unbuckled, Tony twisted around so that he could see her. She looked unconcerned. Or possibly blank. Nothing showed. He was looking at the last wizard of her order, the one hope to defeat the Shadowlord—he could just as easily have been looking at someone's grandmother, parking and waiting to pick the grandkids up from school. He wanted to know what she was thinking but he couldn't see it on her face.

"So, does a gate have to be opened in a specific spot?"

"No. Variables are adjusted for location."

"So you could open a gate here?"

She turned very slowly to face him. "I could."

He really, really hoped she'd add, *But I won't.* But she didn't. "Hey, I just thought of something."

"Don't strain yourself."

She was under a lot of stress, so he'd give her that one. "If you can only affect the gate on the world of origin, how's the Shadowlord going to get home? I mean, sure this is a great world and all, but his stuff's back there and I expect he'll want to go back and forth."

"He probably has the spell set up on the other side ready to go off every twelve hours."

"He's got the gate on a timer?"

"Essentially."

"Cool. Still evil," he clarified as Arra turned to glare at him. "But cool."

"Less cool if he calls through reinforcements."

"Granted."

Henry's BMW pulled into the lot at 8:47. Tony opened his door as he parked and walked around the car to meet him beside Arra. He'd left the-story-so-far on Henry's answering machine and then sent him an e-mail as well as a text message. The whole instantaneous electronic communication thing had very little relevance to Henry—sending multiple copies of things he really needed to know worked best. Things like, *CB is holding the Shadowlord at the studio, Mason and most of the crew are shadow-held and we have to take him out tonight. Meet us there as soon as you're up.*

They not only had to take him out tonight, they had to take him out before the gate opened at 11:15. They had to take him out before he called through reinforcements. Tony hadn't asked Arra what kind of reinforcements were likely to be called through. He didn't want to know.

Henry frowned and Tony remembered he was both bruised and bleeding.

"You've been fighting again."

He shrugged, didn't bother hiding the wince as new bruises rose and fell. "I had to take down three of the shadow-held."

"Girls," Arra snorted, getting out of the car. "So." She looked from one to the other. "What's the plan?"

Tony opened his mouth to protest, but as Henry didn't seem surprised by her assumption, he closed it again. It was the son of Henry VIII, trained in strategy and tactics and, hell, probably the minuet for all Tony knew, who asked: "What do you need us to do?"

"Keep the shadow-held from taking me down." Arra began rolling her shoulders like an old boxer about to go into the ring. "Keep the Shadowlord from preventing my call to the Light of Yeramathia."

"Which is?"

Figuring he wouldn't understand the explanation, Tony hadn't bothered to ask.

Arra frowned at Henry's suspicious tone. "The Shadowlord gave himself over to a dark power, this is its opposite."

That was it? Okay, he understood that.

"A god?" If Henry'd sounded suspicious before, he sounded distinctly un-happy now.

"We've had a little trouble with gods in the past," Tony explained hurriedly before Arra's frown could deepen. "An ancient Egyptian undead wizard tried to call up his god from the top of the CN Tower. Oh, and the year before that, we had demons."

"You never thought to mention that?"

He shrugged. "It didn't seem relevant."

"It isn't. But *you* had no way of knowing that." She turned her attention back to Henry. "Yeramathia is neither god nor demon, only a power. We need to attract its attention. I will draw the calling in the air; the Shadowlord will try and stop me. The only things he controls in this world are the shadows and the shadow-held, but there are plenty of the former and the latter will fight you to the death."

"How much time will you need?"

"As long as it takes to draw the calling."

Tony rolled his eyes. Right. More obscure. "And that'll be how long?"

"Well, it's not a 1-800 number," Arra snapped.

Henry's hand closed over Tony's shoulder before the snapping could escalate. "And if it answers?"

"When it answers," Tony muttered.

"We hope it destroys the minion of its ancient enemy."

"Hope?" Tony began, but Henry's fingers tightened.

"If and hope," Henry said softly as though trying the words on for size. "Battles have been won with less. Do you believe we can win?"

With both of them staring at her, Arra shrugged. "Tony does."

And then they both moved to stare at him.

Oh, crap. No, I don't. I just think that if you have to fight—which we do—there's no percentage in going in believing you're going to lose. It's not like if we lose we can try again later. This is it. All or nothing. One final roll of the dice. The big chimichanga. And that's just fucking great, now I'm out of clichés.

Were they waiting for him to say something?

Apparently.

He sighed, squared his shoulders, and tried to think of something inspiring. "Right. Let's go."

"Not exactly the St. Crispin's speech," Henry murmured.

"The what? Never mind." He raised a hand and cut off the explanation. Knowing Henry, it was likely to be lengthy, boring, and classical. "Instead of walking in the back door like the Three Stooges, how about we split his attention. Henry, remember that up-on-the-roof-through-the-ventilation-shaft thing you wanted to do earlier?"

"Uh, no."

"Good. Now's your chance. Arra, you go in through the front doors, I'll go in through the back. Henry, you take out the shadow-held—bottom line they're still flesh and blood and you're . . ." Even in the dim light of the parking lot, he could see the vampire's eyes darken. ". . . you."

"I think," Henry said slowly, "at some point, he'll send something through that can't be killed by light. Something physical."

"You sound upsettingly happy about that."

The mask slipped. "If it has flesh and blood, I can deal with it."

"And me, I'll deal with the Shadowlord."

His shadow fell over Lee's and the Shadowlord's, wiping out the definition of the attack, leaving nothing but a formless shape of darker gray on the concrete.

"You will?"

It almost wasn't a question. Tony made a mental note to ask Arra about that later—if they survived this. "Someone has to and I'm all that's left. You . . ." He bent and picked up his backpack, swinging one strap over his shoulder. ". . . just dial."

"I have to be in his presence for this to work." Her eyes narrowed. "How do you plan on dealing with him?"

Tony shrugged. "Maybe it *is* my ass." He held up a hand to stop Henry's question and then waved them off in opposite directions, hoping the gesture was fast enough that neither of his companions could see how badly his hand was shaking. "Can we just . . . go!"

Walking over the gravel made so much noise that Tony half expected a couple of the bigger guys on the crew to be waiting for him at the back door. They weren't. No one was. *See, he's cocky. No security.*

He slipped through, took his backpack off and set it safely to one side, then began moving quietly down the London street set. It didn't look much like London, but with lighting, fake fog, a filter or two . . . it probably still wouldn't look much like London. Good thing Mason preferred a lot of tight close-ups.

And speaking of close-ups, the cameras seemed to have been moved to the dining room set. Thankful for the clutter, Tony slipped across the soundstage without being seen although, the closer he got to the set, the harder it was not to be noticed.

Shit. Shooting crew and *construction crew.* More people than they'd planned on. Henry was fast and strong, but he was still only one guy. The more people he had to take out, the more likely someone would be taken out permanently. Dead.

This is such a stupid idea. What the hell was I thinking? You do this, you do that, I'll take out the Shadowlord. First my brain points out that Henry's the one with the training, then it totally shuts down while my mouth flaps. Delusions of grandeur or . . .

Fuck. At least I'm not the only one. Crammed into the eight or so inches between the distant view of the garden and the dining room window, Tony peered onto the set. The dining room table was gone, the cheap Persian rug had been removed, Mason's coffin was up against the opposite wall, and the throne from episode nine's the-writers-are-on-cheap-drugs Charlemagne flashback had been brought out of storage and set up at the far end of the room, leaving the area actually under the gate empty.

On the throne, still wearing the same clothes he'd dropped through the gate in, was the Shadowlord. Problem was, he didn't look like the conquering tyrant Arra made him out to be and he didn't look evil. He looked like he belonged there. Posture, attitude, expression—everything about him said, *This is my right. Serve me.*

He reminded Tony a little of Henry. Of the Prince of Man bit.

Tony felt himself responding. He'd seen something on PBS once that said nine of out ten men were looking for a strong leader to follow. The moment Henry Fitzroy had vamped into his life, he'd known he was one of the nine.

It was a small step from leader to master.

Mason Reed, still in full Raymond Dark costume and makeup, was on his knees to the left of the throne, vogue-ing for the photographer setting up his shot.

Lee was to the right of the throne. Also in character. Also on his knees. As Tony watched, the Shadowlord reached out and ran his fingers through Lee's hair. Eyes closed, the actor leaned into the touch.

Tony felt himself responding to that, too. On a couple of levels. Fingers tightening on the edge of a supporting two-by-four, he decided to go with, *Get your hands off him, you fucking bastard!*

Closely followed by, *I don't get to touch. You don't get to touch!*

Where the hell was Henry?

And Arra?

Were they waiting for him?

Did he have to do everything?

Mason froze as the flash went off and the photographer set up for another shot.

He's documenting his conquest, Tony realized. Both cameras were ready to shoot the set. He could see Peter, Tina, and Sorge wrapped in discussion over at the monitors, Everett was waiting out of shot with his touch-up kit, and everyone not actually working was gathered to one side, watching. Watching the throne. Watching the photographer.

Waiting.

For the gate to open?

No, too early.

For the fight.

For him.

I guess that's my cue.

Yeah, like I'm just going to walk out there . . .

"I know you're here, Tony."

Tony's heart slammed against his ribs. *Fuck!* Excellent timing, he had to give him that.

"I have a part of you in me. You have a part of me in you."

You wish! He fought for control as the Shadowlord's voice filled the sound-stage, realizing the bastard didn't know exactly where he was or there'd be more going on than just talking. He glanced down at his shadow. It quivered. *Not good.*

"We're connected. I can feel your fear. I can feel your need."

Like I need to hear your cheesy fucking dialogue?

"If you're waiting for Arra Pelindrake, I wouldn't bother. She's an old woman. I've destroyed everything she ever cared about. She's nothing. A remnant. She knows she can't destroy me just as she's always known it. If she fights with you, it's only because her guilt is driving her to end it."

There was more along the same lines, but Tony ignored it. No matter what he said, there was a chance Arra could beat him or he wouldn't be here personally making sure she was destroyed. The speech wasn't directed at him anyway, it was meant to undermine Arra's confidence. To make her run. It might even work if he didn't do something soon. He had no illusions about the depth of Arra's commitment to the cause. She was there because he was, motivated, as the Shadowlord said, by guilt. But what to do? Sneak around behind the coffin and ram him with it? Shut off the main power? Weaken the shadows in the dark? No way the Shadowlord hadn't taken care of that, though, it was way too obvious. The main breaker would definitely be guarded. Or welded.

"Shall I show you what's in store for you?"

That was directed at him again although Tony wasn't sure how he knew.

The Shadowlord gestured, Peter called, "Roll camera," and Charlie Harris stumbled out into the center of the set, clawing at his own shadow wrapped around him like a shroud.

And Tony remembered.

He couldn't move, he couldn't speak, and most importantly, he couldn't breathe. It was like being trapped under a pliable sheet of cool charcoal-gray rubber that covered him from head to foot like a second skin, curving to fit up each nostril and into his mouth. Obscenely intimate.

The Shadowlord held out his hand and the gesture drew a wisp of black from Charlie's skull. It sped across the set and into the wizard, who closed his eyes and murmured, "Just taste the terror."

Charlie fell to the floor, heels kicking against the painted plywood.

"Are you learning from this, Tony? Thousands will die this way."

Yeah, yeah. You're not just blowing smoke out your ass. I get it. His hands gripping the edge of the wall, Tony braced himself for the charge. A solid tackle, knock the air out of the son of a bitch, and maybe Charlie'd have a chance.

He was standing, left foot raised, right leg about to push off when Henry dropped from the ceiling.

Right onto the Shadowlord's lap.

The vampire reached out, wrapped his hands around the Shadowlord's head, and twisted.

The resulting flare of darkness threw him back almost to the watching crowd.

Tony froze. *Wizardy protections. You can't whack at him.*

"Deal with him."

As the shadow-held advanced on Henry, Tony remembered *he* was supposed to be dealing with the Shadowlord. But not just dealing with him, dealing with his power over shadow.

How do I stop a shadow?

Know what's real.

Light was real. Darkness was real. Light and dark. Light and absence of light.

Okay, that about does it for the options.

And then he realized he'd already given himself the answer.

You're not just blowing smoke out your ass . . .

⤴ NINETEEN

Tony raced for the back of soundstage, leaped over a half finished set of stairs, and careened around the edge of the London street set.

Unless things had changed after he'd left the studio—changed in reference to the shooting schedule as opposed to changed because there was an evil wizard hanging around—Peter'd planned on shooting the flashback scene first thing in the morning. The fate of the world depended on how much the crew'd got ready before the shadows took them over.

London streets, especially crappy thrown together at the last minute, gray paint on plywood and Styrofoam streets, needed fog. There were two 1400w pro foggers sitting at the edge of the set, a heavy orange one-hundred-and-fifty-foot extension cord curled up beside each of them. The reservoirs were full of fog juice. They were ready to go.

Cables ran everywhere in a soundstage. Praying that the Shadowlord's need to control the lights had kept the whole place live, Tony yanked the lines from the nearest socket, and plugged the foggers in.

With one in each hand, he headed back toward the gate, his palms so slick with sweat that they slid back and forth in his grip. *Don't drop them. Do* not *drop them.*

Over the sound of his new mantra, he could hear fighting.

And laughing.

And screaming.

And a self-satisfied voice enjoying the taste of the pain.

Not hard to figure out what had happened; Henry'd had to hurt someone and the Shadowlord had drawn the shadow back into himself to enjoy it. A clichéd scene that became less clichéd when real people were hurting.

Tony ran faster. And hit the ground hard, his shadow wrapped around his knees.

The fogger flew from his left hand and skidded across the floor, metal chassis shrieking against the concrete. The fogger from his right hit harder, tipped over, and was only just out of reach.

He could see the *fog ready* light on the remote.

All he had to do was reach it.

Dragging his lower body, he clawed his way forward. His fingertips touched metal just as his shadow closed over his face.

You've got a lungful of air! You've got time!

Easy to say. Harder to deal with.

Eyes covered, working in the dark, he scrabbled at the edge of the fogger, fingernails sliding off the casing. Then it moved. And a little more. He stretched past it. Reaching. Touched the remote cable. Hooked it closer.

He'd read once that lack of oxygen created an automatic panic response in the brain.

Like I need another fucking reason to panic!

There were four buttons on the remote.

As he started to thrash, unable to stop himself, needing to breathe, he pressed the largest.

The goddamned thing was too quiet to hear. And his ears were full of shadow. And it came with a fucking microprocessor, so maybe it wouldn't work flipped over on its side.

Then the shadow's grip started to loosen.

Going, going . . . gone.

Arms thrown wide, Tony sucked in a lungful of sweet, moist air. Then another. Then he opened his eyes and started to cough.

Foggers used distilled water and glycerin. It was perfectly safe to breathe except that the brain saw smoke and another automatic response kicked in.

Coughing and choking and telling his brain to shut the fuck up, Tony staggered to his feet, groped for the other fogger, and stumbled with it toward the set. At 7560 cubic-feet-per-minute output—not something he knew; output was stenciled on the top of both machines—the lower half meter of the immediate area was nearly full. There were still places he could see the floor but those places were disappearing fast. Even so, he wanted the second fogger as close to the gate as possible.

The last time they'd needed them, someone—Daniel?—had told him they used a higher density fog juice that kept the fog close to the floor and away from the guts of expensive electrical equipment. But use enough fog, especially between the confining walls of the set, and it would rise. Fill the air.

Fog was visible because each tiny water droplet refracted light. Or reflected light, Tony wasn't positive which. The point was it broke the light up into bits and that broke shadows up into bits. Destroyed their cohesion.

The light was real.

The shadows were an effect.

He thumbed on the fogger as the extension cord hauled him to a stop at the edge of the set.

With no shadows, the Shadowlord had only the shadow-held remaining.

As the set filled, Tony set the fogger down in the covering fog from the other machine.

It felt like he'd been gone for hours, but it had only been minutes.

And not too many of them.

Henry still fought the shadow-held, but he moved too quickly and there were too many of them for Tony to see how the battle was going. Henry would win. Henry was very hard to . . .

A crowbar rose and fell. Impact against flesh and a snarl.

Henry might be hard to kill, but those he fought were more fragile. If he was hurt and the Hunger rose . . . If there was blood and the Hunger rose . . . Tony just hoped Henry would—could—remember that fragility.

Still no sign of Arra.

God damn, h . . .

The hair lifting off the back of his neck, Tony turned toward the throne. The Shadowlord stood staring at him through narrowed eyes. Even at that distance Tony could feel the rage rolling off him.

Man, the air is getting distinctly punky in here.

Teeth clenched, lips thinned to pale lines, evil still looked pretty damned good. "Get him. Turn that thing off!"

Mind you, good-looking evil is still evil, he admitted, backing up.

Mason and Lee rose up out of the fog.

Apparently shadow-held brains had no problem with that whole breathing smoke thing.

Fucking figured.

Mason reached him first. Tony darted left around a blow and realized as both actors followed his movement that they were obeying literally. *Get him.* Then, *turn that thing off.*

All he had to do was keep them busy until Arra ended things.

Right. *All* he had to do. *If* Arra ended things.

He kept moving since closing with one would lead to a beating by the other; dodging, ducking, and finally slamming a bruised hip into the coffin so hard it rocked on its stand. Pain distracted him long enough for both his attackers to reach him. He ducked under Lee's double-handed grab, found himself between the coffin and the wall, and, working with what he had, tipped it over on them.

It hit the floor with force enough to momentarily whoosh the fog away. The lid slammed open. Chester Bane rolled out.

Time stopped.

His eyes snapped open.

And time started up again.

If asked, Tony would have described his boss as strong, powerful, arrogant, controlling, and a little strange. But not fast. He'd have been wrong. He didn't even see the producer move. One minute CB was on the floor, the next he was on his feet with Mason clutched in one massive hand, Lee in the other. White showed all around his eyes, the muscles of his neck stood out like rebar, and he was roaring—no words, just one loud, enraged bellow. It was the scariest goddamned thing Tony had seen all day . . . and given the day he'd had, that was saying something.

Off by the fogger, someone screamed.

Dragged around by the sound, Tony saw the Shadowlord rear back, clutching his right hand to his chest.

To make fake fog, a fog machine's heat exchanger superheated the fog juice and forced the hot mixture out of the nozzle on the front. By their very nature, fog machines got hot. Very hot. It appeared the Shadowlord's personal protection didn't extend to passive attacks by inanimate objects.

Hoping CB would remember he'd need the men he was destroying when this was over, Tony ran for the Shadowlord.

He didn't remember much from his GED, but he remembered some crap about equal and opposite reactions. In order to blast an attacker away, the protections had to apply the same force to the Shadowlord and this time he wasn't comfortably settled on his throne. If Tony went down, the Shadowlord was taking a fall, too.

Unfortunately, magic was one thing and, as it turned out, physics was something else again. Tony slammed into darkness maybe an inch away from his target and was smashed back into the fog.

A fist wrapped in the front of his shirt and dragged him clear.

"Foolish." Only a sliver of gray showed between narrowed lids. The word was almost a hiss. "We could have . . ."

And then the Shadowlord's attention shifted.

Shirt digging into armpits, Tony twisted in his grip.

At the far end of the set, a golden pattern shimmered in the air. As they watched, frozen in place, a new line of light curved around the outer edge.

Tony hit the floor, thrown aside hard enough to slide until he slammed up against the wall. Palms leaving damp prints against the painted plywood, he hand-walked to his feet. When he turned, Mason stood in front of him.

A quick glance showed CB struggling with three of the construction crew and Lee nowhere in sight.

Ducking a swing, Tony tripped on something in the fog. He managed a reasonably coherent, *Not again!* just before impact, then the mist folded over him. A hand closed around the back of his belt as his hand closed around a backpack.

What the . . . ?

Not a backpack, the photographer's camera bag.

As Mason hauled him up, he ripped through the camera bag, finding what he needed by touch. Finally clearing the fog, he squirmed around and triggered the photographer's flash.

The shadow had been in Mason Reed since Friday morning, absorbing all that Mason was. Mason had never met a flashbulb he didn't love. Yesterday, the fan club had delayed him with pictures and it worked again now. Mason's grip loosened, Tony fell free, got his feet under him, and, continually thumbing the flash, kneed the actor in the nuts.

He could almost hear his own giving a little cheer at getting some back.

As Mason dropped down out of sight, Tony ran for the other end of the set, ducking and weaving through the ongoing battle Henry and CB were fighting with the shadow-held. His feet thumped into bodies he couldn't see. Didn't want to see.

The pattern hadn't grown in the last few moments because Arra, laptop open and balanced on one hand, was holding the Shadowlord in place with the other.

"You're only delaying the inevitable, old woman," he snarled as Tony ducked under a flying can of hair spray and slid between them.

"Let him go, Arra. I've got him."

"You?" Simultaneous. From both wizards.

Eyes locked with the one, he snarled, "Fucking bite me! Let him go and finish!" at the other.

He was almost surprised when she did.

But not quite as surprised as the Shadowlord.

"And what can you do?" he mocked, stepping forward.

Tony slid his hands around the other man's face, laced them behind his head, and locked their mouths together. His lips were cool, but Tony was used to that. He changed the angle, made it wetter, more . . . carnal. *We could have* the Shadowlord had said. *We.*

The protective spell didn't kick in.

Hands locked on his waist hard enough to leave new bruises.

Son of a bitch; it is my ass.

Under other circumstances, he'd have found that gratifying. Although, even if evil wizards had been his type, any swelling crotch-side tonight was likely to be edema. Passion, pain—fortunately, all moaning sounded remarkably alike.

As a distraction, it worked because it was unexpected, but it didn't work long.

Darkness flared and Tony found himself on the floor again, his skull cracking hard enough against the concrete to cause stars.

Okay, stars are new.

When they didn't go away, he realized it wasn't stars he was seeing; it was Arra's pattern through the refraction of the fog. Which was dissipating. Either the foggers were empty or the sound stage was just too big.

On the bright side, the Shadowlord seemed to be caught on the lines of light like a fly in a web. That brief bout of tonsil hockey must've given Arra enough time to finish.

Yay, me.

And then again . . .

Torso tight against the light, the Shadowlord flung out his arms, fingers extended. Streamers of darkness began to flow into them. He was calling back the shadows. Releasing the shadow-held. Tony could hear bodies hitting the floor.

He was calling back pieces of himself.

He was getting stronger.

In another moment, he'd be free of the pattern.

Where the hell was Yerma-whoever?

It wasn't working. Arra knew it wouldn't work. Knew it. Had known it. Had always known it. She checked the pattern on the laptop, checked the pattern drawn on the air . . . They were identical. It wasn't her fault.

All your fault.

Caught on the other side of the light, the Shadowlord smiled.

They died because of you, the shadows whispered. *They die when you leave. They die when you stay. They die because you fail them. All of them.*

"Shut up!" A world lived in shadow because she couldn't stop him. This world would fall to shadow because she couldn't stop him. He was right. It *was* all her fault.

The light wavered.

His smile broadened and he jerked back.

You should never have come here. You doomed this world.

She shouldn't have. And she had. Her heart was pounding and her vision began to blur.

At least this time you'll die with them.

Kiril. Sarn. Haryain. Tevora. Mai-Sim. Pettryn. So many others, all dead.

Reflecting back the pattern, his eyes glittered in triumph and she realized he knew the names of the dead as well as she did.

Charlie. Chester. Henry. Tony.

"They're not dead!" All right, from what she'd seen, Charlie very probably was, but the others . . . CB and Henry still fought. Tony was down, true, but moving. Struggling.

They're not dead yet.

She could see Tony. He was close enough to the pattern that the gold tinted his skin and hair. He was trying to sit up.

"You're right. They're not dead yet and neither am I." Snapping the laptop closed, she tossed it aside and spread her arms, a mirror image of the wizard on the other side of the light, pulling her own power in to support the pattern. "And *if* I die, I'm going out kicking your skinny ass."

If you die?

Shadow laughter danced cold air up and down her spine.

A little over seven days spent in Tony's company gave her the words she needed. "Bite me, you son of a bitch!"

Teeth gleaming gold, the Shadowlord jerked back again, far enough this time to find his own voice. "Maybe later."

Fighting for focus, Tony rose up on one elbow and stared at the lines. He was right. It was the pattern that had been drawn on the blackboard in another world seven years earlier. The wizards had been nailed here . . .

. . . and here.

But here . . .

He shook his head, trying to clear it, and nearly puked.

But here . . . the line was wrong.

The Shadowlord cried out in victory.

Tony reached out and tugged a line of light a few centimeters to the right.

Golden light flowed out of the pattern. It covered his skin, ran up under his clothing, and drifted past each individual hair on his head. It felt like . . .

Like . . .

Pain.

As he fell, writhing, he realized he wasn't the only one screaming.

The screams didn't quite hide a familiar soft *sputz*.

Back arched to the point where bone had to be protesting, the Shadowlord rose up into the air. One by one, shadows were wrenched from him and destroyed.

Tony screamed a little louder as that bit of him went. It looked no different than the others, but he felt its loss.

By the time the last of the shadows were gone, Tony's voice had faded to a hoarse rasp, but the Shadowlord's agony continued to fill the soundstage. With the shadows gone, there wasn't much of him left. A translucent figure of a man with golden patterns etched into his skin, his eyes and mouth dark holes in a distorted face.

Flare.

And nothing.

When Tony opened his eyes, he was lying on the couch in Raymond Dark's office. It was a comfortable couch; he'd crashed out on it more than once during seventeen-hour shoots.

Golden flecks of light danced across his vision. He remembered fog.

Right. The London street flashback. Had they finished shooting it?

Then he tried to sit up. Memory rode in with the pain.

Henry's arm was around his shoulder a heartbeat later, supporting his weight. Tony blinked and managed to focus on the vampire. His throat hurt, reducing his voice to a rough whisper. "Is that a black eye?"

"Yes. I ducked a crowbar and your makeup artist nailed me with a can of hair spray."

Frowning hurt, too, so Tony stopped doing it. "Sort of remember seeing one fly by."

"It was an interesting battle. Interesting finish." Henry hadn't been able to get to Tony until the light faded. He'd had to stand, surrounded by the fallen, fighting restraining hands, unable to do anything while Tony screamed. Yeramathia, whatever or whoever Yeramathia was, didn't give a damn what he considered his. "What else do you remember?"

"Golden light. The Shadowlord . . ." He waved a trembling hand. There weren't really words for having seen a man dissolve in light. "I remember pain."

"That's because you were touching the pattern when Yeramathia answered." Arra's voice cut through the memory. She stood, arms folded, by Raymond Dark's desk. Apparently, frowning caused *her* no trouble at all. "What were you thinking, boy? Were you trying to get yourself killed?"

Tony shifted in Henry's grip until he faced her. "I was thinking that your pattern was wrong."

"My pattern?"

"Yeah. Your pattern. I've seen it more recently and it was wrong. So I fixed it."

"You fixed it?"

"Yeah." Her expression had begun to worry him. "No big. I just tugged one line over a bit."

"You *just* tugged one line over a bit?" She was staring at him again, only this time her mouth was open. As Tony was about to point it out, she closed it with a snap. "Right. Well. Next time . . ."

"No." He'd gotten his definite back. "There isn't going to be a next time. We barely survived this time. Go home, Arra, you know you want to. Go home when the timer goes off and start a new order or raise chickens, I don't fucking care." Head throbbing, he let himself sag against Henry's shoulder for a moment. Plenty of time to be butch later. "Just go home and close the gate after you."

"Come with me."

"What?" So much for sagging.

"Be the start of my new order. The Shadowlord has been destroyed, but there remains much work to do on the other side. I could use the help of someone who does not run away from a fight. The help of someone who will not let others run away."

"What?" He squirmed around and looked at Henry, who didn't seem all that surprised. "What the hell is she talking about?"

"She's telling you that you can be a wizard, Tony. If you want to."

"Me?"

"You," Arra answered. "You see what others do not. You reach out where others fear to. You are able to touch power and mold it to your use."

The lack of contractions was beginning to seriously freak him out.

"I saw this in you from the beginning. There is great potential in you. You could become . . ." She paused, snorted, and rolled her eyes. "Well, I'm not promising anything but you could become competent with training and practice."

"Me?"

"We'll work on articulate as well."

"She's serious?"

Henry nodded. "And abrasive. But I believe her."

He could go through a magical gate to another world and become a wizard. He could learn to work the energy of that world, bend it and mold it to his own ends. He touched the memory of the Shadowlord; he could learn to command shadow.

His throat was dry.

Tony swallowed, dragged his tongue across his lips, and got slowly to his feet. Henry helped rather a lot with the latter.

"Arra." A deep breath. "I'd rather have perpetual root canals."

Arra sighed, reached into the pocket of her hooded sweatshirt, and handed Henry a twenty. "I still say it was worth a shot. He's an annoying little shit, but I hate to see that kind of potential wasted."

"He's not wasting it," Henry told her as he pocketed the money.

"Bull. He's a production assistant at a third-rate . . ." CB cleared his throat from the doorway and Arra adjusted for his presence. ". . . second-rate production house."

"Yeah, now," Tony protested.

"He can go far here as well," CB added. "Eventually. Right now, it's 11:12. If you're right about the timer, the gate's about to open."

There were people sprawled up against every solid surface on the set. Most of them were drinking a familiar smelling cocktail—Tony noticed that every prop capable of holding liquid as well as the coffee cups from the office kitchen had been put in service. People looked confused but docile, content to suck back the potion—the potion that he'd made—and stare around them with wide, bruised eyes. A few of the crew were sprawled but not drinking, their eyes closed and their arms lying limp by their sides.

Consequences.

"Are they . . . ?"

"No," Henry told him. "Just unconscious. Probably a couple of concussions. Arra said she'd take care of them."

"Is anyone . . ."

"Charlie Harris and Rahal Singh."

One for the Shadowlord. "Did you . . . ?"

"Yes."

And one for Henry. "Are you okay?"

The corner of Henry's mouth that Tony could see curved up into something not quite a smile. "I've killed before, Tony."

"I know." He tightened his grip on the vampire's arm, not because he was in danger of falling but because he needed Henry to understand that he *did* know. Even if, in true guy fashion, they weren't going to talk about it. Big difference between killing for food or for vengeance or even caught up in Darkness and killing without intending to or wanting to. "You up for comfort food later?"

That evoked an actual smile and an incredulous laugh. "If you are."

"Date." As Arra made her way around the edges of the set, stepping over arms and legs and cables, he noticed a complex pattern drawn in chalk in the center of the floor. "What's that?"

"Memories," CB rumbled from behind him. "Ready to be erased. You and I," he raised his voice to the point where Arra turned toward them, "are not a part of it."

She rolled her eyes. "We've been over this."

"Precedent suggests we have no reason to trust you."

"Does precedent suggest what I have to say to that?"

Then the gate opened and Tony's knees buckled. Fortunately, Henry caught him before he reached the floor. He figured he'd used up his lifetime allotment of smacking into horizontal surfaces.

"You shouldn't be so close."

He struggled back into what was more or less a vertical position. "I need to see this."

As darkness roiled down from an empty place by the ceiling—the Shadowlord's reinforcements coming without being called—Arra lifted both arms over her head and rapidly sketched another pattern in the air. She looked like she always did, but she looked like a wizard, too. Acceptance, Tony realized suddenly. She looked like she'd accepted what she was and what that meant.

Pattern complete, she pushed it forward. There was a sizzle and flash when it hit the darkness. A hiss and a flash as it hit the gate. A distant scream as it disappeared and there was a flashback through the gate so bright Henry threw both arms in front of his eyes. Tony sagged back against CB's momentarily comforting bulk.

He felt the gate snap closed. Arra was still standing there. He must have tensed because CB murmured, "She'll go another time. There are things here that need taking care of."

Right. Of course. "The cats."

"Also the cats." Chester Bane looked out over the soundstage and realized he had been a part of something remarkable. The defeat of an invading evil. The more significant defeat of personal demons. The discovery of a hero in an unlikely place. And the whole damned thing had put them seriously behind schedule. Still, he allowed reluctantly, it could have been worse. They could also be over budget. "Mr. Fitzroy, if you could assist me with . . ."

The bodies, Tony filled in silently.

Blinking away what must have been painful afterimages, Henry nodded at CB and turned again to Tony. "Will you be all right?"

Tony slid sideways until his weight was against the lid of Raymond Dark's coffin. "I'll be fine."

Eventually.

As the two men moved away, another moved in.

Cradling his left arm against his body, Lee stared at Tony for a long moment. *Did people always do this much staring or am I just noticing it now?* He blinked, then asked himself, *"Why not?"* and stared back.

"That was . . ." The actor's brows nearly met over his nose. "There were . . ." He swallowed and, looking as though he was maybe thirty seconds from a total meltdown, jerked his head toward the place where the gate had been. "There was light. What the hell was that?"

"This is television." Tony swept his arm around in a gesture expansive enough to take in both cameras still pointed toward the center of the set. "It was a special effect."

"Bullshit. I'm not stupid, Tony. Or blind. What's going on?" He took a step closer, well within Tony's personal space. "Talk to me."

"All right." He raised a hand to cut off any immediate questions. "But not tonight." He touched his throat. "Hurts. We'll talk tomorrow."

Green eyes narrowed. Wrong color but otherwise a dead man's expression. "Promise me."

"I promise."

An easy promise to make since Arra was already erasing the chalk memories drawn on the floor.

"No, CB says Mason's fine."

Arra snorted as they crossed the soundstage. "I can't say that I'm really surprised. If anyone had ego enough to cope with being shadow-held for so long, it would be Mason Reed." She nodded toward the stepladder. "It's almost time. If there's anything you want to know . . ."

She wanted him to ask about meaning-of-life stuff. She'd been rediscovering her wizard roots over the last three days and wanted him in on it. Tony started to shrug but cut the motion off short as Whitby protested the movement. Both cats had been protesting the indignity of the cat carriers since they'd left the co-op.

"Anything at all," she insisted.

Fine. Tony sorted through unanswered questions searching for one he wouldn't mind having an answer to. There were a lot more of the other kind. "If the Shadowlord had no power here, how did he hold CB?"

"I'm about to leave this world forever and that's it?"

"Yeah. Why? Don't you know?"

Arra snorted and turned toward him at the base of the ladder. "Probably a minor binding spell. The close confines of the coffin helped hold it and hitting the floor broke it. Don't forget to get the gas gauge on the car fixed."

"I won't."

"I've left my laptop down in the workshop."

"It's still working?"

"Apparently it landed on Everett and bounced. But that's beside the point; it has some things on it you might be able to use."

"I'm not a wizard."

She snorted again. "Damned right you're not. Here." She handed him the second cat carrier. "Hold Zazu until I'm up the ladder." First step. Second step.

Not very interesting to look at actually. "It would look a lot more wizardy if you levitated or something."

Third step. "And you'd block this area from the rest of the soundstage? Or maybe you'd rather tell a studio audience where I'm going." Fourth step.

"You didn't have to go through this morning. You could have gone through tonight."

Fifth step. Sixth. "I didn't feel like it. The police have finished with me, I'm out of here."

The RCMP investigation into the "special effect accident" that had killed Charlie Harris and Rahal Singh had been strangely vague considering that they were the third and fourth bodies connected to CB Productions in less than a month. In the end, no charges had been laid and the newspaper coverage had given the show a ratings bump. With any luck, Constables Elson and Danvers would get tired of dropping by before CB got tired of finding them in the building. Unfortunately, Arra's wizardry had had less effect on the insurance industry. CB's enraged commentary on the rise in his rates had probably been heard at the company's head office in Montreal—whole sentences were still echoing around the soundstage.

Tony handed the cat carriers up one at a time, the hand-shaped bruises on his waist reminding him of shadows as he stretched. Arra settled the first carrier on the top of the ladder and the second on the paint platform and looked down at him. No, stared down at him.

Great. More staring. He found a smile that was mostly sincere. "Thanks for the car. And the stuff. And the whole kicking Shadowlord ass."

Arra nodded.

Tony waited.

The gate opened. Zazu went through first—he couldn't see her, but he recognized the yowl. It was slightly higher-pitched than Whitby's. The last he saw of Whitby was an orange and white paw poked through the bars of the crate.

Arra lifted one foot off the step and stopped. "It's going to be one hell of a mess through there."

Yeah, there were wizards nailed to blackboards. He wondered if she could see them from where she was standing.

"Are you sure you don't want to come?"

"I'm sure."

She looked down at that, and finally smiled. "You could be great."

He shrugged. "I'm planning on it."

"Great *and* modest. I'm out of here before the sap level rises any higher. Take care of yourself, kid."

"You, too."

Watching an old woman step off a ladder and disappear in midair was a definite anticlimax. Half decent CGI would have given the scene a lot more oomph.

"You're welcome," he muttered as he folded the ladder and moved it up against the wall. Yeah, getting the car was nice, but would it have killed her to thank him? Not for fighting the Shadowlord; that had nothing to do with her, but she could have thanked him for the backbone he found for her. Without him, she'd have been running until the guilt finally crushed her.

He'd been waiting for her to say something for the last three days, but every conversation they had seemed to end up with her trying to convince him to go with her through the gate.

"I could use the help of someone who does not run away from a fight. Of someone who will not let others run away."

Oh. Hang on.

He'd been a little distracted at the time.

Looking up toward the ceiling, he said, "You're welcome" again but this time he meant it.

"Quiet, please!"

As Peter's voice echoed through the soundstage, Tony crammed the jack back in his ear and turned up his radio.

"Let's settle, people!"

He reached the set in time to call, "Rolling!" with the rest and found a place behind the video village as the second assistant camera called the slate.

"Scene twenty-seven, take two."

Lee grinned as Mason settled his shoulders against the padded satin lining of the coffin and said something that caused the other actor to give a less than bloodsucking undead type snicker.

"Action!"

Left thumb rubbing the scar on his right wrist, Tony watched the monitors as the scene unfolded. Stretched out behind him on the concrete floor, his shadow reached out and held up two fingers behind the shadow of the director's head.

Smoke and Mirrors

∽ ONE

About a third of the way down the massive wooden staircase, the older of the two tuxedo-clad men paused, head up, nostrils flaring as though he were testing a scent on the air. "We're not . . . alone."

"Well, there's at least another twenty invited guests," his companion began lightly.

"Not what I meant." Red-gold hair gleamed as he turned first one way then the other. "There's something . . . else."

"Something *else?*" the younger man repeated, suspiciously studying the portrait of the elderly gentleman in turn-of-the-century clothing hanging beside him. The portrait, contrary to expectations, continued to mind its own business.

"Something . . . evil."

"Don't you think you're overreacting just a . . ." The husky voice trailed off as he stared over the banister, down into the wide entrance hall. His fingers tightened on the polished wood of the railing as green eyes widened. "Raymond, I think you'd better have a look at this."

Raymond Dark turned—slowly—and snarled, the extended points of his canine teeth clearly visible.

"And cut!" Down by the front door, Peter Hudson pushed his headphones back around his neck, peered around the bank of monitors, and up at the stars of *Darkest Night*. "Two things, gentlemen. First, Mason; what's with the pausing before the last word in every line?"

Mason Reed, aka Raymond Dark, vampire detective and currently syndicated television's sexiest representative of the bloodsucking undead, glared down at the director. "I was attempting to make banal dialogue sound profound."

"Yeah? Nice try. Unfortunately, it sounded like you were doing a bad Shatner, which—while I'm in no way dissing the good Captain Kirk—is not quite the effect we want here. And Lee," he continued without giving Mason a chance to argue, "what's on your shoulder? Your right shoulder," he added as Lee Nicholas aka James Taylor Grant tried to look at both shoulders at once. "Actually, more the upper sleeve."

A streak of white, about half an inch wide, ran from just under the shoulder seam diagonally four inches down the sleeve of Lee's tux.

He frowned. "It looks like paint."

Mason touched it with a fingertip and then pointed at the incriminating white smudge down at the entrance hall and the director. "It *is* paint. He must've brushed up against the wall in the second-floor bathroom."

Two of the episode's pivotal scenes were to be shot in the huge bathroom and one of the painters had spent the morning giving ceiling and walls a quick coat of white semi-gloss.

"That's impossible," Lee protested. "I wasn't even *in* the second-floor bathroom and besides, this wasn't there when Brenda delinted us."

"Brenda delinted us fifteen minutes before Peter called action," Mason reminded him. "Lots of time for you to wander off and take a tinkle."

"Oh, no." Lee checked to make sure that the boom was gone, then dropped his voice below eavesdropping range. "*You* wandered off to suck on a cancer stick, I didn't go anywhere."

"So you say, but this says different."

"I wasn't in that bathroom!"

"Look, Lee, just admit you screwed up and let's move on."

"I didn't screw up!"

"All right then, it was a subconscious—and I'd have to say somewhat pathetic—attempt to draw attention to yourself."

"Don't even . . ."

"Gentlemen!" Peter's voice dragged their attention back down to the foyer. "I don't care where the paint came from, but it's visible in that last bit where Lee turns and as I'd like him to keep turning—Tony, run Lee's tux jacket out to Brenda so she can get that paint off before it dries. Everett, if you could take the shine off Mason's forehead before we have to adjust the light levels, I'd appreciate it. And somebody, get me a coffee and two aspirin."

Tony froze halfway to the stairs. As the only production assistant on location—as the only production assistant who'd ever remained with CB Productions and *Darkest Night* for any length of time—he was generally the "somebody" Peter'd just referred to.

"*I'll get him the co . . . shkeeffee, Tony.*" The voice of Adam Paelous, the show's first assistant director, sounded in Tony's ear, pushing through the omnipresent static. *"You get the tux . . ."*

One finger against his ear jack, Tony strained to hear over the interference. The walkie-talkies had been acting up since they'd arrived at the location shoot. It was impossible to get a clear signal and the batteries were draining at about five times the normal speed.

". . . out to wardrobe. The exci . . . shsquit of watching paint dry might kill us all."

Waving an acknowledgment to Adam across the entrance hall, Tony jogged up the stairs. It had definitely been a less than exciting morning—even given the hurry-up-and-wait nature of television production. *And there's not a damned thing wrong with boring,* Tony reminded himself. Especially when "not boring" involved gates to other worlds, evil wizards, and sentient shadows that weren't so much homicidal as . . . actually, homicidal pretty much covered it.

Everyone else at CB Productions—with the exception of CB himself—had no memory of the metaphysical experience that had very nearly turned the soundstage into ground zero for an otherworld/evil wizard/homicidal shadow invasion. Everyone else probably slept with the lights out. After almost two months, Tony was finally able to manage it four nights out of five.

Lee was out of the tux and frowning down at the paint by the time Tony reached him.

"I didn't go into the upstairs bathroom," he reiterated as he handed it over.

"I believe you." Fully aware that he was smiling stupidly up at an explicitly defined straight boy—or as explicit as the pictures the tabloids could get with an extended telephoto lens—Tony folded the jacket carefully so the paint wouldn't smear and headed back down the stairs thinking, in quick succession, *It's still warm.* And: *You're pathetic.*

He slid over against the banister to give Everett and his makeup case room to get up the stairs, wondering why Mason—who was a good twenty years younger and thirty kilos lighter—couldn't have come down to the entrance hall instead. *Oh, wait, it's Mason. What the hell am I thinking?* Mason Reed was fully aware of every perk star billing entitled him to and had no intention of compromising on any of them.

"That man sweats more than any actor I've ever met," Everett muttered as Tony passed. "But don't quote me on that."

Just what, exactly, Everett had once been misquoted on was a mystery. And likely to remain that way as even a liberal application of peach schnapps had failed to free up the story, although Tony had learned more about butt waxing than he'd ever wanted to know.

Jacket draped across his hands and held out like he was delivering an organ for transplant, Tony raced across the entrance hall, out the air-lock entry—its stained glass covered with black fabric to keep out the daylight—sped across the wide porch, and pounded down the half dozen broad stone steps to the flagstone path that led through the overgrown gardens and eventually to the narrow drive. *Time is money* was one of the three big truisms of the television industry. No one seemed to be able to agree on just what exactly number two was, but Tony suspected that number three involved the ease with which production assistants could be replaced.

The wardrobe makeup trailer had been parked just behind the craft services truck which had, in turn, been snugged up tight against the generator.

Brenda, who'd been sitting on the steps having a coffee, stood as Tony approached, dumping an indignant black cat off her lap. "What happened?"

"There's paint on Lee's jacket."

"Paint?" She hurried out to meet him, hands outstretched. "How did that happen?"

"Lee doesn't know." Given that Tony believed Lee, Mason's theory didn't bear repeating. Handing the jacket over, he followed her up into the trailer. The cat snorted at her or him or both of them and stalked away.

"Was he in the second-floor bathroom?"

"No." It was a common theory apparently.

"Weird." Her hand in the sleeve, she held the paint out for inspection. "It looks like someone stroked it on with a fingertip."

It did. The white was oval at the top and darker—fading down to a smudge of gray at the bottom of the four-inch streak.

"Probably just someone being an asshole."

"Mason?" she wondered, picking up a spray bottle and bending over the sleeve.

Tony stared at her back in disbelief. There was no way Mason would do anything to make Lee the center of attention. Not generally, and especially not now, not when at last count Lee's fan mail had risen to equal that of the older actor. And Mason'd always been particularly sensitive to anything he perceived as a threat to his position as the star of *Darkest Night*. That wasn't an opinion Tony'd actually express out loud, however—not to Brenda. The wardrobe assistant was one of those rare people in the business who, in spite of exposure, continued to buy into the celebrity thing. For most, the "Oh, my God, it's . . ." faded after a couple of artistic hissy fits extended the workday past the fifteen-hour mark.

Also, she was a bit of a suck-up, and the last thing he wanted was her currying favor by telling Mason what he thought. Well, maybe not the last thing he wanted—a repeat of the homicidal shadow experience currently topped his never-again list, but having Mason Reed pissed off at him was definitely in the top ten since Mason Reed sufficiently pissed off meant Tony Foster unemployed.

Realizing she was still waiting for an answer, he said, "No, I don't think it was Mason."

"Of course not."

Hey, you brought it up. He picked up a scrap of trim . . .

"Don't touch that."

. . . and put it back down again. "Sorry."

"Are you taking the jacket back or is Lee coming out to get it? Or I could take it back and make sure it looks all right under the lights."

"You could, but since I'm here . . ."

"And as it happens, so am I."

They turned together, pulled around by an unmistakable rough velvet voice to see Lee coming into the trailer.

"There's another mark on the pants." He turned as he spoke.

It looked as if someone had pressed a finger against the bottom of Lee's right cheek and stroked up. Tony thought very hard about cold showers, police holding cells, and Homer Simpson.

Lee continued around until he faced them again, toed off the black patent leather shoes, and unzipped his fly. "I swear it wasn't there earlier."

"The jacket would have covered most of it," Brenda reminded him in a breathy tone Tony found extremely annoying. He held on to that annoyance—it was a handy shield against a potentially embarrassing reaction to Lee stepping out of his pants and passing them over.

Clad from the waist down in gray boxer briefs and black socks, Lee wandered over to the empty makeup chair and sat. The chair squealed a protest. "I have no idea how it happened. I swear I wasn't anywhere near wet paint."

"Of course you weren't," Brenda purred. Lifting the jacket off the ironing board, she handed it to Tony, her heated gaze never leaving Lee's face until she had to lay out the pants. She made up for the loss of eye contact by taking her time caressing the fabric smooth.

Rumor insisted that Brenda and Lee had recently shared a heated moment on the floor of the wardrobe department while Alison Larkin—the head of wardrobe—was off rummaging through charity sales for costumes her budget would cover. Given the intimate way Brenda spread her hand and pressed it down next to the paint to hold the fabric still, Tony had to admit it looked like gossip had gotten it right. Standing there, while she spritzed and then rubbed slow circles over the ass of Lee's pants, he felt like a voyeur.

And he was definitely odd man out.

"Listen, Tony, as long as Lee's here, there's no need for you to stay." Apparently, Brenda thought so, too.

"Yeah, I should go."

"Yes, you should." *Because the moment you're out the door and we're finally alone, I'm going to show that man what a real woman can give him.*

He had to admire the amount of bad fifties subtext she could layer under three words.

"I'll tell Peter you'll be back when Brenda's finished with you," he said, handing Lee the jacket. The expression on the actor's face was interesting—and a little desperate. Desperate for him to leave? Desperate about him leaving? Desperately seeking Susan? What? Tony was getting nothing.

"Are you still here?" *What part of* we want to be alone *don't you understand?*

Well, nothing from Lee. Plenty from Brenda.

"*Tony!*" Adam's voice rose out of the background noise. "*The minute that paint's . . .*" A couple of words got lost in static. "*. . . get Lee back here. We've got a shitload of stuff to cover today.*"

He dropped his mouth toward the microphone clipped to his collar. "Roger that, Adam."

"*The point ishsput to make sure no one's getting rogered.*"

"Yeah, I got that." Most of it, anyway.

Adam had obviously heard the rumor, too, although his choice of euphemism was interesting. Rogered?

"*How much longer?*"

"Jacket's done, pants are . . ." Tony glanced over at Brenda and shrugged apologetically when she glared. ". . . pants are finished now. Lee's dressing . . ." The pants slid quickly up over long, muscular, tanned legs. Feet shoved into shoes and Lee was at the door, mouthing *Sorry, gotta run* back toward the wardrobe assistant. "And we're moving."

"*You're shoving?*"

"Moving!"

"*Glad to finally friggin' hear it. Out.*"

They were almost to the path before Lee spoke. "Yes, we did."

Tony shrugged. "I didn't ask."

"And it was a stupid thing to do."

"I didn't say." Brenda was standing in the doorway watching them leave. He knew it without turning. Feeling the impact of metaphorical scissors between his shoulder blades, he increased the space between them to the maximum the path would allow.

"It was just . . . I mean, we were both . . . And she was . . ."

"Hey." Tony raised a hand before details started emerging. "Two consenting adults. Not my business."

"Right." As the path finally lined up with the front door, Lee stopped. "It's a great house, isn't it?"

"Yeah, it's cool." Tony had been ready for the change of subject—guys, especially guys who weren't exactly friends, had a low level of TMI. Actually, since Lee wasn't the kind of guy to brag about his conquests, Tony was a little surprised he'd even brought it up.

"I asked Mr. Brummel if he thought the owners might sell."

"What did he say?"

"This isn't your average house, boy. You don't own a house like this. It owns you."

Lee's impression of the caretaker's weirdly rhythmic delivery was bang on. Tony snickered. A middle-aged man in rumpled clothes, scuffed work boots, and an obvious comb over, Mr. Brummel—no first name offered—had taken the caretaker clichés to heart, embracing them with all the fervor of someone about to shout, "And I'd have gotten away with it, too, if not for you meddling kids."

But he was right; Caulfield House was anything but average.

Built around the turn of the last century by Creighton Caulfield, who'd made a fortune in both mining and timber, the house rested on huge blocks of pale granite with massive beams of western red cedar holding up the porch roof. Three stories high with eight bedrooms, a ballroom, a conservatory, and servants' quarters on the third floor, it sat tucked away in Deer Lake Park at the end of a long rutted path too overgrown to be called a road. Matt, the freelance location finder CB Productions generally employed, had driven down Deer Lake Drive to have a look at Edgar House—which turned out to be far too small to accommodate the script. Following what he called a hunch, although Tony suspected he'd gotten lost—it wouldn't be the first time—he spotted a set of ruts and followed them. Chester Bane, the CB of CB Productions, had taken one look at the digital images Matt had shot of the house he'd stumbled on at the end of the ruts, and decided it was perfect for *Darkest Night*.

Although well within the boundaries of the park, Caulfield House remained privately owned and all but forgotten. Tony had no idea how CB had gotten permission to use the building, but shouting had figured prominently—shouting into the phone, shouting behind the closed door of his office, shouting into his cell as he crossed the parking lot ignoring the cars pulling out and causing two fender benders as his staff tried to avoid hitting him. Evidence suggested that CB felt volume could succeed when reason failed, and his track record seemed to support his belief.

But the house *was* perfect in spite of the profanely expressed opinions of the drivers who'd had to maneuver the generator, the craft services truck, two equipment trucks, the wardrobe/makeup trailer, and the honey wagon down the rutted road close enough to be of any use. Fortunately, as CB had rented the entire house for the week, he had no compunction about having dressing rooms set up in a couple of the bedrooms. He'd only brought in the honey wagon when Mr. Brummel had informed him what it would cost to replace the elderly septic system if it broke down under the additional input.

The huge second-floor bathroom had therefore been painted but was off-limits as far as actually using it. The painters had left the window open to help clear the fumes and Tony glanced up to see the bottom third of the sheer white curtain blowing out over the sill.

He frowned. "Did you see that?"

"The curtain?"

"No, beyond the curtain, in the room. I thought I saw someone looking down at us."

Lee snorted and started walking again, stepping over a sprawling mass of plants that had spilled out of the garden onto the path. "Probably Mason sneaking a smoke by the window. He likely figures the smell of the paint'll cover the stink."

It made sense, except . . .

"Mason's in black," Tony argued, hurrying to catch up. "Whoever this was, they were wearing something light."

"Maybe he took the jacket off so he wouldn't get paint on it. Maybe that's where he went for his earlier smoke and maybe he did a little finger painting on my ass when he got back." One foot raised above the top step, Lee paused and shook his head. "No, I'm pretty sure I'd remember that." Half turning, he grinned down at Tony on the step below. "It seems I have a secret admirer."

Before Tony could decide if he was supposed to read more into that than could possibly be there, Lee was inside and Adam's voice was telling him to *". . . get your ass in gefffst, Tony. We don't have all fissssking day."*

Fissssking had enough static involved it almost hurt. Fiddling with the frequency on his walkie-talkie as he followed Lee into the house, Tony had a feeling that the communication difficulties were going to get old fast.

"He peeped you. Not the actor, the other one."

"Don't be ridiculous, Stephen."

"Well, he looked like he saw you."

"He saw the curtain blowing out the window, that's all. I'm very good at staying out of sight." Her tone sharpened. *"I'm* not the one that people keep spotting, am I?"

"Those were accidents." His voice hovered between sulky and miserable. "I didn't even know those hikers were there and I don't care what Graham says, I hate hiding."

Comforting now. "I know."

"And besides, I never take the kind of chances you do. Truth, Cassie, what were you thinking, marking him a second time?"

She smiled and glanced down at the smudge of paint on one finger. "I was thinking that since I'd gotten him to take off his jacket, maybe I could get him to take off his pants. Come on." Taking his hand, she pulled him toward the door. "I want to see what they're doing now."

"Raymond, I think you'd better have a look at this."

"Cut and print! That was excellent work, gentlemen." Tossing his headphones onto the shelf under the monitor, Peter turned to his director of photography. "How much time do you need to reset for scene eight?"

Sorge popped a throat lozenge into his mouth and shrugged. "Shooting from down here . . . fifteen minutes, maybe twenty. No more. When we move to the top of the stairs . . ."

"Don't borrow trouble." He raised his voice enough to attract the attention of his 1AD . . . "Adam, tell them they've got twenty minutes to kill." . . . and lowered it again as he pivoted a hundred and eighty degrees to face his script supervisor. "Tina, let's you and I go over that next scene. There'll be a bitch of a continuity problem if we're not careful and I don't need a repeat of episode twelve."

"At least we know there's ninety-one people watching the show," she pointed out as she stood.

Peter snorted. "I still think it was one geek with ninety-one e-mail addresses."

As they moved off into the dining room and the techs moved in to shove the video village out into the actual entryway where it wouldn't be in the shot, Adam stepped out into the middle of the foyer and looked up at the two actors. "You've got fifteen, guys."

"I'll be in my dressing room." Turning on one heel, Mason headed back up the stairs.

"If anyone needs me, I'll be in my dressing room as well." Lee grimaced, reached back, and yanked at his pants. "These may dry faster off my ass."

Mouse, his gray hair more a rattail down his back and physically the complete opposite of his namesake—no one had ever referred to him as meek and lived to speak of it—stepped out from behind his camera and whistled. "You want to drop trou, don't let us stop you."

Someone giggled.

Tony missed Lee's response as he realized the highly unlikely sound could only have come from Kate, Mouse's camera assistant. He wouldn't have bet money on Kate knowing *how* to giggle. He wasn't entirely certain she knew how to laugh.

"Tony," Adam's hand closed over his shoulder as Lee followed Mason up the stairs and both actors disappeared down the second-floor hall. "I saw Mason talking with Karen from craft services earlier. Go make sure she didn't add any bagels to his muffin basket."

"And if she did?"

"Haul ass upstairs and make sure he doesn't eat one."

"You want me to wrestle the bagel out of Mason's hand?"

"If that's where it is." Adam grinned and patted him manfully on the shoulder—where manfully could be defined as *better you than me, buddy*. "If he's actually taken a bite, I want you to wrestle it out of his mouth."

Mason loved bagels, but the dental adhesive attaching Raymond Dark's fangs to his teeth just wasn't up to the required chewing. After a couple of forty-minute delays while Everett replaced the teeth, and one significantly longer delay after the right fang had been accidentally swallowed, CB had instituted the no-bagels-in-Mason's-dressing-room rule. Since Mason hadn't had to ultimately retrieve the tooth—that job had fallen to Jennifer, his personal assistant who, in Tony's opinion, couldn't possibly be paid enough—he'd chosen to see it as a suggestion rather than a rule and did what he could to get around it.

As a result Karen from craft services found herself under a determined assault by a man who combined good looks and charm with all the ethical consideration of a cat. No one blamed her on those rare occasions she'd been unable to resist.

Today, no one knew where she was.

She wasn't at the table or the truck and there wasn't time enough to search further. Grabbing a pot of black currant jam off the table, Tony headed up the stairs two steps at a time, hoping Mason's midmorning nosh hadn't already brought the day to a complete stop.

As the star of *Darkest Night*, Mason had taken the master suite as his dressing room. Renovated in the fifties, it took up half the front of the second floor and included a bedroom, a closet/dressing room, and a small bathroom. Provided he kept flushing to a minimum, Mr. Brummel had cleared this bathroom for Mason's personal use. Lee had to use the honey wagon like everyone else.

All the doors that led off the second-floor hall were made of the same Douglas fir that dominated the rest of the house, but they—and the trim surrounding them—had been stained to look like mahogany. Tony, who in a pinch could tell the difference between plywood and MDF, had been forced to endure a long lecture on the fir-as-mahogany issue from the gaffer who carved themed chess sets in his spare time. The half-finished knight in WWF regalia that he'd pulled from his pocket *had* been impressive.

Hand raised to knock on the door to Mason's room, Tony noticed that both the upper panels had been patched. In the dim light of the second-floor hall, the patches were all but invisible, but up close he could see the faint difference in the color of the stain. There was something familiar about their shape, but he couldn't . . .

Hand still raised, he jumped back as the door jerked open.

Mason stared out at him, wide-eyed. "There's something in my bathroom!"

"Something?" Tony asked, trying to see if both fangs were still in place.

"Something!"

"Okay." About to suggest plumbing problems were way outside his job description and that he should go get Mr. Brummel, Tony changed his mind at Mason's next words.

"It was crouched down between the shower and the toilet."

"It?"

"I couldn't see exactly, it was all shadows . . ."

Oh, crap. "Maybe I'd better go have a look." Before Mason could protest—before he could change his mind and run screaming, he was crossing the bedroom, crossing the dressing room, and opening the bathroom door. The sunlight through the windows did nothing to improve the color scheme, but it did chase away any and all shadows. Tony turned toward the toilet and the corner shower unit and frowned. He couldn't figure out what the actor might have seen since there wasn't room enough between them for . . .

Something.

Rocking in place.

Forward.

Back.

Hands clasped around knees, tear-stained face lifted to the light.

And nothing.

Just a space far too small for the bulky body that hadn't quite been there.

Skin prickling between his shoulder blades, jar of black currant jam held in front of him like a shield, Tony took a step into the room. Shadows flickered across the rear wall, filling the six inches between toilet and shower with writhing shades of gray. Had that been all he'd seen?

Stupid question.

No.

So what now? Was he supposed to do something about it?

Whatever it was, the rocking and crying didn't seem actively dangerous.

"Well, Foster?"

"Fuck!" He leaped forward and spun around. With his heart pounding so loudly he could hardly hear himself think, he gestured out the window at the cedar branches blowing across the glass and lied through his teeth. "There's your shadow."

Then the wind dropped again and the shadows disappeared.

Mason ran a hand up through his hair and glanced around the room. "Of course. Now you see them, now you don't." *I wasn't frightened,* his tone added, as his chin rose. *Don't think for a moment I was.* "You're a little jumpy, aren't you?"

"I didn't hear you behind me." Which was the truth because he hadn't—although the admiring way he said it was pure actor manipulation. Working in Television 101—keep the talent placated.

As expected, Mason preened. "Well, yes, I can move cat quiet when I want to."

In Tony's admittedly limited experience, the noise cats made thudding through apartments was completely disproportionate to their size, but Mason clearly liked the line, so he nodded a vague agreement.

"It's fucking freezing in here . . ."

Maybe not freezing but damned cold.

"Is that jam for me?"

Jam? He followed Mason's line of sight to his hand. "Oh, yeah."

"Put it by the basket. And then I'm sure you have things to do." The actor's lip curled. Both fangs were still in place. "Important production assistant things."

As it happened, in spite of sarcasm, he did.

There were no bagels in the basket but there was a scattering of poppy seeds on the tray next to a dirty knife. Setting down the jam, Tony turned and spotted a plate half hidden behind the plant that dominated the small table next to the big armchair by the window. *Bagel at twelve o'clock.*

Mason had made himself a snack, set it down, then gone to the bathroom and . . .

One thing at a time. Bagel now. Bathroom later.

He reached inside himself for calm, muttered the seven words under his breath, and the first half of the bagel hit his hand with a greasy-slash-sticky impact that suggested Mason had been generous with both the butter and the honey.

"Foster?"

"Just leaving."

All things considered, the sudden sound of someone crying in the bathroom was not entirely unexpected.

As Mason turned to glare at the sound, Tony snagged the other half of the bagel. "Air in the pipes," he said, heading for the door. "Old plumbing."

The actor shot a scathing expression across the room at him. "I knew that."

"Right." Except old plumbing seldom sounded either that unhappy or that articulate. The new noises were almost words. Tony found a lot of comfort in that *almost*.

Safely outside the door, he restacked the bagel butter/ honey sides together and headed toward the garbage can at the other end of the hall, rehearsing what he'd say when Mason discovered the bagel was gone. *"I wasn't anywhere near it!"*

No nearer than about six feet and Mason knew it.

Although *near* had become relative. These days he could manage to move unbreakable objects almost ten feet. Breakables still had a tendency to explode. Arra's notes hadn't mentioned explosions, but until the shadows, she'd handled FX for CB Productions, so maybe she considered bits of beer bottle flying around the room a minor effect. Fortunately, Zev had shown up early for their date and had been more than willing to drive him to the hospital to get the largest piece of bottle removed from his arm. His opinion of juggling beer bottles had been scathing. Tony hadn't had the guts to find out what his opinion of wizardry would have been.

The phrase *special effects wizard* had become a cliché in the industry. Arra Pelindrake, who'd been blowing things up and animating corpses for the last seven years, had been the real thing. Given the effects the new guy was coming up with, it turned out she hadn't been that great at the subtleties of twenty-first century FX but she *was* a real wizard. The shadows and the evil that controlled them had followed her through a gate she'd created between their world and this. The battle had gone down to the wire, but Tony had finally convinced her to stand and fight, and when it was all over, she'd been able to go home—but not before dropping the *you could be a wizard, too* bombshell. He'd refused to go with her, so she'd left him her laptop, six gummed-up games of spider solitaire that were supposed to give him insight into the future, and what he'd come to call Wizardshit 101; remarkably obscure instructions in point form on becoming a wizard.

He wasn't a wizard; he was a production assistant, working his way up in the industry until the time when it was his vision on the screen, his vision pulling in the viewers in the prime 19–29 male demographic. He'd had no intention of ever using the laptop.

And there'd been times over the last few months where he'd been able to stay away from it for weeks. Well, one time. For three weeks. Right after he'd had the jagged hunk of beer bottle removed from his arm.

Wizardry, like television, was all about manipulating energy.

And occasionally bread products.

Mason's door jerked open and without thinking much beyond *Oh, crap.* Tony opened the door he was standing by, dashed into the room, and closed the door quietly behind him. He had a feeling *I wasn't anywhere near your bagel* would play better when he didn't have butter, honey, and poppy seeds all over his hands.

The smell of wet paint told him where he was even before he turned.

The second-floor bathroom.

There were no shadows in this bathroom. On the wrong side of the house for direct sunlight, there was still enough daylight spilling in through the open window to make the fresh coat of white semigloss gleam. Although the plumbing had been updated in the fifties, the actual fixtures were original—which was why they were shooting the flashback in this room.

Weirdly, although this one was thirty years older, it made Mason's bathroom look dated and . . . haunted.

It was just the flickering shadows from the cedar tree and air in the pipes, he told himself.

Whatever gets you through your day, his self snorted.

Bite me.

The heavy door cut off all sound from the hall. He had no idea if Mason was still prowling around looking for him, hunting his missing bagel.

At least if the taps work, I can wash my hands.

Using the only nonsticky square inch on his right palm, Tony pushed against the old lever faucet and turned on the cold water. And waited. Just as he was about to turn it off again, figuring they hadn't hooked up the water yet, liquid gushed from the faucet, thick and reddish brown, smelling of iron and rot.

Heart in his throat, he jumped back.

Blood!

No wait, rust.

By the time he had his breathing under control, the water was running clear. Feeling foolish, he rinsed off his palms, dried them on his jeans, and closed the tap. Checking out his reflection in the big, somewhat spotty mirror over the sink, he frowned.

Behind him, on the wall . . . it looked as if someone had drawn a finger through the wet paint. When he turned, changing the angle of the light, the mark disappeared. Mirror—finger mark. No mirror—no mark.

And now we know where the paint on Lee's tux came from. Next question: who put it there? Brenda seemed like the prime suspect. She'd been upstairs delinting both actors before the scene, she'd have noticed the marks had they already been laid down, and the result had been Lee bare-assed in her trailer. . . . *and let's not forget that she's already familiar with his ass.* He probably hadn't even noticed her stroking him on the way by.

Opportunity and motive pointed directly to Brenda.

Time . . .

Tony glanced at his watch.

"Crap!" Twenty-three minutes since Adam had called a twenty-minute break. Bright side, Mason wouldn't be able to bug him about a rule-breaking snack in front of the others. Slipping out into the hall, Tony ran for the back stairs, figuring he could circle around from the kitchen. With any luck no one had missed him yet—one of the benefits of being low man on the totem pole.

As he ran, he realized Mason had been right about one thing. *It's fucking freezing up here.*

"Why was he in the bathroom? Graham said we'd be safe in there, that they wouldn't be using it until tomorrow."

"Be quiet, Stephen!" Cassie pinched her brother's arm. "Do you want him to hear you?"

"Ow. He can't hear us from way over here!"

"I'm not so sure." She frowned thoughtfully as the young man disappeared through the door leading to the stairs between the servants' rooms and the kitchen. "I get the feeling he doesn't miss much."

Stephen snorted and patted a strand of dark blond hair back into the pomaded dip over his forehead. "Good thing we weren't *in* the bathroom then."

"Yes . . . good thing."

Sunset was at 8:54 PM. It was one of those things that Tony couldn't not remember. He checked the paper every morning, he noted the time, and, as the afternoon became evening, he kept an eye on his watch.

Wanda, the new office PA, showed up at seven with the next day's sides—the half size sheets with all the background information as well as the necessary script pages. Tony helped her pick them up off the porch.

"This is so totally embarrassing!"

He handed her a messy stack of paper. "Don't worry about it, everyone trips. Earlier, I did a little 'falling with style' down the back stairs." The risers were uneven and he'd missed his step, very nearly pitching headfirst down the narrow incline.

"Falling with style is better than falling with skinned knee," Wanda muttered, shoving the retrieved sides under one arm and dabbing at the congealing blood with a grubby tissue. "And how many people saw you?"

"No one, but . . ."

"You saw me." She pointed at him. "And Brenda did." She pointed back toward the trailer. "Because I heard that distinctive snicker of hers. And the Sikh with the potted plant."

"Dalal. The prop guy."

"Whatever. My point, three people saw me. No one saw you and *I'm* bleeding."

"Yeah, well, don't bleed on the weather report. What would we do if we didn't know there was a seventy percent chance of rain tomorrow?"

She snapped erect and glared at him, nostrils pinched so tightly he wondered how she could breathe and talk at the same time. "That's not very supportive!"

"What?"

"That comment was not very supportive!"

"Kidding." Tony tapped the corners of his mouth. "Smiling, see?"

"It's not funny!"

"But I wasn't . . ."

"I'm taking these inside now!"

"Whatever." He wasn't quite mocking her. Quite. Okay, maybe a little. "I'll just be out here cleaning your blood off the stone."

"Fine." Spinning on one air-cushioned heel, she stomped in through the front doors.

"Someone needs to switch to decaf," he sighed. He'd been standing not three feet from the steps when she fell, close enough to hear her knee make that soft/hard definite tissue damage sound, and he had a pretty good idea of where she'd impacted with the porch. Weirdly, while there'd been lines of red dribbling down her shin, he couldn't find any blood on the stones. As embarrassed as she was, she'd probably just bounced up before the blood actually started to flow.

Probably.

The show packed up around 8:30 PM.

"Nice short day, people. Good work. Eleven and a half hours," he added to Sorge as he moved out of an electrician's way. "No way we'll make that tomorrow, not with all those extras."

Tony's grasp of French profanity wasn't quite good enough to understand the specifics of the DP's reply.

➷ TWO

"Hey, Henry, it's Tony." He shifted the phone to his other hand and reached into the back of the fridge. "It's highly likely that we're going to run late tomorrow night . . ." How long had that Chinese takeout been in there? ". . . so I was thinking that I'd better . . ." Opening the container, he stared at the uniform greenish-gray surface of the food. He had no idea what he'd ordered way back when but he had a strong suspicion it hadn't looked like that. ". . . meet you at the . . ." The click of a receiver being lifted cut him off. "Henry?"

"Tony? Sorry, I was in the shower."

"Going out to eat?"

He could hear the smile in the other man's voice. "Is that any of your business?"

"Nope. Just curious." The bologna still looked edible. Well, most of it. He tossed it on the counter and closed the refrigerator door. "We've got extras working tomorrow, so I'll likely be late."

"You say *extras* like you're thinking of calling in pest control to deal with them."

"I'm not, but Sorge and Peter are. They hate working with extras." Tony grabbed a little plastic packet of mustard from a cup filled with identical plastic packets, ripped off the top with his teeth, and squirted the contents out onto a slice of bread. "It might be best if I meet you at the theater. The show starts at ten, so if I'm not there by quarter to, just go in and sit down. I'll find you."

"We can call it off."

"Not a chance. How often do you get to go to the theater in the summer?" Friends of Tony's from film school were taping the play and the high-profile television stars playing the leads for the local cable channel. Opening curtain was at ten because they couldn't get the camera equipment until after their day jobs finished with it. Tony had no idea how they'd convinced the theater or the actors to go along with their schedule but that wasn't his problem. When he'd heard about it, he'd realized it was a perfect show for Henry. Given late sunsets and early sunrises, Henry didn't get out much in the summer. Ripping the slightly green edges off the half dozen slices of bologna, he stacked them on the bread and mustard. "You know where the Vogue is, right?"

"It's on Granville, Tony, practically around the corner. I think I can find it."

"Hey, I'm just checking." He applied mustard to the second slice of bread. "Did you know that the Vogue Theater was haunted?"

"Really haunted or haunted for publicity's sake?"

"Bit of both, I suspect."

Tony took a bite of his sandwich. "Think we'll see anything tomorrow night?"

"I think we'll have to wait until tomorrow night to find out."

"I'm just asking because our last experience with ghosts wasn't much fun." Several innocents had died and, until the whole shadows-from-another-world incident, the experience had provided fodder for the bulk of Tony's nightmares. Well, that and the undead ancient Egyptian wizard.

"Apparently this guy is a lot less interactive," Henry told him dryly. "What are you eating?"

"Bologna sandwich."

"I was thinking I'd have Italian."

"Good night, Henry!" Shaking his head, Tony thumbed the phone off and tossed it into the tangle of blankets on the pull-out couch. "Over four hundred and sixty years old," he commented to the apartment at large. "You'd think he'd learn another joke."

Vampires: not big on the whole contemporary humor thing.

"Seventy percent chance of rain, my ass," Tony muttered as he drove out to the end of Deer Lake Drive and parked behind Sorge's minivan. The rain sheeted down his windshield with such volume and intensity the wipers were barely able to keep up. He turned off the engine, grabbed his backpack off the passenger seat, and flicked the hood up on his green plastic rain cape. Sure, it looked geeky, but it kept him and his backpack mostly dry. Besides, it wasn't quite seven-thirty in the freaking AM—ACTRA rules stipulated a twelve-hour break for the talent but only ten for the crew—he was in the middle of a park, about to head down an overgrown path to a forgotten house—who the hell was going to see him?

Stephen turned from the window smiling broadly. "Listen to the water roar in the gutters, Cass! This'll fill the cistern for sure. Graham's going to be on cloud nine."

"And it's all about Graham being happy, isn't it?" she muttered, rubbing bare arms.

"That's not what I meant." He frowned. "What's the matter with you?"

"I don't know." When she looked up, her eyes were unfocused. "Something feels . . ."

"Different?"

She shook her head. "Familiar."

The trees cut the rain back to a bearable deluge. Carefully avoiding new, water-filled ruts and the occasional opening where rain poured through the covering branches, Tony plodded toward the house. Half a kilometer later, as he came out into the open, and saw the building squatting massive and dark at the end of the drive, thunder cracked loud enough to vibrate his fillings and a jagged diagonal of lightning backlit the house.

"Well, isn't that a cliché," he sighed, kicked a ten-kilo hunk of mud off his shoe, and kept walking.

Finally standing just inside the kitchen door, he shook out the excess water off his rain cape onto the huge flagstone slab that floored the small porch, added his shoes to the pile of wet footwear, and pulled out a pair of moccasins from his pack. Stopping by the big prep table, he snagged a cup of coffee—more practical than most in the television industry, craft services had set up in the kitchen—and headed for the butler's pantry where the AD's office had been set. He shoved his backpack into one of the lower cabinets, signed in, and grabbed a radio. So far, channel one, the AD's channel was quiet. Adam might not be in yet or he just might not be talking—impossible to tell. On channel eight, the genny op and the rest of his transport crew had a few things to say about keeping things running in the rain. Impressed by the way the profanities seemed to make it through the interference intact, Tony set his unit back on channel one, and headed for the conservatory at the back of the house.

Extras' holding.

Tony could already hear them; a low hum as two dozen voices all complained about their agents at the same time.

Passing by the bottom of the back stairs, the servants' stairs, another sound caught his attention. A distant, rhythmic creak. *Er er. Er er.* Like something . . . swinging. Someone had probably left the door open on the second floor. He thought about heading up and closing it, then spotted the black cat sitting at the three-quarter mark and changed his mind. Uneven, narrow, and steep, the stairs had tried to kill him once already and that was without the added fun of something to trip over. A sudden draft of cold air flowing down from the second floor raised the hair on the back of his neck and consolidated his decision. Damp clothes, cold air—not a great combination. Besides, he was already running late.

Sucking back his coffee, he hurried along a narrow hall and finally down the three stone steps into the conservatory.

The house had been deserted of everyone but hired caretakers for almost thirty years and it seemed as though none of those caretakers had cared to do any indoor gardening. The conservatory was empty of even the dried husks of plant life. The raised beds were empty. The small pond was empty. The big stone urns were empty. The actual floor space, on the other hand, was a little crowded.

Over on the other side of the pond, several men and women were changing into their own modern evening dress with the nonchalance of people for whom the novelty of seeing others in their underwear had long since worn off. Ditto the self-consciousness of being seen. Crammed between the raised beds and the stone urns, still more men and women—already dressed—sat on plastic folding chairs, drank coffee, read newspapers, and waited for their turn in makeup.

The two makeup stations were up against the stone wall the conservatory shared with the house. Some shows had the supporting actors do their own face and hair, but Everett had refused to allow it and CB, usually so tight he could get six cents' change from a nickel, had let him have his way. Sharyl, Everett's assistant who worked part-time for CB Productions and part-time at a local funeral parlor, handled the second chair. Curling irons, hair spray, and a multitude of brushes were all flung about with dazzling speed and when Everett yelled, "Time!" Tony realized they'd been racing.

"Not fair!" Sharyl complained as she flicked the big powder brush over the high arc of male pattern baldness. "I had more surface to cover."

"I had a more delicate application."

"Yeah, well, I'm faster when they're lying down." She stepped back and tossed the big brush onto the tray. "You're lovely."

Tony didn't think the man—*white, thirty to forty, must provide own evening dress*—looked convinced. Or particularly happy to hear it.

"Next two!" Everett bellowed over the drumming of the rain on the glass. He waved the completed extras out of the chairs, adding, "Don't touch your face!" Tony couldn't hear the woman's reply, but Everett's response made it fairly clear. "So itch for your art."

Waving at a couple of people he knew from other episodes and a guy he'd met a couple of times at the Gandydancer, Tony made his way over to the card table set up beside the coffee urn. He pulled the clipboard out from under a spill of cardboard cups and checked the sign-in page. It seemed a little short of names.

"Hey! Everybody!" The rain threatened to drown him out, so he yelled louder. "If you haven't signed the sheet, please do it now. I have to check your name against our master list."

No one moved.

"If your names aren't on both lists, you won't get paid!"

Half a dozen people hurried toward him.

Other shows would have hired a daily PA or TAD—trainee assistant director—to ride herd on the extras. CB figured they were all adults and were therefore fully capable of walking from the holding area to the set without him having to pay to see that they managed it. Human nature being what it was, and with two thirds of the season in the can, Tony could pretty much guarantee that someone—or some two or three—would wander off and need to be brought back to the herd while he did his best border collie impression. Snarling permitted; biting frowned on.

It took a moment for him to realize that the scream was not a rehearsal. Extras generally did a lot of screaming on shows starring vampires. Some of them, disdaining the more spontaneous terror of their contemporaries, liked to practice.

On the other side of the conservatory, a half dressed woman clutching a pair of panty hose to her chest, backed away from one of the raised beds and continued to scream. By the time Tony reached her, the screams had become whimpers, barely audible over the sound of the rain.

"What?" he demanded. "What's wrong?"

Conditioned to respond to anyone with a radio and a clipboard, she pointed a trembling finger toward the garden. "I sat down, on the edge, to put on . . ." Taupe streamers waved from her other hand. ". . . and I sort of fell. Back." Glancing around, she suddenly realized she had an audience and, in spite of her fear, began to play to it. "I put my hand down on the dirt. It sank in just a little. The next thing I knew, something *grabbed* it."

"Something?"

"Fingers. I felt fingers close around mine. Cold fingers." A half turn toward her listeners. "Like fingers from a *grave*."

Tony had to admit that the raised beds did look rather remarkably like graves. *Yeah, and so does any dirt pile longer than it is wide.* He stepped forward, noticed where the dirt had been disturbed, and poked it with the clipboard. He didn't believe the bit about the fingers, of course, but there was no point in taking unnecessary chances. Over the last few years he'd learned that belief had absolutely nothing to do with reality.

The clipboard sank about a centimeter into the dirt and stopped with a clunk.

Clunk sounded safe enough.

In Tony's experience, the metaphysical seldom went clunk.

A moment's digging later, he pulled out a rusted, handleless garden claw.

"Was this what you felt?"

"No." She shuddered, dramatically. "I felt fingers."

"Cold fingers." Tony held the claw toward her and she touched it tentatively.

"Okay, maybe."

"Maybe?"

"Fine." Her snort was impressive. "Probably. Okay? It felt like fingers, it's barely dawn, and it's kind of spooky in here, and I haven't had any coffee yet!"

Show over, the other extras began to drift away and the woman who'd done the screaming pointedly continued dressing. Tony tossed the claw back onto the garden bed and headed for the door. Drawing level with Everett, he asked for a time check.

"They'll be ready when they're needed," Everett told him, layering on scarlet lipstick with a lavish hand. "But don't quote me on that."

"I kind of have to quote you on that, Everett. Adam's going to ask."

"Fine." He pointedly capped the lipstick and drew a mascara wand from its tube with a flourish. "But don't say I didn't warn you. Oh, calm down," he added as the middle-aged woman in the chair recoiled from the waving black bristles. "Thirty years in this business and I've yet to put an eye out."

"I put one in once," Sharyl announced and Tony figured that was his cue to leave. Sharyl's mortuary stories were usually a hoot, but somehow he just wasn't in the mood for fun and frolic with the dead. Pausing on the threshold, he glanced back over the room to do a final head count. Party guests and cater-waiters clumped with their own kind, making his job a little easier.

Twenty-five.

Only twenty-four signatures.

A second count gave him the right number of heads and a third confirmed it. He must've miscounted the first time—it wasn't easy getting an accurate fix on the crowd of guests around the central urn. About to turn, he stopped and squinted toward the back garden, a flurry of movement having caught his eye. It had almost looked as if the garden claw had stood on its broken handle and waved its little claw-fingers at him. Except that the claw was nowhere in sight.

Wondering what he actually might have seen—given the absence of the claw—Tony got lost in a sudden realization. If the claw was missing, someone had taken it. *Great. We've got a souvenir hunter.*

Every now and then cattle calls would spit up a background player who liked to have a little something to help him remember the job. With a souvenir hunter on the set, small, easily portable items had a tendency to disappear. During episode seven, they'd lost the inkwell from Raymond Dark's desk. After CB expressed his thoughts about the incident—"No one from that group works again until I get my property back!"—they'd had four inkwells returned. Unfortunately, most of the small, easily portable items from this set belonged to the current owners of Caulfield House, not CB Productions and the odds were good the crew wouldn't immediately realize it if something went missing.

I'd better let Keisha know.

He grabbed a cinnamon bun on his way through the kitchen, dropped the signed sheet in the AD's office, and headed for the drawing room. The original script had called for a ball and the presence of a ballroom was one of the reasons CB had jumped at using the house. Problem was, the ballroom was huge and the number of people it would have taken to fill it—even given the tricks of the trade—would have emptied the extras budget. With episode twenty-two and its howling mob of peasants with torches and pitchforks still in the pipeline, the ball became a smaller gathering and the venue moved to the drawing room.

A huge fieldstone fireplace dominated one end of a room paneled in Douglas fir. Above it, mounted right on the stone, was a massive gold-framed mirror.

Six tall, multipaned windows divided the outside wall and glass-fronted built-in bookcases faced them along the inside. The curtains were burgundy with deep gold tassels and tiebacks—the two colors carried into the furniture upholstery. The room seemed essentially untouched by almost a hundred years of renovation and redecoration. Standing in the midst of this understated luxury were Peter, Sorge, the gaffer, the key grip, and Keisha, the set decorator, all looking up.

"The ceilings are high enough. We can shoot under them," Peter said as Tony joined them.

"We are keeping the cameras low," Sorge agreed. "Keeping the shots filled with the people."

Still staring at the ceiling, the gaffer frowned. "A diffuser under each of them might help."

"Couldn't hurt," the key grip allowed.

Keisha made a noncommittal albeit dubious sound. So Tony looked up.

"Holy fuck." Those were three of the most hideous looking chandeliers Tony had ever seen. In fact, he wasn't entirely certain they could even be called chandeliers except for the dangly bits. Although what the dangly bits were actually made of he had no idea. A certain *Leave it to Beaver*ness about them suggested the same 1950's vision that had been responsible for the redecorated parts of the master suite, the bathroom in particular.

Something.

Rocking in place.

Forward.

Back.

Not that particular.

"I think Mr. Foster has succinctly summed up the situation," Peter sighed and Tony looked down to find all four looking at him. "Did you want one of us for something?"

"Uh, yeah, Keisha mostly, but you should probably all know. We've got a souvenir hunter. There's already a piece of crap missing from the conservatory."

"Crap?"

"Broken end of a garden claw."

"Crap," Keisha acknowledged. "But not our crap either. All right, I'll make sure Chris keeps an eye out and we'll do a double count when we pack up. In the meantime, someone's going to have to get pictures of everything in those cabinets."

"Tony . . ."

Yeah, he knew it. He was usually "someone."

"... get Tina's digital," Peter continued, "and get those shots while we finish setup. We all know how much CB loves unexpected bills."

Only the center cabinet was actually a bookcase. The others were too shallow for books and instead displayed cups and saucers, grimy bowls of china flowers, and the little plastic toys from inside Kinder Eggs—Tony suspected the three-part water buffalo and the working lime-green windmill were the most recent additions to the decor. Behind the water buffalo, he found a yellowed card buffed down to the same color as the shelf by a thick layer of dust. Theoretically, he wasn't supposed to touch.

When he flipped the card over, the black handwriting was still dark and legible.

Finger of a Franciscan monk killed by the Papal Inquisition, 1651. Acquired August 17, 1887.

There was no sign of the finger although on the next shelf he did find half a dozen of the tiny china figurines that used to come in boxes of tea and were required inventory in every cheesy antique store in the country.

He finished up just as his radio sent a spike of pure static into his head.

"Adam, this is Brenda. Lee and Mazzzzzzzzit are in wardrobe."

"Roger that. Everett's on his ..." The last word was lost under another burst of static and some rather impressive profanity from the other end of the room.

"Tony!"

He closed the last cabinet and turned toward the 1AD.

"Send Everett out to the trailer and start moving the extras up here."

"Why does it have to be extras?" Peter muttered as Tony dropped the camera back off at Tina's station. "I hear the Hall of Presidents is closed down for renovations; why can't we borrow their animatronics? Toss 'em in a tux, stick a martini glass in their hands ... Washington would look very feminine in a high collar and some ruffles; he's already in a wig. Who'd notice? But no, we have to use real people. Real people who don't listen, who never know their right from their left, who all want their fifteen minutes, who make *suggestions* ..."

The director's continuing diatribe faded as Tony moved out into the hall heading for the conservatory. Everett, who'd known the talent should be in the trailer at nine, was on the move when he arrived. Sharyl was packing up her case, ready for on-set touch-ups. All that was left was moving the extras.

Humming the theme from *Rawhide* was optional.

With most of the crowd on the correct heading, Tony raced across the kitchen to prevent an unauthorized side trip.

"Hey, where are you going?" Hand flat against the wood, he shoved the door closed before it actually opened.

The actress shrugged. "I was just wondering what was down there."

"Probably the basement." The door felt like ice under his palm. "Just keep moving."

Leaning in closer, she drew her tongue slowly across a full and already moist lower lip. "You're *so* serious . . . No hard feelings?" Her voice dripped single entendre.

"Give it up, love." One of the waiters took her arm, winked at Tony, and started her moving again. "I'd have better luck."

"What?" She shot Tony a frustrated look he answered with a shrug, and then allowed herself to be towed away. "Are there no straight men left in television?"

"You're asking the wrong fag, puss. Besides, he's only the production assistant."

"I know that! I was starting at the bottom."

"An admirable sentiment."

As they followed the rest of the extras down the hall, Tony lifted his hand from the door and stared down at the red mark on his palm. It looked a bit like a letter—a Russian letter maybe, or Greek, or Hebrew. Before he could decide which, it had disappeared. When he touched the door again, it was no colder than any other surface.

"You don't want to be going down there."

He spun around so quickly he had to catch his balance on the door handle. "Jesus!" Snatching his hand off the metal, he sucked at what felt like a burn on the skin between finger and thumb. "Why don't I want to go down there?" he demanded, the question a little muffled by his hand.

"Weather like this, the basement floods. Probably six inches of water down there now." Mr. Brummel's red-rimmed eyes narrowed. "Nasty things in the water. You just be keeping your pretty ladies and gentlemen away from the nasty things."

"What?"

The caretaker snorted and shifted his grip on the black cat in his arms. "Look, kid, we got the original knob-and-tube wiring down there. Damned stuff gets wet and every piece of metal in the place is conducting power. Now, I personally don't give a crap if nosy parkers fry, but I don't like doing the paperwork the insurance companies want, so stay out. You already picked up a spark off the door, didn't you?"

It could have been a spark. "Yeah."

"Well, there, then."

"Isn't all that free-floating electricity dangerous?"

"Yep. And that . . ." He enunciated each word carefully. ". . . is why you don't want to be going down to the basement. Let me see your hand."

Cat tucked under one arm, his fingers closed around Tony's wrist before Tony'd decided how he intended to respond.

The caretaker's second snort was dismissive as he peered at the dark pink splotch. "This is nothing. You aren't even bleeding." His grip tightened to the edge of pain, his fingers unnaturally warm. He leaned in closer, his eyes narrowed, his nose flared—he looked like a poster boy for dire warnings. "You don't want to be bleeding, not in this house."

"Why not?"

"Because we're miles from anywhere." He didn't so much release Tony's wrist as toss him his arm back. "For pity's sake, kid, use your head. These cinnamon buns for anyone?"

"Sure. Help yourself. The uh, cat . . . is it yours?"

"No. I just like carrying it around."

The cat yawned, the inside of its mouth very pink and white against the ebony fur.

Rubbing his wrist, Tony backed slowly out of the kitchen. He didn't turn until he was halfway through the butler's pantry and Adam's voice filled his earjack.

"Graham's not going to like this, Cass. This isn't what I'd call staying out of sight."

She smoothed down the heavy velvet folds of her skirt and smiled. "It's hiding in plain sight. Like the purloined letter."

"What about that feeling you had? The familiar feeling?"

"What about it?" Rising up on her toes, she peered over the heads of the people milling about the drawing room. "It felt familiar."

"Cassie! You just want to meet that actor."

"Well, why not? He's cute. And you're the one who was complaining you were bored." She settled back on her heels, tucked her hand into the crook of his arm, and smiled up at him through her lashes. "This isn't boring."

"It's dangerous," Stephen insisted, but his hand closed over hers and he didn't sound as convinced as he had.

"With all those people and all those lights crammed into one room, there's energy to spare."

"It's not the amount of energy." He glanced around and shook his head. "They're all older than us."

"So frown. It makes you look older."

"They're going to notice . . ."

"They won't." Her smile was triumphant as she waved a hand at the bank of lights. "It's hot enough in here that in a worst case scenario all we'll do is drop the temperature down to a more bearable level. Seriously, they'd thank us if they knew. Come on, he's over by the door."

No one noticed them as they crossed the room. The waiters practiced holding their trays and offering drinks in ways most likely to get them asked back for a larger part, maybe even a part with a name, later in the season. The guests did much the same with bright, animated, but-not-upstaging-the-stars background chatter.

"Cassie, this isn't going to work."

"Well, it won't if you're going to be so negative. Just think 'party guest.'"

"But . . ."

"Concentrate, Stephen!" As they neared the door, she licked her lower lip and dragged her brother around to face her. "Is my face still on?"

He frowned. "I guess. But you overdid it with the eye shadow."

Lee was standing by the door talking to a couple of the extras. It was one of the things Tony liked about him—he didn't have the whole, *I've got my name and face in the opening credits and you don't* thing going on. He was smiling down at the girl now, saying something she had to lean closer to hear, and Tony felt an irrational stab of jealousy. Irrational and idiotic and yes, still pathetic.

"Places, everyone!"

Interesting that Lee seemed to be telling them where they should stand. More interesting that they were standing almost entirely out of the shot.

"All right, people, listen up. This is what's going to happen!" Peter moved out into the center of the room and raised both hands as though he was conducting a symphony instead of episode seventeen of a straight to syndication show about a vampire detective—not so much a symphony as three kids with kazoos. "Mason and Lee are going to come in from the hall and cross the room to the fireplace as you all go through the usual party shtick. You'll all ignore them until Lee calls for your attention, which you will give to him. Mason will then say his piece, you'll listen attentively, reacting silently as you see fit—just remember that reaction because odds are good you'll be repeating it all morning. Do not drop your glass. The glasses are rented. Mason'll finish, and Ms. Sinclair . . ."

A distinguished looking silver-haired bit player Tony had last seen playing Dumpster diver number two in a CBC Movie of the Week, raised her martini glass in acknowledgment.

". . . you'll say your line: 'If you're trying to frighten us, Mr. Dark, you're not succeeding.' Then Mason will reply, 'I'm not trying. Not yet.' And we'll cut. Let's run through once for cameras."

The run-through necessitated a few adjustments in the crowd and their reactions.

"What the hell was that?"

"Astonishment?" the party-goer offered, cheeks flushed.

"Are you asking me?" Peter sighed. "Because if you are, I'd have to say it looked more like indigestion. Gear it down."

The girl divided her attention between the room in general and Lee, smiling in his direction like she knew a secret.

"Let's roll tape on this one." Peter disappeared behind the monitor and Adam moved out onto the floor.

"Quiet, please! Let's settle, people!" He glanced over the crowd and, when he was satisfied, yelled, "Rolling!"

Tony, along with nearly everyone else in a headset, repeated the word. It sounded in the hall outside the drawing room, at the craft services table in the kitchen, maybe even out at the trailers. Then Kate—because CB's budgets never quite extended as far as *second* assistant camera—stepped forward and called the slate.

"Scene three, take one! Mark!"

The boy standing next to the girl who'd been talking to Lee jumped at the crack.

Tony frowned. And he *was* a boy, too. Although his evening clothes fit him like they'd been made for him, he had to be at least ten years younger than anyone else in the room. Well, it wouldn't be the first time someone on the crew had snuck a relative or two in. As long as they behaved themselves, CB was all in favor of extras he didn't have to pay. It wasn't that these two weren't behaving themselves, it was just . . . Actually, Tony had no idea what it was about them that kept drawing his attention. Except maybe that Lee had been paying attention to them.

How often do I have to say this is pathetic before it finally sinks in?

Lee and Mason had barely reached the fireplace when Peter broke off a quiet discussion with Sorge and yelled cut.

"It's no good." Coming out from behind the monitors, he pulled off his headset. "The mirror over the fireplace is flaring out. Sharyl!"

"Yeah?"

"We're going to need to use some hair spray. Tony, take care of it. Meanwhile, Mason, as you come in . . ."

The end of the suggestion was lost as Tony moved away from the director. He reached Sharyl just ahead of a mascara failure and a lipstick problem.

"I swear it's so hot under those lights, it's melting right off my lashes."

"It's actually comfortable where I am, but I can't help chewing my lips while we wait."

Lipstick Problem had been standing near the girl-who'd-been-talking-to-Lee and the boy-who-was-younger.

And why do I care? Tony wondered as he took the offered hair spray with a nod of thanks. He could reach the bottom half of the mirror from the hearth, but the whole area was so supersized he'd need a little help for the rest. The ladders that had been used to set the lights were out in the hall, but maneuvering one through a crowded drawing room would be time consuming. Figuring Peter would appreciate him thinking of and then saving production time, he snagged the director's chair on the way past and set it on the hearth.

The trick was to spray on a nice even coat. Enough to cut the glare but not so much that the audience wondered what the hell was on the glass. And he should probably move the chair in order to safely reach the other end of the mirror.

Yeah, but who wants to live forever?

Plastic bottle of hair spray in his right hand, thumb on the pump, left hand gripping the mantel, he leaned way out and just for an instant dropped his gaze below the line of application.

There.

In the reflection of the far side of the room.

The boy-who-was-younger was in a loose white shirt. Well, white except for the splashes of what had to be blood—had to be because a huge triangular cut in the right side of his neck looked as though it just missed decapitating him. The girl-who'd-been-talking-to-Lee was wearing a summer dress, one strap torn free, the whole fitted bodice as well as her bare shoulders stained a deep crimson. She was also short the top left quarter of her head—her face missing along the nose and out one cheekbone, her left eye completely gone.

He twisted around.

Now that he'd seen them, the glamour—or whatever the nonwizard, dead-people equivalent was called—no longer worked.

Nearly headless. Chunk of face missing.

Their eyes—all three of them—widened as they somehow realized he could see them as they were, not as they appeared. Actually, he kind of suspected his expression was giving the whole thing away.

The vanishing . . . not entirely unexpected.

The chair tipping sideways, as gravity won out and he headed for the floor . . . he had to admit he'd been kind of expecting that, too.

Then a strong hand closed around his arm and yanked him back onto his feet. He fought to find his balance, won the fight, and turned to look down into a pair of concerned green eyes.

"Are you all right, Tony?" Lee asked, one hand still loosely clasped around Tony's bicep. "You look like you've seen a ghost."

～ THREE

"Tony! The mirror!"

Right, the mirror. The mirror where he'd just seen the dead up and animate—or as animate as any extras ever were between shots. Oh, fuck . . . the extras! If that feeling wasn't his blood actually running cold, it was pretty damned close—kind of a sick feeling in his stomach that moved out to his extremities so quickly he thought he might hurl. Traditionally, the presence of extras right before disaster meant a high body count, and dead people in the drawing room certainly seemed like an accurate harbinger of disaster to Tony.

He stared at their reflections in the small part of the mirror still clear of hair spray. They all seemed oblivious to their fate. *Might as well dress them in red shirts now and get it over with!*

"Tony!"

He twisted around to see the first assistant director staring up at him in annoyance.

"Finish spraying the damned mirror!"

It might be damned, he supposed. Damned could explain why it showed dead people. . . .

"Tony?"

Tony looked down into Lee's concerned face and forced his brain to start working again. It wasn't as if these were the first ghosts he'd ever seen. Okay, technically, he hadn't seen the last set—he'd only heard them screaming—but he *was* used to metaphysical pop-ups. Hell, he used to sleep with one. "Can I talk to you for a minute? I mean . . ." A gesture took in the chair, the mirror, and the plastic bottle of hair spray. ". . . when I'm done."

Dark brows drew in, and Lee glanced back at Peter still talking to Mason. "Sure."

Directing Mason—or rather, Mason's ego—took time.

A moment later, Tony was back on the floor. "Those two kids you were talking to . . ." At Lee's suddenly closed expression, he paused. "It's okay, I'm not going to get them into trouble. I know they weren't supposed to be in the scene." Hello, understatement. "I just wondered who they were."

Lee considered it—considered Tony—for a moment then shrugged. "They're Mr. Brummell's niece and nephew. Cassie, short for Cassandra, which she informed me was a stupid, old-fashioned name, and Stephen. They were . . . well, *she* was just so thrilled at being here that I didn't have the heart to turn them in. I warned them that they had to stay in the background, though."

"Yeah, I saw you positioning them. You didn't notice anything strange?"

"Strange?"

"About the way they looked."

"Only that they were younger than everyone else in the room. I'd say mid-to-late teens, no older."

And not going to get any older either. *All right. We're shooting an episode* about *a haunted house* in *a haunted house and that sort of thing never ends well. Real dead people not so big on the happy ending. So what do I do? I get everyone out of the haunted house. And how do I do that?*

Production assistants had about as much power as . . . well, bottom line, they didn't have any power. None. Nada. Zip. And zilch.

He had to call the boss. Since CB remembered the shadows and the Shadowlord, CB would believe him. Announcing to anyone else that he'd seen a ghost—two ghosts—would result in ridicule at best. *"A ghost?"* He could hear the broad sarcasm in Peter's voice. *"Why don't you go see if they'll work for scale; I'm sure CB would appreciate the savings."*

Come to think of it, CB *would* appreciate the savings. And he wouldn't be too happy about losing his chance to shoot in a house he'd already paid a week's rent on. Maybe he could get CB to agree to put the ghosts in the show. They clearly wanted to be involved; maybe official ghost status would be enough to placate them.

"You're going to exhaust the hamster."

"What?"

Lee grinned. "The hamster running around on that wheel in your head. You're trying to figure out how to keep those kids out of trouble, aren't you?"

Close enough. "Yeah."

"Don't worry about it. I'll put in a good word for them. *Darkest Night* isn't quite a solo act no matter what Mason seems to think." They turned together to look at the clump of people grouped around the actor who was standing, arms crossed, glaring at Peter. "You might tell them to keep out of his way, though."

Sure, I'll hold a séance and get right on that. Even if he got hold of CB, how was he supposed to get hold of the ghosts? Glancing around the room, he doubted there was a medium among all the size twos.

"Want to share the joke?" Lee asked as Tony snickered.

He did. And as bad a joke as it was, he even thought that Lee would appreciate it—right up until the back story killed the laughs. As he hesitated, Lee's expression changed; closing in on itself until the open, curious, friendly expression was gone and all that remained was the same polite interest he showed the rest of the world.

"Never mind. I should get back to work before we end up keeping the extras over their four-hour minimum."

Tony couldn't think of a thing to say as Lee flashed him the same smile he'd flashed a thousand cameras and walked away. An opportunity missed . . . An opportunity for what, he had no idea—but he couldn't shake the notion that he'd just dropped the ball in a big way.

A sudden soft pressure against his shins drew his gaze off Lee's tuxedo-clad back and toward the floor. The caretaker's black cat made another pass across his legs.

"Tony!" Ear jack dangling against his shoulder, Adam approached the fire-place. "You get that mirror done?"

He held up the plastic bottle. "It's covered."

"Good. Clean your grubby footprints off Peter's chair, put it back behind the monitors, and . . ." His head dropped forward and he stared at the cat now rubbing against his jeans. "Where the hell did this animal come from?"

"I think it belongs to Mr. Brummel, the caretaker; he was holding it earlier."

"Then grab it and get it back to him. The last thing we need is an unattended animal running around."

One of the extras shrieked with laughter. Both men turned in time to see Mason moving his mouth away from her throat.

"*Another* unattended animal," Adam added wearily, shoving the ear jack back where it belonged. "He's got a bed in his dressing room, doesn't he?"

"It's a bedroom."

"Right. Let's move it with the cat, then; we've got to do what we can to get these people out of here before he talks her into a nooner."

Given that it was the woman who'd put the moves on him in the kitchen, Tony suspected "You want to?" would probably be conversation enough. He bent and wrapped his hands tentatively around the cat. It squeezed through his grip, skittered about six feet away, sat down, and licked its butt.

"Adam . . . ?" Peter's voice.

"Tony's got it." Adam's answer.

A fine sentiment but less than truthful—every time he got close enough for another grab, the cat moved. Once or twice, his fingertips ghosted over soft fur, but that was it. As amber eyes glanced back mockingly and four legs per-formed a diagonal maneuver impossible on two, he had no doubt the cat was playing to its snickering audience. At least it seemed to be moving toward the small door in the back corner of the drawing room.

The library, he thought, as the cat slipped through the half-open door and disappeared. *I'll just close the door and the cat'll be out of our hair.* A sudden burst of static clamped his left hand to his head. *Son of a bitch!*

"*Tony! We've got* sfffft *stored in there. I don't want the cat* pisssssssstnk *on it.*"

Yeah, well, nothing harder to get out than cat pisstnk on sffft. He sighed and kept going.

In spite of the rain, the two long windows to his left let in enough daylight for him to see the cat moving purposefully across the room toward the other door. He could understand why it didn't want to linger. The empty shelves didn't feel empty. They felt as though the books they'd held had left a dark imprint that lingered long after the books themselves were gone. The only piece of furniture in the room was a huge desk and a chair in the same red-brown wood. Tony had overheard Chris telling Adam that it had belonged to Creighton Caulfield himself. The fireplace shared a chimney with the drawing room and over the dark slab of mantel was a small, rectangular mirror framed in the same dark wood. Tony made a point of not looking in it. If there were ghosts in the library, he didn't want to know.

Moving out and around a stack of cables and half a dozen extra lights, he picked up the pace.

The cat slipped out the library's main door, Tony following it out into the main hall. His reaching hand touched tail. The cat picked up the pace, streaking toward the front doors, then turning at the last minute and heading up the stairs. Tony made the turn with considerably less grace and charged up the stairs after it. Three steps at a time slowed to two to one and at the three-quarter mark, as an ebony tail disappeared to the right, he realized there was no way in hell he was going to catch up.

He reached the second floor as the cat reached the far end of the hall. It paused outside the door to the back stairs, turned, and looked at him in what could only be considered a superior way—no mistaking the expression even given the distance—and then disappeared into the stairwell.

Just for an instant, he considered calling the cat to his hand, but the memory of the exploding beer bottle stopped him. While blowing up the caretaker's cat would certainly keep it off the set, it seemed like a bit of an extreme solution. *Not to mention hard on the cat.* Besides, from what he knew about cats, it'd probably head straight for the food in the kitchen where it would be Karen's problem.

Nice to have his suspicions about that creaking sound he'd heard earlier proved right—the upper door to the back stairs *had* been left open.

Mind you, that doesn't explain the baby crying.

The faint unhappy sound was coming from his left. He turned slowly. They weren't using that end of the hall, so he had no idea what was down there. *Gee, you think it could be the nursery?* And the million-dollar question now became: Was it a new ghost or were the two teenage ghosts he'd already seen just screwing around trying to freak him out?

"Tony!"

For half a heartbeat, he thought it was the baby calling his name. Apparently, the freaking-him-out part was working fine.

"Haul asssssssssssstkta wardrobe and pick up Maffffffffffffffk other tie from Brenda."

"I'm on it, Adam." He thumbed off his microphone and started back down the stairs. Investigating phantom babies would have to wait. *And I'm so broken up about that. . . .*

Crossing the porch, he felt someone watching him. The caretaker's black cat sat staring at him from one of the deep stone sills that footed the dining room window.

"Good," he told it. "Stay out here."

Maybe a cat could make it from the second floor and through half of a very large house in the time it took him to cover a tenth of the distance. Maybe it was really motoring. Maybe he didn't much care. Cat weirdness was pretty low on his list at the moment.

As Lee and Mason entered the drawing room for the fourth time, Tony headed for the kitchen and the side door. Tucked into the narrow breezeway linking the main house with the four-car garage added in the thirties, he thumbed CB's very private number into his cell phone. This was the number he'd been given when they'd thought a dark wizard's army from another reality was about to invade. This was the number he'd been told never to use except in the case of a similar emergency. Ghosts weren't exactly on the same level, but the bar *had* been set pretty damned high first time out.

"We're sorry, the number you have dialed is not in service. Please hang up and try your call again."

Great. His direct-to-CB number was worthless. One of the producer's ex-wives had probably gotten hold of it. No chance of getting to him through the regular office number either—not through Ruth the office manager, not by telling the truth anyway. Lying, on the other hand . . .

"Peter wants me to give CB a message."

"Give it to me and I'll pass it on."

"Uh, he said I was to give it directly to CB."

"Tough."

Something more complex, perhaps . . .

"There's been some of the usual trouble with Mason. Peter wants the boss to talk to him. I'm to hand Mason the phone the moment CB picks up."

That might work. When Mason was in one of his moods, CB was the court of last resort.

*   *   *

"Sorry, Tony. CB's in a meeting."

"But . . ."

"Look, Peter'll just have to handle whatever it is on his own. Call back in about an hour."

"But . . ."

"It's a money meeting."

Crap.

Rumor was the police had called during a money meeting when they'd arrested CB's third wife for torching his Caddie after a matinee viewing of *Waiting to Exhale.* CB dealt with it when the meeting was over.

"How long's this meeting supposed to last?"

"How should I know?" He could almost hear Ruth roll her eyes over the phone. "All morning definitely."

"I guess I'll call when we break for lunch, then."

"Why don't you do that."

"Yeah, why don't I." Switching off his phone, Tony stared out at the rain pocking the puddles. "Nothing'll happen before lunch."

He just wished those sounded less like famous last words.

Nothing happened before lunch.

The ghosts stayed out of sight. The baby stopped crying. Flies didn't gather, the walls didn't bleed, and there were no spectral voices telling them to get out. The traditional high body count never happened. Peter finished with the extras, completed the close-ups on the one bit player, and sent everybody home before they legally had to feed them. Although not feeding them was a relative term since craft services looked as though a swarm of locusts had passed through as they exited by way of the kitchen. Their souvenir hunter didn't snatch anything else, but neither was the broken garden claw returned to the conservatory.

"I'm sure I can find a broken claw somewhere to bring in," Keisha sighed, standing over the kitchen sink washing makeup off cocktail glasses. "I'm just glad those tea bag figurines are still there. I could replace them off eBay, but we both know I'd never see my thirteen dollars again."

"Thirteen bucks?" Tony was amazed. Or appalled. He wasn't sure which. "No shit?"

"Shit was up to $72.86 last time I checked. Sure, they call it coprolites, but we know what it is. Are you going to let the cat in?"

The cat was sitting outside the kitchen window languidly tearing at the screen with the claws of one front paw.

"No." He threw the denial as much at the cat as at Keisha. "It lives with the caretaker, so it can just go home. It's not like it's homeless and starving."

And speaking of starving—the caterers had set up lunch in the dining room.

Tony crossed the kitchen toward the butler's pantry, passed the back stairs, glanced up and thought he saw a black tail disappear around the second-floor landing heading for the third floor. He turned back toward the window. The cat was gone. *Next time don't look up the stairs,* he told himself heading through the butler's pantry. *If you don't want to know, don't look.*

He'd barely settled down with a plate of ginger sesame chicken, noodles, and a Caesar salad when he felt a cold hand close over his shoulder.

"Geez, you're a little jumpy."

Considering he'd just dumped his lunch, not really much he could say to that.

"Listen, finish up quick . . ." Adam paused and grinned as Tony scooped another handful of chicken and lettuce off his lap. ". . . and head back to the studio. CB wants you to pick up the two kids playing the ghosts and bring them here." The 1AD cut off Tony's nascent protest. "You did drive today, didn't you?"

"Yeah, but . . ."

"So that look's just because you've got ginger sauce seeping into your crotch?"

"No . . . well, yeah." Setting his plate back on the table, Tony applied a napkin to the warm, wet, fabric and prayed that warm, wet, and pressure wouldn't be enough to evoke a physical reaction. *Oh, yeah, because that sort of thing never causes wood.* He looked up in time to see Lee glance away and realized the actor had seen him spill his food. Tony's brain immediately threw discretion to the wind and added Lee Nicholas to warm, wet, and pressure. "Someone spoke to CB?"

"Peter called him about ten minutes ago." If Adam noticed the strain in Tony's voice, he ignored it. "Why?"

"No reason." It was just going to make getting through Ruth to the boss a lot harder. Hang on; he was going to the studio. Problem solved. While CB had what could charitably be referred to as a slammed door policy, it was always easier to speak to him in person. Where *easier* was generously defined as *taking your life in your hands.*

"Finish eating first."

"Right. Thanks." Might as well since standing up wasn't currently an option.

"CB's not here right now."

"And the kids I'm supposed to pick up?"

Amy glanced around the crowded production office as though the pair of child actors might be hiding in and among the gray laminate desks or the stacks of office supplies. "No sign of them."

"Great. Why doesn't Wanda drive them over when they get here?"

"Because the collate function on the photocopier's broken again and Wanda's helping Ruth with some remedial stapling in the kitchen."

Tony half turned following Amy's gesture and realized that the background thudding was not in fact the sound of a hammer falling but instead the distinctive slam-crunch of a staple forced through one too many sheets of paper. If he'd been paying more attention, the intermittent profanity would have given it away. "So I'm supposed to just hang around here," he sighed. Caught sight of Amy's expression. "No offense."

"Taken anyway." Artificially dark brows drew in as she scowled up at him. "I've half a mind not to tell you what I've discovered."

"If it's about Brenda and Lee; Lee already confirmed it."

"No. Knew it. You should see the graffiti in the women's can. What is it about wardrobe assistants anyway? Didn't Mason boing the last one?"

"Yeah. And *boing?*"

She snorted. "Perfectly valid euphemism. The house is haunted."

It took him a moment to separate the sentences.

"Caulfield House?"

"Yes."

"Is haunted?"

"Yes!" Eyes gleaming under magenta bangs, she all but bounced in place. "Isn't that totally cool?"

The boy-who-was-younger was in a loose white shirt. Well, white except for the splashes of what had to be blood—had to be because a huge triangular cut in the right side of his neck looked as though it just missed decapitating him. The girl-who'd-been-talking-to-Lee was wearing a summer dress, one strap torn free, the whole fitted bodice as well as her bare shoulders stained a deep crimson. She was also short the top left quarter of her head—her face missing along the nose and out one cheekbone, her left eye completely gone.

"Not really, no."

She snorted. "You know what your problem is? You have no imagination! No connection to a world beyond the day-to-day." This time she did bounce. "These are real ghosts, Tony!"

About to argue that there were no such things as real ghosts, Tony suddenly realized that this conversation had nothing to do with him. That he didn't have to be careful about being involved with the weird lest someone trace that weirdness back to Henry, who was helpless and stakeable during the day. Old habits died hard. And weird was Amy's middle name. "How do you know Caulfield House is haunted, then?" He propped one thigh on the corner of Amy's desk.

"Duh, how do you think? I did a Web search. There's been sightings by hikers. Well, sighting," she amended reluctantly. "A young man dressed in white standing in one of the second-floor windows."

And there was that blood-running-cold feeling again. "The bathroom window?"

Heavily kohled eyes widened. "How did you know?"

"Lucky guess. Most movies, the bathroom's haunted," he continued when Amy fixed him with a suspicious glare. "You know, the whole body-in-the-bathtub thing."

"Well, these bodies aren't in the bathtub," she snapped. "Back in 1957, September twenty-sixth to be exact, Stephen and Cassandra Mills' father freaked and attacked them with an ax. They died in the second-floor bathroom. Then he killed himself!"

"How?"

Mollified by his interest, she leaned closer. "With the same ax." She mimed embedding an ax into her own forehead.

So it was entirely possible there was a third ghost. Or a fourth . . .

"Was there a baby, too?"

"You mean . . . ?" More mimed chopping. When he nodded, she sat back and shrugged. "It didn't mention a baby on the Web site. Why?"

"No reason."

"Yeah, right. Like I tell you about a double murder/suicide and you ask about a baby for no reason. Spill."

"I don't . . ."

Leaning forward again, she dropped her voice below eavesdropping levels. "Spill or I tell everyone in the office what you told me about you and Zev on Wreck Beach."

He glanced over his shoulder at the door leading to post production, half expecting the music director to walk through on cue. When he didn't, Tony locked eyes with Amy and matched her volume. "You wouldn't do that because you wouldn't want to upset Zev."

"Hey, as I recall our Zev comes off pretty good in this story. You're the one who stars as the hormonally challenged geek."

Vowing, not for the first time, never to go drinking with Amy again, Tony sighed. Unfortunately, hormonally challenged geek was a fairly accurate description and he didn't doubt for a moment that Amy would follow through on the threat. "All right, you win. I was standing at the top of the main stairs and I thought I heard a baby cry."

"Too cool."

"Not really."

"Really." Throwing her weight back in her chair, she steepled black-and-magenta-tipped fingers together and beamed. The beaming was freaking Tony out just a bit. Amy wasn't usually the beaming type. Scowling, frowning, glowering, yes. Beaming, no. "It's possible that the baby is Cassandra, that she isn't able to manifest the way Stephen does and this throwback to her infancy is all she can manage."

"What the hell are you talking about?"

"Ectoplasmic manifestations. Ghosts, you moron!"

She took a long, almost triumphant swallow from her coffee mug and exchanged it for the receiver as the phone rang. "CB Productions. What? Hang on a sec." Swiveling her chair around, she bellowed toward the closed bull pen door: "Billy, it's your mother. Something about water getting into your comic collection!" There was a faint scream from one of the writers. Amy listened for a few seconds, then hung up the phone. "Apparently, his room in the basement flooded. Anyway, the ghosts . . . Stephen was a year younger, so he'll be stronger. You get points for hearing the baby—provided you heard what you thought you heard—but I suppose it's too much to ask if you've seen the young man in white?"

"You suppose right." Which, technically, wasn't even a lie. "*I* don't suppose you'd be willing to do a little more research on the house? You know, just in case."

"In case of what? The kind of 'oh, no, ghosts are dangerous' crap that shows up in bad scripts? Ghosts are unhappy spirits caught between this life and the next. They can't hurt you, you big wuss."

Someone had scooped a finger of wet paint off the wall of the second-floor bathroom and applied it to Lee's ass. Granted, no one had gotten hurt, but that did prove they could manifest physically. And physical manifestation wasn't good.

"I mean, it's not like they're poltergeists," Amy continued. "They're not throwing things or damaging anything or you'd know about them by now. They're lost and confused and probably lonely. They might not even know they're dead."

They knew. Their reaction to him seeing past the glamour had proved that.

"We're shooting in the second-floor bathroom this afternoon."

"So?" Amy snorted. "It's not like they'll show up on film, and I very much doubt that anyone who works here is sensitive enough to . . . CB Productions, can I help you?"

If they didn't show up on film and he was the only one who could see them . . . No wait, Lee had seen them. Except, Lee hadn't seen them as they were. Did that matter? No. None of this mattered. Bottom line; haunted houses were not a good thing, and he was only a PA; he had to talk to the . . .

"Daddy! Ashley shoved me!"

For the second time that day, Tony felt his blood run cold. He matched Amy's terrified gaze with one of his own. She hung up the phone, and together they turned toward the outside door.

"I did not, you little liar!"

"Did! You just want to get to Mason!"

"He's not even here, Cheese!"

"Zitface!"

"Girls, try to remember this is a place of business."

"And Zitface wants to do business with Mason!" Making kissing noises, a girl of about eight backed into the office both hands raised to ward off the attack of a slightly older girl.

Following them was Chester Bane. The six-foot-four, ex-offensive tackle, who ran every aspect of CB Productions with an iron fist and a bellicose nature to back it up, looked a little desperate. Tony didn't blame him. Ashley and Brianna's mother, CB's second wife, had convinced the girls that Daddy owed them big time for the divorce and they, in turn, had convinced CB. As a result, the man who had once made an opposing quarterback wet himself in fear could deny his daughters nothing. On the rare days they came to the studio, production went right down the toilet. Once or twice other, less easily recovered things went down the toilet as well.

They must be here because we're on location.

Wait a minute.

He was supposed to be picking up the two kids playing the ghosts.

God, no.

As Ashley chased a screaming Brianna through the door leading to the dressing rooms, CB lifted his massive head and met Tony's eyes. "You're driving them to the house, are you? Good."

So much for the power of prayer. "Uh, Boss . . ."

"I promised them they could be on the show. They're thrilled about it." His expression lightened slightly. "Unfortunately, I have paperwork to catch up on." The sound of distant crashes propelled him toward his office. "You'll be the supervising adult of record. Amy has the paperwork. See that they have a good time."

"Boss, I have to talk to you! About the house!"

CB paused in the doorway and considered him for a long moment while Tony tried to make the words' metaphysical emergency appear somewhere in his expression. Finally, as the office lights flickered and faint shrieks of girlish laughter lifted the hair on the back of Tony's neck, he sighed, "Keep it short," before disappearing into his office.

Amy snagged Tony's arm as he moved to follow. "You're not going to tell him about the ghosts, are you? He'll think you're nuts and you'll still have to drive the girls to the set!"

He pulled his arm free. Ghosts on Web sites were one thing. Ghosts in the drawing room talking to the actors were something else again. Hopefully. "You just don't want the terror twins to stay here."

"Well, duh!" They winced in tandem at the distinctive sound of a clothes rack hitting the floor. "I should never have told you about the ghosts."

It wouldn't have mattered, but Amy had no way of knowing that. Although given what was at stake, even if he hadn't seen Stephen and Cassandra large as life and twice as dead, he'd have used Amy's information and tried to convince CB they were real.

CB's office matched him in size and, like him, was functional rather than ornate. The single fish in the saltwater tank glared out at Tony as he passed. The fish had been a recent present from CB's lawyer and the day it was put into the tank it ate the three smaller fish still struggling to live in the murky water—an omen of biblical proportions as far as Tony was concerned. He paused about a meter from the desk, took a deep breath, and decided to get right to the point.

"Caulfield House is haunted."

"So Amy informed me first thing this morning. You're wasting my time, Mr. Foster."

"Yeah, Amy told me, too, but she didn't need to. I saw them—the ghosts."

"You saw them?" When Tony nodded, CB laid both massive hands on his desk and leaned forward. "Is this because of . . . what you could be?"

"The wizard thing? No. Maybe. I don't know." On second thought. "Probably. Point is," he added hurriedly as CB's eyes began to narrow, "I saw them. Stephen and Cassandra, murdered back in '57, standing in the drawing room talking to Lee."

"Mr. Nicholas saw them as well?"

"Yeah, but he didn't know they were dead."

"How did you . . . ?"

"Bits of them were missing."

"And Mr. Nicholas didn't notice this?"

"He wasn't seeing them the way I was. And I saw Stephen standing in the second-floor bathroom window."

"*In* the window?"

"Well, you know, behind the window. I saw him from the front lawn."

"So the house *is* haunted?"

"Yes."

"Well. Thank you for keeping me in the loop, Mr. Foster." He glanced down at the Rolex surrounding one huge wrist. "I'd like both scenes the girls are in shot this afternoon, so you'd best get moving. You may tell Peter I won't be available to take his calls."

Given that Peter had been in a good mood when Tony'd left the shoot, Peter didn't know about the girls. He'd be calling, that was a certainty. And beside the point. "Boss, I don't think you understand. Haunted houses are dangerous."

"In what way?"

He was kidding, right? "In the dead-people-walking-around way! People die in them."

"No, people *have* died in them. Not the same thing. Have you any reason for your fear or are you basing your theory on bad movies and the world according to Stephen King? Have these ghosts done anything that might be considered threatening?"

"They put paint on Lee's tux."

"Annoying, Mr. Foster, not threatening. Anything else?"

"Ghosts stay around for a reason. Usually because they're pissed off about something."

"Like being murdered?"

"Yeah, like being murdered. And they want vengeance."

"So they put paint on Mr. Nicholas' tux?"

"Yes! No. That wasn't vengeance, that was . . . I don't know what that was, but the point is we can't keep shooting in a haunted house."

"Because something *might* happen?"

"Yes."

"You might get hit every time you cross the street. Do you spend the rest of your life standing on the sidewalk?"

"Well, no, but . . ."

"I've paid for the use of this house until the end of the week. If you have nothing substantial to base your fears on . . ." CB waited pointedly until Tony shook his head. ". . . I will not disrupt my shooting schedule because you have a bad feeling and dead people are hanging about the set."

Was the man listening to himself? "Having dead people hanging about the set isn't normal!"

"Normal?" His lip curled. "Being beaten in the ratings by half a dozen so-called real people eating earthworms isn't normal, Mr. Foster. And dead people have got to be less trouble than one of Mason's ridiculous fan clubs."

Tony had to admit that was valid. One last card to play. "Your daughters . . ."

"Are looking forward to this and I will not disappoint them. They've spoken of nothing else for the last ten days."

"But . . ."

"I will *not* disappoint them. Do I make myself clear?"

"Crystal." He'd rather risk his daughters' lives than their wrath. Or at least he'd rather risk his daughters being stroked with paint than their wrath and Tony had to admit he could understand where the boss was coming from with that. Maybe he had overreacted.

Once you turn to the weird side, forever will it dominate your destiny.

So the house is haunted. If I'm the only one who knows, does it matter?

"Is there anything else, Mr. Foster?"

Apparently not. "No, sir. I'll just get the girls."

The girls were standing by the front door, eyes wide and locked on Amy. Who was on the phone. Nothing unusual about that.

"Why don't you two wait for me by my car; I'll be right out."

They nodded and ran.

"What did you do to them?" he demanded as Amy hung up. "And can you teach it to me?"

"I merely looked at them like this . . ."

"That's pretty damned scary on its own."

". . . and told them if they didn't get their grubby hands off my phone I'd put a spell on them so that they'd wet the bed at every sleepover they went on for the rest of their lives."

Checking for eavesdroppers, Tony leaned closer. "Can you really do that?"

Amy sighed. "I'm not surprised Zev dumped you. You are such a geek sometimes."

Right. Of course she couldn't. He couldn't and he was the wizard. In training. In a not-very-enthusiastic-about-the-whole-thing kind of way. Although if it meant easier handling of CB's daughters, it might not hurt to check the more advanced lessons on the laptop.

"Tony?"

"Sorry. Ghosts, girls, I'm just a little freaked. Can you call Peter and give him a heads up?"

"Oh. My. God. He doesn't know?"

Before Tony could answer, a familiar horn sounded in the parking lot. And kept sounding. Throwing a terse, "He doesn't know!" over his shoulder, Tony started to run. How the hell were they hitting the horn? His car had been locked.

⤳ FOUR

With the preteen flavor of the month pounding out of his speakers, and a vaguely familiar blue sedan in his parking spot, Tony pulled in at the end of the line of cars and shut off the engine. "All right, we're walking from here."

Ashley, who'd grabbed the front seat by ignoring screams of wrath and shoving her younger and smaller sister into the back, opened her door, stared down at the ground, and closed her door again. "It's muddy."

"Yeah, so?" Hands braced on either side of the doorframe, Tony leaned back into the car, reminding himself that these were his boss' daughters and the level of profanity had to stay low. Given the delay at the office and an unavoidable side trip for ice cream on the way back to the location—unavoidable if he'd wanted to retain even minimal hearing—they were running embarrassingly late. "It's stopped raining."

"You can't make me walk in the mud. I'll tell my dad. Drive me right to the house."

"I can't."

"Ashes is afraid she'll get all dirty and then Mason'll see she's really a pig," Brianna scoffed from the back. "Oink, oink, oink, oink, oink."

"Drop dead, Cheese!"

"Make me, Zitface!"

"Look, walk in the mud, then blame me when you get dirty," Tony broke in before the insults could escalate. Again. "Mason doesn't much like me anyway, and it'll give you two something to talk about."

Ashley stared at him for a long moment, brown eyes narrowed. "Fine."

"Fine," Brianna echoed mockingly.

With the dignity of eleven years, Ashley ignored her, scooped up her backpack, and got out of the car.

As Tony locked up, Brianna bounded down the road to the path.

"Are you just going to let her do that?" Ashley demanded. "She could get lost!"

"The ruts to the house are a foot deep. I doubt it."

"You have a stupid car." He shortened his stride as she fell into step beside him. "My mom has a better car. My mom's new boyfriend has three better cars. Your car looks like something puked on it."

"Something did." When she turned a disbelieving face toward him, he added, "Old drunk guy outside my building last night. Most of it washed off in the rain."

"Eww! That is like totally the grossest thing I've ever heard."

Tony felt kind of smug about that until he remembered he wasn't twelve. "Hey, I hate to ask, but why do you call your sister Cheese?"

"Duh. Brianna. Bri. Cheese." She shot him a disapproving glare that made her look disconcertingly like her father. "I thought gay guys knew all about cheese."

"I must've missed that part in the manual."

"You got a manual?"

A shriek from Brianna kept him from having to answer. *Memo to self: facetious comments bad idea.* He jogged ahead to find the younger girl balanced on one foot, her other foot bare, the sandal nowhere to be seen.

"The stupid mud ate my shoe!" she announced, grabbing a handful of his T-shirt. "You've got to carry me."

He grabbed her backpack before it could hit the ground and settled it back onto her shoulder. "Walk barefoot."

"Mom says you catch stuff when you walk barefoot."

"Yeah, on sidewalks. Not here. This is a park."

"It's a driveway!" For an eight-year-old, she excelled at implying *you moron* with tone of voice.

"We don't have time for this!" Unfortunately, Amy's expression didn't seem to work when it wasn't on Amy's face. "Fine. I'll carry you." If CB wanted the girls to finish up in one afternoon—and given his personal feelings on the matter, Tony was willing to bet that everyone else involved wanted the same thing—they had to haul ass. He moved around in front of her and squatted slightly. "Climb on my back."

For a skinny kid, she wasn't light. He hooked his hands under her bare knees and straightened.

"You better find my sandal. My dad will fire you if you lose my sandal."

"No, he won't."

"Wanna bet?"

Not really. "Ashley, could you . . ."

"Bite me. I'm so not digging in mud for . . . oh, here it is." To his surprise, she shoved one finger under the strap and dragged it out of the thick, black dirt. "You owe me. You owe me big."

"Fine. I owe you." Hiding a shudder at the thought of what she might demand to even the odds, he jerked his head toward the house. "Now can we walk?"

With Brianna bouncing on his kidneys and Ashley keeping up a running commentary of his shortcomings, the lane into the house seemed a lot longer than it had at 7:30. As they finally drew even with the last of the trucks, two familiar figures stepped out into their path.

"Well, well, Mr. Foster." RCMP Constable Jack Elson smiled and waved a set of sides in a sarcastic salute. "Small world, isn't it?"

Elson and his partner, RCMP Special Constable Geetha Danvers, had been the investigating officers during the series of suspicious deaths that had occurred at CB Productions back in the spring. Although natural causes with a heavy subtext of unlucky coincidence made up the official conclusion, Jack Elson had been convinced there was something else going on and he'd been determined to get to the bottom of things. Unfortunately, since the something else had involved homicidal shadows from another reality, he'd been destined to disappointment.

Because Tony had been instrumental in defeating the Shadowlord, he'd been at the center of the RCMP's investigation. With no one to blame for the nagging sense of justice not quite done, Constable Elson had made his presence felt at CB Productions whenever time allowed—with Tony at the top of his shit list closely followed by CB himself, and then the rest of his employees in no particular order.

Constable Danvers, who'd been considerably more sanguine about the case from the beginning, accompanied her partner to the studio wearing an expression that clearly said, "I'm only indulging you in this because hanging around a television show is kind of cool."

"So we saw the cars out on the road and wandered down to see if the paperwork was in order." During his too jovial explanation, Elson didn't do anything as obvious as block Tony's path but he stood in such a way that it would be difficult to get around him. Especially carrying an eight-year-old. Tony waited silently. First rule of dealing with a suspicious cop—give them nothing new to work with. "And who are these young ladies?"

Second rule—answer questions promptly and politely. And the corollary—lie if necessary. "They're the boss' daughters."

"Visiting the set?" Danvers asked, looking honestly interested.

"We're not visiting," Ashley informed her disdainfully. "We're ghosts."

"Really?" Elson smiled down at Tony in a way that made him think of handcuffs. And not in a fun way either. "You wouldn't be contravening child labor laws would you?"

Before Tony could answer, Brianna lifted her chin out of the indentation she'd dug in his right shoulder, pointed a skinny arm toward Burnaby's finest, and declared, "I can see a booger in your nose."

"Why don't you two go find Peter?" Tony suggested, easing Brianna to the ground.

Shrieking "Peter! Peter! Peter!" she shoved her foot into her muddy sandal and raced after her sister who'd gotten a three Peter head start.

As the director's name died down in the distance, Tony had a strong suspicion it was a suggestion that would come back to haunt him. And speaking of haunting . . .

The police had access to information the general public did not. Information—finding it, having it, passing it along in the way that would do him the most good—had always been Tony's preferred coin. Given that he'd survived everything an increasingly skewed world had thrown at him . . .

"Brianna! No!" Tina's distant protest had a hint of homicide in it.

. . . so far, maybe it wouldn't hurt to do a bit of digging now.

"Great house, eh?" He fixed both officers with his best *"fine, you want to stand there, then I'm going to talk"* expression. "I guess you guys are on top of that whole double murder suicide thing."

"In the house? This house?"

He let himself look smug as he repeated what Amy had told him.

Constable Elson rolled his eyes. "A little before our time."

Memory took him to the top of the stairs and a baby crying. "So nothing more recent?" He snapped back to himself in time to see them both staring.

Constable Danvers raised a questioning brow. "Recent?"

"Maybe he's been hearing things." When Tony scowled, Elson broke out laughing. "Maybe he thinks it's haunted." Waving his hands in the accepted gesture for *ooooooo, spooky*, he headed for the road. "Come on, Dee. I'm so scared. Let's get out of here in case Raymond what's-his-fang has called up more of his dark brethren."

Rolling her eyes not entirely unsympathetically in Tony's direction, Danvers stepped onto the grass at the edge of the drive and followed her partner.

Although he would rather have had an answer to his question, Tony had to admit that giving Constable Elson an exit line he couldn't resist using worked, too. "Probably has all four seasons of *Due South* on DVD," he muttered as he rounded the trailer and nearly slammed into Brenda. She looked terrified.

And it begins . . .

"Ashley and Brianna?" Eyes wide, she grabbed a handful of his T-shirt. "Please tell me the ghosts aren't being played by Ashley and Brianna?"

Okay, not what he'd expected but valid terror nevertheless. "Wish I could."

"Have you ever tried to dress those two? I'd rather put pantyhose on a monkey!"

"And thank you for that image."

"Tony, this is serious. Does Peter know?"

They winced in unison at the crash from inside. "Well, Amy was going to call him." A second, louder crash. "He does now."

"She's staring at me again."

"I think the word you're looking for isn't again, it's still," Lee pointed out, shifting to the right so that Ashley could have a clearer line of sight. "The only time she's stopped staring at you since she arrived was when she was in wardrobe."

Mason shuffled left, putting his costar's tuxedo-clad shoulders between him and the girl. "She's starting to creep me out. I mean, I know what to do when older girls stare at me like that, but she's eleven!"

"So ignore her."

"Easy to say."

Ashley, wearing her turn-of-the-century costume, sat in Peter's chair, stroking the caretaker's cat—allowed back on the set when the girls had screamed down the possibility of its exclusion—her eyes locked on Mason, her bare feet swinging in an inexplicably ominous rhythm. When he moved, she moved. Or she moved whatever currently blocked her line of sight.

In the interest of not having his crew ordered around and his schedule completely disrupted, Peter had told Mason to remain visible.

"Why can't I just lock myself in my dressing room?" Mason had demanded.

"Do you seriously think that would stop her?" Peter'd asked him. "You can suit yourself, but if I were you, I'd stay out where there are witnesses."

In all the time he'd been working on *Darkest Night*, Tony had never seen Mason at a loss for words. Even during an incident with the wardrobe assistant, he'd managed a fairly articulate, *"Get the hell out and tell Peter I'll be there in twenty minutes."* This time, however, he'd opened his mouth, closed it again, and latched on to Lee like the other actor was his new best friend.

Lee clearly found the whole thing amusing.

"Brianna!"

Everyone, cast and crew, turned toward the door as Brenda ran into the foyer.

Sliding to a stop just over the threshold, she swept a wild gaze over the assembled men and women. "Have you seen Brianna?"

Peter paled. "Don't tell me you've lost her!"

Brenda waved the apron she held like a calico flag of surrender. "I only took my eyes off her for a second! When I turned around, she was gone! I thought I saw her running toward the house!"

"Tony!"

Tony felt his heart skip a beat as the director and everyone else turned to stare at him. Had the house claimed its first victim? *At least I warned CB. He can't blame me for this.* Right. Just like no one blamed Bennifer when *Gigli* tanked.

"You brought them," Peter continued grimly. "You find her."

He brought them? Like he had a choice?

"I think we should divide up into search parties," Ashley announced before Tony managed to think of something to say. She stood, crossed to Mason's side, and took hold of his sleeve. "Groups of two, I think. I'll go with Mason."

"No." Mason managed half a step back before he realized Ashley was moving right along with him. "You heard Peter, Tony brought them! Brought you. He's responsible. Adult guardian of record, isn't he? Let Tony do his job. Let Tony find her."

"Tony's a dork," Ashley scoffed.

Tony caught the words, "Am not!" behind his teeth. *Because that would be mature.* "I wouldn't know where to start," he pointed out in what he thought was a fairly calm voice given the circumstances.

From the back of the house came the unmistakable scream of an angry cat.

"Start in the kitchen," Peter suggested dryly.

"I didn't mean to hurt it," Brianna protested, filling her mouth with cheese puffs and wiping her hand on her dress. "It got right in my way and I stepped on its stupid tail! Do you think it hates me now?"

Picking up the bowl of cheese puffs to use as a lure, Tony backed away from the craft services table. "I doubt it. Cats don't have very long memories." Considering how fast it had to have been motoring to get from the front hall to the kitchen, the odds of impact between cat and kid had to have been astronomical. Although considering this particular kid . . . As she reached for the bowl, he took another two steps. And another.

"I just wanted to look behind the door!"

"What door?" Almost out of the kitchen . . .

"That door!"

His hand throbbed. "That's just the basement," he said, trying his best to make it sound like the most boring place on Earth. "And besides, the door's locked. Your father doesn't want us to go down there."

She snorted, spraying bits of damp cheese puff and turned toward the forbidden. "My father lets me go anywhere I want."

Oh, yeah. That went well. In another minute she'd be knee-deep in floodwater and old wiring.

"Tony? Have you fffffffffst her?"

Depended. Define fffffffffst. If it meant *wanted to strangle,* then that would be a big "God, yes."

"That was Adam," he said as Brianna stared up at him through narrowed eyes. "He says since you've been gone so long, Ashley says she'll be the only ghost."

"Oh, no, she won't!"

Wow. If he'd thought the cat could motor . . . Ashley dealt with the resulting tantrum by knocking her sister down and sitting on her until she cried uncle. Tony suspected he wasn't the only jealous adult in the room. Unfortunately, when it was over, the girls backed him into a corner while everyone else was suddenly busy setting up the shot. Since when did it take seven people to check a light meter?

"I *never* said I wanted to be the only ghost!"

"You told me she said that!"

"I'm *so* telling my father on you!"

"Ashley . . ." Struck by inspiration, Tony bent forward and lowered his voice. ". . . Mason's watching. He'll think you're acting like a little girl."

Ashley's eyes widened, her mouth snapped shut, and gathering her dignity around her, she stalked back to Peter's chair.

Tony found Brianna staring up at him with reluctant admiration. "You're such a liar," she said. "Gimme the cheese puffs."

He hadn't realized he was still holding the bowl. Fortunately, the apron covered the accumulated orange stains on the dress.

"Why cheese puffs?" Brenda asked as Peter placed the girls where he needed them. "Why do they even have cheese puffs anyway?"

"In general?"

"No, specifically. Specifically here. Specifically where those two could get at them. Cheese puffs do not make historic stains!"

Tony patted her shoulder in a comforting way. "It's not like we're usually that big on historical accuracy."

Spinning out from under his hand, she glared at him. "I do my best!"

"I just meant it's not that important because the stains can be deleted in post."

"That's not what you said."

"I know."

"They wouldn't wear the shoes and stockings."

"Barefoot works."

"You think?"

"Sure." Why not. It was summer and it wasn't like they had an option. Suddenly certain he was being watched, Tony turned in time to see Lee look away. *Figures. Not watching me. Watching Brenda.*

"My lipstick's all gone!" Had there been a second balcony, Ashley's voice would have carried beyond it. She'd clearly inherited her father's vocal abilities. "I can't act without new lipstick!"

"Tony!"

Ears ringing, he headed out to the trailer to retrieve Everett.

Thing was, when the girls actually settled down to work, they weren't bad.

"Look up at Mason and Lee on the stairs and smile. A little less teeth, please Brianna. Good girl. Now look sad. Good, hold it. Try not to move your bodies, just change your expressions. Can you give me angry? Good work. Now thoughtful. Yes . . . up through the lashes is good, Ashley. Okay, girls, smile again . . ."

The crew held its collective breath as Peter banked as many expressions as possible, shooting cover shots and then close-ups. Tony wiped sweating palms on his jeans and scanned the entrance hall for ghosts. Were he an actual ghost and a television show was in his haunted house filming *fake* ghosts, he'd be showing up in the shot. He'd fade in slowly, so slowly, so subtly that he'd be nearly opaque by the time they noticed him, and then when they did, at the inevitable screams greeting his gruesome appearance, he'd disappear. Poof. A lot more effective than just popping in to say boo.

"Why can't I just appear behind the kids, say boo, and then disappear?"

Cassie rolled her remaining eye at her brother. "Because we're not supposed to be seen."

"But we've been seen."

"Not on purpose."

"Excuse me? Dressing up and pretending to be alive wasn't being seen on purpose?"

"That was different; we were being seen as people." One finger picking at a bit of frayed wallpaper, she peered down the stairs at the television crew. "Something feels . . ."

"Wrong. So you said already." Stephen wrapped his arms around her waist and rested his head on her shoulder.

She reached up and absently set it back in place on his neck. "Wrong. Familiar. I wish Graham was in the house, I need to talk to someone."

"I'm someone."

"I know, love." But her gaze locked on the young man who'd known what they were.

Brianna screamed and dropped to the floor when the light blew, but Ashley stood her ground as bits of hot glass rained down from above, glaring at the smoking piece of equipment like she couldn't believe it was attempting to upstage her.

"Cut!" Peter's voice rose above the chaos. "Is anyone hurt?"

No one was.

"Good. That's all right, then; no one's hurt and I've got what I need down here." He glanced around as though looking for a union steward or a representative from the government's workplace safety committee, who might suggest he have a larger reaction. When neither presented themselves, the set of his shoulders visibly relaxed. "If you're not needed in the bathroom, you can help clean this mess while the rest of us head to the second floor. Everett, Brenda, stay close. Tony, until Adam lets you know we're ready for the girls, keep an eye on them."

An eye? Oh, yeah, like that would be enough. Tony made his way over cables and through the sudden throng of arguing grips and electricians standing by the blown light to where CB's daughters were respectively drumming bare heels against the hardwood and staring at Mason. Before either of them could take off for parts unknown or declare they didn't want to go upstairs or announce they were telling their father about the light, he said, "You two are good."

"No shit?" Brianna asked from the floor.

He crossed his heart. "No shit."

"You don't have to sound so surprised about it," Ashley snorted, actually looking away from Mason long enough to roll her eyes in a disturbingly mature way at Tony. "Our mom is an actress, you know."

"I know." She'd been a minor but reoccurring character in CB's first moderately successful series *Ghost Town*.

"And she says our dad promised he'd make her a star and then ruined her career so she made sure that that bitch Lydia Turrent got caught doing dope and that flushed the show down the toilet."

Didn't know that, Tony thought as Ashley paused for breath.

"Did you like the way I fell?" A small foot drove into his calf with considerable force. "I'm going to always do *all* my own stunts." Brianna held out her hand and allowed him to haul her upright. "I'm not afraid of nothing. The light going bang—that didn't really scare me."

"You probably made it blow up," her sister snorted.

"Didn't. And I didn't do that neither," she added as a cable box slid off the lower shelf of the video village and bounced back down the stairs.

A passing electrician jerked to a stop, the transformer he was carrying nearly yanked out of his arms.

Brianna stepped off the dangling cable. "What?"

The second-floor bathroom had already been lit and a second camera was in place and ready to go. Although Peter hadn't been prepared for CB's children, he *had* been prepared for children. Given that CB had made it quite clear they were to be used only this one afternoon, it was imperative to work as quickly as possible while they were on the set. Considering how long it often took between shots, the half-hour break between the front hall and the bathroom was up to pit standards at any NASCAR track in North America.

As the camera feed was hooked up to the video village out in the hall, the director went over the scene with all four of his actors—Mason standing as far from Ashley as close quarters allowed. "All right, we're going to do the girls' taunting dance once with Mason and Lee in the shot and then the exact same thing with just the two of you pretending that Mason and Lee are in the shot. Then we're going to do it again from the top with each of you individually so we can get close-ups, then we'll do it again from the top with the blood." And then remembering the age of his actors, he added heartily, "But it's not real blood."

"Oh, please," Ashley drawled, "we know it's not real. We're not stupid. Well, I'm not stupid. The Cheese is a moron."

Head cocked to one side, a stubby braid sticking straight up into the air, Brianna ignored her.

Peter took a concerned step toward the younger girl. "Brianna?"

She snorted and frowned up at him. "There's a baby crying."

The silence that followed her announcement was so complete Tony could hear a car passing by on Deer Lake Road way out at the end of the lane. He could also hear a baby crying.

"I don't hear a baby." Peter glanced around at his crew, his gaze moving too fast to actually see any of them. "No one else hears a baby." Statement, not question. They didn't have time for babies.

"I hear a baby!" Her brows drew down into a familiar obstinate expression. In spite of a two-hundred-pound difference, she looked frighteningly like her father. "I'm going to find it!" Head down, she darted toward the door.

Fortunately, maneuvering around the camera and Mouse and Kate slowed her down. Tony caught up at the door as she circled around Mouse and under the camera assistant's outstretched arms and managed to keep her from getting out into the hall. "Why don't I find it for you? Where's the noise coming from?"

Her lower lip went out. "It's not noise; it's crying!"

"Fine. Where's the crying coming from?"

She stared up at him suspiciously. Tony could feel the rest of the crew holding their collective breath. Few things held up a shooting schedule like chasing an eight-year-old around a house the size of some third world countries. Finally, she raised one skinny arm and pointed toward the far end of the hall. "That way."

Yeah, that was where he heard it coming from, too.

"All right. You let Peter set the shot and check your levels. I'll go look and be back before the camera's rolling."

"Yeah, but you're a liar."

"Yeah, but you know I'm a liar, so why would I lie to you?"

He held her gaze as she worked that out—a trick Henry'd taught him.

"The dominant personality maintains eye contact—it's one of the easiest ways to differentiate the hunter from the hunted."

"You mean when you don't have that whole teeth, biting, feeding thing to fall back on?"

"I mean, I am not the only predator in the city."

"Uh, Earth to Henry; how the hell do you think I survived this lo . . . OW!"

After a long moment, Brianna nodded. "You check. Then you don't lie."

"Deal."

Reaching for the door handle, Tony realized that the door at the end of the hall had been divided in half—like the doors of fake farmhouse kitchens in margarine commercials. He could no longer hear the baby crying and since he couldn't hear it, he doubted that Brianna could. Given that she was safely back inside the huge bathroom being fussed over by both Brenda and Everett, he briefly considered lying about having checked.

Except that he'd more or less given her a promise and, staring at the door with the hair lifting off the back of his neck and a chill stroking icy fingers down his spine, he realized that this was neither the time nor place to break his word—although he didn't know *why* and that was definitely freaking him out.

The brass door handle was very cold.

With any luck, the room would be locked.

Nope. No luck today.

He expected a dramatic creak as he pushed it open, but the well-oiled hinges merely whispered something he didn't quite catch as he stepped over the threshold. The sky had grown overcast again, replacing the afternoon light with the soft drumming of rain against the windows. His right hand went back to the light switch, found it where it always was, and flicked the first little plastic tab up.

Nothing happened.

They weren't actually using this space, so no one had replaced the thirty-year-old bulbs.

Tony really wished he believed that.

The air was colder than the air in the rest of the house and, considering the rest of the house had been comfortably cool in spite of television lighting, that was saying something. He could smell . . . pork chops?

There was ambient light enough to see the wide border of primary colored racing cars just under the edge of the crown molding. Light enough to see the hammock strung across one corner and filled with stuffed animals so covered in dust they all appeared to be the same shade of gray. Light enough to see the crib. And the changing table. And that the safety grate had been removed from the fireplace in the far wall.

Light enough to see the baby burning on the hearth. The border suggested it was a boy, but things had gotten too crispy to be certain. Tony's stomach twisted and he'd have puked except there were close to a dozen adults, two kids, and a camera between him and the nearest toilet.

Besides, this was just a recording of something that had happened in the past. He wasn't watching *this* baby die and that helped. A little.

Man, you'd think I'd be used to this kind of shit by now.

He could hear it screaming again.

Or he could hear something screaming.

The room grew suddenly darker.

Tony stepped back and slammed the door. Realized it had separated and he'd only brought the bottom with him, realized the darkness had almost filled the room, spat out the necessary seven words in one long string of panicked syllables, and *reached*. The upper part of the door slammed shut.

The half-dozen people standing around the video village were watching him as he turned.

"What the hell was that?" Peter demanded, sticking his head out of the bathroom.

Wishing that the skin between his shoulder blades would just fucking stop creeping back and forth and up and down, Tony hurried away from the nursery. "Air pressure," he explained, hands out and away from his sides, fingers spread in the classic 'not my fault' gesture. "It slammed before I could stop it."

"If we'd been rolling . . ."

"We weren't," Tina broke in pointedly from behind the monitors, holding up her arm and tapping one finger on her watch.

Peter's eyes widened. "Right. Well, don't just stand there. Haul ass and tell Brianna you didn't see a baby." CB's "one afternoon only" trumped doors slamming, production assistants making lame excuses, and mysterious crying.

Lying in this house might be a bad idea, but—in this case—telling an eight-year-old the truth would be a worse one. Hurrying back to the bathroom, Tony really hoped that whatever weirdness was involved here would take that into account.

"He saw Karl."

"That's unlikely, Cass, no one's ever seen Karl. They just hear Karl. Even Graham hasn't seen Karl."

"*And* he wasn't touching the upper part of the door when he closed it."

Stephen stared at his sister and sighed deeply. "You've never missed that part of your brain before."

"What?"

He waved a hand toward the place the ax had hacked through her head. "The living need to touch things to move them; he's alive, therefore he had to have touched the door. Q.E.D. And where are you going?" he added, hurrying to catch up.

"I need to see what's happening in the bathroom," she told him without turning.

She was wafting, not walking, and that was never a good sign. Cassie was usually militant about them maintaining a semblance of physicality lest they forget how flesh worked—he hadn't seen her so distracted for years. Memories drifted around him. They had no form and less substance, but he didn't like the way they made him feel, so he hung on to what he knew for certain. "Graham told us to stay out of the bathroom while these people are using it."

"It's *our* room."

"Well, yeah, but Graham said . . ."

"Graham doesn't know what's going on in here."

"Of course not, he's just the caretaker, he couldn't possibly . . . Cass!" He sighed again, slipped through a bit of the camera operator, and followed her in under the lights.

"But I want Mason to stay!" Ashley's protest carried easily over the ambient noise of Mason and Lee pushing past various crew members to emerge out into the hall. "He's my motivation!"

"There isn't room." Peter's voice had reached the preternaturally calm stage that seemed to suggest an imminent nervous breakdown—its tonal range so limited it sounded as though it had been Botoxed. "Besides, he's just out in the hall, watching you on the monitors."

To Tony's surprise, Mason, who'd been heading to his dressing room, stopped, sighed, and returned. Since the words "team player" and Mason Reed had never appeared together previously, the crew and his costar stared at him in some confusion.

"If we don't finish today," he muttered, "they'll be back."

Eyes widened and several heads nodded sagely, reassured that Mason's motivations remained vested self-interest.

Lee clapped him on the shoulder and murmured, "Greater love. I'll go get you a coffee."

"She is *not* in love with me," Mason growled, looking a little panicked.

"It's a quote, big guy. I'll be back in a minute," he added to Adam as he turned. "Peter won't even know I'm gone."

The 1AD shrugged. "Just be back when he needs you."

"I need you . . ." Peter's direction drifted out into the hall. ". . . to dance around in that circle a few more times pretending that Mason and Lee are still . . . Ashley, don't turn on the water. Brianna! Don't touch . . ."

All things considered, the soft *phzt* was vaguely anticlimactic.

Standing behind Sorge's left shoulder where he'd have a good view of both monitors, the gaffer frowned. "Sounded like a halo lamp going. I'm starting to think the lines in this house are seriously fucked. We should bring in a second generator."

"And getting CB to agree?" Sorge snorted. *"Bon chance."*

Tony opened his mouth to say it wasn't the lines it was the house and then closed it again. His day was already crap; he didn't need to add the ridicule that would follow any explanation of ax-murdered extras or rotisserie babies. No, better just to stay quiet and right where he was, surrounded by people who wouldn't know a metaphysical phenomenon if it bit them on the ass. Almost literally in Tina's case although the specific piece of anatomy had been higher up.

"Malcolm! Adam!"

The gaffer and the 1AD headed for the bathroom.

"Everett!"

"It's starting to be like a fraternity prank in there," Tina snickered as the makeup artist forced his way through the crowd in the doorway using his case like a battering ram. "How many people can you fit in one bathroom?"

"Tony!"

Hopefully one more.

He squeezed past the camera—extra careful while squeezing past Mouse. Mouse had been shadow-held back in the spring and while under the influence had first locked lips and then worked him over with fists the size of small hams. Theoretically, Mouse—like the other shadow-held—remembered none of his time possessed, but once or twice Tony had noticed him staring and the possibility that some lingering memories remained had made him fanatical about giving the much larger man his space.

With any luck he remembered the beating and not the tonsil hockey; given Mouse's background the beating, at least, had been in character.

Fortunately, although Kate had also been shadow-held, their interaction during that time had been minimal. If she muttered something rude under her breath as he shuffled by her, it had nothing to do with the metaphysical and everything to do with Tony being one of the few people around who had less influence on the show than she did.

The bathroom was definitely crowded. The girls were sitting on the edge of the tub being powdered although they didn't seem to need it. Actually, given the number of bodies and amount of equipment, it was strangely cool.

The nursery had been cool.

Oh fucking great . . .

The girls, Everett, Peter, Adam, Malcolm, Mouse, Kate, one of the electricians—Tony wasn't sure of his name. Nothing and no one in the room who shouldn't be there. Then he glanced in the mirror and saw the two half-dressed, bloody teenagers flickering in and out of focus.

He didn't quite gasp when Adam grabbed his arm. "Tony, the battery in my radio's gone tits-up again. Go drop it in the charger and bring me a new one."

"Sure." Not a problem. Happy to get the hell off the second floor.

Clutching the battery, he pushed his way out into the hall and headed for the back stairs. The main stairs were just a little too close to the nursery. Of course, the back stairs were right across the hall from Mason's bathroom and the crying shadow crouched by the shower stall, but at this point, ghosts that merely rocked and cried were definitely the lesser of two or three or even four evils.

No. Don't even think evil. Don't give anything ideas.

He opened the stairwell door to be greeted by the same soft *er er er er* he'd heard earlier from the kitchen. From here, he could tell that it was actually coming from the third floor. *Oh, yeah, like I'm stupid enough to look up.*

An icy draft pushed him down the first few steps. The light started to dim. He moved a little faster. Missed his footing on the steep, uneven stairs. Started to fall. His feet sliding off every second or third step, his hands desperately grabbing for a guardrail that didn't exist, he plunged toward the kitchen, crashing against the bottom door which flew open. The impact slowed him a little but not enough for him to catch his balance and his out-of-control descent continued until he slammed into a warm and yielding barrier.

Unfortunately, yielding enough he took it with him to the floor.

Heart pounding, fighting to get enough air into his lungs, his body said *familiar* before his brain caught up. No mistaking the flesh sprawled beneath him. Man. Young man. Good shape. Then his brain reengaged. Young man in good shape wearing a tuxedo . . . he lifted his head off the snowy white expanse of dress shirt to see the bottom of Lee's chin. Then the rest of Lee's face as the actor lifted his head and shook it once as though to settle his brain back into place. The green eyes focused.

"Tony?"

"Yeah." One of his legs was down between the actor's thighs, their position a parody of intimacy. He was a little too shaken up to move, muscles doing a fairly accurate imitation of cooked spaghetti as the adrenaline left his sys-tem. No way Lee could know that, though, and he half expected the other man to heave him across the room. Didn't happen. *He's probably winded, too.* "You okay?"

"I think so." Lee shifted slightly and Tony thanked any gods who might be listening for that whole cooked spaghetti muscle thing. "You?"

Him what? A half frown up at him and he abruptly remembered. "Yeah. I'm good. Not *good* good," he added hurriedly in case Lee started thinking he was enjoying this too much. "Just not hurt good." He had a strong suspicion he was making less than no sense.

"What happened?"

"I fell. Down the stairs."

From this angle, Lee's smile was nearly blinding. A warm hand closed around Tony's bicep. "No shit."

"Am I interrupting?"

And there was the expected, albeit delayed, heave. Both men were on their feet fast enough to reassure any onlooker that neither had been damaged by the collision. Except that the only onlooker had arrived after the collision.

"Zev!" Tony ran a hand back through his hair, and flashed a smile he knew was too wide, too hearty, and too guilty at CB Productions' music director and his most recent ex. "I uh, fell down the stairs and Lee was there at the bottom and I slammed right into him. He was just . . . I mean, he cushioned my fall."

"So I saw." A white crescent flashed for an instant in the shadows of Zev's dark beard although his expression remained no more than neutrally con-cerned. "You guys all right?"

"Yeah. Lucky, eh?"

"Very. Nice catch, Lee."

"Sure." His face flushed—although that could have been from either sud-den change in position, going down or coming up—Lee picked two large yel-low Melmac mugs of coffee off the kitchen table. "You guys probably want to . . . uh, you know, talk and I've got to get one of these up to Mason."

Tony took a step toward him, hand outstretched, and stopped as the flush deepened. "You've got dust on the back of your tux."

"No problem. Brenda's dancing attendance on the girls. She can get it." He turned toward the stairs, paused, and visibly changed his mind. "Seems safer to use the other set."

As Lee left the kitchen, Tony spotted Adam's battery—flung out of his hand on impact—over by the sink. When he straightened, battery back in hand, he found Zev staring at him, dark brows almost to his hairline. "What?"

"You fell down the stairs?"

"Yeah . . ."

"And Lee just happened to be there to catch you?"

"Yeah."

"And having saved you, he sank to the floor with you cradled tenderly in his arms."

"It wasn't like that!"

Zev snickered. "Looked like that."

Tony rolled his eyes and pushed past the other man, heading for the butler's pantry and the battery chargers. On the bright side, of all the people who could have walked in on him and Lee in a vaguely compromising position, Zev was the least likely to blow it out of proportion. On the other hand, given their history, Zev was the most likely to tease him unmercifully about it, so he'd just nip that in the bud right now. "I hit him pretty hard, so it wasn't so much sinking to the floor as being slammed into the floor and he wasn't cradling me tenderly or any other way—bits of me were imbedded in his ribs."

"Looked like you were happy there."

Not much he could say to that.

"Looked like he was happy to have you there."

"You're delusional." Since he was there, he changed his own battery and tossed the rest of the fully charged ones into a box.

Hand shoved in the front pockets of his black jeans, Zev shrugged, the backpack slung over one shoulder riding up and down with the motion. "I'm just saying he looked like a man ready for a six-pack."

"What?"

"What's the difference between a straight man and a bi . . ."

Tony sighed and held up a hand. "Okay. I remember the joke. I should never have mentioned that whole crush thing."

"Since we were together at the time, it did seem a bit unnecessary." When Tony turned a worried face toward him, Zev grinned. "Because you know, I'm blind and stupid and would never have noticed on my own even if Amy hadn't discussed it at length."

"Bite me."

"Sorry. You gave that option up."

"You dumped me!"

"Oh, yeah. Nevertheless, biting remains off the agenda."

Back in the kitchen, Tony glanced up the back stairs and, much like Lee had, turned and headed for the main hall, Zev falling into step beside him. "So, unless you dropped by to taunt me with my relationship mistakes, why *are* you here?"

"Ambient noise."

"What?"

"I'm going to play some Tchaikovsky in the foyer and record it, then figure out how the dimensions of the space change the sound. I may be able to use the minor distortions when I score the episode."

"Tchaikovsky?"

"*Onegin.*"

"Who?"

"Ballet based on a novel by Pushkin."

"Hobbit?"

"Russian."

"CB's idea?"

"Your lack of confidence in my ability to make musical choices is why we're no longer together."

"I thought it was my lack of being Jewish?"

"Minor reason."

"Or my inability to understand what you see in Richard Dean Anderson."

"Much larger reason." Grinning, Zev slid the backpack off his shoulder and set it on the floor by the lighting rig in the entrance hall. "Don't you have production assisting to do?"

He did. Adam was still without a battery, although given the radio reception and the fact that most of the crew was standing about six feet away from him, it wasn't likely he could be feeling the loss. "You want to go for a beer after work?"

The music director glanced at his watch. "It's just past six. Technically, I'm after work so it depends on what time you finish up."

"CB said he'd be by to pick the girls up at eight."

Zev winced at the reminder of the episode's guest stars. "They're safely upstairs, right?"

A crash from the second floor answered before Tony could.

"Why are they eating?"

"What?"

"They're eating soup in cups. Why are they eating and not leaving? I want my room back. This is *our* space." Stephen watched his sister pacing, flickering even to his sight as she moved through people and equipment and he added, more to himself than to her, "You'll be fine once they're gone. You'll see."

"So, I just spoke to your father and he says he can't pick you up for a while, so you can stay and finish the scene if that's what you want to do. Or Tony can drive you back to the studio."

Ashley, her gaze locked on Mason, nodded.

"You want to stay?"

Brianna spread her arms and whirled up and down the hall, crashing into people and equipment. "I like being a ghost."

The red splatters were very bright against the hard gloss of the bathroom walls. Cassie touched one finger to the wall and then to the slightly darker splatter on the shoulder of one of the little girls. Faces, clothes, hair, both children were dripping with red. One of them kept licking it off her hand.

Red.

Some kind of syrup.

Red as . . .

She looked down at the crimson moisture on her fingertip. "Stephen, I remember. It's about the blood . . ."

ᔐ FIVE

Brenda had done more than remove the dust from Lee's tux; when Tony found them tucked behind an open door, she seemed to be taking a good shot at removing his fillings with her tongue. There was enough visible movement happening in his cheeks, he looked like he had a pair of gerbils making out in his mouth.

Back in the butler's pantry, Tony jammed dead batteries into the chargers with more force than was strictly necessary. Hey, Lee could play tonsil hockey with whoever he wanted. He was an adult, Brenda was an adult; they had history and so what if Lee had told him earlier that history had been a mistake—nothing like an accidental cuddle with another man to make a straight boy run off and prove his heterosexuality.

He just wished Lee hadn't been so stereotypical.

Oh, no! Gay cooties! Must wash them away with girl spit!

Fuck it.

"Man, what's that battery ever done to you?" Ink-stained fingers with black-and-magenta-tipped nails yanked the battery from his hand and slid it effortlessly into the space. "Aren't men supposed to be better at the whole insert tab A into slot B thing?" Amy demanded as Tony ignored her and moved on to the second charger. "I mean, it's a skill set that comes with the equipment, right? Unless you're having trouble with this because you're having man trouble and we're talking a classic case of displacement."

He glared at her over the final battery. "What the hell are you doing here?"

"Oh, my God, I'm right!" When he took a step toward her, she held up both hands and grinned. "Okay, okay, it's not like my inbox isn't already full of stories of erectile dysfunction."

Tony sighed, determined not to get involved in an argument he couldn't win. "I got you a spam filter."

"What'd be the fun in that? Anyway, I'm here with tomorrow's sides."

"Where's Wanda?"

"Who?"

"Office PA."

"I know who, I was being sarcastic. Bitch sold a movie-of-the-week script to an American network and quit this afternoon. She's moving to LA to become a rich-and-famous writer." Amy's snort carried the wisdom of six years in Canadian television. "Yeah, like that ever happens." She held up her hands again, this time so that Tony could note the black streaks across both palms. "Left me to deal with a printer jam in the photocopier and this crap doesn't wash off. I'd have asked the boss if he minded dropping the sides off when he picked up the girls," she added lowering her hands and looking around, "but I wanted to see the inside of the house. It doesn't look haunted."

Ethereal music drifted in from the front hall. "Sounds haunted."

"That's Zev. He's distorting Tchaikovsky."

"Kinky. So, how long have I got to look around?"

Tony glanced at his watch. "Not long. It's 8:40 now, and when I came downstairs at 8:30, they were almost finished. You go take a quick look; I'd better call CB and find out if he wants me to drive the girls back to the studio."

"Suck-up."

"Adult of record."

"Responsible suck-up."

Cell phone reception in the house still stank and the signal he'd managed to pick up earlier in the breezeway had disappeared. Given the crap radio reception, he didn't think he should move too far away from the building in case Adam needed him. *Maybe the front porch.* It was raining again, so he came back into the kitchen, closed the door behind him, and . . .

Was that three quarters of someone's head?

No.

A flash of bloodstained shirt sleeve?

He was imagining things.

That's my story and I'm sticking to it.

He grabbed a handful of marshmallow strawberries out of the bowl on the kitchen table as he passed. Karen had started to move most of the food back out to the craft services truck, but the marshmallows remained. He wasn't having any problems a hit of sugar couldn't cure.

*   *   *

"Why can't he see us? He saw us before."

"There's more happening now; we can't get enough energy to break through his denial."

"What denial?" Stephen snorted, waving his hand back and forth to no effect. "He already saw us twice, once in the drawing room and once in the bathroom."

"He saw us in mirrors!"

"Okay, but then he just saw us."

"After the mirrors." Cassie closed her fingers around their quarry's arm, but he merely shivered and continued walking. "We need a mirror!"

"There's one on the wall by the kitchen door."

"Stephen! He's walking away from the kitchen door!"

"Hey, no need to get frosted; I'm just trying to help."

"The glass doors in the butler's pantry; you can see yourself in them!" She sped past their quarry and grabbed the pull on the last cabinet by the dining room door. "Help me get this open! It won't do us any good if he doesn't actually look."

"It's not going to make any difference to us."

"Fine. It won't do *him* any good. Now get over here!"

The glass door on one of the upper cabinets flew open with enough force that the glass rattled as it slammed back on its hinges. Tony jumped, recovered, and instinctively reached out to close it. His brain came on-line about half a second behind his hand, but by then it was too late. He could see himself reflected in the glass and, standing behind him, he could see the dead teenagers as clearly as he had in the drawing room. Okay, *not* his imagination. It was suddenly very, very cold in the butler's pantry.

He tossed the last marshmallow strawberry into his mouth, chewed slowly, and sighed. "What?"

The girl—What had Lee called her? Cassie?—made a spinning motion with one finger.

"You want me to turn around?" They were standing behind him. If he turned around . . .

Her motion became a little more frantic.

If he turned around, he'd be able to see it coming. Whatever it was. Which wasn't particularly comforting.

What the hell.

And with any luck, he thought as he turned, *not literally hell.* After all, Lee had spoken to them earlier and nothing metaphysical had happened to him.

They were standing right where their reflections had suggested they would be. Large as life and twice as dead. Or dead twice anyway.

"So?" His voice sounded remarkably steady; given that his feelings about his current situation ranged between terror and barely suppressed annoyance, he was impressed. "Why'd I need to turn around?"

"Reflections have no voice."

"As a general rule—just FYI—neither do dead people."

Cassie rolled her eye, looking remarkably like Amy, considering she was missing a quarter of her face. "Look, I don't make the rules."

"Hey!" He raised a placating hand. "I hear you. You wouldn't believe . . ." A moment's pause. "Actually, *you* might."

"It doesn't matter. You've got to get out of here!"

"What?"

"You've got to get everyone out of the house by sunset!"

Sunset? It was 8:47. Sunset was at 8:53. All those years with Henry had made sunset a hard habit to break. Six minutes. *Oh, crap . . .*

The ghosts kept up as he sprinted through the dining room, fumbling for his radio.

"You believe us?" the boy demanded. "Just like that?"

"I've had some experience with sunsets and things going bump in the dark." And speaking of bump, his battery was dead. *And one more time, oh, crap . . .*

"I'd worry more about splat than bump."

"You're not helping, Stephen!"

"Can anyone else see you?" he asked as he skidded into the foyer.

Zev looked up from his mini disk recorder and frowned. "Pretty much everyone, why?"

Cassie shook her head. "No, just you."

"Great." And to Zev: "We've got to get out of here."

"Well, *I'm* almost done, but you can't just bail on the job."

"Hey, job's almost done." He grabbed the music director's arm and gave him a little shove toward the door. "Why don't I meet you outside?"

"Why don't you switch to decaf?" Zev suggested, twisting free. "It's raining, I'll wait here."

"That ballroom is incredible," Amy announced, emerging from the hall that led past the library and toward the back of the house. "It's bigger than my whole Goddamned apartment!"

"You shouldn't go into the ballroom," Stephen muttered. "There's too many of them in the ballroom."

"Too many what?" Tony demanded. Amy and Zev turned to stare at him. "Never mind. You guys get out of here, I'll get the others."

He'd gone up only half a dozen steps when the girls started down from the second floor dragging Everett behind them.

"We're going to get a facial in the trailer!" Ashley announced when she saw Tony.

"No, no!" Everett protested, struggling to keep up. "I said you needed to wash your faces!"

"Facials!" Brianna shrieked.

Tony got out of their way. If nothing else, the girls would be out by sunset. The girls and Everett. And Zev and Amy. Except Zev and Amy were still standing in the hall! He made a shooing motion toward the door and continued upstairs, pushing past the grinning grip carrying Everett's makeup case.

How many people were still up there? Peter, Tina, Adam, Mouse, Kate, Sorge, Mason, Lee—and Brenda. Given the problems with the lamps, at least one electrician. Chris, the gaffer, had gone out to the truck to check his extra lights and Tony hadn't seen him come back in. One grip following the girls and Everett. Maybe one or two still up there. Hartley Skenski, the boom operator, and a sound tech—there'd been more of the sound crew around before lunch when they'd been dealing with the extras, but Tony could only remember seeing the one by the bathroom. Thirteen, maybe fourteen. Under the circumstances, he'd rather it wasn't thirteen. He really didn't need anything that could be interpreted as an omen.

"I'm not going out there! It's raining and I'll get wet!"

Ashley's voice pulled Tony around. Both girls, Everett, and the grip were standing just inside the closed outer door staring out through the beveled glass into the twilight. Zev and Amy were standing just inside the open inner doors. It was dark enough outside that Tony could see all six reflections. At least there were only six. That was good, right?

Except they were supposed to be outside by now!

"You're running out of time."

"You know, Stephen, your sister's right." Shoulders against the wallpaper, he slid past the ghost and started back downstairs. "You're not fucking helping!"

He'd just stepped off the bottom step when he felt a sudden chill. The air grew heavy and still. The sounds of talking and laughter and cables being dragged along the upstairs hall became distant—wrapped in cotton. No. Given the way the temperature had plunged, wrapped in ice.

"You're too late," Stephen murmured.

Tony snorted. "*Quel* surprise."

A door slammed.

And then another.

And another.

And another.

The sound of the front door slamming echoed through the foyer and as the echoes died, the world snapped back into place.

"The front door was already closed," Tony said to Cassie as he charged past.

She shrugged. "So were all the others."

The girls, actually looking a little scared, had backed into the hall with the grip.

Everett reached for the door handle.

Tony couldn't see his reflection in the glass. Nor could he see the porch, or the rain, or anything at all. It was as if the world had gone from dusk to dark in a heartbeat.

"Everett! Don't . . . !"

Too late. The makeup artist grabbed the handle, turned it, shook it, kicked the base of the door, and then turned back toward his audience. "It's locked. Or jammed."

The inner doors slammed shut, the blackout curtain billowing out into the foyer like a cliché villain's cloak.

It turned out the inner doors were also locked. Or jammed. Or held closed by the evil within the house grown more powerful with the setting of the sun—but Tony figured now was not the time to mention that.

Trapped between the inner and outer doors, Everett pushed while Tony pulled. Nothing.

"What the hell is going on down here?" Peter's voice drew everyone's attention around to the stairs. Tony started to do a quick head count. . . . *eleven, twelve, thirteen* . . .

Which was when the lights went out.

"I guess I should have mentioned that was likely to happen," Cassie murmured under the high-pitched screams of the boss' daughters.

The caretaker's hand stopped about ten centimeters from the kitchen door, his fingers stubbing up against an invisible barrier.

"That's not good." He glanced down at the black cat. "Yep, you were right. I'm sorry I doubted you."

Fortunately, Tina had a small flashlight in her purse and Hartley remembered seeing candles in a drawer in the kitchen.

"What the hell were you doing going through the drawers? Never mind," Peter continued before Hartley could answer. "I don't really care. Go with Tina and bring the candles back here. Everyone else, stay right where you are.

We don't need to spend the rest of the night searching for someone who's wandered off in the dark."

The dark seemed a lot, well, darker, after the small cone of light from the flashlight disappeared through the dining room.

"My cell phone isn't working." Amy's voice.

"Neither is mine." And Zev's.

After the incident in episode five, CB's announcement about cell phones on set had been succinct. *"Next one I find, I implant."* Afraid to find out just *where,* the entire crew had stopped carrying their phones, although Tony was willing to bet that every backpack or bag in the AD's office held one. And that none of them would work.

He jumped about two feet straight up when a small hand grabbed his T-shirt.

"I don't like this!"

"Don't worry." Trying not to hyperventilate, he pried the fabric out of Brianna's grip and wrapped her fingers in his. "It'll be all right."

"No, it won't." Stephen drifted into his line of sight, looking for the first time translucent and traditionally ghostlike. "It'll be bad. And then it'll get worse."

"It's probably just a shift in air pressure." Adam's voice came from about halfway up the stairs. "One of the back doors blew shut."

"The back doors have been shut all day." That had to be Kate, Mouse's second, because it wasn't Tina or Amy or Brenda, the only other women in the house. *Other* live *women,* he corrected silently, wishing he'd taken the time to learn the Wizard's Lamp spell instead of the showier Come to Me.

"Then one of them blew open and the storm took the power out."

"Power in this house sucks." Given the content, probably the electrician.

"The power in this house is ga . . . Ow! Zev! What was that for?" Definitely Amy. "All I was going to say was that the power is gathering!"

"She's right." Cassie joined her brother. "She's guessing, but she's right."

Zev's voice sounded like it was coming through clenched teeth. "Let's try not to scare the G. I. R. L. S."

"We're not deaf." Ashley. No mistaking the nearly teenage snort.

"And we can spell." Brianna sounded better than she had, but her hand remained in Tony's. "And our father's not going to like this!"

No one argued.

"And," she declared triumphantly, "I can hear that baby again."

So could Tony; not screaming this time, but crying. A thin, sad, barely audible sound that drifted down from the upper hall.

Both ghosts turned toward the stairs.

"Karl," said Cassie.

"He's just getting warmed up," Stephen added. Then he glanced at Tony and grinned. "Get it? Warmed up?"

Impossible not to snicker.

"Something funny, Mr. Foster?"

Peter knows my snicker? Now that was disturbing. "Uh, no."

"Too bad, I'm sure we could all use a chuckle. Adam, try to raise Hartley."

"Can't. My battery's dead."

"I thought you just changed it."

"I did."

"They'll be all right," Cassie murmured reassuringly. "As long as they go straight to the kitchen and straight back. It's still early."

"And later?" Tony asked, pitching his voice under the argument going on at the stairs.

"Later . . ."

She paused for long enough that her brother answered. "Later, no one's going to be all right."

"Well, thanks a whole fucking lot for that observation."

Brianna's fingers tightened around Tony's hand, and her small body bumped hard against his hip. "Thanks a whole fucking lot for what observation?"

"Brianna!" Ashley's protest gave Tony a short reprieve. "I'm telling Mom you said fucking!"

"So did you!"

"Did not!"

"Just did, Zitface!"

Other conversations were beginning to quiet as the girls' volume rose. Any minute now Peter was going to demand to know what was going on and Brianna would tell him and then Tony would have to explain why he'd said what he'd said and to who. To whom? *Oh, yeah, grammar and the dead. Let's make sure we get* that *right. . . .* He could almost hear Peter gathering up his authority. And then he saw salvation: "There's a light in the dining room!"

Tina's flashlight.

Hartley emerged out of the darkness carrying a full box of white emergency candles. "I got no way to light them," he said as he reached the hall. "I stopped smoking five years ago now."

Kate hadn't smoked for two, Mouse for almost seven, and Adam for going on six months.

"Oh, for crying out loud." Mason's distinctive tones. He came the rest of the way down the stairs and thrust his hand, holding his lighter, into the narrow cone of illumination. His fingers gripped the blue translucent plastic in a way that dared his audience to comment. No one took the dare. Right at the moment, no one cared if Mason smoked and lied about it. Right at the moment, no one would have cared if Mason set fire to bus shelters and lied about that.

They lit six of the twenty-four candles. Six created a large enough circle of light for comfort but not enough flame to be a fire hazard.

"A fire hazard?" Mason snorted. "It's a twenty-foot ceiling, Peter. What the hell are we going to ignite?"

"This place is rented, and we're going to be careful." The director shut the box on the remaining candles and tucked it under one arm, so pointedly not mentioning the possibility of needing the other eighteen later that everyone heard it.

"Be careful, girls." Brenda motioned Ashley back as she moved in toward a candle. "Keep your clothes away from the flame; we can't afford to replace them."

"Not to mention," Sorge pointed out dryly, "it is a bad thing to have children catch on fire."

Brenda shot him a look that might have done damage given enough light for him to catch the full impact. "That's what I meant."

"I never doubted it."

The baby, Karl, continued crying. Tony glanced up the stairs, wondering if the sound had gotten louder, and realized that Lee was watching him, frowning slightly. Their eyes met and just for an instant, Tony thought he saw . . .

"Everett's lying down!"

And whatever it was, it was gone.

He spun around. Brianna pulled down the blackout curtain and was shining Tina's flashlight between the doors. The beam showed Everett lying on his back, head canted up against the baseboard on the west wall, left arm stretched out, right hand clutching his golf shirt right over the little polo player. "Oh, great! He's had a fucking heart attack!"

"You said fucking."

The door was still jammed shut. "Yeah, get over it."

"Stay back; none of you can help!" Peter's voice stopped the rush. "Tony, is he dead?"

"No," Cassie answered before Tony could.

He turned and gave a little shriek to see her three quarters of a profile also peering through the door about four inches from his shoulder.

"Tony?" Zev. And he sounded concerned.

Face flushed with embarrassment—it had been a distinctly girly shriek—Tony kept his eyes locked on the makeup artist and waved a hand in the general direction of the people behind him. "He's unconscious, but he's not dead."

"How can you tell?"

"I can see him breathing."

"His lips are kind of blue." Brianna flicked the flashlight beam down the length of Everett's prone body. "I like his sandals."

Tony was just beginning to consider stepping away and trying to call the door to him when Mouse's large hand closed over his shoulder and pulled him back. "Move. You too, kid."

She shone the flashlight at the cameraman. The beam gleamed along the length of the light stand he was holding. "Are you gonna break the glass?"

"Yes."

"Cool."

"I wouldn't," Stephen muttered.

Great. With no time to be subtle, Tony grabbed Mouse's wrist. The big man glared down at him. "What about broken glass? You know, shards of it sticking into Everett?"

"Risk," Mouse acknowledged. "But he needs help." He shook off Tony's grip and swung the stand, the heavy base slamming down toward the inner window.

From where he was standing, Tony wasn't even sure it hit the glass although the sound of an impact echoed through the hall. There was a flash of red and another impact as Mouse landed on his ass six feet from the door, the stand bouncing across the hardwood to clang up against the far wall.

"The house won't let you damage it," Stephen told him under the rising babble of voices.

"You couldn't have said that?"

"Would they have believed you?"

Point to the dead guy.

"All right, all right! Just calm down." With everyone used to following Peter's direction, the noise level dropped. "I'm sure we'll be able to get to Everett in a couple of minutes. The guys outside at the trucks are probably working on getting the doors open right now."

The silence that fell was so complete the soft *pad pad* of Ashley shifting her weight from one bare foot to the other was the only sound in the hall.

Then Tina took her flashlight back and snapped it off. "Shouldn't we be able to hear them?" she asked.

"All right; on three."

Chris and Ujjal, the genny op, shifted their grips on four-foot lengths of steel scaffolding pipe.

"One." Karen wiped rain off her face and moved a little to the right, where she had a better line of sight on the kitchen door. "Two. Three."

Impact. A flare of red light and both men were flung away from the house. Karen ducked as a pipe cartwheeled over her head to crash against the side of the truck.

"Told you it wouldn't work." Graham Brummel's voice sounded over the fading reverberation of steel on steel. "House is closed up tight. Won't be opening till dawn and there's nothing you can do from out here to change that. You might as well just do what I said and head home like the rest of the crew."

"Fuck you," Chris snarled as he got to his feet. "I'm not listening to you; you're in on this. I'm calling the cops."

"And why would you need to call the police, Mr. Robinson?"

Chris, Karen, and Ujjal turned. Graham Brummel stepped back into the shadows as Chester Bane moved out into the spill of light falling from the spotlight mounted on the side of the truck. He stood, dry under the circle of his umbrella, and listened impassively as his three employees, growing wetter and wetter, attempted to explain. Finally, he raised a massive hand. "You can't get into the house."

It wasn't a question, but Chris answered it anyway. "No, sir."

"You can't even touch the house."

"No, sir."

"You can't contact the people inside the house, but you believe that they are unable to leave."

"No, sir." He frowned as Karen drove her elbow into his side. "Yes, sir?"

"My daughters are still in there."

Propelled by a hindbrain response to danger, all three of them took an involuntary step back. Karen elbowed Chris again, and he coughed out another, "Yes, sir."

"And the caretaker knows what's going on."

"Yes, sir." In unison this time, powered by relief.

"Where is he?"

"He's . . ." Chris turned, realized Graham Brummel was no longer standing by the front of the truck and frowned. Before he could continue, the sound of a door slamming over by the garage answered the question.

CB made a sound, half speculation, half growl. His employees parted as he strode forward, walked around the truck, and crossed the small courtyard to the garage, the wet gravel grinding under each deliberate step. At the door leading to the caretaker's apartment, he furled his umbrella and handed it back, fully confident there'd be someone there to take it. The door was locked.

He rattled the brass knob for a moment, noting the amount of play in the movement of the door. Then he took four long steps back into the courtyard. Ujjal scrambled to get out of his way.

"Should I call the police?" Karen asked him as he stood, staring at the door.

"Not yet." A sledgehammer wrapped in an eight-hundred-and-fifty-dollar London Fog trench coat would have made much the same sound as his shoulder did hitting the painted wood.

Wood cracked.

"A lock," he said, forcing the brass tongue through the splintered casing and opening the door, "is only as good as the wood around it. Find someplace dry to wait where you can see the house. Come and get me if anything changes."

"Shouldn't we . . ." Chris began and stopped as CB paused, one foot over the threshold. "Never mind. We'll find someplace dry to wait and watch the house."

Two more steps inside, and CB paused again. "Is Tony Foster trapped inside?" he asked without turning.

"Uh . . . yeah."

"Good."

There was a black cat sitting at the top of the stairs. He ignored it. The door behind the cat was also locked.

"You have to the count of three, Mr. Brummel."

The door opened on two. Mr. Brummel didn't look happy, but he was smart enough to move well back out of the way.

"Tell me," CB commanded as he stepped into the apartment.

Graham Brummel snorted. "Or you'll what? Call the cops?"

"No."

The single word carried threat disproportionate to its size.

"You guys know what's going on?"

Brother and sister exchanged a look as identical as injuries allowed.

"Sort of," Cassie allowed at last.

Tony sighed and slid a few steps farther into the dining room. There were about half a dozen arguments going on in the front hall, and so far he hadn't been missed. "'Sort of' isn't good enough."

"It's mostly Graham's theory."

"Graham?"

"Graham Brummel, the caretaker. He's kind of a distant cousin," Cassie explained. "When he got the job as caretaker about six years ago, he began using the blood tie to pull us more into the world. That's why we're aware and the rest aren't."

The rest. Oh, yeah, that sounded good. Tony sank down on one of the folding chairs the caterers had provided and resisted the urge to beat his head against the table. "Start at the beginning."

"The beginning?" She took a deep breath—or seemed to take a deep breath, since she wasn't actually breathing. "All right. The house is . . ."

"Or holds," Stephen interrupted.

"Right; it is or holds a malevolence."

"A malevolent *what*?" Tony demanded impatiently.

Cassie frowned. "There's no need to be rude. You know, we don't have to help you."

"You're right." Not that they'd been a lot of help so far—a little late with the warning. "I apologize."

Mollified, she gave the folds of her skirt a bit of a fluff before continuing. "Graham says it's just a malevolence."

"A piece of bad stuff?"

"Very bad," Cassie agreed. "And it collects tormented spirits. Graham thinks it got the idea from Creighton Caulfield, who collected some very weird stuff. He thinks Mr. Caulfield was the template for its personality."

Tony held up a hand. "So, cutting to the chase—the malevolence, the evil thing in the house wants to collect us?"

"Probably. It hasn't added anything since Karl and his mother and that was almost thirty years ago."

"I didn't see his mother."

Stephen snorted. "Of course, you didn't. Karl's like a night-light, he's on all the time."

That seemed to jibe with Amy's theory of the youngest being the strongest. "And *Mr.* Brummel knew this when CB rented the house?"

"Yes and no. He knew the background of the house, but he also believed that because the house had been empty for so long, the malevolence was dormant."

"Sleeping," Stephen offered as Tony frowned.

"Yeah, I know what *dormant* means. Looks like he was wrong."

"No, he was right. We can feel it now, like we could before, but the feeling only just started up again."

Great. Somehow, they'd screwed themselves. "So shooting here woke it?"

Stephen shrugged and adjusted his head. "Graham says only blood can wake it."

He leaned in closer, his eyes narrowed, his nose flared—he looked like a poster boy for dire warnings. "*You don't want to be bleeding, not in this house.*"

"Yeah, but all the blood we used is fake!"

He'd been standing not three feet from the steps when she fell, close enough to hear her knee make that soft hard definite tissue damage sound, and he had a pretty good idea of where she'd impacted with the porch. Weirdly, while there'd been lines of red dribbling down her shin, he couldn't find any blood on the stones.

"Oh, crap."

"Tony?" Holding one of the candles carefully out in front of him, Zev peered into the dining room. "What are you doing sitting all alone in the dark?"

He wasn't alone and the two ghosts shed enough light for conversation. Probably not a good idea to mention that though. "I'm . . . uh, just thinking."

"Well, think in the foyer. Peter wants us all to stay together."

"In the foyer?"

"He doesn't think we should leave Everett."

As they left the dining room together, Amy's voice rose to meet them. "Look, what we're involved in here is clearly beyond the usual and a séance is a perfectly valid way to contact the restless spirits holding us in this house."

"Restless spirits," Mason scoffed from the stairs. "That's the most ridiculous thing I ever heard."

But he almost sounded as though he was trying to convince himself.

"Do you have a better explanation, then?" Amy asked him. "Does anyone?"

No one did.

"So why *not* hold a séance?"

Tony turned just enough to raise an eyebrow at Cassie.

The ghost shrugged. "Well, the one with the purple hair would be perfectly safe, but make sure the younger girl isn't involved. If she can hear Karl, she could easily get possessed. That's what happened to Karl's mother."

"Not our fault," Stephen muttered. "We were minding our own business and she saw us in the bathroom mirror."

"So she tried to contact us and got grabbed by something else."

"The evil thing?"

"You saw what she did to Karl, what do you think?"

"I think . . ." Which was when Tony realized that the hall had gone quiet. And everyone was staring at him. "I . . . um . . . I think a séance is a bad idea. I mean, if we are being held by restless spirits, by the kind of spirits who'd trap us in the house and keep us away from Everett, do we even want to talk to them?"

Amy rolled her eyes. "Well, duh, Tony. They can tell us why we're here and what we have to do in order to get out!"

"Survive until morning?" Stephen suggested. "And we're not restless, we're just bored."

Karl's crying had gotten louder.

"We're not having a séance." There was a definitive tone in Tina's voice that said this was the final word on the subject. "This is not the time to start playing about with things no one truly understands. Not when we're in the middle of a situation *we* don't understand. And we are most certainly not involving the children in that sort of potentially dangerous nonsense."

"They wouldn't be involved," Amy protested.

"You couldn't get the little one far enough away," Cassie said quietly.

A little too quietly.

Tony turned. He could barely see her.

Stephen glanced down at his nearly transparent hands and grimaced. "Showtime."

The sound lingered a moment after he vanished. It was the only sound. Karl had stopped crying.

A door slammed upstairs.

"I know what you're doing!" A man. Not so much shouting as shrieking in rage. He sounded . . .

Like he's gone totally bugfuck. Tony jumped at the hollow *thunk* of something heavy and sharp impacting with one of the second-floor doors.

Heavy and sharp.

"Back in 1957, September twenty-sixth to be exact, Stephen and Cassandra Mills' father freaked and attacked them with an ax."

Showtime.

"Oh, no . . ." He was halfway up the stairs before he realized he'd started moving. A hand grabbed at his leg, but he shook it off. Voices called his name, he ignored them.

The man—Mr. Mills—yanked the blade of the ax out of the door to Mason's dressing room. Except it wasn't the door to Mason's dressing room; the hall had reverted to pre-seventies renovation carpeting and wallpaper. The small part of Tony's mind not anticipating terror took a moment to note it was an improvement. *And I guess that explains why the lights are back on.*

Mr. Mills staggered sideways as the ax came free and screamed, "You can't hide from me!"

White showed all around his eyes. The skin of his face was nearly gray except for a dark spot of color high on each cheek. Blood oozed out of the cut where he'd driven his teeth through his lip, mixed with saliva, and dribbled down his chin.

Bugfuck seemed a fairly accurate diagnosis.

The door opened across the hall and Cassie stepped out, pulling it nearly closed behind her. Her face was flushed, her hair messy, but her head was intact. "Daddy, what are you . . . ?"

Mr. Mills roared and charged toward her swinging wildly.

Cassie stared at him in astonishment, lips slightly parted, frozen in place.

At the last possible instant, the door behind her opened and Stephen dove out into the hall, one arm around his sister's waist, taking them both out from under the blade of the ax.

Which came out of the plaster and lath a lot faster than it had out of the wood.

Holding hands, Cassie and Stephen ran down the hall and into the bathroom, slamming the door.

"No!" Tony stepped out into the hall. "You'll be trapped!"

Mr. Mills seemed to realize the same thing because he started to laugh maniacally.

"Hey! Crazy guy!"

No response. The ax chopped into the bathroom door.

"Goddamn it, you can't do this! They're your kids!"

Another chop and a kick and the door was open.

Cassie screamed.

He couldn't let this happen. It didn't matter that they were already dead. That this had happened almost forty freaking years ago. He couldn't stand by and do nothing. He raced down the hall and threw his arms around Mr. Mills, hoping to pin the ax to his side.

Mr. Mills walked into the bathroom, swinging the ax, like he wasn't even there.

"Filth!"

The first blow took Stephen in the side of the neck, the force of it driving him to his knees. Cassie screamed again and tried to drag her brother with her into the bathtub. Her father reached past his dying son, grabbed the strap of her dress and yanked her forward. She stumbled and slipped on Stephen's blood. The strap tore. As the pressure released, she spun around just as the ax came down, chopping the chunk out of her head.

Tony really hoped that she wasn't the one moaning as she crumpled to lie beside her brother. He really hoped it was him.

Splattered with the blood of his children, Mr. Mills turned and walked out of the bathroom, Tony backing hurriedly out of his way. Once in the hall, he looked down at the bloody ax as though he'd never seen it before, as though he had no idea whose brains and hair were stuck along its length, then he adjusted his grip and slammed the blade down between his own eyes.

Tony skipped back as the body fell and realized the light was disappearing. "No . . ." He wasn't going to be stuck up here with . . . with . . .

"Tony!"

A light in the growing darkness.

A circle of light.

A hand grabbed his arm and a familiar voice said, "Are you okay?"

"Lee?"

"Yeah, it's me. Come on. Let's get you back to the others, okay?"

He was talking slowly, calmingly. Like he expected Tony to go off the deep end at any moment. As the last of the light disappeared and there was nothing in the upstairs hall but him and Lee and Tina's flashlight, as Karl started crying again, Tony had to admit that the deep end had its attractions.

Lee took his arm as he stumbled and got him to the stairs, where other hands helped steady him as he descended. Once in the hall, he swayed and sank slowly to his knees.

"Amy, get the wastebasket out of the drawing room." Tina's voice.

"But . . ."

"Quickly."

Just quickly enough.

Tony puked until his stomach emptied, then took a swallow of water and puked again. Finally, when even the dry heaves stopped, he wiped his mouth and sat back on his heels.

Wordlessly, Zev handed him a tissue.

He wiped his mouth and dropped it in the bucket. "Thanks."

The music director shrugged. "Hey, not the first time I've seen you toss your cookies."

"Man, you two had a seriously twisted relationship!"

"He had the flu," Zev explained shortly, accepting a water bottle from Amy and passing it over. "You okay now?"

"I think so." Physically anyway.

"What happened?"

Polite "let's pretend Tony's not puking" conversations stopped. Tony glanced around the hall and found all attention directed at him. Not surprising, really—they must've thought he'd gone insane. He sighed. He'd been afraid he was going to have to say this at some point; he'd just hoped to put it off as long as possible.

I could still lie.

Except that he'd figured out what the house—the malevolent thing was up to—and if he couldn't save Cassie and Stephen, there were another eighteen people in danger. Coworkers. Friends. Kids. Lying wouldn't help them.

Another deep breath.

"I see dead people."

Someone snickered. Kate found her voice first. "Bullshit."

"No." Lee came slowly down the stairs, eyes locked on Tony's face. "I believe him."

⌇ SIX

"So, all the time I'm growing up, I heard about my mum's cousin who married a rich guy, had two kids, a big house, and the perfect life except that her husband went nuts and killed the kids and himself. End of perfect life. She dies in the loony bin fifteen years later." Graham took another pull on his beer. "You sure you don't want one?"

"I'm sure." CB leaned forward, the chair creaking under his weight. "Get on with it."

"Yeah, okay. Maybe that story's why it's always been about dead people for me. Maybe not. Who knows? Point is, I never forgot it and a few years back, when I was at loose ends, I decided to go looking for the house. You know; the house where the perfect life ended." He jerked his head toward the window. "That house. I showed up right about the time the last caretaker took a walk out to the highway and stepped in front of an eighteen wheeler. It seemed like a sign—the timing and all—and, next thing I know, I'm employed. A month later, I'm in that second-floor bathroom—the bathroom where it happened, where my mum's cousin's kids got whacked—and I look in the mirror and there's these two dead kids standing behind me. I turn around and there's nothing there. I keep going back to the bathroom and I keep seeing them and I work at it . . ."

"You *work* at it?"

"Yeah, you know, I open up to it. I reach out to the other realm," he added when CB clearly didn't understand. "Never mind, it's not important. Soon I can see them even outside the mirror and soon after that we start talking. They're a little vague at first, after all they've been trapped at the moment of their deaths for years, but the longer we talk the more they remember who they were."

"What does this have to do with my daughters?"

"I'm getting there; you're not going to get what's happening without the background stuff. So while I'm talking to the family—that's the two dead kids in case you lost track—I'm scoping out the rest of the house and spiritually, that's one crowded piece of real estate." A long drink, then he set the bottle down on the table and leaned forward, mirroring CB's position. "Bad stuff leaves its mark, okay? I'm guessing with all the weird crap Creighton Caulfield brought into the house, he got his hands on a piece that wasn't just weird—it was out-and-out evil. Just to be on the safe side, though, I checked to make sure they didn't build the house on some kind of off-limits Indian burial site and they didn't. The First Nations out here, they're on top of that stuff."

"Get. On. With. It." CB growled. Had one of his writers pitched him a plot so heavily weighted with cliché, that writer would be back working the Tim Horton's drive-through before he got to the second act. Cliché applied to his daughters, however, that made a compelling story.

"Right. Now, Creighton Caulfield, he was a piece of work. Nobody liked him and the stuff he liked, well, you don't want to know a guy who likes that kind of stuff, see? And, fed by Caulfield, the bit of bad keeps getting bigger. After a while, it's no longer a mark left by bad stuff, it's reached a critical mass and it's now a bad thing all on its own. By the time Caulfield dies, it's a full-sized malevolence."

He paused, waiting for comment, but CB only nodded, so he went on. "Trouble is nothing's feeding it anymore. Caulfield's gone and nothing's making it any bigger. So it starts working on the new people in the house and a lot more proactively than just lying around and waiting for them to slip on it like some kind of evil banana peel. It finds the weakest link." Snickering, he sat back. "You are . . ."

"I wouldn't." Not a suggestion.

Graham's mouth snapped shut and he sighed. "You know, you should really keep a sense of humor about this or it's going to be a long night."

"A short night for you if you don't *finish* the story."

"What?" Then he found the threat. "Uh, right. So the malevolence finds the person most open to it and kicks him round the bend, but this person doesn't get to go bye-bye until he's offed someone else. The whole damned place, and I use the word damned in its literal sense, is full of murders and suicides and every death feeds the malevolence and makes it stronger, more realized."

"Again, and for the last time—what does this have to do with my daughters?"

"I'm getting there. In the mid-seventies, a woman named Eva Kranby tossed her baby in a lit fireplace and then killed herself. Her husband—another seriously rich guy . . ."

"The Kranby of Kranby Groceries?"

"No idea. Wherever this guy got his money, losing his wife and baby just crushed him, but he wouldn't sell the house. He's living in New Zealand now, but he still won't sell. The house has been empty ever since except for the caretakers. The first guy, he's a total stoner and when the house makes a move he thinks he's having a bad acid trip and takes off. No food for the house. Next guy, he's a religious nut who spends a lot of time praying and finally snaps, goes babbling to his minister about exorcisms and the like and he's gone. Still no food for the house. Next guy, the guy I replace, actually does kill himself, but he does it away from the property. So there's been nothing new coming in for a number of years and hardly anyone to work on, so by the time I get here, in order to keep from just bleeding away energy, the house goes dormant and as long as you're careful not to wake it up, it's perfectly safe. Okay, some parts of it, like the ballroom, can be freak shows in their own right—we're talking a lot of trapped dead in there and you spend any time in with them, next thing you know, you're going to be joining the dance. There was this electrician, back during the first caretaker, got brought in to fix some wiring or something and they found him dead in the ballroom. They called it a heart attack, but it was exhaustion."

"So the house *has* killed after the Kranbys."

"In technical post mortem talk, he wasn't killed, he died—I got the feeling that was the ballroom acting on its own." He frowned. "Mind you, the malevolence was still awake then, so who knows. Not something I'd want to risk anyway. The dead, one at a time, not so big a problem, but you get them in groups and they're like teenagers. Could get up to anything."

"We were going to use the ballroom."

"Yeah, I heard. Good thing you changed your mind." A quick glance at the window and the dark shadow of the house against the night sky. "Or a moot point. Hard to say."

"And, I note, you didn't say. Anything."

"Well, you didn't use the ballroom, did you? I figured as long as the malevolence was asleep, no problem. You got anyone that's too sensitive on staff, and I've seen your show so I'm thinking that's not likely, and they might be getting the whole cold chills and bad feeling about things, but that's all. There's only one thing that can wake the house."

CB waited out the caretaker's pause for effect with barely concealed impatience. It was, as a result, a short pause.

"Blood. One of your people got blood on the house. I warned them not to, so it's nothing to do with me. The house woke up. The malevolence is starving—the energy from the trapped dead is enough to keep it from fading, but that's all—and it doesn't have time to be subtle, so when the sun set, it locked everything down. It'll use what energy it has stored to score big, to get it enough juice to keep it going for years and years. Your guy outside says there's nineteen people in there. It'll use what's in the house already to drive the weak ones mad and they'll do the rest."

"The weak will murder the strong and then commit suicide?"

A long swallow finished the beer. "Yeah."

"How do we stop this?"

"Just like that? How do we stop this?" Brows drawn in, Graham stared across the empty bottle at his audience. "This is the part where you tell me that I'm crazy and that's the most preposterous story you've ever heard."

"I'm in television, syndicated television at that. Your story is derivative but hardly preposterous." Although belief came more from the gate to another world that had opened into his soundstage. "Also, my own people have informed me that they cannot get into the house. Now then . . ." His hands closed slowly into fists. ". . . how do we stop this?"

Pale cheeks paled further as Graham Brummel suddenly realized he was also in a certain amount of danger. "We can't. We can only wait until morning and see who survives."

"That's not good enough."

"Look . . ." All flippancy had left his voice. ". . . I understand. It's your people in there, your kids, but you can't even touch the house right now, so it's a fair assumption we can't get inside."

"Is there a way for the people inside to get out?"

Graham shrugged. "You got me. I'm not inside."

"Theorize."

"Okay. Well, I guess that if someone took on the malevolence and won, then the house'd open up."

Given the plot thus far, that seemed to follow. "Good."

"But that's not going to happen. Your people are sitting ducks. They won't have a clue what's going on and the house is going to work them like the barker works the rubes at a carny. It'll twist them and terrify them and they'll stop thinking for themselves."

"Don't count on it."

"What, because they're television people and they're used to weird?"

"That, too." CB heaved himself up out of the chair and reached into his pocket for his cell phone.

"You can't call in. I thought your people told you that. It's sucking all the power out of . . ." He stopped as CB raised a massive hand, shrugged, and wove his way around the stacks of old newspapers and books to the kitchen for another beer.

His people *had* told him that, which was why he hadn't spent the last twenty minutes on the phone. What he needed now was a second opinion. "Mr. Fitzroy? It's Chester Bane. Mr. Foster seems to have gotten himself into a situation and we could use your insight. No, we're on location . . . Yes, that's right. I'll be waiting for you in the driveway. Thank you."

"If that's a cop you called," Graham muttered, twisting the lid off another bottle as he came out of the kitchen. "They can't help. And *The X-Files* left Vancouver years ago."

"He's not a cop. Now, you . . ."

"Me?"

"What are you? A wizard?" CB stared down at the beer sprayed nearly to the tips of his highly polished Italian loafers. "Not a wizard. What then?"

"I thought I told you. It's all about dead people for me—I'm a medium."

"Ah."

"You believe that, too?"

"Yes."

"Jesus." Dropping back into his chair, Graham took a long drink. "You're either the most open-minded guy I've ever met or the most gullible."

"Do I *look* gullible?"

"Uh, no. Sorry." He rubbed the shadow of stubble on his chin with one hand and under the weight of CB's gaze, began to talk again. "I used to work the carnival circuit till that kind of thing pretty much shut down. Then I did a bit of freelance, but I just don't got John Edward's touch, you know? Say, you're a producer. When this is over, do you think you could . . . ?"

"No."

"Yeah, fine, whatever. I guess you got a right to be cranky; after all, the house has got your kids."

CB walked over to the window and stared at the roofline barely visible through the rain. "The house may have bitten off more than it can chew."

"So . . ." Brianna glared up at Tony through narrowed eyes. ". . . you lied about the baby."

"Yes."

"Was it, like, way gross?"

"Yes."

"Cool."

"All right, just hold on for a minute. You lot . . ." Peter's gesture took in Lee, Hartley, Mouse, and Kate. ". . . can hear Brianna's baby crying. You . . ." A considerably more truncated gesture at Tony. ". . . can actually see it. Saw it. The ghost of it?"

"Yes."

"And other ghosts?"

"Yes."

"And a reenactment of them dying?"

"Yes."

Peter ran both hands back through his hair and sighed. "And we're locked in here because the house is trying to collect us. As ghosts?"

"Probably."

"So it wants us dead, and is planning on driving some of us mad . . ."

"Short drive for some of you," Mason muttered.

". . . and having them kill the rest?"

"That's what it's done in the past," Tony told him, suddenly needing to break the string of one-word answers.

"This is so unfair," Amy muttered, arms folded and chin tucked in tight against her chest. "I should be seeing ghosts. Why do you get to see ghosts? You don't give a crap about other realms. If anyone's going to be a medium, it should be me, not you."

"So you're what?" his mouth asked before his brain could kick in. "A large?"

"Bite me, ghost boy. And," she continued, indignation levels rising, "why do they . . ." Her gesture verged on rude. ". . . get to hear ghosts and I don't?"

It was a rhetorical question, but Tony thought he actually knew the answer. Back in the spring, Lee, Mouse, and Kate had all been shadow-held—not once, but twice. First they'd been ridden by individual shadows sent out to seek information, and then, as the shit really started to hit the fan, they'd been controlled by shadows along with the rest of the crew. Hartley and Mason had also been individually controlled, but Hartley hadn't been at work the day the Shadowlord had come calling and Mason had still been under the influence of his original shadow. Because Hartley was an alcoholic of long standing, his synapses were probably already a little fried before the whole shadow incident, so no surprise it had only taken a single possession to open him up. Mason . . . Tony shot a speculative look at the actor and received a clear, nonverbal *Fuck you* in return. Although Mason *said* he couldn't hear the baby, he had been shadow-held for longer than anyone else.

None of which he was going to mention to Amy.

As for Brianna . . .

He had no idea.

"I mean, Brianna makes sense," Amy went on. "She's a kid and certain energies are attracted to kids."

Oh.

"It's like the baby. The younger the energy, the more power it has. That's why you can hear it."

Heads nodded. Tony wondered if it was the purple hair. *You got purple hair and suddenly you're an expert on the weird.*

"So what do we do now?" Zev asked over the sound of Karl crying.

Finally, an easy question. "We get out of this house."

"And how do we do that?" Mason drawled. "Given that we can't get the door open."

"Uh . . ." They all actually seemed to be waiting for an answer. From a production assistant. Which was weird. Granted, a production assistant who could see dead people, so maybe they thought the two weirds canceled each other out. Tony had no idea. "Why don't we try tossing a chair through one of those tall windows in the drawing room?"

"Oh, no, wait just one minute, Tony." Peter's hands rose into "soothing egos" position. "We should see if *all* the doors and windows are locked before we start breaking things. Windows cost money, and CB'll have my hide if this shoot goes over budget."

"I never thought I'd say this," Sorge murmured, placing his hand on Peter's shoulder, "but if Tony is right and we are locked in with a crazy bad house, CB is the least of our worries."

"If Tony is right," Mason repeated. "Big 'if.' He's a production assistant, for Christ's sake."

"I'm not." Lee stepped forward until he stood by Tony's side. "Neither is Mouse. Neither is Kate. Neither is Hartley." They stirred as Lee named them, but they didn't step forward. "And you know what? It doesn't matter. Getting the hell out of here as soon as possible sounds like a good idea, and since it seems obvious that the guys outside can't get in—or they would have by now," he added pointedly, "—it's up to us." Pivoting on a heel, he headed out of the hall, throwing, "CB can bill me for the window," back over his shoulder. He paused at the edge of the candlelight. "Tina?"

Tina snapped on her flashlight and followed.

"No fair! I want to throw something through the window!" Brianna raced after the script supervisor, Ashley ran after her sister, and the moment after that, the hall began to empty.

"Baaa! Bunch of sheep," Amy muttered. "One person moves and the rest follow." But Tony noticed she picked up a candle and came into the drawing room with the rest.

With the curtains open, the glass in the windows looked like black velvet. Completely opaque and completely nonreflective. When Tina swept the flash-light beam across them, they seemed to absorb the light.

Mouse took the captain's chair from Lee's hand. "I throw harder."

A heavy glass candy dish flew past him and shattered against the window, the pieces skittering across the hardwood floor.

"Brianna!" Brenda's voice sounded a lot like the candy dish looked.

"It wasn't me!"

"I play baseball," Ashley explained as all eyes turned to her. "Third base. It didn't go through the window."

"I throw harder than you," Mouse pointed out. He tested the weight of the chair, then took two long steps away from the window. "Give me room."

"All right, listen up; if you're holding a candle, step back to the far wall, we don't want them blowing out." Moving up next to the cameraman and waving Lee off to one side, Peter indicated where he wanted the candleholders. "Ashley, Brianna—Brianna, don't play with the lamp, it's an antique—you two stay with Brenda."

She jumped at the sound of her name. "I thought Tony was in charge of them."

"Well, right now, you're standing next to them. When that window breaks, I want them to be the first ones out."

Tony couldn't help but notice that final bit of information made Brenda a lot happier about babysitting.

"Everyone else," Peter continued, "make sure Mouse has room to swing. Are we ready?"

"Let's settle down people. Action in . . ." Adam's voice trailed off as he realized what he was doing. "Peter started it."

"I'm the . . ." Peter twisted around to see Mouse frowning down at him from about four inches away. "Right." During half a dozen quick steps to one side, he regained his composure. "What are you waiting for, then?"

The chair had the same effect on the window the candy dish had—none at all. The window had the same effect on the chair except that the pieces were larger and flew farther from the point of impact.

"Son of a fucking bitch!" Mouse yanked the splinter from his arm and tossed it to one side.

Tony watched it tumble through the air, saw the blood glistening on the wood, and knew he wouldn't reach it in time. Call him paranoid, but giving more blood to the house seemed like a very bad idea. Panic spat out the seven words in one long string of sibilants and vowels and the splinter smacked into his hand. He shoved it in his pocket, wiped his hand on his jeans, and realized that everyone had been too concerned with Mouse and/or the impregnability of the window to notice.

"What was that you just said?"

Fuck! Almost everyone! Heart in his throat, he spun around to find Lee staring at him speculatively. There were days he'd give his right nut to have Lee stare at him speculatively. This was not one of them.

"Just, you know, swearing."

"Yeah?" A dark brow rose. "In what language?"

He didn't know. Arra had written out the words of the spells phonetically. She hadn't mentioned the name of the language. Which, as it happened, wasn't the point. And Lee was waiting for an answer.

And waiting.

And . . .

"This is nuts!"

And Tony was saved by the breakdown. As half a dozen other conversations went quiet, Tony turned to see Tom, the electrician, standing alone, his chest rising and falling in a jerky, staccato rhythm.

"This is totally fucking CRAZY!"

"Calm down, Tom." Adam moved toward him, one hand outstretched. "We'll get through this."

"No, we won't! We'll die!" Tom batted Adam's hand away and turned wild eyes toward Tony. "He says we're all going to die!"

Heads pivoted to follow the accusation.

Great. "I said the house was going to try and kill us. Not the same thing."

The same heads pivoted back again to catch the electrician's response.

"Damn right it's not. Because it's not going to kill me." Tom slammed his fist against his sternum. The room had gone so quiet that the hollow thud of impact sounded unnaturally loud. "Me, I'm leaving!" Before anyone could remind him they'd been locked in, he ran for the window.

"Stop him!" Rubber soles squealing against the polished wood, Tony raced to intercept knowing even as he moved he didn't have a hope in hell of getting there in time.

Easily avoiding Adam's grab, Tom shoved Kate hard into Mouse rather than go around her. He was running full out when he hit the window.

He didn't thud at the moment of impact.

He crunched.

Tony skidded to a stop beside the body.

"But . . . I thought I heard the window break," said Amy's voice in the background as he dropped to one knee and felt for a pulse.

"It wasn't the window." Zev's voice.

No pulse. No surprise considering the weird angles and the places the bones had come through the skin . . .

Fuck!

"Mouse! Lift him off the floor!"

"Wha . . ."

"Do it!" When Peter added his support, Tony started breathing again. Peter would remember about the blood. Directors saw the big picture. "Tina! Sorge! Get that drop sheet off the gear in the library!"

Then Peter's hand was around his arm, pulling him to his feet and out of the way as Tina and Sorge raced back with the drop sheet and Mouse laid the body on the plastic tarp and folded the edges up over it.

Then they all stared as the smudges of blood disappeared into the floor.

"Is that bad?" Peter murmured.

"Probably not good," Tony acknowledged.

"Still, the whatever is *already* awake."

"Yeah, but I don't think we should encourage it." Brianna poked the side of the tarp with one bare foot. "Is he dead?"

"Yes, honey." Brenda dropped to her knees and put her arms around the girl, forcing comfort out past what looked to be imminent hysterics. "He's dead."

"Really dead?"

"Really most sincerely dead," Mason told her with exaggerated cheer. "He's the inconsequential character who dies in the first act so we all know the situation is serious."

"That's not funny," snarled one of the grips. Tony thought his name was Saleen but he wasn't sure; the man had only been with CB Productions a few weeks.

Mason snorted. His candle flame flickered. "I wasn't joking."

"And it's not even original!"

Fangs showed below Mason's curled lip.

Brianna poked the body again. "So he's not going to get up?"

"No, honey. He's . . ." Brenda paused. Frowned. Paled. Looked up at Tony. Who didn't understand the question. "What?"

"The g . . . h . . . o . . . s . . . t . . . s."

Brianna rolled her eyes and ducked out of the circle of Brenda's arms. "I got an A in spelling. She wants to know if he's gonna come back as a ghost."

Good question. "I don't know."

"But you knew he was going to die!" Brenda's eyes showed white all the way around and, without Brianna to hold onto, she seemed to be having difficulty holding onto herself.

"I didn't . . ."

The finger she pointed at him was shaking. "You tried to stop him!"

"Yeah, because everything else that hit that window broke." It had seemed like a logical assumption. Well, maybe under the circumstances *logical* was the wrong word, but experience had taught him that the metaphysical followed rules just like everything else.

"All right. Fine. What do we do now?"

She looked a bit maniacal in the candlelight. At least Tony hoped it was the candlelight. Before he could come up with a less inflammatory way of saying *I have no fucking idea*, Amy said, "Silver."

"Hi ho," Mason muttered.

"On his eyes!" Amy handed her candle to Zev and pulled off one of her rings. "We lay silver on Tom's eyes," she announced, twirling it so that it caught the light, "and his spirit won't rise."

Were the shadows gathering around the circle of candlelight growing darker?

"What a crock."

Amy's chin rose and pointed belligerently toward Mason. "So let's hear your plan?"

Had Karl's crying grown louder? Shriller?

"You mean something I didn't learn watching DVDs of *The X-Files*?"

"Bite me! Chris Carter was a surfer boy with delusions and this is valid old world ritual." She removed a second ring and knelt beside the tarp. "Right, Tony?"

Were those footsteps in the library?

"Tony?"

He jumped as Lee touched his arm. *Shouldn't he be back behind me a few more feet?*

He moved, you idiot.

And everyone was looking at him again. Great.

Across the body, Zev frowned. "You okay?"

"Yeah. Just . . ." Just never mind. Things were bad enough without him adding another two cents' worth. "I think it's a good idea. The silver. Amy knows about shit like this. That. You know."

Mason's turn to roll his eyes. "How articulate."

"You're not helping," Peter told him quietly. "Amy, go ahead."

"You know what would be cool?" Ashley said as Amy's hand closed around the edge of the tarp. "If, when she opened that up, if Tom opened his eyes. Really wide."

Amy froze. Everyone in the room considered it.

The silence grew weighted with the possibility.

The hair on the back of Tony's neck lifted as the build of emotion began to escalate into something else. Something they probably wouldn't want to spend the night locked in with. Or more accurately, something *else* they wouldn't want to spend the night locked in with.

"Didn't we do the eyes thing in episode six?" he asked, his voice awkwardly loud. "And again in episode eleven?"

"Cliché," Sorge agreed. "I say so then."

"It was a perfectly valid way to up the emotional stakes," Peter protested in the weary tone of one who had protested before.

The cinematographer dug his thumbnail into the soft wax at the top of his candle. "Maybe the first time."

"The second time, it didn't really happen," Peter reminded him. "It was all in Lee's head. In James Taylor Grant's head, anyway."

"And we were there—why?"

"We were where—why?" And in the same breath. "Brianna, stop poking the body!"

"Why in James Taylor Grant's head?"

"You know why; because he was imagining things!"

"No." Sorge shook his head. "Still doesn't work for me."

"It was six episodes ago!"

"Also eleven episodes ago."

"So you've had time to get over it."

"Still . . ."

"Oh, for crying out loud." Amy flipped back a corner of the tarp and quickly laid a ring on each of Tom's closed eyes.

Tony released a breath he couldn't remember holding as she covered the body again. A small sound by his right side. He turned his head just far enough to see Lee give him a quick thumbs-up, understanding that nothing defused tensions like rehashing creative differences for the seven thousandth time.

Then Lee's gesture continued until both his hands were clapped over his ears. Mouse grunted. Kate swore. Tony fought the urge to do all three and settled on gritting his teeth as every muscle in his body tensed. The lights came up and Karl's screams—which he realized now had stopped for a few moments, leaving the background under Sorge and Peter's argument empty of sound—became shrieks of panic and pain.

Fortunately, it had been a large fire and a small baby.

The faint, distant sound of a woman's voice singing nursery rhymes grew more distinct as the shrieking stopped, but he seemed to be the only one who could hear her and even he lost the thread of the song under Brianna's shrill demands to be let go.

"I want to go see the baby!"

She fought against Zev's grip, driving her fists into his shoulders, but he had her held too closely for her to put much force behind the blows. And too closely for her to use her feet, Tony noted. Smart guy, given that he was on his knees. Tony doubted he had a cup on under his jeans. At least he never had while they were dating.

"Let go! Let go! Let go!"

Zev murmured something against her hair that Tony didn't catch.

" 'Cause Tony said it was way gross and I want to see!"

Both brows rose, but he quickly schooled his expression and brought her face around until he could stare deep into her eyes, his tone calm and reassuring. "It's not real, you know. It's just bits left over from a long time ago."

She sniffed and stopped fighting him. "Like television?"

"Just like television. The house recorded what happened and now it's playing it back."

"Trying to fool us and make us think it's real?"

"That's right."

"But we know it's not real."

"Yes, we do."

Shoulders squared and chins lifted among the listening adults. Out of the mouths of babes—they *knew* it wasn't real.

"Stupid house."

"No argument from me." When she answered his smile with one of her own, Zev stood, scooping her up and settling her weight on one hip. "Let's get out of here." For the benefit of the others in the room, his gaze flicked down to the body and back up again.

Tony's heart stopped at the sight of a red-brown streak across Zev's cheek and then started beating again when he realized it had been left by some of the fake blood still in Brianna's hair. *No way. We don't lose Zev. Or Amy. Or . . . fuck. Who says I get to choose?* And even thinking about choosing put him in a Meryl Streep space he'd just as soon not have visited.

"Leaving is a good idea." Amy, now holding her candle and Zev's, started for the foyer.

How had the foyer become their safe place? Because they'd spent more time shooting in it and it had become familiar? Because it was a big empty space with fewer nooks and crannies for the weird to hide out in? Maybe because it was the last place things had been normal. Or what passed for normal during the long, overcaffeinated hours of television production.

"Mason?" Ashley tugged on the actor's tuxedo jacket. "Are you okay?"

"Fine. I'm fine. Just a headache."

It had to be one hell of a headache, Tony conceded, because when Ashley took hold of his hand, Mason's fingers closed around hers almost gratefully.

"Our contract says no smoking in the house," Peter told him as he followed the actor and the little girl out of the drawing room. "So if you feel the need to light up . . ."

"That's not it!"

It was something, though. Mason wasn't a good enough actor to entirely smooth out the ragged edges in his voice.

"Are we just going to leave him here?" Lee asked, pausing by the tarp and Tom's body.

Tony shrugged. "If he wants to join us, he knows the way."

"That's . . . ghoulish." One corner of Lee's mouth curled up. "This is me not laughing. Do you think he will?"

"No. If Amy's rings don't work, and if I actually understand what the fuck is going on, he should just keep running into the window over and over."

"One show and then immediately into reruns."

"Yeah, doesn't take much to go into syndication around here."

"Still not laughing." Although he sounded close.

"Me either." It felt so strangely right, standing there, together, staring down at the first casualty, making the kind of bad jokes that guys made when things got dangerously whacked, that Tony began to get just a little freaked. Fortunately, he had an easy out. "Brenda's waiting for you."

Brenda was standing by the door, doing a Lady Macbeth with her hands.

Next to her stood Saleen, who had the only candle still in the drawing room and was clearly waiting for the three stragglers to leave. Just as clearly as Brenda was waiting for Lee.

Lee said nothing for a long moment, although Tony had the feeling things were being said just beyond the range of his hearing. Like Lee was talking at a level only dogs could hear. Or something. Then he snorted, sounding almost amused, and crossed to tuck Brenda up against his side. While she didn't exactly relax, the time frame extended on her obvious air of "I'm five minutes from a total breakdown."

"Move your ass," Saleen snarled at Tony, standing alone by the corpse.

Was it his imagination or had Karl's crying picked up a mocking undertone?

With half a dozen candles burning and light reflecting off the polished floor and the high gloss on the wood paneling, the hall was almost welcoming—where *almost* referred to its being as good as it could get while trapped inside a homicidal house.

Tina stood by the inside door, shining her flashlight beam down into the entry. "Everett's still breathing, but he doesn't look good."

"He's never looked that good to me," Mason muttered. "Oh, come off it," he continued over half a dozen protests. "It was the perfect straight line; everyone was thinking it."

Most of the men, and Amy, nodded.

"I don't like that he's been in there so long." Tina brought her left wrist up closer to her face and frowned. "Damn, my watch isn't working. What time is it?"

No one's watch was working—although the hands and numbers on Amy's were still glowing in the dark.

"What difference does that make if it's not telling time?" Adam asked her.

She shrugged. "It's comforting."

"So what do we do now, eh?" Hartley asked, shifting his weight from heel to toe, arms wrapped around his torso.

"We survive until morning," Peter announced in the same no-nonsense tone he'd use to call for quiet on the set. "All of us."

"All the rest of us," someone said. Tony thought it might have been Pavin, the sound tech, but he wasn't sure.

"Yeah, and we stop listening to *him*!" That was definitely Kate. Arms folded in the more aggressive version of Hartley's position, she glared at Tony. "If it wasn't for his stupid idea of throwing stuff through those windows, Tom would still be alive!"

A little stunned by the accusation, it took Tony a moment to find the words. "I never said he should throw himself through!"

"Your idea to go into that room, so you put him in there. Your idea to throw stuff, so you planted the seed in a desperate man."

"Seed? What seed? And he didn't seem desperate to me."

"You're not denying it, then!"

"What?" Oh, crap. He hadn't. He hadn't thought he needed to, but from all the creased brows and narrowed eyes, it looked like Kate wasn't the only one who thought he was responsible for Tom's death. *Some of us will go crazy and kill the rest. Great. And guess which list I'm on.* As Kate stepped forward, he took an involuntary step back. *So I'm thinking it's too late for us to become friends.* As Mouse joined her, he stepped back again. And once more for luck.

"Leave him be, Kate."

Mouse was on his side?

"Can't blame Tony for Tom's death. Might as well blame Lee for going into the room first."

The narrowed eyes and creased brows fixed on Lee.

"Or Ashley for throwing the dish."

Creases began smoothing out. No one in the crew could blame a little girl. Or more specifically, they'd learned there was no percentage in blaming CB's daughter—even for things she was guilty of.

"Or me for throwing the chair."

And that killed the accusation cold. Tony was relieved to see that no one was suicidal enough yet to throw accusations at a man capable of bench-pressing a Buick.

In the awkward silence that followed, Tina picked up Everett's makeup case and carried it over to where Brenda and Lee were standing. "Brenda, why don't we get the girls' makeup off?"

"I'm wardrobe."

"So you're saying you can't do it?"

"No, I just . . . I mean . . . Fine." She pulled away from Lee so reluctantly Tony almost heard duct tape releasing. "Brianna, you're messier, so you should . . . Brianna?"

"Cheese!" Ashley reached past Zev and grabbed her sister's shoulder, shaking animation back into her face.

Zev gently but firmly separated them and then knelt. "What is it, Bri?"

"The baby's stopped crying."

"But that's good, right?"

She frowned. "I don't think so."

Neither did Tony. Previously, when Karl stopped crying, it signaled the beginning of a flashback. Cassie and Stephen, Karl's own death . . .

The lights in the hall came on. There was furniture—a couple of high-back chairs, a half-moon table with a vase of white tulips, an Oriental rug.

And Tony was alone.

Except for whoever was screaming, "Charles, don't!" up on the second floor.

The second floor still seemed to be in darkness, so whatever was going to happen was going to happen out here.

And there they were.

Ladies and gentlemen, if I could direct your attention to the top of the stairs. Charles was wearing a uniform. The woman with him wore a gray suit—snug, tailored, and obviously expensive. Tony didn't know much about women's fashions, but it looked like the one Madonna wore in *Evita*. Charles had his hands wrapped around her upper arms and was moving her slowly backward. She was crying, begging him to stop, but he almost seemed not to hear her, his face terrifyingly blank.

That's great. I can hear her and he can't?

Crap. He's going to throw her down the stairs. Knowing it was futile, Tony ran for the stairs anyway.

But they descended two, three, four steps down the long staircase and still no push.

Charles stepped down so they were both standing on the fifth step. "You want to hang around with your *friends* while I'm gone," he said quietly, emphasis making the gender of the friends clear, "you go right ahead." Then he lifted her and slammed her onto one half of the rack of antlers hanging on the wall. Fabric tore and the longest prong emerged out through the front of the gray suit.

"Okay, I'll believe that madness gave him strength," Tony protested, to the house, to the ghosts, to keep from screaming, "but there's no way those antlers would stay on the wall with a full-grown woman—even a short one—hanging off them!"

Which was when the antlers came off the wall and bounced down the stairs, the gurgling, thrashing woman still attached. Tony glanced down as Charles did to see that she'd come to a twitching stop halfway through his legs.

"Fuck, fuck, FUCK!" He danced back.

Stopped dancing in time to see the big finish to Charles' dive over the banister. Heads really did sound like melons splitting. The Foley guys would be pleased.

The lights went out. Became candlelight again.

And he was no longer alone.

"Stop staring at me," he muttered, trying to catch his breath.

"They think you've gone crazy."

"Jesus fucking Christ!" He jumped back as Stephen and Cassie appeared suddenly in front of him.

"And that's not helping," Stephen pointed out.

"Thanks. No shit. Where the hell have you two been?"

"It took us a while to manifest again after we died and then we were stuck in the bathroom while the others took their turns."

The siblings were just translucent enough for Tony to see that no one had, in fact, stopped staring.

Some of them would go crazy and kill the rest.

Lunatic.

Or victim.

Now, he might be reading too much into expressions he could barely see—given the ghosts and the candlelight and all—but it seemed as though everyone had changed their mind about which description best suited him.

⬭ SEVEN

"I'm not crazy."

"You're reacting to things that only you can see, and you're talking to nobody."

"I'm reacting to old murders being replayed, and I'm talking to Stephen and Cassie." Tony jerked his head toward the brother and sister. Stephen was watching the exchange with some interest, but Cassie's gaze flicked all around the hall—her single eye working overtime to cover the whole area while both her hands clutched at the translucent fabric of her skirt. Given that she'd been brutally murdered years before and had apparently relived the incident numerous times since, he wondered just what remained for her to be uneasy about. "What's the matter?"

"She's listening for the music," Stephen answered when his sister didn't. "The ballroom creeps her out."

"You're talking to ghosts," Zev sighed.

"Yeah."

"And that doesn't sound crazy to you?"

"Zev . . ."

"I'm not saying it's not all true—my personal beliefs to the contrary, weird shit is definitely happening here tonight—but you have to admit it sounds crazy."

"He's right."

"Shut up, Stephen!" Tony turned to glare at the ghost as Zev's reassuring smile tightened.

"Case in point."

Tony ran a hand through his hair. He hadn't exactly been ostracized since his reaction to the last reenactment, but everyone seemed uncomfortable having him too close, forcing him out toward the edges of the light.

"In situations like this . . ."

And that was certainly using the phrase "like this" in its loosest sense.

". . . people look for someone to blame. You're setting yourself up to be that someone." Zev closed his hand around Tony's arm and squeezed gently. "You know you are."

"Yeah, and I also know I can't not tell you guys what's going on. In a situation *like this* . . ." Okay, maybe Zev was trying to help and maybe the sarcastic emphasis wasn't entirely called for. So what. ". . . I can't be the one who decides what's important information and what's not. Not when nineteen . . . eighteen lives are at stake."

"Seventeen."

"Everett's still alive." Suddenly unsure, he glanced over at Cassie who nodded. "Yeah, still alive. Eighteen."

"I'm not disagreeing with you, Tony, I'm just . . ." He paused and sighed again, his grip on Tony's arm tightening. "I'm just saying you should be careful. Emotions are fraying."

"He's right."

"Cassie agrees with you."

Zev nodded at the space to Tony's right. "Thank you." Tony pointed left. "She's over there."

"Stop it! Stop it now!" Brianna's protest rose up and over and temporarily obliterated Karl's crying. As Tony turned, he noticed everyone's attention locking on CB's younger daughter, grateful for the distraction. "You're pulling!"

"Fine." Brenda stepped back, lip curling. "Then we'll just leave your hair like it is."

"No! I want it braided!"

"Then you have to hold still."

"I won't! Not for you! You suck!"

"No . . ." The pause went on just long enough that everyone leaned forward slightly, waiting for Brenda's response. ". . . you suck!"

Brianna's chin lifted and her eyes narrowed. "No, you! And I'm telling my father you didn't take care of me!"

"Don't tempt me!" The wardrobe supervisor held up her right hand, finger and thumb barely apart. "I'm this close to taking care of you!"

Zev released Tony's arm. "I think I'd better get over there before Brianna gets strangled."

"Don't hurry."

"Give the kid a break, she's just scared and acting out."

"I guess." Although it didn't look like any definition of scared Tony'd ever seen. Not unless she'd been scared eighty percent of the time she'd ever been at the studio. "I never knew you were so good with kids."

"Yeah, well . . ." He turned back just far enough for Tony to see a dark brow rise. ". . . we weren't together long enough for you to find out."

"Zing and ouch!" Amy stepped into the space Zev had vacated and they watched him cross to Brianna's side, taking the blue plastic comb from Brenda's hand as he passed. "This is why you should never date someone from work."

No surprise that she conveniently ignored having encouraged them both. "Should you be standing here? Aren't you afraid I'll finish going crazy and kill you?"

"Because you're seeing ectoplasmic manifestations?" She snorted. "Man, I'd love to see a ghost. What do they look like?"

"I don't know . . ." He shrugged and took another look. ". . . dead. Cassie's missing a chunk of her head, and Stephen's neck has been hacked into. Their clothes are covered in blood and . . ."

"And what?"

"Nothing." He'd just realized that Stephen wasn't wearing pants under the bloodstained shirt—with all the blood and them being ax murdered and, well, dead, he'd never noticed it before. They were both watching him when he lifted his eyes off Stephen's bare legs. "Hey." He spread his hands. "None of my business."

Amy looked in the same direction and frowned. "What?" she demanded, repeating the question again, significantly louder, when Tony didn't immediately respond.

With Brianna happily submitting to Zev's hairdressing, everyone now snapped their attention around to Amy.

"We're just talking," she sighed. "Get a collective life."

"Not entirely a bad idea." Peter pushed himself away from the wall under the stairs and walked out to the center of the hall, visibly becoming "the director" as he moved. "Listen up, people, it's going to be a long night if we just sit here, so let's try and come up with something a little more proactive."

No one spoke.

"You could kill yourselves now. Then you wouldn't have to wait for bad stuff to happen."

No one except Stephen. Tony decided not to pass his observation on.

"Anyone?" Peter pivoted on one heel. "Adam? Tina? Sorge?" With two shrugs and a nontranslatable mumble as a response, he threw up his arms. "Oh, for God's sake, we create this kind of crap. If this was an episode of *Darkest Night*, how would we resolve it?"

"If this was an episode of *Darkest Night*," Amy snorted, "we'd all be red-shirts. Well, except for Mason and Lee—because they've got to be back next week and probably the kids since the last one of us standing sacrificed him or herself to save them. The only sure thing about this many people trapped in a haunted house is that the body count is going to be high." She swept a disdainful gaze around at her silent audience. "What? You know that's the way it would go down."

"All right, fine. Maybe," Peter snapped, over the chorus of muttered acknowledgments. "And now you've made your point, let's rewrite the script in such a way that we all survive."

"Oh, a *rewrite*. You should've said. I think . . ." Black-and-magenta-tipped fingers tapped her chest somewhere around Hello Kitty's left ear. ". . . that if there's a thing in the house attempting to collect us, we should destroy it, thus freeing the ghosts and ourselves."

New silence. Speculative this time. Tony was amazed that no one said anything about the *thus*. He, personally, was standing too close to comment safely.

"That sounds . . . simple enough," Adam admitted after a long moment.

"Too simple," Saleen scoffed.

"What? It can't be simple?"

The grip pointedly folded muscular arms. "If it's been around since before the house was built, how do we destroy it? And how do we even find it?"

"It's in the basement," Tony and Stephen said simultaneously. "The caretaker warned me away from the stairs," Tony continued on his own as Stephen made "fine, go ahead if you're so smart" faces. "And when I touched the doorknob, it gave me a shock."

"Oooo, a shock." Saleen recoiled in mock horror.

Tony ignored him; so far there'd been plenty of real horror to pay attention to. "The shock made a weird mark on my hand."

"So let's see it," Amy demanded, grabbing his wrist.

"Other hand. And it's gone now."

"Convenient." Saleen again. He was rapidly working through the goodwill he'd built up by waiting in the drawing room with the candle. Not that it much mattered, given he was almost as big as Mouse.

"What kind of mark, Tony?" Peter asked, brow furrowed.

"I don't know."

"Big surprise." And a change in the chorus as Saleen handed off to Kate.

"So." Ashley moved out of Mason's shadow, stepped to Peter's side and folded her arms, sweeping the group with an expression eerily reminiscent of her father. "Let's go to the basement and kick ass!"

Adam joined her. "Works for me."

"No." Kate shook her head as she stood. "Do you really want to go face-to-face . . ."

"It has a face?" Amy asked him. Tony shrugged.

". . . with something that makes people kill each other from a distance? You don't know what it's capable of up close!"

Saleen moved to stand by Adam. "Only one way to find out."

"Fine." Tina took Ashley's hand and pulled her away from the two men. "But the girls aren't going."

Ashley's struggles only proved what almost everyone else in the room already knew. When Tina made up her mind, she couldn't be moved. Figuratively. Physically. "But it was my idea!"

"I don't care." Tina's tone challenged and went unopposed. "The girls and I are staying here. I don't want to leave Everett alone again."

Brianna seemed to be considering making a run for it but settled as Zev's hand closed on her shoulder. "Okay, fine, but if I have to stay with Ashes, Zev has to stay with me."

"Then Mason's staying with me." Still held securely by Tina's side, Ashley reached out her other hand and grabbed Mason's jacket.

"Mason's . . ."

"No, that's all right." Mason twitched his jacket free but moved close enough so that Ashley could tuck her hand in his elbow. "If she needs me, I'll stay."

Tony could almost hear responses to that considered and discarded.

"All right, then," Adam declared, squaring his shoulders. "Who else is coming?"

"I'm not going near the basement." Brenda's hands were back to performing a full-out Lady Macbeth as Sorge joined the other two men.

"Too obvious," Mouse muttered.

"He's right." Kate moved closer to her cameraman. "Why would it let us know where it is?"

"Why would it care?" Saleen demanded.

"Maybe it doesn't care if we know where it is because it wants us to face it," Pavin said, getting to his feet. Tony wondered if the sound tech had always had that slight twitch. Was it endemic to the sound department? Although Hartley's twitch wasn't exactly slight . . . "It wants us down there in the wet with the wires," Pavin continued. "Old, frayed, cloth-wrapped wires. And then, when we're all standing knee-deep in the flood, it'll turn the power back on and drop a wire in the water because if it can close the doors it can surely do that, and we'll all be electrocuted. Or one of us'll snap and pull the wire into the water, and we'll all be electrocuted. You know how you die when that happens? Soup."

And that pretty much killed the charge to the basement.

"Okay," Amy said after a long moment of soup-filled silence. "Then we protect ourselves here."

"Wouldn't moving into an actual room make more sense?" Tony asked.

"In there with Tom?" Kate snapped, glaring at him.

Tina's glare was less personal but more potent for all that. "I'm *not* leaving Everett."

Guess not.

"We need salt. Lots of salt." Amy drew a vaguely circular shape in the air. "We draw a circle of salt around us and the evil can't get in."

Tony was about to point out that, first of all, he didn't think the evil wanted in and, secondly, if it was permeating the house, it was kind of a moot point since inside the circle would be as much a part of the house as outside the circle, when he realized the salt might calm a few fears and calm was a good thing. He'd be willing to bet that very few people went crazy calmly. "I saw some salt in the kitchen."

He was starting to get used to the staring.

"You want me to go get it, don't you?"

"Not alone," Kate muttered, brows drawn into a deep vee. "I don't trust you alone."

"No one goes anywhere alone," Peter amended pointedly. "It's not safe. Someone has to go with you."

And a whole new silence descended.

"Me!"

"Me, too!"

"Neither of you," Tina informed the sisters, who shuffled and muttered but obeyed.

"Oh, for . . ." Amy rolled her eyes with enough emphasis the gesture was visible even in the candlelight. "I'll go."

"No." Peter was as adamant as Tina had been. "You know what's happening . . ."

Hang on. Tony frowned. *He* knew what was happening. Amy just spent a lot of time on Web sites called creepycrap.com.

". . . you have to stay here."

He didn't much like the implication they could afford to lose him but not Amy. Not that he wanted to lose Amy, but he didn't much like the idea of losing *him* either.

"I'll go with him."

Lee. It was the first thing he'd said since they'd left the drawing room, and Tony turned to stare at him in surprise.

"Lee, no . . ."

The expected protest from Brenda, but why the hell were Zev's eyebrows up?

"Look, someone's got to go and if Lee's willing, fine." Peter waved down further protests. "We'll get nothing accomplished if we stand around arguing all night. Tina, lend Lee your flashlight."

And what? I can see in the dark?

"I don't know." She pulled it from her pocket and peered down at the purple plastic. "It's looking dimmer . . ."

"That doesn't matter. They can't walk and keep a candle lit."

A valid point, but if the flashlight's batteries died, they'd be screwed, and given the way other batteries had been lasting . . . or not lasting . . . "Maybe we should take a candle anyway, just in case."

"NO!"

Multiple voices, all unthrilled about the prospect of a night spent trapped in the dark.

The kitchen seemed farther away than it had been barely hours earlier. The flashlight was definitely dimmer, the circle of light Lee kept pointed at the floor in front of them almost a brownish yellow—like a dirty headlight. They were walking close together—for comfort, for security, Tony had no idea why—and the sleeve of Lee's tuxedo jacket kept brushing against his bare arm, lifting the hair on the back of his neck, then taking a direct route to his groin.

His whole body remembered the feel of the other man sprawled beneath him in the kitchen.

Here's a thought, you pathetic geek, try to act like a mature adult in a dangerous situation instead of a horny fifteen-year-old.

"This reminds me of a job I had in high school," Lee said quietly, sweeping the flashlight beam up one wall, across the ceiling, and down the other. "I worked with the animal control guy clearing raccoons out of cottages in the spring."

Tony glanced at the actor and snickered. "You worked in tuxedos?"

"Only if we had a formal complaint."

That got the groan it deserved.

Back behind them, he could hear another argument starting up in the hall, but although he could tell it was an argument from the volume, he couldn't make out any actual words. They hadn't gone that far. He should have been able to hear words.

Their footsteps sounded strangely muffled, like the hardwood was absorbing the sound.

Yeah. Strangely—like that should come as a shock.

He felt like he should say something, discuss the situation, maybe bat around a few ideas for getting them the hell out of there, but he couldn't think of a thing to say that hadn't already been said.

"So, you and Zev aren't seeing each other anymore?"

Okay. That was unexpected. "Uh, no. We . . . uh . . . aren't."

"But you're still friends."

"Sure." Not a question, but he answered it anyway.

"How do you guys do that; stay friends? I mean, if a man breaks up with a woman, they don't slide immediately back into friendship afterward."

Tony snorted. "Are they usually friends before?"

"Not usually, no." Lee sounded a bit rueful. "But you and Zev; I see you guys together and . . ."

"Is that a problem?" Tony asked when the sentence continued to dangle.

"What? No, of course not. Like you said: two consenting adults, none of my business."

Had he said that? Oh, right, about Brenda. Who was not Lee's friend.

And you are?

Ah, but I'm not fucking him.

He was still trying to figure out just what he meant by that and whether his answer had any relevance at all to his question when the light went out.

The jacket sleeve stopped stroking his arm as they froze in place.

The muted clicking was less than comforting as Lee turned the flashlight on and off. Finally: "I think the battery's dead."

The darkness was so complete it had weight and wrapped around them like a heavy blanket. Eyes open, eyes closed, it made no difference.

"This could be a problem."

"You think?"

"There's a couple of lanterns and some matches in the cupboard in the conservatory."

A third voice.

"Jesus fucking Christ!" Heart in his throat, Tony whirled around, stumbling into Lee, who reached out blindly, caught his arm, and steadied him. Cassie looked as sheepish as possible, given she was barely a pale gray sketch on the air. Stephen, equally translucent, shrugged not at all apologetically. "You followed us!"

"We came with you," Stephen amended.

"There's no point in staying with the others," Cassie said reasonably. "They can't see or hear us and they're boring."

Which was when Tony realized she wasn't looking at him but staring at Lee with the kind of besotted expression he was only too familiar with—except it usually came with two eyes and an entire head.

"They followed us?" Lee repeated.

"They did."

"The ghosts?"

"Yeah. They think the others are boring. They say there're lanterns and matches in the conservatory."

Stephen nodded and adjusted his head. "Graham found them one day when he was snooping around."

"Caretaking," Cassie corrected archly.

"Yes, well, he found them. He left them there."

"Then all we have to do is find the conservatory," Lee said before Tony could ask just what exactly Graham had been snooping around for, had he found it, and was it likely to now bite them on the ass.

"I'll take you!" Cassie wafted past.

"Only Tony can see you," Stephen muttered as he followed. "She thinks he's cute," he added as he drew even with Tony's ear. "She's the one who painted his butt."

"I figured. You okay with that?" A jealous brother would be such fun under the circumstances. Particularly given how close the siblings were—had been.

"Why should I care?"

Tony decided not to mention the whole lack of pants thing. He ran his hand down Lee's arm, found his hand—*I'm at the end of his arm? What else was I expecting to find?*—and tucked it into the crock of his elbow. "All I can see is the ghosts, but I'm assuming they can see the house, so I'll follow them and you stick with me."

Lee's fingers tightened, just for an instant, then loosened to the minimal contact he no doubt felt was required when a straight man touched a gay man.

And that was minimal contact on the floor in the kitchen?

Shut up!

He didn't need the house to drive him crazy, he was doing a fine job all on his own. With any luck, mass murder wasn't next after inappropriate sexual fantasies and self-chastisement. Verbal self-chastisement. Not the physical kind.

If his sense of distance had seemed off before, it was totally screwed now as he followed the pair of pale forms through total darkness. His feet never entirely left the floor, the soles of his running shoes sliding over the hardwood with a series of soft squeaks as treads scraped urethane. Lee's dress shoes made an answering shush-shush that seemed to indicate he also intended to remain grounded. Given the total lack of light and their lack of planning in not being in contact with a wall when the light went out, the floor underfoot was all they had to be sure of.

Tony was beginning to think that they should have arrived *somewhere* and was beginning to worry that they hadn't when the hard/soft crash of body slamming into an opened door derailed his train of thought. The impact jerked Lee's hand off his arm.

"Son of a fucking . . ."

"Lee?" He grabbed for the other man. As his fingers closed around familiar fabric, he started breathing again.

"I seem to have found the kitchen." The wet velvet voice sounded rougher than usual. "Or at least the kitchen door."

"Is he hurt?" Cassie drifted in close and stared up at where Lee had to be. *Too bad they don't actually throw enough light to be useful.*

Stephen shot his sister an exasperated eye roll. "Don't worry, he's fine."

Yeah, dead guys walking around were great judges of *fine*. "Are you okay?"

"I think so. Although if I've given myself a black eye, tomorrow's shoot will be interesting."

Tomorrow's shoot. *He thinks we'll get out of this.*

Of course he does, he's in the credits. The guys in the credits always survive.

Maintaining his grip on Lee's jacket, Tony reached out with his other hand and defined the rest of the kitchen door. "If we turn left here, the conservatory's about seven or eight meters straight ahead. If I keep my hand on the wall, we'll know when we arrive and avoid falling down those three steps."

"I'd have told you about the steps," Cassie murmured. "And we're sorry about the door."

"Why was that our fault?" Stephen demanded.

And that was the peanut gallery heard from. "Lee?"

The arm inside Lee's jacket had no give to it, the muscles tensed, the joints locked. "Tony, I don't hear the baby anymore."

Now it had been brought to his attention, he couldn't remember having heard Karl the entire time they'd been standing in the kitchen doorway.

The lights came up and Tony was all alone. He moved his hand before he thought to wonder if he was still in real-world contact with Lee. *Stupid, fucking . . .* "Lee, I know you can hear me—I'm in another replay. I've got lights now, so I'll walk to the conservatory and the cupboard and wait there until the replay stops. Stephen and Cassie are stuck in the bathroom for the duration and you can't see me to follow, so stay right where you are. Don't move. I'll come back with the lanterns as fast as I can." He tried to sound reassuring, but the scream from the conservatory distracted him a bit.

By the time he covered the seven meters, the gardener—he assumed it was the gardener given the location and the overalls—was lying on his back on an old wooden bench while an elderly woman in a dark brown dress and sensible shoes sawed off his right leg. From the way he was twitching, Tony didn't think he was dead. When she got through to the bone, she switched to a hatchet.

Good solid swing considering her age.

Right leg. Left leg. Left arm. Each piece—thankfully—removed much faster than in real time. As she hacked through each bone in turn, the sound was a lot less brittle than Tony had expected. He made a mental note to mention it to the sound guys. CB didn't want to pay for his own Foley studio, so they usually bought what they needed from independent artists. None of them had quite gotten the wet crunch right.

The extended dismemberment should have upset him more than it did. Maybe he'd become desensitized by the parade of axes and burning babies and antlers. Maybe the past had lost its ability to affect him, given that in the present a person he actually knew was dead and he and another seventeen were in danger of dying. Maybe the whole old lady sawing and hacking thing was just so over the top, he found it difficult to believe it was real and, frankly, he'd seen blood done better. Spurting arteries were unfortunately forever tied to Monty Python marathons on Comedy Central. Whatever the reason, he found he was standing, arms crossed, drumming his fingers on his elbow and wishing she'd hurry the hell up.

He almost cheered as the head finally came off—but no, now she had to bury the pieces. One piece in each of the raised beds.

Damn. That extra *could* have felt fingers. Sure, there was no way that the actual hand remained buried in the dirt, but since metaphysical action was still going on . . .

And on.

He sighed and leaned against the cupboard.

Grunting a little with the effort, she dropped the gardener's head into the large urn in the middle of the room. Tony frowned at the muffled squelch. Hadn't he ended up with an extra background player when he'd done the final head count around that urn this morning? An extra head in the head count. Cute. A malevolent thing with a sense of humor—like that made it so much better.

Then the old woman was suddenly at the cupboard, reaching through him for the handle. He jerked to one side, far enough to get free of her arm but not so far he couldn't scan the shelves. No lanterns, not in this time, but that didn't matter as long as they were there when he got back to the present.

There was, however, a brand new box of rat poison.

She ripped open the little cardboard spout and tipped a generous portion into her mouth.

Modern rat poison contained warfarin—a blood thinner. The rats ate the bait, scuttled into the walls, and bled to death internally. It was a slow, painful, terrifying way to die. Emphasis on slow—which was why Tony even knew about it. The writers had wanted to use rat poison to deal with the crime *du jour* in episode eleven but had ditched the idea when they found out how long it would take. Pre-warfarin, the active ingredient depended on the brand of the rat poison but throughout most of rural Canada arsenic-of-lead predominated.

Eyes so wide bloodshot red showed all the way around pale brown irises, the old woman swallowed a second mouthful.

And then forced down a third.

Teeth clenched so tightly Tony could see a muscle jump in her jaw, she managed to keep all three down as she walked back to the bench and sat primly down on the blood-soaked wood, knees together, feet crossed at the ankles.

Tony had no way of telling how long after that the vomiting blood began, but once started, it continued for some time. Continued until the old lady was lying in a puddle of her blood and the gardener's combined, protruding tongue white, skin faintly blue. Her open eyes were staring directly at him and for a moment, just before she died, she frowned slightly—almost as if she could see him standing there.

And *that* was the most frightening thing he'd seen so far.

Then it was dark. Dark and completely silent. He couldn't hear the rain on the glass, but whether that was because it had stopped raining or the house prevented the sound from entering, he had no idea. Half afraid he could still feel the old lady's eyes on him, he fumbled for the clasp of the cupboard as Karl started crying again.

How weird that the sound of a baby in a fire was comforting?

Pretty damned weird actually.

"Tony?"

Lee's voice much, much closer than the kitchen. He shrieked as fingers stubbed up against him.

"It was taking so long. I, uh . . . I got worried about you, so I followed the wall." And except for the desperate way he clutched at Tony's arm, he'd have sold it. "Did I startle you?"

"Startle me? I almost fucking pissed myself!"

"Way too much information." The chuckle was slightly strained but, still, an award-winning performance considering he was leaving bruises.

Tony was just as happy to have the contact maintained—and for a change the thought of Lee touching him in no way evoked a sexual response. Or at least not much of one. It was actually kind of encouraging that his dick was taking a mild interest since, mere moments before, terror had driven his balls up to sit on his shoulder.

Cupboard open, he found something that felt like he thought he remembered lanterns looked on the top shelf. Carefully holding the round middle section, he shook it gently. Liquid sloshed.

"Kerosene?" Lee asked.

"Let's hope so."

His other hand finger-walked along the shelf until he touched a greasy box. It rattled when he nudged it. "I think I found the matches."

He had a lantern in one hand. He had matches in the other. Time passed. This chuckle sounded legitimate. "You have no idea what to do, do you?"

"Yeah, well, lanterns—not so big in my life."

"Never a Boy Scout?"

"No." He tried to keep the disdain from sounding in his voice and didn't quite manage it. Back when he was on the street, he'd had a scoutmaster among his regulars. Every week, like clockwork, after his scout meeting . . .

"Lucky for you, I was. Don't move." The grip on Tony's arm moved down to his hand and then up the lantern. Glass clinked against glass. "Chimney's got to come off." Glass against wood as, still holding the lantern with one hand, Lee set the chimney in the cupboard with the other. "Wick has to be turned down into the kerosene." His fingers brushed Tony's as he steadied the lantern. "You're holding the matches?"

"Yeah."

"Okay. Bring that hand over . . . Got it." It took a moment's fumbling to get the box open. "Do you have your eyes closed?"

"What?"

"It's so dark, I just wondered . . ."

"No." When he closed his eyes, he could see the old lady staring at him as she died. "You?"

"No."

Tony thought about asking what Lee saw on the inside of his lids. Decided against it. Had a feeling, considering what had gone down last spring, he knew what the answer would be.

"Okay, the wick's damp. Let's light this sucker."

The first match fizzed weakly but didn't catch.

The second flared; a painfully bright, two-second orange-red point of light. "Third time lucky."

Since the only reply that occurred was *"Three men on a match,"* Tony kept his mouth shut.

The third match caught and held. Cupped in Lee's hand, it descended to a piece of cloth sticking up from the bottom of the lantern.

And then there was light.

He watched as Lee fiddled with a small metal wheel for a moment, put the top glass bit back on, and then he switched his grip to the wrapped wire handle. "All right, then."

"Yeah." Lee visibly relaxed as he slid the box of matches into his pocket. "There's a second lantern," he said, lifting it out of the cupboard. "And a two-liter can of kerosene that's barely been touched."

And four mouse traps.

And a box of rat poison.

Foreshadowing, Tony sighed. *The sign of quality horror flicks.* Except this wasn't a movie, it was real life. He squinted at the packaging.

"Problem?"

"Nope." It was a new box and if the doors opened at sunrise the house didn't have time for the warfarin to work. And how disturbing did life have to get for *that* to be reassuring?

Pretty damned disturbing.

"Tony? Lee?" Adam. Not close. The 1AD had probably moved only as far as the edge of the candlelight since his voice—a voice that could carry over half a dozen separate conversations, background construction noise, and a posse of hysterical Raymond Dark fans—was barely audible. "What the hell . . ." A few words got lost in the distance, making the whole thing eerily reminiscent of the problems with the walkie-talkies. ". . . so long?"

Lee half turned, pulled around by the reminder that they weren't alone. "We need to get back."

"Yeah."

They were halfway through the kitchen when Tony remembered what they'd originally come for. "Salt."

"What?"

"Amy's protective circle."

"Right. Do you think she knows what she's talking about?"

"I think it can't hurt."

Lee's answering expression was so carefully neutral it was obvious he heard the subtext. And just as obvious, he wasn't going to mention it. Hope was a fragile thing at the best of times and locked up in a psychotic house, it took a beating.

Craft services had left a large box of small salt packets and other condiments on the counter by the door. Tony set the lantern down by the box—Lee was carrying the spare and the kerosene—and folded in the cardboard flaps. As he tucked it under his arm, three packets slid out and hit the floor. He bent to pick them up and froze. "Son of a bitch."

"What?"

The cables running out of the generator hadn't been packed up before the doors slammed closed. He was so used to spending his working day stepping over and around a web of cable that it hadn't even occurred to him to question their continuing presence or how impossible it would be to close a door on them. *Under the circumstances, maybe impossible isn't the right word.* The cables ran up to the door and stopped. Tony grabbed one and pulled to no effect. They hadn't been severed. They just stopped. "They're still going through the space," he muttered. "When is a door not a door . . . ?"

"When it's a jar?" Lee's tone had distinct hints of *let's humor the crazy man.*

"When it's a metaphysical construct."

"Say what?"

He sat back and glanced up at the actor. "This door was created by the house to lock us in. The actual door is still open."

"Can we get out through it?" Lee frowned down at the point where the cables met the wood.

Good question. Eyes closed to keep perception out of the equation, Tony ran his fist along the top of the cables and punched out at the space they had to be using. "Ow." To give the house credit, that was one *solid* metaphysical construct.

"Tony! Lee!" Adam again. A little closer.

"We're on our way! We have to get back," Lee added, dropping his volume and nodding toward the salt. "If we can't get out the door . . ."

"Yeah." He rapped his knuckles against it again. Still felt solid. "I guess. Listen, why don't you light the other lantern, take the salt, and go back to the others. I'll catch up. There's something I want to try."

"I'll stay . . ."

Lee wanted to stay with him and he was sending him away. Maybe he should just tell him about the whole wizard thing. Which would lead to telling him about the whole shadow thing. Which would not be a good thing. "No. We've been gone so long they've got to be getting a little freaked."

"Uh-huh."

What the hell did that mean? Tony wondered as Lee set about lighting the other lantern. *If you want to know, dipshit—ask!*

Yeah, like that was going to happen.

Lee tucked the box of salt under his arm, much as Tony had done. "Don't take too long."

That was it?

Apparently.

As Lee left the kitchen, Tony turned his attention back to the cables and attempted to clear his mind of everything but his immediate surroundings.

He thinks I'm a freak.

And the longer they were stuck in this freak show of a house, the more evidence he'd have to support that theory.

So since this is our best way out, can we get on with it!

The door was only a physical seeming of a door. It made sense that he couldn't put his hand through something physical. Visualizing the back porch and the bucket of sand that had been left there for the smokers, he raised his right palm toward the space he couldn't see and snapped out the seven words.

Sixteen cigarette butts later, he stopped.

"That's not normal."

"Pot, kettle, black, dead people." He sat back on his heels and tried to flick a butt back outside. It bounced off the door and hit him in the forehead. Okay. He'd proved something here. Wasn't sure what, but it might be useful later. Brushing his experimental data off his jeans, he stood and faced his own personal Greek chorus. "What?"

"I think that's our question," Stephen snorted. "What *are* you?"

Why not. It wasn't like they could pass the information on.

"I'm a wizard."

Tony braced himself for the inevitable Harry Potter references.

Cassie frowned. "Like Merlin?"

And let's hear it for those who died before J. K. Rowling was born. "Yeah, sort of."

Stephen nodded down at the mess on the floor. "Is that all you can do?" he asked, realigning his head.

"So far." It wasn't all he'd attempted, but it was all he could do with any certainty of success.

"It doesn't look very useful."

"Bite me."

"Pardon?"

"Never mind." There were two unopened boxes of bottled water on the floor by the table. He set the lantern on top and carefully lifted them into his arms. It wouldn't hurt to bring back a bribe. "How many more of those replays to go?"

"Three. The ballroom, the drawing room, and the back stairs . . ."

"Let me guess." He could still hear a faint creaking sound over Karl's crying. "Someone got pushed and the someone who did the pushing hung themselves."

"Isn't it hanged?"

"Does it matter?" The lantern's flame flickered as he passed the basement door. Had his hands not been full, he didn't think he could have resisted trying to lift the latch. "Just as dead hanged or hung."

"You're getting just a little blasé about this, aren't you?" Cassie sounded almost insulted.

He shrugged and cut the motion short as the lantern rocked. "They're just recordings of past events. They can't hurt me."

"Maybe not you."

"Maybe not yet," Stephen added.

⟿ EIGHT

"All right, let me just make sure I understand this. Tony, your daughters, and sixteen people from your show, including both your lead actors, are trapped inside a haunted house. This man . . ." Henry nodded toward Graham Brummel, who lifted his beer in salute. ". . . says the house contains a malevolence that feeds on the trapped dead and is looking to add our people to its buffet table. We can't get in, they can't get out, the windows have been blanked, and all phones are nonfunctional. All they have to do is survive until dawn, but the house will spend the night working on their fears, attempting to drive at least one of them insane enough to kill the rest. Is that it?"

CB's attention remained directed out the window at the roof of the house. "Yes."

Henry sighed and ran both hands back up through his hair. "This isn't good."

"But you believe it?"

He turned to face the caretaker, one red-gold brow raised. "Of course."

"Oh, for cryin' out loud!" Graham jumped to his feet and began to pace back and forth over the minimal floor space in front of his recliner. "What is with you people? I mean, first the big guy, now you. How can you possibly buy into this kind of a cock-and-bull story?"

"Isn't it true?"

"Yeah, of course it's true, but what difference does that make? Haunted houses. Malevolent things. You should be in deep denial." He kicked at a yellowing stack of tabloids as he paced. "You should be making up something about how the doors all swelled in the rain and some weird air pressure thing is holding them closed and the rain is affecting the cell phone reception and you don't just calmly *believe* this kind of shit! I mean, if I tell you I'm a medium, you're supposed to tell me I'm a fake!"

"Are you?"

"No! But that's not the point. You two are really freaking me out!" The mouth of the beer bottle jabbed toward CB. "He was bad enough on his own." And back to point at Henry. "You are seriously upping the weird stakes here, and given my life just generally, that's saying something."

Henry stared at him for a long moment, contemplated dropping all masks just to see what would happen, and finally allowed his better nature to prevail. "I'm grateful you called me," he said at last, joining CB at the window, dismissing the other man entirely. "But I'm not sure what you expect me to do."

"Offer an experienced interpretation. Take advantage of any opening that lends itself to your . . . particular strengths. It also struck me that you're a little possessive and unlikely to allow the destruction of someone you consider to be yours."

"And if I find a way to get Tony out . . ."

"My daughters, and my employees, will be freed as well."

"You guys have done this kind of thing before!" Vampire and producer turned together.

"You have!" Bloodshot eyes narrowed speculatively.

"You guys are like what? Some kind of otherworldly Starsky and Hutch?"

"How many of those has he had?" Henry asked, nodding toward the bottle.

Graham snorted before CB could respond. "Oh, no, you can't blame the beer. I know how it is! Your show, the whole leading his people through the darkest night toward the dawn, it's based on real life."

CB blinked. Once. "The show is a work of fiction. Any resemblance to persons living or dead is purely coincidental." When Henry glanced up at him, he shrugged and added, "Usually."

Before Graham could continue—which he looked ready to do—a pair of feet in work boots pounded up the stairs and a heavy fist banged out a three-beat rhythm on the door.

"CB? Boss? You better get out here; something's happening!"

"The cat tipped us off. It was sitting on the porch rail there and then it had a little freak-out."

"Cat?" Henry glanced down at the black cat being soothed in Graham's arms. There'd been a black cat up in the apartment, stretched out along the back of the sofa. He hadn't seen it leave . . .

"I got two." Graham's tone suggested he was bored with the explanation. "Same litter, eh." He shrugged, the cat riding the motion. "I named them both Shadow since they don't come when I call."

"*What* was the cat reacting to?" CB snarled as attention shifted to the cat.

"Sorry, Boss." And attention shifted around again within the crowded shelter of the back porch. "That." Ujjal pointed at the empty butt bucket. "There was a good pack and a half in there before, but one by one they just up and whooshed through the door."

"Whooshed?"

"Well, they didn't make the *whoosh* noise or anything, but yeah." The genny op shrugged, fully aware of how the story sounded. "It was like something on the other side of the door was pulling them in."

When CB raised an eyebrow in Henry's direction, Henry nodded. Tony could call the butts from the bucket to his hand. Therefore, until another explanation presented itself, he was going to believe this had been Tony. But this was the first Henry'd ever heard of him moving them through a closed . . .

"The cables." When all eyes turned to stare blankly at him, he pointed. "Look at the cables. The whole bundle is still running into the house."

A couple of heads nodded, but they were clearly continuing to miss the point. Cables were like background noise for this lot.

"The door is closed . . ." He frowned, thinking out loud. "The cables are running through a closed door, except that's impossible, so the space they were running through must remain regardless of how it appears."

"But you can't move them." Ujjal yanked at the bundle. "It's tight, no play at all. There's no hole—it's like it goes to the door and stops." He blinked. "You're right. That's not possible."

"So we just think the door's closed?" Karen asked, twirling a piece of red licorice as she squinted down at the porch.

"It doesn't matter." Chris cautiously poked a finger toward where the space should be. Ten centimeters out, a small red flare slapped his hand back. "We can't get to it."

"We can't," Henry agreed. "But power can obviously go through it."

Ujjal snorted. "I'm shut down. There's no power in these cables." A pause just long enough to connect the dots. "Should I start the generator, Boss?"

"That kind of depends," Graham said before CB could answer. "How big a mess will it make if it overloads and blows up?"

"My generator is not going to overload."

"I'm betting it will if you try and send power into that house while it's locked down. You can bet against me if you want to, though—that's why I asked about the mess."

"The generator won't deliver the kind of power I meant. You . . ." Henry whirled toward Graham, knew he was moving at more than mortal speed by the way the man's eyes opened, but he didn't care. They were stalking a solution here. "When you talk to the ghosts . . ."

"He talks to ghosts?" Chris repeated incredulously.

". . . you're using a type of metaphysical power . . ."

"Of what?"

". . . and that power can obviously go through the door."

"Obviously?"

". . . because a metaphysical power moved the cigarette butts through the door."

"That's not exactly obvious."

"You call your cousins to the door and you tell them to tell Tony . . ."

"Tony talks to ghosts?"

". . . what he has to do to defeat this thing."

"*What* thing?"

Henry turned just far enough to glare at Chris.

Who paled and took a step back. "Never mind."

"Look, I might be able to do that," Graham admitted slowly. "But even if they can make some kind of contact with this Tony person, I don't know what to tell them. I don't *know* how to destroy this thing."

The cat in his arms yawned.

"I don't like that Tony was left on his own in the kitchen." Kate ripped open another packet of salt and glared across the circle at him as she passed it to Amy. "How do we know he was working on a way to get the back door open?" Her lip curled. "We only have his word for it."

"Why would he lie?" Amy asked as she added the salt to the circle.

"Same reason anyone lies. He wants to control the situation."

"Yeah, and he's sitting right here." Tony handed Amy another half dozen packets. The group had insisted she be the only one to draw the protective circle, but given that they actually wanted it finished before morning, there were no proscriptions on who could open the hundreds of tiny paper containers. "You want to know something, just ask me."

"Because you've been so open and forthcoming about stuff," Kate snorted.

"Hey, I told you about the ghosts." Who weren't back from their latest trip to the bathroom. When the lights came up and his coworkers disappeared, and someone sounded as though they were choking on glass in the drawing room—he'd stayed sitting right where he was until the lights went out again. The house, or more specifically the thing in the basement, could just do that whole not-at-all-instant replay without him from now on.

"He did tell us about the ghosts," Peter acknowledged, glancing up from his own pile of packets. "And at some risk to his reputation."

"What reputation?" Brenda demanded. "He's as strange as she is! Uh, no offense," she added hastily, lowering the arm pointing toward Amy.

"And yet, I'm offended."

"But I just . . ."

Lee tightened his arm around Brenda's shoulders. "Let it go," he told her quietly.

"Because you can't win," Amy added.

"Amy."

She rolled her eyes but allowed Peter to have the last word.

"So." Kate shuffled around on the floor until she was staring directly into Tony's face. "I'm asking. If you were just trying to get the back door open, why did you send Lee away?"

"I figured you could use the salt and the lantern."

"You didn't want him to see what you were doing."

Yeah, that, too. "I didn't think he needed to wait since you guys were waiting for the salt."

She waved a packet at him. "And this is *so* useful."

"Kosher salt." They were the first words Hartley had said since before Tom died. He paled as everyone turned toward him. "The salt on *The X-Files* ep . . . p . . . p . . . pisode," he stammered. "It was kosher."

And everyone turned to Zev. Who sighed. "How the hell should I know? I never watched *The X-Files.*"

"You swore," Brianna pointed out.

"Yes, I did. Don't eat the salt."

"I'm hungry!"

"You just ate . . ." Habit drew his gaze down to his watch. He sighed again. ". . . not that long ago. You're not hungry, you're bored."

"She's not the only one," Mason muttered.

Tony tuned out the overlapping litany of complaints and concentrated on opening salt packets. A circle large enough to enclose seventeen people required significant seasoning.

". . . there, see, everything's okay." The light of the second lantern lapped out of the library. The low murmur of sound became Adam's voice and broke up into words. "Just keep moving out into the hall and we'll be back with the others in no time."

After some discussion, Peter had sent Adam, Sorge, Saleen, and Mouse to bring the company's canvas chairs out into the hall. Amy had agreed they'd be safe enough to use inside the circle since they didn't actually belong to the house.

Mouse emerged first carrying four of the chairs, then Sorge with two, Adam with the lantern, and Saleen with the last two.

"Don't worry," Adam continued. "I'm right here and the light's not going anywhere. See, there's the other lantern right where we left it. Just go over to the edge of the circle and put the chairs down carefully."

It was clearly meant to be comforting. Comforting who, that was the question.

Mouse dropped the chairs, jumped back at the noise, bumped into Sorge, and leaped ahead. "Don't!" he snarled.

And that seemed to be the answer.

"Mouse got a little spooked in the library," Adam explained, splitting his attention between his audience and the cameraman. "Mouse, why don't you pass the chairs into the circle?"

"Pass the chairs?" His eyes were wild, his hands were visibly trembling, and damp circles spread out from the underarms of his faded *Once a Thief* crew shirt.

"Yeah, the chairs. Pass them to Hartley and . . . uh, Mason so they can set them up."

"I don't set up chairs," Mason muttered.

"I've got it." Tony pushed his pile of salt packages over in front of Tina and stood.

Mouse shook his head, graying ponytail making a *swoosh, swoosh* sound against his back. "Tony avoids me."

Tony didn't even bother to check and see if everyone was staring at him. *What's the point?* He just tugged the chair from Mouse's hand and opened it, fully conscious of people edging away. *Oh, yeah, the big guy's going crazy, but you'd rather displace onto the little guy.* Actually, he couldn't fault them for that. He'd faced Mouse under the influence of the metaphysical, and the evening had included a couple of cracked ribs, significant bruising, and some tongue he'd just as soon forget. Fortunately, the repetitive motion of passing over the chairs seemed to be calming the big guy down. Probably Adam's intent.

He shifted position slightly so he could overhear the 1AD's murmured conversation with Peter.

". . . don't know what set him off. He said the library was full of dark and until I loaded him down with half the chairs, I was afraid he was going to bolt."

"The lantern didn't go out?"

"Hell, no, he was just freaky."

"High-strung is not a description I'd have ever applied to Mouse." Peter shoved his hands in his pockets.

"It's the house. The situation."

They turned to look at Tony who suddenly got very busy setting up the last chair. Mouse could hear the baby and Mouse had started to freak. Kate was not only talking a lot more than usual but was getting distinctly paranoid. Lee . . .

He glanced over at Lee as he shoved the chairs into a tighter pattern.

Lee had Brenda plastered up against his side.

Those who'd been double shadow-held were starting to fall apart. Even Hartley, only a single, had picked up a stutter. Mason, however, seemed fine. He seemed no more obnoxious than he ever was—although he *was* voluntarily spending time with Ashley.

Bottom line, both actors had picked up distractions. And both of them were, well, actors.

*   *   *

"I don't know about this . . ."

"I do." Henry stayed hard on Graham's heels, herding him up the muddy lane toward the road. "You don't know how to defeat the evil in the basement."

"Yeah, I mean no, but . . ."

"Neither do I. That doesn't change the fact that we need to defeat it." A gust of wind blew a scud of water off the firs. Henry avoided most of it. "Your research suggests that Creighton Caulfield interacted with the manifestation—that this was the purpose of the séances and the psychic investigators he had to the house."

Graham wiped water off his face, slicking thinning hair back over his skull. "Well, yeah, but . . ."

"So Caulfield could be the only person who ever put together the information we need. Information to defeat this thing and save the lives of those people trapped in the house."

"I guess so, but . . ."

"We're going to get that information." He gestured at his BMW. "Get in the car."

"Whoa! Hang on!" Graham stopped by the passenger door, both hands raised, brows drawn in. "I can't just call up Caulfield's ghost; it doesn't work that way. I mean, I could stand on his grave playing *Who Who* on a trumpet from now until doomsday, but if he's not hanging around, it won't do anybody any good. The dead have to want to talk to me."

"Good." Henry's eyes darkened as he stared across the roof at the caretaker. "Get in the car."

Graham did as instructed. Buckled his seat belt. Asked, "What are you?" as Henry pulled out onto Deer Lake Drive.

"Someone who plans to get what's *his* out of that house."

"Yeah. Okay. But what . . ."

Henry glanced over at his passenger.

". . . never mind." He sank down in his seat, head drawn into his shoulders, knees up, one thumb scraping mud off the side of his boots. "So, where are we going?"

"To talk to someone who knew Creighton Caulfield."

"What's this supposed to do?" Stephen asked, drifting back and forth across the curved line of salt.

"Lend a little peace of mind to the people inside the circle," Tony told him quietly. "Calm them, make it harder for the house to work on them."

"Oh." He blinked. "Good idea. How does it work?"

"Power of suggestion."

"I don't understand."

"You don't have to."

But it *was* working. The six chairs were clumped together in the center holding Mason, Ashley, Tina, Peter, Sorge, and Pavin—who had a bad back and couldn't sit on the floor. Around them in a loose circle, backs to the chairs, were Adam, Saleen, Zev, Brianna, Kate, Mouse, Lee, and Brenda. Amy was slowly walking the circumference, holding the largest blade of her Swiss army knife out over the salt and singing softly under her breath.

Tony, placed at her starting point so she'd know where to finish, couldn't hear the actual words but the tune sounded disturbingly like Painted Ponies. Disturbing because Amy and Joan Baez went together like reality TV and actual dramatic content. When she reached him, she drew what looked like an infinity sign in the air with the knife point.

"There. It's closed. Negative energy can't get in. We're safe." She snapped the knife blade shut. "If you want to leave the circle at any time, let me know and I'll open a door."

"Isn't this just a little tree-of-life tote bag for you?" Tony murmured under the rising sound of relieved conversation. Stephen drifted into and out of the circle again looking bored.

"Bite me. I'm a well-rounded, multifaceted person."

"Uh-huh. You're making this up as you go along, aren't you?"

Her eyes narrowed. "Do you question my kung fu, Grasshopper?"

"I would if I knew what the hell you were talking . . ." He could hear music. But Karl was still crying.

"Tony?"

"What the fuck is happening now?" Kate. And Mouse didn't look happy. Tony could only see a bit of Hartley's hair on the other side of the chairs, but the boom operator never looked happy, so he wasn't sure actually seeing his face would help. Lee untangled himself from Brenda's arms and slowly stood.

"I hear music." Brianna launched herself to her feet, but Zev dragged her back.

"I think you all do," he said, looking around the circle and finally settling on Tony. "What is it?"

Tony, in turned, looked to Cassie, who had backed into her brother's arms, her remaining eye wide and frightened.

"It's the ballroom."

"What's so bad about the ballroom?" he demanded.

"There's a lot of people in there," Stephen explained. "So it's strong. It pulls. Cassie got lured in there once, just after Graham brought us back." His arm around her waist pulled her closer still. "I almost didn't get her out. If it had been going, with the music and all, I think we'd still be there. When Cassie told Graham about it, he closed the doors and told us to stay away from it. Really helpful after the fact."

"Why can we hear it *and* Karl?" Tony waved a hand around the hall, still dark and full of his muttering coworkers. "The replay hasn't even started yet."

"I told you, it's powerful."

"But contained?"

"I guess. If the doors are closed. We're going up to the bathroom now, it's *our* place. We're safe there." The last sentence hung in empty air.

"Tony? Hey!" Amy grabbed his arm and jerked him around to face her. "You want to share with the living?"

So he told them.

Amy paled. "I left the ballroom doors open."

"Are you sure?"

She was.

"Is anyone *surprised*?" Mason snapped.

As it happened, no one was.

"I want to go dancing," Brianna whined.

"Tony . . ."

And the soundtrack of his life started playing the *Mighty Mouse* theme. "I'm on it."

He was almost to the edge of the lantern light when he realized voices were yelling about breaking the circle and that he hadn't brought a light of his own. He lifted his left foot, about to turn. The replay started before it hit the floor.

The music was suddenly a lot louder and vaguely familiar. People were talking and laughing, the clink of glassware suggesting expensive booze of some kind was flowing freely. Champagne, maybe. People who lived in houses like this weren't the type to open a few two-fours for friends. Faintly, he could hear the rhythmic pattern of dress shoes against a wooden floor. Step. Step. Slide.

No point in going back for a light, so he trotted out of the foyer and down the hall.

Turned out that the sound of dancing was muffled because the ballroom doors were closed.

He frowned.

Except Amy was sure she'd left the doors open.

All right, they were open in his time but not in the replay. And that was no help. In order for Graham's protections to work, they had to be closed in his time. Which he wasn't exactly in.

Great.

The music faltered. It was live, not recorded.

Someone in the ballroom banged on the closed doors.

Which weren't only locked, they were barred.

On this side.

He reached for the bar but couldn't touch it.

The music stopped.

Muffled thuds. A lot of padded somethings hitting the floor.

Bodies?

You think? He could hear coughing, choking, what might be a little thrashing. And he could smell . . .

The lights in the hall were electric and they looked new, the wires surface-mounted along the moldings. Henry had found him an apartment in Toronto with the same surface-mounted wires, surface mounted because the building had started out with gas lights. Apparently, so had this house. If the electric lights were new, then the gas lines were probably still in place.

Three guesses about what's killing the people in the ballroom, and the first two don't count.

Someone had opened the gas jets. Since all the murdering someones had, so far, stuck around for the actual deaths, Tony'd have been willing to bet that they'd barred these doors and gone back into the ballroom through the service door, locking it behind them with the key. Not that it really mattered.

A whole ballroom full of dead people. No wonder it was powerful.

And in his time, the doors were open.

The music started up again although the odds were good it wasn't exactly *live* anymore. Other replays had stopped with death. This one kept going.

Had it reset to begin again or were the dead dancing? Given the night so far, he'd bet on the latter.

He was standing in front of the doors in his time as well as in the replay—he'd established that movement was timeless beyond a doubt in the conservatory. Which was a good thing because right now doubt would be a bad thing. Eyes closed so as not to be distracted, he clung to an image of the open doors, held out his hand, said the seven words, and *reached*.

The doors are already closed, memory insisted.

Yeah, well, if it was easy, everyone would be doing it.

Once again, Tony could hear people talking and laughing, but it didn't sound like they were having a good time. Although he couldn't hear actual words, the voices had a nails-on-a-chalkboard kind of timbre and the laughter carried more than a hint of desperation. Step, step, slide had become shuffle, shuffle, drag.

He stepped forward.

Something brushed past his hip.

Something from his time because nothing in the replay could touch him.

Oh, crap!

Hand. Words. *Reach!*

He opened his eyes just as the door slammed shut. Just in time to see a pale, corpse-gray hand snatched back from the front of Brianna's pinafore. An almost familiar pattern glowed gold against the wood.

CB's younger daughter turned and glared at him, squinting a little in the lantern light radiating out from behind him. "I wanted to go dancing!" she shrieked, and kicked him in the shin.

"Brianna!" Zev rushed past. "Are you all right?"

"I wanted to dance—and he closed the door!"

"Tony couldn't have closed the door, he's not close enough." He grabbed her wrist and pulled her hand away from the brass door pull. "And you don't want to go in there, it's all . . ." He glanced up at Tony. "Full of dead people?"

Tony nodded.

"I want to see dead people!"

"No, you don't."

"Do, too!"

"Tom . . ."

"Tom is boring, he's just lying there!" She folded her arms. "I want to see the gross dead baby, or I want to go in there and dance with dead people!"

"Why don't we . . ."

"No!"

"Cheese!" The odd acoustics in the house had no luck at all in muffling Ashley's voice. "You get your skinny butt back here, or I'm telling Mom you put those pictures of her in her underwear up on the Net!"

"Did not!"

"So?"

Brianna yanked herself free of Zev's grip and charged past Tony back toward the entrance hall, the darkness between the lanterns of less concern than getting to her sister. "I'm gonna rip your tongue out, Ashes!"

"They're really very nice kids," Zev murmured as he passed.

"Sure." Tony turned to see Lee standing behind him with a lantern. "Zev thinks they're nice kids," he said, suddenly at a loss for words.

"That's because Zev likes kids. And Zev's never picked up a prop they've broken, then *fixed* with a tube and a half of Crazy Glue, and then gotten his picture in the tabloids brandishing a four-and-a-half foot cross in a hospital emergency room."

"It was a good picture."

"That's little comfort." Lee stared past Tony at the ballroom doors. "I can still hear the music."

"Yeah. Me, too." Although it was faint, distant. Distorted. "We should get back."

He didn't understand the moment of silence that followed his suggestion.

"Right." Lee turned as Tony came even with him and they fell into step. "Tony, why do you think I can hear the baby?"

He asked like he had a theory. Like he knew and he was just asking Tony to confirm his suspicions. Had he started to remember the shadows?

"Why me and Mouse and Kate and Hartley? Oh, and you . . . of course."

The pause was disconcerting.

Why "of course" me? None of the shadow-held remembered the experience and Arra had wiped the memories of everyone on the soundstage after the final battle. Lee was asking like he thought Tony knew the answer and just wasn't telling. If the shadow-held were more sensitive to the stuff the house was throwing at them, did that mean the house was restoring their memories?

"Why do you ask?"

"Last spring Mouse and Kate and Hartley all had lapses of memory, somewhat like mine. I had an . . . incident on the set. So did you. I thought it might be connected."

"I guess it might be." That seemed safe enough.

"I'm pretty sure Mason is hearing things, too. Remember that friend of his that showed up on the set just before the gas leak?"

They'd gone with the traditional explanation for a group of disoriented people whose memories had just been magically wiped. Had to have been a gas leak. Also the traditional explanation for a ballroom of dead people as it turned out.

"His name was Michael Swan," Lee continued, before Tony could answer. "I asked Mason about him, and he had no idea who I was talking about. Everyone else remembered him, though."

Mason had been shadow-held at the time. Of course he wouldn't remember.

Just like Lee didn't remember the actual weird shit—a shadow from another world in his body, the Shadowlord after his body—only the stuff around the weird. Unfortunately, he seemed to have gathered enough pieces to start trying to put two and two together. Fortunately, since two and two made five in this instance, it was unlikely he'd come up with the actual answer.

Suddenly realizing he was about to step out of the circle of lantern light, Tony stopped and turned. Lee was standing about five paces back, watching him. "What?"

"You changed since all that happened."

"Changed?"

"You're more confident. You're interacting with CB. And you don't . . ." He paused and brushed his hair back off his face, almost as though he wasn't sure he wanted to continue. ". . . you don't watch me like you used to."

"What?"

"You used to . . . there was this expression . . . I mean, every time I turned around you were . . ." He shrugged. "I guess I got used to it."

"Sorry." Tony had no idea what he was apologizing for, but it was all he could think of.

"Yeah. We should get back."

"Sure."

Four or five steps in an uncomfortable silence, then, "Did I mention everyone's a little pissed at you because you broke through the circle?"

"No."

"Well, they are."

A little pissed was a bit of an understatement. Kate was ready to throw him to the wolves and nothing said seemed to calm her down.

"He's putting us all in danger! We need to get rid of him!"

"And how do you suggest we do that, eh?"

Shut up, Sorge. You're not helping. Tony shot a whose-side-are-you-on glance at the DP, who answered with a Gallic and totally noncommittal shrug.

"We lock him away somewhere safe," Kate insisted. "Where he can't hurt us."

"He hasn't done anything to hurt us!" Amy snapped.

"Oh, yeah? How do you know? How do you know he didn't arrange all this? He sees things we don't. We only have his word for what's going on."

"She's right!"

Brenda. Big surprise. Tony shuffled a little closer to Lee. While Brenda hadn't been shadow-held, she was more than keeping up in the freaking-out department. Plus, lately, it seemed that she didn't much like him although he didn't . . . *Right. I'm an idiot.* He would have shuffled away again, but Lee grabbed his arm. Comfort? Restraint? Tony had no idea. *He misses the way I used to look at him? What the hell's up with that?*

"Maybe Tony woke the house! On purpose! Have any of you morons even considered that?" Kate swept a narrowed gaze around the circle and Tony realized that more than one of their companions *was* thinking of it. Lee's grip tightened slightly. "Tony broke the circle," she continued, volume rising with every word. "He *wants* one of us to go crazy and kill the rest. That way we won't think it's his fault!" She lunged at him, but Adam caught her.

"I like Tony!" Brianna declared as Kate struggled to free herself from Adam's grip. She took two steps forward and pinched a fold of Kate's stomach.

"OW!"

"She pinches with her fingernails," Ashley commented from her place inside the curve of Mason's arm.

"You little bitch!" The fury of Kate's attack dragged one arm free of Adam's hold.

Brianna ducked under the swing and wrapped herself around Kate's lower leg.

"OW!"

"And she bites."

Zev took a blow that knocked his yarmulke half off his head, but he managed to get his hands under Brianna's arms and drag her away.

Eyes narrowed, managing to look dangerous in spite of age, size, a turn-of-the-century pinafore, and the fact she was essentially dangling from Zev's hands, Brianna jabbed a finger toward Kate and snarled, "You say one more mean thing about Tony and my dad will fire your ass!"

"He can't fire me if we're all dead!"

"Wanna bet! My dad fires dead people all the time!"

News to Tony but, given CB, not completely unbelievable.

"Does not!"

"Does, too!"

"Does not!"

"Does, too, infinity!"

"Does . . ."

"Hey!" Ashley moved away from Mason—who looked astonished at being left—to stand with her sister. "She said infinity!"

Kate glared at the two girls for a moment, then turned and growled, "You're hurting my arm."

Adam smiled tightly. "Seemed preferable to the alternative. Have you calmed down?"

"I'm *fine!*"

Oh, yeah. And we all believe you, too.

After a long moment, Peter nodded and Adam released her.

Okay, some of us believe you.

"We're in this together," Peter reminded them as Kate rubbed her arm and scowled. "Lynching Tony . . ."

Kate perked up.

". . . metaphorically speaking," Peter sighed, "just because he knows things strikes me as cutting off our noses to spite our face." He frowned. "Faces. I don't believe he's lying to us and I consider myself an excellent judge of character. Shut up Sorge."

The DP's mouth closed with an audible snap.

"But since you brought it up . . ." He turned to Kate. "The house, the thing in the house . . ."

"In the basement," Amy added.

"Right, the thing in the basement wants us dead so that it can feed off us..."

"According to Tony," Kate sneered.

"Granted. But why do you think Tony would want one of us to go crazy and kill the rest?"

Nostrils flared, she tossed her head. "Because."

"Oh, yeah, that's a good reason."

Mason's dust-dry delivery set off a wave of laughter. It sounded more relieved than amused, but Mason preened at the attention and it was almost back to business as usual.

"He's always going off on his own!" Kate insisted, trying to reclaim her audience.

"And he shouldn't be," Peter agreed. "None of us should. If we leave the circle—once Amy has resealed the circle," he added pointedly, "we go in pairs. At least in pairs."

"Not going anywhere," Mouse muttered.

Kate ignored him, jerking her chin toward Tony. "Who's going to want to go with him?"

"I will."

"Oh, yeah." She curled her lip in Lee's direction. "Big surprise, *you've* been running around with him all night." Her observation dripped innuendo.

Heads turned. Eyebrows rose.

Tony—and, from the look on her face, Brenda—waited for Lee to release his arm and leap away but the actor only said, "Then he's hardly been going off on his own, has he?"

"That's not..."

Lee shook his head, a lock of dark hair sweeping across his forehead. "I can hear the baby, Kate, and the music—and so can you and..."

"So can I!" Mason announced.

Heads turned again.

Mason's chin rose and his face stiffened into what Amy had once referred to as his patently portentous expression. After Tony'd looked it up, he'd agreed with the description. "I've always heard the baby," he said, Raymond Dark's fangs adding a surreal touch. "But I felt I should remain as neutral in this situation as possible."

Amy snorted and asked what they were all wondering. "Why?"

"Because you thought we'd laugh at you!" Brianna kicked him in the shin.

"Don't you touch him!" Ashley launched herself at her sister just as Karl stopped crying.

Tony froze as the lights came up—gas this time, not electric—and he was standing alone in the entrance hall. He could feel a kind of pressure that had to be Lee's hand on his arm. What would happen if he pulled away? Would Lee hold on? Would he have to let go? Tony didn't want to know the answer enough to try it. The house was absolutely silent and then, very faintly, he heard a series of thuds, some panicked profanity, and one final crash. Then, more silence.

Help, I've fallen and I'm not getting up again.

Educated guess, where educated meant "let's attach the sound to the worst case scenario": someone had been pushed down the kitchen stairs and had landed without Lee Nicholas to cushion the impact. Broken neck, temple slammed down on the corner of the kitchen table, impalement on a rack of salad forks—it didn't much matter; he was more concerned with what was going on with the live people in the house during his absence.

The replay continued to run, but death number two seemed to be happening quietly. And slowly. Tony ran through video production specs as he waited. *SD video is transmitted at SDI rates of 270, 360, or 540 Mbps; HD video is transmitted at the SDI rate of . . . of . . . crap.* He hadn't remembered on his final exam either. When reviewing Wizardry 101 got him no farther than: *In the manipulating of energies the price of intent is often greater than the price of manipulation*—which had made no sense the first time around either—he settled on counting backward from one hundred in French.

At *quarante-deux*, the lights went out. Lee was still beside him but standing now with his arms folded as he, and everyone else, listened to Peter, who was clearly coming to the end of some lengthy direction. Kate was scowling, Brianna was sulking, Ashley looked triumphant, and every other face Tony could see wore the default expression common to those who worked in television production and spent most of their professional careers waiting for a thousand and one details to line up so they could do their jobs. No one seemed to have noticed he was gone.

"Does everyone understand me, then?" Peter raised a finger. "We're in this together. I don't want to hear accusations and no one wants to hear how certain people used to have a starring role in a network police drama."

Mason opened his mouth and closed it again as the finger jabbed toward him.

"Good." A second finger rose. "Most importantly, no one goes anywhere alone. Not Tony. Not me. No one." He looked around, gauging reaction, and frowned. "Where's Hartley?"

⌒ NINE

"Look, no one's more in favor of all this cultural crap than me, eh, but I thought you wanted to save your friend."

"The Lambert Theatre is haunted."

"No shit. Medium with an Internet connection, remember?" Graham slammed the car door and waited for Henry to join him on the sidewalk before he started walking toward the theater. "We got some poltergeist activity—you *don't* want to talk to those little shits—and repeat appearances of dark figure in a long coat suspected to be Alistair McCall, an actor who died during a performance of *Henry V.* The reviews said it wasn't the best death scene he'd ever done."

In spite of circumstances, Henry grinned. "Harsh."

"Yeah, well, we weren't there; they might've been right. So do you want me to try and talk to McCall, is that it?"

"If it *is* McCall, he was around at the same time as Creighton Caulfield, and they likely moved in the same social circles—Caulfield was nouveau riche and McCall was a local celebrity."

"Okay, sure, that's fine if it is McCall, but what if it isn't?"

"Then get what information you can."

"The dead don't usually like crowds." Graham nodded at the people milling about under the marquee. "And this lot doesn't look like they're leaving."

"They're not. There's a late show tonight."

"Yeah, so . . ."

"So you'll have to concentrate a little harder to ignore any distractions, won't you?" Henry wrapped his hand around the caretaker's elbow, the movement as much threat as restraint.

Graham glanced down at Henry's fingers, pale lines against the dark green fabric, and shrugged. "Okay. So we're what? Just going to walk right on in?"

"Yes."

"Because you got tickets?"

"Not exactly."

They slipped past two young women checking their watches as they discussed unlikely methods of revenge, pushed past a clump of slightly younger men who could only be first-year film students from the way they were pontificating, and went around the smokers desperately topping up their nicotine levels before they had to go inside. The clothes of all three groups were such an eclectic mix that neither Henry's white silk shirt and jeans nor Graham's workman's overalls looked out of place.

Muscles, tattoos, and a clipboard blocked the open door.

Henry smiled up at her, carefully keeping it charming. "Henry Fitzroy. Tony Foster."

The charm slid off without penetrating. She checked her list. Drew two lines. "Go in and sit down if you want. We'll be starting late—camera two's stuck in fucking traffic."

"Any idea how long it'll be?"

"If I fucking knew that, I'd be doing a fucking dance of joy," she snarled. "Sit, don't sit. It's all the same to me."

The Lambert had been built just before the turn of the century when money poured into Vancouver from timber, mining, and fleecing unwary treasure seekers heading north to the Yukon gold rush. A group of the young city's most upstanding and wealthy citizens, stung by a federal study that said Vancouver led the Dominion in consumption of alcohol, vowed to bring culture to the frontier and, with their wallets behind the project, it took only five short months from breaking the ground to the first performance on the Lambert stage.

A hundred years later, a similar group ripped out screens, projection booths, and drop ceilings and restored the theatre to its original glory. In order to sell local wines in the lobby during intermissions, the restored Lambert had a liquor license.

Henry appreciated the irony.

"Jesus." Graham tipped his head back and stared up at the gilded Graces and cherubs dancing across lobby's ceiling. "That's a bit over the top, eh?"

"Well, when you're spending government money, why not go for Baroque."

"What?"

"Never mind." The lights on the stairs leading up to the balconies were off. It therefore seemed reasonable to assume that the balcony wouldn't be used during the performance and would offer them the privacy they'd need. Henry dragged Graham across the lobby. "Come on."

"We're not supposed to go up there."

"Then we'd better not get caught."

Graham didn't seem to find that comforting. Frowning, he stopped at the bottom step. "The lights are off."

"You talk to the dead and you're afraid of the dark?"

"That's not . . . Oh, never mind." He threw a nervous glance over his shoulder, pulled his arm from Henry's hand, and sprinted for the second floor, the muffled thud of work boots on carpet drowned out by Radiogram's new CD playing over the sound system.

Henry met him at the top of the stairs.

"Oh, sure . . . beat the old . . . man." He sagged against the flocked wallpaper and panted.

"You should exercise more."

"You should . . . mind your own . . . damned business." Pushing himself upright, Graham headed for the main balcony. "If we're going to . . . do this. I want . . . to sit down."

The balcony was deserted, but Henry noted the cables leading to the empty spot waiting for the delayed camera two. Down below, half a dozen crew members ran around attending to last minute details. On the stage, a pair of actors Henry didn't recognize—although Tony had assured him they'd been famous in their day—worked on blocking. The seats were about three quarters filled, the audience not yet restless but becoming loud.

Loud was good. Loud would cover the conversation Graham Brummel was about to have with the dead.

"Well?"

The replica turn-of-the-century red plush seat protested as Graham dropped into it. "Well, what?"

"Is he here?"

"Sure. But that's the wrong question. The right question is; does he want to talk. Actually . . ." Graham scratched thoughtfully at his comb-over. ". . . the real question is, will he say anything I can understand. The dead are not usually what you'd call articulate. Now these days I can't get them to shut up, but I still had to work on Cassandra and Stephen for a couple of weeks before I could get anything and I had a blood tie there."

"Here, you have me."

"That and thirty-two seventy-five'll buy you a two-four." He sighed. "I could use a beer."

"You've had plenty. Call. Or concentrate. Or do whatever you have to."

"You've got no friggin' idea how this works, do . . ." Twisting around, he looked up at Henry and froze. "Yeah. So like, I'll just, um . . ."

As little as he wanted to, Henry dialed it back. Masked the Hunter. Destroying this annoying little man would not help free Tony and the others. *More's the pity.* Closing his fingers over the back of Graham's chair, he waited.

"I'd still like to know, why me?"

"Like attracts like. Look, there's a whole shitload of myth about you. Okay, not you, specifically, but about your kind. It's all around you . . ." Tony spread his arms. *". . . like a metaphysical fog. I bet that's what the ghost's attracted to. I bet that's what pulls him to you."*

Tony's theory, expressed between visits from the last ghost Henry'd had to deal with, had made a certain kind of sense. Like was drawn to like. *Except, of course, when opposites attract.*

That wasn't helping.

Fabric began to tear under Henry's fingers and he snarled softly in frustration.

The temperature in the balcony plummeted.

"He's here." Graham's announcement plumed out from his mouth.

"I figured."

A tall figure began to take shape in the place where camera two would rest. The lack of light in the balcony made it difficult to see defined edges, dark bleeding out into dark. It almost seemed as though the pale, middle-aged face cupped by the high formal collar of the early part of the century floated, sneering and unsupported.

"He's complaining about the theater. I don't think he means the building, I think he means . . ." Graham waved toward the stage. "That stuff."

"Why couldn't I hear him?"

"Because you're not a medium." Graham snickered. "You're short enough I bet you're barely a small. What?"

The ghost frowned.

"I think he thinks I'm brave talking to you like that because you walk in darkness. Jesus, the lights are out. Who doesn't?"

Alistair McCall, once given five curtain calls for his Faust, and Henry Fitzroy, once Duke of Richmond and Somerset, exchanged an essentially identical expression.

"Yeah, yeah, Nightwalker. What the hell is a . . ." Whites showed all the way around Graham's eyes as he slowly turned and gazed up into Henry's face. "Oh, boy, oh boy—I knew you were strange from the moment I laid eyes on you, but you're a *vampire?*"

Henry smiled, and this time he didn't bother being charming. "Ask him about Creighton Caulfield. We haven't got all night."

"Hartley's gone?" Brenda's eyes were painfully wide and both her hands were wrapped around Lee's arm in a white-knuckled grip. "The house! It's the house!" she shrieked as Lee closed his hand over hers—not so much for comfort, Tony was just petty enough to observe, but to try and force her to loosen her hold. "It's eaten him!"

"No, it hasn't!" Amy snapped. Then she frowned and turned to Tony. "Has it?"

He shrugged and glanced over at Stephen and Cassie, who'd finally rejoined them. Cassie still looked a little twitchy—which would have seemed reasonable given the dance music still playing a counterpoint to Karl's crying except that she was dead and therefore should, in Tony's opinion, be beyond twitchy.

"The house doesn't eat you, it uses the energy of your death," Cassie told him, smoothing down her bloodstained skirt and glaring at Brenda. The *you're an idiot* was clearly implied.

Tony repeated Cassie's statement, trying to keep the implication a little less obvious. "And since no one else is dead," he added, "Hartley can't be. It's been murder *then* suicide since the beginning."

"So he's probably just gone off looking for a drink," Peter sighed.

Arms folded, Kate shifted her weight from foot to foot. "Or he's gone off looking for someone to kill!"

"Who?" Amy demanded impatiently. "We're all here."

"So he wants us to go looking for him and when we're separated, then he kills one of us."

Heads nodded agreement.

"Yeah . . ." Amy pursed her lips, giving credit where credit was due. "That sounds reasonable."

"Tom wasn't a murder/suicide," Mouse muttered mournfully.

Tina shot him a flat, unfriendly look. "Stop saying murder/suicide around the children."

Safely out of the way beside Zev, Brianna rolled her eyes as Ashley pulled her ears out from between the script supervisor's hands. "First of all, not a child," the older girl snorted. "And second, it's not like we don't know the words. We watch *Law and Order*, you know."

"How can you avoid it?" Adam snorted.

Heads nodded again.

"Tom was kind of a metaphysical accident," Amy reminded them. "He didn't intend to kill himself, so his death is different."

Kate's lip curled. "If one death can be different, what's to say others can't be?"

More nodding.

"Hartley wants a drink," she continued, "so the house, the thing . . ."

"In the basement," Amy interrupted.

"Fine. The thing in the basement convinces him that a bottle of rubbing alcohol is just what he's looking for and the next thing you know, he's poisoned himself."

Amy spread her hands. "Come on, guys. This is Hartley we're talking about. He's perfectly capable of drinking a bottle of rubbing alcohol and poisoning himself without any help from a thing in the basement."

The nodding continued.

The circle was beginning to look as though it contained an assorted variety of bobblehead dolls.

"So do we go looking for him?" Tony asked.

"Oh, you'd like that, wouldn't you? Go off all alone. Come back and tell us stuff we're expected to believe. If all we have to do is survive until morning, then I think we stand a better chance if we use a little duct tape on Tony and keep him from wandering off." Kate patted the roll of tape hanging off her belt. "Who's with me?"

"No one is duct taping anyone," Peter told her. "Not unless I say so."

"Unless *you* say so?"

Stephen wafted closer to Tony as the shouting started. "It likes this. It likes anger. It likes any strong emotion," he added thoughtfully as Sorge shoved Pavin, Mouse shook Kate as she tried to lunge at Peter, and Amy, Adam, and Saleen were attempting to outshout each other—the three clumped together but yelling independently. Tina, Zev, Mason, Lee, Brenda, and the girls were being shoved toward the far edge of the circle. "Anger's easiest for it to use, though."

"Yeah?" Tony jerked back away from Kate's flailing arm. She wasn't flailing at him, but he still wanted to avoid impact. "How do you know?"

"How do I know what?"

He turned and glared at the ghosts. "How do you know what *it* likes?"

Cassie rolled her eye and stepped forward. "It feeds off our death, remember? We're its prisoners as much as you are. We've just been here longer, so we know more."

"Stockholm Syndrome."

"What?"

He frowned. "Helsinki Syndrome? Never mind. The point is; how do I know you haven't gone over to its side? How do I know I can trust you?"

"It's working on him now," Cassie muttered.

Stephen snorted. "You think?"

"It is not! It's more likely you two are working with it than with me against it because you and it are . . . OW!" Tony clutched his crotch with both hands and stumbled back through Stephen. Gripping her arms, Mouse had lifted Kate off the floor, freeing her feet to swing. In spite of the pain—or maybe because of it—Tony felt more clearheaded than he had in a while. Clearheaded and cold. "Man, you are fucking freezing!"

"Heat is energy." Stephen adjusted his head. "We don't have energy to spare."

Heat . . . "You used the heat from the lights to look real this morning."

"The lights and the people. We . . ."

"Is that relevant?" Cassie interrupted, sounding remarkably like Amy. She waved a bloody hand at the rest of the crew. "I mean it was fun and all, but right now you need to do something about this!"

While Tony'd been distracted, the darkness had thickened around the circle of light cast by the lantern. It felt . . . *anticipatory* seemed the only—if clichéd—choice. Within the circle, the old arguments went on and new ones had started. Mason and Lee stood nearly nose to nose, yelling about fan sites. Brenda was on her knees between them—the tuxedo jackets covering just what exactly she was doing there—with Zev hauling at her shoulders trying to pull her away. Tina had left the circle and was banging on the front door demanding that Everett wake up. Her pinafore over her head, Ashley sat cross-legged on the floor singing "Danny Boy" at the top of her lungs.

That's a bizarre choice for an eleven-year-old . . .

It looked as though everyone had slipped over the edge, Tony realized as he slowly straightened. He had no idea how the hell he was supposed to haul everyone back.

"I HAVE TO PEE!"

Okay, not everyone.

Brianna stood in the center of the circle, hands on her hips, and as the echoes of her announcement died down, she glared at the suddenly quiet adults. "I have to pee, now!" Not quite as loud but just as penetrating. One bare foot lashed out . . . "Shut *up*, Ashes!" . . . and "Danny Boy" died. "Did you hear me? I have to PEE!"

"I think they heard you in Victoria," Amy winced.

"Do they have bathrooms in Victoria?" Brianna demanded. " 'Cause if they do, I want to go there! Right NOW!"

"Okay, okay . . ." Zev stepped up behind her and patted her shoulder. "I imagine there's a number of bathrooms in a place this size." He looked around expectantly at the others, and Tony remembered that the music director had only been at the location for about half an hour before the house closed down. "Right?"

"Yes and no," Peter admitted. "There're six bathrooms, but only the one in Mason's dressing room has been approved for use."

Amy opened her mouth to say something rude, but Zev stopped her with a raised hand and allowed his smile to say it for him. "Given the circumstances, trapped in a haunted house and all, I think we can ignore that rule."

"Sure, if we're planning on not getting out. But this was one of CB's directives, and I'm not leaping from the frying pan into the fire. I think I'd rather stay in the frying pan."

"She'll pee in the frying pan," Ashley warned ominously.

"Fine." With no time to argue, Zev surrendered. "We'll use the bathroom in Mason's dressing room."

"You won't," Tina told him, taking Brianna's hand from his. "*We* will. I think . . ." She swept her gaze around the circle, allowing it to momentarily alight on the other three women and Ashley. ". . . that we should all go. All us girls. Together."

"No!"

"Oh, for Christ's sake, Mason." As Amy lit the second lantern, Tina turned a withering glare on the star of *Darkest Night*. "Grow up and learn to share."

"Fuck you," Mason muttered. He pulled a battered cigarette out of the inside pocket of his tuxedo jacket and held out his hand for his lighter. "It's not about sharing," he said as he lit up, staring at Tony over the flame. "It's about shadows."

"She'll pee on the shadows," Ashley giggled.

"I'll pee on you, Zitface!"

"Try it, Cheese!"

Brianna lunged out to the end of Tina's arm.

"Enough!"

Everyone stared at Zev, impressed, as both girls quieted.

Then all heads swiveled toward Tony.

He sighed. "There's something in that bathroom," he began.

"Richard Caulfield," Cassie interrupted. "Creighton Caulfield's only son. He was retarded. We think he lived in that room his whole life."

"We know he died in it," Stephen added.

"He's not like the rest of us. He doesn't . . . um . . ." She frowned and sketched circles in the air.

"Replay?" Tony offered.

"Yes, he doesn't replay. He's just . . ." Unlike her brother's, her head remained in place when she shrugged. "He's just there."

"Tony?" Lee's voice had risen on the second syllable. He closed his hand over Brenda's and moved it off his arm, frowning at her while he did. "That hurt."

Her lips twisted into a bad approximation of an apologetic smile. "Sorry."

Lee's smile was no more sincere. "Sure."

What the hell is up with those two? And then Tony realized that no one else had noticed as they were all—like Lee—waiting for him to elaborate on Mason's shouted *no*. "Uh, it's safe. It's . . ." He glanced at Mason, who sucked back half an inch of cigarette. ". . . shadowy, but safe."

"Who cares!" Pulling Tina along behind her, Brianna headed for the stairs.

"Wait!" Amy came forward with the lantern and swung it three times over the line of salt. "Okay, it's safe to step over now."

Stephen snickered and wafted back and forth over the line until Tony turned to glare at him. He knew Amy was spouting bullshit, but the section of salt the women were stepping over did look duller than the gleaming line that made up the rest of the circle. "Believing is seeing," he muttered thoughtfully.

"What?"

"Christmas movie, Walt Disney Pictures, 1999, John Pasquin directed and . . . never mind, long after your time."

"Brenda?" Amy paused on the outside of the circle. "You coming?"

"I'll stay with Lee."

"No, you won't," Tina said from the bottom step. "Get out here."

"But . . ."

"Now! He won't run off with someone else while you're gone."

"Why's the guy in the hat looking at you?" Stephen asked as Brenda reluctantly joined the others.

Guy in the what? Oh. Zev. Tony had no idea.

"Cassie?"

She smiled down at her brother from the stairs. "I'll be right back."

"What is it," Peter asked as, up on the second floor, the door to Mason's dressing room opened and closed, "about women going to the bathroom in groups?"

Every man in the circle shrugged.

Stephen adjusted his head.

As they reached the end of the lane, Henry could hear the three remaining crew talking inside the craft services truck, their hearts beating just a little more quickly than normal. He was impressed at how well they were continuing to react to some rather extraordinary circumstances. Was it because they were in television and used to thinking of the unusual as normal and the bizarre as something to get on tape? Was it because Arra's spell to erase their memories of the battle at the soundstage had a lingering, dampening effect? Was it because no stronger reaction would be permitted with CB on the scene?

Or because no stronger reaction was necessary with CB on the scene . . .

The executive producer of *Darkest Night* stood by the back porch, hands in the pockets of his trench coat, head sunk low between massive shoulders. If will alone could have forced the door open, his attention would have reduced it to a pile of kindling and a few bits of twisted metal.

He turned his head, and only his head, as Henry and the caretaker emerged into the light. "Well?"

"Graham spoke to an actor named Alistair McCall," Henry began.

"An *actor*?" CB snorted. "That's just what we need, another damned ego on legs."

"This one actually seems to *be* damned; at least by one of the looser definitions of the word." A quick gesture stopped Graham from speaking as Henry met CB's gaze Prince of Man to Prince of Man. "More importantly, he used to go to séances at this house while Creighton Caulfield was still alive."

The tense line of broad shoulders relaxed slightly. "Go on."

"He says Caulfield started out collecting grotesqueries—the finger of an alleged witch killed during the Inquisition, the skull of a cat that had supposedly been sacrificed in satanic rituals, a vial of dust and ash said to be the remains of one of the bloodsucking undead."

CB raised a single brow.

Henry shrugged. "Probably not."

Both men ignored the strangled choking sounds coming from Graham.

"Anyway, around 1892, Caulfield stopped collecting things and started collecting books. McCall said that some of those books made him very uneasy."

"He said some of them were warm," Graham added, shuddering.

CB's brow lifted again.

"It's possible," Henry told him. "Some books have the kind of contents that require a specific construction." He had, in his personal collection, a grimoire that recorded twenty-seven demonic names. The names were true—he had no desire to discover how the author had acquired them—and both the vellum pages and the thicker leather they were bound in maintained a constant body temperature. Blood temperature. Skin temperature. He'd taken it from a man who was using it to call demons into the world at about the same time as Caulfield had begun to collect the books that made McCall uneasy. He'd been told his was one of the last three true grimoires remaining. There was no reason Caulfield couldn't have gotten his hands on one of the other two.

"With the books," he continued, "came the séances. Séances and spiritualism in general were very popular at the time."

Graham snorted. "Yeah, well, you'd know."

Again, they ignored him.

"According to McCall, Caulfield was interested in contacting something he called Arogoth."

"Arogoth?" CB repeated, punctuating the name with a disdainful snort.

Henry shrugged. "Since the name seems to have no power, I suspect it's one that Caulfield made up. That whatever this thing was, it had no name—so he gave it one."

"Not a very original one. If one of my writers suggested such tripe, I'd take away their Lovecraft."

"So Caulfield was derivative. So what?" Graham demanded. "He was also more than dabbling in darkness." Hands fisted on his hips, his gaze flicked between Henry and CB fast enough to dislodge his comb-over. "And stop ignoring me!"

"Sorry. Would *you* like to continue?"

"No." Defiance wilted under CB's attention. "It's okay." The toe of one scuffed work boot dug a trench in the damp gravel. "Henry here's doing good."

"Thank you. But Graham's right," Henry admitted. "Caulfield was more than dabbling. According to McCall, the séances were often violent. The temperature in the drawing room would plummet, the darkness would thicken, and the spiritualists he used were never the same again. One of the more reputable died. The doctors called it a brain hemorrhage, but McCall—possessing a unique hindsight given his current condition—said he thought that something she'd contacted had overloaded the woman's brain. After a while, spiritualists refused to come to the house."

"And who can blame them, eh? If they were expected to talk to the thing in the basement." Graham frowned and scratched thoughtfully between the buttons on his overalls. "Except, it might not have been in the basement then."

"It makes no difference where it was, only where it is. How do we . . ." CB glanced back toward the house. ". . . they defeat it?"

"Caulfield kept a journal of his research. The séances, and the things he found out from books—he was determined to control the dark power found . . . acquired . . . stumbled over . . . who knows."

"And this journal is where?"

"Probably long gone."

"But there're ghosts in the house," Graham added, before Henry could continue, "who were alive when the journal was there. Servants."

"Servants." CB turned his attention back to the house, his expression dismissive. "What makes you think they knew anything about what their employer was up to?"

It was Henry's turn to raise a brow. If CB thought his housekeeper remained ignorant about any aspect of his life, he was being deliberately blind—which was, in Henry's long experience, the best way to deal with a good servant, the fiction of ignorance maintained by both halves of the relationship. "I think there's a very good chance they'd be curious about what their employer spent so much time and effort on, but we also have to consider that these ghosts died under . . ." He considered and discarded a number of words. ". . . familiar circumstances. One of the maids pushed one of the male servants down the kitchen stairs and then hanged herself from the third-floor landing. They were the first murder/suicide the house evoked and it may have been able to reach the maid because she'd read the journal. Tony has to talk to her."

"So now he's a medium, too."

Henry smiled at the weary lack of surprise in CB's voice. "No. But we know he saw Graham's cousins, so we stopped by his apartment and got this." He tugged at the strap hanging from his shoulder and swung Tony's laptop case into view.

"Is that . . . Arra's?"

"It is."

"And she left something on there that will help?"

"I have no idea, but there's eighty gig of magic instruction on here, so I'm hoping that there's something he can adapt."

"Adapt? Why does that not fill me with confidence?"

"He's a smart guy. He'll figure something out."

"Out. Yes. This may out his abilities to his companions. Have you considered that he may not want that to happen?"

It was Henry's turn to stare at the building. He could hear the five lives in the driveway—CB, Graham, the three crew—but nothing from the house. No life, no death—nothing. This house, this Arogoth, was attempting to poach lives on his territory. His lips curled back off his teeth. "Under the circumstances, what Tony does or doesn't want doesn't much matter. He'll do the right thing."

The silence pulled him around. Even with the Hunter masked, those who could meet his gaze were few. With the Hunter so close to the surface . . . Henry could think of only two others who would even attempt it. After a long moment, CB nodded and looked away. "What happens now?"

"Graham will call his cousins to the door, then they'll go to Tony and tell him about the servants and the journal."

"I've pulled them pretty much into the here and now, you know? If this Tony can see them, they can get . . ." Graham frowned. "Unless the house being awake is giving them trouble." He stepped back as both vampire and executive producer turned on him. "But probably not. You guys can just go back to ignoring me."

"Tony," Henry continued, emphatically doing just that, "will pull the laptop into the house, and use the information on it to find a way to talk to the maid. She'll tell him what was in Caulfield's journal, he'll use *that* information to either defeat the darkness in the basement or work around it and get the house open."

"There are a great many *ifs* in this plan."

"Got a better one?"

CB snorted. "I foresee one other problem," he said, not bothering to answer Henry's question. "Will the laptop work inside the house? According to my people, equipment batteries were draining rapidly all day."

Henry patted the laptop case. "Ah, but this doesn't run on batteries."

"Magic?"

"Apparently."

CB stepped away from the porch and indicated that Graham should approach. "Then let's begin."

As Graham sidled past him, he paused, and peered up into the taller man's face. "He's a vampire." The merest hint of a glance back at Henry. "Did you know he's a vampire?"

"Yes."

"And that doesn't bother you?"

"You speak to the dead."

"Yeah, but I don't suck blood."

"I have only your word for that."

Brianna stepped past the lantern sitting on the threshold—the compromise between all of them crowding into the bathroom and privacy. "Okay, next. And don't worry, the boy's mostly scared about strange people coming in his room." She glanced around at the half circle of silent faces. "What?"

"What boy?" Ashley snapped.

"The boy whose room it is, Zitface." The younger girl rolled her eyes. "He's not even a little bit gross. I want to see the baby."

"Just hang on a minute." Tina cut off both Ashley's reply and any potential attack on her sister. "There's a boy in the bathroom?"

"Yeah, but you can see through him, so . . ." She pursed her lips and blew a disinterested raspberry.

"You can see the ghost of a boy in the bathroom?"

"Duh."

"Oh, my God! Oh, my God!"

Releasing her hold on Ashley, Tina grabbed the wardrobe assistant's arm, keeping her from bolting. "Brenda, calm down."

"Calm down? Calm down! How am I supposed to calm down! There's a dead person in the bathroom!"

"There's going to be another one right here if you don't shut the hell up," Kate growled.

Amy stepped forward and leaned over the threshold. "I don't see anything."

"Maybe that's because you're in on it, too." Kate folded her arms as Amy leaned back to glare at her. "Well, you could be!"

Brianna shrugged. "She doesn't hear the baby neither." She cocked her head. "I don't hear the baby."

"Maybe you're too far away?"

"You can always hear the baby."

Kate's lip curled. "Unless Tony's playing ghosts again."

"Oh, for fuck's sake and for the last time!" Amy snapped. "Tony has nothing to do with this! You don't know him. Until tonight, you've hardly ever spoken two words to him. You're totally losing it."

"That's not helping," Tina warned as the two younger women moved closer together.

"You people are all nuts!" Whites showing all the way around her eyes, Brenda jerked her arm free and ran for the door of the suite.

Tina swore and raced after her.

The other four watched as the script supervisor crossed the dressing room and disappeared into the darkness of the bedroom. They winced in unison at the soft hard crash of flesh and furniture hitting the floor. After a moment, Tina limped back into the light, alone.

"I lost her in the dark, but I think she made it to the hall. I'm sure she'll be able to see the light of the other lantern coming up the stairs. She'll head right for it."

"She'll head right for Lee," Amy snorted.

Kate snickered an agreement.

"Do we go after her?"

"I'll go."

Tina grabbed Brianna's arm on her way by. "No, you won't."

Ashley pushed past Amy still standing by the bathroom door. "You guys can do what you want, but I'm going to pee. Any boy shows up and I'll slap him stupid."

"She will, too." Brianna tugged experimentally on Tina's grip, and relaxed against her side when it became obvious she was going nowhere. "She slapped Stewie so hard his nose bled. It was pretty gross."

"Brenda will be fine." Tina's tone suggested that the wardrobe assistant wouldn't dare not be.

Amy shoved her hands into the front pockets of her black cargo pants and rocked forward on her toes. "You know, that sounds a lot like famous last wo . . ." Tina's expression froze her in place. "Never mind."

She hadn't expected it to be so completely dark. Eyes open so wide they hurt, Brenda bounced off the side of the dressing room door and out into the hall. Arms outstretched, swaying in place, she tried to get her bearings.

There was someone with her in the hall.

Someone angry.

Too terrified to scream, she turned and ran.

Stumbled.

Found her balance.

Kept running.

Her left side slammed into something that moved and she grabbed at it as she fell. Wood. Smooth wood. And a handle. The door to the back stairs. It was open, swinging out into the hall. She'd run the wrong way, but she could get down the stairs to the kitchen and then find the others. Find Lee. Lee would make it right.

Eyes narrowed, Amy moved out to the edge of the lantern light. "Did you hear that?"

"It was the toilet." Tina folded her arms and glared at her companions. "I thought I told you no flushing until we were all done? With the power off, we only have the water in the lines."

"Toilets don't thud."

"Like someone chopping?" Brianna asked brightly. "Whack. Chunk."

"No . . ."

"It was the toilet," Tina repeated. "Keep the girls from running off while I use it."

"I'm not going anywhere," Ashley muttered as Amy took hold of Brianna's arm. "Don't touch me."

"It wasn't the toilet," Brianna insisted.

Kate nodded in agreement. "Sounded like an ax."

The stairs were narrow enough she could touch both sides. She moved as quickly as she could on the steep uneven footing. Stumbled again at the bottom when suddenly there were no more steps. Groped for the table. Hand walked along the long side. Off the end. One hand still holding on, she reached for the wall.

Her fingers brushed something solid.

Something cold.

The basement door.

It was in the basement.

"Lee!"

Tony shook off the sound of Stephen and Cassie's death in time to see Lee leap to his feet and cross to the edge of the circle, stumbling over Adam's legs and ignoring the 1AD's creative cursing.

"Brenda?"

Very faintly, from nowhere in particular, they heard a terrified, "Lee!"

"Brenda!" He paced the edge of the curve. "Where the hell is she?"

"She's not upstairs."

"No shit!"

Mason shrugged and lit another cigarette. "Fine. So you don't need my help."

Pivoting on one heel, Lee recrossed the circle. He looked, Tony thought, like he was trying to catch her scent. *Or I've just spent way too much time with Henry.*

"Brenda!" And across again. "I'm going after her."

"You don't even know where she is," Pavin muttered.

"And you're not taking the lantern." Mason hooked his foot around the base and slid it closer to his chair.

"Fine." Lee dropped to one knee by the box of candles. "I don't need the damned lantern, but I *am* going after her."

"No one's going anywhere," Peter began, his hands spread and his voice reasonable.

"She's in trouble."

"You don't know that." Reason began shading toward annoyance, but Peter managed to pull it back. "She just went off to use the bathroom."

"Yeah, and since she's calling for me, I suspect she's not using it now!" He snatched the lighter from Mason's hand and lit the candle. "I'm going to go . . . uh . . . ." The candlelight threw his puzzled expression into sharp relief.

Tony understood his hesitation. The house had stretched and twisted Brenda's voice so that it could have come from anywhere.

Glass broke.

"Dining room!"

"Step over the salt! Over it! Ah, Jesus, right through it . . ."

Snatching up a candle, Tony followed.

She thought the light was from the hall, but it was a candle, on the floor and shielded so that had she come out of the butler's pantry at any other angle she wouldn't have seen it.

Light glinted off glass.

"Hartley?"

Sitting on the floor by an open cabinet—one door hanging at a crazy angle—the boom operator straightened and lowered the now empty bottle.

The rush of relief was so great she had to grab the back of one of the dining room chairs. Trust Hartley to find the booze in an empty house. "I'm so glad to see you," she murmured as he stood, still holding the bottle loosely in one hand. "I thought I was following Lee's voice, but I guess I wasn't."

"Leesh not here." He staggered toward her and, although it was hard to tell for sure because his eyes were just at the edge of the small circle of light, he didn't seem to be focusing very well.

"Are you drunk? Because you know what CB said . . ."

The bottle smashing against the edge of the table cut off her comment.

"Brenda!"

"Lee?" She pivoted around her grip on the chair . . .

* * *

It was so dark in the dining room it looked as though Hartley had drawn a line of shadow across Brenda's throat. Tony didn't exactly find lines of shadow comforting, but they were infinitely preferable to the way the candlelight reflected off the liquid that flowed glistening down over the wardrobe assistant's chest.

Brenda's eyes widened. Her hand came up to clutch her throat. She gasped. Gurgled. Crumpled.

Lee surged forward, the movement blowing out his candle, and caught her before she hit the floor.

Tony stared past the two of them at Hartley, who was turning the broken bottle so that the dark stain gleamed in the flickering flame of the candle melted onto the floor.

Murder.

Suicide . . .

Crap!

This wasn't a replay. This was real life. Real death. Really happening.

Lee was yelling. Voices out in the hall were answering. Tony somehow managed to get to Hartley's side without his candle blowing out.

The boom operator looked over at him, blinked, and stammered, "Hate that d . . . d . . . damned music." Then he tossed the broken glass aside and bent to pull another bottle from the cabinet.

Jamming his candle into one arm of the candelabra on the sideboard, Tony launched himself onto the older man's back. The rush of air blew both candles out.

Graham sat back on his heels and swiped at the beads of sweat on his forehead. "They're not answering."

"Keep calling. They might just be distracted. We have no idea what's happening in there." Henry frowned down at the medium's expression. "Do we?"

"Know someone named Brenda Turpin?"

Old wood shuddered as CB stepped up on the small porch. "She works for me."

"*Worked* for you," Graham corrected matter-of-factly. "She's dead."

"Trapped?" Henry asked. "Like the others?"

"Well, I didn't feel her leave . . ."

"But you felt her die?"

He nodded. "And it wasn't pretty."

"It never is."

∽ TEN

Tony was just as glad that Hartley's howling protests were drowning out most of the noises Lee was making. Unable to see anything in the pitch-black dining room, he fought to hold down the struggling boom operator.

"What is going *on* in here?"

As Tina's irritated question followed the light from the second lantern into the room, Tony shifted back and pinned Hartley's arms with his knees. The howling stopped and Lee's cries faded to pained gasping for breath. It might have been Lee . . .

It might have been Brenda.

"Holy crap." Amy's quiet observation held horror enough that Tony managed to twist around to see the women grouped in the doorway staring down at Lee holding Brenda crumpled across his lap. Tony could only see the curve of his back and Brenda's legs, but Lee looked broken and Brenda far too still.

"Lots of blood!" Brianna pushed between Amy's and Tina's hips. "Is she dead?"

"I don't . . . she isn't . . . I can't . . ." Lee shook his head, hair flicking back and forth with the violence of his denial, then he curled even more tightly around the body.

Not Brenda.

The body.

Amy stepped forward as Peter, Zev, and Adam pushed in from the hall. Zev took one look at the tableau and grabbed the girls, pulling them back out of the dining room.

"I already saw!" Brianna protested.

"Then you can get out of the way," Zev told her calmly. "Ashley, Mason stayed in the circle; maybe you should go sit with him so he's not alone."

"Her heart's not beating," Amy murmured over the sound of Ashley leaving. "It was fast, Lee, there was nothing you could do. The carotid artery was cut. Wound like this, you bleed out in less than three minutes."

"How do you know?"

Tony could hear hope in Lee's question and maybe, just maybe, a slight relaxing together of all the bits and pieces he'd become.

"I saw it on a television show." Amy sat back on her heels, and Tony could just see her face over the black line of Lee's shoulder. Somehow the magenta hair and heavily mascaraed eyes lent weight to her explanation. This was death. Goth girls knew about death. Right?

"It was the same situation," she continued solemnly, "except it was a gunshot and not a wardrobe assistant, but the same wound. Bled out in less than three. There was . . ." She gripped his shoulder, the black tips on magenta nails disappearing against his jacket. ". . . nothing you could do."

"Why was there nothing Tony could do, then?" Kate drawled. "He's supposed to be on top of all this."

She's right. I know what's happening. I'm the one talking to the ghosts. I'm the one with the metaphysical powers. I should have gone after Hartley.

"Hello." Amy ground out the word through clenched teeth. "He's sitting on the perp."

"Too little, too late. And I think . . ."

"No one gives a flying fuck what you think!" Without rising or releasing her hold on Lee's shoulder, she swiveled around. "Peter!"

Given the director's reaction, Tony could imagine Amy's expression.

"Yeah. Right. Uh, Kate, be quiet, you're not helping. Lee, let Brenda go, and we'll carry her in and lay her beside Tom."

"What do we do with Hartley?"

And once again, Tony found himself at the center of attention.

Hartley, his right cheek flattened against the floor, glared up at him with one bloodshot eye.

"Duct tape."

"Kate, that's not . . ." Peter paused and Tony all but heard everyone considering it. "Actually, that's a good idea."

Once Mouse arrived in the dining room, Hartley stopped struggling. Given their relative sizes, there wasn't much point and Hartley was generally not an aggressive drunk. Tony slipped back and let the larger man flip Hartley over and effortlessly cocoon his arms to his sides.

"Why'd you do it? Why'd you do it?" Mouse moaned the words over and over as he moved down Hartley's body and began to tape his legs together. No longer needed, Tony stood and backed away. He didn't understand the look Mouse shot him. He wasn't sure he wanted to. The cameraman had been double shadow-held. *If Mouse snaps, we're fucking doomed.*

"Why did he do it?" Tina wiped tears off her cheeks with the flat of her hand, unaware she was repeating Mouse's quiet mantra. "I can't remember Brenda ever saying more than two words to him."

"It wasn't him," Tony reminded her wearily. He stepped back as Adam and Lee lifted Brenda—Amy covering her face and the ruin of her throat with Lee's tuxedo jacket. "It was the house. Nothing that's happened here tonight is anyone's fault. The thing in the basement is using us. Manipulating us."

"And there's nothing we can do?"

"Survive until morning." He wasn't aware he was clutching his throat until he saw the direction of Kate's scowl. Forced his hand back to his side. Put them both in his pockets just in case.

"You didn't cover his mouth," Peter observed as Mouse hauled Hartley upright and slung him over his shoulder, duct tape creaking ominously.

"Nose is plugged."

"And you're afraid he'll suffocate?"

"Let him," Kate muttered as Mouse grunted an assent.

"All right. That is it from you!" Tina blew her nose and turned on the younger woman, her words emerging with the kind of distinct enunciation achieved only by nuns and senior NCOs. "I am sick and tired of your attitude, young lady. From now on, you will either have something constructive to say or you will keep your mouth shut. Am I understood?"

Even the house seemed to be waiting for Kate's answer.

Tony had gone to a Catholic elementary school and lessons learned under the steely-eyed glare of the older nuns lingered. Apparently, Kate had also had involuntary responses installed by the Sister Mary Magdalenes of the world.

"Yes, ma'am." Strangely, she looked almost peaceful as she turned to follow Tina into the hall.

She knows who's in charge, Tony realized, stepping out of Mouse's way. He picked up the two candles, his and Hartley's, and waited for Peter, who held the lantern, to leave the room.

But the director stood staring down at the dark puddle on the floor, apparently unaware that the others had left. He moved the light back and forth, mesmerized by the reflection of the flame. After a long moment, he sighed. "That's way too much blood, people. Let's try and keep it realistic."

"Peter?"

"You may know what's happening, but you're not responsible for any of this, Tony." His voice was low, too low to be overheard by anyone more than an arm's length away. "I am. That's why I get the big bucks."

Peter, as much as Tina, was the voice of reason. She couldn't hold them in place alone. He couldn't slip.

Tony snorted. "CB pays big bucks?"

The older man started, stared at him for a moment, then snorted in turn. "Relatively speaking. Come on, they'll need the light."

They left Hartley lying inside the circle of salt staring sullenly at the ceiling. The pair of candles lit so Peter could carry the lantern into the dining room were left burning, the second lantern blown out so as not to waste the kerosene, and everyone followed Brenda's body into the drawing room.

They set her down next to Tom. Lee's hands were visibly shaking as he released her shoulders and straightened. Although Adam moved to join the others, he remained standing over her, facing away from the group, the back of his dress shirt a brilliant white like a beacon reflecting the lantern light.

I should go to him. He needs . . . Except that Tony had no idea what he needed.

It was Mason who finally broke the tableau. Mason, who had made vested self-interest a cornerstone of his personality, stepped forward until he stood shoulder to shoulder with Lee and offered him a cigarette.

Lee looked down at Mason's hand, up at his face, and almost smiled. "No thanks, I don't smoke."

"Good." He slipped the cigarette back into his jacket pocket. "Because it's my last one."

Almost became actually and Lee's teeth flashed as he shook his head. "Jackass."

"And I thought you gay guys were supposed to be the sensitive ones," Amy muttered, so close to his ear her breath lapped warm against his skin.

He'd have suggested she bite him, but given the distance . . .

As Lee turned, he almost seemed to be searching for something. Someone. His eyes locked on Tony's face just for an instant and, for that instant, flashed . . . relief? Tony was too distracted by the dark stain dimming the brightness of his shirtfront to be sure. By the time he looked up again, Lee was moving away from the body and Amy was moving toward it and Zev's hand was around his arm. A quick squeeze. And gone.

"Is anyone going to say words over the body?" Amy asked as she worked off her two remaining rings.

"No one said anything over Tom," Adam pointed out.

"Yeah, well, Tom took us by surprise."

"And we expected *this*?"

Amy's arched brow was answer enough. She waited. "Fine. I'll do it." A deep breath. A glance down at the bodies, the rings jingling in one hand. "To the living, death sucks. But to the dead, it's just another stop on the journey. Have a nice trip."

"That was . . ." Tina began.

". . . stupid," Ashley finished. "Because they're not going anywhere, they're just trapped in the house like all the other dead people."

"You think you can do it better?"

"I never said that."

"Then shut up."

"You shut up."

"Girls . . ." Tina's voice held obvious warning. The phrase *clear and present danger* chased itself around Tony's head.

Amy rolled her eyes and dropped to one knee, lifting the edge of Lee's jacket off Brenda's face with one hand and dropping her rings on the dead woman's eyes with the other. "Anyone else goes," she murmured, "and we're going to have to hope silver plating works as well."

Foreshadowing, Tony thought. And he could see the word on a couple of other faces. *Just what we need.* Movement at the far end of the room caught his eye, and he turned, expecting to see Cassie and Stephen but instead seeing only the faint gray outline of the mirror. He'd managed to be elsewhere when Peter had ordered the hair spray cleaned off after finishing the cocktail party scene. Given the length of the room, he was surprised that the lantern light reached that far. On second thought, he wasn't sure that it did.

Movement in the mirror had nothing to do with movement in the room. Shapes offered other shapes something. Tea. Little cakes. Faces, made indistinct by distance, formed and reformed as cups rose and fell and dropped to the carpet when the convulsions started.

"Is that how we left him?"

Amy's question snapped his head back around so quickly he nearly kinked his neck. Tom's left hand lay by his side, the fingers curled up so that chewed fingernails pointed toward the ceiling. His right rested palm down on his thigh. Under the tarp, his head flopped a little to one side. Tony couldn't remember how they'd left him.

"Who looked that closely?" Adam muttered, more or less voicing Tony's thought.

"I think it would be cool if he walked around," Brianna sighed. "You guys never did zombies yet."

"Episode after next," Amy said without looking up.

"Seriously?" Mason didn't sound thrilled. Tony couldn't blame him. The whole walking undead thing was just too easy to parody. Once Sara Polley took up arms against an army of animated corpses, zombies were done to death—at least on the Canadian side of the border.

"Writers were finishing the final draft when I left the office."

"Peter . . ."

"Not now, Mason."

Amy nodded, having come to a decision. "Of course that's how he was. I'm sure."

She almost sounded sure.

That would have to be good enough.

"You have a safe trip, too." She lightly touched Tom's shoulder before she stood, then tugged her Hello Kitty T-shirt down and headed for the door. "Let's get back into the circle and this time, let's *all* stay there."

"Brianna, Ashley, come on." Zev tugged the girls into motion and everyone else followed behind; walking slowly like mourners leaving a funeral.

Which, Tony supposed, was what they were. Amy was right, Tom had taken them by surprise and they hadn't so much mourned him as feared for themselves. Brenda, they grieved for.

He watched Lee's bowed shoulders, found himself wondering just how much the other man grieved, and almost hated himself for it.

"Tony?"

"Right. Sorry." He hurried to catch up to Peter and Adam.

"Isn't this great?" the 1AD muttered. "We have our own morgue. It's like we're being punished for inflicting yet another gumshoe with fangs on the viewing public."

"This seems a little extreme for bad television," Peter sighed.

"Episode nine."

"Even for that."

The silence waiting for them in the hall seemed weighted. The people waiting, numbed. Amy knelt by Hartley, everyone else stood around the outside edge of the circle.

Peter pushed past. "What is it?"

Amy's voice had lost most of its highs and lows. "He's dead. It looks like he puked and choked on it."

"You're sure?"

"I watched a lot of *Da Vinci's Inquest*." Her lip curled. "And besides, it's pretty obvious."

"Eww, puke." Even Brianna seemed to have lost her interest in the ghoulish.

"Right. All right." Peter visibly pulled fraying bits back together. "Saleen, Pavin, carry him into the drawing room beside the others. Don't even start with me," he continued as the sound tech opened his mouth to protest. "Half the time it's like you two aren't even here. Amy . . ."

"Earrings." Her hands rose to the first of four silver hoops in her right ear. "I'm on it."

Sorge led the way with the lantern, then Amy, then the body. No one said anything. No one followed.

"At least it was his own vomit," Adam observed thoughtfully as the body passed.

Tony would have laughed, wouldn't have been able to stop himself from laughing, except that the lights came up and Karl started shrieking as he burned.

Some of the moisture beading Graham's forehead was rain. Most of it wasn't. Breathing heavily, he sat back on his heels and shook his head. "Still nothing. They're there. I can feel them, eh, but it's like they don't know where I am."

"The house." CB made it an accusation, not a question.

"Yeah, sure, probably. So what? There's nothing I can do. I need a beer." He started to stand but Henry's hand came down on his shoulder and held him in place.

"When we're done, you can drink yourself into a stupor if you need to." Henry reached past the medium with his other hand. "Try again while I'm in contact with the house."

"And that'll do what?"

"Like calls to like."

"Yeah. Okay." Graham watched the pale fingers approach the closest point the house allowed. "It'll just throw you off."

Hazel eyes darkened. "Let it try."

"At least Karl doesn't take too long." Cassie rubbed her arms, hands ghosting over the rivulets of blood without disturbing them. "I need to get out of this bathroom."

Stephen snorted. "It's not Karl that takes the time, it's his mother. And what a way to go; poking her eyes out with knitting needles might not have even killed her."

"I think *it* made sure she was dead."

"Well, yeah." He sat down on the edge of the tub, the blood splatters from their deaths evident on porcelain and paint. "Did it seem faster this time?"

"Karl?"

"The time between us and Karl."

"I don't know." Cassie reached out and lightly touched her reflection in the mirror. Her face was whole and she never tired of looking at it.

"It seemed faster to me. I think *it's* speeding things up, putting more pressure on them now that they've started to crack. I mean, we barely pulled ourselves back together after dying when we were back in here again. And there's two more dead."

"I know." Her eyes were . . . were . . . "Stephen, what color were my eyes?"

Her brother shrugged and fixed his head in one practiced motion. "I don't know."

"Blue?"

"Sure."

"Gray?"

"If you want."

"Stephen!"

"Karl's stop . . ." Stephen didn't so much stand as he was suddenly on his feet. "Can you feel that?"

Cassie frowned and turned from the mirror. "It's Graham. He wants us."

"It's more than Graham!" Eyes wide, he reached for her and was still reaching an instant later in the kitchen. "How did we get here?"

A young man, his head lying in a spreading puddle of blood, appeared and disappeared by the corner of the table.

"Cassie, look! Colin's being pulled out of sequence!"

"Graham's never done that . . ." Only their lack of substance kept them from slamming into the wall by the back door. ". . . before." She spun around to face the door, parts of her moving faster than others, legs swirling unsubstantially in an effort to catch up. "All right, we're here. Stop shouting!"

Power surged up his arm, locking his muscles into agonizing rigidity. The house fought to force him away. He fought to remain in contact. The flesh between suffered.

It burned.

And it froze.

And it melted off his bones.

"I've got them."

Henry heard the voice, couldn't quite comprehend the words. Knew they were important, couldn't remember why.

Then warm points of contact on each arm. Warm and painfully tight.

The slow and steady beating of a mortal heart beneath his cheek brought him back to himself. He could hear blood moving purposefully. Feel the gentle rhythm of mortal breathing. Feel solid muscle, below, beside, almost all the way around him. Smell expensive cologne over meat. He opened his eyes.

He was lying across CB's lap, cradled in the big man's arms. It was an unexpected position, but it felt surprisingly safe—which was a good thing since leaving it seemed to be temporarily out of the question. "What happened?"

CB smiled, dark eyes crinkling at the corners, but before he could speak, another voice broke in.

"You were kind of vibrating inside this red light, not making any noise, but it looked like you were screaming. The boss grabbed your arms, and when the red light tossed him away, you came too."

Chris. Henry managed to turn his head and saw the three members of the production crew standing and staring down at him. Teeth clenched, feeling more like throwing up than he had in four-hundred-odd years—a remarkably effective way of keeping the Hunter at bay—he flopped his head back around until he could see CB again. "You knew the house would push you away."

"And I figured I'd take you with me." This close, his voice was a bass rumble in the depths of a broad chest.

"That explains why my arms hurt."

"Indeed."

"I wouldn't have been able to get loose on my own." No point in lying about it.

"So I surmised."

"Are *you* all right?"

"He put a dent in the side of the generator truck."

"I own the generator truck, Mr. Singh; I can dent it if I choose."

"Sure, Boss."

"Why are you three still here? There's nothing you can do."

After a long moment, Henry heard feet shuffling in damp gravel. Chris cleared his throat. "Well, there's weird shit going down and we wanted to see how it ends."

"Besides," Karen added, "those are our friends trapped inside that house. Just because we can't do anything now doesn't mean we can't do something later."

"Commendable. For now, I suggest you get out of the rain."

Ah. Right. Rain. After a while it became such a normal part of life on the West Coast it was easy to ignore. Henry rubbed a dribble of water off his cheek against the smooth fabric of CB's trench coat.

"We'll be in the craft services truck if you need us, Boss." And much more quietly as they moved away, voice barely touching innuendo, "You think they want to be alone?"

CB, Henry realized as the other man shifted beneath him, hadn't heard. Probably for the best. He was comfortable, recovering in this position that parodied passion, and had no wish to be tossed aside as smart-ass employees were summarily dealt with.

"Old Arogoth," he said after a moment, "is really starting to annoy me."

"You've felt its power. Can Tony defeat it?"

Henry could lie and make CB believe him, but they'd moved past that back in the spring. "I hope so."

"If he gets my daughters out . . ."

Carefully pulling himself up into a sitting position, Henry watched the other man's face as he stared up into the night sky, rain beading against mahogany skin. Conscious of the scrutiny, the ex-linebacker lowered his head and met the vampire's gaze. Henry could read no promises in his dark eyes, none of the futile bargains with death he'd heard made a thousand times.

"If he gets your daughters out?" he asked softly. Curious.

Broad shoulders shrugged. "I'll thank him."

"Okay . . ."

Both men turned toward the caretaker, the contact between them stretching to fill the new space.

". . . Cassie and Stephen'll tell your friend Tony to come to the door and get his laptop, but they won't be able to do it right away. They got dragged back to the bathroom and they'll have to wait until the replay is over."

"Replay?" Henry asked as he got carefully to his feet. When he swayed, a warm hand closed around his elbow and steadied him.

Graham shrugged. "Yeah, well, *replay*'s what Tony calls it. The deaths the house has collected are running over and over—they're powering the malevolence . . ."

"Arogoth."

"Yeah, whoever." Another shrug. "These replays, they're throwing off enough dark energy to drive even the most stable person nuts. It's how the malevolence does it; throws all kinds of dark and spooky crap at you until you break. Just, usually, it does it slower because it has more time."

"And my girls are in the midst of that?" CB's grip tightened. Had Henry been a mortal man, it would have done damage. "Of violent death replaying over and over?"

"Kind of. But not really. So far, only Tony is experiencing it."

"So far?"

Sitting splay-legged on the porch, sagging back against the lower part of the railing, Graham shrugged a third and final time.

When Tony opened his eyes, he could still see Charles' broken body superimposed over Zev. He reached out and gently tugged the music director a little to the left.

"What?"

"You don't want to know."

Zev thought about it for a moment then nodded. "All right."

Things had settled after Hartley's body had been taken away. Tina had split up the basket of food she'd brought down from Mason's dressing room after the bathroom break and everyone sat quietly eating. With everyone holding tightly to the normalcy of food, Tony doubted they'd even noticed he'd been gone.

"Tony! You have to go to the back door!"

He jumped as Stephen and Cassie appeared directly in front of him. Jumped again as Cassie grabbed for his arm and the cold raised gooseflesh from the edge of his T-shirt to his wrist. As they began to talk, overlapping each other's sentences, it spread.

". . . and if Lucy read the journal, she might be able to tell you how to deal with the malevolence."

The lights came up with a scream, and from the conservatory came the wet crunch of limbs being hacked off.

Tony wrapped his arms around his torso, shivered, and waited. And waited.

As he recalled, the old woman did a thorough job. Dismembered. Buried. Was that the sound of a shovel? Finally, rat poison.

This time, when the entryway reappeared, lantern lit and smelling ever so faintly of sweat and vomit, Amy's hand came out of nowhere and impacted with his face.

"Ow!"

"Sorry." Except she didn't look sorry; she looked disturbingly disappointed that she wasn't going to be able to hit him again. At least the numbness she'd been wrapped in since Hartley's death had disappeared. "We thought you'd been possessed."

His cheek throbbed. "I was waiting out another replay!"

"Well, yeah. We know that now."

"I mentioned it at the time," Zev pointed out.

"I wanted to stick you with pins." Brianna smiled at him over the edge of her muffin. "But Zev said no. The poopy head."

Just Zev? Given the evening so far, stupid question.

"Well, what did they say?"

"Say?" If the second replay was identical to the first, the gardener had been quickly unconscious and the old woman had said nothing as she methodically hacked him to pieces.

Amy rolled her eyes and her arm twitched. "The ghosts you were obviously listening to before you went away."

"Oh, them!"

"Oh, them," she repeated sarcastically. "Messages from beyond the grave should never be taken lightly! Share!"

"I need to go to the back door."

Kate snorted. "The hell you do."

"A friend of mine—Henry," he added to Zev, who nodded, "has my laptop there."

Kate snorted again, this time adding a sneer. "And this is exactly the situation that needs a game of spider solitaire."

Arra used to tell the future with spider solitaire. This didn't seem to be the time to bring that up.

Tony stepped to one side so that Amy no longer stood between him and the bulk of their companions. "Graham Brummel, the caretaker, is a medium." When everyone accepted that without throwing things, he continued. "He told Cassie and Stephen that one of the ghosts who died while Creighton Caulfield was still alive may know how we can deal with the thing in the basement. I need my laptop so I can figure out how to talk to that ghost."

"Why?" Peter asked, crossing his arms. "You've been talking to the brother and sister all along."

"Because the caretaker is their cousin and he redefined them as individuals, pulled them away from . . . uh . . ."

"Death?" Amy offered.

"Yeah, death."

"So your laptop came with software for talking to the dead." Peter used the tone he saved for dealing with unfinished sets, unlearned lines, and extras in general. "You got lucky, Tony. All I got on mine was a copy of Jukebox."

They were clearly not going to let him leave until he explained. No point in making a run for it since the light faded to total and complete darkness just past the curved line of salt. Granted, he could just wait for the next replay and move through the lit halls of that earlier time, but given the varying edges the group seemed balanced on, he couldn't guarantee he'd survive the experience. He really didn't want to be the headliner in the next murder/suicide.

On the other hand, the explanation wasn't likely to win him any friends.

"We're waiting, Tony."

While only Kate looked actively hostile, even Amy, Zev, and Lee—the three who'd been on his side throughout—looked impatient. Well, mostly Lee still looked shattered, but the impatience was there as well.

We know you're hiding something from us.

Spill.

He took a deep breath. Tom was dead and Brenda was dead and Hartley was dead, so in comparison . . . "Arra left me the laptop . . . her laptop. She left lessons on it. Lessons on how to be a wizard."

"Say what?" Amy spoke first, but they all wore nearly identical expressions of incredulous disbelief.

"Arra was a wizard." He had to take another deep breath before he could manage the corollary. "I'm a wizard."

"Harry Potter," Brianna announced.

"Gandalf," her sister added.

"Fiction," Mason snapped as Sorge muttered something in French that sounded distinctly uncomplimentary.

"That's not like some strange euphemism for gay, is it?" Adam demanded.

Tony's turn for incredulous disbelief. "For what?"

"Because we all *know* that."

"No. Wizard. Like Harry Potter." He gestured at Brianna. "And Gandalf." And at Ashley. Finally at Mason. Seven words. Mason's lighter lifted off his thigh and slapped into Tony's hand. "And it's nonfiction." He tossed the lighter back to Mason, who instinctively caught it, then let it slide out of his hand onto the floor. *Yep, it's covered in wizard cooties.* "According to Arra, it's just a slightly left-of-center way to manipulate energies."

Brianna dove for the lighter. "I want to manipulate energy!"

"It's not something everyone can do."

"I'm not everyone!"

"Why doesn't Tony check you out later," Zev suggested, pulling the lighter from her hand.

Amy's hands were on her hips. "So Arra was a wizard?"

"Yeah."

"Did CB know?"

"Yeah."

"And you're a wizard?"

"Sort of."

"And does he know about you?"

"Yeah."

She smacked him hard on the arm. "So why the hell didn't you tell me?"

"CB didn't want any of this to get out." CB hadn't actually said Tony couldn't tell people. They'd been in full agreement on that. He glanced around the circle of staring faces. "You know how weird people can get about this kind of thing."

"What kind of thing?"

"You know, telling people you're a wizard."

"He has a point," Sorge murmured, nodding.

"His head points," Amy snapped. "Hello! Haunted house! People dying! I think at that point CB might have let you mention . . ."

Dance music drowned out her last words.

The lights came up.

Great. The ballroom.

Before he could decide what to do—should he put himself physically in front of the doors in case Brianna slipped the leash again—he heard laughing from the drawing room.

That couldn't be good.

Brenda and Hartley danced out into the hall. Like Cassie and Stephen, Brenda remained drenched in blood. Hartley had lost the duct tape and was remarkably light on his feet. Tom shuffled gracelessly behind them; his broken bones an apparent handicap.

Who the hell is coming up with the rules for this shit?

Both men shot him somewhat sheepish looks as they passed.

"Come and dance with us," Brenda purred over Hartley's shoulder. "Just let the music pick you up and carry you along."

"I don't think so," Tony snarled.

"I'm not talking to you, asshole."

Oh, crap . . .

He turned and could just barely make out the translucent forms of Kate and Mouse and Lee and Mason. The shadow-held. And Brianna—whose youth made her susceptible to the other side. Currently, the side he was standing on.

"Don't let anyone leave the circle." Loud enough to be heard over the music. Loud enough to be heard over any shouting going on back in the real world. Loud enough to be heard across the divide. Loud enough they realized he was serious. "Sit on them if you have to!"

"Leeeeeee . . ." Brenda sang the vowels. "You want to be with me, don't you? You let me die. You owe me."

"Cheap shot," Tony growled, placing himself between her and the actor.

She smiled; her teeth red. "He's mine, not yours."

"You'll have to go through me to get him."

"Through you . . ."

He stood his ground as the ghosts danced closer.

". . . all right."

"Dancing. We should all go dancing!" Smiling broadly, Mason grabbed Ashley's hands and began to swing her around. "Everything will be fine if we just go dancing."

She tried to pull away. "Tony said . . ."

"Tony's a PA, what does he know?"

"Let go of me!"

"We're going, d . . . AMN it!"

Stephen's hand passing through his arm had been cold. This was so much colder it was almost pain with temperature. Ice shards in his blood. Muscles tensed past stillness into trembling. The taste of copper in his mouth as he fought to breathe.

Tony's legs folded and his knees slammed hard against wood. He jackknifed forward, gasped in pain, managed to fill his lungs. Coughing, hands braced against the floor, he looked up to see Tom leaving the hall with Brenda and Hartley dancing behind.

"No! It's not fair!" The internal struggle to turn the dance was evident on Brenda's face. "I could have had him!"

The call of the ballroom was too strong. Cassie and Stephen were safe in the bathroom. Their place. Brenda and Hartley hadn't yet had a replay to anchor them in the dining room and Tom . . . who the hell knew.

He could hear Brenda protesting until the lights dimmed and he knelt, coughing and shivering at the edge of the lamplight.

"Tony?"

Amy. Beside him. Unable to straighten up, he got his head around. She'd dropped to one knee and was studying him like she was on the bomb squad and he was liable to explode at any moment. "Is everyone okay?" he coughed.

"Are *you* okay?"

"I asked first." It wasn't much of a smile, but she seemed to appreciate it.

"Well, Mason's a little bruised. Ashley got freaked by the whole 'take me dancing' number and kicked him in the nuts. Did you know she plays soccer?"

He didn't.

"Yeah, well, his Beckhams are a little bent, let me tell you. Mouse curled up in a ball. Zev stopped Brianna from running by lifting her off the floor, and the rest of us did what you suggested and sat on Lee and Kate. And by the way, it totally sucks that I seem to be without any psychic sensitivity."

His eyebrows may have risen. He was still so cold he couldn't tell for sure. "You have *no* kind of sensitivity."

"Bite me." Shuffling closer, she tucked her hands under his arm. "You're freezing. What happened?"

"Ghosts. Brenda and Hartley and Tom. The ballroom called them and Brenda and Hartley danced through me."

"Danced?"

"I think it was a two-step."

"How the hell do you know what a two-step looks like?"

"Square dance club." He tried to keep all his weight from sagging into her grip and almost succeeded.

"Gay square dance club?" she grunted, heaving him back onto his heels.

"Duh. I went with an ex."

"I can't think of another reason . . . What's that on the floor?"

Exposed as he lifted his left hand, silver glinted against the wood.

She stopped him from bending forward. "You'll break your nose. I'll get it."

Four rings. Two earrings. The metal slightly frosted.

"I don't think they're working anymore."

"No shit. *I* think I'll just tuck them out of sight." Suiting action to words, she slipped them into the lower pocket on her cargo pants and stood. "Right. Let's get you on your feet."

"Actually, I'm fine down here."

"You going to crawl to the back door, then, Mr. Merlin?"

Right. The back door. Tony sighed and let her help him to his feet. He couldn't stop shivering, but other than the lingering chill, he seemed fine. He didn't want to turn and face the voices behind them—rising, falling, accusing, whimpering—but he knew he didn't have a choice.

"I won't need the other lantern."

Conversations stopped. Kate scowled at Saleen and Pavin until they let her go. Mouse remained curled in a fetal position on the floor—best possible reaction for a guy who once won a fistfight with a bear as far as Tony was concerned. Sure, the bear was handicapped by not actually having fists, but that was pretty much moot. Sorge stood next to Mouse. Face red, Mason still cradled his dignity; Zev had both girls now and was glaring protectively. Lee sat flanked by Peter and Adam, his lashes wet ebony triangles, his bloody dress shirt in a pile beside him on the floor. Unfortunately, Brenda's blood had soaked through to the white T-shirt he'd worn beneath it.

Shit! Where's Tina?

Then he saw her over by the door, tears glistening on her cheeks as she stared down at Everett.

"Is Everett . . . ?"

She shook her head without looking up. "He's still breathing."

Well, yay. Funny thing to cry about.

"You won't need the other lantern," Amy prodded, adding a sharp elbow to the ribs.

"Yeah, uh, the replays are coming faster, so I'll just move while the lights are up."

Peter shook his head. "You're not going alone."

"Peter . . ."

"Tony." His smile held no humor and very little patience. "Let me rephrase that in a way you'll understand. You're not going alone."

"Fine. Amy . . ."

"She stays here. Same reasons as before. Lee . . ."

"No way, he's . . ." . . . *falling apart.* But Tony couldn't actually say it.

As he stepped closer, Peter lowered his voice—not so low he couldn't be heard because right now secrets were the last thing they needed but low enough that an illusion of privacy could be created. "Lee needs something to do. He needs to not sit around . . ." Words were considered and discarded in the pause. ". . . thinking. Besides, he's gone out on all your other excursions and you've both always come back. Right now, that seems like a good omen to me."

"Yeah, sure, but . . ."

"You'll take the second lantern." Slightly better than normal volume now. Director's volume. "You'll get your laptop. And you'll come up with a way to get us all out of here."

Even Tom and Brenda and Hartley? Something else he couldn't actually say.

Maybe Peter read the thought off his face. "All of us," he repeated. "Get moving. Lee! You're going with Tony."

Propelled by Peter's voice, by the normalcy of Peter telling him what to do, Lee stood.

Tony surrendered. Even with the replays moving faster, they'd be back long before the ballroom started up again.

"You sure?" he asked quietly as Lee came to his side.

"Peter's right. I have to do something."

"Carry the lantern?"

"Sure."

They were at the door of the dining room before Tony realized they should have gone the other way. He stopped on the threshold, but Lee grabbed his arm and dragged him over.

"It's just a room with blood on the floor. That's all." And if his grip was tight enough to stop the blood from moving in Tony's arm . . .

Tony added that to the growing list of things he couldn't say.

"She'd be pissed about the blood."

She. Brenda. A quick glance down at the dark not-quite-puddle. "On the floor?"

"No. On the shirt."

"Oh. Right."

"She was always at us not to get the clothes dirty because CB never gave wardrobe enough money for them to buy more than one set."

"Technically, she made the mess."

The answering snicker sounded just on the edge of hysteria and Tony decided that maybe he'd better skip the manly banter for now. As they moved into the butler's pantry, he suddenly remembered his backpack, stored in the AD office back just after dawn and forgotten. "I've got a shirt with me if you want to change."

"Into what?"

"Out of . . ." He waved at Brenda's blood.

"Oh. Right. Thanks." Lee's movements had none of their usually fluidity as he set the lantern on the granite countertop. "I wish that damned baby would shut the fuck up!"

Karl had pretty much become background noise, tuned out the way they all tuned out traffic and elevator music and provincial politics. But he was a convenient excuse.

Reaching under the counter, Tony dragged out his pack and pulled out a black T-shirt. "It may be a little tight, but it's clean," he said as he straightened. And froze. Lee'd stripped off his shirt and was scrubbing at a fist-sized stain on his skin with the crumpled fabric. The lantern light painted the shadows in under muscles and gilded the upper curves. He kept his chest waxed for the show—body hair gave the networks palpitations—but Tony had no difficulty filling in the patch of dark curls he knew should be there.

He was having trouble breathing again.

Bright side, he wasn't cold.

"I was going to a play after work with Henry," he said hurriedly, one arm stretched awkwardly out offering the change of clothes.

"Henry?" Lee raised his head. "Your *friend*?"

"*Just* my friend now."

Strange exchange. Weighted even.

What the hell is happening here?

He was still holding out the shirt. Lee was staring past it with a . . . Tony had no idea what to call the expression on the other man's face, but the green eyes locked onto his with an almost terrifying intensity.

Then his back was up against the counter, the edge of the granite digging in just over his kidneys. Lee's hands were holding his head almost too tightly, fingers wrapped around his skull like a heated vise, and Lee's mouth was on his devouring and desperate, and Lee's body was pressing against him, and there was a rather remarkable amount of smooth, heated skin under his hands and Jesus, people reacted to death in the weirdest damned ways! Tony knew that the worst possible thing he could do was respond, but he wasn't dead and he *was* responding . . .

And the lights came up.

ꙮ ELEVEN

TECHNICALLY, since he hadn't moved, he had to be still kissing Lee. Except that he was also up against the counter in the butler's pantry with his mouth working and his elbow braced in a plate of insubstantial cakes. He could feel . . .

No, he couldn't.

Damn!

Lee'd probably jumped back. It didn't matter if it was an Oh-my-God-what-the-fuck-am-I-doing reaction or if he'd realized Karl wasn't crying or he'd sensed a different reaction when Tony'd turned his head to look at the cakes—the point was they were no longer in physical contact.

He stayed where he was for a moment, catching his breath—the other reaction would just have to take care of itself—then, in as steady a voice as he could manage: "I'm in a replay. It's happening in the . . ." Bathroom, nursery, stairs, conservatory, ballroom; he counted down the recent replays. "... draw-ing room. From the hall it sounded like someone convulsing, but I didn't go in, so it might, um . . ." He struggled to bring his brain back on-line, but talking made him think of his mouth, which made him think of Lee's mouth, which made him think of what Lee'd just been doing with his mouth, which made him wonder why he'd stopped and . . . *Jesus H. Christ! At the risk of betraying the side, getting some is not the issue right now!* "Look, it's not very long, so I'll head for the kitchen while I've got the light. You can wait here or you can follow."

As he finished talking, he started moving; pleased with the way he'd fi-nally managed to sound almost as though nothing out of the ordinary had happened. Where nothing out of the ordinary *didn't* include convulsions by the long dead in the drawing room, of course. If Lee wanted to deny swapping spit, then Tony would give him that chance.

And if he doesn't?

Twenty-four hours earlier—no, twelve—Tony'd have given his right nut to have Lee Nicholas suddenly decide to change orientation. He even had a cou-ple of scenarios all worked out where *he* was the reason. One of them involved kiwi-flavored lube and ended rather spectacularly in Raymond Dark's satin-lined coffin back at the studio. Right at this moment, however, it was a com-plication he didn't need. Unrequited lust was a situation he was used to dealing with—start requiting and God only knew where things would end up.

Actually, it was fairly obvious where things would end up. . . .

For chrissakes, Tony, get your mind out of your freakin' pants!

The moment the replay ended, he was going to beat his head against the wall a time or two. Not only a fine physical distraction, but this talking to himself in the third person had to be stopped.

Although a kettle steamed on the stove—had apparently been steaming while that killer tea was being served in the drawing room—the kitchen was deserted and the back door closed. Apparently closed. And apparently closed doors hadn't stopped him before. All he had to do was . . .

Problem.

Cassie had said that Henry would leave the laptop on the bucket the butts had been in, but that would mean he had to get a horizontal laptop through a vertical opening barely five centimeters wider than the laptop was deep. Someone had to hold the laptop up on its side, facing the opening.

Pity he hadn't thought of that while Cassie and Stephen were still around.

"Henry! Henry, can you hear me?"

If Graham could communicate with the ghosts of his cousins because of a blood tie, he should be able to communicate with Henry. Blood had tied them for years.

"Hen . . ."

Darkness.

And Karl.

". . . ry!"

No answer. Or not one he could hear anyway. After all, Henry was the metaphysical being—Vampire, Nightwalker, Bloodsucking Undead. He was just a production assistant helping to put together a second-rate show at a third-rate studio. Reaching out, he trailed his fingertips over the wall, touched the edge of the doorframe, and couldn't go any farther. He leaned his weight against the barrier and almost felt the power gathering to stop him. It felt substantial.

And the vaunted wizard power of copping a feel off the thing in the basement was no friggin' help at all. Fortunately, there was another way. An already proven way.

"Cassie! Stephen! I need you in the kitchen!"

"What's wrong?"

Not the ghosts. No mistaking that brushed velvet voice. Although the lantern light throwing Lee's shadow against the door pretty much made identifcation a gimmie.

"The door's only open this much." Tony held his hands about five centimeters apart as he turned. "Laptop's this wide." His hands separated. "It's got to be up on its side or I can't get it through the space."

"And why do you need the ghosts?"

"They can talk to the caretaker."

"You can't talk to Henry?"

"Can't seem to."

The borrowed T-shirt was tight. He'd seen Lee in tight T-shirts before but never in *his* tight T-shirt. It made an interesting difference where *interesting* referred to interest being taken independently by parts of Tony's anatomy. Dark strands of hair fell down in front of the actor's face, free of the product Everett had used to slick it back. Tony had a vague sensory memory of gripping a handful of hair as an invading tongue probed for his tonsils.

Lee's gaze bounced around the room like his eyes had been replaced by a pair of green-and-white super balls—stove, window, door, wall, cabinet, sink, floor, ceiling—alighting everywhere but on Tony's face. "Look, about what happened; I uh . . . I mean it was . . . There was just . . . Brenda . . ."

And then he stopped.

Man, actors suck at the articulate without writers behind them.

And by the way, Brenda? *Thanks for bringing her up. Nothing like being the substitute for a dead wardrobe assistant.*

Tony was half inclined to let Lee sweat. Fortunately, his better half won—but only because the part of his brain connected to his dick thought that a sweaty Lee Nicholas was a good idea and he was trying to discourage it. "You were freaked. I get it. It's cool." Rush to finish before Lee could protest. Or agree. Or say anything else at all. "But if we *have* to figure out what was going on . . ." With luck, his tone made his preference clear. The last thing he wanted to do was sit down with Lee and discuss *feelings*. ". . . can it wait until after we get out of this house?"

Maybe relief. "And until then what? Denial?"

"Hey, we're guys—we're all about denial."

Definitely relief. And most of a smile.

So Tony smiled back.

"I said; what do you want?"

Startled, he stepped back and brushed against Stephen's arm. The sudden cold took care of any residual "interest" and snapped his attention back to the problem at hand. "Sorry. I was . . . uh . . ."

Stephen rolled his eyes. "Don't tell me. I don't want to know." His voice rose. "Cassie, back off! We don't want it to know we're moving around!"

"It doesn't know?" Tony asked as Cassie reluctantly lowered her hand and drifted around to check Lee out from the rear. Cassie was distracted, but Stephen sounded nervous. No, more than nervous. Afraid.

"It doesn't seem to." He patted the front sweep of his hair with the heel of one hand. "As long as we do nothing to attract attention to ourselves, things should be okay. But it's safest in the bathroom."

"Safest?"

"That's our place. Until Graham came, that's where we stayed. But it was asleep when we started being us again, and now it isn't." The other hand patted down the other side of his hair. "And it's more awake now than it was. So . . ." He half shrugged, the motion not quite enough to dislodge his head. "It's already keeping us here—we can leave the bathroom, but we can't leave the house. And, you know, we keep dying. We don't want to know what else it can do."

Made sense. "So, what attracts its attention?"

Arms folded, Stephen nodded toward his sister. "Stuff that uses energy. Anything physical, like the paint, or making it so others can see us like we did this morning."

"Contacting your cousin?"

"No. That doesn't pull any energy from *it*," Cassie explained, finally joining them at the door. "It pulls it from Graham."

From what Tony could remember of the caretaker, he didn't seem to have much energy to spare.

*   *   *

Wiping sweat off his forehead, Graham sat back on his heels and sucked in long, slow lungfuls of humid air. "This Tony kid," he said after a moment, "he needs you to turn the laptop on its side or it won't fit through the door."

Henry flipped the computer up on one edge. "Like this?"

"Yeah and line it up like the door was open this much." He held his thumb and forefinger apart, both of them shaking.

"Like this."

"Like that. Okay . . ." Wrapping one hand around the porch rail, he hauled himself up onto his feet. Henry could hear his heart racing. "I need a beer."

"When we're done."

"Done what? Done this? Done the next thing? Guy could die of thirst around you," he muttered, then added quickly, his heart beating faster still. "Not that I want you to think about being thirsty."

"You're right. You don't."

"It's just you might be a little more sympathetic because you're still not looking a hundred percent after having been knocked on your ass and . . ."

"Shut up." Tony was just inside the door. Less than a body length away and he might as well have been on the other side of the world. So close, the song of his blood should have been an invitation. But Henry sensed nothing but the power keeping them apart.

The power that had, as the caretaker so elegantly put it, knocked him on his ass.

The computer case creaked in his grip. It took an effort to let go and a greater effort to stop the growl rising in his throat.

When the laptop quivered, he loosened his hold further so that it barely rested against his fingers. It inched forward, stopped on the edge of the bucket, and then disappeared. Mortal eyes couldn't have seen it move, and Henry barely made out a silver blur disappearing through what seemed a solid door. His fingertips were warm and so was the galvanized metal.

After a moment, Graham sagged against the rail and started to cough. "It's like yelling across the friggin' Strait of Juan de friggin' Fuca, but I think he's got it."

"You think?" Not quite a snarl.

"Okay, okay, he's got it."

"Good." Rising, Henry dusted off his knees and then moved down off the flagstone slab, moved in such a way it would be obvious to anyone watching that the power wrapped around the house gave him no trouble at all. Didn't make him want to tear through it and yank Tony free. Didn't remind him of pain.

"So." Arms folded, feet planted shoulder-width apart in the damp gravel, CB scowled at the door. "We have done all we can."

"You know," Graham snorted, pivoting shakily toward the driveway, "when you make pronouncements like that, there's bugger all anyone else can say."

"Good."

"I can't find anything about talking to the dead."

"How about conversing with ghosts?" When Tony glanced up, Amy shrugged. "Hey, it's all about what you punch into the search engine. Also, try necromancy."

He frowned. "How do you spell that?"

He wasn't surprised she knew. Sitting cross-legged, the laptop on the floor in front of him, Amy on the other side of the laptop, he typed in the word.

No results.

Nothing for connecting with the dead.

Nor connecting with the spirit realm.

"I don't think there's anything in here."

"Try spirits all by itself. Broaden your search parameters," she added impatiently, reaching for the computer. "Give it to me, I'll do it."

"Don't . . ."

Too late. She jerked it out from under his hands and spun it around. "Tony! You're playing spider solitaire!"

"It's a glamour!" he snapped, spinning it back. "It makes you believe . . ."

"I know what a glamour is," she told him, emphasis adding volume. "I have a complete set of *Charmed* on DVD!"

The silence that followed accompanied raised brows and general expressions of disbelief.

Amy flashed a sneer around the circle. "Hello. Vampire detective? It's not like we can claim the creative high ground here!"

Tony glanced up in time to see Mason open his mouth, but before any sound emerged, the lights came up and all he could hear was Stephen and Cassie dying while the band in the ballroom played a waltz.

"That was 'Night and Day'," Peter told him when the house returned to lamplight and Karl. "Cole Porter wrote it for Fred Astaire and Ginger Rogers in *The Gay Divorcee*. We all heard it this time. Well, all of us except Amy, Zev, and Ashley. Why not those three?"

"They're not Fred and Ginger fans?"

"Hey, Fred's brilliant during that number. 'Night And Day' is one of his choreographic peaks."

"Not the point, Zev." Arms folded, Peter glared down at Tony. "Try again. Why not those three?"

"How would I know?" Tony was afraid the question sounded more than a little defensive. Still, a little defensive was better than the can of worms he'd open with *"Because they were never shadow-held."*

"You'd know because you know lots of things, don't you, Tony?" Kate shoved Pavin away from her with enough force that he slammed into Sorge and the two of them nearly went over. "Lots of things you never thought to tell us before people started dying."

"I couldn't have stopped it. Any of it."

Her lip curled. "But you're a wizard." Bent fingers tapped out patterns in the air. "Oooo!"

"At least *he's* more than a pain in the ass," Amy spat as she stood.

"Put another record on," Mason drawled, shaking free of Ashley's grip. "Bitch, bitch, bitch, yap, yap, yap. Who the hell cares what he knows as long as he gets us the hell out of here before I end up spending eternity doing an undead rumba!"

"I haven't heard a . . ." Tony began, but Mason cut him off.

"It doesn't have to be a fucking rumba. Just type, okay?"

Brianna poked Zev. "What's a record?"

"It's like a great big CD."

She snorted. "No one cool uses CDs anymore."

"They're like from another time," Ashley agreed with a disappointed look up through her lashes at Mason.

Tony let the argument about music downloads wash over him—on one level grateful the others were distracted. The less time they spent chewing at their situation the better, especially since they seemed to invariably end up chewing on him. Meanwhile, Ashley had given him an idea.

Time.

The replays were like pieces of time trapped by the malevolence. Mosquitoes in amber if *Jurassic Park* could be trusted. He had a certain amount of confidence about the science in one, very little in two, and none at all in three—even with the return of Sam Neil.

Time had its own folder on the laptop.

Time, Determining.

Look at watch, he snorted and scrolled down.

Time, Keeping Track of Passage.

If I tossed a couple of dozen Timexes through the gate, I could make a fortune.

Time, Finding More.

Time, Traveling Through.

That might do it. If he'd had a little more time, he could have learned more spells and been better prepared. *Ah, who am I kidding; if I'd had more time,*

I'd have gone clubbing. He double-clicked and found himself staring at a single word on the screen.

Don't.

Oh, ha ha. Back a screen.

Time, in a Bottle.

Not going there.

Time, Speaking Through.

Possibly.

There were two subfolders. Speaking with the past. Speaking with the future. He double clicked the first option.

"Warning: Speaking with the past can cause paradoxes and time splits. Changes made will never be for the better. Do not attempt to send a message to yourself to get yourself out of your current situation."

So much for that idea.

"Okay, I found something under Elementals. Apparently, they're a kind of spirit that are always around and there's a way to contact them." He felt like a total idiot talking about this, but they'd all insisted on knowing what he was about to do.

"Secrets get people killed," Kate had snarled.

Even Zev had nodded.

"So I have to go to the back stairs where Lucy Lewis is in order to cast the spell." There, he'd said it: *spell.* Could he sound any geekier? "Because I got her name from Cassie and Stephen, it should be easy enough to manage." Where *easy* was a distinctly relative term. Easier than trying it without her name, one hell of a lot harder than snatching illicit snack food from Mason. "At first I thought I was going to have to work with a banishing demons spell, but . . ." Oh, crap. Did he say that out loud? Apparently, yes. "What?"

"There is a spell to banish demons on that thing?" Sorge asked, nodding toward the laptop.

"Yeah."

"Then why haven't you banished it?"

"Banish Lucy's ghost?"

The DP rolled his eyes, hands curling into fists as he visibly searched for the English words. "Banish the thing in the basement!"

"Oh." Good question. He only wished his answer didn't sound so much like he was scared shitless. Which he was—but the actual reason was equally valid. "Because I don't know that the thing in the basement is a demon, and if I go down there and I try to banish it and the spell doesn't work, then it knows we're on to it and we've blown our one shot. I need more information before I face the big bad. I need to know what's in Caulfield's journal."

"Ghosts aren't elementals," Peter informed him.

Obvious much? "I know, but . . ."

"You're using a spell for an elemental on a ghost."

"Yeah, but I know her name, so if I slot that into the spell, it should take me to her, and if it doesn't work, there's nothing Lucy can do to me. She's just a captured image." Totally ignoring any indication Stephen or Cassie had given to the contrary because, well, why the hell not. "If I try something in the basement and it doesn't work, I've just poked the big bad with a stick."

"So?" Peter spread his hands like he'd be the one throwing magical energies around. "Worth trying. We're already up shit creek."

And, hey, heads were nodding again.

They just weren't getting it.

"All right . . ." Tony reached for an explanation from their world. ". . . let's say the thing in the basement is CB in his office. His power extends through the soundstage and out onto location; he's sitting there quietly running our lives. Now, suppose someone who knows nothing about him goes into his office and pokes him with a big fucking stick! What happens to that person?"

"Is this a real stick or a metaphorical stick?" Adam asked before anyone could answer Tony's question.

"Pick one."

"I was just wondering because if it was a real stick, it'd likely end up shoved where the sun don't shine, and if it was a metaphorical stick . . . What?" Adam glared around the circle. "Okay, if it was a metaphorical stick, it'd have the same result, only metaphorically."

"I think he just likes saying the word," Tina sighed.

"So," Peter broke into the murmured round of agreement, "if you try this banishing thing on the thing in the basement and it doesn't work because you don't have the particulars, you could end up dead."

"Yes."

"For crying out loud, Tony, why didn't you just say so?"

He shrugged. "I didn't want to give Kate any ideas." It sounded stupid saying it out loud and he braced himself for Kate's reaction.

To his surprise, she merely scowled and stomped across the circle to sit on the floor by Mouse, snarling, "I hate ballroom dancing."

Under the circumstances, he couldn't blame her. "Because I've got to put myself on an elemental plane to do this . . ."

"Put yourself on a jet plane. Just stop talking about it and do it," Mason muttered.

". . . I need someone with me to anchor me and pull me back if I can't get back on my own."

"Yank physically or metaphorically?"

"Adam!"

"Both." He didn't look at Lee, but the rest of them did.

"No." Lee shook his head, dark line of hair arcing across his face. "Not this time. I just . . . I mean . . ." Arms folded across the borrowed T-shirt, he stared down at the polished toes of his shoes. "Between the baby and the music, I can't . . . That is, I might . . ." The sound he made was far too dark to be called laughter. "I don't fucking know what I'm likely to do."

And he, in turn, was so very definitively *not* looking at Tony that every head swiveled around like they were forcing a tennis match between two players who refused to step onto the court.

"What happened in the kitchen?" Peter asked suspiciously.

"Nothing!"

Pavin rolled his eyes. "Tony probably put some kind of faggot whammy on him."

Zev handed Brianna over to Tina and stood. "Watch who you're calling a faggot."

"Trust you guys to stick together!" The sound tech rolled his eyes. "You know why faggots stick together? Not using enough lube."

It could have gone either way.

Tony could feel the darkness outside the circle of lamplight waiting. Waiting for anger. Waiting for pain.

Then Zev laughed. He glanced over at Tony, who had a sudden X-rated memory of a Sunday afternoon, a distinct lack of planning, and the less than adequate contents of his refrigerator.

It was fairly obvious what they were laughing about, at least in a general sense. First Amy, then Adam, then one after another the others joined in. Lee laughed last and when Tony caught a glimpse of his face, the word that came immediately to mind was, *"Actor."*

The laughter edged toward hysteria but never quite crossed the line.

"God, no wonder you two broke up," Amy gasped at last. "You're too warped to sustain a relationship."

"I don't get it," Brianna complained.

And that set everyone off again.

At least Tony thought it did. Right about then, the lights came up.

The music from the ballroom didn't seem as loud, but that might have been wishful thinking. Entirely too clichéd for laughter to be the solution.

When he got back, Peter had come to a decision.

"Amy's going with you this time. The girls don't want Zev to leave . . ."

Whole conversations Tony was just as glad he wasn't around for in *that* statement.

". . . and there's no one else . . ."

"Hey!"

". . . except for Ashley, who has any kind of resistance to this place. We don't want to lose you." One corner of Peter's mouth curled up as Kate growled the expected denial into the deliberate pause, then he continued, "Once you find out how we can fight the thing in the basement, get back here as quickly as you can. We're all getting just a little tired of this."

"And bored!" Brianna added, rocking from side to side, arms rolled up in her pinafore. "Bored. Bored. Bored. The walls don't even bleed."

"Hey," Mason glared down at her. "How about you don't give this place any ideas."

"Hey," Zev repeated, glaring up at the actor. "How about you don't give *her* the idea that she can give this place ideas!"

Amy took hold of Tony's arm with one hand and waggled the second lantern with the other. "Hey, how about we get out of here."

"Sounds good."

They'd gone about five meters when Adam yelled, "Follow the yellow brick road! Ow! What? They're off to see the wizard."

"They're off with the wizard, you moron."

"Don't turn around," Amy sighed as the girls began singing "Ding Dong the Witch Is Dead." "You'll only encourage them. Zev's got a good voice, though," she added thoughtfully a moment later when Zev joined the song.

"Yeah, *that* I knew."

"What?"

"Never mind." The emphasis had tied the comment to a previous conversation with Lee. He'd expected Lee to be at his side. Sure, they'd been thrown together in more than an actor/production assistant kind of way by a homicidal piece of architecture, but they'd been connecting. Amy was a friend, but he'd still rather have had Lee. . . .

Oh, crap.

Maybe all that wanting did put some kind of a fag whammy on him.

Wizards affect the energies around them. That was what Arra always said. Well, she'd said it once anyway. He was a wizard—since he was heading off to do wizardry, it seemed a little pointless to deny it—but he was untrained. Maybe he was affecting the energies around Lee without even realizing it. Warping reality to fit his own desires.

"You're thinking about Lee, aren't you?"

"You can tell?"

"Duh. You're wearing your patented 'thinking about Lee' expression. One part panic, two parts horny. It's totally obvious."

Great.

*   *   *

"I don't want to leave the bathroom."

"What?" Cassie stared at her brother in disbelief. "One of the first things you said when Graham called us back to ourselves was that you hated this place."

"That was then, Cass. That was before it was awake. I don't want it to notice us."

"It can't . . ."

"It might." He took her hands and led her over to the tub, pushing her gently until she sat down on the edge. Then he dropped to his knees and laid his head on her lap. "I know we're dead, but we're not like the rest—we're not just mindlessly haunting the place we died. We're aware. Of things. Of each other. If it found out, it could take that away. I don't want to risk that. I don't want to stop being."

"Oh, Stephen." She stroked his hair, could almost feel the silky strands under her fingers, could almost feel the heat of his cheek through the thin fabric of her skirt, could almost feel the desire that had gotten them into this mess in the first place. Almost. She thought of telling him that they weren't really *being,* but since she couldn't have told him what they were, she didn't bother.

Dead, yes. But also together. She didn't want to lose that either.

They'd done everything they could for Tony and his friends. Maybe it wouldn't hurt to stay in the bathroom for a while.

It was their turn to be murdered again anyway.

"All right . . ." As the lights dimmed, and Karl started crying, Tony shook the sound of the ax impacting out of his head. "I have to get this done before we cycle around to her replay."

"Whose replay?"

"Lucy Lewis. The servant. The one who might know about the journal," he expanded when Amy continued to stare at him uncomprehendingly.

She leaned a little closer. "You know, it's totally weird when you do that."

Okay, not uncomprehending, lost in her own headspace. "Do what?"

"Walk in the ghost world." Apparently satisfied with what she saw, she leaned away again. "I mean, you're here, but you're so not. It's freaky. And not in a good way. It was like following a sleepwalker to the kitchen."

They were standing at the bottom of the back stairs.

"Sorry."

"Why? It's not like you're doing it on purpose." Artificially ebony brows dipped in. "You're not doing it on purpose, right?"

He opened his mouth.

"Good, I didn't think so, but you know. So why do you have to get this done before we hit Lucy's replay? And why her? Why not the dude she pushed down the stairs?"

"Since Lucy did the pushing, she was probably more corrupted by the thing in the basement."

Amy glanced over her shoulder toward the basement door.

"Come on. She's on the second floor. Be careful on the stairs."

"Can you do a wizard light?" Amy asked as they began to climb.

"It's called a Wizard's Lamp. And no."

Her snort held several layers of derision. "Why the hell not?"

"Okay, Arra said that the energy to control . . . things . . ."

"Things? Is that a technical wizard-type term?"

"Bite me. The energy comes from the wizard. Why would I suck power out of myself to do something a flashlight or a lantern could do just as well?"

"Batteries are dead in the flashlight and what if the lamp blew out?" She waved it just enough to make the shadows dance. "You just suck at being prepared, don't you?"

Yes. No. And second-guessing would get him nowhere. "I should have anticipated this?"

"Hey, you're the wizard. You're the one on speaking terms with the great unknown. Besides, a Wizard's Lamp would be enormously . . ."

Wasted. The lights came up—although they weren't as bright on the back stairs as they were in more public areas of the house. *I guess there's no point in wasting power on the servants.*

"Amy, this is 'old lady chops up the gardener' time. It takes her a while, so we'll just climb to the second floor and wait." He slowed down; hoping Amy would keep pace with him and not go charging on ahead. It might have been his imagination, but he thought he could hear the damp thunk crunch of the ax going through bone in time to the music from the ballroom.

Dah dah dah da-dah, da-dah, thunk crunch.

And then again, since he'd never imagined dismemberment in waltz time before, who knew?

The second floor landing consisted of a wall of linen cupboards and an even steeper set of stairs leading up to the third floor and the servants' rooms. The narrow window was as dark and unreflective as every other window in the house and the hanging bulb with the iron shade threw shadows very similar to the lantern.

Dah dah dah da-dah, da-dah, thunk crunch.

No, he wasn't imagining it.

"You know, Amy, I just had a thought." He gave her enough time to make a derogatory comment before continuing. "It's possible that the extra who went all hysterical this morning did feel fingers. I'm pretty sure I remember the old lady burying the gardener's right arm in that spot. Yeah, I know it's not still physically there—but maybe it was kind of a ghost grope. So it's also possible no one actually rabbited the claw. The gardener just reclaimed it."

Just.

As applied to not only dead but dismembered gardeners.

When did he start living such a weird, freakin' life? Oh, right, when Vicki "I know best" Nelson pulled him in off the street to donate blood to a wounded vampire.

He wasn't sure whether or not he should be deeply disturbed that CB had called Henry for help. Bright side, Henry wasn't alone at the theater plotting revenge for being stood up *and* he'd delivered the laptop *and* if they happened to finally need a member of the aristocratic bloodsucking undead to storm the barricades from the outside, they had one on hand. Not-so-bright side . . . well, it was hard to nail down anything resembling a decent reason, but Tony wasn't entirely happy with the thought of CB and Henry doing that buddy thing.

"Tony?"

The light levels hadn't changed significantly. Amy's sudden appearance right in his face was one of the more startling things he'd seen tonight.

"Why the frowny face?" she asked, clearly pleased with his reaction. "You worried someone hoofed it out of here with the gardener's actual hand?"

"No," he told her, opening a narrow drawer and balancing the laptop across it, while trying to reclaim a little dignity. "If they had, we'd be playing 'ghost rampages across city for missing body part' instead of the standard 'haunted house tries to eat the souls of trapped and eccentric group.'"

"Ghosts don't rampage."

"This one would."

"And if this plot is so standard, shouldn't we be doing a better job of getting the hell out?"

"Maybe we're not eccentric enough."

"Please, you're eccentric enough all on your own."

"Me?"

"Hey there, Mr. Wizard, you're the one with the magic lessons on a laptop that seems to show nothing but spider solitaire . . ." Reaching out, she tried, unsuccessfully, to move the cursor. "And eww . . . Why is your touch pad so sticky? Never mind." A raised hand cut him off cold. "I don't want to know. Just tell me how to haul your ass back out of the spell and . . . What's that noise?"

"The *er er* creak?" He glanced away from the screen just long enough to catch her nod. "When I heard it this afternoon, I thought it was the door to the stairs moving back and forth."

"The door isn't moving, Tony."

"I know."

"Is it . . ." Her voice dropped dramatically. ". . . one of the ghosts? And I can hear it? Why can I hear it? I mean, it's great, but why?"

"Maybe the house has finally worn down your natural cynicism."

"As if."

Contradictions wrapped in attitude, that was Amy. "Okay, maybe proximity. Take your boots off."

Amy set the lantern on the floor and took a handful of black parachute cloth in both hands, lifting the wide legs of her cargo pants to expose gleaming black ankle boots laced in glittering pink. "Off?"

"Off. According to this, I have to write runes on your bare feet to anchor you."

"Cool." She sat on the bottom step and began undoing the laces.

"It's July. Don't your feet get hot in there?"

"No. Besides, do I look like the little strappy sandal type?"

She really didn't. Her socks matched the laces. Her toenails matched her fingernails—magenta and black.

"That's a lot of work for something no one's ever going to see," he mentioned, dropping to one knee and taking her left foot in his hand. Her toes curled in anticipation as he pulled the top off the magic marker with his teeth.

"No one's asking you to do it," she told him. Squinted. "Tony, is that supposed to be an anchor?"

He leaned back and studied the black lines on her pale skin. "What's wrong with it?"

"I'm the anchor, so I have anchors? That's not magic."

"It's symbolism." He bent over her other foot.

"Big word. Do you have any idea of what you're doing?"

"Honestly?"

She leaned back on her elbows and tipped her head up toward the *er er* sound. Dark brows dipped in, and Tony could see her remembering Tom and Brenda and Hartley. After a long moment she sighed and met his eyes. "No. Lie to me."

He squeezed her foot gently before he released it. "I have complete confidence in my metaphysical ability to pull this off."

"Liar."

"Ow!" Blinking away the pain, he stood. "Why the hitting?"

"You lied to me."

"You told me to!" Tony was amazed to discover that when Amy stood up, she was considerably shorter than he was. And he wasn't exactly tall. A quick glance over at her boots explained the discrepancy. "How the hell do you walk in those?"

"None of your damned business. Now let's do this before you go ghost walking again."

The hand rubbing gave her away. Right over left, left over right—she looked like a goth punk Lady Macbeth. Since she didn't have anything to feel guilty about, it had to be fear. Since he didn't have anything to say she might find even remotely comforting, he kept his mouth shut and pulled off his T-shirt.

"It's a cheat note," he told her as he copied the symbol on the computer screen onto his chest. "Because I've never done this before."

"The line under your right nipple needs to curve up more." She stepped toward him, bare feet slapping against the linoleum. "Let me."

"No, I have to do it." Good thing he didn't have much chest hair. "Better?"

"Yeah." Half a step back. "You ever think of getting your nipple pierced? You could go shirtless and wear a chain between it and your eyebrow."

It was a good thing he'd already moved the marker away from his skin. "Not exactly my style."

"You don't *have* a style."

He was about to disagree when he noticed Karl had stopped crying. "Amy, the ballroom's about to start. We'll just sit down . . ." He dragged her down beside him onto the step. ". . . and not go anywhere . . ." The fingers of his left hand linked with her right. ". . . and we'll be . . .

"Crap."

Eyes open, sight fought with sensation, so he kept his eyes closed and concentrated on the feel of Amy's hand. Or more specifically on the pain of Amy's grip.

In spite of the greater distance from the ballroom, the dance music maintained the same volume it had in the front hall. Something humming along was new. It wasn't Amy. And it wasn't him. Certain Amy had no intention of releasing him, he risked a glance up the stairs. Nothing.

Probably Lucy.

Which meant the captured dead were beginning to overlap.

Which meant . . . actually, he didn't have a freakin' clue what that meant. Probably nothing good.

He swore as a sudden drop in temperature ratcheted Amy's grip tighter, the pain snapping his eyes open. In ballroom time, he was alone on the landing. "Whatever it is, breaking my fingers will not help!"

Amy apparently disagreed.

The music paused. Downstairs, the dead died again. The music restarted. "It's almost over. I'll be back in a minute."

It felt like about five minutes. *Yeah, and if you think time is subjective trapped in a car with a vampire who likes boomer music, try being trapped in a haunted house without a working watch.*

Watching for him to focus, Amy started talking pretty much the instant he could see her. "Tony, it was so cool! She was hanging right above us!"

"Who?"

"Well, I'm guessing it was Lucy Lewis . . . okay, her spirit—not actually her because of the whole translucent thing—but damn! I felt like Hayley Joel Osmond!"

"Osment."

"Whatever. Point is, I saw a ghost!"

"Trust me—after a while, less thrilling." He worked the feeling back into his fingers as he dropped off the step, back onto one knee, and pulled the top off the marker. "Let's do this."

"I wish I could talk to her."

"Well, you can't."

"Hang on. You just drew a circle on the floor in Magic Marker."

"Not much gets by you, does it?"

"CB is going to have your ass."

"If he can get it out of this house, he's welcome to it." As Amy made a series of totally grossed-out faces, he capped the marker and stood. "I need you to count slowly to a hundred and sixty, that's three minutes."

"Thanks for the math lesson, Einstein. A hundred and eighty is three minutes."

"Fine, count to a hundred and eighty. When you get there, grab the back of my jeans—don't touch skin—and haul me out of the circle."

"Me, I'm not the wizard, but that sounds a little dangerous."

"It is. A little." Arra's notes weren't specific on just how much. "But just to me, you'll be fine. It's the emergency exit procedure."

"Great. I'll be fine. What's the nonemergency exit procedure?"

"That'd be the second half of the spell."

"Then why not . . ."

"Because the laptop won't be coming with me, and I don't have time to memorize it."

"Tony . . ."

"Three people are dead, Amy."

"Yeah." She sighed and cuffed him on the back of the head. "Go on."

He stepped into the circle, bent, and set the laptop on the third step where he could see the screen. The first part of the spell was a string of seventeen polysyllabic words spaced to indicate the rhythm with room left to add the elemental's name if known. Arra had helpfully added a phonetic translation. The second part was also a string of seventeen polysyllabic words—not the same seventeen, not that it mattered since he was unlikely to remember the first seventeen. It was, essentially, hopefully, a more complex version of the Come to Me spell aiming for a totally different result. Trying not to think of exploding beer bottles, Tony began to read.

When he inserted "Lucy Lewis" between the dozen or so clashing consonants that made up most of the words, his lips twitched. It sounded like Jabba the Hut's dialogue.

Garble, garble, garble, Han Solo. Garble.

Concentrate, dipshit!

Lesson one: The spell guides the wizard. It is the wizard who manipulates the energies. With time and practice, the wizard will find such guides unnecessary.

Someday, he'd have to go back and read lesson two.

Garble. Garble. Garble.

Jesus, it's cold . . .

All except for the pattern drawn on his chest. *That* was almost uncomfortably warm.

Contact.

She'd have been cute when she was alive. Not very tall, brown hair, hazel eyes behind small round glasses—he thought there might have been a scattering of freckles but with all the swelling and discoloration, it was hard to tell. The *er er* sound was the creaking of the rope Lucy had hanged herself with.

Had PBS ever done a series on hanging? He didn't think so, but he knew he'd seen something about the way most suicides changed their minds when the rope started to tighten, that no matter how determined they started out, faced with slow strangulation they clawed trenches into their own skin trying to get free. Lucy hadn't.

Worst part, there was someone home behind the eyes.

Trapped.

"Can you hear me?"

"Yes." Barely a word. The rope had destroyed her voice.

Great. If he wanted any hope of understanding her, he'd have to keep this to one-word answers. "My friends and I are trapped in the house and we need your help to get out. Did you read Creighton Caulfield's journal?"

"Some."

"Does it contain information about the thing in the basement?"

She shuddered violently enough to start her swinging. "Yes."

What makes the dead shudder?

"Can we use the information to defeat it?"

"Don't."

"Because you don't think it'll work?"

The laughing was worse than the shuddering.

This was taking too long and he didn't know what questions to ask. No way he could get the information one word at a time. "Do you know where the journal is?"

"Now?"

Of course now—no—wait, her now was a hundred years ago. No way the journal would still be there. Except during her replay, he was there, too. In the same time as the journal. His chest burned, his head started to ache, and he had a sudden insight about that *Don't*.

"Okay, now."

Even given distortions, the look she shot him quite clearly said, *I may be dead, but you're an idiot.* "Hidden."

"Caulfield hides it? Where?"

"Don't."

Very helpful. "Appreciate the warning but we don't have a choice. Where does . . . did Caulfield hide the journal?"

"Li . . ."

Something grabbed his jeans.

". . . bra . . ."

Pain blocked out the last syllable. When it faded enough for him to speak, he was propped up against the wall of shelves with the taste of copper in his mouth and a splitting headache. "Ow."

"Ow my ass." Boots back on, Amy squatted in front of him. "You had convulsions."

"Didn't plan to."

"You bit through your lip."

Talking hurt. "I know."

"You scared me half to death."

She flicked him just above the navel. His skin felt tight, sunburned. "Ow."

"Suck it up. Did you find out what you needed to know?"

"I think so."

"If your head wasn't so damned hard, you'd have a cracked skull, so be sure."

"I'm sure."

"Let's hear an amen from the choir!" She reached out to help him up. "Come on, get dressed and we'll tell the others."

The others had moved into the butler's pantry. Amy flatly denied panicking when they returned to the hall and found a scattering of salt and two disks of warm candle wax.

"We needed a better way to keep people from wandering during when Fred and Ginger take center stage," Peter told them, beckoning them through the dining room. "This room is small, we can block both doors, and no one's died in it."

"What about Everett?" Tony asked as everyone shuffled closer together to make space for two more. With fifteen people crammed into the butler's pantry, small was an understatement.

"I convinced Tina that Everett wasn't going anywhere."

"What about the circle of salt?" Amy demanded.

"Keeping evil spirits out is going to have to take a back seat to keeping actors in," Peter snorted. "I can work with the possessed, the dead are a little beyond my skill. What the hell happened to Tony?"

Amy rolled her eyes. "He didn't stick the dismount."

"I don't really care what that means." Turning back to Tony, Peter folded his arms. "What did you find out?"

"Well, she wasn't a big talker . . ." Head to one side, he lifted an imaginary rope.

"The dead can dance, but they can't talk?"

"I'm not making up the rules. I'm not even sure there are rules. Back when Lucy killed herself, the journal was hidden in the library. I'll have to find it and read it during her replays."

Crammed in between Kate and Saleen, Mouse began to shake, eyes wide and cheeks pale. "You can't go into the library," he moaned, twisting both hands in his T-shirt. "The library is haunted!"

Her head pillowed on Zev's backpack, Brianna managed to combine a yawn with an expression of complete disdain. "The whole house is haunted, you big baby!"

⤳ TWELVE

"All right, that's it for me," RCMP Constable Danvers rolled her chair away from the desk and stretched. "Bad guys caught, paperwork filed electronically and redundantly, government satisfied—I'm heading home for a shower and four blissful hours of shut-eye before I have to get up and get my darling children off to day camp." She balled up a scrap of paper and tossed it at her partner. "Jack! Hello, Earth to Jack! You planning on staying here all night?"

"I'm just checking into something that Tony kid said."

"What, this afternoon out at the house?" When Jack grunted an affirmative, she ran over everything she could remember of the conversation. "He asked about that murder/suicide from the fifties."

"Uh-huh."

"So you looked it up?"

"I looked it up."

"You don't have enough to do?"

"He got me curious."

"Uh-huh." Like all good cops, Jack could get a little obsessive and over the last few months she'd gotten used to dropping in on CB Productions—studio or location shoots—when the mood took him. She had no idea what he thought he was doing, but she trusted his instincts and Lee Nicholas was easy enough on the eyes she didn't begrudge Jack the time.

"It went down pretty much the way Tony told it. Father went crazy, axed his two kids and then himself."

"And . . . ?" They'd been working together long enough that she knew when the story wasn't over.

"And then he asked if we'd heard about anything more recent."

"And you gave him grief about ghosts. So?" Jack looked up from his computer and Geetha stifled a sigh. He was wearing his bulldog expression, the one he wore when he was hard on the heels of a hot tip. The one that said RCMP Constable Jack Elson always got his man. *If he doesn't make detective in the fall, I'm asking for a transfer to Nunavut.* "I know I'm probably going to regret this, but what did you find?"

"November 17, 1969, Gerald Kranby bought the house."

"Kranby of Kranby Groceries? The largest independent chain west of Winnipeg? Best in the west? Fresh or frozen, Kranby keeps costs do . . ." His new expression cut short her commercial moment. "Sorry. It's late, I'm a little punchy. That Kranby?"

"Yeah, that Kranby. In the early seventies, his ten-month-old son, Karl, was killed."

"Murdered?"

"Set onto a roaring fire like a Yule log."

"A Yule log being something you Christian folk burn at Christmas?"

"That would be it."

"Hey, I'm all about context." She stacked her fists on her desk and rested her chin on top. "Did they nail the perp?" When he winced, she grinned. "Just trying to sound hip, dude."

"Don't. And they didn't have to look far. His mother was lying beside the fire with burned hands and knitting needles in her eyes."

"Knitting needles? Plural? She put her baby on the fire and killed herself with knitting needles?" The shudder was only half faked. "That's very twisted."

"Or she tried to get the baby off the fire and was killed by whoever had put it on."

"That's a theory." One her partner clearly didn't believe. "Official line?"

"Murder/suicide. The nanny found the bodies when she came back from the kitchen with snacks. The cook and gardener were both in the kitchen at the time. Kranby had a rock-solid alibi and no one had a motive."

"Please, Kranby was a successful businessman. They always have enemies."

"And that's what Kranby said. But here's the odd bit . . ."

"Odder than Yule logs and knitting needles?"

". . . Kranby said that someone was piping ballroom dance music into his house."

"So he suspected Baz Lurman. *Strictly Ballroom* . . . it's a movie," she continued when Jack stared at her blankly. "You have got to start watching something besides crappy science fiction. Let me guess; the dance music drove his wife mad."

"That's what he said. In her statement, the nanny agreed that Mrs. Kranby had been getting increasingly nervous of late and had mentioned that she was afraid of the man with the ax."

"The man with the ax?"

"Chris Mills killed his teenage children with an ax."

Geetha blinked and sat up. "And Chris Mills would be the father who went crazy?"

Jack nodded.

"That happened a little over a decade before Kranby bought the house." She knew what he was implying. And she was staying as far away from it as she could.

"That's not all."

"Oh, joy."

"I went down to records and I pulled everything we had on the house. March 8, 1942, Captain Charles Bannet killed his wife Audrey and then took a dive over the second-floor railing onto his head."

"Well, that's . . ."

"Not all." Jack ran one hand back over his scalp, brushing his hair up into pale yellow spikes, and fanned the papers on his desk with the other. "Constable Lui-tan, the officer who wrote up the report about the Bannets, did some research of his own. January 12, 1922, Mrs. Patricia Haltz, a wealthy timber widow, hacked her gardener into pieces and then swallowed a fatal amount of rat poison. February 15, 1937, thirty-nine people—hosts, guests, and band—died at a Valentine's Ball. Official verdict was a gas leak, but Luitan's notes mention that two of the entrances were barred from the outside and the third was locked. The host had the key in his pocket."

Habit replayed the scene. "That ballroom's got glass all down one wall. Okay, it's February so the windows are closed, but you'd think someone would have tried tossing a music stand or something."

"Yeah. You'd think." Then he waited.

Cops learned two things early on. The first was that, occasionally, coincidences were just that. No more and no less than the laws of probability winning out. A suspect with both motive and opportunity wasn't automatically guilty. The second was that while a suspect with both motive and opportunity wasn't *automatically* guilty, the odds were good. Coincidence be damned.

"You're seeing a link between what happened to the Kranbys and the earlier deaths, aren't you?"

"Man with an ax. Ballroom music. Weird piling on weird."

"You need some sleep."

The corners of his mouth twisted up into a fair approximation of a smile. "Not arguing. There's people who say that Caulfield House is haunted."

"There's people who say the moon landings never happened." She shoved her chair out and stood. "There's people who swear to all kinds of strange shit. Some of them are even straight at the time. Come on, let's get out of here."

"I . . ." Jack stared at his monitor a moment then he shrugged and shut down. "Yeah, you're right."

"I often am." Waving good night to the team processing a very stoned hooker, Geetha herded her partner out of the squad room. "Mind you, I'm not arguing that it's weird, all those deaths in the one house."

"That wasn't all of them. In the twenties, Creighton Caulfield's aunt, who inherited the house, died, along with a visitor, after drinking cyanide-laced tea." A pause to sign out with the desk sergeant, then Jack continued as they headed out the door and across the street to the lot for personal vehicles. "In 1906, one of Caulfield's maids, a Lucy Lewis, shoved a male servant down the stairs and then hung herself."

"Hanged."

"What?"

"I think that when people do it to each other or themselves, it's hanged."

"Okay, hanged herself."

She grinned, hearing his eyes roll in the tone of his voice. "That's a lot of dead people. Why isn't this better known?"

Standing by his truck, Jack rubbed a thumb and forefinger together. "Money talks. Money also tells you to shut the fuck up."

"Yeah, I guess." Geetha unlocked her driver's door—probably the only car on the lot without an electronic key—and paused, one foot up on the running board. "What happened in the teens?"

Jack leaned out and stared at her over the top of the driver's side door, hair and skin the same pale gold under the security light. "When?"

"The nineteen-teens. Death every decade up to the seventies except for in the teens."

"Right. Well, according to Constable Luitan's notes, in 1917, a year after his only son died—of natural causes," he added quickly before Geetha could ask, "Creighton Caulfield disappeared."

"Disappeared?"

Jack nodded.

She snorted. "Well, that's clichéd." When he clearly had no idea of why, she rolled her eyes. "For a haunted house."

"Who said the house was haunted?"

"You . . ." Her brows dipped as she ran over the conversation. "Okay. Fine. Get some sleep, Jack."

"And you."

But she sat in her car for a moment, watched him drive away, and remembered the expression on Tony Foster's face when Jack had jokingly asked if he thought the house was haunted.

Knew that Jack remembered that expression too.

Tony hadn't liked the library when he'd gone into it earlier and he liked it less now. There were shadows lingering in corners and on empty shelves that had nothing to do with the light thrown by his open laptop sitting on the hearth. After last spring's adventure, lingering shadows were not on his list of favorite things. These weren't the same kind of shadows. And that didn't help. Hell, if even Mouse could sense bad shit in the library, where did that leave him?

Sweat ran down his sides and the pattern burned into his chest itched under the onslaught of damp salt.

"I am Oz, the great and powerful!"

The library seemed unimpressed.

"Right. And don't look at the man behind the curtain." He had no idea of just what exactly he was doing, but at least, this time, he was only risking himself.

"*Look, Peter, the replays are happening so close together now that anyone who goes with me—Amy or . . . you know . . .*"

To give Peter credit, he didn't pretend not to know.

"*. . . is going to be on their own. I mean, I'll be there, but I won't . . .*"

A raised hand had cut him off. "*I get it.*"

"*If the thing in the basement figures out I'm looking for Caulfield's journal, it could try to stop me.*"

"*How?*"

"*No idea, but if it's got half a brain, it'll go after the . . . the um . . .*"

"*The nonwizard.*" Peter nodded. "*Very likely.*"

"*So I think I should do this by myself.*"

"I agree."

"Come on, Peter, you can't . . ." Tony went back over the conversation. *"Wait; no argument?"*

"No. And Tina wants you to check on Everett while you're out there."

The lights came up—midafternoon by the lines of sunlight not pouring through the matte-black window glass—and Tony could hear convulsing and china shattering next door in the drawing room. There were books on the shelves, but the room looked dusty, unused. Felt unwelcoming. Not to the Amityville *"Get out!"* level, but it wasn't a room he'd linger in by choice.

With *A True and Faithful Relation of What Passed for Many Years between John Dee and Some Spirits* snuggled up next to *The Confessions of St. Augustine,* he suspected the shelving would give an actual librarian heart failure. He wouldn't have minded taking a look at a scuffed copy of *Letters on Natural Magic,* but his fingers passed through the spine as though it wasn't there. Or more specifically, he wasn't there.

During the previous replay, while dance music had filled the house and he'd had to force himself to stop moving to the beat—"Night and Day" was back at the top of the play list—the shelves had been filled with leather-bound books on law and business. Anything that might have belonged to Creighton Caulfield was long gone. Anything except the huge mahogany desk that continued to dominate the far end of the room.

People had clearly died in the drawing room years earlier than they'd died dancing since these books were obviously Caulfield's. There were as many in French and German as in English and a depressing number of them looked like journals. Who'd notice one more? The perfect hiding place. Tony was up on the ladder peering at the badly worn titles on a set of three dark-red volumes when the lights went out.

Fade out the past. Fade in the present.

"Ready camera one," he sighed as he climbed carefully to the floor. "Take two."

It seemed a safe assumption that the darkness lingered where the really nasty books had been. Most of them were clumped around Caulfield's desk—which emanated a distinct nasty all of its own. Retrieving his laptop and setting it down on the seat of the desk chair, Tony told himself he'd best make the most of the ten minutes or so he had until Lucy's replay and his one chance to find the journal during its own time.

The top of the desk and the drawer fronts had all been refinished to a high gloss and as he reached for the center drawer's ornate brass pull, his reflection shot him a look that clearly asked if he was sure he wanted to do that.

"I'm sure I don't."

The drawer was locked. Using the cheap pocket knife attached to his key ring, he applied lessons learned a lifetime ago at juvie and jimmied it open. There may have been a spell on the laptop that wouldn't scratch the finish, but he didn't have the time.

Didn't care much about the scratches either.

The drawer was empty.

All the drawers were empty.

No secret compartments. Nothing taped to the bottoms.

He stuck his head into the empty right side. Nothing. Left side. Something gleamed. Fingertips identified it as a square of glossy paper. It had probably fallen from a higher drawer and moisture or time or both had stuck it to the side wall. Edge of the knife behind it . . .

He caught it as it fell and held it by the monitor.

Photograph. A smiling woman sitting on the front step of the house, one hand raised to push dark hair off her face, the other holding a laughing baby on her lap. Most of the writing on the back had been lost against the side of the desk. The only word Tony could read clearly was Karl.

Up in the nursery, Karl stopped crying.

"Crap."

He shoved the picture in his pocket as the lights came up.

"Son of a . . ."

Eyes closed, stomach heaving, he scrambled backward away from the desk, bouncing off discarded drawers and the chair. He didn't stop until his shoulder blades slammed into the lower edge of the nearest bookshelf.

During all of the other replays the house had apparently been empty of everyone but the dying. Not this time.

Tony opened his eyes.

There was no one at the desk.

Except that he'd seen Creighton Caulfield sitting there. His head had practically been in the man's lap. Tony's left shoulder and Caulfield's left leg had been occupying the same space.

Vomiting was still an option as he stood.

Caulfield *had* been at the desk. He'd been . . .

"Fuck!"

He'd been writing.

In the journal?

No way of knowing. *Sure, now I want to see him, where is he? This is worse than Stephen and . . .*

He ran for the hearth and the mirror.

In his present, a light film of dust covered the glass. Here, in a memory of 1906, it gleamed. It was about a third the size of the gilt-framed mirror in the drawing room and appeared no more metaphysically revealing.

Raise your hand everyone who thinks that's relevant . . .

Deep breath. One foot up on the hearth. Left hand flat against the stone just to one side of the inset mantle. Tony arranged himself so that he wouldn't be staring at his own reflection, and looked into the glass.

Creighton Caulfield sat at his desk writing in what could be a journal. The distance and the angle made it difficult to tell for sure. Frowning in concentration, Tony leaned a little closer.

And Creighton Caulfield looked up.

Fuck!

Tony jerked back instinctively and glanced toward the other end of the room. No one. Heart pounding, positive Caulfield had been staring right at him, Tony took another cautious look in the mirror.

Nothing had changed.

Caulfield continued to sit, pen motionless over the page, staring toward the hearth.

Calm down, he's just thinking.

His head cocked at a sound Tony couldn't hear—actually, he couldn't hear much of anything over the damned dance music—Caulfield smiled and placed his pen back in what looked remarkably like the inkwell that had gone missing from Raymond Dark's desk. He closed his journal and stood. Tony adjusted his angle. Picked up the journal, still smiling, and headed . . .

Right for me.

Tony backed up as far as he could and still maintain the reflection.

Not for me.

For the hearth. His face filled the mirror. His eyes were a pale, pale blue with the same edge-of-insanity stare a husky had. Tony was not a big fan of crazy-looking dogs. Liked crazy-looking people a lot less, though. Even ones who'd been dead for decades.

Yeah, like that matters.

The sudden vertigo was unexpected. The library twisted and pitched, slid several degrees sideways, and the floor came up to slam Tony in the knees.

Where he already had bruises from his visit with Lucy.

The actual vomiting was new, though.

Fortunately, his last meal had been some time ago and the puddle of warm bile barely covered a square foot of floor. He was still kneeling, back arched, dry heaving like a cat horking a hairball when the lights went out.

Suddenly, forcing his stomach up his esophagus became less important.

His laptop was at the far end of the room.

There was a limit to how far the light from even a magical laptop could travel.

He was alone, in a haunted library, in the dark.

Except it didn't seem to be as dark as it should be.

"Amy?"

No answer, just the almost echo of a nearly empty room.

"Stephen? Cassie?"

Nada. Just Karl crying and the band playing on.

Since he was still fairly certain he was alone, precedent suggested that the extra light making it possible for him to see his surroundings wasn't a good thing. *Okay, so maybe I shouldn't have skipped over that protection spell . . .*

It was the mirror.

It was glowing. It was glowing like a computer monitor. The mirror was picking up the light of the monitor aimed at it from the far end of the room and reflecting it back. Which was impossible.

Vampires, wizards, ghosts . . . Your life is a freak show and this *you find impossible?*

So what had just happened? He'd been staring into the mirror and suddenly, with Caulfield all up close and personal with the glass, the world went wonky. Odds were good it had something to do with the mirror. Like the mirror had . . .

. . . moved.

"I'm an idiot."

And the benefit of an empty room was that no one agreed with him.

The mirror had moved. Specifically, Caulfield had moved the mirror. Why would a man carrying a journal he kept hidden in the library move a mirror?

Making a wide circle around the desk, still a little weirded out by the whole Caulfield experience, Tony retrieved his laptop and with it balanced in the curve of his left arm examined the mirror frame. And if he was more than a little careful about not looking in the glass, who was going to know?

There had to be a hidden latch.

If he could get it open and expose the hinges, he had complete faith in his demolition ability. If he could get the mirror off the wall, next time Lucy went swinging he could stand behind the desk and use it to read the reflection of the journal entries. In spite of what Henry seemed to think, the odds were good that the exposed pages wouldn't contain detailed instructions on thing-in-the-basement removal, but any information was more than he had now.

About to run his finger along the edge of the frame, he had a sudden memory of one of the gaming geeks at film school yelling at the screen during *Name of the Rose.*

"Check for traps!"

Everyone had roared with laughter when Sean Connery'd fallen through the floor a second later. Best part of a long and boring movie as far as Tony was concerned, given the distinct lack of Connery and some skinny kid actor doing the nasty.

"Homoerotic subtext, my ass." Setting the laptop down, he pulled his keys from his pocket and opened his knife. "Where was the action?"

The blade caught about an inch from the bottom on the left side, but no amount of wiggling it made anything happen. The light was so low and the wooden frame so dark he couldn't see exactly what was stopping the knife.

"Stephen! Cassie!"

The dark didn't seem to matter to them. Maybe they could spot what he was missing.

"He's calling us."

"I know." Stephen turned away from the mirror and smiled. He almost looked relieved. "But so's Dad."

"He's not . . ."

Stephen raised an eyebrow.

Just on the edge of hearing. More a feeling than a sound. Their father calling them back to the past. Back to the ax. Their wounds disappeared as they faded and the two voices became one.

"I guess death's a decent excuse." Tony winced as the impact of ax against door seemed to shake the whole house. On the bright side, he had the afternoon sunlight back and could actually see what he was doing. Could see cracks too regular to be actual cracks in the side of the frame.

The mirror was the same in his time as it was now. Same mirror in the exact same place on the stone. So although he couldn't touch this mirror, he could touch the mirror in his time. The same way he could reach out for the door to the ballroom. Right?

Who the hell do I think I'm asking?

Only one way to find out.

From the sound of the screaming, Cassie and Stephen had reached the bathroom.

He pressed his thumb down on the wood between the cracks.

Oh, right. Traps . . .

Didn't seem to be any.

Well, that's . . . good.

The piece of frame under his thumb depressed slightly, then swiveled away. At least that's what he thought it did. He closed his eyes quickly as sight and touch veered off in different directions.

His fingertips found a finger-sized hole in the midst of metal parts.

Put your finger in the hole and pull the latch back.
And I'll never play the piano again.
But a knife blade fumbled in by touch didn't work. Neither did a key.
Put your finger in the hole and pull the latch back.
Would you shut the fuck up, I heard you the first time.

A final thud from the second floor. He cracked an eye to determine that yes, the lights had gone out. Karl and the band started up almost instantly.

In the light of his laptop held up to the frame, he could see that a two-inch veneer of wood had opened to expose the latch works. Mechanism. Thing. He squinted and tried for a slightly different angle. There seemed to be something *in* the finger-sized hole. Something pointy.

Something pointy that glistened.

"Oh, give me a fucking break," he muttered as he maneuvered his knife blade back into the hole and scraped a little of the glistening away. In the slightly blue light from the monitor, the drop of liquid on the edge of the steel looked purple.

Apparently, it took a blood sacrifice to open the mirror.

This blood was fresh.

Creighton Caulfield had just opened the mirror.

Yeah, about a hundred years ago!

With Karl ready to hit the fire, if he was going to do this, he didn't have time to dither. Not that fear of having his soul sucked out his finger was exactly dithering.

It hurt precisely as much as he thought it would. And, oh great, he'd just exchanged bodily fluids with a crazy dead guy from the beginning of the last century. *Kind of makes all those condoms seem a bit redundant.*

And closely following that thought: *Henry's going to be pissed.*

But the mirror swung open, exposing a shallow hole in the stone about a foot square and maybe four inches deep.

No problem to get the mirror off the wall now. I just ream on the hinges and . . .

In the hole was a book.

Or maybe I should just grab Caulfield's journal while I'm here.

Out of replay or not, Tony half expected his fingers to pass through the book, but they closed around the worn, red leather. It should have smelled of mold or mildew, but it didn't, it smelled like smoke—made sense he supposed, it *was* in a chimney. The leather felt greasy and a little warm. And it was heavy. Heavier than it looked anyway. A quick flip of thick, cream-colored pages showed notes and diagrams written and drawn in thick black ink.

Nowhere inside or outside the book did it say that this was Creighton Caulfield's journal.

But then, it didn't have to.

Tucking the book under his arm, Tony closed the mirror just as the lights came up and Karl started to scream.

Tony almost joined him. Creighton Caulfield's reflection stared at him from just behind his right shoulder. Heart pounding, he spun around, but there was no one in the library, no one standing behind him close enough to touch, and, when he turned again, no one in the mirror.

It wouldn't have been so bad, but the son of a bitch had been smiling.

"Brianna's gone!"

"What?"

Zev yanked Tony the rest of the way into the butler's pantry, cast and crew scattering back from their entrance. "The girls were sleeping over there under the counter. I went to check on them and she was gone. So's the second lantern."

Tony glanced at Ashley still curled up on a pile of discarded clothes and then stared at Zev in disbelief. "You had got fourteen people in a six-by-ten room. How the hell could she just grab a lantern and leave?"

"Look, it's late. People are tired and that damned music is distracting."

Wait.

"You can hear the music now?"

"Yeah." He winced. "The trumpet's off a semitone."

"She probably went to the bathroom." Tina lit another two candles and handed them to Kate. "There. This room is lit. I'm going after her."

"I'm going with you," Zev declared.

"Maybe she went to look at the burning baby," Ashley offered sleepily. "She's always boring yack yack yacking about it."

"She's your sister." Tina frowned down at her. "You should be worried."

Ashley snorted. "As if. She once rode a polar bear at the zoo."

No one in the room assumed it was a scheduled ride.

"How did she get into the polar bear enclosure?"

"No one knows."

Mason did a fast soft shoe, his white shirt gleaming almost as much as his smile. "Maybe she went dancing." He started humming along with the band.

"Stop it!" Eyes wild, Mouse grabbed his shoulders and shoved him into one of the canvas chairs, which rocked and creaked with the force of the landing. "Stay there! Don't move! Nobody move. They can't find us if we don't move!"

From the total lack of reaction, Tony realized that this was just more of the same. Mouse was dealing with Mason, having apparently worked the no-longer-entirely-stable actor into the scary movie playing out in his head. Kind of the inmates running the asylum, but if it worked . . .

The situation had clearly deteriorated while he was in the library. The thing in the basement had made significant inroads into the minds of the shadow-held. So far, no one seemed about to do its evil bidding—unless its evil bidding involved dancing in an enclosed space—but things didn't look good. Pavin and Saleen sat one on either side of Kate, who was scowling—no big surprise there—and the sound tech held a prominently displayed roll of duct tape. Lee stood by the far wall, arms wrapped around his torso, head down, eyes closed. He seemed to be muttering under his breath but didn't look likely to either make a run for the ballroom or commit mass murder. Or commit mass murder and *then* make a run for the ballroom.

"Tony!" Peter pulled him around. "What about your ghost buddies? Can they find her?"

"I haven't seen them since they told me about the laptop. I called, but they didn't answer."

Hope faded, but he rallied quickly. "All right, we'll do it without them. Tina, Zev; take the lantern and check the bathroom. While you're up there, check the burning baby room."

"I believe it's called a nursery," Tina snorted.

"Fine. Call it what you want. Then Adam, Sorge, and I will take the candles and . . ." As Peter opened the door, the candles blew out. "Shit."

"Anyone want to bet that's going to keep happening?" Amy muttered.

No one did.

Tony set his laptop on the counter, opened it and powered up. "This doesn't throw a lot of light, but it's a small room. If Tina and Zev check upstairs, I can make it to the ballroom on the replay light."

Shooting a disdainful glare at Mason as he passed, Lee moved out of the shadows in the back of the room. And Tony really hated that imagery. "*I'll* go with you."

"No. You can't. It's too dangerous. The ballroom already wants you."

"I'll be fine."

"You'll stay right here," Peter told him, one hand against the borrowed black T-shirt.

Lee sneered at the director's hand but moved back against the wall.

"I'll go . . ."

"No." Tony threw Amy the book. "Go through this, see if there's anything useful."

"You found Caulfield's journal?"

"Duh."

"I don't see where it says it's Caulfield's journal. How do you know?"

How did he know? "When I hold it . . ." He frowned. "There's power there. When I hold it, it feels like my laptop."

Lip curled, Amy rubbed her hand against her pants. "It feels like it needs a facial."

A couple of Henry's oldest books, the dark ones, the one the demon had wanted way back when, were made of human skin. "Don't go there," he advised as she flipped pages. "Tina." He stopped the script supervisor on her way to the door. "Do you have a mirror in your purse?"

Running full out, Tony made it to the ballroom before Charles impaled his wife. One of the double doors hung open just far enough to allow an eight-year-old access.

"Brianna!" But he doubted she could hear him over the yelling in the front hall and the now constant music. Tina's compact ready in one hand, Tony sidled sideways into the ballroom. No point in opening the door any further. No point in asking for trouble.

And speaking of trouble . . .

He thought he could hear Brianna's voice, but the music was louder now, even though it wasn't the ballroom's turn. He couldn't see her; there were too many boxes stacked in the way. Apparently while Charles and the missus were in the house—*living* in the house, since they hadn't actually gone anywhere after they died—the ballroom had been used for storage.

Movement to the left.

More boxes.

To the right, a glint of gaslight on expensive jewelry and the rhythmic patter of hard-soled shoes against the floor.

Except, of course, there was nothing there but more boxes.

The replays were beginning to bleed into each other more and more.

So. He'd ignore any distractions, grab the kid, and haul ass back to the butler's pantry. It was *good* to have a plan. Of course, it would help if he knew where in the room the kid was because this replay wasn't one of the longer ones and the last thing he wanted was to be stuck in here in the dark. Brianna's voice rose, and the string section very obviously screwed up a few bars.

It seemed she was with the band.

Logically—as much as logic could be applied to this fun house—the bandstand would be at the far end of the room.

The boxes were stacked in no particular order and it seemed to take forever to race through the maze. *I can't believe mice fucking enjoy this!*

Certain he heard a familiar protest . . .

"My father will do you!"

. . . he opened his mouth to call her again and remembered just in time there was power in a name. Henry'd taught him that years before Arra'd further complicated his life. Sure, he'd yelled it once, but that had been in the hall and okay, maybe they'd been using each other's names all night but there was still no point in gifting it to the ballroom. Fortunately, there was an option.

"Cheese!"

The indignant, high-pitched descant shut off. He might have been reading too much into it, but a certain bounce as the music carried on suggested relief.

"Tony?"

Clearly, no one had taught Brianna the name thing.

She didn't sound close. Had he gotten turned around?

A heartbeat later that was the least of his problems as the lights went out.

But Brianna had one of the lanterns!

And in a room the size of the ballroom, that meant bugger all. She was standing maybe three meters away in the center of a small circle of orange-red light, the lantern on the floor at her feet, both hands balled into fists and planted firmly on her hips. "What did you call me?" Her eyes had orange-red highlights.

"That's not important," he said as he trotted toward her, "we've got to get out of here."

"No. I'm not going nowhere until they do what I say!"

"They?" He grabbed for her arm, but she scooped up the lantern and skipped back out of his way.

"Them!" A determined finger jabbed toward the wall. "I want to hear something good!"

Flipping open the compact with one hand, Tony grabbed and missed with the other. In the minimal light, he could just barely make out the band.

Brianna stomped into the reflection, took up a position directly in front of the band leader, and screamed, "I want something good NOW!"

Holy shit! Was that Creighton Caulfield at the piano?

No.

Great. I'm losing my mind.

Another grab. Another miss. It was like chasing a pigeon.

"*Tony . . .*"

He jerked back, away from the voice. It sounded a little like Hartley. Right, he didn't have to worry about the house discovering his name. The house knew his name. Hell, with Brenda on board the house knew what size jeans he wore.

"*Tony . . .*"

Too far away now to see the reflection of the band. But there was definitely something there. Something between him and Brianna. A couple of somethings. They might have been waltzing.

"Cheese, we've got to go."

"Don't call me that!"

"You're right. I shouldn't. You should come here and kick me."

"I'm not stupid!"

"I never said you were."

"Tony . . ."

Crap.

Mrs. White with the ax in the conservatory. Just after he'd arrived in Vancouver with Henry, Tony'd bought a box of cereal that came with a free CD-ROM of Clue. In the current situation, it wasn't at all comforting that he totally sucked at the game.

Now that he had light, he could see the reflections of the couples dancing between him and Brianna. Couples he didn't know.

"Tony . . ."

"Fuck!"

Hartley was behind him, grinning his fool head off at the reaction he'd evoked. Behind Hartley; more dancers. They all turned to look at him as they drifted by. It wasn't the ballroom's turn, but with him and Brianna standing in the midst of things, that didn't seem to matter.

"No! The way I want or I'll tell my dad!" Lantern on the floor, arms in the air, Brianna was dancing.

Her reflection was dancing with Brenda.

Sure, warn your kids about strange men and never say a thing about dead wardrobe assistants.

"Bri, come on!"

"I'm dancing."

She said it like she thought he was an idiot. Brenda laughed.

Two steps toward her seemed to put him four steps back. Eyes closed, eyes open, it didn't help. Brianna kept dancing—one little girl alone in a big room—and no matter how much it seemed like he was running forward, he kept moving toward the door.

"Tony . . ." Hartley. Pulling him by his name. He didn't remember Hartley's eyes being such a pale, pale blue.

The mirror showed more ghosts now between him and Brianna than between him and the door. The ballroom's replay was next. If he didn't get Brianna out before it started, she wouldn't be leaving alive. He didn't know how he knew that, but he'd never been more certain.

Great. Why can't I be certain of things like lottery numbers?

He stretched out his hand.

Were little girls more fragile than glass? The beer bottle had shattered into a hundred pieces.

Don't think about the beer bottle, you idiot.

Seven words. Shouted. Demanding.

Brianna screamed as she flew across the ballroom into his hand. Not fear. Not pain. Rage.

Little girls weighed a lot more than beer bottles. They both went down. Tony grunted as a bony elbow drove into his stomach, got an arm around her waist, and started dragging her backward toward the door. They were close. He could feel the edge of the ballroom behind him.

"Tony . . ."

Hartley had moved out in front of him.

"Oh, sure, *now* you don't want me to leave."

Brianna kicked and bit, but he hung on. He had no idea where the mirror was, but he didn't need to see what was going on.

"Tony . . ."

Brenda joined the chorus.

"Tony . . ."

And that was Tom finally heard from.

"Tony . . ."

Fucking great. The whole room.

What's next, chanting in waltz time?

Yes.

He fought the pull of his name. He wasn't going farther in. He was leaving and he was taking CB's youngest with him. He just had to break their concentration for a moment . . .

"My father is going to fire your ASS!"

There should've been a light bulb, the idea was that good.

"Look, ballroom people, I know you're dead but just think for a minute." He jerked his head to one side as a flailing fist tried to connect with his nose. "Sure she's young, full of potential power you can use, but do you honestly want to spend an eternity of trapped torment with a tired, obnoxious eight-year-old!"

"I am NOT noxious! You're noxious! And you SUCK!"

The last word echoed and there was good chance, given proximity, that his ears were bleeding.

On the bright side, as the echoes died there was a stunned pause in the chanting.

Tony scrambled backward, dragging Brianna with him. The instant he felt his butt cross the threshold—so not questioning how his butt knew the difference, but hey, go butt!—he rolled back, cleared his legs, cleared Brianna, and slammed the door.

Things thumped against the other side.

"Yeah, yeah, give it a break." Maintaining his hold on the girl, he got to his feet, dragging her upright with him. "Are you okay? Nothing broken?"

"I wanted to DANCE!"

Over the years with Henry, biting had become a sexual thing for Tony. That changed.

"OW!"

Brianna dove for the doors. He caught her again, favoring his bleeding hand.

"Hey, bigger, stronger, smarter here! You're coming with me, so you might as well make it easy on both of us. OW!"

So much for reason. However, actually carrying a fighting eight-year-old was the next thing to impossible. One option left.

"If you come quietly, I'll take you to see the burning baby."

"Liar!"

"Cross my heart."

"And hope to die?"

"Not in this house."

She thought about that for a moment. "Deal."

"Good. Now let's get back to the butler's pantry before we lose . . ."

The light.

And the lantern was in the ballroom.

"I can't see anything." She sounded more than a little put out.

"Nope. Me neither."

"Wait, turn this way." Small hands tugged him around. "What's that gray thing coming down the hall?"

Didn't seem to be a lot of point in making something up. "I think it's the gardener's right arm."

The snort sounded remarkably like her father. "Is it supposed to be scary?"

"I have no idea. If we hold hands and I keep my other hand on the wall to guide us . . ." He pressed his fingertips against the paneling. ". . . we can't get lost."

"Yeah, right."

"Just walk."

He felt her twist around. "It's following us."

"Of course it is."

Zev met them in the entry hall with the other lantern. A quick glance showed the arm remaining beyond the edge of the light, scuttling back and forth and not looking at all frightening. Still, points for the attempt.

Passing the lantern to Tony, Zev dropped to his knees and gathered Brianna into his arms. "You're safe!"

"I was dancing." *And this bozo dragged me away!* was clearly audible in her tone. *My father is going to fire his ass* was evident in her body language.

"You can dance later. When we're out of here," Zev amended hastily, tightening his hold. "The important thing right now is that you're safe!"

"I'm safe, too."

He looked up and smiled, and Tony couldn't remember a good reason why they broke up.

"Were you looking for us?"

"No."

The pause as he straightened and took Brianna's hand went on just a little too long.

"What?"

"Lee's missing."

Frankly, Tony didn't have the words.

Brianna did.

"What's he missing? Because if you started doing something without me, I'm telling!"

⟿ THIRTEEN

"How the hell could you just let him walk out?" Tony demanded of the room at large. "You knew the thing in the basement was getting to him!"

"We didn't *let* him do anything!" Peter snapped, dabbing at a bit of blood running from the corner of his mouth. "Kate managed to grab a brass candlestick out of that lower cabinet, coldcocked Saleen—he probably has a concussion, thank you for asking—kicked Pavin in the nuts, and charged the door. Thank God, Mouse wrapped himself around her leg screaming *Don't go!*, or we wouldn't have been able to subdue her."

Gray, duct tape shackles wrapped around Kate's wrists and ankles, and she glared up at him over the linen napkin they'd used as a gag. From the way her jaw kept working, Tony suspected she was chewing her way free.

"So what you're saying is, you traded Lee for Kate."

"What?"

Good question. While his brain wondered if he wanted to get fired, his mouth rephrased and repeated. "You saved Kate and just let Lee waltz out of here."

"Wasn't a waltz," Mason said thoughtfully while Peter looked stunned. "I could show you a waltz that would make you weep. I'm exceptionally graceful. I could have been a professional dancer."

Ah the hell with it; he'd survived without a job before. His head snapped around and he glared at Mason. "No one cares."

"Tony . . ."

"Shut up, Zev."

Tony had shoved Brianna at Zev and raced back to the ballroom the moment he'd heard Lee was missing. He'd run on instinct through the pitch-black mess, bounced off at least one wall, may have kicked through something numbingly cold. Arriving seconds before the ballroom's replay, he'd placed himself in front of the barred doors. He wouldn't be able to see Lee, but he'd be able to grab him if he tried to push by.

He hadn't. Although Tony could feel the dead brushing up against the door at his back . . . Heard his name whispered, called, caroled, sung, and rapped with a painful lack of skill. Rap that bad *had* to have been Tom. Heard nothing that gave any indication things in the ballroom had changed during the replay. That Lee had reached the doors before him.

Or used one of the other two.

Damn!

The door into the garden required leaving the house, so it was off limits. Obviously. The door the servants used that led into a hall off the kitchen, however . . .

When the replay'd ended, Zev had been there with the lantern and a worried frown—the worry obviously for him, the immediate cause of the frown a little less obvious. He'd followed as Tony raced around to the servants' door. Padlocked.

The replay was over and Lee wasn't in the ballroom.

Which was of dubious comfort since he wasn't in the butler's pantry either.

Mouse cowering, Mason dancing, Kate taped—no Lee.

"Did you just tell me to shut up?" Zev.

"Who the hell do you think you are?" Adam.

"Jesus, Tony, chill." Amy.

"Me, I never trust him." Sorge.

"Now, let's all just calm down." Tina.

All five simultaneously.

Pavin was moaning about his balls. Saleen sat quietly, holding his head. He could hear Ashley and Brianna talking but lost content in the mix.

Peter held up a hand and the babble dimmed. Ginger brows dipped as he fixed Tony with a basilisk stare. "I'll make some allowance for the situation, Mr. Foster . . ." Mr. Foster. CB talk. Peter used it when he was emphasizing he was the boss under the boss. ". . . but I will not be accused of trading my costar for a number two camera. And *you* should try to remember you're a *production assistant.*" Emphasis suggested he might not be for much longer.

"No."

"Excuse me?"

Tony stretched out his hand, said the incantation, and the Caulfield journal slipped out of Amy's fingers, across five feet of crowded pantry, and slapped into his palm. "Until we're out of this house, I'm the wizard who's trying to save everyone's ass."

Silence. Even Kate stopped gnawing and muttering.

Peter glanced from Amy's hands to Tony's, his eyes tracking the trajectory of the book. Everyone else merely stared. Sure, he'd moved Mason's lighter way back when, but that was small stuff. A book looked impressive. It was the most impressive magic any of them had seen him do. Even Amy had only seen him talking to empty air and then convulsing. Hell, back when he'd been shooting up, he used to do that all the time.

"And after?" Peter asked at last.

"After?" Tony's shoulder's sagged; he was tired and Lee was gone. "Fuck, can we just worry about during?"

The director nodded. Once. "Sure."

He'd probably never work in this town again. Hard to get worked up about it at the moment, but he had a strong feeling he'd regret that whole mouth first, brain second thing later. "All right. Lee. If he didn't answer the call to the ballroom, where did he go?"

"He didn't go in to see Brenda. I stuck my head in the drawing room before I met up with you," Zev expanded when the mention of Brenda brought puzzled frowns.

Amy wiped the hand that had been holding the journal on her pants and folded her arms. "He's not in the kitchen. He went out the door that leads that way, so I used the monitor and just kind of looked without leaving the pantry. I leaned." She tilted a little, illustrating. "If he's been, you know, possessed, I don't want to end up dead. Like Brenda."

If he's been possessed . . .

Tony couldn't think of another reason why Lee'd leave the others and go wandering around in the dark. Especially when he considered the way he'd been acting. What with the kissing and all.

"So he could be in the conservatory, the library, or up on the second floor." In a house this size that was a lot of territory to cover. "We've got one lantern, a computer monitor, and candles that blow out the moment we open the pantry doors."

"Why not while they're lit in the pantry?" Tina wondered.

Amy shrugged. "Maybe the thing in the basement is hoping we'll burn ourselves down."

"Nice," Zev snorted, smacking her shoulder.

Amy smacked him back. "She asked." And to Tony. "Bet you're wishing you'd learned that Wizard's Lamp now."

"He can make light?" Tina folded her arms. "Then why isn't he?"

"Because I can't," Tony told her, wondering just who exactly she'd been asking. "There's a spell in the computer, but . . ."

"You learned the talk-to-Lucy spell," Amy reminded him.

"No, I didn't learn it, I just performed it. Half of it." He held up his shirt, so the others could see the burn.

Tina's expression softened. "Does it hurt?"

Only when I slam an eight-year-old into it. "Yes."

Zev acknowledged the burn and moved on. "But what harm could making light do?"

"Well . . ." Stretching the fabric out a careful distance from blistered skin, he pulled down his T-shirt. ". . . the first attempt at a spell's always tricky, so I could blind myself." Okay, that received more in the way of thoughtful consideration than sympathy. "Or I could blind everyone still alive in the house."

"The amount of light may be moot," Peter announced suddenly, hands shoved deep in his pockets, weight back on his heels. "I'm not sure we should go looking for Lee. Remember what happened when Brenda found Hartley," he continued when all eyes turned to him. "Lee's safer if no one finds him. Remember, it's murder and then suicide." He stressed the second word. "No murder; no suicide. And we're *all* still alive." Met Tony's gaze. "Oh, wait, you have powers that will protect us from Lee, don't you?"

He could lie. He wanted to lie. He was a *good* liar.

"No. But there's safety in numbers. We'll search for him in groups."

Peter nodded toward the lantern. "Group. Except you probably have a plan to retrieve the lantern you left behind."

Because he was the wizard who was going to save their asses. He sighed. That had to have been the world's shortest coup. "Look, I'm sorry. You know, Lee . . . Brianna . . ." Except he *had* saved Brianna; that should count for something. "Anyway . . ." He punctuated the truncated apology with a shrug.

Peter's eyes narrowed. "So you don't have a plan."

Oh, for . . .

"No, I don't have a freakin' plan, all right? The lantern's in the ballroom and at the speed the replays are happening, I don't want to open the ballroom door and risk being caught with it still open when its turn comes around again."

"I think I have a solution to that." Amy crossed the room and pointedly took the journal back. Tony suspected there'd be an apology in her future as well. "There are these symbols that keep the thing in the basement's power contained. They're all over the house, probably all that's kept it from murder/ suiciding its way across the lower mainland." She flipped the book open to a page of what looked like random squiggles she'd marked with a doubled-over piece of tape. "If you copy this symbol here from wall to wall across the threshold of the ballroom like a barricade, then those dead dancing fools—since they're part of the thing's power—they won't be able to cross."

"Are you sure?"

"Yes, absolutely. Mostly. Caulfield's notes are a little . . . undetailed."

Brianna pulled a water bottle away from her mouth with a pop of releasing suction. "Why don't you draw the symbol thingie in front of the hand?"

"What hand?"

She pointed with the bottle. "That one."

It had come through the door as far as the wrist, gray and translucent fingers combing the air.

"It's come to take me dancing," Mason announced over the perfectly understandable screaming. He jumped to his feet and would have run to meet it except Mouse's sudden hysterics knocked him over backward, slamming them both onto the chair he'd been sitting on and crushing it. Kicking himself free of the wreckage, he dove onto the wildly thrashing cameraman, fists and feet flailing into flesh as he accused the other man of never taking him dancing.

"Well, that settles that," Zev muttered. "Mason's reality has left the building."

The arm was through the door to the elbow. Barely an inch or two of hacked bicep remained outside the room.

As the others dove to break up the battle—Mouse having found a direction for his hysteria in violence—Tony grabbed Amy's arm. "What symbol exactly?"

A black-tipped nail tapped what looked like a three-dimensional sketch of a croissant. "This one."

Given her previous answer, it seemed pointless to ask again if she was sure. Besides, it looked a lot like the mark the basement door had left on his hand. And like the mark he thought he'd seen as he closed the ballroom doors. Maybe all the doors had them.

All the doors but the two leading into the butler's pantry.

Great choice of room, guys.

He didn't have a pen.

The arm scuttled toward Ashley, who drew her bare feet up under the edge of her pinafore and screamed. The sound was piercing, echoing around the enclosed space like shards of glass. Even the arm paused.

He didn't have time to find a pen. Using the tip of his tongue, he licked the pattern onto the palm of his left hand and made a grab for the stump end of the arm.

The cold burned, but he could feel resistance under his fingers, so he tightened his grip and whipped it back out through the door.

"Here!" Amy shoved a small plastic tube into his other hand. "Mark the threshold before it comes back."

"And that'll help how?" he demanded, staring down at the lipstick. "It's a ghost hand; it can go through the wall!"

"No, it can't or the ballroom doors wouldn't keep the dead contained!"

That actually made sense. Mostly.

Dropping to his knees, he twisted up half an inch of magenta cream. "Hold the book where I can see it."

"Why don't you . . ." She whistled softly as he raised his left hand. Fingers and thumb were curled in toward his palm—touching neither palm nor each other. Tendons stood out across the back in sharp relief. "Ow."

"Yeah."

It wasn't a particularly difficult symbol compared to some Arra had loaded onto the computer. Although as far as he knew, none of Arra's lessons involved precision copying while racing the return of a disembodied ghost arm. Trying to balance speed and accuracy, Tony laid out the pattern end to end on the floor in a slight curve from one side of the door to the other.

"So," Amy murmured by his ear, voice pitched to carry over the roaring and swearing and shrieking behind them. "This is the arm the little old lady chopped off the gardener?"

"One of." A sharp impact against his shoulder spun him around in time to see Amy shove Adam back into the battle. She apologized and adjusted the angle of the book.

"Kind of makes you wonder who the Addams family chopped Thing off of," she mused as he continued drawing.

"Hadn't occurred to me."

"Oh, please. You see a hand chugging around and you don't think Thing? I loved those movies."

"First one didn't suck. The second . . ."

"The second was brilliant. I mean it so speaks to all us outsiders who were told by brutal authority that sleeping in a cabin with gum chewers and gigglers was for our own good." When Tony shot her a look of blank incomprehension, she sighed. "You must've had some kind of a camp experience when you were a kid."

The lipstick left a ridge of color on the floor as he pressed just a little too hard. "I had a couple of friends who were drag queens."

"That's not what I meant."

"I know." He finished the last line of the last symbol, rocked back on his heels and up onto his feet. "I guess we'll know this works if the arm doesn't come back."

"What if it's heading for the other door?"

"Uh . . ."

Between them and the other door was a roiling mass of bodies. Brianna appeared momentarily above the mix of arms and legs and torsos wrapped around what—given the size and the work boot—could only be Mouse's foot. Tony half expected her to yell "Yee ha!" as she disappeared back into the fray.

". . . it doesn't move very fast."

"Good thing," Amy acknowledged philosophically. "What about your hand?" She lightly touched the pale skin. "It's freezing!"

"No shit."

"Ghosts need energy to manifest, so the cold is indicative of them sucking power."

"Yeah, Stephen said something like that earlier."

"Stick it down the front of your pants."

"What?"

"Your hand—stick it down the front of your pants. It's the warmest place on your body."

Footwork Mason would have been proud of kept him from scuffing the pattern as he backed away. "Yeah, and I'd like it to stay that way."

"Well, you're not sticking it down the front of my pants."

"Damn right, I'm not." He stuck it into his right armpit, sucked air through his teeth at the cold and watched as Amy darted forward and dragged Kate out from under Mouse's descending ass just in the nick of time. Kate's snarl was incomprehensible, but the attempted kick in the head with her bound legs was fairly easy to understand.

Amy patted her shoulder. "You're wel . . ."

He lost the end of the word in the next replay. The good news: this time there'd been a little more time between the ballroom and the drawing room. The arm had to be using energy now that it was out of its piece of history so that could be why the replays were spreading out again. The bad news: well, actually that was more of a disturbing question. The gardener had been cut into six pieces. What else was out there moving around?

The plate of little cakes was back on the pantry counter. Last time he'd been here . . .

He couldn't believe he was just standing here when all he wanted to do was tear the house apart looking for Lee.

The good of the many outweighs the need of the one.

And thank you, Mr. Spock, for your two cents' worth. Stupid, goddamned, sanctimonious Vulcan . . .

The familiar sound of duct tape being ripped from the roll accompanied his return to the present pantry and seemed to indicate that the battle was nearly over. The slightly less familiar sound of duct tape being ripped from Mouse's legs—with accompanying bellow—suggested there were still a few loose ends to tie up. And a lot less hair on Mouse's legs.

"*Reste alongé!*"

Light glinted off the ornate, brass candlestick as Sorge raised it above his head. It was on the way down before Tony realized where it was headed and it was close enough to part Mason's hair when he called it to his hand.

"Sorge! Sorge!"

The DP's eyes were wild as he glared first at Peter's hand on his arm and then up at Peter.

"Beating Mason to death is not the answer! Trust me, if it was, I'd have done it months ago!"

"*Il reste toujours alongé de* won't!"

"In English. Please."

"I say, he won't lie still!" He smacked his palm against Mason's chest. "I make him lie still!" He scanned the room and his eyes locked on the candlestick still in Tony's hand. "Give me that!"

"Sorge, look, the guys have got him taped."

"Taped?" His brows drew in and he shook his head. "No, we can't tape. The light, she is all wrong."

"No, no, *duct* tape."

His focus moved to the bands of gray around the cuffs of tuxedo pants and dress shirt. "Ah."

Mason craned his head up and stared at the tape as though he was seeing it for the first time. "You can't do this to me! Don't you know who I am? It's all about me! I'm Raymond Dark! You have no show without me!"

"We have no show if you go for a wander and get killed," Peter told him, shaking out a match to the linen napkin gagging Kate.

"My agent is going to hear about this!"

He was sounding remarkably lucid. Apparently Peter thought so, too, because he paused and peered into Mason's face, napkin ready. "If you lie quietly, I won't gag you."

"And the tape?"

"The tape stays."

"Because I've been captured by vampire hunters and I'm lying quietly, listening to their plans."

Okay, so much for lucid.

"Why not." Peter pocketed the napkin and patted Mason's shoulder. "Please don't mention that to the writers," he muttered as he stood. Turned. Frowned down at both techs, Brianna, Zev, and Adam, who were sitting on Mouse. "Why isn't *he* taped?"

Saleen held up the empty cardboard roll. "We've got electrical, but it won't hold long enough for us to get enough around him."

"Wonderful. You couldn't have taped him first?"

"Oh, sure, criticize." His lower lip went out.

Brianna bounced on Mouse's wrist. "I have to pee!"

"Big surprise the way you sucked back that bottle of water," Ashley sniffed from within the circle of Tina's arms.

"I have to pee NOW!"

"Fine." Shoulders squared, a man facing the inevitable, Peter pointed at Tina. "Tina, take the lantern and . . ."

"No!" Ashley tightened her grip. "Mason's gone mental, so Tina stays with me!"

"Whatever, Zev . . ."

But when Zev shifted his weight, Mouse got an arm free. Tears streaming down his face, the big man grabbed the back of Saleen's shorts and very nearly started the whole fight again before Zev wrestled his arm back to the floor.

"All right, Amy, you take Brianna upstairs. Zev, move *carefully* around to hold down both arms. Adam, once Zev's in place, you go with her. Check the bathroom for Lee—maybe he's just taking a piss. Tony, do the lipstick writing in front of the other door."

"I want Tony to go with me!" Brianna opened her mouth to shriek, but Tony clamped his good hand over it.

"Bite me," he warned, "and I'll pull your brains out your nose. No more shrieking, the room's too small and everyone's on edge."

Her nostrils flared dangerously over the edge of his hand, but she nodded. "My father would fire you if you pulled my brains out my nose," she growled when he uncovered her mouth.

"Yeah? Well, right now, on a scale of one to ten, that's about a minus two. I'll go with you . . ." *Because the needs of little girls trump the needs of possessed actors. I'm sorry, Lee.* ". . . but first I'm securing this room."

"No, *me* first."

"You want your sister to be safe, don't you?"

Brianna shot him a look that suggested he was out of his mind, but after a moment reluctantly nodded. "Yeah, whatever."

He stepped over Mason, and crouched by the other door. The door that led to the kitchen. The door that Lee had gone through when he left. The door he was not charging through, racing off to the rescue. *You can't go after him right now, so try concentrating on the immediate problem.* How long would it take an arm to get around the first floor? Hopefully, a few minutes longer.

"Amy . . ."

And she was there with the book.

No longer distracted by a battle behind him, the copying went a little faster. When he finished, he handed Amy the flattened lipstick. She sighed, capped it, and handed it back.

"Hel-lo! I still gotta pee!"

"Fine." One hand clamped on her shoulder, Peter gestured toward the supine cameraman with the other. "Tony, take Zev's spot on Mouse. I'll keep Sorge from braining Mason . . ."

"And I do the same for you," Sorge muttered, staring down at Mason, who smiled and said, "What the vampire hunters don't know is that it's my show, so it's all about me. It's always all about me."

Peter nodded at his DP. "Thank you. Zev, go upstairs with Amy and Brianna and Adam."

Hang on. Tony stepped forward and bumped up against Mason's leg. "I thought I . . ."

"No. You're staying here. I'm not having the boss' youngest daughter escorted through a haunted house by a PA who keeps zoning out. Unless you can protect them with your magic power."

Man, he just wasn't going to let that go. Tony sighed and surrendered, moving around to where Zev had Mouse's arms laid out over his head with a knee on each forearm and a good grip above the elbow. The moment they got back from the can, he was heading out for the other lantern and the moment after that, they were going to find Lee.

Brianna stomped one bare foot. "I want Tony!"

Peter smiled down at her. "Tough."

"My father . . . !"

"Isn't here."

Her brow furrowed and she glanced around the room, gaze finally lighting on her sister.

Ashley's shrug got lost in the depths of Mason's jacket. "He's right. And there's like arms walking around, so stop being such a pissant, Cheese."

"But Tony said he'd show me the burning baby." Volume dialed down to a whine. "He promised."

"You promised?" Tina's head snapped around like a bad horror effect. "You promised to show an eight-year-old a burning baby?"

Although they were a good four feet apart, Tony leaned away from the force of the script supervisor's affronted gaze. "It got her out of the ballroom," he muttered defensively, then turned his attention to the girl. "Look, Bri, Peter's right." Probably too late, but it never hurt to suck up. "I can't protect you if I zone out, but I can still be dead weight here."

"You're not dead!"

"It's a . . . never mind. Zev can show you the baby."

"No, he cannot!" Tina snarled.

"If I don't see the baby . . ." Volume ratcheted back up again. ". . . you'll all be sorry!"

No one doubted it.

"Show her," Peter said, eyes rolling.

"You won't be able to see it," Tony reassured Zev as he choked, "but I'm pretty sure she will." Given that everyone had seen the hand, it was possible that Zev would also see the baby. Since that hadn't occurred to Zev, Tony wasn't going to bring it up. "Just open the nursery door, give her a three count to look, and then close it. Don't let her go in and don't keep the door open any longer."

"Do I want to know why?" Zev asked, taking Brianna's hand.

"No." He popped the top off Amy's lipstick with his teeth, and beckoned Brianna closer with his nearly useless left hand. "Pull your apron thing out tight." He carefully drew the symbol on the fabric. "There, that might help."

She peered down her nose at it. "With what?"

"I have no idea."

"Brenda is going to have a fit!" Mason giggled. As all eyes turned on him, he sighed dramatically. "Yes, I know, an out-of-character comment. Unless, of course, one of the vampire hunters' name is Brenda, in which case it's a perfectly valid . . . Hey! Don't stop looking at me! I'm acting here! I'm the star!"

Tony had assumed that the killers were always the ones the house had driven over the edge. If the common urge to brain Mason was any indication, apparently not.

"The kitchen sink's closer than the bathroom," Amy sighed, taking Brianna's other hand. "Why can't she just pee in that?"

Even Mouse stopped weeping long enough to look appalled.

"What? You've never done it? You're guys; you pee in corners for chrissake!"

"*I* am not a guy," Tina reminded her, "and this child is not peeing in the sink."

"But . . ."

"No."

"What is it with people and bodily fluids?" Amy demanded. "Healthy urine is safe to drink."

"Why do you know that?" Zev asked as Adam picked up the lantern. He shook his head when it looked like she was about to answer. "Never mind. I don't actually want to know."

Lantern high, Adam paused, his hand almost to the doorknob. "What if the arm didn't go around to the other door? What if it's waiting in the dining room for this door to open?"

"It's an arm," Tony said after a moment. "I don't think it's that smart."

"It's an arm," Zev repeated. "We shouldn't even be having this conversation."

"Just stay inside the pattern. That's what's stopping it, not the door."

"What if Lee's waiting in the dining room?"

Where Hartley killed Brenda.

"Then slam the door and Brianna can pee on someone's foot."

Hanging between Zev and Amy, Brianna looked intrigued.

Door open.

No arm.

No Lee.

"If Lee goes after them, do you think they can stop him?" Tina asked as footsteps started up the stairs.

"Zev and Adam can handle him," Peter told her, leaning against the counter. "He's an actor, for crying out loud."

"He's a costar," Mason muttered.

"What happened to lying quietly and listening to the vampire hunters' plans?"

"Right."

Tina tightened her grip on Ashley. "I can't believe you're allowing that child to look at a burning baby."

"It's not a real baby," Tony offered. "It's a ghost baby."

"She'll be traumatized."

"Perhaps," Peter allowed. "But better a supervised visit than have her go charging off on her own again. I think CB'd rather get her back traumatized than not at all."

"The Cheese doesn't have nightmares, if that's what you're worried about. Mom says she's like Dad; sensitivity of a post." Ashley pulled out of Tina's arms and stuffed her hands in the pockets of Mason's tuxedo jacket. "Me, I'm like Mom. I'll have screaming nightmares about that arm coming right at me for years. And years. It'll probably stunt my growth." She shot Mason a challenging look through her lashes. "I'm very sensitive."

Mason nodded. "So am I. But then, I'm a star. I thought we were going dancing; why am I tied up?"

"Captured by vampire hunters," Peter sighed, fondling the napkin.

"Right."

Tony shifted position to give a different set of bruises a chance to ache and saw that Mouse, who'd been lying quietly under the weight of three men, was staring up at him, his eyelashes clumped into damp triangles. "You okay?"

"You've been avoiding me."

So not the time to go into this. "No, I haven't."

"Yeah."

"I'm right here."

The big man sighed. "Not now, before."

"I haven't." He looked up to see he was once again the center of attention. "Really. I haven't."

"Ever since I kissed you."

Crap.

"He's not himself."

Peter leaned back, folded his arms and crossed one ankle over the other. "Sounds like he's having a lucid moment to me."

"He's not."

"Did I hurt you?" Mouse's lower lip trembled.

"No," Tony reassured him hurriedly. "No, you didn't hurt me." And just to reassure everyone else. "He didn't kiss me either."

"Kissed you in the bus shelter."

Sorge snickered. "Bus shelter? That one of those gay euphemisms?"

"Kissed you when the Shadowlord controlled me."

And crap again.

"Okay, he's definitely delusional," Tony sighed. And given the condition Mouse had been in for most of the evening—the irrational terror, the weeping—it would have been believable except . . .

"Oh, sure, acting like you're the only one to remember the Shadowlord! You're just a cameraman. He liked me best."

Mason's current condition made him less than reliable as backup except . . .

"The Shadowlord?" Kate spat out the last of shred of damp napkin. "I remember that son of a bitch!"

And Tina—who spent fourteen-hour days keeping track of dialogue changes and shot numbers and continuity while half a dozen people clamored for her attention and a dozen more built and brought to life Raymond Dark's world around her—put the pieces together. "I wonder," she said softly, "if Hartley and Lee would remember this Shadowlord. What else aren't you telling us, Tony?"

"What else?" Best defense—good offense. "What do you mean what else?"

"You didn't tell us you were a wizard."

"I told you!"

"Somewhat after the fact. And since this is apparently a new thing," she added, folding her arms, "I find myself wondering about the circumstances of your discovery and just where these particular people and the Shadowlord fit in."

"The Shadowlord made me kiss Tony," Mouse sniffed.

Saleen finally looked interested. "Kinky."

"If the Shadowlord wanted to kiss someone, he should have kissed me," Mason muttered indignantly.

"The Shadowlord can kiss my ass!" Kate barked.

"Tony?"

"I'm sure both Mason and Kate are very kissable." Great. Humor; not working. Tina was clearly not going to let it go. "Look, it happened way back in the spring. It's not important now." He waved his still not entirely usable left hand around the room—both a gesture and a reminder. "We've got other stuff to worry about."

Right on cue, a door slammed in the distance and multiple pairs of feet pounded down the stairs. Adam yelled for Amy. Then they were in the dining room. Then the pantry door opened. The three adults charged in, Brianna riding Zev's hip.

"We didn't see Lee," Adam began, setting the lantern on the counter. "Although this one . . ." He jerked his head at Amy. ". . . went for a bit of a wander."

"I went to the front door," Amy snorted. "I checked on Everett. And the good news is he's still breathing. We skipped across the hall to Lee's dressing room *together*." She threw the emphasis at Adam. "He's not there." Suddenly realizing her audience wasn't paying full attention, she frowned. "What's wrong?"

"Seems that Tony only came partway out of the wizard closet."

Amy glanced over at him and he shrugged, hoping he looked like the rational one in the room.

"Does the term *Shadowlord* mean anything to you?" Tina asked her.

"Not to me." She glanced over at her companions. Adam and Zev shook their heads. Brianna yawned.

"Mason, Mouse, and Kate all remember a Shadowlord."

"Yeah, and they're loopy."

Go, Amy. Point out the obvious.

Tina shook her head, denying that was the end of the matter. "Tony as much as admitted there was something to it."

He had? Why the hell had he done that?

"It happened last spring," Sorge put in.

"Last spring?" Amy rolled her eyes. "Please, a lot of strange shit happened last spring. Just before Arra left, everyone was having those weird memory lapses."

"Not everyone," Tina said slowly, thoughtfully. "Lee lost about eight hours. Kate lost nearly forty-eight. Mouse got into that fight that broke his jaw but doesn't remember it. Hartley fell off the wagon. And Tony had that little fit in the soundstage."

"Tony?"

And that little fit gave him the perfect excuse. He just had to convince them that he'd lost his memory, too. Unfortunately, the lights came up and

Lucy Lewis pushed a nameless fellow servant down the back stairs before he could begin.

Tony didn't know why Saleen thought the electrical tape wouldn't hold Mouse; it seemed to be holding him just fine. A quick glance to the right showed that Mouse was weeping again, Saleen and Pavin were looking bruised, and Mason had a rising goose egg on his forehead. He thought about apologizing, but since he had no idea if he'd been responsible, he decided to let it go.

"The boy in the bathroom didn't even notice the thing you drew. He's hiding 'cause he's scared of his daddy." Crouched by his head, Brianna fingered her apron as she murmured into his left ear. "Karl's mommy didn't like it. 'Cept she couldn't see it because she had sticks in her eyes. The baby was way gross. I saw a movie just like it once."

"This isn't a movie."

"I know. If it was, there'd be popcorn and I wouldn't be . . ." She yawned. ". . . bored."

"So you're back." Peter took Brianna by the shoulder and pulled her away.

Since he'd obviously been talking, there didn't seem to be much point in denying it. "What's with the tape?"

"Just don't want any surprises."

"Surprises? What kind of surprises?"

"You tell us, Tony. Last spring, two people died."

"I had nothing to do with that!" How could they possibly connect that to him? "Amy? Zev?"

"A man who cheats on his wife will cheat on his mistress," Amy muttered unhappily.

"What the hell is that supposed to mean?"

"It means you lied to us," Zev told him, looking betrayed. "And if you can lie about one thing . . ."

"You mean about being a wizard?" Neck aching, he let his head bounce back on the floor. "I didn't exactly lie. I mean, you never asked if I was a wizard."

"I asked how you got a hunk of beer bottle embedded in your arm. You said you were just goofing around."

"I was."

"With a spell?"

"Yeah, but I didn't exactly *lie*."

Before Zev could respond—although his opinion of Tony's answer was pretty clear from his expression, Peter stepped between them. "We want the truth about what happened last spring, Tony."

"Because nothing says trust us like electrical tape," Tony muttered, struggled a moment, and glared up at them. "What about Lee? Lee's still out there!"

"Before we go after Lee, we want the whole story."

"Why? The shit that went down last spring has nothing to do with the shit that's happening tonight."

"If the Shadowlord was here, he'd take me dancing," Mason muttered.

Tony winced. "Okay, some people are more . . . uh, *open* to the house because of it, but that's all."

"You don't think it might have been helpful to know that?"

"No." Maybe. "Lee . . ."

"You want to go after him? Talk fast."

Seemed like he didn't have an option.

"You messed with our memories!" Tina clutched at the front of her blouse with one hand and balled the other up into a fist. Appalled or angry—it looked like it could go either way. Tony knew what he was voting for.

"I didn't. Arra did."

Amy snorted. "Oh, that's so much better."

"Your memory didn't even get messed with," he reminded her. "You and Zev had already left the studio."

"Yeah, and that's another thing; how come I got left out!"

"You weren't left out. You'd just gone home."

She tossed her head. "Oh, sure, you say that now."

"How do we know he's not still lying?" Peter asked Sorge as Tony tried to figure out Amy's damage. "Gates to another world, invading armies of shadows . . . this is the kind of crap our writers keep coming up with."

"No, it's crappier."

"Not as clichéd as that story about the gas leak, though. I can think of half a dozen shows that've used it to explain away stuff with no explanation."

"True."

Tina leaned between them. "He messed with our memories!"

And he left out the part about Tina providing snackies for the bastard son of Henry VIII, too. In fact, he'd left Henry out entirely. He and Arra and CB had saved the world all on their own.

Backhanding both Peter's and Sorge's chests to ensure she had their attention, Tina added, "What's to say he won't mess with our memories again?"

"Hey! I had nothing to do with that decision. It was all CB and Arra!"

Her eyes narrowed and her upper lip curled. "We only have your word for that."

"So we keep him tied?"

Peter shrugged. "I'd feel safer."

Oh, for . . . Tony bounced his head on the floor a couple of times.

"What about the second lantern?" Peter asked. Sweat beaded the five o'clock shadow on his upper lip. He wasn't as calm as he sounded.

"We could go get it," Adam suggested. "We only have his word that the ballroom's dangerous."

Oh, man. Tony lifted his head again. "Brianna, what's in the ballroom?"

"Dancing dead people. And a really gross band." She thoughtfully scratched the back of her right leg with the toes of her left foot. "And Brenda. She danced with me."

"That's it. Untie me immediately. What kind of place is this where a wardrobe assistant can go dancing but not a star!"

Peter hurriedly shifted over so that he was in the actor's line of sight. "Mason, we just need to work out a few parts of the shot with the vampire hunters."

"But . . ."

"You know how your fan mail increases when we tie you up."

"Right."

It did, too. Tony couldn't see why. Mason tied up did nothing for *him*, but forty-year-old straight women were into the damnedest things. Shifting position, he discovered that the tape around his wrists might have stretched just a little. Rolling his wrists together, he kept working at it.

"All right." Peter squared his shoulders. "I think we should leave the lantern in the ballroom and go looking for Lee." He didn't sound completely convinced, but it was a start.

"It's a big house," Tony reminded him. "You'll need . . ."

"You'll need to be quiet." The director waved a napkin at him. Kate had recently been regagged with another in the set. The abusive profanity had nearly drowned out Tony's story. "Adam, Zev, you're with me. Amy, light a couple of candles after we're gone and work on the journal."

"What about the gardener's arm?"

"I think we can handle one ghostly arm."

"Tony had to handle it the last time."

"And we haven't seen it since, have we?"

"Peter . . ."

"No, Mr. Foster." Peter's smile was tight and uncompromising. "I think we'll manage to save our own. . . ."

Asses, Tony finished silently as the lights came up and Cassie and Stephen's father started swinging his ax.

When the lights went out, Zev was cutting the tape around his ankles with the knife attached to his key chain.

"Lee's in the basement."

"How do you know?"

"The door was open."

"Open!"

"It's all right, it's closed now. The gardener's hand closed it. But not before we heard Lee calling for you."

"For me?" Why was Zev rolling his eyes?

"He sounded . . ." Adam paused to search for a description clearly not in his vocabulary. "Well, he didn't sound happy," he finished at last.

"I told him he was no hero," Mason sniffed.

"When?" One question, multiple voices.

"Just before he left. He said he was going off to be a hero. I said he was only a costar. He told me to fuck myself. And then he left. Rude bastard."

Peter ran both hands back through his hair, exhaling as he brought them down, and clasped them together. "Why didn't you mention that before?" he asked wearily.

Mason rolled his eyes. "Well, it's not about me, is it?"

⤜ FOURTEEN

"Why would Lee go down in the basement?" Tony demanded, ripping the severed pieces of electrical tape off his wrists.

Amy snorted. "Because he's possessed by an evil house?"

"Yeah, that was a gimme." Throwing the tape aside, he stood. Now he knew where Lee was, he wanted nothing more than to go charging off to the rescue. Challenge the thing in the basement to single combat for the hand of the fair . . . okay, not fair . . . and not a maiden either, but the challenge to single combat stuff still stood. Except, he wasn't the hero. Hell, he wasn't even the costar. He'd survived on the streets by brokering information, and—although he hated taking the time because of the whole Lee-very-likely-in-mortal-danger thing—there was just too much information here he didn't have. "What does the *house* want Lee to do down in the basement?"

"To get beer out of the fridge?" Adam shrugged as attention turned to him. "What? It's why I go to the basement."

"And very not relevant in this case," Peter snapped.

"Well, excuse me for trying to help."

Tony wanted to pace, but there wasn't enough room. "It can't want his energy, that's what the ballroom's for."

Brianna looked up from searching through Zev's backpack and blew a raspberry. "The ballroom's stupid."

"If the thing in the basement set up the ballroom as the big bad, it's not that impressive," Zev agreed, taking his earphones out of her hand before she could completely unspool them. "You two got out really easy."

"It wasn't *that* easy," Tony protested.

"You're a production assistant who knows one spell; you're not exactly . . ."

"Raymond Dark," Mason muttered.

Mason had a point. Raymond Dark always won through no matter how great the odds stacked against him because if he lost, there wouldn't be a show. But no one was writing a script filled with coincidence and handy FX for Tony.

"Who told you the ballroom was the big bad?" Amy asked, her brow furrowed.

"Stephen and Cassie."

"The dead-as-doorknobs duo."

"Yeah, so?"

"Ignoring the whole dead-people-maybe-not-a-reliable-source, maybe the ballroom is bad for them *because* they're dead. Brianna says it sucked in Brenda . . ."

"And Tom and Hartley," Tony added, remembering. "And Stephen said something about it almost getting Cassie once."

"It's like the ballroom is a big tornado." She sketched spiraling visual aids in the air. "And all the replays are little tornados and the big tornado, just because of its size, keeps trying to suck the little ones into it. Although not actively *trying* as such."

"That makes sense." And that was almost the scariest thing Tony'd run into all night.

"So it's bad for the ghosts, not so bad for the living."

"And if the door is open?"

"Tornado spreads throughout the house and again, all the little ones are sucked in. But it only works one way because Brenda and Hartley and Tom got in through a closed door. It wants the energy of the living—that's why it's calling—but it can't suck it up unless it can keep them in there dancing until they die."

"Please tell me you're not working on a script," Peter muttered.

Amy ignored him. "So it's not the ballroom we should be worrying about. It's the basement. It always was."

"So you could have stopped him if you'd gone to the basement door instead of the ballroom."

Tony glared over at Mason, still taped but now propped up against the lower cupboards.

The actor shrugged. "I'm just saying."

"We need the other lantern back," Tina announced in a tone that offered no room for argument. "Tony can't go down in the basement with our only reliable source of light."

"Because he might not be coming back," Peter agreed.

"Because the thing in the basement wants Tony specifically."

"Say what?"

Zev sighed. "Lee was calling for you, remember. It's just using Lee as bait. As soon as it had full possession of him, it took him away. It didn't use him to strangle Tina."

"Why me?" Tina wondered, fixing him with a worried stare as she leaned away.

"Nothing personal. You were just closest."

"If you're having a problem with me, Zev, we should talk about it."

"There's no problem." He made soothing gestures with his hands. "It didn't use Lee to strangle Peter or Sorge either."

Or Mason, who, in Tony's opinion, had to be the odds-on favorite. Although, since Mason was also at least partially possessed, he was probably safe. "But why would the thing in the basement want me?"

"I don't know," the music director sighed. "Could it be because you're a wizard?" *You moron* rang out so clearly it was more text than subtext. "If it can take you out, we're sitting ducks."

"There's three dead with his help," Adam muttered. "How much worse can it get without him?"

"Look around. You do the math."

"Doesn't matter." Tony had all the information he needed. Lee as bait was a different matter than Lee possessed. As long as no one made themselves available as the murder half of the murder/suicide, a possessed Lee was safe. As bait, the danger he was in would escalate until Tony arrived to save the day. Night. Whatever. Point was, Lee needed him.

Amy grabbed his arm and hauled him away from the door into the kitchen. "And what'll you do when you get to the basement?" she demanded.

"Call Lee into my hand and get the hell out. It'll work!" he added as her brows disappeared under the fringe of magenta hair. "It's how I got Brianna out of the ballroom."

"Point one . . ." The first finger of her free hand flicked into the air. ". . . does this spell have a weight limit? Because Brianna's eight and Lee, as you very well know, is not."

"What's that supposed to mean?"

"It means Lee isn't eight," Zev snapped. "Lay off the defensive crap—we all know how you feel . . ."

Heads nodded. "You should, like, get a room," Ashley muttered.

". . . even the thing in the basement knows how you feel."

"You're like a puppy when he so much as talks to you," Tina told him.

Sorge nodded. "If you have a tail, you wag it."

Puppy feelings? "I do not."

Zev rolled his eyes. "Yeah, you do. Now answer the question."

Question?

Oh, yeah; weight limit.

"I don't know. Brianna was the heaviest I've ever moved."

"Cool." Brianna bent Zev's sunglasses case open until the hinges started to crack.

"And was it easy?" Amy demanded.

"Sure."

She smacked him hard on the back of the head. "No. Not really."

"So you don't know that you could move Lee." Zev pried his case out of Brianna's fingers.

"And I'm not going to find out standing here." He was bigger than Amy, not by a lot, but bigger. Adam stepped between him and the door. Okay, not bigger than Adam. "Get out of my way. Lee needs me!"

"He needs you thinking with your head," Amy told him, hauling him away from the door. "Not your . . ."

"Amy!" Tina's gesture took in both girls.

"Weiner," Brianna offered calmly.

"It's called a penis." Ashley sneered at her sister. "Only babies say . . ."

The lights came up and Karl started to scream.

"I'm going for the other lantern," Tony told the now empty pantry. There was resistance as he started to turn. "Amy, let go of me. You're right, it won't help Lee if I go charging to the rescue unprepared, but I can't be a part of any plans right now and it'd be stupid to waste the light." After a moment, the resistance disappeared. "This isn't a long replay," he said as he walked to the other door, sliding his feet along the floor lest he step on someone. "I promise I'll come right back with the lantern."

And the moment we're out of this, he promised himself silently as he closed the pantry door behind him and started to run. *I'm learning shield spells and lightning bolts. Maybe fireballs. Don't wizards always use fireballs?*

He couldn't believe his feelings for Lee were that obvious.

Had Lee noticed?

Learning the mess-with-the-memory spell was looking better and better.

He didn't need both of the ballroom doors open, so he whipped out Amy's lipstick and began to block the right side. Fortunately, he could open his left hand almost all the way; a raised ridge of skin gave him the necessary symbol etched in white across the flesh of his palm. Finishing the last curve and dot required the final bit of color gouged out of the tube on his little finger. Although his left hand continued to ache, he found he could hold the lipstick against the pressure and the return of manual dexterity banished a fear he hadn't acknowledged.

Karl stopped screaming just as he opened the blocked half of the ballroom door.

His experience with this sort of thing was limited, but the tiny orange speck of light over by the bandstand probably meant the lamp was nearly out of fuel.

"*Tony* . . ."

He had a feeling he should be a little more distracted by ghosts of workmates calling his name while "Night and Day" played in the background. Hand outstretched. First three words of the incantation . . .

"Tony!"

Lee's voice. Distant. Desperate. Afraid. It wrapped around Tony's heart and squeezed.

Now that was a definite distraction.

Brenda slamming up against an invisible barrier and screaming jealous curses no more than four inches from his face—that was almost expected.

"I had him!" she shrieked, the wound gaping in the translucent ruin of her throat.

"I know."

"He likes girls."

"Yeah, *live* girls."

"Tony!"

Save me.

The good of the many, he reminded himself and fought his way back to focus. The lantern slapped into his hand and he almost dropped it. "Son of a . . . !"

"Was it hot?" For a dead wardrobe assistant, all Brenda's sarcasm facilities seemed intact. "Did you burn yourself?"

Strange; still a third full. "Nearly. Thanks for asking."

Hard to tell for sure, given that she was a gray sketch against the darkness, but she looked confused by his response. "I win in the end, you know. Me."

"You're dead. Not my definition of winning."

"He'll be dead with me. Dancing. Forever."

"What? Lee dies after the thing's destroyed me? Not so easy as that."

"Easier. You'd let Lee slit your throat or cave in your skull or rip out your heart and never lift a hand to defend yourself because it's him."

The third option, maybe.

"But that's not what it waaaaaaaaaaaaaaaaaaaaaaaaaaaaaaaaaaaaa . . ."

Hartley spun her away from the door. Danced her howling across the ballroom until she faded in the darkness, the ballroom door slamming shut in Tony's face. Slamming shut. He hadn't shut it. Maybe Brenda'd been about to tell him the secret weakness of the thing in the basement. Maybe she'd been about to taunt him with Lee's breakfast preferences. Either was as likely in Tony's opinion. Dead or not, Lee was still between them.

The same way Brenda would always be between him and Lee.

Except that there *was* no him and Lee, for fuck's sake, because Lee was straight—random kissage aside—and possessed by the thing in the basement. There'd be no Lee at all if he didn't get the lantern back to the butler's pantry and figure out a way to get him back.

Glaring down at the lantern—responsible for the delayed rescue—he realized the wick was almost burned away. Two turns of the wheel on the side and he was rewarded by a sudden increase in light. Eyes watering, he made his way back to the pantry.

Kissage.

Lee possessed by the thing in the basement.

Oh, crap, not again . . .

Aspects of this were becoming frighteningly familiar.

As he entered the dining room, he caught a glimpse of something moving by the bottom of the door leading to the butler's pantry door.

Gray. Translucent. And rolling!

The gardener's head came out from under the table into the circle of light and rolled, wobbling, toward the entrance hall.

Eyes and ears for the thing in the basement. The only possible reason for it to be there—where the word *reason* was stretched to the limit. The head had been eavesdropping on the plan to free Lee .

Tony got between it and the door.

It smiled and kept coming.

It? He? Did a ghost head have gender?

Not important right now . . .

I really don't want to do this.

Not that he had a choice.

He relicked the pattern onto his left palm and grabbed the head as it went to roll through his legs.

"Zev! Dump your backpack and bring it to me!" Yelling helped the pain. "Amy! Quick, another lipstick!" Although not significantly.

The pantry door slammed open.

"Tony? What the . . ."

"Your backpack . . ." Fingers pressing into the gardener's skull, he set the lantern on the dining room table and ran toward Zev. ". . . is it empty?"

Zev glanced down at the pack dangling from one hand. "Yeah, I ditched . . ."

"Tony, here!" Amy shoved Zev farther into the dining room and thrust another tube into Tony's free hand. "It's Tina's!"

"Zip the backpack shut and hold it up!" This lipstick was pale pink—easy to see the symbol against the black fabric and over the black plastic zipper. Easy to tell why Amy had disavowed it. With both Amy and Zev holding the pack steady, he finished the last curve. "Open it!" Slam-dunked the head into the pack. "Close it!"

The sides of the pack bulged, but the symbol held.

"More of the gardener?" Amy asked, breathing a little heavily.

"Yeah." Tendrils of pain extended from his hand to his shoulder. "I think . . . I think it was spying on you."

"On us?"

Peter's question drew Tony's attention to the doorway. It seemed that everyone but Mason, Mouse, and Kate were crammed into the narrow space, watching.

"Yeah, on you." When expressions remained mostly skeptical, he added, "Can you think of another reason a head would be hanging around outside the door?"

No one could.

No surprise.

"Me, I seen better heads," Sorge remarked thoughtfully. "More realistic."

Tony stared at him in astonishment. "This head *is* real!"

The DP shrugged as he turned to go back into the pantry. "Maybe it's the lighting."

"Weird that there's no weight," Zev murmured as he held the backpack out an arm's length from his body.

"It's captured energy, not substance," Amy snorted. She poked the bag with one finger. "You know, if people weren't dying, this would be so cool."

"You'd think so. Can I put it down?"

Curled around his left arm, Tony nodded more or less toward the table. "Sure. Whatever."

"Are you all right?"

"Uh . . ."

"Let me look." Zev gently pushed Tony up into a more vertical position. His eyes narrowed. "That can't be good."

Tony's hand had curled back in on itself and his lower arm was tight against his upper, tight in turn against his torso.

"How does it feel?" Amy asked.

"Like frozen flames are lapping at my skin."

"Ow. Mixed metaphors. That's gotta hurt."

Zev laid two fingers against Tony's forearm and snatched them back again almost immediately. Two red marks remained behind for a heartbeat. "This is just a suggestion, but I don't think you should grab anything else. This kind of cold is going to do some serious nerve damage if it hasn't already."

"Just tell me it was worth it and that you have a plan."

Amy picked up the lantern and led the way to the pantry. "We have a plan."

"Really?"

"No. We've got nothing. But," she continued as they stepped over the lipstick line and closed the door behind them, "I did find out that the thing in the basement has a name. It's A . . ."

Tony slapped his good hand over her mouth. "Don't! Names have power. We don't want to . . ."

"Attract its attention?" she snarled, dragging his hand away. "Because I think it knows we're here. I mean, ignoring the story thus far with us locked in and three people dead, it's sending body parts to spy on us!"

"Speaking of body parts; where's the head?" Peter asked.

"In the dining room."

"Is that safe?"

How the hell should I know? "Sure. It's contained. Look, you don't have a plan to save Lee, so we're going with mine."

"Which is?"

"I'm charging to the rescue."

"With a useless wing?" Amy snorted. "Good plan."

His mouth twisted into something he suspected looked nothing like a smile. "Only one we seem to have."

"Tony?"

It took him a moment to place the voice—he was getting just a little too used to ignoring people calling his name—and a moment after that to notice Tina holding out a pair of caplets on the palm of her hand.

"For your arm."

"Thanks." He swallowed them dry then drank half a bottle of water after, just because. Odds were good, they'd do nothing for the pain in his arm but what the hell, they couldn't hurt.

"There's what?" Adam wondered, frowning. "A crapload of ghosts in this building, right?"

"Given that crapload isn't an exact number, yeah."

"So why is the thing in the basement sending the gardener to mess with us? He's in friggin' pieces."

"Well, it's obvious." Mason looked superior as attention turned to him. "He's a servant."

Tony shook his head. "Lucy Lewis is a servant."

"Yes, but she's all tied up."

"The guy she pushed down the stairs . . ."

"Maybe the pieces take less energy to control than the whole body," Amy suggested, her eyes gleaming in the lantern light. "If the thing in the basement is feeding off the energy of the dead, it's going to want to give as little back as possible."

"I was just about to say that." Mason's lip curled. He was still wearing Raymond Dark's teeth and Tony felt a rush of longing at the sight. If only Henry were here. Inside. Independence be damned, he'd give up control to Henry in a minute.

The heels of Mason's shoes thudded against the floor as he lifted his legs and let them drop. "Why am I tied up again?"

"You're not," Peter sighed. "You're taped."

"And I find I'm getting just a little annoyed about it." He sounded annoyed. He sounded, for the first time in a while, like Mason Reed.

Her hands shoved deep into the pockets of his tuxedo jacket, Ashley padded across the room and crouched beside him, peering into his face.

"Your father is going to hear about this," he muttered, struggling with the tape around his wrists.

Ashley's smile lit up the room. "He's back!"

"You're sure?"

"She knows," Brianna sighed before her sister could answer. "She's in love. Makes me want to . . ."

Probably puke, Tony thought as Charles started yelling at the top of the stairs. Hurl, upchuck, and ralph also contenders. He slid down the cupboards and sat cross-legged on the floor trying to work some feeling that wasn't pain into his left arm. He had to believe Lee wasn't in any immediate danger. He had to believe it because Amy was right—in a way. It wasn't that he couldn't use his arm; it was more that until it stopped hurting quite so damned much, he couldn't think of anything else. No way could he maintain enough concentration to pull Lee into his hand.

Inadvertent imagery very nearly made him forget the agony in his arm.

The lights dimmed and the present crowded back into the butler's pantry, just in time for him to see Mason get to his feet.

"There's tape debris on my cuff links."

"I'll help." Ashley began picking happily at one sleeve, Mason watching her with an *it's the least I'm entitled to* expression.

A little more disconcerting, considering, was seeing Mouse on his feet, staring through a . . .

"What the hell is Mouse looking through?"

"It's the viewfinder off his camera," Amy told him, dropping down on the floor beside him. "Zev detached it when we were upstairs taking Bri to the can. Isn't it brilliant?"

"Isn't what brilliant?"

"Zev's idea. You know how cameramen are always walking into war zones with this weird idea that nothing they see through the camera can hurt them?"

"Yeah, and then they get shot."

"Sometimes, but that's not the point. The point is, Mouse is a cameraman and now he has a camera to look through, he's completely stabilized."

"He has a viewfinder."

Amy shrugged. "Seems to be enough."

Since Mouse was coming his way, Tony sure as hell hoped so. Large, bare, hairy knees poked out to either side of him as Mouse squatted.

"We have to talk."

"Now?"

"No. When we get out."

"About."

The big man chewed on a scarred lip. "Shadows," he said at last.

"Yeah. Sure." He watched Mouse rise and move away. *And if I'm really lucky, I'll have to sacrifice myself to free everyone else.*

"I'm not sure it's just the viewfinder," Amy murmured. "I think the thing in the basement is pulling back, depossessing. I mean, Mouse seems fine and Mason's his usual arrogant nondancing self."

"What about Kate?"

Kate was still taped and gagged.

"Well, we tried releasing Kate, but since there seemed to be a good chance she'd try to kill someone, we gave it up as a bad idea."

"Funny that the thing in the basement's still holding on to her."

"Yeah . . ." Amy picked at a bit of chipped nail polish. "I'm not so sure we can blame the thing. She's always been a bit . . . prickly."

"Prickly is hardly homicidal."

"Yeah, true, but now she's motivated."

"Tony . . ."

He pushed himself up onto his feet as Peter approached. Had a feeling he needed to be standing.

". . . we talked it over while you were ghost walking and decided that if you want to go charging down to rescue Lee, we'll charge after you." Peter's gaze flickered over to Tony's arm and away.

Okay. Hadn't expected that. Apparently, all he needed to have done to be taken seriously from the beginning was cripple himself. A near concussion and a couple of magical brands were apparently no more than par for the course.

"You look all sappy," Amy sniggered in his ear as Peter continued.

"Not all of us, of course. Tina will stay here to look after the girls . . ."

"And I'll be . . ." Mason trailed off, cleared his throat, and started again. Shoulders squared. Declarative. "I'll be helping her."

"With these girls, she'll need the help."

The almost gratitude in Mason's eyes was almost enough to make up for the kick Brianna landed on his shins. Almost.

"And if you phase off again . . ." Peter shrugged. "Well, we can still hear you, so just keep talking."

"I don't think that'll be a problem. The conservatory's up next and we have the gardener's head in a backpack. Part of the program's missing. It can't reboot."

"Computer metaphor?" Zev asked him, grinning.

Tony grinned back. "Best I could do on short notice." Fuck, maybe it *was* all about Mason because with him up and about, the mood certainly had changed. They were all working together again. The "us" defined against Mason's "them." If the basement had taken Mason instead of Lee, they'd be out of here by now. He managed to move his lower arm about two inches from his upper. His fingernails still looked kind of opalescent, but he could feel his fingers. He kind of wished he couldn't, but the pain breaking up into specific areas was probably a good thing. "Okay, then. Let's . . ."

The door leading to the kitchen began to swing open.

Everyone crowded to the far end of the room. Behind Tony.

And given the size of the room and the numbers in the crowd, having everyone behind him pushed Tony to within about three feet of the door.

Sure. Now *you're all fine with the wizard thing.*

The lantern light extended just far enough to illuminate Lee's smiling face. No one moved.

Tony's heart beat so hard the burn on his chest ached in time.

"Lee?"

Might have been Peter. Might have been Adam. Tony wasn't sure.

Green eyes gleamed. As Lee opened his mouth, Tony answered for him.

"No. That's not Lee."

His smile had too many angles. Tony knew Lee's smile and this wasn't it.

"The thing in the basement," Lee said mockingly, "wants to talk to you."

No need to be more specific. They all knew who he was referring to.

"Why?" Tony demanded.

"I don't know."

"Give it up. For all intents and purposes, you *are* the thing in the basement."

"Why, so I am." One long-fingered hand brushed back through the fall of dark hair. "But I don't want to talk to you in front of an audience—talk about a tough room. Unfortunately, you refused to be lured, so I had to go with the direct approach. Come downstairs and face me."

"And if I don't?"

Lee's hands started to tremble and the velvet voice roughened. "I think you know the answer to that."

"If you don't go with him, the thing in the basement will hurt Lee!"

Tony sighed. "Yeah, Tina, I got it."

"Well, pardon me for wanting to be clear about things," the script supervisor muttered.

This time the smile was almost Lee's.

Tony looked past him, into the darkness of the kitchen, at the edge of the ceiling over the door, down toward the floor at his feet—anywhere but at the smile that almost *wasn't* Lee's. "Let me talk it over with the others."

"Why? You know you're going to come with me."

"Let's pretend I have a choice."

"All right." Dark amusement flashed in the depths of the green eyes. "Let's pretend. You talk. I'll wait."

Tony turned, stepped back toward the pack, and motioned for the others to huddle around him.

"If you go down there and the thing in the basement destroys you, what the hell are we supposed to do?" Amy demanded.

"Thanks for caring."

"You know what I mean!"

"If it destroys me, you stay in here and do anything you have to in order to survive until sunrise."

Adam shook his head. "How do you know it'll let us go at sunrise?"

"It's traditional."

"In order for a thing to become a tradition, it has to happen more than once," Zev pointed out, dragging Brianna back into the huddle and away from Lee.

"In every movie . . ."

"This isn't a movie!"

Tony closed his eyes and counted to three. "Look, you'll just have to trust me on the sunrise thing. Besides, I think I'll be okay. Brenda implied it didn't want me destroyed."

"Why not?"

"She didn't say." Technically, she'd only said that the thing in the basement didn't want Lee to destroy him. It could still want to do the nasty itself. Since he was going into the basement regardless, Tony didn't see a lot of point in mentioning that. "Does anyone have a mirror? I left Tina's in the ballroom."

"Honestly, Tony, you should be more careful when you borrow something!"

"I'm sorry."

"I'd had that compact for years."

"It's still there; you can get it in the morning."

"Oh, sure." Her nostrils flared. "*If* I survive. Well, even if I were willing to lend you another mirror, I don't have one."

"Amy?"

"Please." She tucked a strand of black-tipped magenta hair behind her ear. "I look this good when I leave the house and it lasts all day."

After a long moment, Mason sighed and pulled a small silver compact out of his pants pocket. "I like to check my touch-ups," he explained as he passed it over.

"You always look wonderful!" Ashley gushed up at him.

He nodded. "True."

All eyes tracked Tony as he slid the compact into his front pocket. He leaned farther into the huddle and murmured, "Let the gardener's head out while I'm gone. I want to see how the thing in the . . ." Screw it, life was too short. ". . . the *thing* reacts to a replay."

"Mouse and Mason?" Zev asked.

Glancing over at the actor and the cameraman, he didn't immediately understand Zev's point. Mason ignored him—business as usual—Mouse peered at him through his viewfinder. Oh. Right. The possible return of the crazies. If the replays began again, would the house then feel it could expend the power to repossess? If Mouse and Mason didn't remember how far they'd fallen apart, could they make the decision to risk it again?

Did he have the right to risk them—all of them; a crazy Mouse was a dangerous roommate—for the sake of information that might not be relevant?

Might be, though.

No way of telling.

"Tony?"

"Ask them first." The good of the many. *Yeah, like that'll apply to Mason.* He touched the hard ridge of the compact, and straightened.

"So you going, then?" Sorge asked.

"Of course he's going," Peter answered. The director reached across the huddle and clasped Tony's forearm. "Bring Lee back to us. We can't lose him now; he's pulling in as much fan mail as Mason is."

"More."

As Mason sputtered, everyone else craned their heads to stare at the thing that was Lee.

He shrugged. "Small room, and Peter's voice tends to carry. Are you coming, Tony?"

"No," Tony muttered under his breath as he turned, "just breathing hard. Ow!" He scowled at Amy as he rubbed his bad arm. "What the hell was that for?"

"So not the time to make jokes!"

"Can't think of a better time." Picking one of the lanterns up off the counter, he waved it toward the kitchen. "Let's go."

"Don't want to be alone in the dark with me?" Lee asked as the pantry door closed behind them.

"Stop it."

"You don't think your attraction to me might have caused me to ask myself a few questions about the way I'm living my life?"

"Yeah, right," Tony snorted. "With one bound, he was up and a gay? I don't think so."

"Perhaps you're selling yourself short."

"Perhaps you should shut the fuck up."

He could hear the creaking of Lucy's rope up on the third floor. Karl crying. The band playing on. Aware of each sound momentarily before it faded to background again.

The basement door was open. The memory of touching the doorknob spasmed through Tony's left hand and the new pain burned a little of the rigidity out of his arm. Eyes watering, he realized that *no pain, no gain* was quite probably the stupidest mantra he'd ever heard. And that whole wizard being able to feel power thing truly sucked.

As he followed Lee down the basement stairs, the lantern light seemed to close around him, as though the darkness was too thick for it to make much of an impression. Old boards creaked under his weight as he hurried to keep up, not wanting to lose sight of the other man.

The splash as he stepped off onto the concrete floor came as a bit of a surprise. So did the cold water seeping in through his shoes. Apparently Graham Brummel hadn't been kidding about the basement flooding. *Great. And the thing knows, because Lee knows, about tossing live wires into the water and making soup.*

He'd half turned back toward the stairs before he realized he'd moved. He didn't want to be soup. But then, who did? A rustling from above caught his attention and he lifted the lantern. The light just barely made it to the top of the stairs. The gardener's hand rose up on its wrist and flipped him the finger.

Looked like they hadn't released the head.

On the bright side, he could hear neither Karl nor the band. The silence was glorious. Muscles he hadn't realized were tense relaxed.

"Cold feet, Tony?"

"Yeah. Cold and wet."

"You're perfectly safe. I don't want to hurt you."

Not Lee, he reminded himself. *Also, big fat creepy evil liar.* Wrapping his left hand carefully around the handle of the lantern, he slid Mason's compact out of his pocket and quietly thumbed it open. He almost pissed himself as Lee's hand closed around his elbow.

"Come closer."

"I was *going* to."

"You're still standing at the foot of the stairs."

"I know! I said I was going to." He took a deep breath, hated the way it shuddered on the exhale, and allowed Lee to pull him forward. The basement smelled of mold and old wood and wet rock.

He stumbled once on a bit of cracked concrete, but Lee's grip kept him on his feet. Hurt like hell, since he was gripping the left arm but better than falling when falling would have extinguished his light. "Thanks."

"Like I said, I don't want you hurt."

"I wasn't thanking you."

Amused. "Yes, you were."

Not amused. "Bite me."

At least the reflection of the lantern light off the water pushed the darkness back a little farther. Enough to see Lee if not the actual basement. Under the circumstances, it didn't exactly help to see Lee, but it was nice to know he wasn't alone. Of course, Lee all by himself wasn't alone. He suppressed most of a totally inappropriate snicker.

"Care to share the joke?"

"It's not really very funny."

The sound of them splashing forward bounced off hard surfaces, nearly but not quite an echo. Made sense; big house, big basement. Tony was pretty sure he could hear water . . . not so much running as dribbling . . . somewhere close.

"So, is there a laundry room down here?"

"Yes."

"Wine cellar?"

"There is."

"Bathroom?"

"No."

"That's too bad because all this wet is reminding me that I could really use a chance to piss."

"Too bad."

He snorted. "Yeah, well I've walked through worse, so how are you going to stop me if I just whip out and let 'er rip?"

Lee's grip tightened way past the point of pain. Tony's hand spasmed. The lantern fell. Without releasing his hold, Lee bent and gracefully scooped it out of the air just before it hit the water, straightened, and hung it back over Tony's fingers.

Teeth so tightly clenched he thought he could hear enamel crack, Tony held the lantern as securely as possible and yanked his arm free. He staggered, would have fallen but slammed up against a stone pillar instead, forgave it for new bruises, and collapsed against its support. *Right. Taunting the thing in the basement—bad idea.*

Gaining a little more movement in his left hand—bad trade.

"I don't *want* to hurt you."

"Yeah, I get the emphasis." His voice sounded almost normal, which was good because he hadn't totally ruled out screaming as an option. "You don't want to, but you will."

Lee continued walking to where the edge of the light lapped up against a section of the fieldstone foundations then he turned and spread his hands. "I have a proposition for you."

Déjà vu all over again. "What is it about evil," he wondered aloud, "that makes it so damned attracted to my ass?"

The thing raised Lee's eyebrows into a painfully familiar expression. "Excuse me?"

"You, the Shadowlord . . . Is it something I'm doing? Because if it is, I'll stop."

"What?"

"My ass," Tony sighed. "Your interest."

Understanding. Then disgust. "My interest in you has nothing to do with your body or your perverse and deviant behavior."

"Oh." Wait a minute. "You shove people off the sanity cliff and then pull a *Matrix* battery thing on them and I'm a deviant?"

"What are you babbling about?"

"Little trouble keeping up with contemporary culture? Here, I'll translate. You drive people crazy and then you feed off their deaths. You have no business calling me a deviant."

"Homosexuality is against the law of nature."

Tony felt his lip curl. "You're one to talk; you're a thing in a basement!"

"I am a power!"

"Yeah, big power. So you've killed a few . . . dozen people." He kicked at the water. "You're still stuck in a flooded fucking basement."

Lee shuddered and his nose started to bleed.

"Okay, I'm sorry." Jerking away from the pillar, Tony took a step toward Lee. "I'm sure it's a very nice basement."

"Enough."

"Right."

"Or I may just kill him now." The shudders grew more violent.

Would another step closer make it better or worse? "I said I was sorry."

"You'll consider my offer?"

"So *make* an offer."

"I want you to join me."

"Say what?"

"With your power added to ours, we could be free."

Ours? Things in the basement? Plural? Listening for a second presence, Tony remembered the mirror. He glanced down, adjusted it to pick up Lee's reflection, saw movement to the actor's left—looked up at a blank fieldstone wall—looked down, made another adjustment, and saw something looking back.

Sort of.

The wall was in constant movement. Roiling. A description he honestly thought he'd never use. Features appeared and disappeared, pushing out from the stone and reabsorbing a moment later. Eyes. Nose. Mouth. It was as if someone with a scary sense of proportion had animated one of those abstract paintings Henry liked so much—where the proportions were already a little frightening.

"You're very quiet."

"Just a little surprised," Tony admitted. When it spoke, the features appeared in the standard arrangement. The mouth even moved although Lee still did the actual talking. Tony couldn't shake the feeling he'd seen the face before.

"Why surprised? I've been helping you. The journal was a tad . . . convenient, wasn't it? I left it there in the library for you."

He *had* seen the face before. He'd seen it every day they'd been on location hanging against the red-flocked wallpaper over the main stairs.

"Creighton Caulfield?" Seemed Graham Brummel's theory that Caulfield was the template for the thing's personality came up just a bit short.

On the wall, brows connected to nothing in particular drew in as Lee said, "You've only just figured that out?"

"Excuse me for being distracted by being trapped in a haunted house with dead people—including," he added, "a few that weren't dead when the doors closed!" He waved the lantern for emphasis since if he moved his other hand, he'd lose the reflection in the mirror.

Caulfield looked a little confused. "Well, yes, but . . ."

"So I'm thinking that if you want me to join you, you'd better assume I know nothing and make with the backstory."

The face on the wall couldn't sigh, but Lee could. "Did you even *read* the journal?"

Tony actually felt his ears grow warm and the water lapped a little higher on his calves as he shuffled his feet. "A friend's reading it."

"A friend?"

"I'll get to it! I just haven't had time."

"I left it for you."

"So you said." Best defense, good offense. "I'm finding that hard to believe since you stuffed it behind that mirror almost a hundred years ago."

"Fine." Lee and the reflection of Caulfield in the tiny mirror snorted—although only Lee made the actual noise. "I left it there for someone *like* you. Someone like me."

"I'm nothing like you!"

"You thought you were the first?"

"The first what?"

"Heir to ancient power."

And the anvil dropped.

⟿ FIFTEEN

"So you're a wizard?"

Lee drew himself up to his full height, the movement echoed by an upward surge of the features roiling on the wall. "I am nothing so tawdry!"

"But you said . . ."

"I did not."

A quick glance down into the mirror showed that Caulfield's reflection looked as offended as Lee did. Tony, who'd been forced to embrace his inner wizard in a big way over the last few hours, tried not to feel insulted. "Whatever. My bad." Although he didn't try too hard.

"Your what?"

"Just forget it." Tony's left hand ached, the weight of the lantern pulling his fingers away from his palm and, in turn, his lower arm away from his upper. Probably a good thing in both cases, but the pain was distracting. Unfortunately, if he wanted to keep an eye on the thing Caulfield had become, he couldn't switch the lantern to his other hand as he very much doubted his left hand had recovered enough to manipulate anything as small as Mason's touch-up mirror. "So if you're not a wizard, what are you?"

"We are Arogoth!"

Tony closed his teeth on his initial reaction to the pompous declamation—*Dude, you sound like an alt-rock cover band*—but the snicker slipped out before he could stop it, before he could remind himself of what the consequences would likely be. And who'd suffer them.

Lee went to his knees in the water, features twisted in pain, mouth open in a silent scream.

"I'm sorry!" He surged forward and, as the collection of powers trapped in the wall surged out toward him, realized that touching the darkness would be a really bad idea. Only one step away from the pillar, he jerked to a stop. Lee remained on his knees, writhing. In the mirror, Caulfield's face had disappeared from the roiling darkness, leaving nothing but threat. "I said I was sorry, damn it! Leave him alone!"

"Do not mock me!"

Bright side; if Caulfield wanted to use Lee's voice, he had to ease up on the punishment. Ease up. Not stop. It was pretty fucking amazing how much punishment the human body could take and still keep talking.

"I wasn't!" Growing frantic, Tony searched for something he could use to reach the other man without putting himself in danger of being absorbed. "I'm tired, that's all!" There was nothing near him but the stone pillar. And nothing on the stone pillar but a nail about head height. *Yes.* Twisting around, he looped the lantern's wire handle over the nail, spun back, and *reached* for Lee.

With his left hand. Nerves shrieked as he spread his fingers. Tony just barely stopped himself from shrieking along with them.

Fortunately, there wasn't much distance to cover. Fortunate, because although there wasn't exactly a weight limit, the heavier the item the more it took out of him and Tony was running near empty. Also fortunate because Lee wasn't an eight-year-old girl and the less time he had to accelerate before impact, the better. Tony hit the water, sucking back a scream as the other man slammed into the burn on his chest. As they fell, his left arm wrapped around Lee, holding the actor close.

So close he could feel Lee's heart pounding within the cage of his ribs.

So close he could smell the faint sweet iron scent of the blood dribbling from Lee's nose.

Was this what Henry felt? So intimately aware of another's life?

So desperately needing to protect it.

He lost his grip on the mirror but somehow managed to keep both their heads above water. Up close and personal, it was numbingly cold. Under the circumstances though, numbing was good. He finally folded his legs and settled Lee on his lap. Snarled, "If you kill him, you've lost your leverage."

Lee went rigid. And not in a good way.

"If you kill him, I'll destroy you," he continued. "I don't care who else you throw in my way. I don't care if I have to die to do it. I will take this house apart, brick by brick, and I will wipe you off the face of this Earth."

A shudder. Then the dark head tipped back against his shoulder and green eyes focused on his face. "You mean that."

"I do." And he did. At that moment, he'd have thrown the world away to keep Lee safe. *How will Lee live with no world?* the more rational part of his brain wondered.

Shut up.

"Then it seems we may be able to come to an arrangement." And just like that, with a second shudder, all evidence of pain disappeared from Lee's face. "Release me."

There didn't seem to be any point in holding on, although it took Tony a moment to convince his arm of that. Or maybe it just hurt too much to move it. Who knew? Eventually freed, Lee bent forward and splashed a handful of water against his face, rinsing the red streaks from his mouth and chin.

"Me, I'd have left the blood." Tony braced himself as the other man moved against his lap. "You don't know what's pissed in this water." His bladder was giving him some definite ideas in that direction himself.

No real surprise when Lee . . . or specifically, Caulfield . . . ignored the comment. He probably knew exactly what was in the water and didn't care. It wasn't his body after all. And the bastard had borrowed it without permission.

Tony pulled his legs back out of the way as Lee stood. As Caulfield walked the body back to stand by the wall, he groped around the floor for the mirror.

"Were you planning on remaining down there?"

His fingers closed around metal and glass. "Just need a moment to catch my breath."

"You're weakening."

"Still got enough going to kick your ass," he muttered as he crawled back to the pillar and used it to get to his feet. "So, what kind of an arrangement did you have in mind? You know, with the joining you and all."

"Simple. You join me and I will release your coworkers and the object of your unnatural lust."

"He has a name."

"So?"

Yeah, okay. Probably didn't matter much. "I join you in the wall?" An eternity of roiling. Hard to resist.

"With you as a part of us, I will be free."

"You said that earlier. Free how?"

"Free of this place. Free to go where we will. Free to do as I will."

"Will some of that *doing* involve unnatural acts?" He flipped the compact open again, and rubbed the glass against his jeans. Wet denim didn't exactly help clean up the reflection.

Lee's brows drew in disapprovingly. "Not the kind you enjoy."

"Duh. I meant that whole murder/suicide thing you've got going upstairs."

"The whole murder/suicide thing, as you put it . . ." His lip curled. ". . . will be unnecessary. As we will be free to move from this house, I will not need to contain the dead as nourishment."

"But there'll be dead? Dying?"

"Of course. I will gain power and we will make a place for myself."

Caulfield seemed to be having a bit of an identity problem. Seemed like he wasn't completely merged with the original darkness. Or after being stuck in a damp basement for almost a hundred years, he'd gone completely bugfuck. Oh, wait. Odds were good that being bugfuck was what had brought Creighton Caulfield to the basement in the first place.

"Okay, if . . ." Tony stopped as Lee's face went blank. He looked down at the mirror and saw that the roiling had progressed to writhing. The darkness had become thicker, nearly obscuring the fieldstone wall completely, and Creighton Caulfield was very nearly defined as a separate presence. It almost seemed as though he'd been pushed out of the darkness by its more aggressive movement. His features actually held together as a face on a head over a body, cheeks and shoulders held a faint tint of color and . . . oh man, the old guy was naked. Obviously naked.

A quick glance over at Lee showed a similar response—although less blatant given the generous coverage of a pair of wet tuxedo pants.

Response to?

A replay. Had to be. Replays fed the thing in the basement and since it was definitely reacting positively to whatever was going on, Amy and Zev must've released the head and let the cycle start up again. The memory of pain tried to force Tony's arm back up against his body, but he fought it and won.

Breathing heavily, sweat burning in the broken blisters on his chest, he studied the image in the mirror. Caulfield arched out from the wall, spine bowed, only hands and feet a part of the darkness. The position looked painful. Given Caulfield's reaction, it either wasn't, or that was part of the attraction.

It's like porn for elderly masochists. And it would *be the gardener's replay; it's one of the long ones.*

Eyes narrowed, head cocked to one side, Tony could nearly see Caulfield without the mirror. The faintest translucent image of a man bowed out from the wall; easy enough for those who didn't know—who didn't believe—to dismiss it as a trick of the light.

He returned to the reflection, hoping Caulfield wasn't heading for a big finish because that would put a distinct bend in his sex life for some time to come.

Unfortunately . . .

Great. Something to look forward to. Tony sighed silently as Caulfield snapped back into the darkness and began to roil again within it. He could hear that future conversation now.

Damn, there it goes again. Is it me?

No, I was just thinking of this evil old guy I saw once . . .

Of course, if he wanted Lee to survive this, that particular problem was unlikely. A very minor bright side.

"So." Lee's arms made a pale band across the black T-shirt as he folded them. "Have you made up your mind?"

Seemed that Caulfield—both on the wall and in Lee—planned to ignore what had just happened. Worked for Tony. Forgetting would be harder, but ignoring he could do. "If I join you, then Lee and the others walk away?"

"Yes."

He snorted. "Like I can trust you."

"As a gesture of good faith, I no longer possess the other actor or the two who use the camera. And besides . . ." Lee spread his hands and mirrored the smile that appeared briefly at the surface of the darkness. ". . . when you become a part of us, there is a chance you will be able to influence our actions." And his hands crossed over his chest. "It is the only way for you to save him."

"Yeah. I got that a while ago." Tony fought the urge to scratch at his blisters. "So why does freedom ring after I join in? What difference will I make?"

"Unfortunately, I made a slight miscalculation and did not have substance enough on my own to give Arogoth existence independent of this house. Together, we will."

"You're sure of that? Because a hundred years stuck to a basement wall—not appealing."

Lee's smile twisted into a darker curve. "It had its moments. The taste of death is sweet as you will learn. If you'd die to preserve this man, think how much better to live forever."

"Forever?"

"Yes. As Arogoth, immortal devourer of death!" Not even the use of Lee's talent could pull that line back from the brink, and Caulfield seemed to realize it. His eyes closed briefly before disappearing into the churning mix of features. Obviously trying to save face, Lee scowled and pointed. "Choose."

"What choice?" The pain in his arm was constant enough to almost ignore as he reached for the lantern. "I have to tell the others what I'm doing or they'll be down here trying to pull off some half-assed rescue attempt."

"That is . . ." Lee paused and Tony got the impression that Caulfield was shuffling through what he knew about the people who put together *Darkest Night*. Without perspective, they seemed like an insane bunch—twelve-to-seventeen-hour days making a vampire detective believable . . . at least for forty-three minutes at a time. "Fine. Tell them."

"They'll try and talk me out of it." He carefully bent his fingers around the handle and then more carefully still lifted the lantern from the nail. "They'll try and convince me there's a way we can beat you."

"Convince them there isn't."

"Easy for you to say." His gesture with the lantern made shadows dance, made it seem as though the whole basement was roiling. Roiling. He just couldn't get enough of that word. "Well, come on, then."

"Come . . . ? Ah." Lee leaned back against the wall. Not the piece of wall where Arogoth was contained and Caulfield's features continued to surface but a section of fieldstone empty of everything but a little mold and mildew. "I don't think so. This one stays with us while you are gone."

Tony froze. "No," he snarled. "He goes with me."

"He stays."

"The hell he does."

"Exactly."

Bugger. "If he stays, how can I be sure you aren't hurting him?"

"You can't. And I can hurt him while he is with you—or have you forgotten already?"

Not something he was likely to forget in a hurry. "But if he's with me, I'll know you're hurting him and I'll know you're a lying sack of shit. I want him with me."

"You don't always get what you want." There was nothing of Lee in that smile at all. "Best hurry back."

"I don't . . ."

"Have much time." No mistaking the threat.

"Lee, if you can hear me, I'll be back for you." Without waiting for a response, Tony spun on one heel and splashed toward the stairs. Although he hated leaving Lee in Caulfield's control, hated leaving him in the dark, his protests had more to do with convincing Caulfield to keep his hostage in the basement. Had he not protested, the—well, *thing* still seemed to apply—the thing would have grown suspicious about why he didn't want Lee upstairs. Didn't want Lee in a position to be Caulfield's eyes and ears.

When the splashing wasn't quite enough, Tony matched his breathing to the rhythm of the other man's lungs so that he couldn't hear him receding farther and farther away. Shoes and socks squelching, he climbed to the kitchen just in time for Karl to stop crying and the ballroom's replay to begin.

Just for a moment, he missed the quiet of the basement. If he never heard "Night and Day" again, it would be way too soon.

"*Tony . . .*"

"Give me a break." Spinning on his heel, spraying dirty water as he turned, he stuck his head back into the stairwell. "Hey, you want to tell your ghostly minions that the plan's changed. Because the name calling is really fucking annoying!"

"*Tony . . .*"

"Oh, right. I forgot." Caulfield was just a little too distracted during replays to respond. Where *distracted* meant getting his metaphysical rocks off. Pot, kettle, black on that whole unnatural lust thing. Eyes rolling, Tony headed for the kitchen sink. He couldn't connect with anyone alive during the replay anyhow and he *really* had to take a leak.

The door to the butler's pantry opened as Tony reached for it. They'd clearly been waiting for him. All eyes were locked on his face as they shuffled back to give him room to enter.

"You're wet," Mason pointed out, moving fastidiously farther away.

"Basement's flooded."

"Chest high?"

"There was a bit of sitting," he admitted, sagged against the counter and twisted the top off a bottle of water.

"Where's Lee?" Peter demanded.

"In the basement, still possessed." A long swallow. "Creighton Caulfield is a part of the thing."

"So it worked."

He turned to stare at Amy in confusion. "What worked?"

Mouse shuffled back against the far wall as Amy waved the open journal. "The last entry." She glanced down and read: "*I go to become great. I go to become immortal. I go to become . . . the name you won't let me say.*"

"Well, he hasn't quite *become*," Tony snorted. "Not yet anyway. He wants me to join him—them—and finish the project, or he'll kill Lee. If I join him, you all go free."

"Including Lee?"

"So says the thing in the basement." He waited while everyone in the room thought about how easy production assistants were to replace.

"What are you going to do?" Tina asked at last.

Tony took another mouthful of water, swallowed, and shrugged. "Save Lee. Save you guys. Save the day."

Zev's hand closed around his arm. "You're going to join him?"

"Not if I can help it."

"You have a plan."

He smiled wearily at the music director. "I got nothing. Amy, he implied that the journal would explain all. What have you got?"

"Um, okay . . ." She turned a couple of pages. "He started out as a collector of the weird. Grave dirt, cat skulls, mummy bits . . . not really unusual for a man of his time."

"How are you knowing that?" Sorge asked, his tone more intrigued than suspicious.

"Amy knows her mummy bits," Tony told him. "Go on, Amy."

"Anyway, later . . . Why are you squirming?"

Fabric squelched as he flexed his butt muscles against the edge of the counter. "Wet underwear."

"Okay, didn't really want to know. The stuff Caulfield collected led to books to look the stuff up in, to verify it, and then he started collecting the books. Then he found a book that convinced him that . . ." She bent her head to read again. "*That there is a world beyond what fools admit. There is power for those who dare take it. There is power here.*"

"What an idiot," Mason muttered.

"Except he was right," Tony said thoughtfully. "All that nasty shit he collected . . ."

"I'm guessing waxy buildup of evil," Amy agreed. "And that's when he started calling in the mediums, trying to contact this power. You know he had a developmentally handicapped son, right?"

"He's in the bathroom," Brianna added, crawling backward out of one of the lower cabinets clutching a silver salad fork.

"Well, one of the mediums—one of the ones who survived—thought that spirits were attracted to those kind of brain waves, so Caulfield started using his son."

"Using?"

"That's all it says."

"I think we can fill in the blanks," Zev growled.

"He never hit him." Brianna patted Zev on the arm. "But he was scary. Really, really scary. Except I wouldn't have been scared."

"I don't doubt that for a moment," Zev muttered, taking the salad fork away.

Tony frowned. "It likes fear, strong emotions." There had to be a way he could use that.

"Looks like the fear was enough," Amy continued, "because contact was made. Meanwhile, Caulfield had been using his books to research how to hold the power when he found it. Thus the pages of mystic symbols."

Tony held up his left hand. His palm throbbed and the skin under the pattern itched like crazy. "This was what he used to hold the power here in the house."

"Yeah, kind of like a roach motel. Nasty energy checks in, but it doesn't check out. He used a bunch of the other symbols to get it all gathered up in one place. He's not writing for the ages here, so he's kind of obscure, but I think he believed that the more of it he gathered in one place, the more real it would be."

"Half an inch of water spread over an entire room is harmless," Saleen announced unexpectedly. "Put that water in a bucket and you can drown someone."

"Exactly!" Amy shot Saleen an approving smile. "Caulfield used his own blood to gather this thing up. *My heart pounding with anticipation, I opened a vein and dipped in the brush made to the specification in the ancient text. Chanting and breathing the fumes of . . .*"

"*Reader's Digest* version," Tony interrupted. "I don't have a lot of time and there'll be another replay blowing through in a minute."

"Okay, he burned some herbs, lifted some bad poetry out of an old book, painted on the basement wall in blood and all the power scooted there and what was abstract gained enough substance to become . . . stract. Defined. Sort of like catching a demon in a pentagram. Then his son died . . ."

"Of what?" It might be important.

"It doesn't say."

"He was scared," Brianna offered. "Really, really scared. He's still scared."

"He died of fright?"

She shrugged, dismissing the concept. "He was too scared to go away. That's why he's there."

"Without his son, Caulfield couldn't access the power he'd trapped in the basement, so he went looking for a way to draw it into himself. He figured he found one. And then . . ." Amy held the journal up again. "We're back at the last page. *I go to become . . .*"

"Except the stuff he wrote on the wall held him as well as the power and probably that's what kept them from completely merging as well. He thinks that with me added to the mix, we'll be strong enough to break the spell, merge and emerge, and become that name."

Sorge rolled his eyes. "If it isn't that name yet, why can't we say it?"

"We don't want to lend it definition."

"What the hell does that mean when it's home?" Adam demanded. Then he raised a hand as all eyes turned to him. "Never mind. Don't really care."

"With you in the mix, what makes Caulfield think he'll be in charge?" Peter wondered.

"He's read the right books and he's had a hundred-odd years to work out what he'll do. I'm winging it. And I've used a lot of energy tonight already."

Brianna poked him in the leg, then held out her other hand. "Sugar?" Her fingers peeled away from a damp, crumpled paper package.

"Where did you get that?" Zev asked, plucking the package off her palm and examining it. Tony wondered what he thought it might be. What dangers it might contain.

"From the box with the salt."

"You haven't been eating it, have you?"

"Duh."

"Maybe that explains why Ashley's asleep . . ."

Covered with Mason's coat, her head on Tina's lap, Ashley murmured at the sound of her name but didn't rouse.

". . . and this one's still bouncing off the walls." He handed the sugar to Tony. "Will this help?"

"Can't hurt." He ripped it open and poured the sugar into his water bottle. "Bri? Can you get the rest of the sugar out of the box?"

She drew herself up and saluted. "I'm on it!"

The box was by the other door. *Sugar rush,* he thought as she raced toward it. *Use it wisely.*

"So he's like physically stuck to the wall?" Amy wondered as Brianna raced back with a double handful of packages.

"No. It's more like he took himself down to his component atoms and mixed them with the power he'd already trapped on the wall."

"Component atoms?" Peter looked hopeful. "So there's a scientific explanation for all this?"

Pouring more sugar into the water, Tony wondered what explanation Peter had been listening to. "Not a chance. Caulfield was a wizard, although he doesn't like the word. Instead of an Arra, he found the wrong book."

"If there's a book, then there must have been other wizards."

"Yeah, I'm not unique. It sucks to be me." He took a swallow of the sugar water, made a face, and took another. "The way I see it, I have two options. I join with Caulfield to save you all, hoping that something outside the house will be able to stop our combined power before it destroys the mainland and kills everyone living on it." And everyone unliving on it. Caulfield didn't know about Henry now, but he would the moment Tony joined up. "*Everyone* means you lot as well," he added.

"So if you go join up now," Tina said thoughtfully, "you're not really saving us, just delaying the inevitable."

"Yeah." He took another swallow. "Sucks to be you, too."

"And the second option?" Zev prodded.

"We destroy Caulfield. We remove the writing on the wall. We disperse the power."

Amy closed the journal. "You mean destroy the power."

"I mean disperse. You can't destroy energy, you can only change it." He glanced around the room. There were half a dozen degrees in here; one of them had to have been in something useful. "Right?"

"He's right," Saleen answered. Pavin nodded agreement.

Let's hear it for tech support.

"Great. So how do you destroy Caulfield?" Amy asked. "Snatch him away from the power?"

"He's not in this reality anymore. I can't touch him."

"Use the flypaper on your hand to grab him."

"Flypaper?"

She shrugged. "Roach motel, flypaper; amounts to the same thing."

Tony glanced down at the mark and thought of how much it would hurt to snatch up a handful of Creighton Caulfield. Good thing his pants were already wet. "I can't. If I get too close, he'll pull me in."

"So you need something out of this reality that can destroy him from a distance?" When he nodded, Amy snorted. "Good luck."

"You have an idea," Zev said softly, eyes locked on Tony's face. "But you don't like it much."

Flexing his left hand, Tony grinned at his ex. "I don't like it at all. But I think it'll work."

"All right." Peter's tone suggested he was bringing up a point that they'd all missed. "How do you destroy Caulfield without him hurting Lee?"

"I'm going to need a little help with that."

"We're here for you," Amy declared. Most heads nodded.

"Not from you guys," he said as the drawing room replay began and he was alone in the pantry with that damned plate of tea cakes. "I'm playing a wild card." Because they could still hear him, he explained.

". . . the paint's buried in our gear in the library," he finished as the lantern light came up again. "So it's going to have to be dug out."

"Saleen, Pavin . . ." Peter jerked his head toward the door. "Take the other lantern, get the paint."

"On it!"

"They'll need to pull energy from something," Tony said as the door closed. "Someone."

Amy raised her hand and waved it. "I volunteer!"

No one looked surprised.

"It might be dangerous."

"Please." Her grin widened. "Danger is my middle name."

"I thought your middle name was . . ."

"And unless you want your e-mail address written on the wall of every virtual truck stop on the Web, you'll hold that thought."

"What's your plan for removing the writing on the wall?" Tina asked before Tony'd entirely decided that would be a bad thing.

"Don't have one exactly." He shrugged. "But there's a lot of water down there."

"No." Tina shook her head. "Water won't work. Not on ancient bloodstains. Trust me on this; I have two sons who grew up playing rugby."

"The cleaner." All eyes turned to Sorge. "The cleaner we use to clean off the blood on the walls in the upstairs bathroom. During the scenes the girls do!" he expanded when no one seemed to get it. "We splash the walls with the fake blood, but we have to clean it off again. The cleaner, she is guarantee to cut through anything. Old. New. Fake. Real. There are six different warning on the label about the contents."

"And you sprayed that around the girls?" Zev asked him, visibly appalled.

Sorge looked affronted. "Not me. I don't clean locations, I design fantastic scenes that are ignored during award times. But there is a spray bottle also with the gear in the library."

"Sounds like it'll work. Thanks, Bri." Tony accepted another bottle of sugared water from the girl and frowned. "Crap. I won't be able to spray the wall."

Peter rolled his eyes. "And why not?"

"He's not sure he'll survive destroying Caulfield."

Attention flicked from Zev—who stood arms folded—to Tony, who was looking pretty much anywhere but at Zev.

"Is that true?" Peter asked him.

"I should survive." Another long swallow helped him ignore Zev's expression. "I just won't be in any condition to do much else, so someone needs to be available to haul my ass out of the water."

"Me."

Surprised, Tony glanced over at Mouse. Thought of the last time the big man's hands had been on him. Banished the thought. "You sure you're okay?"

The cameraman shot a wary glance at the journal and nodded. "And Lee?"

"Yeah, he'll likely need to be hauled as well."

Adam stepped forward. "That'll be me, then."

"Good. Okay, now for the spray . . ."

"Hello!" Amy waved her hand.

"No. Mouse and Adam can charge in after the fact, but whoever is spraying is going to have to be with me. Close to the thing. If we don't do this at the same time, I'm not positive that one half of that thing can't heal the other. Besides, you've already got something to do."

Her lower lip went out. "Well, yeah, but I'll be done by then."

"You might also be unconscious."

She perked up at the thought. "There is that."

"Me."

"You're . . ."

Peter folded his arms. "In charge. I'm there to see that the thing keeps its half of the bargain and lets my costar go."

"I don't know . . ."

"I do." Zev moved closer to Tony. "It should be me."

"Zev, Peter's plan might . . ."

"We have history. I've come with you to say good-bye. Caulfield's a product of his time as well as his ambition; first of all, two men are going to throw him off and second, he's not going to consider another fag to be a danger to him. You're going to need all the edge you can get."

"Actually, yeah." He sighed. Did it make him a bad person if he'd rather have Peter in danger than Zev or just a good friend? "We could throw Caulfield a bit off his game. But the bottle . . ."

"Will be duct taped to his back." Mason included them all in his smile. "Episode eight. That asshole who tried to stake me in my own office had the stake duct taped to his back."

"Oh, for the love of God, Mason . . ." Peter paused, reconsidered, and started again. "Mason, that didn't work."

"Because I saw the reflection of the stake in the mirror. There are no mirrors in the basement and that thing sure as hell isn't Raymond Dark."

All Zev would have to do was walk across the basement by his side. He wouldn't have to turn. He wouldn't ever expose his back. Tony swallowed more sugar water. "Damn. That might just work."

"Don't tell the writers," Peter muttered. Tina snickered, then stroked Ashley's hair as she stirred.

"One problem." Mouse scowled at no one in particular. "No duct tape."

No duct tape? Well, that was practically unCanadian. "The electrical . . ."

"No." Sorge shook his head. "If we wrap electrical tape so it holds a bottle, Zev won't be able to get it off."

"You need duct tape? Why don't you use some of mine?"

Positions shifted until everyone could stare down at Kate sitting propped and taped against a lower cabinet.

"You chewed through another gag?" Amy sounded impressed.

"Please." She spit a bit of damp fabric to one side. "My boyfriend is a terrible cook; I've eaten worse and smiled while I did it."

Two napkins down, Tony had no doubt that she'd eaten anything set in front of her. The smiling part was giving him a little trouble, though. "Used duct tape . . ."

Kate snorted. "Will work fine. It'll peel off itself just like it does off the roll.

You'll lose the layer that's against me, but that's all. And stop bloody worrying," she snapped as no one stepped forward. "Sitting around with our thumbs up our collective butts while people get possessed and other people die makes me kind of cranky, but I'm fine now. We have a plan."

"You still sound cranky," Tina pointed out.

"Always sounds cranky," Mouse grunted.

"Yeah, yeah," she muttered as he pulled open his pocketknife and knelt by her feet. "Bite me, you big rodent. One more thing, though. The tape's not going to stick to fabric. It'll have to be attached to . . ."

Mouse pulled the final layer of tape off skin.

". . . son of a fucking bitch! . . . Zev."

Zev looked understandably less than thrilled. "If it's under my shirt, how will I reach it?"

"We'll have to cut the back of your shirt away. Tina . . ."

Tina pulled a pair of nail scissors out of her purse and handed them up to Amy, who advanced on the music director's shirt with a gleam in her eyes.

"And then we'll tape down the edges of your shirt so it doesn't flap and then we tape the bottle to you."

"Is a big bottle," Sorge observed with a grin. "Why don't you just stuff the bottom down the back of his pants?"

Amy paused in her advance, glared at the DP, and handed Tina back the scissors. "Well, aren't you just a big bunch of no fun at all."

The door leading to the dining room opened. Saleen came in first carrying the paint followed by Pavin with the lantern. "We got it."

"Great." Peter smiled approvingly at them. "Set it down and go back for a spray bottle of cleaner."

"We didn't see any spray bottles."

"It's in there." Sorge walked the length of the butler's pantry and paused with his hand on the door. "Come. I'll go with you."

Pavin held out the lantern. "Why don't you go by yourself?"

"I don't want to. Come on. Varamous."

"That's not French," Saleen muttered as he set the can of paint on the counter and turned to follow Sorge and the sound tech out of the room.

"Me, I'm a man of many talents," the DP said as the door closed.

Tony drained the last of the sugar water and slid off the counter. "Okay. Open the paint can and then put it outside the door in the kitchen. Amy, wait by the can. When the guys get back with the cleaner, Zev and Adam and Mouse get ready to meet me by the basement door. Wait until you hear me coming down the back stairs and then move. Delays will be . . ." He could feel sweat dribbling down his sides. ". . . not good. Make sure the spray bottle is on a tight, hard spray—all we have to do is cut through the blood pattern, break it up. We don't have to completely erase it. The rest of you . . . If this goes completely to hell, the pattern on the floor will keep anything from coming in; you'll have the laptop and the candles for light and all you have to do is stick it out until morning."

"What if Caulfield sucks you in?" Amy asked.

"You die and I spend eternity as part of a three for one that even our writers would consider over the top, where the other two parts are a hundred-year-old naked homophobe and evil waxy buildup."

Amy's smile came nowhere near her eyes. "Dead sounds better."

"Yeah, no shit."

Tony went upstairs while Lucy Lewis killed her coworker and waited by the second-floor bathroom while she hanged herself. When the only light on the floor came from the lantern in his hand and Karl started crying again, he went into the room.

"Cassie? Stephen?"

He didn't know where they'd been for the last—impossible to tell exactly how long since he'd seen them, without a watch and only the very subjective replays to determine the passage of time, but it had been a while.

"Guys? I need to talk to you. It's important."

Nothing. Big white empty bathroom.

He sighed and crossed to the mirror. Not so empty anymore. Not so white. The mirror showed Cassie and Stephen sitting on the edge of the tub and the walls covered in splashes and sprays and dribbles of blood. Too much blood for a double murder? Even considering that head wounds bled like crazy? Maybe every replay left its mark. And wasn't that depressing.

"Guys, I can see your reflection. I know you're there." They were looking at him. But only in the mirror. Cassie looked sad. Stephen stubborn.

Fine.

"The thing in the basement wants me to join it, and it's holding Lee hostage to make me. I think we can beat it if one of you two helps me to save Lee."

Cassie glanced away. Stephen lifted his sister's hand off his leg and wound their fingers together. He couldn't have said *"Mine"* more obviously if he'd said it out loud.

Tony counted time by his heartbeat. He had to convince them before the next replay started. Before their replay started.

"If I can't save Lee . . ." Try again. "If Lee dies, I die with him. You guys are dead. You have to admit that alive is better. Together and alive. Because, him and me, we won't be together if we're dead." Yeah. That was articulate—not!

Entirely possible all that sugar water had been a bad idea as he couldn't seem to maintain a coherent thought. Time to pull the big guns. Time to use the magic word . . .

"Please."

"If we help you, it'll know we have more than the existence it allows us."

He turned. Cassie sat alone on the tub, the fingers of her right hand, the fingers wrapped around her brother's hand, fading into nothing. Her single eye locked on his face, willing him to understand.

"If it knows we're awake and aware . . ."

"It'll kill us again." Stephen was there now. "It'll take away the little bit of life we have. Is that what you want? Because we're dead, we don't count for as much as the living?"

Yes.

No.

Damn.

"If you're dead, then what you have isn't life, is it?"

Stephen's eyes narrowed and when he rose, he looked menacing for the first time that night. "Get out."

Remembering what a glancing touch against his shoulder had felt like, Tony backed toward the door both hands raised. "I'm sorry!"

"Not good enough." Then he jerked to a stop, his head dislodging.

Cassie stood, still holding her brother's hand, his arm stretched tautly between them. "He's right, Stephen. What we have isn't life."

"All right, not life." He settled his head. "But we have each other and we can't risk losing that. *I* can't risk losing that! Can you?"

"We don't know that we will. But if we don't help, we know that Lee will die?"

She'd made it a question. Tony answered with a nod. "It hasn't noticed you yet, right?"

"Because we've been staying in our place." Stephen spat the words at him. "Here. Together."

"You were walking around earlier and it didn't notice you."

"Before it was awake!"

"And after."

"We were lucky. We can feel it. We can tell that it's awake. It has to be able to do the same."

"Why?"

Stephen frowned. "What?"

"Why does it have to be able to do what you can do? It can't move around, you can. It can't communicate without possessing someone's ass, you can."

"How does it communicate with someone's ass?"

Tony's turn to frown. "That's not what I meant, I meant . . ."

"What do you want us to do?" Cassie interrupted.

Free hand holding his head in place, Stephen whirled to face her. "Cassie!"

She shrugged, broken sundress strap swaying with the motion. "I'm just asking."

"I need you to draw this symbol . . ." Tony held up his left hand, palm out, and both ghosts leaned away. "Oh, shit, you can't, can you?"

"I don't think . . ." Her single brow drew in. "It pushes at us. What is it?"

"It's complicated. It's kind of a protection. A protection against the thing's power, but you're a part of that power."

"Only while we're dying." She studied the symbol. "But *this* it would definitely notice. And if we had anything to do with it, it would notice us."

"Told you," Stephen grunted.

Cassie glanced over at him, her expression unreadable, then turned back to Tony. "The symbol would protect Lee from the thing? Keep it from hurting him?"

"It should."

"Should?"

"Should. No chance of a rehearsal. We have to go live and hope it works, but that doesn't matter because you can't." He slammed his fist into his thigh. "Shit! Fuck! Damn it!"

"You want this done with the paint, like before? Right?" When Tony nodded, the sudden rush of hope making it impossible to speak, Cassie nodded with him.

"I like Lee. He's cute."

"It's dangerous." Stephen almost wailed the word, and the skin on Tony's arms pebbled into goose bumps.

"It's a little paint," Cassie argued. "It's no more than what I did this morning. Where is Lee?"

"In the basement."

"Are you insane!"

"The door will be open," he told them quickly before Stephen could continue. "So you'll be able to go downstairs. There's an open can of paint in the kitchen and you can suck energy out of Amy to use it. You don't need much right? Just for a little symbol like this. She says it's okay. Actually, she's looking forward to it." He was almost babbling but couldn't seem to stop. "And the shit won't hit the fan until the next replay after yours, so first you get the paint then you wait until Karl stops crying then you flick the symbol onto Lee just before Karl starts screaming and then, as Karl's replay starts, you get sucked back here . . ." He tapped the wall. ". . . to safety."

"No." Releasing Cassie's hand, Stephen folded his arms. "Not in the basement. No way."

"But . . ."

"I said, no!"

"Tony . . ."

He looked past Stephen to Cassie.

". . . go away. I need to talk to my brother."

Yeah. That would work. Cassie wanted to help, he could see that, and Cassie was the only person, living or dead, Stephen would be willing to listen to. Except . . . He paused in the doorway. "How will I know?"

Her expression said, *trust me*. The shrug that went with it, not so confident.

"Stephen . . ."

"No."

"If we don't help, Lee will die."

"And if we do help, what happens to us?"

"If we each stroke on half of the symbol, maybe nothing. But maybe something. And that's good because nothing has happened to us since we died. We're as trapped now as we were before Graham woke us. Except now we know it."

"But . . ." He started to shake his head, remembered, and caught her hands in his instead. "I can't lose you. I can't." When she sat back on the edge of the tub, he sank to the floor and buried his face in her skirt. "I can't. I won't. And there's more!"

She freed a hand and stroked his cheek. "More?"

"Have you thought of what happens to us if Tony destroys it? What happens to us if we're not trapped here anymore?"

"We move on."

He lifted his head then. "Where? Because, you know, there was sinning."

The corners of her mouth trembled up into a smile. "I remember."

"So, I'm thinking we're better off here." His smile suggested he'd found definitive reasoning.

"Maybe if we save Lee, the sinning won't count for as much. And if we don't save him . . ." Her fingers remembered the soft silk of Stephen's hair. "If we don't save him and Tony still destroys the malevolence, well, that won't look good for us if we move on. Given the sinning and all."

"No."

She sighed. Or she thought she sighed; her fingers, it seemed, had a better memory than her lungs. "I'm going to help Tony. So if we do move on . . ."

"No."

But that "no" was less definite. And he'd stopped smiling.

*   *   *

Waiting outside the bathroom door, Tony flicked open his pocketknife. His left hand had only just regained enough strength to grip it while he poked the point of the blade into the tip of his right index finger.

Here's irony for you . . .

Caulfield seemed to think the answers Tony needed in order to understand the metaphysics of the situation were in the journal. The journal told them that Caulfield had used his own blood to trap the accumulated power against the basement wall. After folding the knife and slipping it back into his pocket, Tony pressed his thumb against the ball of his finger, just under the cut, and squeezed out a steady supply of blood as he painted over the symbol on his left palm.

He'd only just finished, cut finger in his mouth, when Karl stopped crying.

Quiet on the set.

Action . . .

∽ SIXTEEN

Mr. Mills staggered back as the ax came free and screamed, "You can't hide from me!"

Tony didn't watch as Cassie and Stephen came out into the hall and then ran, hand in hand, for the bathroom. He knew he wasn't seeing them alive, that their reality was a nearly severed neck and three-quarters of a head, but to see them appear alive, to see their last few moments and to know they'd be trapped replaying those moments over and over—well, it was fucking tragic, that's what it was.

It was supposed to stop with death. Maybe there was a judgment, maybe there wasn't—Tony had seen enough weird shit he was unwilling to commit—but the point was: end of something, start of something else. Cassie and Stephen didn't end, didn't start, didn't do anything but sort of exist. And maybe that *sort of* was better than risking the alternative, but Tony didn't think so.

Maybe he should just stop thinking about it. He'd had his chance to convince them.

He winced. Twice. Ax into flesh. Ax into bone. Funny that the impact of the ax—an impact that wasn't particularly loud—made more of an impression than the screaming. Actually, Karl had pretty much desensitized him to screaming. Karl, and before Karl, Aerosmith.

Splattered with the blood of his children, Mr. Mills turned and walked out of the bathroom. Once in the hall, he looked down at the bloody ax as though he'd never seen it before, as though he had no idea whose brains and hair were stuck along its length, then he adjusted his grip and slammed the blade down between his own eyes.

Tony took a step forward as the body fell, held out his left hand, his own blood glistening on his palm, and he reached. Energy never went away and bottom line, the ghosts were captured energy.

Line below the bottom line, this was really going to hurt.

But he couldn't think of another way.

It was all a matter of manipulating energy. Any and all types of energy, if Arra's notes could be trusted. It was, in the end, what separated the wizards from the boys. Or maybe, more accurately, those who were willing to risk losing the use of an arm from those who'd come up with a less debilitating solution. And, man, he'd sure like to talk to that other guy . . .

The ax slapped against his hand as the lights dimmed. His fingers didn't so much close as spasm around the handle. *Well, whatever works.* When the replay ended, he couldn't see the ax, but he sure as hell could feel it.

The pain was . . .

Definitively pain.

The kind of pain that, should he actually survive this, he'd compare to every other pain for the rest of his life.

You think that *hurts? I once pulled a ghost ax out of its time and walked through a haunted house with it.*

Except he wasn't exactly walking. Or doing anything but trying to suck enough air into his lungs to stay conscious.

Come on, feet, move!

A deeper breath. And then another.

A guy can get used to anything in time.

Yeah, but he didn't have time. Or not much of it anyway. He had to be in place in the basement before the next replay started.

Okay, don't think about the basement. Think about one step. Just one.

One step didn't hurt any more than standing still. Neither did two or three.

Now just get to the back stairs. Straight hall. Easy trip.

He could do that. Hell, he'd once walked to Wellesley Hospital in February with two broken ribs, a fat lip, and only one shoe. To this day, he had no idea where his other shoe'd gone.

Now down the stairs. This should be easy, gravity's on your side.

Wait.

He needed a test. Some way of making sure that the energy he held continued to act like an ax. It'd be piss useless if it didn't.

Instead of down, he went up. And gravity was a bitch.

Lucy's rope had crossed the lower edge of the third floor just slightly off center. The stairs were so steep he could reach the lower edge of the third floor from four steps up. If he could reach it from four, he wasn't going for five. No point being stupid about this. Sucking in a lungful of air, he willed his arm to work and swung the ax.

He felt the blade cut into the wood.

Felt the burn of a severed rope whistle past his cheek.

Felt dead weight just for an instant roll against his legs.

Staggered back down the four steps, panting; small quick breaths that didn't hurt quite so much.

Heard a voice destroyed by a noose murmur, "Thank you."

And felt a lot better.

For just a moment, he had the strong feeling it was 1906 and he was a chambermaid, but since that was a huge improvement on what he had been feeling—pain, pain, and, well, pain—he could cope. He still felt as though his left arm had been dipped in acid and then rolled in hot sand, but whatever Lucy was doing—Lucy being the only chambermaid he knew from 1906—it gave him a little distance from the feeling. It got him down the stairs and across the kitchen to where Mouse and Adam and Zev waited with the second lantern.

When he joined them, the double circle of light expanded to include Amy sitting cross-legged just outside the butler's pantry by an open can of white paint. She shook her head at his silent question.

It took them a while to recover from their own murder.

There was still time.

"Come on, Zev."

As the music director came forward, Tony grinned. "Is that a bottle of cleaner in your pants or are you just happy to see me?"

Adam rolled his eyes and handed Mouse five bucks as Zev reached back and touched the bottle crammed into the top of his jeans. "What about us?" the 1AD asked. "When do we charge to the rescue?"

"You'll know," Tony told him.

"You sure?"

"It'll be obvious."

"Obvious how?"

"I'm thinking, screaming."

"Yeah." Adam forced a hand back through thick hair, standing it up in sweaty spikes. "Listen, if this thing's been around for so long, what makes you think we can beat it?"

Time for the big, last minute motivational speech.

"Duh. We're the good guys. Zev, can you get the door? My hands are full."

Lantern in one hand. Ax in the other. Of course, no one could see the ax.

Zev made a clear decision not to ask and opened the basement door. He frowned as Tony stepped over the threshold. "What's that on your cheek?"

"Rope burn."

"Do I want to know?"

"I doubt it." He shifted over as Zev joined him on the top step. "Stay to my right, by the lantern. And remember," he added as they began to descend, "anything Lee can hear, it can . . . Fuck!"

Lee's face appeared in the darkness at the bottom of the stairs looking for an instant like it was on its own, floating unattached. "I was beginning to think you weren't coming back to us."

Tony shrugged and tried to pretend he wasn't carrying an invisible ghost ax. Lucky break that Lee—Caulfield—couldn't see it either. He hadn't been one hundred percent certain about that, but given the total lack of reaction, it seemed *no one* could see it. "I told you it would take a while to convince them."

"But convince them of what; that's the question. Hello, Zev."

"Lee."

"Not Lee," Tony growled.

"Close enough." The green eyes narrowed, pupils dark pinpricks in the direct glare of the lantern. "Why are you here, Zev?"

"The odds are good that you . . . your body . . . will need a little help leaving after Tony does his thing." He waved a hand, the gesture managing to encompass all the possibilities inherent in the word *thing*. "And besides . . ." His eyes narrowed in turn. "I had no intention of allowing Tony to go through this alone."

"So you're here to hold his hand?"

"I'm here to hold anything that might make it easier for him."

Lee fastidiously brushed a bit of muck off his dress pants. "The depth to which moral rot has penetrated this age astounds me. Perversions accepted as normal behavior."

Tony turned just enough to grin at Zev. "You never said anything about perversions."

"I didn't want to get your hopes up." He shrugged philosophically. "There may not be time."

"Fair enough."

"Stay with him, then, if you must," Lee snarled. *And be the first to fall!*

That had to be some of the loudest subtext Tony'd ever heard and, given the volume of the subtext over the course of the night, that was saying something. "You go first." He motioned with the lantern. "I want you out where I can see you so that I know you're not mucking about with Lee's body."

"I do not muck about!"

"Muck about, torture. Potato, potahto. Move."

Lee pointedly turned and began wading across the basement.

"Since when do you quote Gershwin?" Zev murmured as they descended into the water.

"Sometimes I like to embrace the stereotype." The water felt warmer than it had. Tony really hoped that was because his legs were already wet.

"Gilbert and Sullivan?"

"Not in a million years."

"That's a pretty halfhearted embrace, then."

"I gotta be me."

The thing seemed closer to the stairs than it had been, but, as it was a part of the foundation, Tony was fairly certain it hadn't moved. As Lee took up his old place by the wall, Tony realized that with both hands full, the mirror in his pocket was about as useful as last week's *TV Guide*.

"Hand the lantern to your friend . . ." The final word dripped with distaste. ". . . then come forward and merge with us."

"Dude, you make it sound so dirty." He motioned for Zev to step back, splashed closer to the pillar and hung the lantern on the nail. "Less likely to take damage if I leave it here."

"Dude?" Lee's lip curled. "Your speech patterns are strange."

"You'll have time to get used to them." He never thought he'd miss the sound of Karl's crying. Or rather the sound of Karl not crying to mark the beginning of the next replay. They had to fill the time and they had to fill it in such a way that they didn't seem to be stalling. He stepped in front of Zev and leaned in. "So, I guess this is good-bye."

A faint smile within the bracket of the dark beard as Zev silently agreed to take one for the team.

Give one?

Whatever . . .

Physical incompatibility had *not* been the reason they'd broken up. Tony finally had to pull back from the kiss lest he miss the next replay entirely. Also, he needed to leave a few brain cells functioning.

Lee's lip had been curled before, but it had enough lift in it now to give Raymond Dark a run for his money. "Perversions!"

"Protesting too much?" Zev looked smug.

"He doesn't want you." Lee's voice, Caulfield's disgust.

"I think *he* means me," Tony murmured.

"Yeah, I got that."

Caulfield spread Lee's arms. "He wants this!"

Zev snorted. "Who doesn't?"

That seemed to throw him for a moment. "He settled for you!"

"Duh."

"Hey!" Tony palmed the mirror under the cover of his protest. "I didn't settle! I didn't!" he repeated as neither Caulfield nor Zev seemed to believe him. He could only hope Lee wouldn't remember any part of being possessed. "Wanting something does not keep you from being content with something else. I like hot dogs, but I'm happy with . . ."

"Blintzes?"

"Don't start."

He had the mirror now. Was that a flicker of gray on the edge of the lamplight? Two translucent figures waiting for their cue? Or was it hope and nothing more? "I want Lee standing over here with Zev before I come to you."

"Fine." The actor took a step forward, away from the wall. Room enough behind him for a ghost to do a little finger painting.

Or a pair of ghosts.

Lee took another step, shuddered, and stopped.

Good luck. Rough rasp of a voice in his head and the sudden return of pain as Lucy Lewis snapped back to the stairwell, to her place during the replay.

Tony checked the reflection in the mirror . . .

Eyes in the roiling black bulged out toward him.

Then formed a face. And a head. And a body. Caulfield defined.

And without the mirror?

The faintest hint of a pink and naked shape arcing out from the wall.

No way of knowing if Lee was protected.

No way of knowing if Lee was about to die.

Even if they managed to delay Caulfield until the next replay, he'd never be able to hold onto the ax.

Now or never.

Never.

Now.

Teeth clenched, Tony stumbled closer to the wall, somehow got his arm raised over his head, and put everything he had left into snapping the ax forward, not so much releasing it at the right moment as forcing his fingers to straighten and hoping momentum would do the rest. The ax became visible as it embedded itself in Creighton Caulfield's head.

Lee screamed.

They hadn't . . . He wasn't . . .

Tony splashed toward him. Didn't seem to be getting anywhere. Streams of cleanser were going by awfully high.

Oh, wait, I'm on my knees.

He didn't remember falling.

His left hand hurt up his arm, across his shoulders and chest, and all the way down to his right hip. Waves. Of. Burning. Pain. The gardener's arm and head had both been smaller and he'd held them for a lot less time. Lucy's presence had masked the damage, allowed him to get this far, but hadn't stopped it from happening. Water was cool. Water would help. He started to topple forward.

Wait.

That wasn't Lee screaming. Tony forced his eyes to focus. Lee was also on his knees, staring into the water like he couldn't believe what he saw, lower lip caught between his teeth and dripping blood. But he wasn't screaming.

So who was?

Right. Naked writhing guy with ax in head. Eyes wide in the streams of darkness running down his face, Caulfield pulled an arm free and grabbed for the ax handle. His fingers passed through the shaft.

His other arm came free on its own. Spat free.

Then his feet.

Seemed that the accumulated power wasn't too happy about having been trapped.

Tony scrambled backward as a decomposing body dropped face first into the water. Bobbed up. Rolled over. Head split open, no sign of the ax.

He screamed as hands grabbed his shoulders.

"It's me." No mistaking Mouse's voice or size.

Right, the cavalry.

"Let's move it, people, I think that wall's going to blow!"

Adam's voice.

"Lee?" Tony twisted as Mouse lifted him out of the water.

Mouse shifted his grip, the pressure making a strong nonverbal argument that squirming would not be tolerated. "Puking."

Puking was good. At least he *thought* puking was good. "Alive?"

They were climbing the stairs. The big guy could really motor when he had to.

"The dead don't puke."

"Didn't some freelancer pitch that title for episode nine?"

"No."

Tony was fairly certain that he'd been kidding, but when he started to explain that to Mouse, he found himself passing out instead.

"Something just happened." Henry stepped out onto the front path and frowned at the front of the house.

Graham joined him, rubbing at the rain running down his neck and under the collar of his overalls. "Yeah, I felt it, too."

"Felt what?" CB demanded. His tolerance for obscurity had never been high and what little there was had clearly already been used up. "Is it over?"

Vampire and medium exchanged a glance. Finally, Graham shrugged. "Unfortunately, there's only the one way to find out and you're still fucked up from the last time."

Henry's eyes narrowed. "I'm fine."

"You usually got those big purple bruises around your eyes? Nope. Thought not. And you keep rubbing your temples when you think no one's looking. Bet it's been a while since you had a headache."

Henry snarled softly.

"Long while. So it's up to me." He scrubbed his palms against his thighs, walked up the path, reached out, and touched the edge of the porch.

Flash of red light.

And he was lying at Henry's feet. "Are you all right?"

"I'm fine," he muttered as he put his hand in Henry's and was set upright again. "It's not over."

"What's not over?"

The three men turned slowly.

Jack Elson stood in the driveway at the edge of the light.

"Cop?" Graham asked quietly.

"Cop," Henry replied at the same volume.

CB drew in a deep obvious breath and let it out slowly before meeting the advancing RCMP officer halfway. "My night shoot is not over. Can I help you with something, Constable Elson?"

"No, not really. I was just driving by and I saw some cars were still parked out on the road, so I thought I'd come in and find out if there was a problem."

"I see." And included in those two words, was the certain knowledge, shared by everyone who heard them, that Deer Lake Drive didn't actually go anywhere, which made just driving by . . . unlikely.

"Not as many cars as there were."

"We don't need as large a crew at night."

Elson smiled in a hail-fellow-well-met kind of way that set Henry's teeth on edge. His father used to smile like that. "I assume your permits for a night shoot are in order?"

"We've been shooting at this location all week," CB told him.

"But not at night."

"No, not at night."

"So your permits?"

"Are inside."

There was an undercurrent of warning in the producer's voice that Elson ignored.

"All right." His smile broadened. "Let's go take a look."

"The doors have swollen shut in the damp."

Blinking rain off pale lashes, Elson shot Graham an incredulous glare before turning his attention back to CB. "Damp?"

"Yes. Damp. My people are working on getting out."

"There're no lights."

"Constable Danvers." CB nodded as a second figure appeared in the driveway—nodded politely enough but with an edge of impatience in the movement.

Elson turned to scowl at his partner. "What are you doing here?"

"I could ask you the same question." She shrugged and stepped up beside him. "But I won't. After all that research you did, I had a feeling you weren't heading home."

"So you followed me?"

"I didn't have to follow you, Jack. I knew where you were going. There're too many unanswered questions here for you to stay away."

"Research?"

Both constables turned to face the producer.

"There've been a number of unusual occurrences in this house over the years," Danvers told him, ignoring the signals her partner was shooting her. "After speaking with Tony Foster this afternoon, Constable Elson took a look at our records and found a list of murder/suicides as long as your arm." She paused, dropped her gaze to the arm in question, and amended, "Well, as long as my arm anyway. Funny how these sorts of things start piling up in one place."

"Yes. Funny." CB didn't sound particularly amused.

"So you're not here to check our permits."

It wasn't a question, but Elson answered it anyway, lips curved into a tight smile. "Might as well look since we're here."

"I get the strong impression you're here off duty."

"The Horsemen are never off duty." Danvers glanced over at Henry as though somehow aware he was the only one of the four who knew about the blood rising in her cheeks. "Heard the line in an old movie once; I've always wanted to say it."

"Yeah, now you've said it," Elson sighed. "What do you mean there're no lights?"

"What?"

"When you arrived, dogging my heels, having not followed me, anticipating my interest . . ."

A raised brow cut off the list.

". . . you said there were no lights."

"Oh. Right. There're no lights on in the house." One hand gestured gracefully toward the building. "If they're in there, shooting, why is it so dark?"

"Because we've been shooting day for night and the windows are covered in blackout curtains." CB's words emerged clipped of everything but bare fact. If Henry had to guess, he'd say that at the end of a long night of waiting and worrying about his daughters, CB was beginning to get angry. Too practical to lose his temper at the house, fate had just given him a pair of targets. Given that the last time Henry'd seen CB angry he'd lifted a grown man by the throat and thrown him across a soundstage, it might be a good idea to intervene.

"Blackout curtains? Okay. And you've probably got an explanation for that flash of red light that knocked . . ." Elson paused, the question in his stare unmistakable.

"Graham Brummel," the caretaker muttered.

". . . Mr. Brummel here five feet back onto his ass?"

The fabric of CB's trench coat rippled as he settled his shoulders. "You saw that?"

"'fraid so."

The faintest growl and Henry was there, left hand wrapped around CB's right wrist, holding the big man's arm to his side.

"I saw it, too. From the driveway." Danvers' eyes locked on the muscles straining under CB's coat, the movement obvious even in the darkness.

"What the hell is going on here?" Elson demanded, his attention having snapped instinctively to the greater threat. "You were there. Now you're here. No one can move that fast."

Henry kept his smile just to the safe side of dangerous. "Obviously, since I did, someone can. I'm very fit." Feeling the pressure against his grip ease, he let his fingers slide off CB's heated skin. Holding Constable Elson's suspicious gaze, his eyes darkened. "I suspect what happened to Mr. Brummell was a result of weather. We've had a fair bit of lightning and old houses like this can acquire quite the buildup of static electricity."

"Static electricity?" The suspicion began to fade slightly. "Yeah, I guess that could . . ."

"What a load." Danvers' attention flicked from CB to Henry and back to CB again. "I'm thinking that either one of these cables you guys are running in from your truck here isn't properly grounded and you've created a hazardous environment—in direct violation of any number of workplace safety regulations—and that's what's screwed up the doors, or the house is haunted, has grabbed your people . . ." One slim finger jabbed toward a broad chest. ". . . including your daughters—who we saw entering the house this afternoon—which is why you've lost your vaunted cool, and that red flash was the house keeping you—all of you—the hell out. Were you not listening when I said we've done the research? Why don't you tell us what's really going on?"

"Vaunted cool?" Elson muttered.

"Not now, Jack."

"I think you're confused, Constable Danvers." CB's voice had returned to its usual masterful tones. "My studio is shooting a haunted house episode in this building. The house, therefore, is haunted because I choose it to be."

"Uh-huh." She rocked back on her heels, eyes narrowed. "And the murder/suicides?"

"Not in this episode."

"Not in *any* episode." Emphasis dared him to deny he knew about the incident she referred to.

"Ah. You're referring to the unfortunate deaths of Mrs. Kranby and her infant son?"

"And the others. In the thirties, a number of people were killed during a dance. During her time in the house, Mrs. Kranby heard dance music. In the fifties, Christopher Mills killed his two children and himself with an ax. Mrs. Kranby was terrified of a man with an ax that no one else ever saw."

"So you're saying that during her postpartum depression, Mrs. Kranby thought the house was haunted because of its unfortunate past?"

"No, that's not what she's saying." Elson, who'd been staring at his partner in disbelief, moved to stand beside her, shoulder to shoulder. "She's saying we're going to stick around until those doors open."

"Hauntings aren't against the law," Graham pointed out, folding his arms and moving up the path to fall in at Henry's right.

"No one said they were. But, since we're here and since it's our job to know what the hell is going on, I think we'll stay."

"You're wasting your time."

"It's our time." Eyes narrowed, Elson's expression dared all three men to try and run them off. When no one took the dare, he flashed them a triumphant grin. "Now, if you don't mind, just so we're dotting the i's and crossing the t's, I'm going to go try to open that door."

"You saw what happened to Mr. Brummell."

"I did."

CB stepped out of the way. "Then be my guest."

Graham tried and failed to hide a smirk as the pair of RCMP constables walked past.

A moment later, he tried and failed to hide a snicker as light flared red and Constable Elson swore, stumbled back, sat, and squashed an overgrown plant by the side of the path.

"Didn't go far," he murmured as Henry moved up beside him.

"I suspect that paranormal ability affects the amount of force used—got a lot, go far. None at all . . ." He nodded at the constable. ". . . don't."

"Yeah, but CB made some distance when he got zapped earlier."

"CB is a law unto himself."

Graham glanced back at the producer still standing by the end of the path somehow managing to dominate a scene that involved a haunted house, a shocked police officer, a medium, and a vampire and nodded. "I hear you. Satisfied?" he asked as the two constables passed again going the other way.

Elson glared at him but turned a less readable expression on Henry. "Static electricity, eh?"

"It's an explanation."

"Not a good one." He took Constable Danvers' arm and headed for the driveway. "We'll be waiting over here if you need us for . . . anything."

"Go ahead. Say it. Tell me I've lost my mind."

Rubbing the back of his neck in the hope of getting the hair to lie down, Jack stared up at the dark silhouette of the house. "I wish I could."

Geetha ignored the house and watched him. "You're glad I said it because you couldn't."

"Not glad." His mouth twisted into and out of half a smile. "I *know* there's something going on with these people. There was something going on last spring and there's something going on now. Something that isn't . . ." His hands sketched words in the air.

"Normal?"

"Close enough. And, although I'd rather you'd spoken to me before you info dumped on them, I'll hold my opinion on your mental state—and my own—until after those doors open." Folding his arms, Jack nodded toward the cluster of men on the front path. "Or until they tell us what's really going on."

"Is that why we're over here? So they can talk among themselves?"

They were close enough to the edge of the light she could see the glint of a pale eyebrow rising. "Yeah. That's one of the reasons."

And he wanted her away from them before she said anything else that might make it look like RCMP Constable Jack Elson believed in something other than crime and punishment, but she was too tired to take the bait. "The greasy one's right, though. If the house *is* haunted, that's not a crime."

"Granted."

"So why are we here?"

"We? Why are you here?"

"Because you are."

"Right." He rubbed the hand that had been in contact with the house against his sleeve. "I like to . . . I mean, I need to . . . We're supposed to . . ."

"Know?"

"I'm betting that Tony Foster is in the thick of it."

"Of what, Jack?"

"Yeah, that's the question." He sighed, unfolded his arms, and folded them again the other way. "I hate it when I know there's *something* and I don't know what it is."

She turned and stared at the three silhouettes on the path. "Bet you we could find something if we ran Graham Brummel."

"Sucker bet."

"A few misdemeanors, that's all. Nothing big. Oh, and a fraud charge down in Seattle that got tossed." Graham exhaled loudly. "Never take financial tips from a dead guy." A quick glance at Henry. "No offense."

"As, technically, I'm not dead; none taken."

"What? You're not dead? I thought you guys, you know . . ." He stuck out his tongue and let his head fall to one side. Before Henry could respond to an image unlike that of any unanimated death he'd ever seen, Graham jerked his head upright and said, "Wait, I should've tried this before. I just look at you on the spirit level . . ." His eyes unfocused. "Holy shit." Skin blanched gray, he snapped back to the here and now. "You're . . ."

Henry smiled.

"Mr. Fitzroy is not our problem," CB growled. Graham started at the sound and stuffed trembling hands deep into his overall pockets. "Our two overly diligent police officers are." His attention landed on Henry. "Can you take their memories?"

"Wipe them out like Arra did?" Henry shook his head. "No. Even . . ." He shot a glance at the caretaker. ". . . fucked up as I am, I could make them forget me, but they'd remember terror and darkness and the night and given that they're police officers and trained to both notice and investigate things like that and because they're already looking beyond the obvious—which is rare even for the police—I can't guarantee it would hold. Unless I took them both to bed—which I suspect would cause Constable Elson more trouble than anything else he might discover."

"Together or separately?"

A slow pivot on one heel. "Pardon?"

Graham shrugged, clearly wishing he'd kept his mouth shut and just as clearly unable to stop himself. "Would you take them to bed . . . you know, together or separately."

"Now, I'm offended."

"Sorry."

"When that door opens," CB said pointedly, "there will be at least one body, maybe more. There will be an investigation. Can Tony use Arra's information to erase the memories of the people inside the house?"

"I very much doubt it." Since, as far as Henry knew, Tony's one sure spell involved retrieving snack food without rising from the couch, erasing multiple memories would very likely be beyond him.

"So they'll know about his abilities and during the investigation . . ."

Henry nodded. "It'll come up. Especially if it's his abilities that get them out of the house."

"He'll either be the next amazing fucking Kreskin," Graham sighed, "and his life'll be hell, or he'll be stuffed in a loony bin. Trust me on this," he added when Henry and CB turned, frowning. "The world's not kind to the psychically abled. They tend to read the psychic as psycho, if you know what I mean."

"Unfortunately, yes."

"Fortunately, yes," Henry corrected deliberately. "I think we're looking at this the wrong way." He waved the other two quiet and began to build the ending as though he were building the final chapter in one of his books. "When the doors open—at sunrise, if not before—your people will come out of the house claiming it's haunted. That they saw ghosts. That they were under an attack by a malevolent thing in the basement. They won't be able to prove any of it, though, and the general public will think they're nuts. And given that they're television people, they won't get the benefit of the doubt. Everyone knows television people are slightly crazy."

"Is this true?" CB wondered.

Graham nodded. "Common knowledge around Hollywood North, that's for damned sure."

"Now then, put hallucinating television people in a house with a history of gas leaks and what do you have?"

"Probable cause of crazy. What?" Graham demanded as eyebrows raised. "I watch a lot of Law and Order."

"Who doesn't?" CB wearily asked the night. "Suppose my people say nothing at all about hauntings or ghosts or things in the basement? Suppose they collectively agree on a more plausible story?"

"It won't matter; even if they could agree on a story—and most groups that size can't agree on where to have lunch—there's no way they'll all be able to maintain it throughout a police investigation."

"The truth will out?"

"And not be believed."

His next question was less rhetorical. "Did we not use a gas leak to explain what happened at the studio last spring?"

"There's a reason it's a classic," Henry reminded him. "And I'm guessing—given that the police know the other deaths in this house were murder/

suicides—that the actual cause of your wardrobe assistant's death will be obvious. People were trapped in a house. They all went a little crazy. Someone went a lot crazy and killed someone else."

"And that someone is probably dead, too," Graham added. "If the house stays to the same MO."

"So the actual crime committed becomes an open and shut case. Why did they go crazy?" Henry spread his hands. "Not our problem. What exactly caused the doors to jam shut? Also not our problem. One of the people trapped did amazing magical things? But we've already established that they all went a little crazy, so no one can be considered a reliable witness."

"But these two . . ." Graham nodded toward the driveway. ". . . think something is up."

"And it's one thing to tell us what they think is going on and another thing entirely to put it in an official document. They're not stupid, they've proven that already. If they find out what actually happened, who can they tell? Not only is there no empirical proof, there's no way to get it."

"Whoa. What about you? You're walking, talking, empirical proof, eh?"

"They don't know about me."

Graham snorted. "You're standing right there." As Henry's eyes darkened again, he backed up a step. "Oh. Right. They don't *know* about you. And no one who does is going to say anything. Not a word. Lips are sealed. Hey, I talk to the dead; who am I to point fingers, right?"

"Right." The masks were back in place. The smile held only the faintest hint of warning. "Given that there's been a death, the sooner the police are involved, the better our people . . ." CB's people except for Tony. ". . . your people . . . look. And given that these particular police are already somewhat sympathetic to the situation . . ."

"Sympathetic?" CB growled.

"To the situation," Henry repeated. "And if they do mention anything about hauntings, well, there's no faster way for anything else they say to lose credibility with the powers that be." A quick glance at the house. "The judicial powers that be."

"Yeah and what about the press?" Graham demanded. "Friggin' tabloids'll be all over something like this."

Henry glanced up at CB, one eyebrow cocked. After a moment, CB smiled. "Of course. Given the right slant, this may even provide *Darkest Night* with a bonanza of free publicity. May even jump our ratings. If there's a chance that ghosts are real, why not vampires?"

"You might want to go easy with that."

"Of course."

⟿ SEVENTEEN

Tony regained consciousness slowly, pulled out of a comforting darkness by the suspicion that while he was gone, people had been sticking red hot needles into the left side of his body. When he forced his eyes open, Brianna's face swam into focus.

"He's awake!" she yelled without turning her head.

Amy's face appeared almost immediately behind her. "You okay?"

"Maybe. You?"

"I didn't even go out." She sounded disappointed. "I just got woozy. Define *maybe*."

"Define *okay*."

"Not about to kick it."

Fair enough. "Not sure," he told her in turn. "Help me sit up."

Relying on Amy and Brianna's help, he ended up slumped against familiar lower cabinets. Still in the butler's pantry, then. Not good. Expressions on the half circle of faces staring down at him seemed to support that conclusion.

"The doors are still locked." The voice of doom from above.

He blinked up at Peter. "It didn't work?"

"Worked," Mouse told him before Peter could say anything more. "Caulfield's rotting. The wall's clean. Cleaner," he amended, clearly remembering he was speaking of a fieldstone foundation.

Peter's lips were thin, white lines. "But the doors are still locked."

"Okay." Tony managed to raise his right hand. "Let me think about this. Caulfield's gone . . ."

Mouse shot a hard look at Peter and nodded.

". . . the symbols that held the accumulated power to that specific spot on the basement wall are gone . . . Lee!"

"Lee's fine," Zev told him, handing him a bottle of water. "All right, he's not exactly fine, but he's back. He's himself. Tina and Mason and Ashley are . . . dealing with him."

Comforting. Zev had been going to say comforting, but changed it to dealing at the last moment. Tony could see another pair of legs in dark trousers tucked in behind Mason, but he couldn't see Lee. He wasn't sure he wanted to see Lee as long as he knew Lee was fine. Back. Himself.

"Lee is not your concern," Peter interrupted his train of thought, looking thoroughly pissed. "Your job is to figure out why the hell the doors are still locked!"

"Right." He could do that. It would keep him from thinking about Lee. Stalling for time while he got things straight in his head, he took a swallow of water and almost spat it out. Zev had dumped sugar into it. "Okay," he muttered, shooting his ex a *thanks for the warning* glare. "The power was cohesive down there for a long time. Maybe it stayed together even without the symbols—maybe it chose to stay together. It was definitely a separate thing from Caulfield, so maybe it had a kind of consciousness. It could go wandering off through the city, but it's choosing to stay as a part of this house."

"Why?"

The lights came up. The band played "Night and Day." In the ballroom, the dead danced.

"Because the house is feeding it," Tony sighed, knowing that although they couldn't see him, they could still hear him. "The ghosts are still trapped."

"If it's not trying to add us to the collection anymore, then we just sit tight and wait it out." Peter glared at Mason and Mouse, who did their best to look sane. Kate glared back. "It can't be that long until sunrise."

"Probably not." Not knowing was making Tony a little edgy. Edgier. Was Henry still outside?

"They're not our responsibility; they've been dead for years."

It took Tony a moment to realize just who *they* were and switch back over to the problems inside the house. After four-hundred-and-fifty-odd years—some of these later ones, very odd—Henry knew enough to get out of the sun. "Brenda and Hartley and Tom are trapped, too."

"You know, we only have your word for that."

"And mine." Brianna folded her arms, every line of her body daring Peter to argue. "I danced with her."

"Fine." He sighed impatiently. "Brenda, Hartley, and Tom are trapped, too."

"And Karl's still crying. I can hear him."

As Brianna pressed up against Tony's side, he felt something crumple in his pocket. The photograph of Karl and his mother. "I can hear him, too." He pulled the photo out and handed it to Amy. Multiple dunkings in icy water hadn't improved its condition any, but it was still painfully obvious who it . . . they were.

"So we have to free the ghosts." Amy left the *duh* silent but obvious as she passed the picture to Peter.

He studied it for a moment, looked up, realized everyone was waiting on his word, and sighed again. "Fine. We free the ghosts." His gaze locked on Tony's. "What do we do?"

"I don't know."

"You don't know?" Peter repeated and threw up his hands. "Great. Does *anyone* know?"

No one seemed to.

Tony glanced down at the top of Brianna's head, and frowned. "According to the journal, Caulfield used his son, Richard, to connect with the power and Richard is haunting the master suite bathroom."

"Are you going somewhere with this, Tony," Amy asked, peering into his face, "or are you just reiterating random bits of information?"

"He doesn't replay. All the other ghosts replay," he continued as the expressions he could see ranged the short distance from puzzled to confused. "Even Stephen and Cassie keep getting sucked back into the loop of their death although they're aware the rest of the time. Richard doesn't. And he's always there. Even Mason was aware of him."

"Hey." The qualifier got the actor's attention. "What do you mean, *even* Mason?"

"He means you're generally considered too smart to get mixed up in any supernatural nonsense," Peter interjected smoothly.

"Oh."

Amy reached out and poked him in the leg. "Get to the point, Tony."

"Richard Caulfield is the key."

A moment of contemplative silence.

Then Adam asked what they were all wondering. "The key to what?"

"To freeing the ghosts, starving the thing, and getting us the hell out of Dodge."

Peter took the photograph from Amy. The way he was staring at it made Tony realize he probably had kids of his own. For a long moment, the distant sobs of a dead baby were the only sounds in the butler's pantry. Finally, Peter shoved the photograph into Tony's hand and jerked his head toward the door. "So, what are you waiting for? Go turn your key."

Right. Because, of course, it was his job to be the hero. They'd already established that. His left hand and everything attached to it was pretty much unusable with only minimal movement in the fingers *and* his entire arm felt as though someone had peeled all the skin off before seasoning it liberally with chopped jalapeños, but, wizard or not, he was just a PA and crap jobs landed like sediment down there at the bottom of the totem pole. Standing hurt. Hell, breathing hurt. He was working his way up to feeling really remarkably sorry for himself when a high-pitched voice slammed the door on his pity party.

"I'm coming with you."

"Bri."

She looked up at him and said very slowly and very pointedly, "He's not scared of *me*."

But he'd been terrified of his father and Tony was a man. Younger, thinner, and with more piercings, but still . . .

"Okay. Sure." He expected Tina to protest, but she was still too busy mothering Lee to even notice. "Can you carry the lantern?"

"She can, but she probably shouldn't." Zev picked up the lantern off the counter just before Brianna's hand connected. "I'll come along, too."

"So will I."

"No." Peter physically put himself in Amy's path. "Caulfield might be gone, but this house remains dangerous. The fewer people we have wandering around, the better."

Amy jabbed a finger toward Brianna. "No fair! She's the boss' daughter and you're letting her wander around!" Her mouth closed with a sudden snap. "That sounded about six, didn't it?"

Tony and Zev nodded in unison.

"Brianna's going because the boy isn't afraid of her. Tony's going because this is his show . . ."

Oh. Well, that sounded significantly better than *Tony's going because we don't want to endanger anyone more significant.*

Stop being such a whiny ass, he told himself.

But my arm hurts.

Deal with it. You're still the only one who can do this.

". . . and Zev's going because Tony looks like shit and I'm not sure he can make it up the stairs without help," Peter continued. "You . . ." He jabbed a finger toward Amy. ". . . are not going. We're all going to sit here and stay out of Tony's way. The last thing he needs on his plate right now is another rescue."

Shoulders slumped, Amy shoved her hands into her pants pockets. "Fine. Whatever."

"So, go!" Peter waved at the door and Tony, who'd been staring at him in astonishment, shuffled forward, feeling good about being appreciated. *Feeling good* being a relative term and nothing twelve hours of sleep and a kilo of painkillers couldn't fix.

Cassie and Stephen were waiting in the dining room, held out of the butler's pantry by the line of lipstick symbols on the floor. As Zev pulled the door closed, they rushed forward looking . . . looking as happy as Tony'd ever seen dead people look. Well, except for Henry, who was really more undead than dead.

"It worked!" Stephen spun around them faster than mortally possible. "I wrote half and Cassie wrote half. We put it up between his shoulders and it worked!"

Tony hid a smile. Stephen sounded as though the plan had been his idea from the start. *Teenagers*. He thanked them after he explained to Zev and Brianna that they were there. No more talking to empty air. "You saved Lee. I'm sure of it."

"No problem. And the thing is gone. There's a whole different feeling in the house now. Different even from when it was asleep. It's still . . . I mean there's still *something*, but it isn't aware anymore. We're more aware than it is. And we're still us." He took hold of his sister's hands and spun her around. Stopped, settled his head, and grinned. At her. As though she was the only person in his world—which, technically, Tony supposed she was. "We're still here. Together. Only the bad stuff has changed. And you look awful."

"Yeah. You should see it from this side."

Cassie seemed happy, laughed with her brother, allowed him to spin her around, but, for the first time, seemed the more reserved of the two.

"You're still replaying," Tony reminded him as they left the dining room.

"True. But we're used to that." Stephen dismissed his reoccurring death with a jaunty smack on his sister's ass. She shot him a look Tony couldn't translate. "Once you're gone and there's no people in the house, it'll happen less and less and then what remains of the thing will probably go to sleep again and we'll be left alone. Not completely alone, because Graham will be here, but left alone. No one bothering us."

"You don't mind being dead?"

"Hey, I guess I'm used to that, too."

"Where are you three going?" Cassie asked as they reached the stairs. And the way she asked told Tony why she hadn't joined her brother's slightly manic celebration. She knew it wasn't over.

"To talk to Creighton Caulfield's son. Cassie wants to know where we're going," he explained to Zev, grabbing the back of Brianna's pinafore with his good hand. "We're staying together," he told her as she glared up at him. "That means no running off."

"So walk faster!"

The ghosts floated backward in front of them, up the stairs.

Stephen snorted. "Why do you want to talk to Richard? He's not exactly a sparkling conversationalist."

"Creighton Caulfield was a part of the thing in the basement." Tony's arm hurt all the way down to his legs. Both legs. And his feet. And all ten toes. "Caulfield's dead."

"Yeah, we know. We helped, remember? So you're what, off to offer Richard your condolences?"

The stairs were killing him. "No."

"Then why?" Stephen demanded, impatient with anything getting in the way of his good mood.

Cassie smoothed down her skirt, her fingers carefully arranging each gather. "He's why we're here." She seemed to be confirming something she'd known for a while even if she'd only just realized she'd known it.

One hand holding his head in place, Stephen spun around toward her. "What are you talking about?"

"Creighton Caulfield's son, Richard, is why we're still here. They . . ." A chill breeze as she gestured. ". . . are going to talk to him about us—about all of us—moving on."

"NO!"

Tony froze. Zev and Brianna went up one more step, half turned, and stopped as well. They might have started back toward him, Tony wasn't sure. His eyes were locked on the ghost. "Stephen . . ."

"We helped you!"

It was like the scene in Scrooge's rooms in *A Christmas Carol* when Marley's ghost shrieked, and suddenly the slightly comical dead guy looked a lot more dangerous.

"We risked everything to help you and now you're doing this? I knew it! You're trying to destroy us!" Hands outstretched, fingers crooking into translucent claws, Stephen dove toward him.

Tony didn't know if he was going for his throat or about to drive his hands into his chest and squeeze his heart—both classic ghost-goes-in-for-the-kill possibilities—but he did discover that under the right conditions—like, oh, threat of imminent death by severely pissed ghost—his left arm moved. Hurt like hell, but it moved. He smacked his branded palm into the side of Stephen's head, flinging him across the entrance hall. Tried to blink away the fireworks exploding inside his own skull, then positioned himself in front of the other two as Stephen came shrieking back.

Cassie was there first.

"It's over," she said softly. "We had each other for so much longer than we should have, but it's over."

"NO!" When he tried to go around, she blocked him again.

She glanced back at Tony over her shoulder, her face at such an angle that she looked whole and beautiful. "Go on. I won't let him stop you."

"What's happening?" Brianna demanded.

"Stephen's pissed. Cassie's keeping him from hurting us." Tony grabbed Brianna's free hand and motioned for Zev to start moving again. "We have to get there before the next replay," he explained as they half dragged her up the stairs between them. "The sooner we finish this the better."

"But it's you and me against everyone else!" Stephen's protests followed them up to the second floor—lost, disbelieving, and painfully young. "You and me, Cass! It *can't* be over! We did what he wanted! Why is he doing this to us?"

"He's doing this for us. It's time to move on to someplace better."

"You don't know what you're talking about! Get out of my way, I have to stop . . ."

As the door to Mason's dressing room closed and cut off the argument, Tony hoped Cassie was right. He could be sending them to hell for all he knew. Did he have the right to choose for them?

"They chose when they agreed to help in the basement," Zev said quietly. "They decided to risk moving on no matter what might happen to them."

"How did you . . ."

He smiled and shook his head. "When you feel something strongly—like, say, guilt—it's all over your face."

Brianna nodded agreement.

"Not just when I'm thinking about Lee?"

"All the time."

"Well, that's . . . embarrassing."

Zev nodded. "Most of the time, yeah. Come on." He held the lantern up and led the way to the bathroom, pausing on the threshold to let Brianna push past.

Tony stopped beside him and peered into the small room. "Where is he?" He squinted along the line of Brianna's pointing finger. There was something . . . something too big for the space between the toilet and the corner shower unit. A shape. A shadow. No. Gone.

"You really can't see him?" Zev murmured.

"I really can't." Then, "Can you see him?"

"No. It's just that Brianna can and you can see everything else, so . . ." The music director shrugged. "Seems strange."

"As compared to what?"

"Good point."

He could hear a snuffling sound, but he couldn't see . . .

"Stop seeing the bathroom."

"What?"

Squatting by the shower in the boneless way of small children and elderly Asian men, Brianna rolled her eyes. "Stop seeing the bathroom," she repeated.

He took a step into the room. "How do I do that?"

The look she shot him suggested he was stupider than she'd ever suspected. "Pretend it's not there."

Right. Sure. He could play let's pretend. Let's pretend he didn't still wake up aching for the feel of teeth meeting through his skin. Let's pretend Lee had kissed him in the butler's pantry because he'd wanted to, not because of some weird mix of guilt and being possessed. Let's pretend that the something between the toilet and the tub had plenty of room because neither toilet nor tub were there.

Actually, he sucked at let's pretend.

"Tony?"

And he didn't want to know what was showing on his face. A raised hand to answer Zev's question and another step into the room. No toilet. No shower. Focus on the something between them. Just the something.

He might suck at let's pretend, but he aced obsession.

Brianna was talking to Caulfield's son, so Caulfield's son was obviously there . . .

. . . sitting on the floor, leaning against the side of a big old wardrobe that filled the corner where the shower . . .

The scene wavered.

. . . that filled the far corner of the dingy room. The walls were gray, the floor some kind of early industrial tile, and if he'd had a cigarette, the smell would have reminded him of nights spent crouched in doorways on the Yonge Street strip. Hard to forget the smell of old urine walked on by expensive shoes.

Blond, blue-eyed, and somewhere between twelve and twenty, Richard Caulfield had Down's syndrome. Tony was no expert, but he'd known people with Down's syndrome and this didn't look like it was that severe a case. Certainly not lock-the-kid-in-a-room severe. Still, in a hundred years he supposed the definition of severe changed and, not to forget, he'd already determined that Creighton Caulfield was bugfuck. Evil and bugfuck.

Bare feet peeking out from under a white-and-blue-striped nightshirt, Richard hugged his knees, rocked, and cried. Every now and then, he wiped his nose on the fabric stretched over his knees. That explained the snuffling sound.

Brianna, crouched in front of him, was telling him about what had been happening down in the butler's pantry. ". . . and like Ashes keeps falling asleep because she's a total loser until Mason, he's the actor I told you about, he stopped being a spaz and they untied him and then she was all over him again and the real creepy bit is that he seems to like it now."

Ashley's adoration would act like an anchor, redefining Mason's unpossessed self. Mouse had his viewfinder. Mason had a fan. Kate had her temper. And Lee, who'd been through so much more, Lee probably had a whole lot of therapy to look forward to.

"Get down." Brianna's voice cut through his reflections. "You're too tall and you scare him."

So Tony crouched. "Hey, Richard."

Richard tried to push back farther into the space.

"It's okay." He held out his hand, expecting Richard to cringe away, not expecting a grab that flipped stubby fingers through his with no contact. The wail of despair brought tears to his own eyes.

"What's wrong?" Brianna demanded.

Tony wasn't sure if she was asking him or Richard, but he answered anyway. "He's lonely. He's been alone up here for a long time." Resting one knee on the floor, he glanced down at the throbbing pattern on his left palm, cupped his left elbow with his right hand, and lifted. The fingers of his left hand brushed the warm, damp skin of Richard's cheek, trailed down, and were suddenly clutched so tightly that he literally saw stars.

"Easy," he gasped. Richard seemed to understand. The pressure eased off a bit. Most of the stars faded. "Good. Thank you."

"Ank ou."

"Hey, you can talk!"

"Risherd Cawfud."

"That's your name!" Brianna punched Tony. "That's his name!"

"No hit!"

To Tony's surprise she looked abashed at Richard's protest. "Sorry."

"S'okay. Richard . . ."

"Risherd Cawfud."

"Right. Richard . . ."

"Risherd Cawfud."

Okay. Rewrite and try again. "You don't need to be afraid anymore."

New tears. And a tighter grip.

"OW!"

Richard cringed back but continued to cling to Tony's hand. "Shurry. Shurry! No hit!"

Brianna understood immediately. "Tony's not going to hit you!" Her voice lowered to a near growl, and Tony was, once again, reminded of her father. "No one is ever going to hit you again!"

And like her father, it was impossible not to believe her.

"Not hit?"

"Never again! Tony . . ."

"No hit," Tony agreed as reassuringly as the pain allowed. "Come on." He started to stand and thanked any gods that might be listening when Richard scrambled up onto his feet with him. "It's time to go."

"Go where?" Brianna asked as Richard wiped his nose on the back of Tony's hand and stared trustingly at them both.

Good question.

Where did the dead go? Questions of religion aside.

A snail trail of snot glistened on the back of Tony's hand.

Glistened.

I'm an idiot.

Where did the dead always go?

"Go into the light."

"Cliché much," Brianna muttered.

Richard looked worried. "No leave room."

"You don't have to." When Tony smiled, Richard smiled with him. "All you have to do is walk into the light. It's right here. It's been here all along." He stepped closer to Brianna so that Richard could look past him.

His eyes widened and his smile with it. "Light."

"Yeah."

The one thing all the replays had in common was light. He'd thought, while it was happening, that it was just the difference between the small circle of light thrown by the lantern or the candles or his monitor and the gas or electric lights of the past. In his own defense, while it was happening, he'd had other things on his mind. But the light had been exactly the same for all the replays. Richard didn't replay, but the light was exactly the same in his room.

Wiping his nose one more time, Richard shuffled forward. Tony moved with him, teeth clenched, trying not to scream as the movement pulled his arm out away from his body. As he turned, pivoting to follow, the light grew until there was only light and Richard Caulfield silhouetted in front of it.

It was like the world's cheesiest special effect. All it needed was that Czechoslovakian women's choir that seemed to be wailing in harmony on every soundtrack recorded in the last twenty years.

The extended dance version of "Night and Day" just didn't have the same effect.

Tony could only see Richard, but he could feel the crowd passing by. As they brushed against his injured arm, falling to his knees and screaming was starting to feel more and more like a good idea. Richard held him in place.

There might have been voices and some of the touching might have gotten a bit personal, but he couldn't be sure over the distraction of his arm.

Distraction.

Yeah. When distraction meant constant bone-grinding, blood-boiling agony. He wanted to snatch his hand away, but he couldn't. After so many years alone in this room, it had to be Richard's choice.

The outside edges of the light started to close in. A gentle tug.

"Come with."

"I can't." A harder tug that should have hurt more than it did. "It's all right.

You won't be alone. You won't ever be alone again unless you want to be. But you have to go into the light."

"Risherd Cawfud."

Tony managed a smile. "I'll remember."

The band stopped playing and the light condensed into a brilliant globe that lingered for a moment with the touch of Richard's fingers against Tony's palm.

Then it was gone.

"Do you see that?"

"See what?" CB asked as the two RCMP constables rejoined them on the path.

"The um . . ." Elson gestured with one hand and then stopped, fully aware that no one—not the three guys they'd joined, nor the three people who'd just come out of one of the trucks, nor his partner, nor, hell, himself—was looking at anything other than the brilliant white light rising up from the house. "The that."

"Yes, Constable, we see it."

"Okay. Good. What is it?"

"If pressed, I'd have to say it's a shocking absence of originality."

Something hummed.

Something sparked.

And the lights came on.

They were standing in the bathroom of the master suite.

The light over the sink was on.

"What the hell just happened?" Zev demanded. "Are you two all right?"

Tony glanced at Brianna, who shrugged. "Yeah, we're fine." And then added, surprised. "Really." His left arm no longer hurt. The symbol was still there on his palm, etched into his skin like a scar, but everything worked. Muscles, ligaments, bones, joints, those stringy things that attached stuff . . . tendons, that was it. Everything. No pain. The absence left him a little light-headed.

Light-headed.

The light.

It had to have been the light. Or some kind of freaky coincidence, but Tony preferred to think he'd sent Cassie and Stephen and Richard and Tom and Hartley and, hell, even Brenda to a place where good things happened.

They could hear shouting downstairs.

"We should join the rest of them." Zev gestured with the lantern. Brianna took his other hand and led the way out to the hall.

As Zev flicked the hall light on, Tony paused.

He could hear . . .

"You guys go on, I'll be down in a minute."

"I don't think . . ."

Then they all heard: "Ashley! Brianna!"

"DADDY!"

Zev shook his head as Brianna yanked her hands free and raced for the stairs. "I should go with her, so he knows we weren't letting her wander around alone."

"Go on. I'll be fine." Tony could see that the other man didn't entirely believe him—or more specifically didn't believe him at all but decided to give him the benefit of the doubt. He watched until Zev disappeared down the stairs then turned and headed the other way.

Paused at the door to the bathroom, flicked on the light, glanced in. White walls. A scuff on the floor from where the camera had been set up. Not where the noise was coming from. He left the light on.

At the door to the back stairs, he recognized the sound.

Er er. Er er.

When he opened the door, Lucy Lewis was sitting on the lowest step leading to the third floor, the noose around her neck, the end of the rope—the rope he'd cut with the ax he couldn't see—hanging against the upper bib of her apron.

He frowned. Thought about it for a moment. "You died before Richard did."

She nodded, toying with the end of her rope.

The light levels hadn't been the same in all the replays. They'd always been different at the back stairs. Not as bright. "You weren't under the control of the thing when you pushed that guy, were you?"

"No." Her voice sounded a little better now the pressure on her throat had been relieved. More like the engine on an old truck and less like a working cement mixer. "He said he loved me and then he met this girl from town . . ."

Oldest story in the book. "You gave the thing the murder /suicide template. Two dead for the price of one."

She shrugged.

A glance down the back stairs showed nothing but a patch of kitchen floor. And a black cat. "So *he's* gone?"

A nod and an adjustment that reminded him of Stephen. They'd barely been gone for ten minutes and he was missing them already. And they *had* gone into the light with the rest. Of course they had. They hadn't been responsible for what they'd done that last afternoon of their lives and if they were, well, they'd certainly paid. He asked, but Lucy shrugged.

"Not part of my story."

Yeah. That was helpful. "Okay, your story's still . . . uh . . . in progress because . . . ?"

Her hand closed around the dangling rope. "I need to make amends."

"You saved my ass. I don't think I'd have made it to the basement if you hadn't come in and diverted the pain. And if I hadn't made it to the basement, we'd all still be stuck here. That's amends where I come from."

"You're not enough."

"Way to pander to the old ego."

"What?"

"Never mind. You think God . . ."

"Not God. Me. *I* need to make amends."

Ah. That was different.

She waved the cut end of the rope at him. "This will help, thank you. I can do much more now than if I was just hanging around."

Joke? He wasn't sure. She looked perfectly serious. "If the rope's cut, how come I can still hear it creaking?"

"The house remembers."

Before he could decide if that was something he should seriously freak out about, the stairs were empty. "So, um, maybe I'll see you again?"

"*You know where to find me.*"

Fair enough.

The night caught up to him as he started down the stairs. By the time he staggered past the cat, events were sitting on his shoulders and bouncing, trying to drive him to his knees. He grabbed the edge of the kitchen table. Heard shouting. May have heard his name although his ears didn't seem to be working properly. Or they weren't connecting to his brain properly. There seemed to be a lot of high-pitched howling going on. He stumbled toward the back door. It was open about four inches to allow the bundles of cable access to the house.

"Ha!" he said to no one in particular as he grabbed the edge and yanked it open.

A step out into fresh air.

Another step.

More voices.

Another step and he was falling.

Either I'm walking crooked or the porch is.

Funny thing, he didn't hit the ground.

"I've got you."

Not the voice he was expecting. He blinked and, like he was suddenly Samantha Stevens and that whole blinking thing actually meant something, the world came rushing back. The man holding him was blonder than Henry. Bigger, too. Smelled like stale pizza and . . . law enforcement.

"Constable Elson."

"So you can talk."

"For years now." He was oddly comfortable cradled across the lap of an RCMP officer. *Not going to think about* that *too hard.*

"You know, since I busted my butt to keep you from landing chin first in gravel, you think you could lay off the smart-ass for a minute?"

Seemed fair. "Sure."

"What the hell happened here?"

Best to stick to the basics. "The doors wouldn't open."

"That door *was* open."

Tony turned his head just far enough to see the cables running up over the porch and into the kitchen. Then he turned it back. Jack Elson had very blue eyes and they were locked on his. Not at all hard to tell what he wanted. "You want the truth." Given his current state of exhaustion, Tony found it impossible to stop his lips from twitching.

"Do *not* tell me I can't handle the truth!" Elson snapped.

Fortunately, he didn't have the energy to laugh for long. Even more fortunate that he didn't have the energy for hysterics because he sure as hell was due. He half expected the constable to dump him onto the driveway but he didn't. Finally he managed a long, shuddering breath, and said, "*I* can't handle the truth right now. Can I tell you later?"

The blue eyes narrowed and examined his face.

Tony tried to look trustworthy but gave it up after a second or two as a lost cause.

"That depends on when later is."

"Not now?"

After a long moment, narrow lips curved, pale stubble glinting in the porch light.

Something growled.

No. Tony knew that sound. Some*one* growled. "Henry."

"Your partner is calling for you, Constable Elson."

A familiar pale hand reached down, took hold of Tony, and lifted him to his feet. Then the arm attached to the hand went around his waist and effortlessly kept him standing. Constable Elson rose under his own power, eyes locked on Henry's face. Given his reaction, Tony could tell without looking that Henry had the Prince of Man thing going full blast and would, in a heartbeat or two, slide into Prince of Darkness. Not a good idea. Not tonight. Not here. Not now. He just wasn't up to it. So he said, "Call me. You have my number."

A long look, and a nod, and Elson trotted off to where Constable Danvers was directing a crowd of police and EMTs. Ah. Not howling. Sirens.

Glad to have that explained, he turned in Henry's grip. "So you're still here."

"Obviously."

"It must be nearly dawn."

"Nearly. I have forty minutes."

Tony actually felt his heart lurch. "You can't . . ."

"It's all right. I'll wrap up in the blackout curtain in my trunk."

"In your trunk?"

"It's a big trunk, it's lightproof, and once I'm in it, it can only be opened from the inside. I've made some modifications."

"You were prepared for this?" Relief made his knees weak. Well, relief on top of everything else.

"This? Not likely. But I was prepared." Henry pulled his keys out of his pocket and offered them discreetly on his palm. "Can you drive me back to the condo's garage?"

"Sure."

"Think about it for a moment, Tony. Can you?"

If he didn't . . . "Of course I can."

"You look terrible."

That didn't exactly come as a surprise. "You look kind of off peak yourself."

"It was an interesting night."

His tone suggested Tony let it go. Reluctantly, Tony did.

The keys were cool and heavier than they looked. Which reminded him. He moved so that Henry's body blocked him from the milling crowds out front and he stretched out his left hand toward the house. Caulfield's journal slapped against the pattern on his palm.

"Impressive."

"Thanks." He hadn't doubted for a moment he'd be able to do it. Had known where the journal was, touched the shape of its power, and had called it to him. It hadn't even hurt. Much. He'd come a long way in a short time from bagels and honey. "You need to take charge of this. I don't trust anyone else with it."

Henry's lip curled at the touch of the leather. "It feels familiar."

"I think Caulfield found what was intended to be another grimoire like the one you have, but it hadn't been written in yet, so he made it his own." He frowned at Henry's expression. "I think!"

The expression changed; quickly enough that Tony knew he'd called it close to right. "Of course you do. I have to go."

"I know."

"You're all right?"

"I'm fine."

The hug drove the breath out of his lungs and gave him some indication of how much Henry had worried. Then he was gone, moving up the driveway in such a way that it was hard to watch him. Even with practice. Another man would have seen only shadows. Tony knew the difference.

He frowned as Henry was suddenly very visibly standing at CB's side. The big man put his hand on Henry's shoulder for a moment, nodded, smiled, and then Henry was gone.

Henry and CB?

Tony didn't like the look of that. His hand tightened around the keys.

Sure Henry came to the set on occasion and maybe he'd helped defeat the shadows last spring, but CB was his. CB Productions was his. Not Henry's.

What the hell had been going on out here?

"So the spirits have done it all in one night."

He grinned and met Amy halfway.

"I brought your laptop out."

"Thanks." Tucking it under his arm he fell into step beside her.

"I think he likes you."

"Who?"

"RCMP Special Constable Jack Elson. You guys going to get together?"

"I don't date straight boys."

"Right. They're taking Everett to the hospital," she said, breaking the chaos swirling around them into chunks. "Tina made some calls and she's going with him."

"Good."

"You should maybe think about a trip yourself. You look like crap."

"Maybe later. And thank you."

"There're cops swarming all over the bodies. They seem to get what happened with Brenda and Hartley, but Tom's giving them palpitations. Good thing there's a full body print of him on that window."

"Word."

"Brianna won't let go of Zev's hand, and Mason's actually being kind of sweet to Ashley. Although I think he's using her as a distraction, so he doesn't grab a smoke in front of witnesses. He's a star, you know, got to keep up appearances."

Mason was still wearing Raymond Dark's fangs. Ashley was still wearing Mason's jacket.

"Whatever works."

She snorted. "You're feeling mellow."

"It's not mellow, it's exhaustion. You know, that moment of clarity just before you puke?"

"And wouldn't that be the perfect end. Speaking of perfect ends, what have you got on your ass? And don't get too excited about the perfect bit," she added through a yawn. "It was just a convenient segue."

Between twisting and dragging his jeans around, he managed to see a small heart. Two pieces. Drawn in white paint, each line thick at the top and then trailing off at the end.

I wrote half and Cassie wrote half . . ."

"So what is it?"

"I'm pretty sure it's a happy ending."

She bumped her shoulder with his. About as sucky as Amy got. Four-hundred-year-old vampires hugged. Amy bumped. "Speaking of, I think someone wants to talk to you."

He turned instinctively toward where Zev and Brianna stood by CB.

"Idiot." Amy took hold of his shoulders and turned him toward Lee sitting in the open back of an ambulance, a blanket draped over his slumped shoulders.

"He doesn't . . ."

She shoved him forward. "Yes, he does."

Yes, he did. That was obvious when Tony came closer.

"You okay?" Stupid question. The man was sitting in an ambulance.

"I guess. I don't know. They want to check me out. Thanks for . . . uh . . ."

"The T-shirt?" Tony offered hurriedly. He had no idea of how much Lee remembered of the basement, but he wasn't going to be the one to bring it up.

Lee stared at him for a long moment, then he smiled. There was nothing of Caulfield in it. Tony felt his heart start beating again as a fear he hadn't been willing to admit was banished. Since leaving the house, his heart had been having a rough time of it.

"Yeah. For the T-shirt."

"All right, Mr. Nicholas, let's go." The EMT began to step up into the ambulance, got a good look at Tony, and paused. "Has someone seen you?"

"Seen me?"

"Have you received attention from emergency personnel?"

Tony wondered if she always talked like that or if Lee's presence was making her self-conscious. "No."

"Wait right there." She pointed to a spot about a meter from the back of the ambulance. "There'll be another team along shortly. Now, Mr. Nicholas . . ."

Lee raised his head. "Could you give us a minute?"

She hesitated.

"Please."

And melted.

"But no more than a minute," she warned as she moved just out of eavesdropping range.

Lee took a deep breath. Hesitated. Visibly remembered their time limit and said quietly, "When I kissed you. I wasn't kissing Brenda's ghost."

Tony blinked, but it was still Lee. "Good," he managed. "And, you know, eww."

"Yeah."

That howling was back in his ears again. Not a siren this time. "So what happens now?" he asked as the EMT tapped her watch and pointedly climbed on board.

Lee shrugged. "The show goes on."

"I meant . . ."

His smile held regret and something a little lost as the doors closed. "I know."

Smoke and Ashes

 ONE

Although both moon and stars were hidden behind cloud, the night was not as dark as it could have been. The light from streetlamps bounced off pale concrete, providing illumination enough to make the two men walking along the empty sidewalk clearly visible.

The dark-haired man shoved his hands deeper into the pockets of his brown suede jacket. "I know we didn't have much of a choice, but I don't like how that ended."

"It ended the way it had to end," the blond replied with a weary smile. And if his teeth were just a little too white and preternaturally long, there was no one there to note it. They might have been the only two men alive in the entire city. Their footsteps should have echoed . . . that's how alone they seemed.

"I don't like circumstances making my choices for me."

"Who does?"

"You don't seem to be having any trouble."

"I've just had a lot more practice at hiding . . ." His voice trailed off and, frowning, he looked up.

"That's it. Good. Lee, follow his gaze. A woman screams and . . ."

A plaid flannel body pillow, clearly weighted, dropped down onto the sidewalk about three feet in front of the actors.

". . . and the unfortunate lady lands. Cut!" Peter Hudson moved out from behind the monitors, pulling off his headset and tossing it back in the general direction of his black canvas chair. Tina, his script supervisor, reached out and snagged the set just before it hit the pavement, her left hand marking the place she'd stopped lining her copy of the script, her eyes never leaving the page. "Mason, I liked the same old/same old thing you had going during the dialogue," he continued as he reached the pillow. "It was a nice counterpoint to Lee's whole mortal indignation thing."

"Nice?" Mason Reed—aka Raymond Dark, syndicated television's most popular vampire detective and star of *Darkest Night*—folded his arms, and curled a lip to expose one fake fang. "That's the best you can do?"

"It's after midnight," Peter sighed. "Be thankful I can still come up with nice. Once Angela adds the echoing footsteps in post, I think the scene'll play . . ." The sound of large machinery revving up reduced the rest of the director's observation to moving lips and increasingly emphatic gestures.

Still standing on the top of the ladder from where he'd thrown the body pillow—Peter liked to be certain about lines of sight—Tony Foster caught one of the gestures aimed at him, clambered down, and ran over to the director's side.

"I want one more take before we bring in Padma!" Mouth by Tony's ear, Peter all but screamed to make himself heard. "Deal with it, Mr. Foster!"

"How?"

"Any way that'll get my footage!"

Any way.

Yeah. Tony headed for the construction site. Like he didn't know what that meant.

Promoted back in August from production assistant to TAD, trainee assistant director, Tony found himself in October still doing much the same thing he'd been doing as a PA—which surprised no one, him least of all, since Chester Bane, the notoriously frugal head of CB Productions, hadn't yet gotten around to hiring someone to do his old job. Still, TAD meant he was now moving up in the Directors Department with a raise in pay and a clear, union-sanctified path to the director's chair. Not necessarily a short path, but he was on it and that was the main thing. Since he'd been in the business less than a full year, he really had nothing to complain about. Besides, CB's penny-pinching ways ensured that he was learning a lot more than he might have on a show with a larger personnel budget.

And on a show with a larger locations budget, he'd have never learned how to take advantage of roadwork in order to get a normally busy Vancouver street cleared of traffic without having to go through all the hassles at city hall or pay off-duty police officers to safely keep it that way. Half the permits. Half the money spent. Digging for a sewer line guaranteed empty streets for blocks away from the actual machinery and city hall had been more than willing to halve the inconvenience to Vancouver drivers.

There was, of course, a downside. They'd been working around the noise—construction seemed to follow the same "hurry up and wait" schedule that television did—but that machine . . .

Backhoe, Tony realized as he drew closer. . . . seemed to be settling in for a long roar. Sure, they could remove the sound in post, but Peter hated looping dialogue. Mostly because Mason wasn't particularly good at it, and the results always looked as though a big rubbery monster was due to stomp Tokyo.

Any way didn't include actually talking to the construction crew. The foreman had made it quite clear earlier in the evening that they needn't bother. He had a job to do and no fancy-assed, la-di-da television show was going to put him off schedule.

With that attitude in mind, Tony stopped about six meters from the backhoe and watched the huge bladed bucket bite through the asphalt. After a moment, he noticed that the operator worked in what was essentially an open cab. Noticed, after a moment more, that her line of sight didn't extend as far down as the keys dangling off to one side of the double bank of bright yellow-and-black levers.

That could work.

Turning on one heel, he started back toward the trailers. There was always the chance the operator might glance down—it was a small chance, but given the size of the biceps on the woman, he wanted to make sure there wouldn't be the slightest possibility she'd even begin to contemplate the thought of considering him responsible.

Call him a coward, but those arms were the size of his thighs.

Besides, he didn't need to see the key. He knew where it was. Knew the shape it occupied in the universe. Okay, maybe *the universe* was going a little far, but he had local space nailed.

"Mr. Foster?"

He had to strain to hear Peter's voice in his ear jack.

"Any time."

Now seemed good. He concentrated and closed his fingers around a handful of keys as, behind him, the backhoe sputtered to a stop.

Wizardry, according to Arra Pelindrake, the wizard from another world who'd left him a laptop with instructions both detailed and annoyingly obscure, was all about focus. New spells required words or symbols or embarrassing contortions—Tony suspected that the wizards of Arra's world were either double-jointed or had a vicious sense of humor. After a while—where *a while* generally referred to years of practice—the words, symbols, and contortions could be replaced by the wizard's will.

Back in the summer, Tony had discovered that trying to keep a location crew alive in a haunted house could condense *a while* into one high-stress night. These days, if he wanted something to come to him, it came. Other spells were a different story. He was still trying to forget what happened the first time he tried a clean cantrip on his bathroom. Nothing said, *Hey, I'm a weirdo!* like having a date attacked by scrubbing bubbles.

As far as other spells were concerned . . . Well, there were surprisingly few places in and around the lower mainland to practice Powershots, given population density and the expected explosive results, but just in case he ever had to blast his way out of another haunted house, he had the theory nailed.

He reached the craft services table in time to see Lee—one hand still shoved in the pocket of his leather jacket, the other wrapped around a Styrofoam coffee cup—flirting with Karen, the craft services contractor. As Lee dipped his chin and looked up at her through a fringe of thick, dark lashes, she giggled. Actually giggled. Not a sound Tony'd ever connected to Karen before. Laugh, yes. Also swear like a sailor. But giggle? No. Lee's answering smile and a murmured comment Tony wasn't quite close enough to hear brought a flush to her cheeks, the rosy color under the freckles clearly visible in the double set of halogen spotlights aimed at the table.

"When you're ready, Mr. Nicholas!"

In answer to Peter's summons, Lee winked, drained the cup, tossed it into the nearer of the two garbage cans, turned, and half smiled as his gaze swept over Tony. Then the gaze kept sweeping, that half smile the only acknowledgment he gave.

Tony watched him walk back to where Mason and Peter were standing by the scene's starting mark. The shadows following hard on the actor's heels were nothing more than the result of solid objects blocking the path of both natural and artificial light. No otherworldly shadow warriors dogged his footsteps. The chill Tony felt on the back of his neck was a fall breeze, a warning that winter, such as winter was in British Columbia, was on its way. If the dead were walking, they weren't walking here. Everything was so aggressively normal it was almost possible to believe he'd imagined Lee screaming, his body tortured from within by an insane dead wizard. Almost possible to believe he'd imagined Lee sitting in the back of an ambulance and admitting that . . . well, essentially admitting that when he'd kissed him, he'd been fully aware of whose lips were involved.

Of course, he'd also said that the show had to go on.

That had been August. It was now early October. The show had been going on for nearly two months and was getting very good at it. Unlike a lot of actors, Lee had always been friendly with his crew and that "friendly" had always extended to Tony. Nothing about that had changed; he treated Tony no differently than he treated Keisha, the set dresser, or Zev Sero, the music director. The kiss and the confession were safely buried under what Tony thought was one of Lee's better performances.

Since the ladder and the pillow had been moved away from the shot, Tony assumed that Peter was doing this last take without his assistance. The backhoe keys slid off his fingertips into the garbage to lie hidden under a half-eaten muffin. Watching the boom operator—a skinny, middle-aged man named Walter Davis, who'd replaced skinny, middle-aged Hartley Skenski, who hadn't made it out of that haunted house alive—Tony reached for a handful of marshmallow strawberries.

"Those things'll kill you, you know."

One of them took a shot at it.

Coughing and blowing bits of soggy pink marshmallow out of his nose, Tony glared up into the amused face of RCMP Constable Jack Elson and contemplated several responses that would get him fifteen to life. When he could talk again, self-preservation prodded him to settle for a merely moderately sarcastic, "Aren't you out of your jurisdiction?"

Constable Elson, like CB Productions, was based in Burnaby—a part of the Greater Vancouver area about ten miles east of the city.

The constable shrugged. "I'm off duty. Heard you lot were out on the streets, thought I'd come down and take a look."

"Quiet, please!" Adam Paelous, the first assistant director, began the familiar litany. "Let's settle, people!"

Tony jerked his head back toward the trailers and started walking. Smiling slightly, Jack followed, snatching a couple of cookies off the corner of the table as he passed. He'd been around often enough in the last month or so that Karen, usually pit bull protective of the show's food, no longer tried to stop him and, even more disturbing, sometime in the last few weeks Tony had started thinking of him as Jack.

"Rolling!"

Half a dozen voices, including Tony's, echoed the word.

"Scene 19a, take three. Mark!"

The crack of the slate bounced off the buildings a couple of times and finally disappeared under the distant profanity of the road crew.

As Peter called action, Tony figured they were far enough away and murmured, "Okay, fine, now you're here, what are you looking *for*?"

Jack grinned. "It's been almost two months since you were found next to a dead body. I figured you were about due."

He was probably kidding.

The RCMP constable had been unhappy about the verdict of Accidental Death after the Shadowlord had come and gone, but that was nothing on the way he'd felt when Tony'd finally forced open the doors to Caulfield House on that August night. He'd seen the kind of weird-and-wonderful that even television writers would have had a hard time making people believe, and what he'd seen, combined with a good cop's ability to sift out the bullshit, had left him with no choice but to believe Tony's promised explanation. He'd believed it. He just hadn't liked it much.

Given his adversarial history with the police, Tony still wasn't sure why he'd told Jack and his partner Geetha Danvers the truth about what had happened in the house—slightly edited of personal information and back story. Maybe he'd hoped that it would keep them from hanging around and scowling suspiciously at all and sundry. It had worked on Constable Danvers, not that she'd been the scowling suspiciously sort to begin with, but it had done sweet fuck-all to get Jack Elson out of his life.

"Look at them." The constable gestured with a cookie, including actors and crew in the movement. "They're acting like nothing happened."

They were acting like the backhoe was quiet and that meant they could shoot, that was all they cared about. Except that wasn't what Jack meant. Peter, Adam, Sorge—the director of photography—Mason, and Lee; they'd all been in the house. Karen and Ujjal, the genny op, had been outside trying to get in. Or get the others out. The rest of the crew had been involved only to the extent that they'd heard the stories.

Tonight they were all working to get the scene in the can as though nothing had happened.

Tony's turn to shrug. "It's been a while."

"That shouldn't matter." Jack had taken to an expanded reality like a fangirl who knew her favorite actor was in town. Now that he believed, he suspected the supernatural of lurking around every corner. Sometimes he even spotted it. Sometimes he called Tony.

"What's about six centimeters high and can take a bite out of a car bumper?"

"What?"

"I think I saw one in the impound yard. Maybe more than one."

Finally recognizing the voice, Tony'd rolled over and squinted at the clock. *"It's three in the morning."*

"Does that matter? Do these things only come out between midnight and dawn? What are they?"

"How the hell should I know?"

"You're the . . ." Elson's voice—he'd still been Elson then, not yet Jack—had dropped below eavesdropping level. *". . . wizard."*

"Yeah. Wizard. Not a database for things that go bump in the night."

"So you won't tell me."

"It's three in the morning, for fuck's sake!"

"Why do you keep repeating the time?"

He'd sighed. "Because it's three in the morning."

In a just world, Jack would have gotten discouraged by now. Or distracted.

"Bunch of hikers just spotted a Sasquatch up by Hope—probably not a real one," Tony added quickly. "We're old news." A shadow moved just at the edge of the light, and he rolled his eyes. "Well, to everyone but you and him."

Him. Kevin Groves. Their very own tabloid journalist.

Fortunately, after the house incident, Mason had hogged the spotlight, and for Mason it was all about Mason. Unfortunately, Kevin Groves had apparently heard the bits of truth nearly buried under ego.

To his great disappointment, after official statements were taken—and with three dead under mysterious circumstances, official statements *were* taken—no one really wanted to talk much about what had happened. They seemed almost embarrassed about having been a part of a paranormal experience, given the kind of people to whom those sorts of things generally happened. In the public perception, haunted houses came just under alien anal probes and slightly above thousand-year-old lizard babies. Group gestalt insisted on a rational explanation for everything that could possibly be given one and refused to admit to the rest, leaving Kevin Groves lurking unfulfilled around the soundstage and being regularly escorted off location shoots.

However, it was clear that an unwillingness to talk didn't mean that anyone had actually forgotten the experience. No one ever seemed to be under a certain place on the soundstage between 11:00 and 11:15 AM or PM and Tony's *abilities* were used whenever they'd save a few moments or dollars. Television people dealt with the surreal on a daily basis and had managed to work a couple more bits in with little difficulty.

It helped that Tony had been a PA back in August, bottom man on the television totem pole, so anything too bizarre coming from his position wasn't exactly hard for them to ignore.

"I wouldn't be so fast to dismiss Mr. Groves, if I were you," Jack observed around a final mouthful of oatmeal raisin. "It mostly got lost in all of Mason Reed's posturing, but don't forget that there were interesting things said about your actions that night."

Tony sighed. "Yes, I have vast and incredible powers."

"You talk to dead people."

"So? I also talk to my car and the bank machine."

"Dead people talk to you."

"What, you never caught an episode of *Crossing Over* back when it was on six or seven times a day? Apparently, dead people talk to everyone."

"You . . ." He waved a hand.

Tony raised an eyebrow, the movement attaching a certain smuttiness to the unspoken part of the constable's observation.

Jack snorted, refusing to be baited. "The word wizard *was* mentioned."

"Yeah, so were the words mass hallucination and gas leak. If I'm such a mighty wizard, don't you think I'd have better things to do than stand around on the edge of a construction zone at one o'clock in the morning?"

"What, and give up show business?" Brushing cookie crumbs off his jacket, Jack grinned, golden stubble glinting in the spill of light from the streetlamp. The grin made Tony nervous.

It was supposed to. And knowing that didn't help.

"I'll go have a word with Mr. Groves."

"I can't stop you."

"You know, you're not as dumb as you look."

Since "*neither are you*" would be an enormously stupid thing to say, Tony bit his tongue as the RCMP officer walked toward the reporter.

"Cut! Good, that's got it!"

"*Tony.*" Adam's voice in his ear. "*Go get Padma.*"

The conversation with Jack had moved him nearly back beside the trailer shared by makeup and wardrobe. He leaned in through the open door and saw it was empty but for Padma Sathaye, the victim of the week. Ready for her scene, she was sitting in the makeup chair, absently rocking it back and forth with the pointed toe of one shoe, and reading an Elizabeth Fitzroy romance novel. *Sweet Savage Seas*, Tony noted; one of the older ones.

"Padma? They're ready for you."

She murmured a distracted reply, read for a second longer, and then closed the book around a folded piece of tissue. "I'm afraid I have a bad addiction to trashy romance novels," she told him apologetically as she stood.

"Who says they're trashy?"

"Pretty much everybody."

"I don't."

"But you wouldn't be caught dead reading one."

"I've read a couple."

The caked blood kept her from smiling too broadly. "How very sensitive new age guy of you."

He shrugged and stood to one side to let her pass. He'd read them because Elizabeth Fitzroy was the pseudonym of Henry Fitzroy, once Duke of Richmond and Somerset, bastard son of Henry VIII, vampire, and one of his exes.

Sort of ex.

Sort of . . . not.

Henry Fitzroy—Prince of Man, Prince of Darkness—was just a little on the possessive side. As far as he was concerned, Tony would always be one of his.

Mostly, that was all right by Tony. He liked to keep things friendly with all his exes. Hell, he saw Zev all the time at work and they still occasionally hung out. It used to be like that with Henry. Even a couple of months ago, he'd have given the vampire a heads up on this night shoot so they could hang together for a while, but things had cooled between them since the incident with the house.

Since it had become obvious that Henry'd developed some kind of connection with Chester Bane.

Okay, strictly speaking, things hadn't so much cooled as Tony'd cooled things.

He didn't like Henry becoming a part of his daytime life. He might be Henry's, but this show, this job, was his—and Henry could just piss off and stop bonding with his boss.

He wished he had the guts to ask CB if they were still in touch.

Following Padma across the street, he noted Everett, the makeup artist, standing by the video village, a gallon of fake blood at his feet. Beside him, Alison Larkin from wardrobe sketched costumes in the air, her every gesture threatening to drench the immediate area in coffee. As far as Tony knew, she'd never lost a drop. He placed the genny op, light techs, sound techs . . . the greater part of his job on location was knowing where people were so he could find them if needed.

Jack and Kevin Groves seemed to have left the area. Probably not together. Hopefully not together. Unless Jack had arrested the reporter for loitering with intent.

No. Not even then. Jack knew enough that Tony wanted the reporter nowhere near him for any length of time even if that time involved handcuffs. And not in a fun way.

"Come on, people, let's move!" Adam's voice set the crew in motion. "We've only got the street for one more night and second unit's got it all tied up!"

Padma laughed at something Lee said as she arranged herself on the pavement and Mason smacked his costar lightly on the arm. Peter shuffled the two men into position, Adam called for quiet, and they were rolling again.

Raymond Dark and James Taylor Grant stared down at the body that had just landed at their feet.

They weren't the only ones.

Tony's gaze flicked up to the rooftop.

Something else was watching . . .

Wonderful.

It was like having fucking gaydar for the supernatural.

"So I have to be careful now because I'm a player?" It was one of the last conversations he'd had with Henry before he'd stopped returning the vampire's calls. *"What was I before?"*

Henry's eyes had silvered slightly, a sign that the Hunger was near the surface. "A victim. But there's enough of them that you had a chance of being lost in the crowd. Now, you stand out."

He'd very nearly responded with something stupidly cliché about how he thought he'd been more than just a meal to the other man. Stomping hard on his inner drama queen, he'd snarled, *"I'm not saying I don't appreciate your help, but I've been taking care of myself since I was fourteen."*

"You survived . . ."

"Yeah, my point. Before you came along to hold my dick, I survived just fine."

"Things are different now."

"And that gives you the right to bite down on the rest of my life?"

"What?"

The conversation had deteriorated around then, but the point was, if Tony was sensing a supernatural watcher on the roof, he was probably sensing Henry playing Mother Hen of the Night. Sure, he hadn't told Henry about the shoot, but Henry had new contacts in the business now.

He flipped a finger in the general direction of the feeling.

"CB Productions, can I help you? Uh-huh. Uh-huh." Tucking the phone under her chin, Amy waved her left hand in Tony's general direction while she doodled on a message pad with her right. "No, I'm sorry, that's not possible."

He crossed to her desk during the other half of the conversation and noted that up close her fingernails weren't a uniform black. Each nail also wore a tiny, white stick-on skull.

"Look . . ." She methodically scratched out what she'd already written. ". . . why don't I just put you through to our office manager? Okay. Just stay on the line." Pushing the hold button, she hung up the receiver and frowned up at Tony over the blinking red light. "What are you doing here? You're working second unit tonight."

"CB wanted to see me." Tony glanced around to see that Rachel Chou, the office manager, was noticeably absent. "Shouldn't you find Rachel?"

"Why?"

He nodded toward the phone.

Amy snorted. "She's not in the office today. That asshat can stay on hold until she gets back for all I care."

"Nice." Tony picked up one hand and took a closer look at the nails. "Skulls glow in the dark?"

"Uh-huh."

"Hair, too?" White strips of hair bracketed her face. They seemed slightly greenish next to the matte black of the rest.

"Please; too tacky." Lids lowered, she tipped her face up. "But my eye shadow does."

Wondering why glow-in-the-dark hair was tackier than glow-in-the-dark eye shadow—and skulls—he leaned forward for a closer look.

"Don't do it, Amy. He'll make you watch old black-and-white movies."

"Don't do what?" Tony demanded, turning in time to see the door to post close and Zev start across the office.

"She looked like she was about to make an unhealthy commitment."

"As if. And what's wrong with black-and-white movies?" Amy leaned to the right so she could see the music director.

Zev grinned within the shadow of his dark beard. "He keeps pausing so he can comment on the way they used to set up scenes."

She jerked her hand out of Tony's grip. "Is he kidding?"

"No, but . . ."

"Dude, you've got to work a little harder at getting a life."

"I used to have one." Tony nodded toward Zev. "He broke up with me."

"Yeah. Quel surprise."

Shoving his hands into the front pockets of his jeans, Zev frowned thoughtfully in Tony's general direction. "I thought you were doing second unit tonight?"

"I am."

"CB wants to see him." Amy's tone suggested last requests, last meals, last rites.

"Why?"

Tony shrugged. "I don't know."

They turned as one toward the closed door of the boss' office. The scuffed wood gave nothing away.

"He's just running over the stunt with Daniel," Amy murmured.

"Daniel's not doing the stunt."

"Gee . . ." Eyes rolled. ". . . I can't see why not. Daniel'd be so convincing as a not very tall, gorgeous Indian woman."

"Well, the not-very-tall would give him a few problems," Zev reflected, measuring a space some two meters from the floor.

Daniel was the stunt double for both Mason and Lee. He also acted as coordinator for any stunts performed by outside talent. "Why is it when Frank writes an episode," Tony wondered, "we always need to hire a stuntwoman?"

They turned toward the bull pen. From behind that closed door came the rhythmic sound of someone reading aloud.

Zev frowned. "Maybe he thinks the only way he can get a date is with someone used to risking her life."

"Frank dating?" Amy shuddered. "My mind just went to the scary place."

In the awkward silence that followed, Tony heard maniacal laughter. He might've been worried except it clearly came from one of the writers.

"Not a specific scary place," Amy amended quickly.

They both turned to look at Tony. Amy was the exception to the general rule that those who'd been in the house ignored what had gone on and Zev, as an ex, had certain rights and privileges involving shared history and exploded beer bottles.

"So." She picked at the edge of a skull, then looked up hopefully. "Seen any dead people lately?"

He'd nearly seen Henry keeping tabs on him the night before. But Henry, not being exactly dead, just differently alive, didn't really count. "No."

"But you'll tell me if you do?"

At the edge of his vision, Tony could see Zev shaking his head almost hard enough to dislodge his yarmulke. "Sure . . ."

Zev sighed.

". . . I promise."

"Brianna has been asking after you."

"Brianna? Really?" From the expression on CB's face, that clearly sounded as stupid as Tony suspected. Brianna had been asking for him pretty much every time she spoke to her father. "Uh, in what context?"

CB's eyes narrowed as he leaned back, his leather office chair creaking ominously under his weight. "In what context do you imagine, Mr. Foster?"

"Boss, I swear I never told her she was a wizard!"

"So you've said previously. And, once again, I believe you." He steepled fingers the size of well-muscled bratwurst. "However, as Brianna does not, I think it's time we move on."

"Move on?" Tony cleared his throat and tried again an octave lower. "Move on?"

"Yes."

No. He was not going to teach CB's youngest daughter how to be a wizard. First, wizardry was a talent more than a skill, and while Brianna had proved sensitive to the metaphysical, he had no idea if that equaled talent. Or what, exactly, did equal talent, for that matter. Second, he was still teaching himself how to be a wizard and, frankly, as a teacher, he sucked. Scrubbing bubbles and one pissed-off cater-waiter had to be incontestable evidence of that. Third, giving this particular eight-year-old access to actual power would be like . . . his mind shied away from comparisons and settled on: the height of irresponsibility. No one, including her father, could control the kid now. And fourth, he'd rather have toothpicks shoved under his nails.

Mouth open to lay everything but the last point out in front of CB—not smart to give the big guy ideas—he closed it again as CB continued speaking.

"I have a friend putting together a PBS miniseries for Black History Month, so I called in some favors, and he gave my ex-wife a sizable part. She's taking both girls to South Carolina with her. Shooting ends December twentieth. You have until then to come up with a permanent solution."

The pause lengthened.

"Was there anything else?"

Like invasions from another world or a waxy buildup of evil?

"Um, no."

"Good."

"Permanent solution. Permanent solution." Tony paused, one hand on the door leading out to the parking lot, frozen in place by the sudden memory of his mother sitting at the kitchen table twisting her hair onto multicolored rollers shaped like bones. A home perm. And the permanent solution had totally reeked. He remembered because they were called *Tonys* and his mother used to tease him about being a hairdresser.

Later, like around the time he hit puberty, his father stopped finding the hairdresser jokes quite so funny—Warren Beatty's enthusiastically hetero performance in *Shampoo* conveniently ignored.

His father was no longer a problem given that they hadn't spoken to each other for about ten years.

Brianna's father, however . . .

The door jerked out of his hand, and he stumbled forward, slamming up against a solid body on its way in.

His way in.

Tony recognized the impact. And the black leather jacket he was currently clutching with both hands. "Lee." Two fast steps back. He stared down at his arms still stretched out . . . *Right. Release the jacket.*

"Tony."

Just for a second, Tony was unsure of what Lee's next words were going to be. Just for a second, it almost looked as if the show was over for the day and reality was going to get its time in. Just for a second. Trouble was, a second later Lee pulled his hail-fellow-well-met actor-face back on.

"You okay? I didn't realize there was someone standing there."

"Well, why would you? You know, solid door and all and you not having X-ray vision." X-ray vision? Could he sound any more geeklike? "I was just leaving."

"Right. You're doing second unit work tonight."

Everyone seemed to know that. Were they posting his schedule now or what?

Lee shifted his motorcycle helmet from under his left arm to under his right but didn't actually move out of the doorway. "So you were here to . . ."

"Meeting. I had a meeting with CB."

"Good. I mean, it was good?"

"Yeah. I guess. Still dealing with Brianna's reactions in the . . ." Shit. Never bring up the house thing with Lee.

The actor-face slipped. "In the house?"

Unless he brings it up first. "Yeah. In the house."

Lee's eyes closed briefly, thick lashes lying against his cheeks like the fringe on a theater curtain. Only darker. Not gold. And without the tassels. Tony realized he was babbling to himself, but he couldn't seem to stop. They hadn't been alone together, standing this close, since, well, since the house. For a moment, he hoped that when Lee opened his eyes, the actor-face would be gone and they could maybe start dealing with what had happened.

Lee had to make the first move because Lee was the one with the career he could lose. It was Lee's face plastered on T-shirts worn by teenage girls and forty-year-old women who should know better. Tony was a TAD. Professionally, no one gave a crap about him.

The moment passed.

Lee opened his eyes. "Well, I have to say that it's been nice running into you and all, but I need to get to my . . ." Dark brows drew in, and he waved the hand not holding the helmet.

"Dressing room?"

"Yeah." The smile was fake. Well done, but fake. "My memory sucks some days."

Tony reflected the smile back at him. "Old age."

"Yeah." The smile was still fake, but the regret flattening his words seemed real. "That has to be it."

Tony squinted up at the top of the building, trying to count the number of people standing at the edge of the roof. Sorge's request for a steadicam had been overruled by the budget, so there should only be two: Leah Burnett, the stuntwoman doing the fall, and Sam Tappett, one of Daniel's safety crew. Two. Not a hard number to count. Most nights he could even do it with his shoes on. So why did he keep getting three? Not every time—because that would have made sense. Every now and then, he thought—no, cancel that, he was *sure*—he could see a third figure.

Not Henry.

Not tonight.

Not unless Henry had been growing an impressive set of horns in his spare time and had then developed the ability to share his personal space with mere mortals. The same actual space. Sort of superimposed.

Welcome to the wonderful world of weird.

Déjà vu all over again.

The question now: should he do anything about it and, if so, what?

It wasn't like his spidey-sense was tingling or something in his subconscious was flailing metaphorical arms and wailing *Danger, Will Robinson! Danger!* He didn't have a bad feeling about things, and he had no idea if this was a threat or some kind of symbolic wizard experience. Maybe it was something all wizards saw on top of buildings at—he checked his watch—11:17 on Thursday nights in early October and he'd just never been looking in the right place at the right time.

Still, as a general rule, when he saw things others couldn't, the situation went south in a big way pretty fucking fast.

Unfortunately, none of the second unit crew had been in the house. They'd heard the stories, but they didn't know. Not the way those who'd been trapped and forced to listen to hours of badly played thirties dance music knew. If he told Pam, the second unit director, that he intermittently saw a translucent, antlered figure on the roof, she'd assume controlled substances and not metaphysical visitations.

Tony hadn't done hard drugs since just before Henry pulled him off the streets. Point of interest; he'd never seen big, see-through guys with horns while he was shooting up.

He glanced down as a gust of wind plastered a grimy piece of newspaper to his legs. Evening weather reports had mentioned a storm coming in off the Pacific, and the wind was starting to pick up, sweeping up all kinds of debris as it raced through the artificial canyons between the buildings. Before he could grab the newspaper, another gust whirled it away and slapped it up against the big blue inflated bag Leah would land on.

If Daniel thought it was too dangerous, he'd cancel the stunt regardless of the shooting schedule. Tony hurried over to where the stunt coordinator was checking the final inflation of the bag.

"It's getting kind of windy."

"Yes, it is."

"Four stories is a long way to fall."

"Uh-huh." He straightened and bounced against the side of the bag. "That's why they call it a high fall."

"Yeah, it's just that falling four stories the wind'll have longer to throw her off . . ." As Daniel turned to look at him, Tony sputtered to a stop. "But you've taken that into account."

"I have." Stern features under dark stubble suddenly dissolved into a smile. "But I thank you for staying on top of things. It never hurts to have another person thinking about potential problems." He unclipped the microphone from his collar. "Hey, Sam, what's the wind like up there?"

"Little gusty. Not too bad."

"What's Leah think?"

During the pause, the antlered figured came and went and came again. It almost seemed to wave when Leah did.

"She says she's good to go whenever you give the word."

"We're ready down here. Pam, we can go any time."

"Glad to hear it." Pam's voice in the ear jack. "Let's have a slate on the scene and get started!"

Tony backed away from the bag as Daniel's people took up their positions. Since a high fall relied 100 percent on the stuntie's ability to hit the bag safely, the stunt crew were essentially there to deal with a miss. Tony wouldn't have wanted to see the backboard so prominently displayed were he about to jump off a roof, but, hey, that was him.

"Quiet, please, cameras are rolling."

A repeat of "Rolling!" in half a dozen voices rippled out from the director's chair.

"Scene 19b, high fall, take one. Mark!"

"Action."

Far enough away now, Daniel's voice sounded in Tony's ear jack. *"On three, Leah. One . . ."*

Up on the roof, Sam would be echoing the count, fingers flicking up to give visual cues.

A gust of wind blew a bit of dirt in Tony's eye. He ducked his head just in time to see that same gust about to fling a ten-centimeter piece of aluminum with a wickedly pointed end into the bag.

"Two."

Impact wouldn't make anything as simple as a hole. At that angle, at that speed, it was going to be a gash. And a big one.

"Three."

The *wham whoosh* of impact and applause from the crew covered the sound of aluminum slapping into Tony's palm. The jagged piece of debris had probably blown down from the construction site. *Revenge of the backhoe.*

"Cut!"

He looked up as Leah climbed down off the bag, Daniel, grinning broadly, reaching out a hand to steady her. The fall had clearly not been a problem; the high heels, on the other hand, were giving her a little trouble. She was smiling, definitely happy, but less overtly euphoric than a lot of stunties were after nailing a four-story fall.

She didn't look like Padma. She looked like a stuntwoman wearing the same costume over some strategic padding.

So much for the magic of television.

It took a moment for Tony to realize she was staring at him.

No, not at him. At the piece of aluminum still in his hand.

As though she'd suddenly become aware of his attention, she lifted her head. Lifted one dark, inquiring brow.

Even the see-through guy with horns sharing her space seemed interested.

⤳ TWO

Night shoots always threw Tony's sleeping patterns out of whack. When a guy his age got off work, he was supposed to go out and do things. He wasn't supposed to drive straight home and fall over. It wasn't just wrong, it was old. It was what old guys did.

Except there wasn't a whole lot to do at 2:30 on a Thursday morning in beautiful downtown Burnaby.

Cradling a bag of overpriced groceries from the 7-Eleven, Tony kicked the door to his apartment closed and shuffled into the tiny kitchen. The shuffling was necessary because he'd started sorting laundry back on Monday, hadn't quite finished yet, and didn't want to start again from scratch because he'd mixed the piles. The bread and milk went into the fridge. He tucked the bottle of apple juice under his arm and carried the bag of beef jerky and the spray cheese into the living room—where *living room* was defined as the part of the long rectangle that contained an unmade sofa bed instead of a stove, a fridge, and a sink.

The television remote was not in the pizza box under the couch. It finally turned up on top of the bookcase by the window, half buried in the pot with the dead geranium. Raising it in triumph, he settled back against the pillows, sprayed some cheese on a piece of jerky, and started channel surfing with the mute on.

Replay of a hockey game on TSN, end of hurricane season on *Outdoor Life*, remake of *Smokey and the Bandit* . . .

"Which after *The Longest Yard* and *The Dukes of Hazzard* pretty much proves there is no God," he muttered, jabbing his thumb at the remote.

. . . some guy eating a bug on either the Learning Channel or FOOD—he didn't stay long enough to see if it came with a lecture on habitat or a raspberry vinaigrette—three movies he'd already seen, two he didn't want to see, a bug eating some guy on either Discovery or Space, someone knocking at the door . . .

His thumb stilled.

Someone knocking at *his* door. Carefully. Specifically. Trying not to wake the neighbors.

It didn't sound like Henry's knock. He checked his watch: 2:57. Besides the vampire, who did he know who'd be up at this hour? Even tabloid journalists eventually crawled back under their rocks for a nap. It wasn't Jack Elson or his partner; the police had a *very* distinctive knock.

Might be Conner, that friend of Everett's he'd met while visiting the makeup artist in the hospital. They'd gone for coffee but hadn't been able to hook up since—Conner worked in the props shop at one of the other Burnaby studios, and his hours were as insane as Tony's. Maybe their schedules had finally matched up.

Of course, Conner'd have no way of knowing that.

Unless Everett had told him.

Hell, if he was going to imagine hot guys, why not drop all the way into fairy-tale land and assume it was Lee, no longer conflicted and unable to deny the blistering passion between them? Okay, for passion substitute a couple of possessed kisses—but they'd been pretty damned hot.

Another knock.

Of course, I could just get off my ass, walk a few meters, and find out. Dropping the spray cheese down in a pile of blankets by the jerky, Tony headed for the door.

There was a spell on the laptop called "Spy Hole" that allowed the wizard to see through solid objects. The first time Tony'd tried it, he'd given it a little too much juice and gotten way too good a look at Mr. Chansky across the hall in apartment eleven. Talk about being scared straight. The experience had convinced him that sometimes the old ways were the best. Leaning forward, he peered through the security peephole.

Leah Burnett.

And the translucent overlay of the big guy with antlers.

She grinned up at the lens and lifted a bag of Chinese food into Tony's field of vision.

All right. She had his attention.

Stepping back, he opened the door.

"Hey." She waved the bag. "I thought we should talk."

"All three of us?"

"Three? If you have company . . ."

"No." He just moved enough to stay solidly in her line of sight, blocking her view of the apartment. "You, me, and the guy sharing your space."

Dark eyes widened. "Guy?"

"Big guy." He held his hand about half a meter over her head.

"Really? What does this *guy* look like?"

"Hard to say, he's a little fuzzy. Got a rack on him like Bambi's dad, though."

"And you can see him right now?"

"Not right now. He kind of comes and goes."

"Uh-huh." A quick glance up and down the hall. "Maybe we should discuss this inside."

"Got something to hide?"

"Just trying to keep you out of trouble with your neighbors."

That seemed fair. Besides, there were precautions in place in case he was actually in any danger from her. Them. Although, given the Chinese food and all, he doubted it. Opening the door all the way, Tony tucked himself up against the wall and beckoned the stuntwoman in.

The glyphs painted across the threshold were supposed to flare red and create an impenetrable barrier if danger approached—it had taken days of fine-tuning to stop them from going off for the pizza girl, Mr. Chansky, and the elderly cat who lived at the end of the hall. As Leah stepped into the apartment, they flared white, then orange, then green, then a couple of colors Tony suspected the human eye shouldn't actually be able to see. The pattern slammed out to fill the doorway, turned gray, and fluttered to the floor.

Leah brushed at the shoulder of her jacket, the pale ash smearing across the damp fabric. "Sorry about that." Her nose wrinkled as the smell of burned cherries momentarily overwhelmed the smell of the Chinese food. "What did you paint those on with, cherry cough syrup?"

"Yeah." When she stared up at him in astonishment, he shrugged. Carefully. His head felt like he'd just been hit repeatedly with a rubber mallet. "Cherry was the only flavor that worked. And," he added, hoping he sounded like he believed it was possible, "I will fireball your ass if you try anything."

"Like what?"

"Sorry?"

She pulled the door out of his hand and closed it. "What are you expecting me to try?"

He had no idea, so he followed her farther into the apartment.

"I suppose I should be impressed that a guy your age actually sorts his laundry," she, muttered stepping over a pile of jeans and up to the kitchen counter, where she set the bag down, shrugged out of her jacket, and started opening cupboards. "Ah. Plates." And a moment later, "Cutlery?"

"In the drawer by the fridge."

"Right. It's mostly plastic."

"They were free."

"Fair enough." She handed him a full plate and stepped over socks and underwear and stood staring at the rest of the apartment. "Daniel told me you were gay."

"Yeah."

"Way to work against the stereotype."

"What?"

Her gesture took in the walls, the floor, and most of his furniture. "It's beige."

"It was beige when I got here."

"You have a flag tacked up over the window."

"I'm a patriotic kind of guy."

"The only thing on the wall is a poster for *Darkest Night*."

"It was free."

"I figured. You seem to have spent everything you've made in the last year on that entertainment center."

"Look . . ." Tony pushed the laptop to one side and set his plate down on the small square table. ". . . if you're here on some weird makeover thing, I don't want my apartment redecorated or my life rearranged."

"You sure?"

Her smile changed the whole shape of her face. Made her look years younger. Made her eyes sparkle. Made her look like someone he'd like to get to know. Really well. Made him want to slide the sweater off her shoulders, push back the dark curls and . . .

. . . he suddenly noticed that the translucent antlered guy looked a lot more solid. Except for the horns, and the weird way his eyes had no whites, he seemed to be human. His skin tone was a little deeper than Leah's—a regular coffee instead of a double double—he had a lot of long dark hair twisted into dreads, and he was naked. And, although it was difficult to tell for certain, given that he and Leah were still sharing the same space, remarkably well hung.

What the fuck?

Tony shook his head and Leah was once again just a not very tall stunt-woman eating chow mein in his living room. Alone. No overlay of antlered guy. Eyes narrowed, he took a step back and raised the plastic fork. "What was that?"

"A test." She caught a bean sprout before it fell off the edge of her plate. "Ninety percent of men fail it."

Tony did the math. "Well, good for me. I'm really most sincerely gay."

"And yet you still can't afford a gallon of periwinkle paint?"

"Yeah, well here's a thought . . ." He moved a pile of old sides—the half-size sheets with all the background information for each day's shoot as well as the necessary script pages—and sat on the steadier of his two folding chairs. ". . . unless that guy is your inner interior decorator, how about you let the beige thing go and tell me what the hell is going on?"

She thought about it for a moment, then nodded and sat on the edge of his bed. "You're a wizard."

Tony just barely managed to resist coming back with, *I know I am, but what are you?* It was just past three in the morning, for fuck's sake. He was a little punchy. He swallowed a mouthful of beef fried rice and said: "You're . . . ?"

"Not." A wave of her fork, dangling a piece of overcooked bok choi, cut off his reply. "It's complicated. Maybe you should call your teacher, and I'll only have to go through it once."

"My teacher?"

"Mentor. Whatever you call the senior wizard in charge of your education." Dark eyes sparkled again. "I'm assuming that in this brave new millennium you don't use the word *master.*"

"What makes you think I have a teacher?"

Leah sighed. "You're young. Far too young to be on your own."

"Surprise." He spread his hands.

Brows rose. "What happened to your teacher?"

He pushed chow mein around his plate. "I thought we were going to talk about the naked horny dude."

Fortunately, only a little rice went up her nose. When she finished laughing and snorting and blowing her nose on the crumpled handful of toilet paper Tony'd brought from the bathroom, she said, "His name is Ryne Cyratane. It means: He Who Brings Desire and Destruction. He's a Demonlord."

"Oh, man." The fork bounced as he dropped it on the table. "Not again."

"Excuse me?"

"A few years ago, some friends of mine stopped a Demonlord from coming through in Toronto."

"Coming through?"

"Yeah, there was this lesser demon writing the Demonlord's name on the city in blood and . . ." He frowned, trying unsuccessfully to remember the specifics Henry had told him about how they'd finally defeated it. "It got complicated, but he didn't make it."

"Obviously." Her tone went beyond dry to desiccated. "Well, there's no need for you to worry about this one. I've got him contained." She stood and pulled up her sweater.

"Nice tat."

"Thank you." It circled her navel, row after row of black glyphs spreading almost up to the edge of her ribs like ripples moving out from the point of impact. "It's a Demongate. As long as I live, the gate stays closed and my lord is denied reentry to this world."

"Your lord?"

"Long story."

"Okay. Reentry?"

"He was here about four thousand years ago. For almost five hundred years, worshiped as a god, he ruled a territory in what's now Lebanon. Ish. Same general geography anyway, near as I can figure. He had a temple, he had handmaidens, he had a lot of sex."

That would be the desire part, Tony figured.

"Then something came up—he's never said what—and he created a gate to return to the hell he came from. It took a lot of power. To get it, he killed everyone in the village and, with their blood, anchored the gate in his sole surviving handmaiden."

And that would be the destruction. Tony leaned closer. The tat wasn't black. Not exactly. It was a very, very dark red-brown. "You're the handmaiden."

"Handmaiden, priestess, lover; I was his . . ."

"Girlfriend?" He winced at her expression. "Sorry. I was just channeling *Young Frankenstein*, you know when Frau Blucher is explaining and . . . Never mind. Sorry. Totally inappropriate interruption. I'll just, uh, be quiet now."

She waited a moment longer.

Tony picked up his fork and ate some more rice and tried to look like there was some *other* idiot in his apartment who couldn't keep his mouth shut.

"I was his most beloved." Leah continued at last. Her fingertips lightly stroked the edges of the pattern, raising goose bumps on her skin. "He cut the gate into my flesh, glyphs written in the blood of my people, because he intended to return but would be unable to open the gate from the other side. Gates from the hells have to be opened from our side or we'd be overrun by demons in a heartbeat."

"And they have to be asked in?" Then he remembered that he'd said he'd be quiet and he shrugged apologetically, but she seemed resigned to the interruption.

"You're confused, that's vampires."

It didn't seem like the right time to correct her. Henry went where he wanted. "Why didn't this Ryne Citation . . ."

"Ryne Cyratane."

"Right. Why didn't he just leave the gate open?"

"Because that would have been just asking for another Demonlord to come along and try to take it over. And, before you ask, the wizard who had opened the original gate was long dead."

"Dead wizard." Yeah, that sounded encouraging. "Nice."

"Probably not. Anyway, Ryne Cyratane figured that I'd be able to stand what he'd done to my people for just long enough for him to finish up his business at home and then grief and guilt would cause me to take my own life. Should I be stronger than my grief, it wouldn't much matter because time was on his side and a human life is pitifully short to the demon kin—and, back then, pitifully short was even shorter. Unfortunately for his plans, he made a small error—although, to be fair, I was squirming a bit while he incised the protection runes." She traced the outer ring. "He intended to protect the gate from me, to keep me from defacing the pattern, thus destroying the gate and preventing him from returning, but he ended up writing in a much more powerful and general protection.

"The gate protects itself and, in protecting itself, protects me. I can't be injured because that would affect the gate. I can't age because that would affect the gate. I am held as I was the day he left this world."

"Four thousand years ago?" And that would make her . . . "You're four thousand years old?"

She shrugged and sat back down on the end of the bed, retrieving her plate and looking to be in her mid-twenties at the absolute outside. Jeans. Sweater. High-tops. "More or less. Probably closer to thirty-five hundred. You lose track after a while."

Given the whole vampires, wizards, other worlds, sentient shadows, trapped ghosts deal, he saw no reason to doubt her. Precedent suggested the world was about a hundred and eighty degrees weirder than most people suspected and, these days, nothing much surprised him. Besides, hers wasn't the kind of story a sane person would make up. On the other hand, she did fall off buildings and set herself on fire for a living, so perhaps sanity wasn't a given here.

"So . . ." He groped his way back to the beginning of the story. ". . . this Ryne Cyratane slaughtered everyone you knew?"

"Every single person. Even called the goatherds in from the hills."

"I don't want to bring up old shit, but . . ." Tony pushed a cashew around his plate until it slid off the edge, bounced across the table, and off onto the floor. Only then did he look up and meet her gaze. "He slaughtered everyone, and you don't seem too upset by that."

"What do you expect?" Her shrug was perfect twenty-first century ennui. "It happened a very long time ago. I've dealt. You should have seen me right afterward, I was a mess." She widened her eyes, raised both hands, fingers spread, and shook them from side to side. "I was the crazy lady who lived in the wilderness for about three hundred years. One day I was a warning to misbehaving children, next thing I knew I was being fished out of the Nile by the servants of a priest of Thoth. He cleaned me up, brought me back to my-self. *He* was a wizard." Her eyes unfocused and the corners of her mouth curled into a smile as she examined the memory. "And kind of cute in a shaved head, totally fanatical sort of way."

"What happened to him?"

"He got a little too ambitious and the governor fed him to the crocodiles."

Crocodiles? Tony wished the threats on *his* life were so mundane. "Couldn't have been much of a wizard."

"They were very large crocodiles. And there were a lot of them."

"What happened to you?"

Attention snapped back onto Tony's face. "Do you really want the whole life story? Because until the last couple of centuries, it's been pretty much centered in and around the beds of powerful men."

It'd been more than that—frighteningly more—Tony could see a bloody history lurking behind Leah's glib comment. But he could also see she didn't want to share. Not a problem. He didn't like handing out every detail of his back story either. "So this demon has been trying to get back through the gate for thirty-five hundred years."

Dark brows drew in. "No. What makes you say that?"

"Well, he's . . . you know." He waved at where the translucent image would be and realized it hadn't been around since Leah's little orientation "test."

"Oh, that. We're connected, of course, but after all this time he knows I'm not going to kill myself, so he lives his own life. He's probably hanging around the gate right now because of the Demonic Convergence."

"Say what?"

"The reason I'm here."

"Right."

"And he's usually around during sex."

Tony raised the fork again.

She grinned and rolled her eyes. "Stop panicking, we've already established that's not going to happen. But if it did, the energy created while I adjusted your lifestyle would go through the gate and into my lord—as long as he's close enough to the gate at his end."

"The Demonlord gets off through you?" That sounded just a little ethically kinky.

"Not exactly off. He gains power from sex. Always has. The man/woman variety only, though . . ." Her voice picked up a slightly mocking tone. ". . . which seems kind of limiting for a demon powered by sexual energies, but there you go."

"You're feeding him? With sex?" Scratch the qualifier. Tony liked to think he didn't judge, but there was a definite ethical kink in the stuntwoman's lifestyle.

"Well, he *was* my god," Leah reminded him pointedly. "And," she continued before he could respond, "there've been benefits on my side over the years. Like . . . the years. And a certain . . ." Dark eyes gleamed. ". . . vitality."

"He slaughtered your people!"

"You're going to have to let that go," she sighed.

"Why?"

"Because it's ancient history, it's not important, and we have bigger problems."

"Bigger?"

"The Demonic Convergence." Tony could hear the capital letters in her voice. "Energies are aligning. Powerful energies. Powerful enough to crack the barriers between here and the hells."

He had to agree that didn't sound good. "Hells? More than one?"

"Many more."

"Well, isn't that just fucking great?" All at once, Chinese food seemed trivial. He put down his fork. "And these energies are powerful enough to open a Demongate?"

Her hand dropped to cradle her stomach. It was the same gesture Tony'd seen pregnant women make and in this context that creeped him right out. "Not this gate. Like I said, it's protected. New gates will be created. Okay, not really gates, more like access points that can be exploited just long enough for something to come through."

"One to a customer?" That sounded good.

She nodded. "But there could be hundreds of them."

That didn't. "Hundreds?"

"Rough estimate." When her expression grew reassuring, Tony figured he must have looked as stunned as he felt. "But don't worry, most of these holes will only go through a few layers, just to the closest hells. The convergent energy has to hit the same spot over and over before we get to anything much bigger than imps." She got up, walked into the kitchen, and set her empty plate in the sink.

Empty. She'd kept eating while she was telling him about demons and Demongates and slaughter. *I guess she really has gotten over it. It's just a story to her now.* Maybe someday the Shadowlord and the house would be just stories to him. Maybe. Probably not. Thirty-five hundred years was a lot longer than he'd get. He watched her rinse the plate, set it on the counter, and turn to face him.

"Well?"

"Well what?"

Her expression slid from reassuring to impatient. "Don't you have questions?"

"Yeah. A couple." Understatement. He had so many questions he could barely drag one free of the mess. "Okay. Imps. They're not a problem?"

"Without a wizard they can be one hell of a problem, pardon the pun, but you should be able to deal with any that manage to get through."

"*Manage* to get through?"

"Didn't I tell you?" Leah's sudden smile had so much wattage behind it, her Demonlord made a brief, translucent appearance, flickering in and out again before Tony fully realized he was there. "We'll be smoothing out reality's potholes before anything can come through. I'll find them," she added when he shook his head, "and you'll close them."

"I don't know how!"

"I do." She all but patted him on the head as she passed on her way back to the sofa bed. "I just needed a wizard to implement the knowledge."

Just. As far as Tony could tell the word *just* didn't belong in any sentence spoken since Leah had walked through his door. Just thirty-five hundred years old. Just got a Demongate on the old tum. Just a Demonic Convergence. Just imps. Just needed a wizard. Wait a minute . . . "How did you know?"

"Know?"

"That I was a wizard?"

"I felt you use your power when you kept that piece of flying metal from puncturing the bag, of course. Over the years I've become attuned."

"To power?"

"Among other things." Her expression as she looked up from rummaging in her purse was subtly smuttier than anything Tony could have ever managed. He felt his ears grow hot. Hotter when he realized she was doing it on purpose.

"Stop it."

"Sorry. Bad habit. Sugarless gum?"

"No, thanks." She seemed more amused than contrite. "Hang on; I thought the . . ." He waved a hand in the general direction of her stomach. ". . . the gate thing was supposed to protect you."

Her hand slipped under her shirt again. "It does."

"Then why did you need me out there saving your ass tonight?"

"What makes you think that you weren't there because I needed you to be?" Three and a half millennia of confidence in the question.

"Well, I . . ."

"They tried to burn me at the stake once—well, actually, they tried a number of times, but in this particular instance, it rained for eight days. The wood was too wet to light, and finally one wall of my cell washed away and I escaped."

"I'm surprised you didn't just . . ."

"Fuck my way free? Devout Dominicans; a little too fond of barbeque but devout. They weren't interested. So . . ." She stood and slowly walked over to stand beside his chair, pushing a pile of laundry out of the way with the side of her foot. She wasn't exactly looming over him—she wasn't exactly tall—but she was so *there* that he had to fight the urge to move away from her, to give her space. ". . . are you going to help me out or not?"

"Help you close up imp holes made by a Demonic Convergence?" He was amazed he got that sentence out with a straight face.

"This isn't funny."

Okay. Maybe not entirely a straight face.

"If a shallow hole isn't filled in and the convergent energies keep hitting it and making it deeper, then something a lot more demonic could get through. If that happens, people will die."

That took care of the smiling. "I figured." Nikki, Alan, Charlie, Rahal, Tom, Brenda, Hartley . . . "They always seem to."

"Yeah, they do." Her palm cupped his cheek for a second and he saw thousands of years of people dying while she lived on. He'd have jerked back, but she was gone before he could move, sitting once again on the end of the sofa bed. It had happened so fast he could almost convince himself he'd imagined it. In fact, he had every intention of convincing himself he'd imagined it.

"So . . ." She leaned back on her elbows, crossed her legs, and kicked one sneakered foot in the air. ". . . what happened to your teacher?"

And here they were back at the beginning. And why not answer? It seemed he owed Leah a confidence or two. "She went back to her own world."

"Her own world. Another world?" Leah asked when he nodded. "Not a hell?"

There were wizards nailed to a blackboard. "Not exactly."

"Damn." Apparently, after living for so long, nothing much surprised her either. Tony appreciated how much that simplified things. "Reality's getting a little crowded."

"Tell me about it."

"Now." Her foot kicked out and pointed. "Your turn."

So he told her. About the Shadowlord because that was tied up with the whole wizard thing but mostly about Arra and how he hadn't wanted to leave and she hadn't been able to stay. "But she left a lot of information on her laptop about how to be a wizard and I've been . . ." He stopped when Leah raised a hand. "What?"

"You're learning how to manipulate cosmic energies from a home study course designed by a wizard from another world?"

"Yeah."

"Unbelievable."

"What is?"

"Her cosmic energies aren't your cosmic energies."

"What?"

"She's not from *this* world."

"Duh."

Gripping the edge of the sofa bed, Leah sat up and leaned toward him. "Okay, I'll try and make this simple. It's all about energy, right? This Arra did teach you that?"

"Yeah." He tried not to sound defensive and had a feeling he was failing miserably at it.

"So the energy of her world has to have been different from the energy of this world because the whole . . ." One hand rose to sketch a circle in the air. ". . . world is different. Different planet. Different stars. Her energy pattern is therefore *different*. Following me so far?"

"Yeah."

"So, on this world she had to adapt everything she knew to fit a new pattern. To make a square peg—her—fit in a round hole. What worked for her here won't necessarily work for you. You are not a square peg. You're a round peg. The hole is also round. You need to find a teacher who knows what's going on in this world."

Beginning to get pissed about the distinctly patronizing tone, Tony reached out for the spray cheese and the container slapped into his hand. "I seem to be managing."

"What is *that*?"

She sounded more appalled than impressed. Not the reaction he'd expected but then, he reminded himself, she claimed to have met wizards before. "It's a can of spray cheese." He turned it so she could see the label. "I was eating it on beef jerky."

"On beef jerky?" Leah rummaged around in the blankets, pulled out the open bag of jerky, stared at it, and shuddered. "I can see I've got my work cut out for me. Never mind, we'll deal with your eating habits another time."

"Hey, I'm not the one with a demon in my belly!"

"Oh, for crying out loud, I didn't eat him! And I certainly didn't cover him in . . ." Leaning forward, she snatched the can out of his hand. ". . . an edible cheese product. Doesn't it worry you that the manufacturers feel they have to define it as edible?"

"No."

"Fine!"

"All right, then!"

Leah glared down at the can in one hand and the bag in the other and her lips twitched. Then her whole body. Just for a moment, Tony was afraid that spray cheese and beef jerky were the secret ingredients Ryne Cyratane had been holding back and now, with them both in close proximity, the gate was opening. Then he realized she was trying not to laugh.

Then she wasn't trying anymore.

She laughed like they hadn't been talking about demons and wizards and the possibility of people dying. She laughed like this moment, the moment when laughter overwhelmed her, was the only moment that mattered. Tony smiled as he watched her; it was impossible not to.

It was just as impossible not to join in.

They almost managed to stop a couple of times, then one of them would wave the can of spray cheese and they'd lose it again. Finally, they ended up lying side by side on the sofa bed, gasping for breath.

"Oh, yeah. I needed that." A long breath in and she sat up, twisting just enough to look back over her shoulder at him, pushing dark curls off her face. "Was it good for you?"

Tony ignored her, frowning as he tugged a familiar plastic bag out from under her butt. "You've crushed my jerky."

The brow he could see lifted in a decidedly smutty manner. "Is that what you crazy kids are calling it now? Damn." And the brow dipped down. "Is that the time?"

He squinted toward the TiVo. 4:46. He had to be up for work in three hours and fifteen minutes. "Fuck."

Her turn to ignore him. He was kind of amazed by that actually, all things considered. "I've got to get some sleep." She slid to the edge of the mattress and stood. "I've got a two o'clock call for a CBC Movie of the Week."

"Stunt?"

"It's what I do." Scooping up her purse, she hung it on her shoulder and headed for the door. "If you're finished with work before sunset—they want the light for the shot, reflections on the water and all that artistic crap—can you come by VanTerm? I'll leave word with security."

"Hang on!" He jumped to his feet and followed her. "That's it? We eat chow mein, you tell me we're having a Demonic Convergence with a high chance of imps, and then we just go off to work?"

"Unfortunately, saving the world doesn't buy the groceries." Rummaging in the depths of her bag, she pulled out a slightly crumpled card and passed it to Tony. "My cell number. Call if you're going to be late or you can't make it."

"And?"

"And we'll reschedule. This isn't going to go away; we've got lots of time to fix it."

"Yeah, but when did it *start?*"

"A week ago, Monday afternoon at 2:10."

"Really?"

"No. And yes. Approximately." He could hear her smile even though he couldn't see her face. "You really are gullible for a wizard."

"Maybe." Reaching out, he stopped her from opening the door. "But one thing before you go; are you here, in Vancouver, because this is where the convergence is happening, or is it happening here because it's where you are?"

Her expression was almost proud when she turned, like she was about to praise a puppy. "You're smarter than you look."

"Thank you. You didn't answer the question."

"This . . ." A light, almost reverent touch against her stomach. ". . . is the second oldest and most powerful continuously running bit of magic in the world."

"What's the first?"

"I'm not allowed to say."

"Seriously?"

"No, I'm just bullshitting you again." A firmer pat on the sweater above the tat. "This is the oldest."

He literally felt his heart start beating again. The way his life had been going lately, if there *was* an older bit of magic in the world, he could expect it on his doorstep at any time. "That's a sick sense of humor you've got there; I can see why you were a demon's favorite handmaiden."

"Sticks and stones . . ." Ryne Cyratane flashed as she smiled. ". . . won't actually touch me."

"Lucky you. So if you're walking around with the oldest magic in the world, then the convergence is here because you are? Nothing personal," he added when she nodded, "but I wish you were somewhere else."

"Too late now. Things have started. And when I say things, I am, of course, referring to the Demonic Convergence eating holes through our reality into a myriad of hells. Bright side, though, with a wizard in the immediate area, the world stands a better chance." Dark brows lifted as she grinned. "You wouldn't wish a worse chance on the world, would you?"

He made a show of thinking about it but didn't fool her.

"You're a good man, Tony Foster." Taking hold of his shoulders, she kissed him gently on both cheeks and murmured something in a language he didn't know. "Sumerian blessing," she told him, stepping away. "Roughly translates as 'the gods help those who help themselves.' I left out the part about the goats. Redo the wards before you go to sleep—they won't stop a Demonlord, but they might stop lesser demons."

"Might?"

"Should."

"*Should*'s not a lot more encouraging."

"Best I've got."

Ryne Cyratane flickered again as Leah went out the door. Head half turned, he seemed to be paying more attention to Leah's surroundings than to his handmaiden although, since Tony was trying to get a better look at his ass, there may have been subtleties missed.

He had just enough cough syrup left to reset the wards. Finished, he closed the file on the laptop, powered down, and closed the door.

They won't stop a Demonlord, but they might stop lesser demons.

He locked the door, put the chain on, and shoved a chair up under the handle. One thing he'd learned over the years—it didn't hurt to take precautions and not taking them often hurt a lot. Where hurt could be defined as, *Oh, look, here I am back in the ER.*

He could still catch two hours and forty minutes of sleep if he fell over right now. When the paper bag the Chinese food had come in rattled as he tossed it onto the counter, he realized that they hadn't eaten the fortune cookies. He grabbed one and cracked it.

The blow from sunlight is more unexpected than the blow from darkness. That was new. "Cookie guys must have gotten themselves a new Magic 8 Ball," he said. Shoving the slip of paper in his pocket, he stripped off his clothes and dropped onto the bed. As he leaned across to get the light, something crinkled under his elbow.

Somehow a copy of *TV Week* magazine had gotten shoved under the bottom sheet. It had been folded open at "Star Spotting" and the photo of Lee and the blonde du jour. It looked like they were coming out of a club. She had both hands wrapped around Lee's arm, her gaze following the strands of long, pale hair blowing up into his face. He looked like he was saying something clever to the crowd of paparazzi, his hand holding a shape in the air.

"Wizards see what's there," Tony told the picture.

He wasn't touching her. He wasn't looking at her. She was an accessory.

A smoke screen.

A lie.

"Yeah." The magazine hit the far wall and fluttered to the floor. "Bitter much?"

He left the television on a blue screen with the sound off. A high-tech night-light for people who knew there were things to be afraid of in the dark.

"Hey, Tony, I got an e-mail from Brianna."

Tony lowered his coffee and peered blearily across the office at Amy. He must be getting old. Two hours and forty minutes of sleep just didn't do it for him anymore. "So?"

"You want to know what it says?"

"No."

"It says, 'Tell that jerk-face Tony to check his e-mail.' You know . . ." She leaned back in her chair and flicked an eraser at him. ". . . you might want to try and establish a relationship with someone your own age."

He realized he should have gotten a larger coffee as the eraser bounced off his forehead. Except that he didn't think they made a larger coffee. "We don't have a relationship."

"No? Then why'd you give her your e-mail?"

"I didn't."

"Sure you didn't. You look like shit, by the way. Late night?"

"Very."

"Hot date?"

"Not even remotely."

"Cold date?"

Henry's body temperature was several degrees below normal. Tony wondered why his brain decided to throw that into the conversation. "No date."

"Ah, so you stayed up drowning your sorrows. Dude, I'm there."

Amy had gone off again with Brian—her on again/off again boyfriend—just after the incident in August. She insisted it had nothing to do with what had happened that night, but Tony still felt vaguely guilty even though nothing had specifically happened to Amy. Of course, given that it was Amy . . . well, that might have been the problem.

Tuning out Amy's litany of dating woes, he negotiated a maze of papier-mâché tombstones and headed for the soundstage.

He wasn't sure how he made it through the morning.

Mason's close-ups.

Lee's close-ups.

Padma's close-ups.

The same lines, over and over.

Sorge's anticipated rant about matching light levels between studio and location.

"Welcome to the thrilling and exciting world of syndicated television."

Peter half turned. "What was that, Mr. Foster?"

Oh, shit. Had he said that out loud?

"I . . . um . . . was just . . ."

"Why don't you go make sure Raymond Dark's office is ready?"

"Right."

The next scene would be one of the first scenes in the episode, the scene where Padma's character arrived to hire Raymond Dark, someone or something in an advanced state of decay having been lurking about her windows at night. People who worked in the entertainment industry got very blasé about the dead walking.

*   *   *

"This isn't *just* a stalker, Mr. Taylor. Stalkers don't shed parts of their body . . . Sorry."

"'Don't shed body parts behind the hedge,'" Peter called from behind the monitors. "I like the emphasis on *just* and we're still rolling."

"This isn't *just* a stalker, Mr. Taylor . . ."

Tony let the words wash over him. And over and over, and the moment Peter called lunch, he dropped onto the office couch and closed his eyes.

"Late night?"

No mistaking that crushed-velvet voice. He opened his eyes to see Lee gazing down at him from a little over an arm's length away. For one damn-the-torpedoes moment Tony thought about asking, *Afraid I'll drag you down here with me?*—but sanity prevailed and he said only: "Very."

"Hot date?"

Been there, done that, had the conversation once already today. "Not even remotely."

"Hey, too bad."

Oh, no. You don't get to be all happy my love life sucks. "Bite me."

"Pardon."

Oh, shit. Had he said *that* out loud, too? So much for sanity prevailing. Miss a few hours' sleep and his sense of self-preservation took off for parts unknown. He shoved his fist in his mouth to block a yawn and, when he could talk again, said, "Sorry. I'm so out of it, I don't know what I'm saying."

"Sure."

What was that supposed to mean?

"Pleasant dreams."

Or that, he wondered as Lee walked away.

Worrying about it probably kept him awake for all of three or four minutes. He tossed. He turned. He realized he was probably dreaming about the time Lee suddenly acquired an impressive and familiar set of antlers. Usually, that kind of awareness woke him up but not today. He heard Leah's voice say something about feeding on sexual energies, and he settled back to enjoy the show.

"Tony!"

No.

"Come on, wake up."

Not going to happen. Not now. Not when . . .

"I haven't got time for this shit."

He didn't have a whole lot of choice about waking up when he hit the floor. Rolling over onto his back, he glared up at Jack Elson. "What?"

"I've got a body I want you to look at."

"What?"

"They found a construction worker just down from where you lot were shooting last couple of nights, torn to pieces."

Tony took the RCMP constable's offered hand and allowed the larger man to drag him up onto his feet. "Sucks to be him, but what's that got to do with me?"

"Something bit his arm off."

⤳ THREE

"Cougar. Didn't they have one in Stanley Park a couple of years ago? Probably ran out of house pets to eat out in the suburbs and wandered into the city."

"Coroner ruled it out."

"Bear, then."

"No."

"Really big raccoon." When Jack took his eyes off the road long enough to glare across the cab of his truck, Tony shrugged. "Raccoons can be pretty damned big. I saw one once about the size of small dog."

"You sure?"

"About what?"

Jack downshifted and accelerated through a changing light. "About what you saw. Maybe it wasn't a raccoon."

"You think I saw a small dog?"

"Don't tell me what I think."

"Fine." Tony sighed. "If you don't think I saw a raccoon, what do you think I saw?"

Another glance across the cab. "You tell me."

"Oh, for fuck's sake; sometimes a raccoon is just a raccoon!" He sank down as far as the seat belt strap would allow.

Tony hadn't wanted to go look at a dead body, particularly not a dismembered dead body, and he'd half hoped that CB would refuse to allow him the time off. Although CB hadn't been happy about losing his TAD for the afternoon, he was well aware of the benefit of remaining in the RCMP's good graces and he'd waved off Tony's protests that he was needed on the soundstage with one massive hand. *"As difficult to believe as it may be, Mr. Foster, I believe production can continue for a few hours without you."*

"Boss, there's no PA out there yet. I'm it."

"So if an errand needs running, someone on the soundstage will have to run it."

Tony'd opened his mouth to point out how unlikely it was that grips or electricians or carpenters would do any such thing and then closed it again when CB added: *"They'll do it for me."*

Yes, they would. Because no one who worked for Chester Bane would be suicidal enough to refuse although they'd tell themselves they were doing it because it never hurt to do the boss a favor.

Which was also true.

As Jack pulled into the underground parking at Vancouver General Hospital, Tony's stomach growled. "You made me miss lunch," he muttered.

"You may thank me for that," Jack told him, turning off the truck. "Come on."

The city morgue was in the basement near the end of a long hall made narrow by a line of gurneys, wheelchairs, and a locked filing cabinet. Cramped conditions along the outside walls of the outer office made the reason for outsourcing the filing cabinet clear. A middle-aged Asian woman, wearing the end-of-her-rope expression common to professionals who fought with bureaucracy on a daily basis, sat at one of the cluttered desks forking noodles out of a Styrofoam bowl.

"Dr. Wong."

She waved the fork in Jack's general direction and continued chewing.

"This is the witness I mentioned earlier. Should we just go on in?"

Fork tines pointed toward the set of double doors in the back wall.

"Thanks. We won't be long."

A large hand between Tony's shoulder blades got him moving again in spite of his brain locking things down by suddenly repeating *dismembered dead body* over and over as though it had just realized what that meant.

"Elson."

Jack paused in the doorway, leaving Tony staring into a harshly lit room at a bank of stainless steel drawers familiar to anyone who'd ever turned on a television set.

"If he pukes, you clean it up."

Jack snorted. "If he pukes, he cleans it up."

"Hey!" He turned just far enough to glare back through the open door at the doctor. "I'm not going to puke."

"Yeah." She plunged her fork back into the noodles. "That's what they all say."

And then the door was closed and Jack was walking across the room and opening a drawer.

Pulling it open.

Exposing the dead body.

The dismembered dead body.

For him to look at.

Look at the dismembered dead body.

"Oh, for Christ's sake, Foster. You've seen bodies before."

"I know."

"So get your ass over here."

It wasn't so much the body, it was the morgue and the drawer and the smell—the place smelled like the grade ten biology lab just before the whole fetal pig fiasco; he'd dropped out a week later—the combination made it creepier than he was used to.

Creepier than a dead baby in a backpack, its life sucked out by an ancient Egyptian wizard? Creepier than a man bouncing off a window, every bone in his body broken? Creepier than watching a wardrobe assistant gurgle out her last breath through the ruin of her throat?

Well, if you put it that way . . .

At least this guy was likely to stay dead.

Fingers crossed about that whole staying dead thing, Tony walked over to the open drawer.

He didn't recognize the construction worker, but then he hadn't seen any of them naked so that might be a factor. The left arm was missing about ten centimeters below the shoulder, the edges of the wound ragged, the end of the bone crushed. "Where's the arm?"

"No one knows."

"Nice."

"Probably not. Losing the arm didn't kill him; whatever took it also broke his neck. What do you see?"

"Dead guy missing an arm."

"Tony."

"Seriously. That's all I . . ."

"What?"

Frowning, Tony walked around the drawer and stared at the construction worker's other side. Head cocked, he spread his fingers and tried to match the tips of the first three and his thumb into a line of gouges ending in deep punctures. "Is there a set just like this on the guy's back?"

"Why?"

Wizards saw what was there. "Because if there is, it's how it held on while it bit the arm off."

There was a set of identical punctures in the guy's back.

"It?" Jack demanded.

Tony shrugged. "Your guess is as good as mine."

"Probably not!"

Yeah, okay. That was valid. He took another look at the body. Something with three fingers and impressive claws had definitely bitten the poor bastard's arm off. And that was all he had.

Not an imp, though. Not unless the Demonic Convergence imps were bigger than the regular kind, and Leah's attitude had implied they weren't. She'd said he wouldn't have any trouble dealing with them and, although his ego was plenty healthy, he suspected he'd have a little trouble dealing with whatever the hell had been snacking on construction workers.

Worker.

So far.

Great. This meant there was something going on in Vancouver besides the Demonic Convergence. And Henry. *Yeah, we're a happening kind of place.*

"If you've got something, Tony, spit it out."

He rubbed the edge of the stainless steel table with his thumb. "It's not about this."

"For Christ's sake, try and stay focused. I've got a dead man here, and . . ." When Jack's voice trailed off, Tony looked up to find the constable's pale eyes locked on his face. "It's more weirdness, isn't it? There're two sets of weird going on. This . . ." He waved a hand over the body. ". . . and whatever you decided didn't do this."

"It's nothing."

"Oh, no. This is something so the other thing, it doesn't get to be nothing until I say it's nothing."

Tony ran over that in his head and wasn't sure where he ended up. "What?"

"Talk. Or we stay in here until you do."

"So this Demonic Convergence thing, it started a week ago but it isn't responsible for this?"

"No. Probably not." Jack's expression suggested he be more definite and since hanging around in the morgue was beginning to freak him out, that seemed like a good idea. "Definitely not," he amended.

"Demonic Convergence says demons to me, and a demon could have done this."

"Yeah, but there's barely even been enough time for it to wear reality away to the point where imps could get through." Tony was improvising now off very little information, but Jack didn't need to know that. "No way the Demonic Convergence had anything to do with this unfortunate man's death."

Jack stared at him for a long moment and then slammed the drawer. Fortunately, the seals absorbed most of the sound. "So what did?"

"I have no idea."

"Layers of hells?"

"Yeah."

"But if hell exists, then . . . just, no."

Tony braced himself as the truck briefly lifted up onto two wheels while taking the exit off Lougheed. "If it helps, it's not hell like a church-sponsored hell. It's hell like a really shitty place to be stuck in, so why not call it hell. If you live there, you probably call it something like Scarborough."

"What?"

"It's a Toronto thing."

"Then no one outside of Toronto cares." Palming the wheel around, Jack hit the gas and set about trying to break the sound barrier heading south on Boundary Road. "So I can expect demons as this Convergence goes on?"

"First, demons would be a long shot even if there was no one around to take care of things. Second, I'm on it."

"Is that a 'no'?"

"That's a no. Although there might be a few imps."

"Imps?"

"Sort of small, mostly harmless demons."

"Can I shoot them?"

"How should I know?"

"You're the wizard. How long is this Convergence going to last?"

"No idea."

Like many very fair men, Jack turned almost purple when upset. Tony took pity on him before he blew an artery. "I'll check some stuff out, okay? When I have answers, you'll have answers."

"What kind of stuff?"

"Wizard stuff."

"This is totally insane."

"Don't blame me, you're the one who decided to go all Nightstalker. You know, a little denial can be a lot healthier."

"Not in my line of work. I'm after the truth." He narrowly missed running down a young woman pulling a two-meter-high Dutch windmill on a dolly and sighed. "That sounded inanely pompous, didn't it?"

"Had a certain Fox Mulder–like quality to it, yeah."

The truck rocked to a stop in front of the studio, momentum fighting brakes hard enough that Tony's face nearly impacted with the dashboard. From his sudden vantage point, he could see other vaguely oily scuff marks. His face hadn't been the first. He supposed it was encouraging that Jack's driving hadn't been aimed specifically at him—he'd been starting to think he inspired a certain lunacy behind the wheel. Some kind of wizard leakage thing.

"I'm fine, thanks for asking," he muttered as he straightened, fumbling for the seat belt.

"You're welcome. You've got my cell number?"

"Yeah." Jack's card was in his wallet right next to Leah's. The cop and the stuntwoman. The RCMP and the Demongate. Small world. He jumped out of the truck and turned to close the door.

"Hey." Jack leaned toward him. "If you find out what killed that guy, you call me."

"I'll call," Tony sighed. He closed the door and looked in through the open window. "But whatever it is, you won't be able to arrest it."

"I can arrest anything I can get a pair of cuffs on," Jack snarled, slammed the truck into gear, and roared off. Traffic stuttered to give him room, and Tony had an instant's unobstructed view of the other side of the street . . .

. . . and Kevin Groves. The tabloid reporter looked like he'd just won a lottery.

"How long until we can shoot at UBC?" Eyes rolling, Amy beckoned Tony over. "You have got to be kidding me! Who? That can't take more than a . . . What, them again? Right. Fine. If anyone cancels, will you call me? Thank you." She dropped the phone onto the receiver and sighed. "Once again, UBC is standing in for every alien city in syndication. You'd think it was the only place in the lower mainland that looked science fictiony."

He balanced half his butt on the edge of her desk. "So why do we want to shoot there?"

"Giant mutant plants escape from a genetics lab and start blinding people. Raymond Dark goes in at night when they're doing whatever plants do at night."

"Like Day of the Triffids."

"What?"

"RKO movie with Howard Keel and Janette Scott. Although I think it was a meteor shower that actually blinded people. They mention it in the *Rocky Horror Picture Show*." Frowning, he reached for a plastic six-legged octopus and got his hand slapped.

"So there are no new ideas in television. Quel surprise. Not." She moved the octopus out of his reach. "No one will notice we stole it."

"I'll notice."

"Yeah, and if you spent more time learning wizard shit and less time watching Movie Central, you might be useful."

"For what?"

"That's the question, isn't it?" Leaning back in her chair, she laced her fingers over the line of skulls embroidered onto her raw cotton shirt and smiled. Tony mistrusted the smile. "So, an afternoon off with the new boyfriend?"

And that was why. "You're delusional."

"I just want you to be happy."

"We were at the morgue."

"Cool. Why?"

"He wanted me to look at a body."

"Kinky. Pre-or post-autopsy?"

Tony couldn't remember any stitching, so he guessed. "Pre."

"Kinkier."

Before the conversation could devolve further, they were distracted by a young woman fighting to get a Dutch windmill through the front doors and into the office. She looked familiar.

"This is the last one they have," she gasped over the noise of balsa wood and canvas hitting the floor, "so it better be the right one."

"They?" Tony asked, ducking a flimsy-looking blade. "Windmills R Us?"

"Prop shop over at Bridge," Amy explained. "We borrowed it. And before you ask, I suspect it was part of some bucolic alien landscape."

"I was actually going to ask if they know we plan on burning it down in a blatant *Frankenstein* rip-off."

"With any luck, that would be a big fat no and, according to the writers, it's not a rip-off, it's an homage. Krista, this is Tony, our TAD. Tony, this is Krista, the new office PA."

"Hey!" Krista waved a hand in Tony's general direction. "I don't suppose you could help me get this onto the soundstage."

"Through there?" He glanced toward the scuffed door that led to the hall that led to the soundstage that led to the show that CB built. Lined with racks of extra costumes, the hall was barely wide enough for one and not even remotely wide enough for one and a windmill.

"Well, duh."

"Not possible. You'll have to take it outside and go around to the carpenter's door."

Krista looked at the windmill and then at the bloody knuckles she'd acquired getting it into the office. "You're fucking kidding me."

"He really isn't," Amy told her cheerfully.

The new PA's brows drew in, stretching the blue crescent moon on the left side of her forehead. "This is a test, isn't it?"

As Amy shook her head, Tony leaned close and murmured, "You're lucky. The last two got sent to Starbucks."

"Bad?"

"One of them's still there."

"Right." She took a deep breath and began to force the windmill back outside.

"Need some help?"

"No, thanks. I've got it."

Tony backed toward Amy's desk as something cracked. His view was blocked by the base of the windmill, so it was impossible to tell what.

"Get out of my way, you fucking asshat," Krista's voice snapped out like a whip.

Or who.

"I think I'm starting to like her," Amy said, grabbing for the phone. "She has a way with words. CB Productions."

"I definitely like her," Tony growled as Kevin Groves came into the office cradling his left arm. Anyone who recognized Groves for the fucking asshat he truly was, was a person worth knowing. "Hey," he waved a hand in front of Amy's face. "I'm out of here."

She nodded at him and began explaining the company policy regarding their actors and reality shows. As far as Tony knew, CB didn't actually have a company policy. Amy just enjoyed maligning the intelligence of reality show producers on CB's dime.

"Tony Foster." Groves' voice matched his looks: thin and unmemorable.

"Can't talk." Tony spun on one heel, rubber squealing against tile, and headed for the exit. "Have to work."

"Just a few minutes of your time."

"No."

"Why were you out riding with RCMP Constable Jack Elson?"

"Ask him."

"Is it true you're lovers?"

Tony turned in the open doorway and laughed in Groves' face. "You know, you should ask Constable Elson that—but wait until I'm there so I can watch you get your ass kicked."

"I just intended to get your attention." Groves took a step closer. His jaw worked at a wad of gum. Spearmint from the smell. He was holding up his PDA, the record icon flashing. "Were you with him today because of the construction worker who was killed last night by your location shoot?"

"*My* location shoot?"

"Fine. By the show's location shoot. By the location being used by the television program known as *Darkest Night*. Whatever. Do the police believe that supernatural forces are responsible for the removal of the man's arm?"

Groves knowing the arm had been removed was better than him knowing it had been bitten off, Tony supposed. Over one of the reporter's polyester-clad shoulders, he saw Amy stick her head in Mason's office. "Are you on cheap drugs?" he asked conversationally.

"Do you use drugs to heighten your senses?" Groves asked in turn.

Tony smiled as Jennifer, Mason's personal assistant, emerged. Part of

Jennifer's job was to protect Mason from unwanted press attention. When she was in a good mood, she extended that protection to the rest of the studio. His smile widened as one set of impeccably manicured fingers clamped down on Groves' shoulder and the other reached low to give the wedgie to end all wedgies.

He joined in Amy's applause as Jennifer frog-marched the reporter across the office by the grip she maintained on the waistband of his tighty whiteys—which was now considerably higher than his waist.

"Foster!" Not surprisingly, Groves' voice sounded shriller than usual. "Does this have anything to do with the Demonic Convergence?"

He stopped applauding and ducked quickly through the door, closing it behind him before Groves could see his face.

"Demonic Convergence?"

Too late to hide his expression from Lee, who'd apparently been lurking in the hall, one arm draped nonchalantly over a rack of faux Gypsy-wear.

"Tabloid reporter." Tony shrugged, hoping he sounded a lot more dismissive than he felt. "That sort of shit's his stock in trade."

"Like haunted houses."

"Sure." Shit. Not sure. The last thing he wanted was for Lee, who knew damned well haunted houses were real, to start thinking they were about to be involved in an actual Demonic Convergence. Which they were. Tony worked his way past a pair of gorilla suits wondering how the hell Groves had known about the DC. Had Leah spoken to him? And if she had, why? And if she hadn't, how else . . . ?

"Tony!"

He turned just far enough to see that Lee had followed him. Given his ongoing obsession with the actor, not noticing that kind of proximity had to be healthy. Healthier had he not been distracted by the thought of Leah taking Kevin Groves, of all people, into her confidence, but lately he'd take any emotional stability he could get.

"Well?"

From Lee's tone of voice, he'd missed half of an entire conversation. "Sorry. I wasn't listening."

"Yeah. I noticed." And Lee wasn't happy about it. Another time, a time when Tony didn't have an immortal stuntwoman, a gung ho RCMP constable, and a Demonic Convergence to deal with—*and let's not forget there's also something out there that reduced a grown man to snack food*—Lee's unhappiness at his lack of attention would be bringing on a case of the warm fuzzies.

Another time.

Right now, he had rather a lot on his plate. Did Jack expect him to go hunting the snack-food-reducing monster? Because that so wasn't going to happen.

"Tony!"

"Right. Sorry. Distracted."

Lee sighed and ran a hand up through his hair. "I was just asking if there was anything in what Groves said. That you were out with Constable Elson because a construction worker got killed."

He wanted to be a part of it—whatever it turned out to be. It was obvious in his voice, in his expression, in his body language. Everything said: *Let me help you.*

Oh, yeah, like Tony was going to let *that* happen. In the last six months, Lee had been possessed three times and there was no way in hell—any hell— that he was going to add to that list.

Let me help you.

Why?

Because I seem to have a deep-seated metaphysical death wish I'm not even aware of. Maybe it stems from my repressed sexual identity, but since that's tied up with you, too, I guess I'm in the right place.

No fucking way. He was not going to be responsible for Lee getting wham- mied yet again. Tony managed a near approximation of a smutty grin and flashed it in the actor's general direction. "Hate to admit it, but Groves was right. I was with Constable Elson because we were having hot Mountie sex in the cab of his truck."

Long pause.

Lee stared.

Tony kept grinning.

Finally, Lee sighed again, the exhalation a type of surrender. "CB let you off work for that?"

"Yeah, the boss is all about keeping the cops happy." He started walking again. Once in the soundstage, Peter'd have them both back at work and this conversation would be over. "Just be thankful Jack's not interested in your ass, or he'd pimp you out, too."

"You call him Jack?"

"When I call him other things, he reminds me he's armed."

"Tony . . ."

Tony sped up just enough to keep Lee's hand from landing on his shoulder. *Goddamn it!* The red light was on, and they were stuck together at the end of the hall, waiting for the camera to stop rolling in a space barely a meter square. They were *not* going to talk about the Demonic Convergence. He was not go- ing to give Lee the chance to talk him into changing his mind, then somehow put himself in danger, and confuse the hell out of both of them when Tony had to ride to the rescue. Again. "So, how's the blonde?"

Lee frowned. "Which blonde?"

"You can't keep track?"

"Sure, but . . ."

"The one you took to the latest premiere." Hands curved out in front of his chest indicated her dominant features. "Nice picture of the two of you in *TV Week*."

"Ah, yeah . . . Judith. She's fine. Great."

"Rented?"

"Jesus, Tony." Lee rolled his eyes. "No, she was not fucking rented."

"Borrowed?"

"Where do you go to borrow a blonde?"

Tony snorted. "Probably not the same place you do. So how was the movie?"

"What movie?"

"The one you went to with the borrowed blonde."

"Obviously, not great; I don't remember it. How was the morgue?"

Nice try. "What morgue?"

"The one you went to with *your* borrowed blond."

"Before or after the hot Mountie sex?"

"Look, Tony, if you don't want me to have any part of this—whatever this is—all you have to do is say so."

A long moment passed, and it was as if all that guy banter hadn't happened. They were back at the Demonic Convergence part of the conversation.

Tony'd never noticed before that the red light made a noise when it went off. Sort of a faint *plock*. "I don't want you to have any part of this," he said, yanked open the door, and stepped out onto the soundstage.

He hadn't expected to be done with work by sunset, let alone have time to get from the studio to VanTerm before Leah finished her stunt. But at 5:50, almost an hour before the sun actually went down, he was in his car and heading west on Hastings, squinting behind the shield of his dark glasses.

VanTerm was a container terminal up on Burrard Inlet. Eventually, everyone shooting any kind of shipping scene in the Vancouver area ended up there because its layout made it easy to crop the shot. For the short time Tony'd been paying attention, it had stood in for San Francisco, New York, New Jersey, Singapore, Gotham City, and at least two alien planets, not to mention the half-dozen times it had actually played itself. It was the UBC of shipping locations.

He turned right on Victoria Drive, drove more or less the speed limit to Stewart Street, turned left and then right onto the terminal grounds.

"I'm here for the CBC shoot." He fumbled out his Director's Guild Card, but the middle-aged security guard in the box barely looked up from his laptop before waving him through.

Berth three was past the reefer yard, past the container yard, jutting out into the inlet across the end of the jetty that also held berths one, two, and four. Tony parked by the first truck—freshly purple, the CBC logo bright and shiny on both sides and across the back—locked his car, and started walking. Quickly. It was still a bit of a hike and he wanted to make sure he saw Leah take her dive. It was more of a stunt than CB would ever be willing to pay for—even if the season one *Darkest Night* DVDs sold as well as Olivia in marketing predicted. Since Olivia in marketing was ten thousand or so in debt to a bookie named Icepick Ernie, no one put much faith in her ability to pick a winner.

They had four cameras set for the shoot. One up on the back end of the container ship to catch the fall from above, one in a Ports Canada Police boat about ten meters out, and two on the jetty. The two on the jetty were, Tony was happy to notice, one model older than the cameras used by CB Productions.

"Let's hear it for government spending," he muttered, hands in his front pockets as he watched the second unit director set the shot. "Repaint the trucks before you replace the equipment."

Still, hard to argue with the kind of pull that got clear skies and a totally killer sunset in a city that got roughly three hundred days of rain a year. When the CBC wanted a sunset, they got one.

A familiar voice shouting his name turned his attention away from the water. "Daniel?"

CB Productions' entire stunt team jogged over, grinning.

"What are you doing here?"

Daniel patted his radio. "I'm on the safety crew. You don't honestly think I can support a family on the hours I get from CB, do you?"

"I thought your wife supported your family." Daniel's wife was in advertising. Tony wasn't exactly sure what that meant, but it had, at one point, involved Daniel bringing in packages of wieners for everyone on the shoot.

"Ouch. Way to kick a guy in the nuts." But he was still grinning when he said it, so Tony decided not to worry about insulting a man who had black belts in three martial arts and who cheated death for a living. Okay, maybe not death, not most of the time, but he definitely cheated soft tissue damage on a regular basis. "So, you're done early today."

"I am that."

"You here to see Leah's dive?"

"Yeah." Tony nodded up at the container ship. "She going from the back end there?"

"It's called the stern, you ignorant git."

"Looks stern. Also high."

"And this is one of the smaller ones. There's ships out there today that can carry up to and above 8,000 TEU—this one, I'd say no more than 4,000."

"No shit."

"You have no idea of what I just said, do you? TEU stands for twenty-foot equivalent unit and . . . uh, never mind. Essentially, this may look big, but there's lots bigger." He waved a hand; a *Blue's Clues* bandage wrapped around one finger. "Approximately seven meters, railing to surface, into water approximately fifteen meters deep."

"Deep enough?"

Daniel snorted. "More than. And cleaner than usual, too. Ports Canada guys on the boat were saying it was highest tidal backwash they'd ever seen up the inlet. Swept all sorts of crap out to sea."

"And that's good?"

"Very. Hitting a hunk of crap that floated in past the cleanup crew is always a frightening possibility—where always means not today."

Not today, not for Leah, Tony thought as Daniel took on the unmistakable characteristics of someone listening to voices in his head. Coincidence or Demongate? He didn't have enough information to answer that. He really didn't want enough information to answer that, but then, it sucked to be him.

"Divers are in the water." Daniel clapped him on one shoulder hard enough to rock him back a step. "We're ready to go. I'll talk to you later."

"You know you've got a burning windmill in your future, right?"

He paused, half turned. "*Frankenstein* rip-off?"

"Homage."

"That's what they all say."

True enough, Tony admitted as Daniel jogged back to join the rest of the safety crew on the jetty. The sunset had painted the tops of the waves red-gold and burned highlights along the edges of the ship. Leah, wearing a short blonde wig and a shorter red dress, was standing at the rail talking to a heavy-set man with a gleaming shaved head and a down vest. Probably the show's stunt coordinator. As Tony watched, she glanced down and lifted a hand to acknowledge the divers, then positioned herself with her back to the rail. She had to be on a box. She wasn't that tall.

Bald-and-gleaming moved back to stand by the camera.

The entire crew gathered itself up.

"Rolling!"

Tony repeated the word silently as it bounced up and down the jetty. As it faded, he knew the director would be telling Bald-and-gleaming that Leah could go when she was ready.

Leah's arms went out; she jerked back and went over.

Seven meters later, she hit the water butt first, folded just enough to take the heavy slap off her back. From the pumped fist rising up over the video village, the splash, lit by the setting sun, was everything the DP wanted.

He couldn't see her surface, the edge of the jetty was in the way, but he heard her.

"Damn! That's cold!"

He joined the crew's applause and moved closer as the divers swam up to help her to the aluminum ladder Daniel had just lowered into the water. The strappy red high heels seemed to be giving her a bit of a problem, but hands reached down to pull her the rest of the way. She accepted their congratulations with a coy and dripping curtsy, waved toward the director's double thumbs up and again to Bald-and-gleaming. By the time she got to Tony, she was wrapped in a thermal blanket.

"You okay?" he asked, falling in to step beside her.

"Please. Went out of the crow's nest once on a pirate ship in the Caribbean— 1716, it was. Now *that* was a fall."

"I thought you said you spent your time in the beds of powerful men?"

She winked at him from under a dripping fringe of wet wig. "What do you think I was doing in the crow's nest?"

"Keeping watch?"

"I had my eyes open if that counts."

Tony followed her up into the makeup wagon where she sat, still wrapped in the blanket so that a middle-aged Japanese woman could work the wig off without ripping the lace that attached it to her face.

"Tony, Hama. Hama, Tony."

The makeup artist nodded without looking up.

"Tony works over at CB Productions."

"The vampire show?"

"That's the one."

She looked up then. "Everett Winchester still with you?"

"Yeah. But don't quote me on that."

Hama grinned at Everett's signature line. "Tell him I said hi. All right, that's it." She tossed the wig onto the counter where it looked like blond roadkill. Drowned blond roadkill. "Get into dry clothes, and I'll take out the pins."

Her own hair still up under a net cap, Leah left the towel in the chair and slipped in behind the set of shelves that separated makeup from wardrobe. It was a layout Tony was familiar with and therefore just a bit on the cheap side for any other show. Still, with only Leah on camera, there wasn't a lot of point in bringing out two separate trailers.

"So, you the boyfriend?"

Given the peal of laughter from behind the shelves, Tony didn't see much point in answering.

Hama raised a delicately arched brow. "Apparently not."

"We're just . . ." Then he paused. What were they? Friends? Not yet. Metaphysical accidents? Closer, but hard to explain.

"We're compatriots," Leah declared, emerging from behind the screen in jeans, a white T-shirt, and a yellow hoodie, dress dripping from one hand and a pair of yellow high-tops in the other. "Partners in crime. *Paesano!*" She dropped back into the chair and drew her feet up to lace on the sneakers as Hama took the pins out of her hair. Released, it fell in thick black curls reaching just below her shoulders.

"Your mouth is open," she snickered, looking up from tying her second shoe. "What?"

"How the hell do you fit all that hair . . ." He waved at the wig on the counter. ". . . under that?"

"Magic."

Tony believed her.

Bouncing out of the chair, she zipped up the hoodie and turned just far enough to kiss Hama on the cheek. "You are a wizard of the makeup chair. I've stair falls next week. Will I see you there?"

"You will."

"*Bueno!*" She scooped the strap of a plaid shoulder bag up and over her shoulder, and grabbed his arm, not quite dragging him out the door. "Come on, Tony, I've got to sign off, then we can go."

"The stair fall's for the same movie?"

"Yep. Hell of a way to make a living, eh?"

"Then why do you do it?"

"Are you kidding? It's the most fun I've had with immortality since the thirteenth century." She raised a hand. "Don't ask. And the money's nothing to sneeze at. I mean we're talking $500 a day base rate plus, for this shoot, the CBC increase of 25 percent. I get called for a big budget movie and the increase can be as high as 130 percent—you should maybe learn some basic physical protections and think about it."

"No, thanks, I want to direct."

"Of course you do. Hey, I'm starving. The moment I finish the paperwork, let's head for some food."

"We're eating?"

"And talking. I think you proved last night you can handle both."

Last night. Right. "Where's . . . ?" He gestured at the space over her head.

"Ryne Cyratane? Probably as far from the gate as he can get. He's like a cat, hates water. Shit. Shoelace. Hang on."

Tony, who'd taken a couple of extra steps, turned as she dropped to one knee. The sunset was behind her, the last of the light unexpectedly bright. He raised a hand to shade his eyes, and saw something move. At first he thought it was the Demonlord, then he realized it was significantly more solid and was swinging a human arm directly through the space Leah's head had just occupied.

She dropped flat, warned by the swish or the smell or both, and rolled away from a kick that would have disemboweled her had the claws made contact.

Disemboweled anyone else.

As Leah rose to her knees, he thought he saw a familiar breadth of translucent bare shoulders behind her although with the sun in his eyes it was hard to tell for certain. "Do something!"

"Do what?" There were scales and horns and whoa! Teeth!

"Wizard it!"

Right.

He folded the middle two fingers of his right hand in and swung his right arm back and then around and over his head. He was supposed to shout the eleven words of the spell clearly and distinctly, but clear and distinct got dumped in favor of speed. Things that were mostly serrated edged were fucking motivating! As long as the arm motion and the words finished as the same time it should . . .

Energy surged up from his feet, roared through his body, and blew out of his outstretched arm, arcing between forefinger and little finger then blasting forward.

The sudden flash was impressive.

"Tony?" Leah scrambled across the asphalt toward him. "Are you all right?"

Good question. Bits hurt. Hardly surprising since the spell had knocked him back on his ass. He blinked away brilliant blue afterimages. "I think I broke my tailbone."

"Yeah . . ." She slipped an arm behind his shoulders and levered him up. Fortunately, her Demonlord seemed to have taken a powder because being cuddled by them both would have been too weird. ". . . and your fingernails are smoking."

One last narrow wisp of smoke drifted off into the twilight from the ends of both blackened nails. "Ow."

"Well put. What do you call that?"

"Arra called it a Powershot." His fingers felt scalded, but he could use his hand. "What the hell was that thing?"

"*That* was a demon."

"A demon? Like a Demonic Convergence demon? Like nothing to worry about because we'll only have to deal with imps? That kind of a demon?"

"It shouldn't be here!"

"No shit!"

Still supporting most of his weight, she glared down at him. From this close, Tony could see a tiny scar at the edge of her right eyebrow. "Quit yelling at me! It's not helping!"

He could also see that she was really most sincerely freaked and that threatened to send him into strong hysterics. When thirty-five-hundred-year-old immortal stuntwomen got freaked, it was time for the rest of the world to fucking lose it. Fortunately—for some weird definition of *fortunately* he didn't want to go into right now—he was too exhausted to start up the whole *oh, my God, we're all going to die* thing. After a couple of deep breaths, he managed a fairly calm, "What happened to it?"

"Ash."

"And the arm?"

Leah nodded toward a long, narrow lump of black on the pavement. "It got just a little overcooked."

"But the demon is ash?"

"The demon was other, the arm was flesh."

That almost made sense. Tony struggled to sit up a little straighter, but someone seemed to have snuck into his body and replaced all his muscles with marshmallows. "I don't feel so good."

"Considering the way you just blew your wad, I'm not surprised."

"Nice imagery."

"Thank you. Can you . . ." Approaching voices cut her off and suddenly it became necessary he sit up on his own as Leah withdrew her arm and stood. "Oh, no, here comes the cavalry. They must've seen the flash. You get that arm packed up and let me deal with them."

Deal? Tony managed to brace himself on one hand and turn enough to see three men approaching from the jetty. Then Leah crossed into his line of sight, hips moving to an ancient rhythm. She laughed in answer to something one of the men said, a low, throaty sound that held heated suggestion.

And if even he could feel the heat, the odds were very high that none of the three men were now paying any attention to anything else.

You get that arm packed up.

Yeah. Right. Like that was the sort of thing he did every day. Well, actually, given the content of *Darkest Night*, he'd done it a couple of times helping out the set dresser. He rolled up onto his feet, swayed for a moment, and staggered back to the makeup trailer, where he begged a garbage bag from the box on the counter.

"Are you feeling all right?" Hama asked as she handed it over. "You don't look so good." Her eyes narrowed. "You should be a medium beige and you're down to a light ivory."

"I'm fine. Just a little tired."

"You need more protein and less pizza. Especially if you're going to spend time with Leah."

"I'm not spending that kind of time with her." He'd just rest for a moment longer against the open door.

"Uh-huh."

"I'm gay."

"I'm generally fairly cheerful myself," she said dryly. "Trust me about Leah and red meat. Now close the door and go; you're letting cold air in."

It wasn't easy finding the remains of the arm. The banks of overhead lights shining down on the stacks of containers created nearly impenetrable shadow and, half blind, he almost tripped over it before he saw it. It looked like a long lump of charcoal roughly carved into the shape of an arm—a slight bend in the black where the elbow might be and little stubby fingers on one end. Given that the construction worker's other hand had been relatively normal, he had to assume the stubbiness occurred after death. Had the Powershot burned the fingers away? Or had the demon snacked on the end of his weapon?

"Demon snacks. Right. Why can't I ever spend time thinking about cars or getting laid, like a normal guy?" He sighed as he shook out the garbage bag. It was one of the small white ones made for garbage pails under the sink and it smelled vaguely of mint.

The scar on the palm of his left hand twitched as he dropped heavily to one knee beside the arm, and he hesitated, fingers spread out about five centimeters over the burned flesh.

"Problem?" Leah's voice behind his right shoulder.

"The last time I picked up an arm, it wasn't . . . fun." Hello, understatement.

"Well, this one's pretty much pure carbon, so I don't imagine it'll give you any . . . Oh, my God! The fingers moved!" She snickered as he threw himself back so quickly he toppled over and pulled the garbage bag from his hand. "Kidding. Here, I'll get it."

"You seem to be feeling better," he muttered from the asphalt.

"There's nothing like a little slap and tickle to remind a girl of what's important." Slipping the bag over her hand, Leah bent and scooped up the arm like she was scooping an enormous turd. An enormous burned turd. With fingers. Stubby fingers. "I'm going to be feeling better than you will for a while," she added, straightening. "You just ripped that energy right out of your guts, didn't you?"

"I guess." Feet, legs, guts eventually. Tony rolled up onto his knees as Leah closed the bag and reached into his pocket for the twist tie Hama had given him. A narrow piece of paper fluttered to the ground, a small line of white against the dark asphalt.

"What's that?"

"Fortune from last night's cookie." He picked it up and turned it over, leaning back just a little to bring it out of shadow. "*The blow from sunlight is more unexpected than the blow from darkness*. That demon just attacked you in the last of the sunlight," he said slowly as he got to his feet. "And I'd say that was unexpected."

Leah rolled her eyes. "You got a fortune cookie that really tells the future?"

"You've got a tattoo that's a Demongate."

"So you're saying stranger things have happened?"

"You're holding an arm."

She glanced down at the bag. "Good point."

"Can I ask you something?"

"Sure."

It took almost more effort than he had available to pull his car keys out of his jacket pocket. "Can you drive?"

Tony didn't notice the rip in the side of her hoodie until they were going into the steak house and he stumbled. Leah turned to steady him, and he saw the fabric gape. "Looks like that demon almost got you."

She glanced down at the sweater and shrugged. "It's the *almost* that matters; I can't be hurt, remember? Unfortunately, that doesn't extend to my clothes. The important thing is that I ducked at exactly the right moment and you were there in time to blast the little bugger into dust."

"Not so little," Tony grunted. "And not an imp!"

"Would you let that go?" She maneuvered them around a table, toward the back of the restaurant. "So there was a lot of convergent energy hitting the same spot early on, and something a little bigger than an imp got through. It happens."

"Is it likely to happen again?"

She flashed him a sunny smile. "Well, if it does, you'll be there to deal with it, won't you?"

"You said imps," he muttered. "That wasn't an imp."

"And speaking of how much size matters . . ." She waited until she'd helped him into a high booth against the back wall and they were holding laminated menus before she continued. ". . . you might want to dial your Powershot down a bit. I think you're going to lose those nails."

The nail on his pinkie had begun to curl. It wasn't painful when he poked it, but it wasn't a pleasant feeling. Sort of a condensed memory of the energy surge.

When he looked up, Leah was shaking her head. "You don't know how to dial it down, do you?"

Tony thought about lying, but there was an arm in his trunk, and transporting detached, carbonated body parts made lying seem a little pointless. "That was the first I ever did. I'll get better with practice."

"Uh-huh. He'll have the sixteen-ounce T-bone," she told the waitress.

"I can't eat a . . ."

Both women turned to stare at him. Leah's gaze flicked down to his fingernails.

He had the sixteen-ounce T-bone.

All of it.

And two baked potatoes with sour cream and chives.

And a side of creamed corn.

And a side of fried mushrooms.

And three huge pumpernickel rolls with butter.

And two beers.

Once he got started, he barely paused to breathe.

Leah had a lot less of the same things.

"So," she said at last when he set the gnawed bone on the plate and sat back with a satisfied sigh, "you got lucky."

"Lucky?" Maybe wizards had a second stomach. He should have felt sick, but he only felt comfortably full. In fact, he felt like dessert. He yawned. And a nap.

"You got lucky with your first Powershot. You didn't blow off your hand."

"And I saved your ass," he reminded her, through another yawn. "Stress the negatives much?"

"Sorry." The dimples flashed. "You did, indeed, save my ass. You got lucky."

"Isn't that what happens around you? My day ends early enough to let the only person who can save you arrive in time to save you?"

"Yes, but . . ."

"I see no buts."

"You've just eaten enough for two people . . ."

"Why is that bad?"

"You needed to replace the energy you used."

"But that's normal for a wizard, right? It's not bad. Demons running around VanTerm are bad. But, like you said, I dealt, so that's good."

"Fine." She rolled her eyes. "If you want bad, I have a hole in my favorite hoodie!"

Tony grinned as Leah shoved her hand through the hole and waved it at him. "You're right, that's . . ."

He stopped grinning.

She frowned. "What?"

"Your T-shirt."

She twisted and looked down, pulling the yellow fabric aside. There was a smaller hole in the T-shirt.

And under that, the very tip of the demon's claw had lightly scratched Leah's skin. Her finger shook as she traced the tiny burgundy beads of dried blood on the centimeter-long scratch. "No. That's impossible. I can't be hurt."

"That's not exactly *hurt*," Tony began but she cut him off.

"You don't understand. That's blood!"

The scratch was barely visible from across the table. "Not much . . ."

"My blood!" Leah spat the words out through clenched teeth. "I haven't seen my blood in thirty-five hundred years!"

"You must have . . ."

"No!"

Other people in the restaurant were beginning to turn and stare. "Come on. We need to go."

"Where?"

"Back to my place." All of a sudden he didn't feel like dessert. Her eyes were wild and he wondered just how close the "crazy lady in the desert" was to the surface.

"What are we going to do about this there?"

Good question. Too bad he didn't have an answer. Wait . . . "We can start by reading *your* fortune cookie."

∽ FOUR

"I have to say that I'm not surprised you lost the fortune cookie in this mess."

Tony sat back on his heels in time to see Leah shake her head at the pair of boxer-briefs dangling between thumb and forefinger, then toss them to one side. She'd calmed down a lot in the car, and by the time they got to the apartment, she'd either got a handle on things or slid so deeply into denial she was living in Egypt. Tony wasn't sure which, but that was okay because he didn't care which. Whatever worked. "I told you, I was sorting laundry."

She prodded a pile of jeans with the toe of one sneaker. "Historically, most people sort laundry in order to do laundry."

"I was going to get to it."

"When you get down to a pair of paint-stained sweats and a T-shirt you got free from a promo guy?"

"Pretty much, yeah." He smothered a yawn with the back of his hand and nodded toward the kitchen. "The garbage is under the sink. Try there."

"You said you didn't throw it out."

"I didn't throw it out on purpose." Shoving a pile of old newspapers out of the way, he dropped to his belly to look under the sofa bed. Dead batteries. *Firefly* disk two. Blue silk tie. One dress shoe. *Where the hell was the other one?* Assorted balled-up socks. Empty Timbit box. Three issues of *Cinefex*. As the cheap parquet floor warmed under him, it got harder and harder to stay focused. Empty sample bottle of guava-flavored lube. Empty beer bottle. Unopened can of generic cola. No fortune cookie.

Clutching the can of cola, he shuffled backward until his head cleared the bed frame, dragged himself up onto his knees with a handful of mattress, and allowed his upper body to collapse onto the bed.

Something crinkled.

Setting the can aside, Tony rummaged in the tangle of sheets. "Found it."

Leah stared down at him in disbelief as she turned from the sink. "You slept with it?"

"Calm down, we're just good friends." Although the packaging had maintained physical integrity, the cookie within had been crushed. He got himself up on his feet just long enough to shuffle around and sit down on the edge of the bed. Then he reached out and dropped it into her hand.

Her other hand moved to cover the scratch on her side. "This is foolish."

"Maybe."

"Yours could have meant anything. It didn't have to refer to the demon; that could have been coincidence."

"Could have. But I doubt it. Wizard," he added with a shrug when she glanced at him.

Crumbs whispered against each other as she shook the package, the motion hiding the way her fingers had started to tremble. "Yeah, but this is my cookie, and I'm no wizard."

He understood why she was delaying; a certainty she had held for her whole life had changed and, given the length of her life, that was saying something. Change could be terrifying. He understood; he just didn't have a lot of patience with it since these days his life changed every twenty minutes. "Would you just open the damned thing?"

She hesitated a moment longer, then caught the edge of the plastic between her teeth and ripped. A small strip of paper spilled out of the pile of amber crumbs on her palm.

"*Ambitious change requires help; timing is everything.* Oh, yes, very clear and extraordinarily anticlimactic." Eyes rolling, she dusted the crumbs off into the sink. "That could mean anything."

"It could mean that your Demonlord is getting ambitious and is using the Demonic Convergence to send through minions with the ability to kill you so that the gate opens and he can come through."

"Minions?"

"Demonic minions."

"Yes, I got that." She sat beside him on the bed, dark brows drawn in. "The rest of it, though—you're really reaching."

"I'm really not." Grinding the heels of his hands into his eyes only blurred his vision. The steak seemed to be wearing off. Tony patted the blanket until he found the cola, popped the tab, and took a long swallow. "When you were attacked," he told her, feeling the sugar and caffeine hit his bloodstream, "when that demon drew blood—such as it was—he was there, Ryne Cyratane. I saw him."

"So? I told you last night he'd be close because of the Convergence." Her hand went back to her side. "He had nothing to do with this."

"He likes sex, he hates water. You were with me so that takes care of the sex, or lack of sex, and you were still close to lots of water. He had to be in that parking lot with you for another reason."

"Tony . . ." The paper crinkled slightly as she waved it. ". . . this is a fortune cookie fortune. It's a mass-produced platitude. Ambitious change could mean anything."

"You said he made a mistake on the spell. He's had thirty-five hundred years to figure out how to fix it. He can't get through himself . . ."

"Why not?"

"How the hell should I know? He can't because he didn't, but he can send . . ."

"Minions?"

"Yeah. He's got motive *and* opportunity, and all the pieces fit."

"Based on a fortune cookie."

He snatched the paper from her, crumpled it up, and threw it at a pile of T-shirts. "Wizards see what's there."

"You're learning to be a wizard from a correspondence course. Did it ever occur to you that you're seeing the wrong thing?"

"Okay. Fine. What do you think's going on?" They were sitting side by side. Not looking at each other.

"Ryne Cyratane would have nothing to do with this."

"With hurting you?" When she didn't answer—and given that the Demonlord had carved those runes into her flesh using the blood of her people, Tony figured she didn't really have an answer—he asked, "Would he let another Demonlord use the gate?"

"No."

No question there.

"Then since he's still around, he's got to be the one trying to open it. He probably figured out a way to direct the convergent energy to one spot."

"Okay, fine, you have all the answers . . ." Leah twisted around to face him, eyes narrowed. "Why did that demon bite the construction worker's arm off?"

Tony sighed. "Duh. Demon."

He downed half the can of cola while she thought about it.

"It explains everything."

"Yeah."

"I bet you're feeling pretty smug about figuring this out," she muttered at the toes of her high-tops.

He assumed she was actually talking to him. "Not really. It was kind of obvious." For a long moment the soft squeak of his fingers rubbing the cola can was the only noise in the apartment. "I guess you're feeling kind of betrayed."

"Well, yes!" After contemplating her shoes a while longer, she lifted her head and pushed her hair back off her face. "And no." Her laugh was a bit shaky, but to Tony's surprise, it wasn't faked. "I mean, he is a Demonlord, after all. He did slaughter everyone I knew, so this isn't exactly out of character for him. It just took him a while to make his next move."

"Maybe time runs differently where he is."

"Probably not. He was never very bright." One hand slid under her clothes to stroke the tattoo, and she smiled. "The sex was great, though."

Tony stared at her with as much astonishment as he had the energy for. "And that makes everything okay?"

"Well, no, not okay; but it puts it in perspective, doesn't it? So," she continued before Tony could respond, "assuming that he'll try it again as soon as he's used the convergent energy to open a new hole, how do we keep these minions of his from killing me?"

"And releasing a Demonlord into the world."

"That's part two. You'll excuse me . . ." Her hand moved around from the tattoo to the scratch. ". . . but I'm more concerned about part one."

Since keeping Leah alive would keep the Demonlord out, Tony decided there was no point in calling her on that. They needed a plan. And while they were planning . . . "Can he hear us?"

"No. He says he gets impressions of my life, but our only real conduit is sexual energy."

"Good." Hang on. "He *says*? You have conversations?"

"Sometimes, when he's right up by the gate, I enter a meditative state and we talk."

"Sometimes?"

"Postcoital."

Why did he even ask? "All right, we're not totally helpless; I dusted the demon with the arm."

"And got knocked on your ass," Leah reminded him. "It's been what? Three and a half hours, and you're still too wiped to get it up again."

"I could so . . ." Actually, no, he couldn't. Not even thinking of Lee in his motorcycle jacket and chaps got a response.

"That was a metaphor, Tony."

Her expression suggested she knew what he'd been thinking. He could feel his ears go red. "It doesn't matter. I've got time to recover . . . for another Powershot," he added hurriedly as she grinned. "It'll take him a while to get another minion through, right? So we just have to stick with the original plan. We find out where the weak spot is, and you teach me how to close it down."

"No."

"Why not?"

"If Ryne Cyratane is sending demons through to kill me, my going anywhere near the weak spot would be like waving a steak outside a lion's cage. It might provide enough incentive for a breakout—resulting in a really bad time for the steak."

Tony fought his way through this second metaphor—which was, at least, not about sex. "Fine, you don't have to go near the weak spot. You tell me where it is, teach me what to do, and I'll deal."

"It's not that simple."

He sighed. "It never is. All right, what do we do? How do we stop your Demonlord from opening the gate?"

"We keep me alive."

"Yeah, I got that."

"Seriously, that's all we have to do." She reached out and touched his arm. "I teach you how to send the demons back without destroying yourself, and every time one shows up, you zap it."

"That sounds simple. Or not," he amended when her expression threatened bodily harm.

"One question: what'll the demon be doing while I'm zapping?"

"Trying to kill me." Her expression added a clear and succinct *You idiot.*

"Or trying to kill me, and you can't stop it because, guess what—oh, yeah—it can kill you, too. I'm thinking we need some backup." Leaning forward, he could just barely reach his jacket hung over the back of a kitchen chair. He pulled his cell phone from his pocket, turned to Leah, and grinned. "Who you gonna call?"

She looked confused. "I'm not calling anyone."

He sighed. "No one watches the classics anymore."

"Nelson."

"Nice phone manner, Victory. You always bark at your clients?"

"Good to hear you've regained consciousness, Tony."

"I wasn't . . ."

"You weren't? Then you had another reason for not calling?"

"I was . . ."

"Busy? Hang on a sec." Her voice faded slightly as she moved the phone from her mouth. "Drop the pins and step away from the doll."

"Vicki?"

"Yeah?"

"Are you working?" Victory Nelson had once been a much-decorated Toronto cop; now she was a vampire P.I.—just like Raymond Dark only without the sidekick, the contrived plots, and the need to keep the violence under PG-13. Tony heard a couple of muffled thuds and some moaning.

"It's no big. These guys are total wannabes. What can I do for you?"

"I have a friend with a bit of a problem."

"Is this friend another wizard?"

Oh, crap. She knew. He hadn't called because he hadn't known how to tell her and make it sound believable. "How . . . ?"

"Henry told me, idiot."

Right. Because Henry still considered Tony's life to be his. His Henry's, not his Tony's. God, he was too tired for this. "No, she's not a wizard. She's a stuntwoman and an immortal Demongate."

"Cool."

"Not really." He outlined the problem.

Vicki let him talk without interruption. "Okay," she said when he finished. "Here's what you do . . . You listening?"

"Yeah. I'm listening."

"Stop acting like an ass and call Henry."

"I'm not . . ."

"Bullshit. Look, I'm not saying he's not indulging in a bit of testosterone-fueled assness as well, but one, he's out there in Vancouver and I'm not. Two, he owns a grimoire. Maybe more than one. He understands the whole demon thing. And, three, he needs to know what's going on, unless you'd rather he found out that you were dealing with demons in his territory and didn't tell him."

"I don't think . . ."

"I know."

Tony waited and when she didn't say any more, he sighed. Of course she heard it, even three thousand miles away. She could hear the blood moving through the hand holding the phone.

"You know I'm right."

He sighed again. "I guess."

"Tony . . ."

"Fine. You're right. Happy?"

"Ecstatic. Let me know how it turns out. Unless, of course, I find out on the news and then you needn't bother."

"Because then I'll be dead."

"That's not as much of an excuse as it used to be. Now . . . you call Henry, I'm going to grab a bite."

The background moaning grew louder.

Henry paused outside the door to Tony's apartment. He could feel the power painted around the frame. He could smell the cherry cough syrup. It seemed that in the weeks since they'd talked, Tony's studies had progressed. And adapted.

Tony had always been adaptable. It had helped him survive on the street. It had helped him accept that the world held wonder and darkness beyond the barriers most people thought marked the edge of reality. It had certainly helped him working in an industry that created yet another reality and very nearly believed in it.

Yes, adaptable was good.

Young, arrogant, prickly, possessive; not so much.

And if Tony didn't exactly go out looking for trouble, he certainly seemed to call it to him.

A noise pulled Henry's attention to the far end of the hall, and he turned in time to see an overweight tabby slip out of the last apartment. The cat's owner kept the door open on the safety chain so that the cat could wander in and out at will. Henry had never met the owner, but he and the cat had come to an understanding months ago.

The tabby's yellow eyes narrowed; he raised his tail and sprayed the wall just outside the apartment door.

Mine.

Henry sighed and raised a hand to knock. That was exactly the sort of welcome he was anticipating.

He could feel a life on the other side of the door. Hear a heart beating. Feel power . . . When the door opened, he smiled. It was more of a warning than a threat. "Leah Burnett?"

She was no more than five foot five, Mediterranean looking—south side of the inland sea. Almost, but not quite, Arabic. Under black-and-yellow clothing she had the kind of curves most women in this age dieted away. Thick dark hair fell in soft curls just past her shoulders, framing a face with full lips, high cheekbones, and dark eyes narrowed in a frown.

"You're Henry Fitzroy?"

"I am." He could feel old power clinging to her like smoke. No, not merely old. He was old. This was ancient.

"I thought you'd be taller."

At six feet, his father had been huge—even before his girth had expanded to fit his ego. At five six, Henry was more typical of his century. "Sorry."

"No, it's all right. I like a man I can look in the eye without getting a crick in my neck."

And she *was* looking him in the eye. Wondering what she was trying to prove, he let a little of the mask fall and a little of the Hunger rise.

She smiled in a way that told him she knew exactly what she saw. Then she drew her tongue over her lower lip, leaving it glistening, and tossed her hair back off her face to expose the curve of her throat. Looking up at him through thick lashes, she drew in a deep breath and exhaled a challenge.

Henry felt himself respond and only barely managed to keep himself from moving toward her. He dragged the Hunger—both hungers—back under control and asked, "Should we be doing this in the hall?"

She laughed and stepped aside, her power masked as his was. "Tony's asleep."

The wards on the doorframe stroked against him as he stepped over the threshold but made no attempt to keep him out. Leah seemed satisfied with that as she closed the door, and Henry wondered just how sensitive to Tony's wizardry she was.

"Did he tell you he dusted a demon this evening?"

"Dusted?"

"Well, specifically ashed. He called it a Powershot. Took a lot out of him," she added quietly as they stood together looking down at the young man on the bed. "How much did he tell you on the phone?"

"He told me your history. Your pertinent history with the Demonlord," he added when she snorted. "He told me of the Demonic Convergence, and he told me how this Demonlord is planning to use it to kill you."

Pushing her hair back off her face, she nodded. "Demonic minions. As long as the spell controlling the Demongate holds, they shouldn't be able to hurt me, but they have."

Minions. He could hear Tony in the word. "May I see the spell?"

Moving away from the bed, she unzipped her hoodie and raised her T-shirt. "Be my guest."

It was an amazing tattoo. Even . . . no, *especially* knowing what it was. He dropped to one knee to get a closer look. And frowned. "I have seen the language of the damned," he said softly, head cocked to one side as he followed the curve of the characters, "and this writing I do not recognize."

"There is more than one hell, Nightwalker." She matched his formal cadence. "And more than one heaven, I suspect."

"Blasphemy."

The two fingers she placed under his chin were warm, and he allowed her to lift his head. "A religious word. And a strange word coming from a man whose church believes him soulless and damned. I say there is more than one hell and I am in a better position to know. By the time your lord was born, I had been carrying mine for over a thousand years."

"Your *lord* is . . ."

"I *know* what he is. You take yours on faith."

"Mine is not trying to kill me."

"His . . ." And she grinned, breaking the mood, suddenly looking no more than the young woman she appeared to be. ". . . minions would."

Again with the minions. Henry strongly suspected Tony had provided it. "The church does not think of itself in that way."

"Yeah, like that matters."

She had a point. "They would kill you as well."

"Oh, they've tried."

Which brought them neatly around to the matter at hand. Holding her hips, he moved her around so that he could see the wound. It was small, a minor flaw on the smooth curve of café-au-lait skin and only barely deep enough to bleed. Not worth noting had it not been the first blood drawn from this body in over three thousand years. Bending closer, he drew in a long, slow breath. The scent of her blood was familiar; neither the demon that had attacked her nor the demonic power that enveloped her had marked it. The scent around the blood, her scent, was almost smoky and he found himself wanting to taste. To lick a moist line along the curve from hip to ribs. Could he feed? Would the protective power perceive the threat or the seduction?

The flesh of her hips was warm and yielding under his grip. The air between them began to heat. Henry caught the scent of her arousal and growled low in his throat. She wound her fingers into his hair and subtly shifted her weight to bring bared skin closer to his mouth.

The growl snapped Tony fully awake. One moment he'd been dreaming of driving his car from the backseat and the next he was up on his elbows staring at Leah and Henry at the foot of his bed.

Actually, Henry on his knees, his hair wrapped around Leah's fingers, his mouth about to descend to skin was pretty damned hot. Tony could feel his body responding like it always did when Henry got the vampire mojo going. His responses had gotten a bit kinky after all those years of teeth and, under normal circumstances, he'd be more than happy to lie here and watch while they went at it.

Unfortunately, the word normal had sweet fuck all to do with his life.

"Not a good idea, Henry."

Oh, yeah, interrupt a vampire when he's about to chow down. Not the best way to live a long and happy life. Henry's eyes were dark, and he had the whole Prince of Darkness thing on full blast.

Too bad.

Their history helped him hold Henry's attention but only just. "Ryne Cyratane is in the building and he doesn't look happy." In fact, for a guy who supposedly fed off sexual energy—and there was enough floating around that Tony strategically draped a fold of blanket over his boxer-briefs as he sat up— the Demonlord looked decidedly unhappy. Possessive even. Possessive and pissed. Tony recognized the expression even when he could see the wall of his apartment through it. "Henry! I'm guessing he doesn't like to share with other powers! He's already sending demons after Leah; it won't help her if he starts sending them after you, too."

Henry's lips drew back off his teeth.

Great. Vampire, prince; they both saw the whole thing as a challenge.

"Leah! Turn it off!"

Yeah. Like that was going to happen. Her head was back, her skin practically glowed, and even he was starting to find her tempting.

Henry was after blood. Leah was after sex. Together, they'd make a bad situation worse. As far as Tony could see, there was only one thing to do. He picked up a pillow and threw it as hard as he could at the vampire's head.

The next instant, he was flat on his back, Henry's hands around his wrists, Henry's body driving his down into the thin mattress. Tony's hips bucked up as Henry's teeth closed through the skin of his throat and concerns about demonic interference abandoned ship . . . along with pretty much anything else resembling cognitive thought.

"Oh, please, there's no need to be embarrassed, it's not like I've never seen ejaculate before."

"Make her shut up," Tony muttered as Henry handed him a glass of juice.

"How?"

"I don't know, vamp her or something."

"I don't think we want to go there again."

Tony wasn't sure he *could* go there again. At least not for a couple of days. Provided those days included thirty-six hours of sleep and a lot of liquid. He handed the empty glass back to Henry, wrapped the sheet and the shredded remains of his dignity around him, and stomped off to the bathroom to clean up.

The shower helped. Although he had to brace himself against the tile to keep the water from pounding him down onto his knees.

Afterward, wrapped in his one thinning bath towel, he wiped the mirror clean and studied the mark on his neck. It was . . . noticeable. In spite of the coagulant in Henry's saliva, the actual bite within the impressive bruising still seeped blood. Fortunately, in the almost empty medicine cabinet, he had one sterile pad remaining from the exploding beer bottle incident. No gauze, but there was a rolled-up tensor bandage with very little *tense* left that should do, provided he kept it fairly loose.

Tomorrow . . .

Crap.

He didn't think he even owned a turtleneck.

"Tony?"

Henry outside the bathroom door. Worrying.

"I'm okay."

It seemed a little pointless to balk about being seen in a towel, all things considered, so Tony squared his shoulders, stepped out into the hall and across it to his closet. He'd have gone back into the bathroom to dress except Henry needed a few moments in there. Leah was out of sight, so she had to be in the kitchen end of the room where the angle was too tight to see or be seen from the hall. He pulled on jeans—Henry had destroyed his last clean pair of underwear—a T-shirt and a sweatshirt over that, then socks and shoes. Dressed, he walked into the living room and quickly stripped the bed, throwing the bedding onto a pile of dirty laundry in the corner and folding the mattress up into the sofa. It was a little stiff; he didn't close it often. The two cushions went back on as he shoved debris that had been under it out of the way with the side of his foot.

There.

That ought to help bring things back to what passed for normal.

He turned to find Leah standing behind him. "Could you not fucking do that!"

"Sorry." She offered him a large glass of what looked like chocolate milk. "It's an instant breakfast. I dropped a couple of packages from the craft services table into my purse."

"That's not . . ."

"Please, it's a CBC show. Think of it as your tax dollars at work."

It didn't seem worth it to argue. Tony sat at one end of the sofa and took a cautious swallow. "It's a little slimy."

"How old was your milk?"

"Oh, ha." Another swallow. He frowned as she pulled a chair out from the table and dropped onto it. "Are you . . . um . . . Tall, dark, and naked is gone, did you . . . um . . ."

"Get off?" She crossed her legs and smiled at him. "Don't worry. I took care of it. Although, if truth be told, you guys almost took care of it for me. Woof!"

His blood pressure was too low to raise a decent blush. "Could you not talk about it?"

"At all?"

"Ever."

"You know, you're weirdly prudish for someone with a Nightwalker as a lover."

"It's not . . . it's having an audience." A memory of a night in an alley off Charles Street back in Toronto surfaced. "No, it's having *you* as an audience."

"Hey. You will never find a more appreciative audience than me. Although the audiences for this live sex show I was in back in London in . . ." Dark brows drew in, and the yellow toe of the sneaker in the air drew circles. ". . . 1882 were great."

"At the Midnight Lily?"

Tony was childishly pleased to see her jump as Henry appeared behind her. "The what?"

"The Midnight Lily—was that the name of the club?"

"Yes . . ."

Henry nodded thoughtfully and walked past her to sit on the other end of the couch. "I thought you looked familiar."

Rolling his eyes, Tony reached for the remote. "I'll just watch a little TV while you two trade flashbacks."

Then the remote was gone. "I don't think so." The fingers of Henry's other hand gently touched the rough bandage on his neck. "You took a chance."

Shaking his head hurt. "Not much of one. You never really damage what you consider to be yours." He was impressed by how nonchalant he sounded about the whole thing.

"A good thing you stopped us, then." Fingertips lingered a moment longer, then withdrew. "A good thing you saw the danger."

"Yeah, well, wizard. We see what's there."

"True." Henry sat back against the sofa cushions. "And occasionally what isn't there."

It might have been wiser to just let that go but, given what he'd already survived tonight, Tony was feeling a little reckless. He turned and faced Henry, eyes narrowed. "Are you telling me you're not doing CB?"

"And are you deciding who I can and cannot feed from?"

"You have the whole damned lower mainland. CB, the studio, that's mine!"

"Your employer might argue that."

"Are you two always such drama queens," Leah demanded, "or is this special for me? And," she continued before either of them could respond, "while it's painfully obvious you two are dealing with the kind of personal shit that would give Dr. Phil reason to retire, this isn't the time. Let's concentrate on the important thing here. Me. You," she pointed at Henry, "are here for backup. Tony seems to think you'll be useful—the brawn to our brains and beauty combination although there was some mention that you might have access to information we can use. I doubt you're going to know anything about demons I don't, but, hey, better safe than sorry. Also, given what you are, and given how stupidly territorial vampires can be, I'd rather have you with us than against us. You . . ." Her finger moved to Tony. ". . . need to conserve your strength. Between that spell you threw earlier and your ex's feeding habits, you haven't got energy to spare for arguing." She paused just long enough to ensure she had their full attention. "Now then, who has a plan?"

"I think," Tony said slowly, "we should bring Jack Elson in on this."

One red-gold brow lifted as Henry drawled, "Now, do I say anything about you and Constable Elson?"

"There *is* no me and Constable Elson; the man is straight!"

"You're doing it again," Leah snapped.

"Fine." The look Henry shot her would have caused strong men to run. Leah rolled her eyes. "Why Elson?"

Tony finished swallowing the last mouthful of liquid breakfast. "I have an arm in my trunk."

"This is a human arm."

"And he's what? Only four hundred and sixty-ish?" Leah shot an anime-sized look of wonderment in Tony's direction. "What amazing deductive powers!" And to Henry. "I have to know; how did you work it out?"

"It smells like burned pork," Henry told her dryly, not rising to the bait. "Not to mention, it's wearing the remains of a watch. From what you said about Tony dusting a demon, I had assumed it was a demonic arm."

"We wouldn't need Jack for that." Tony yawned and nodded toward the arm. "This got bitten off a construction worker. Jack took me to see the body this afternoon."

"Why?"

"Because he doesn't believe in giant raccoons and he wanted some answers."

"I'm moderately disturbed by how much sense that makes," Henry muttered. "And you think we should give this arm to him?"

"Sure. He can put it with the rest of the body."

"And you don't think that would cause more questions?"

"Well, we'd . . . I'd . . . answer his questions. Mostly. He knows what's going on. I mean, he knows there's stuff going on. I told him about the Demonic Convergence." Tony yawned again. "He's still at least one version of the script behind, but it won't take long to bring him up to speed."

"I wasn't actually thinking of questions from Constable Elson," Henry pointed out. "I was thinking of the coroner and the victim's relatives. It might be best if they continue to believe that the arm was bitten off by a wild animal and eaten. Another urban myth of man-eating cougars in the city would be preferable to an investigation. Modern forensics can be remarkably thorough."

"Let me guess, you've been watching *CSI*." This time, Tony yawned so widely his jaw cracked. "Besides, we'll need Jack to work backup in the daylight."

"Demons don't . . ." Henry began and stopped.

"The last one did. Which leaves us kind of screwed if you're all we have."

"Thank you."

Crap. "Sorry. That was . . ."

"Tactless," Leah offered. "But true."

Henry nodded, graciously acknowledging the point. "And you think Jack Elson can stop a demon?"

"He has a gun."

"Will a gun have any effect on these creatures?"

Forgetting the wound in his throat, Tony shrugged and ground out, "I have no idea," through gritted teeth.

"Then perhaps we'd best not involve Constable Elson until we know more. Why don't you start by telling me *exactly* what happened this afternoon."

"I've got it." Leah lifted a hand to cut off Tony's protest, but he hadn't actually planned on one. Exhausted, he sagged back against the sofa cushions half listening to the immortal stuntwoman tell Henry about the demon attack but mostly thinking how *immortal stuntwoman* sounded like a cool idea for a show and wondering if he should pitch it to CB.

Hell, at some point someone had to have thought that *vampire detective* was a good idea.

"Tony?"

"I'm awake."

"Of course you are."

Leah's eyes were so dark a brown he could barely make out where the irises ended and the pupils began. "What?"

"Henry's going to get rid of the arm."

Tony shot Henry, still standing by the arm, a thumb's up. "How?"

"Leave that to me," Henry said quietly. "Leah knows a better way of returning the demons to hells, one that won't nearly kill you. She'll teach it to you. But not tonight," he added. "Tonight you need to regain the energy you spent." *And the blood you lost.* Tony felt his heart beat just a little faster. Henry's eyes darkened slightly, aware of Tony's response.

"You're doing it again," Leah sighed.

"You are not totally without fault here," Henry told her, masking the Hunger. "Your presence is provocative."

"Why, thank you."

"What about more construction workers?" Tony asked.

Dimples flashed as Leah turned her attention to him. "I'm very much in favor of construction workers."

"Yeah, funny. Remember the arm. That demon that attacked you killed someone else first."

The Vampire and the Demongate exchanged nearly identical glances.

Tony sighed. Figured that he'd be the only one who thought of the little guy. "If either of you says the words *collateral damage*, I'm going to be really pissed."

"Tony . . ."

Henry cut her off. "If we concentrate on keeping Leah alive, on keeping the gate from opening for this Demonlord, we prevent mass slaughter. With the demons focused on her, there will, hopefully, be few other lives lost." Henry's tone suggested this was the last he was prepared to say on the matter.

Can't make an omelet without breaking eggs. God, I must be tired if I'm thinking in bad clichés. "So tomorrow I learn a better way to return demons to hell and then I become Leah's bodyguard for the duration of the convergence. As each demon pops out and attacks, I send it home. If it attacks at night, are you willing to make sure I stay alive long enough to do the spell?"

"I am."

"And if it attacks in the daytime . . ."

"It is ultimately your choice if you involve Constable Elson."

"Sure it is." Both Leah and Henry looked as if they wanted to respond. Tony ignored them. "Okay, I'm seeing one big problem here. I already have a job."

Henry folded his arms. "I will talk with CB."

"And get me some time off."

"It seems like the best idea."

"With pay."

"You have a high opinion of my powers of persuasion."

"Am I wrong?"

"No. And now, you need to sleep. Where do you keep your clean sheets?"

Tony glanced around the room at the piles of laundry. There were fewer of them than there had been, but that was only because they'd been unsorted over the course of the evening. "I only have one set."

"Then we won't worry about it." Henry crossed the apartment at close to mortal speed and knelt by the sofa. "I don't suppose one night without sheets will hurt you."

Tony nodded. "Once I was pissed off about having no sheets, then I met a man with no blankets." When the only response was confusion, he sighed. "It's a variation on the shoe/feet thing." The confusion deepened. He waved a hand; hardly his fault if he was being profound and they were being dense. "Forget it."

"I don't think that'll be hard," Henry murmured, slipping one arm under Tony's legs and the other behind his back.

"Hey, don't . . ."

Henry ignored him and straightened. Big surprise. Tony squirmed a bit but nothing he could do was going to change the fact that he was being held in Henry's arms like an overgrown infant. "I hate it when you do this."

"I know. Leah, would you fold the bed out, please?"

"Sure thing. I'm good with beds."

Too tired for innuendo, Tony let that go. Besides, it seemed to be the simple truth. In a remarkably short time, he was shoeless but still dressed and stretched out under a blanket.

"Okay, it's a long shot, but what if another demon attacks tonight?" he asked as Henry turned off the overhead lights.

"These are lesser demons, not the Demonlord himself. They may not even be able to get through your wards and, if they can, I'm sure I can at least slow them until you wake."

"At least slow them?"

"Good night, Tony."

"So . . ." Leah pushed a curl back off her face. ". . . what do we do while we're waiting for dawn?"

"I suggest you sleep." Henry nodded toward the bed. "Tony won't even know you're there."

"And you?"

"I'm going to get my laptop from the car and do some work."

She slid out of her sweater. "You can do that; work with me lying right over there?"

"I am perfectly capable of maintaining control regardless of your provocation—however involuntary that provocation is most of the time."

"Maybe together we could provoke Ryne Cyratane into making a fatal mistake."

His lip curled, showing teeth. "Since the only person in this room likely to be a fatality is Tony, I'd have to say no, thank you."

FIVE

Tony was chasing a penguin around the *Darkest Night* set when the phone rang. Which was when he realized he was dreaming. Given his experience in television, penguin chasing was a distinct possibility; a phone ringing on the soundstage was not. The last time it had happened, Peter had promised to castrate the next recipient of an incoming call, and he'd promised it with such sincerity that even the women on the set had been nervous.

It was almost fortunate that Arra's gate reopening had destroyed cell phone reception, downgrading the threat to a moot point.

As the penguin shuffled off past Raymond Dark's coffin, Tony dragged himself up out of sleep and groped amid the debris on the bedside table. Lukewarm liquid splashed onto his shoulder as he attempted to answer the half empty can of cola. When he finally found the handheld, he sank back against the pillows.

"What?"

"Mr. Fitzroy just explained your situation, Mr. Foster."

None of his three functioning brain cells allowed him to mistake CB's less-than-dulcet tones. "Uh . . ."

"He seems to think that it will be too dangerous for you to be Ms. Burnett's bodyguard at the same time as you're being my TAD."

"Demons . . ."

"Yes. Mr. Fitzroy mentioned that there may be demons and, as I'd just as soon not have demons on my soundstage disrupting my production schedule, you may have the time you need to deal with them."

"Thanks, Boss, I . . ."

"Don't make a habit of this, Mr. Foster."

"No, I . . ."

"And while you're sitting around waiting for something to attack Ms. Burnett, I suggest you answer your e-mail."

"Boss, I won't exactly . . ."

But he was talking to the dial tone. Wondering what Henry had said, or more importantly, what CB had heard, Tony tossed the phone down onto the tangle of blankets on the bed beside him.

The tangle snorted and swore in a language he didn't recognize.

Three guesses who and the first two don't count.

He grabbed one of the tangle's rising curves and shook it. When it gave under his fingers and kept shaking on its own, he snatched his hand away. "Hey! Where's Henry?"

"He left about an hour ago . . ."

Tony squinted toward the entertainment unit. 6:55. Sunrise was at 6:49. He must have called CB from his car.

". . . he said I should wake you, but I figured the wards would give enough warning."

"Why didn't he wake me?"

Leah's head and shoulders emerged from beneath the covers. "Hey, you guys have issues I'm not going near." When she stretched, Tony had an epiphany.

"You're naked!"

"I hate sleeping in my clothes."

He was still in his jeans and T-shirt although someone had removed his socks and sweatshirt.

"Relax." She yawned. "Although I've contaminated your space with girlie bits, your honor remains safe."

"It's not my . . ." Taking a deep breath, he sat up and swung his legs out of bed. "I just think you got naked a little fast."

Warm fingers patted his arm. "Sweetie, I've gotten naked a lot faster."

Okay. Should've seen that one coming.

Another deep breath as he shifted his weight forward. He seemed fine. Internal fluid levels had to still be low, but he wasn't feeling faint or light-headed. In fact, he was feeling pretty good. If he had to, he could probably toast another demon.

Three. Two. One.

When something with horns and scales missed its cue to break down the apartment door, Tony stood and made his way past the piles of laundry to the bathroom.

The bite on his neck still looked like hell. A hickey of the damned. In all the years he and Henry had been together, Henry'd never lost control like that.

Issues.

Yeah. Right.

Leah was up and dressed by the time he got out of the shower. The bed had been reconverted into a sofa and she was stuffing clothing into a pillowcase. "I've got a washer and dryer. You can do some laundry at my place."

"Your place?" Had he missed something?

"You didn't think we were staying here, did you?"

Tony shrugged.

It seemed to be the answer she'd expected because she grinned and tossed the stuffed pillowcase down beside its equally stuffed mate. "Get together everything you can't leave behind. We'll grab some breakfast on the way."

"So those files your wizard mentor left you, they're cued to you, right?"

Tony resisted the urge to glance toward the laptop case in the back seat, keeping his eyes on the road instead. "You booted up after I fell asleep?"

"I was curious. All I got was spider solitaire."

"She used it to tell the future."

"It?"

"Games of spider solitaire."

"Well, who hasn't used *that* excuse to justify not working? Hash brown?"

"Sure."

Leah lived out in Sullivan Heights and the fastest way there from Tony's apartment was to get onto Lougheed and head west. When they crossed Boundary, Tony had to remind himself not to turn. It was weird driving almost right past the studio on a Thursday morning.

I should be there. They need me.

Or worse, they don't really need me and I should be there so they don't find out.

"Did you see that?"

"See what?" Caught up in his concerns about remaining employed, Tony had no idea what Leah'd seen.

"There was a spot back there, by the gas station, where the rain wasn't."

He glanced over at her, but the back of her head didn't tell him a lot. She'd twisted around in her seat and was staring out the window, back the way they'd come. "Say what?"

"I saw an interruption in the rain. Some demons don't like to get wet."

Tony snorted. "Man, are they converging in the wrong place." And then the program loaded. "Hang on! There's another demon through?"

"Looks that way. Drive faster," she commanded, throwing herself back into the seat.

"What? No! I can get off Lougheed on Douglas and back on at Springer."

Leah turned to stare at him. He could feel incredulity hit the side of his face as he changed lanes. "And do what?"

"If there's a demon back there, it might eat someone. Or part of someone. I can't let that happen."

"So if we go back and wave me around like bait, and you Powershot it, what happens then?"

"No one gets eaten."

"Yeah, but you're out on your ass for another twelve hours. You're too wiped to learn the new spell and you're not able to protect me. Then, during those twelve hours, another demon shows up and eats me, opening the Demongate and ending the world as we know it."

"If it eats you, will the gate open inside it? Ow!" He rubbed his thigh where she'd smacked him.

"If you drive faster, we'll put more distance between us and it, and it'll take that much longer to find me. During that time, you can learn how to send it back to hell so that, when it finally catches up, you'll be able to save me without taking yourself out of the fight."

They were almost at the off ramp.

"I can't just let a demon run around loose."

"You can't just let a Demonlord into the world either."

Valid point.

Past the ramp. Too late to go back.

"If someone else dies . . ."

"Better them than me."

He fought the urge to hit the brakes and skid to a dramatic halt. It was the kind of reaction that would look great on screen and accomplish absolutely nothing in real life. He wanted to snarl, *It isn't all about you!* but, until the Demonic Convergence was over, it was. He wanted it to be about imps again. He'd kind of been looking forward to that.

"All right." Deep breath. No option but to deal. A little more gas and they were matching speeds with the fastest car on the road. "Why won't this new thing you're going to teach me knock me on my ass?"

Her seat creaked as she shifted her weight, tucking her knees up to brace her feet against the dashboard. "You'll be manipulating energy instead of just hurling it."

"Say what?"

She sighed impatiently. "Well, I'm no wizard, but that Powershot of yours looked like the magical equivalent of picking up the biggest rock you can find and crushing your enemies with it. Of course you're exhausted afterward; you're also looking at pulled muscles, back trouble, and probably hernias."

"Hernias?"

"Magical equivalent of. What I'm going to teach you is more like rolling the rock to the edge of a cliff and pushing it off as your enemies pass under it. There's a lot less effort involved and the result is the about the same."

"Really?"

"No, not really." Slouching as far as the seat belt would allow, Leah propped her yellow high-tops up on the dash. "It's actually a pretty lousy analogy and only applies to the amount of power involved. Powershot, lots. My way, less."

"Yeah, but you said you're not a wizard . . ."

"No, I'm not. I'm just the one who stands to be eviscerated if you don't get it right." She gave his leg a patronizing pat, her fingers lingering just a little too long. "And then the world as we know it ends."

Yeah. Yeah. No pressure.

Leah's condo was in a clump of high-rise concrete towers overlooking the TransCanada and a railway ravine, and it wasn't hard to understand why she objected to his beige. Her walls were shades of yellows, oranges, and reds. Her furniture was large and heavy and predominately wood and leather with cushions the same shades as the walls softening the angles. Every piece looked sturdy enough to take the weight of two moving adults.

From the sparsely furnished second bedroom on the north side of the corner unit, Tony could almost convince himself he could see Simon Fraser University high on the heights of Mount Burnaby—where *height* was a relative term given the actual peaks of the Rockies less than an hour's drive to the east.

He couldn't see any interruptions in the rain.

"All right." Leah opened the bottom of the white silk shirt she'd changed into after an impressively quick shower and, pushing her black track pants dangerously lower on her hips, stepped closer to the gooseneck lamp they were using as a spotlight. "The innermost circle of runes defines the actual gate. All you have to do, because we're not talking about creating an actual gate as much as reminding reality that demons don't belong here, is burn these four into the air . . ." One finger, a careful distance from skin, indicated the runes in question. ". . . each rune more or less an equal distance from the other, with the demon in the middle of the pattern. When you finish the fourth rune, reality will reset itself and no more demon."

With his nose so close to her skin, she smelled like soap and cinnamon. Or cinnamon soap. Which was a weird choice, but it suited her. "*All* I have to do?" Tony muttered, peering at the intricate tattoo.

Leah chose to ignore the sarcasm. "Because the demon doesn't belong here, you don't have to be specific about its name or its ultimate destination. Once you weaken the barrier, it'll snap back to where it belongs. It's a variation on what we were going to be doing before Ryne Cyratane upped the stakes— only then you'd have been pushing the runes through the weak spot to reinforce it."

"Yeah. Okay." The individual runes were a lot more complex up close than they were when they were just a part of the larger pattern. "What happens if I screw one of these up? Squiggle when I should spiral?"

"Probably nothing . . ."

The *probably* was a little worrying.

". . . although if, by chance, you re-create an entirely different power definition . . ." She shrugged, the curve of her belly rising and falling with the motion. "Maybe death. Destruction. Perpetual reruns of *The Family Guy*."

"Hey, that show's a classic!"

"Every now and then," Leah muttered, flicking Tony on the top of the head with one finger, "I think, why not let him in? How much worse could things get? You'd better draw the runes on paper first."

"Sure." He straightened. "But what did . . ." Tucked into the front pocket of the laptop case, his cell phone played the *Darkest Night* theme; Zev had made a digital file available to anyone in the studio who wanted to use it. Tony suspected he was hoping it would get picked up as a download by one of the big online ring-tone sites, but so far there were no takers. Flicking the phone open, he checked the display. "It's Amy."

"Who?"

"Assistant office manager at the studio. I should take it."

"Why?"

"It might be about work."

"You're a TAD." Leah allowed her shirt to fall closed. "Nothing you do is more important than learning how to keep me alive."

Since she put it that way, he answered the phone.

"Tony?" Amy had conspiracy in her voice. "You okay?"

"I'm fine, why?"

"Because CB said you weren't coming in today. Or tomorrow. CB. The boss. He didn't show up at your place last night and beat you into a coma, did he?"

"No. Why would he?" Did Amy know something about CB's feelings toward him that he didn't?

"Why would he carry your messages unless he was feeling, like, mondo guilty?"

"I asked him for some personal time."

"Personal time?" Amy snorted so vehemently, he had to move the phone away from his ear. "Loss of consciousness is CB's definition of personal time. It's not . . ." She lowered her voice dramatically. ". . . the other stuff is it?"

"The other stuff?"

"This isn't a secure line, nimrod."

"It isn't a line at all."

"Exactly my point. Well?"

And who was to say that Kevin Groves wasn't crouched in a bush outside the studio attempting to intercept his phone calls? It was the kind of sneaky, underhanded, not exactly legal thing that tabloid reporters did, wasn't it? "It's sort of the other stuff."

"Bastard. Just so you know, if you have any . . ." Her voice moved away from the phone. "CB Productions, please hold." And back. ". . . extracurricular fun without me, I will kick your ass up onto your shoulders."

"It's not . . . fun." He said the last word to no one in particular.

Leah sat down and pushed the lamp out of her line of sight. "So Amy, the assistant office manager at the studio, knows you're a wizard?"

"Yeah."

"And your boss knows?"

"Well . . ."

"Well," she mocked, fingers tapping out annoyance on the polished table-top. "Most people who have, let's say, *unusual* powers don't go talking about it to all and sundry since all, and particularly sundry, don't usually deal well with unusual."

"Thing is, we were trapped in a haunted house together."

"All three of you?"

"No, CB was outside."

"But he knows?"

"He knew before, during the Shadowlord thing."

"So Amy and your boss . . ."

The *Darkest Night* theme interrupted.

Tony glanced down at the screen. "It's Zev. He's the music director at the studio."

"Does Zev know?"

"He was in the house."

"Along with how many other people?"

"Not many."

"Good."

"About thirteen."

Dark brows rose almost to her hairline. "About?"

"Three of them died."

"Yay." Her fingers stilled.

It's when the drums stop that you have to worry. The *Darkest Night* theme looped back to the beginning and kept playing.

"Tony, answer the damned phone."

The conversation with Zev paralleled the conversation with Amy minus the speculation about a coma and the final threats.

"You'll call me if you need me?"

"Sure."

"And you'll be careful?"

"Count on it."

"Because you're an annoying pain in the ass, but I'm used to you being around."

"I'm used to being around. Don't worry." As he hung up, Leah slid a sheet of blank paper in front of him.

"Practice," she snapped, handing him a pencil. "Before someone else . . ."

The *Darkest Night* theme.

Once.

Lee's cell number.

Tony had, of course, memorized it even though he'd never used it. He stared at the phone, but Lee had obviously reconsidered calling.

"Earth to Tony." One bare foot kicked him, not particularly gently, in the shin. "Let's try and remember we're on the clock here!" Leaning back, she re-exposed the Demongate. "Now that your fan club has checked in, can we get on with this?"

"Sorry." He peered at her belly, put pencil to paper, and stopped. "Look, when you said, burn these four runes into the air, what did you mean?"

"You know." The tip of one finger sketched invisible circles. "Draw them in the air with lines of energy."

"Okay." He remembered Arra creating golden lines of power as she called on light to banish shadow. "I don't actually know how to do that."

"Everything in here is about energy. There's just nothing specifically about energy."

"Well, that's useless." Leah pushed a curl away from her face and tried to shove Tony away from the laptop. "Look up drawing."

Tony flicked the same curl away from *his* face and refused to be shoved as he scrolled up the file list.

Drawing, of the Dark.

Vaguely familiar but not helpful.

Drawing, Down the Moon.

Also familiar. He opened the file.

This is woman's magic. You don't need to know it.

Then why the hell did you list it, you crazy old . . .

Drawing, Blood.

"What did she think she was training," Leah snorted, "a wizard or a para-medic?"

"So she was a bit rushed when she put this together."

"A bit rushed? Da Vinci was a bit rushed when he was finishing the *Mona Lisa*. This wizard of yours seems more like a complete incompetent." Her breath hit the side of his head, warm and impatient. "You scroll; I'll stop you if I see anything useful."

Storms, Calming.

Poison, Checking for.

Water, Purifying.

Demons, Banishing.

"Hold on. Right there." One fingertip tapped the screen. "You have a spell to banish demons." The fingertip moved to tap him on the forehead. Hard. "You think maybe you should have mentioned that? Just in passing, perhaps?"

"I forgot it was there." He jerked away before she could tap him again and opened the file.

Calling demons is among the stupider things you can do with your power. I am inclined to allow stupidity to be its own reward; however, it is possible that someday you may need to clean up another's mess. Begin by drawing six drops of blood from the idiot who called the demon. Do it quickly before the corpse cools.

"This is useless." Leah straightened, turned, and dropped onto the edge of the table. "These demons weren't called, they're being sent. There's nothing we can use in there . . ."

"It says we should use an unnatural rope to hold the fiend."

"And then do what with it? Why don't I just kill myself and save them the bother?" Dragging both hands back through her hair, she began to pace. "I can't believe this wizard of yours would leave out something so basic."

Tony scrolled up and down the list one more time and frowned. "Hell, if it's all that basic, maybe there's something about it in the instructions."

The sudden silence was so complete, he could hear the traffic passing on the TransCanada six stories down and almost a half a kilometer away. He twisted around on his chair to find Leah staring at him from across the room. "What?"

"There's instructions?"

"Yeah. I didn't read them, but . . ."

"You didn't read the instructions? Of course you didn't," she continued before he could answer. "You just opened the spell list and started trying things out, didn't you?" While he was thinking about denying it, she closed the distance between them and smacked him on the back of the head. "Men!"

"Hey!"

Leaning back she flashed him a narrow-eyed glare. "Hey, what?"

"Nothing." It just seemed like a bad time to go into the whole gender stereotyping thing.

"Good. Now then . . ."

He could feel every one of those thirty-five hundred years leaning over his shoulder with her.

". . . let's have a look at the instructions, shall we?"

Power, Responsibilities of.

Power, the Focusing of.

Her finger touched the screen. "That's got subdirectories."

"On it." The next layer down had been divided into basic, intermediate, and advanced. As Tony moved the cursor onto advanced, Leah's hand closed around his wrist and moved it back to basic. "I thought we were in a hurry."

"We are. But as much as I don't want to be killed by a demon, I'd also rather not be killed by you. Start at the beginning. Read fast."

Fortunately, the lesson was, well, basic and it seemed he'd been instinctively doing most of it already. The rest of it seemed simple enough. When he mentioned that to Leah, she snorted.

"Lots of things seem simple when you read the instructions, but it's an entirely different story when you actually try to hook up the DVD player."

Fair point. "It doesn't seem that complicated, though. Mostly, I just have to shift my internal focus to external."

"Do you even know what that means?"

Tony pushed his chair out from the table and stood, forcing her to take a couple of steps back. "It's sort of like choking up on the Powershot."

"Choking up on the Powershot?" Muttering under her breath, she moved around until she stood behind him. "Your keen grasp of description fills me with confidence."

"I need to practice."

"You think? Make it fast and don't destroy my apartment."

"Your faith is underwhelming," he muttered, bouncing lightly on the balls of his feet and shaking the tension out of his arms. He could do this. He called things to his hand by knowing where they were, by being aware of the space they defined. According to Arra's notes, focus meant being aware of the space *he* defined and pulling in energy to fill it. That was the part he'd been doing instinctively.

Once he had the energy, all he had to do was pick a spot outside his body, shift the focus to that spot, and re-form the energy in his chosen pattern. Like writing with sparklers, only the images would stick around longer. Arra's notes suggested he practice with a neutral symbol, something that could only be what it was.

Okay.

Right index finger extended—best not toss the scar on his left hand into the mix until he had a better grip on what he was doing—he picked a point about halfway to the window, refocused until his right eye started to water, and began burning his chosen symbol onto the air.

Leah's curtains caught fire.

Crap! That wasn't supposed to happen. Glancing down at the laptop, he checked the screen. No, definitely not supposed to happen.

He opened his left hand. The fire arced toward it.

The curtains separated at the char line, the lower third dropping to the floor.

Tony coughed, smoke pluming out on his breath. Back in his teens, although he couldn't afford the habit, he'd bummed the occasional cigarette from other guys on the street. The coolest guys could always make the biggest plumes of smoke. Apparently, for wizards, the cigarette had become optional—although he wasn't sure that the present circumstances were any healthier.

He was sure blowing out a nice big plume, though.

Leah crossed the room and picked up the burned fabric. Ash crumbed off between her fingers, drifting to lie like dirty snow on the hardwood floor. She stared at the ash, at the curtain, and finally at Tony. "Damn. What did you do?"

"It was an accident."

"*After* the accident. When you put the fire out."

"Oh." He coughed again. There was a little less smoke this time. "I called it to me."

"The fire?" Still holding the piece of curtain, she started back toward him. "You called the fire toward you?"

"It's just another kind of energy, right?"

"Yeah. Right." Her fingers left dark gray smudges behind when she patted his arm. "You just keep believing that, okay?" A wave of the ruined curtain for emphasis. "Try dialing it back this time."

"It?" One last puff of smoke as punctuation. "You want me to do it again?"

"Curtains can be replaced," she reminded him as she returned to her place out of the line of fire, "I can't. Once more, with less feeling."

"I don't think . . ."

"Good. You think too much and we're running out of time. Do what you just did, only less."

"Less. Right." Tony wiped damp palms on his thighs, extended his finger again, and very carefully refocused. To his surprise, a bright blue light burned in approximately the right position and then went out. Okay, almost there. He needed less less. *That's more, right?* Licking dry lips, he tried again. The blue light burned longer. *A little more.* And again. This time the light maintained; became a line; the line bent into a circle; the edges of the circle sputtered, but the shape held. Within the circle, two dots of power for eyes. The curve of a smile.

It was slightly lopsided but recognizable.

"What is it?"

Or not.

"It's a happy face." Even when he turned away, the power he'd used to create the symbol hung in the air. It was bone useless but way cool. "I told you it would be . . ." His voice trailed off as the sound of laughter filled the condo.

Tony whirled around, both hands up, expecting some kind of demonic clown charging in from the balcony. There was only his happy face, all blue and glowing and hanging in the air. Given the way it was laughing, it seemed to be very, very happy indeed.

"Simple," Leah said, raising her voice enough to be heard. "You said it would be simple. I think you meant to tell me that you were simple. And when I say simple, I don't mean that you're easy, I mean that you're . . ."

The *Darkest Night* theme joined the laughter to drown out her last word.

Since he couldn't think anything else to do, Tony answered his phone.

"Tony! There's something in the soundstage! It's ripping the place apart. There's crashing and screaming and . . ."

"Lee!"

"No, it's Amy, you ass!"

He knew that. "I meant . . ."

"I don't give a good goddamn what you meant! Get in here!"

"What . . ."

But there was only the dial tone. Over by the window, the happy face kept laughing.

Shoving the phone back in his backpack, Tony hung it over one shoulder as he ran for the door. "The demon's at the studio!"

"Tony! Wait!"

"Forget it, Leah. You want your body guarded, you come with me."

"I intend to." She grabbed his backpack and dragged him around. "But you can't leave that thing hanging in my condo!"

The happy face kept laughing.

Tony stretched out his left arm and sucked the energy back through the scar. He had the giggles all the way to the underground garage.

Leah's driving made it difficult to practice the four runes he needed to know. He'd taken half a dozen pictures of the tattoo with the camera on his phone and, with his knees pressed against the dash and the phone open on his knees, he tried to memorize the swoops and curls as he sketched.

Tried to sketch.

"Leah!"

"You want to get there in time or what?" Considerably over the 100K limit, she cut in and out of westbound traffic in order to maintain her speed.

The TransCanada was a slightly less direct route back to the studio, but it had no lights and they were making amazing time—even considering the amount of lateral movement. Flung right then left, Tony wondered again why every time something metaphysical came down, he ended up in a car with people who drove like complete maniacs. Henry, Arra, Mouse, Jack, Leah . . .

"Hey!" The car started to hydroplane on the wet pavement, the back end fishtailing for about thirty meters before Leah got it under control. Tony caught the phone before it hit the floor but lost his pencil. "We're not all immortal here!"

"Trust me. I'm a professional stunt driver."

"They aren't!" The drivers of a late '90s Buick and a little imported hybrid flipped them off in quick succession. Hoping Leah's protective coating would work against road rage, he bent to find the pencil. He'd just about decided to take off his shoulder belt when he heard the siren and straightened so quickly he cracked his head on the dash. "Shit. Is that for us?"

"Seems to be. Are you crying?"

"No. My eyes are watering, I hit my head. You're not stopping!"

"Neither is the demon at the soundstage."

Good point. He wasn't looking forward to explaining it to the police but, still, a good point.

"If it is a demon." She slid between two transports, passed on the right shoulder, and somehow ended up back in the left lane.

"What do you mean if?" Tony demanded.

"If it's a demon, why is it at your soundstage? Why isn't it hunting for me?" As they passed the Kensington on ramp, an unmarked car squealed onto the highway in front of them, siren also wailing, the light on the dash just barely visible through distance and rain. "They're trying to cut us off!"

He grabbed the wheel before Leah could change lanes. "No. Follow them."

"Are you insane?"

"They're not slowing down, and the car behind us has fallen back."

"I lost him."

"No." There was no mistaking Jack Elson's pale blond hair in the unmarked car. "I know these guys."

Leah shot him a quick glance. "Your Mountie buddy?"

"Eyes on the road! My Mountie buddy and his partner," he expanded when his heart started beating again. An East Indian woman was driving and he was willing to bet she had to be Constable Danvers regardless of how much ethnic recruiting the RCMP did.

"I forgot to add them to the list of the people who know what you are, didn't I? Why didn't you just tell the papers?" she continued before he could answer. "It'd save time."

As the two cars sped toward the studio, he tried to remember if he'd told her about Kevin Groves. And what it was *about* Kevin Groves that he'd intended to tell her. "Well, technically . . ."

"I don't want to know."

They fishtailed off the ramp onto Boundary, squealed tires through the gate of the industrial complex, and sprayed gravel in tandem as they pulled up in the parking lot at CB Productions.

Jack was out of the car, gun in his hand, before the gravel hit the ground again. "When they called in your plates, I figured something was up. What is it?" he demanded, falling into step as Tony sprinted for the building.

Tony hesitated, wondering if Jack had kept his partner in the loop. Television cops never kept secrets from their partners. "There's a demon ripping up the soundstage!"

"A what?" Danvers yelled as the four of them pounded in through the office doors.

"A demon!" Tony skidded to a stop as the dozen or so people in the office turned to stare.

He stared.

They stared.

"Jesus, Tony . . ." Amy's brows dipped to nearly touch over her nose. ". . . what the hell happened to your neck?"

"Not important." Trust Amy. He couldn't stop himself from touching the bite as he hurriedly counted heads. "Not everyone's out."

"Such a grasp of the obvious," she said to the room at large. "This is why I called him."

"Amy." Tina's tone suggested that was enough. "A few people got out the back," the script supervisor continued, rocking the new and teary assistant set decorator in the circle of her arms. "There's a few still in there."

"CB?"

All heads turned toward CB's office as though they were on a single string.

"He went in as we came out."

Of course he had. Tony took a quick mental inventory of CB's office but could think of nothing that the big man could use as a weapon.

"Okay." Deep breath. A quick, purposeful crossing to the door—made slightly less purposeful by the people milling about in his way.

"You brought the cops?" Zev asked, pushing through to his side.

"They brought themselves." He reached for the door and paused. This wasn't a case of reacting to an attack, blasting before he could consider the consequences; this was deliberately going after a demon. Deliberately going after something with teeth and claws and attitude. *Try not to look like you're nearly pissing yourself.*

You went after the thing in the basement, a little voice reminded him.

Did you miss the part about teeth and claws? he asked it.

A quick glance back over his shoulder. "You guys don't have to . . ."

Jack reached past him and shoved the door open. "Move!" he snapped.

So he moved.

They ran in single file between the double racks of costumes—a wizard -in-training, two RCMP officers, and an immortal stuntwoman/Demongate bringing up the rear. It sounded like the punch line of a bad joke. All they needed was a duck. Tony'd been a little afraid that either Zev or Amy would follow, but they both seemed to have more sense.

The door to the soundstage was closed.

When Tony reached to open it, Jack stopped him, hand without the gun wrapping around his wrist. "You don't just go charging in! Listen first."

Leah raised an eyebrow in Tony's direction, sharing her amusement. "The door's soundproof. We might as well go charging in."

"Fine. We . . ." Jack used his weapon to indicate that *we* in this case meant him and Danvers. ". . . go in first."

"Good idea."

The constable fixed Leah with a pale stare. "Who the hell are you?"

"Leah Burnett."

"And?"

"I'm a stuntwoman."

"Let me rephrase. Why are you here?"

"I don't even know why *we're* here," Danvers muttered.

"Believe it or not . . ." She pointed at Tony. ". . . the safest place I can be is next to him."

"Not," Jack snorted.

Tony could feel momentum slipping away. Once it was gone, he was afraid he'd never be able to force himself onto the soundstage. Ignoring the others, he yanked open the door and charged through, heading for the area under the gate.

The Demonic Convergence was happening on the lower mainland because Leah and the oldest spell in the world currently lived here. But she didn't have the only spell around. It might not even be the strongest. It sure as hell wasn't the freshest.

Looking for that nice, fresh demonic feeling?

Oh, man, I seriously need some downtime with my brain.

In the last few weeks, the set under the gate that had brought Arra Pelin-drake into this world and then taken her out again had been the living room of grieving parents, a medieval dining hall, and a veterinary office—anything they could fit into the space without moving the walls or windows. CB disap-proved of unnecessary rebuilding.

The end wall had been reduced to a jagged bit of framing and a dangling piece of plywood. Standing surrounded by debris, one sleeve ripped from his suit jacket and the exposed arm hanging limp by his side, CB shook a length of pipe up at the lighting grid. "Get your scaly red ass down here so I can kick it back to whatever overblown special effect it crawled out of!"

A shriek of tortured metal from above.

One of the big lamps plummeted toward the floor.

Time was supposed to slow as certain death approached. That was the theory. Total bullshit as far as Tony was concerned. The lamp exploded against the painted concrete floor; CB dove out of the way, swinging the pipe to deflect a shard of glass away from his leg, and Tony barely had time enough to realize he should do something. No time at all to think of just what he should do.

The sound of another lamp ripped from the grid made one thing clear; he had to get the demon down.

Tony held out his hand and called.

The demon was about the size of a ten-year-old but remarkably heavy for all that. The impact knocked the breath from them both and for a moment they sprawled together on the concrete, arms and legs tangled in interspecies intimacy. Then it blinked orange eyes, and a mouth, far too wide for the face that held it, opened.

Black teeth.

Shiny and black like that lava rock Tony could never remember the name of.

Lots and lots of black teeth!

Pain flared in his left shoulder, something squeezed around his right leg, and the demon's head snapped forward.

Fuck! Teeth!

Four shots jerked it back far enough for Tony to get his left leg free. He kicked out, hard. It reared back, hissing and snarling, still attached by the tail wrapped around Tony's leg. He kicked it again, a little lower, and black claws on the hind legs shredded his jeans below the knee.

Jack took another shot. The tail whipped away. Danvers grabbed his shoulders, dragging him up onto his feet.

"Why are you wrestling with it?" Leah screamed, crouched behind a yellow chaise lounge. "Get those runes in the air!"

Tony ducked as the demon launched itself over him, heading for Leah. Ducked a little lower as it returned the other way, arms and legs flailing as CB yanked it back by the tail.

It folded back on itself, squirmed free, and leaped straight up.

If it regained the high ground . . .

No way in hell he remembered the runes.

So we stick with what we know.

Miraculously still standing, Tony made a mental note that a Powershot released inside was blinding. Hopefully, *temporarily* blinding.

"Mr. Foster!"

Patterns of blue light danced across the inside of Tony's lids. At least, he thought he had his eyes closed. "Yeah, Boss?"

"Was that you?"

"Yeah."

"Did you hit it?"

"I don't know."

"Is anyone being disemboweled?" Sarcasm dripped from Leah's voice.

It seemed that no one was.

"Well, isn't that lucky." Not so much dripping now as flowing freely.

"What was that?" Jack's voice, demanding an answer.

"The demon? Or Tony's pyrotechnical answer to the demon?"

"Hey!" He turned toward where Leah's voice put her. "We were all screwed if it got back into the light grid."

"Damned right." Danvers this time. Nice that someone understood.

A hand closed around his arm and by blinking rapidly he could almost make out the silhouette of the person attached to the hand. At least he hoped it was the person attached to the hand.

"You're bleeding." Danvers again.

"He should count his blessings he's alive to bleed." Leah, closer now, sounded distinctly unsympathetic. "What happened to the plan, Tony?"

"You guys had a plan?" Jack didn't sound like he believed her.

"There's a way to send the demons back where they came from without wiping out our best defense."

"If this ash is all that remains of the demon, he's out of the picture." CB. From near the floor. "Except for a few minor punctures, I believe Mr. Foster—whom, I assume, you were referring to as our best line of defense—is fine."

"Tony, can you see yet?" Leah. Right in his face.

He could sort of make out shapes, but he got a little dizzy when he turned his head. "Uh . . ."

"No. He can't. We can. He can't." Probably Leah's hand on his cheek. The fingers were trembling a little. "Someone had better grab him before he cracks his skull open on the floor."

On cue, Tony felt his knees buckle.

"I've got you, kid." A dark Jack-shape with blond highlights.

"These holes look clean, and they're not as deep as they could be." Danvers, as she pulled his shirt off and started working on the punctures in his shoulder. Tony was starting to really like her. "Damp denim seems to make decent body armor. I don't think he did much damage to your leg either. Is there a first aid—Thanks."

No mistaking CB's presence up close and personal. There was a sudden lack of open space in the immediate area.

Jack shifted his grip to give Danvers a better angle on the shoulder. "So what's wrong with him?"

"You mean besides the holes? It was the Powershot. Not the smartest thing to do."

Jack answered Leah's question with one of his own. "Who *are* you?"

He'd keep asking until he got an answer, like the world's biggest red serge-wearing terrier. Given Leah's earlier opinion of all and sundry, and given that Jack was definitely one of the sundry, the odds were good she wasn't going to tell him. The trick was figuring out how much of the truth would shut him up.

"She's a demonic consultant," Tony told him, trying not to think about what Jack's partner was doing to his shoulder.

"A what?"

"Demonic consul . . . OW!"

"Sorry."

"It's okay." And it was. The flash of white light accompanying the pain seemed to have cleared his vision. Where *cleared* meant he could see people standing around him and pretty much figure out who they were. Beyond about three meters, things were still a little fuzzy—like his focus had been pulled so he had no depth of field—which likely meant there'd be something with teeth and scales charging in from the fuzzy any minute now.

"Tony?"

Or not.

Lee gradually came into focus as he came closer. Then came into focus a lot faster as he broke into a run and dropped to one knee.

"What happened?" he demanded, his hand closing around Tony's wrist.

Tony opened his mouth, but Jack filled the words in. "It's the aftereffects of frying a demon."

"You're hurt!"

"It's uh . . ." He glanced over at the blood-soaked pad in the RCMP officer's hand and decided not to bother with the whole manly denial thing. "Yeah."

"It's not as bad as it looks." Danvers' matter-of-fact tone made it convincing. Given that it was his blood, Tony wasn't entirely convinced, but Lee seemed to be.

Seemed to be glaring at Jack.

Who still held Tony cradled against his body while Danvers finished with his shoulder.

Lee was glaring?

Tony had no idea how Jack was responding, but something in the way his grip shifted and the way muscles moved in his chest, made Tony think he felt amused.

"How are the others, Mr. Nicholas?" CB's bulk reappeared like a mahogany wall at the end of Tony's feet, the force of his personality enough to break through Lee's . . . well, to break through whatever the hell was up with Lee.

"Fine. They're good." The actor sat back and turned, visibly distancing himself from the scene on the floor—although his fingers maintained their grip. "Mouse thinks the gaffer's nose might be broken."

"And Mason?"

"Would be on the phone to his agent if there was a phone around to be on."

"I'll speak with him in a moment."

"I can't say that I blame him, CB."

"Demons." Jack ignored Lee's reinstated glare, but there was nothing that suggested amusement this time. He shifted Tony's weight onto his partner, who caught it, steadied it, and raised a skeptical eyebrow when Tony muttered, "I can sit on my own."

"What about them?" CB demanded as Jack got slowly to his feet.

"She said *demons*. As in more than one. They had a plan to send the *demons* back where they came from. That . . ."

All eyes turned with his gesture to the smear of ash on the floor. Tony could just barely make it out. ". . . isn't the end of this. Is it?"

And all eyes turned to Leah.

Who looked at him.

His stomach growled.

∽ SIX

"How long is this Demonic Convergence going to last?"

"I don't know."

"You don't know?" CB repeated Leah's answer as a question, an eyebrow raised for punctuation. There were rumors that eyebrow had once caused a loan manager to wet himself—a rumor that Tony, having more than once been on the receiving end of said eyebrow, was inclined to believe.

Leah proved to be made of sterner stuff, but then she'd already survived plagues, the Inquisition, disco. . . . "Information on the last Demonic Convergence was passed on as an oral history for centuries before finally being written down by an insane monk in 332. He was a little vague on duration."

"Rather an important point, don't you think?"

"As a matter of fact, I do." She matched his dry, sarcastic tone precisely and then sat back and crossed her legs. "Fortunately, we know that the Convergence is of limited duration, just not exactly how limited. My best guess would tie it to the moon through one full cycle. A month, no more. Maybe a little less."

"And your worst guess?" CB growled.

She shrugged. "The planets change position slowly and the stars slower still."

"You're saying this could last years?"

"It could."

"Demons could be dropping into my studio for years?"

"Or the one Tony destroyed could be the only one you'll see. There's no way of knowing for sure."

Liar, Tony thought. He was impressed by how much like a consultant she sounded and less impressed by how heavily edited the story had become. She hadn't mentioned that the demons were only coming through because a Demonlord was directing the convergent energy. Nor had she said anything about being an immortal Demongate, confident that Tony would keep her secret. Since he'd already lied for her once today, he supposed she had reason for the confidence. After all those years with Henry, he was good at secrets. And given that the residue of Arra's spell seemed to be exerting a stronger pull than Leah, the whole Demongate thing seemed a little less relevant than it had.

"I have a question!" Perched on the edge of CB's desk, Amy waved her hand above her head, the charms hanging off the polished bicycle chain she wore wrapped around one wrist glinting under the fluorescent lights. "How does one become a demonic consultant? Exactly?"

Amy hadn't been included in the *we* when CB'd growled, *"We need to talk."* When those who'd been involved in the battle—plus Lee who'd arrived on the scene before anyone thought to adjust the story—followed CB into his office— where *followed*, in Tony's case, meant hanging off Jack's arm and more or less putting one foot in front of the other—she'd invited herself along, dragging Zev behind her. Tony was glad they were there. Although the odds were good Zev would have understood, keeping Amy out of the loop had limited survivability, and even CB seemed to realize it would be easier in the long run to let her stay.

"I have a better question," Constable Danvers sighed, rubbing the bridge of her nose. "Who the hell is going to believe all that damage in the soundstage was caused by a deranged fan?"

"Drugged fan," Lee corrected. He'd suggested the cover story.

"Whatever. Drugged, deranged; no one will buy it."

"Mason did," Lee reminded her. Mason had been thrilled to think that one of his fans had gone berserk and trashed the soundstage. Mason was thrilled to believe pretty much anything that made it all about him.

"Once Mason starts talking about it," CB explained, "everyone else will believe it, too."

"Like he'll give them a choice," Amy snorted.

CB nodded. "My point exactly. You should use the tools you have to hand."

Everyone turned to look at Tony.

"You calling me a tool?" he roused himself enough to mutter.

"Yes."

So much for humor.

"I shall sum up, then." CB leaned back in his chair, which creaked alarmingly under his bulk. "We are in the midst of a Demonic Convergence of indeterminate length. The demons are attracted to this building because of . . ."

Tony hoped no one had noticed the slight pause—where *no one* referred to the RCMP officers who hadn't been told about the gate or Arra or the Shadowlord when they were told about what had happened in the house. Given that they'd been standing on the front lawn when the heavens opened, the story of the house had been unavoidable, but—so far—Tony'd managed to avoid filling in the whole metaphysical backstory.

". . . the residual energy; energy most likely connected to Mr. Foster's abilities."

That's right. Make it believable. Blame me.

"Ms. Burnett," CB continued, "who has made a study of demonology . . ."

No one seemed to have any trouble believing in a stuntwoman as a student of demonology.

". . . just happened to have recently contacted Mr. Foster to inform him about this Demonic Convergence and to instruct him on how to return said demons to the hell they came from—although, as circumstances have forced Mr. Foster to fry both demons he has already faced, whether or not he *can* return them remains theoretical."

Tony rubbed the bandage on his shoulder. Nothing much about this seemed theoretical to him. His whole body ached.

"Because both demons have been reduced to ash, we have no proof should we decide to make the story public, so rather than be mocked by those who have not shared our experiences, we are maintaining that today's incident was caused by a drugged fan of Mason Reed's. Constables Danvers and Elson will support that story in their reports."

"I can't believe we're going to falsify a report!" Constable Danvers punctuated each word by banging the back of her head against the wall.

CB laid both hands flat on his desk. The fingers of the left hand started to tremble. Muscles tensed in the arm the demon had dislocated and Jack had snapped back, and the trembling stopped. "Given that you arrived here in an official capacity, the report is unavoidable. You may, of course, choose to tell the truth."

Danvers looked at CB, she looked around the room, and, finally, she looked at her partner. Who shrugged. Jack had been remarkably quiet since he'd brought up the point about multiple demons. Tony wondered what he was thinking. His partner seemed to be wondering the same, but after a long moment, she sighed and muttered, "Fine. But what happens if these things go public? You know, suddenly show up on the six o'clock news climbing the Lions Gate Bridge?"

"They don't show up on camera," Leah told her.

"Why not?"

"They don't have souls."

"What?"

"A camera steals a piece of your soul," Leah explained. "Demons have no souls, so they don't show up on camera."

"That's total bullshit."

A raised hand cut off the murmur of agreement. Leah leaned toward the constable, smiling slightly. "Why *don't* demons show up on camera, then?"

"Because they . . . I mean, they . . ." When no one seemed willing to help, Danvers' shoulders sagged. "I can't believe I'm even having this conversation." *Bang. Bang. Bang* against the wall.

Jack reached out and grabbed her shoulder, stopping the motion. Once she'd stilled, he stepped past her, swept a narrow-eyed gaze around the room—which would have been more effective had most of the people in the room not recognized it as having been inserted for effect—and finally locked his eyes on CB. "As long as demons are attracted to your soundstage, for *whatever* reason . . ."

Translating the emphasis, Tony could see another "talk" with the constable in his future. Probably accompanied by shouting.

". . . you'll have to close the studio."

Zev hummed a few portentous bars of music under his breath.

Amy moved off CB's desk and out of the line of fire as the producer smiled. "I have an episode and a half of a show still to shoot, Constable. I *have* to do no such thing."

"People are going to get hurt. Someone's already been hurt. Someone besides Tony."

"It was the gaffer," Tony murmured. "He's the guy who sets the lights to get the effect the DP wants," he expanded when Jack turned to glare. "When things get weird, it's good to hold onto the stuff you know. Not you, personally," he added quickly. "Us you."

"Did you get hit on the head?"

"I don't think so."

"Check." Jack's attention relocked on CB. "Your gaffer's nose is broken. He's on his way to the hospital. You were lucky no one was seriously hurt. Or killed. You're closing the studio."

"I am contractually obligated to provide twenty-two episodes of *Darkest Night* within a specific time frame," CB told him. "If I close the studio, this won't happen, and we will be in violation of our contract. There will be no season two. My people will be let go. Most will not be able to find new work as many of the network shows that were filming in Vancouver have moved back across the border."

"So you think your 'people' . . ."

That was the most sarcastic set of air quotes Tony had ever seen.

". . . would rather be exposed to demonic attacks than unemployment?"

"Speaking as one of his people . . ." Perched now on an arm of the couch, Amy waved again. ". . . definitely."

"You are not the average employee," Jack pointed out.

"I am," Zev broke in before Amy could respond. He shuffled forward to the edge of the couch cushion. "I vote we finish the season."

Jack stared at the music director for a long moment. "Why are you even here?" he asked.

A nod toward Amy. "I came in with her."

"That's not helping your case, you know that, right?"

"Yes, but . . ." He winced and fell silent as Amy smacked him on the arm.

"And," Jack continued, "as I understand things, neither of you spend much time out on the soundstage where the demons are going to be."

"I do." Lee rose slowly off his end of the couch and moved until he stood face-to-face with Jack. "And I say we don't close the studio."

Tony had a feeling that, right at that moment, Lee would say black if Jack said white. He cleared his throat and was more or less gratified when it drew everyone's attention back to him. "Look, I'm going to be here anyway . . ." He tried to sit forward like Zev had, found he didn't have the energy, figured *screw it* as he fell back, sagging slightly into the warmth Lee had left. ". . . and it would be a lot easier on me if I didn't have to waste time and energy . . ." A short rest for emphasis before he finished. ". . . keeping friends and coworkers from being eaten while I deal."

"Eaten?" Amy and Zev together. Lee came in a little late.

"We've got a dead guy without an arm in the morgue. Killed by a demon who ate the arm." Jack folded his arms triumphantly.

He didn't know the arm hadn't been eaten, and since he was helping Tony make his point, Tony wasn't planning on mentioning it.

"So . . ." CB steepled his fingers and peered over the mahogany triangle at his TAD. "You think I should close the studio."

"No." Leah jumped in before Tony could get his mouth open. "I don't think you should close the studio." She stood and spread her hands, looking earnest. "We don't know how long the Demonic Convergence will last." Tossing her hair back over her shoulders, she adjusted her posture subtly. "There's no reason to risk putting so many people out of work. Tony will be here. I've taught him everything he needs to know."

The simple statement sounded pornographic.

Lee, who was closest to her, made a sound low in his throat. CB and Jack leaned in.

Ryne Cyratane flexed translucent muscles and ran his hands down Leah's arms.

"Then it's settled." CB's voice slipped past Barry White and headed toward registering on the Richter scale. "We'll keep the studio open."

Jack nodded, absently drying his palms on his thighs. "That sounds reasonable."

"Nothing about this sounds reasonable," Danvers muttered. "What the hell are you talking about, Jack?"

"She's the demonic consultant." A nod and an appreciative smile toward Leah. "We're out of our depth—we should listen to her."

"You're out of your mind."

Charms chimed as Amy waved. "I'd like to second that, except I want the studio open, so I won't."

All right. Enough was enough. If Leah didn't want her secrets told to all and sundry, she needed to lay off taking advantage of all and sundry. Tony frowned at Lee. Especially this particular sundry. "She's using demonic sex appeal to convince you."

Leah's dark eyes widened, and her lower lip went out. "Tony!"

"Do you have proof of this accusation, Mr. Foster?"

"No, but . . ."

"Then don't make it."

"Hello! Wizard!" He tried to stand and fell back onto the couch. His second attempt was more successful but only because Zev helped. "Okay. Wizard. Let's assume I know more about what's going on here than . . ." The room shifted out of focus and back in again. ". . . than not-wizards, okay? And let's assume that I can . . ." Whoa. His head felt like a raw egg balanced on a strand of cooked spaghetti. ". . . I can . . ."

"You can barely stand, Tony." Lee didn't sound particularly sympathetic, but then Lee was as enthralled by Leah as Jack and CB.

Okay, forget the room. Focus on Lee's face. You're good at that. He was. But

it had never been so hard before. His brain attempted to toss in a smutty innuendo but didn't quite manage it. "Behind her . . . there's a big . . . a big
naked . . ."

On *naked*, Lee turned his attention back to Leah.

Crap.

Tony's knees gave out, and Zev was a second late keeping his head from
bouncing off the floor of CB's office.

"That sounded like it hurt." Amy frowned down at him.

Way to state the obvious.

"He needs to see a doctor."

Constable Danvers was rapidly becoming one of Tony's favorite people.

"No, he just needs rest. A Powershot uses a lot of personal energy, and
that's not something a doctor can fix. No wonder he's babbling." Leah sounded
convincing. Tony would have been more convinced if, when his head fell to
one side, he hadn't been looking through a bare foot. An enormous bare foot.

"What happens if another demon attacks before he recovers?" Jack demanded.

"We're screwed."

Tony wondered if he was the only one who heard, *You're screwed.*

"I can shoot it."

"That's sweet, but bullets will only slow it down. All you can do is hope
Tony recovers and that from now on, he does things *my* way."

Tony was starting to think Leah had some serious control issues. He closed
his fingers around Zev's wrist. "All . . . about . . . sex."

As darkness claimed him, he heard CB snort. "Welcome to the wonderful
world of television, Mr. Foster."

He came to, stretched out on the couch in CB's office, all his attention on the
vegetable soup in a Styrofoam bowl steaming on the coffee table beside him.
Ignoring the spoon, he grabbed it with shaking hands and downed it in four
swallows. Or, more accurately, three, since a good portion of the fourth he
coughed out his nose.

A familiar hand passed over a wad of paper napkins.

"Where's everyone gone?" he asked when he could talk.

"Back to work." Ryne Cyratane had vanished and Leah looked no more
than normally attractive. "Your friends on the force have reports to file and a
nonexistent drugged fan to pretend to track down. Your coworkers are finishing the day's pages—well, except for Mason Reed, who leaked news of the
incident to the press and is now giving interviews."

Tony snorted out an alphabet noodle; an F or maybe an E deformed by its
passage through his sinuses. "The studio's staying open."

"Yes."

"The demons will come here."

"Yes."

"Because the gate is putting out the kind of residual power that attracts them more powerfully than you do."

"Yes."

"If there're people in the studio, the demon won't just check out the gate, realize it's not you, and go hunting as instructed by its boss. It'll try for a snack and make itself obvious. If it's distracted by a meal, it'll be easier for me to send it home." His subconscious had put the pieces together while he'd been out. "You're setting up the people here as bait."

She stared at him for a moment, then she smiled. "Only during business hours. Your vampire can still deal with it after dark. More soup?"

"Sure." Tony drank, slower this time, and considered his options. His brain felt like it was wrapped in barbed wire. It hurt to think and, as far as he could tell, he didn't actually seem to have any options. Sucked to be him. "I could tell them."

"About what?"

"About them being bait. About you being a Demongate. About the Demonlord's plan to kill you and take over the world. I could tell them everything."

"And that would accomplish what?" she asked reasonably, crossing the office and perching on the edge of the coffee table so she could stare earnestly into his face. "CB has very good reasons for not shutting the studio down. I agreed with him, so I helped him convince your friend Jack. Yes, your crew will be in a bit of danger, but if you get your head out of your butt and learn how to deal with the demons, it's all incidental anyway. You'll send them back before they do any damage."

"Yeah, tell that to Ritz."

"Who?"

"The gaffer." He waved at his nose.

"Your gaffer's name is Ritz?"

"Probably not, but that's what he goes by."

"Right." She tucked a strand of hair behind her ear. "If you'd been here, instead of at my place . . ."

"I was protecting you!"

Leah ignored him. ". . . Ritz wouldn't have gotten hurt."

"So what happened was my fault?"

"It was no one's fault." Leaning forward, she patted his knee. "Tony, this is working out perfectly. The gate obviously has a more powerful signature than I do or that demon wouldn't have come here first."

First. He frowned. First? "That wasn't the first demon."

Leah wrapped a curl around a finger. "Well, no, but . . ."

"And the first demon didn't come here first."

"Ah!" She held up a cautioning finger. "We don't know that."

"It killed a guy, ripped off his arm, and *then* came after you."

"It probably came to the studio at night when there was no one here, then it found my scent at the stunt site where it killed the construction worker. It was the next day before it found me. If there'd been a wizard in the studio prepared to send it back . . ." Her voice trailed off dramatically.

"I'm seeing a problem with that."

"I'm not saying it was your fault that man died."

"Yeah. Bite me. Let's consider the word *probably*."

She frowned as she went back over what she'd said. Then she rolled her eyes. "Fine. But the second demon definitely came here first—even though we drove right by it—so the odds are certainly in favor of the first demon having done the same thing. Demons at this level aren't known for independent thought. They're just big scary, scaly killing machines. Fortunately, this lot has been given a mission, so there's less random killing."

"That's comforting." Tony's head hurt, his shoulder was throbbing, the soup had barely taken the edge off his hunger, and at some point while he was in la-la land, his torn and bloody clothes had been replaced by geek wear off the costume rack. He couldn't decide if he was pissed off, resigned, or just hungry, and he was doing it all while wearing polyester. "So I'll be sitting under the gate, 24/7 until the convergence is over."

"You'll have breaks between demons. It takes time to divert enough convergent energy to get a demon through even a thinned barrier, and I can't imagine that my lord will be able to pop them out any closer together."

"He's not still your *lord*! He's trying to kill you!"

"Sure, now, but he's been my lord for thirty-five hundred years. It's not going to be an easy habit to break."

"And you like using his power."

"Well, duh."

Kind of a hard response to argue with. Tony wasn't sure if he admired her honesty or was appalled by it. Bit of both, probably. He dropped his head into his hands and scrubbed at his face. "I took out demon-with-the-arm last night and red-and-toothy this morning, that's barely twelve hours apart."

"No, it's closer to twenty-four. Demon-with-the-arm acquired the arm the night before he attacked us," she reminded him. "And look at the bright side, when you're not sending demons back to hell, you can do your job and, more importantly, collect a paycheck. You couldn't work or get paid if you were still following me around."

He didn't really have an argument for that either. "My laundry is at your place."

Sensing the win, she smiled. "I'll deal with your laundry."

"Yeah." The edge of the Styrofoam cup flaked apart under his fingernails. "Look, the only way I can see ruling out that probably—as in probably the demons will come here first—is if you're here with me. Then the demons will *definitely* come here first."

Her hand dropped to her side, and the smile disappeared. "Tony, I bled."

"So?" When he moved, the adhesive tape holding the gauze pad over the hole in his shoulder pulled at sensitive skin.

"The demons can hurt me."

"Yeah, well, big scary killing machines, remember? You got off easy." There were three deep scratches under his polyester pant leg. "We both did."

Leah's eyes narrowed. "Are you being deliberately stupid, or did you hit your head harder than I thought? They're the *only* thing in the world that can hurt me!"

Ah. "So, given the chance, you'd rather they weren't given the chance?"

"And a second brain cell comes online!"

He supposed he could understand her reaction. Except . . . "You came to me so that I could help you deal with the Demonic Convergence, and now you're putting other people in danger."

"Oh, no!" Both hands went up, palms toward him. "Don't put that on me. I came to you so we could spackle the weak spots and maybe deal with a few long-legged beasties that'd scuttled in from the closest hells. I never intended to face down demons. And people? People are in danger every time they step into the shower. Do you know how many household accidents happen in the bathroom? Should they stop showering? Or what about the chance of choking and dying? Should everyone stop eating? These demons are the *only* things that can hurt me, and I don't think it's unreasonable that I should avoid them!"

"But they can't *only* hurt you! You've lived for thirty-five hundred years; don't you think shorter lives should be protected because they are shorter?"

She sat back and frowned. "No."

Actually, he should've seen that coming.

"Look, let's forget about me for the moment and talk about you. You're a wizard, and wizards pretty much have three options." She flipped up a finger. "An ascetic life of learning." A second finger. "World domination." A third finger. "Or supporting the greater good. What's it going to be?"

"World domination."

All three fingers snapped down. "Wrong answer."

Was it fair that she could go for so long without blinking? Finally, he looked away and sighed. "Do I get a big red W on my chest?"

"Why would I know about your skin problems?"

"Just asking."

Her expression bordered on triumphant as she patted his arm and stood. "You really shouldn't waste any time learning those runes. CB says you can stay here and use his office."

"Me? Where are you going?"

"To get your laundry." Tone and expression together suggested that if he was all that stood between the world and demonic domination, the world was doomed.

"Right. Laundry." He watched her walk to the door. "Leah?"

She paused, holding the door handle.

"What if you're wrong? What if the next guy doesn't come here first? What if it goes after you?"

She chewed the corner of her lower lip, looking a lot younger than someone who'd seen her entire village slaughtered thirty-five hundred years ago. Then she tossed her hair back over her shoulder and smiled. It wasn't a particularly believable smile, not when one hand dropped to rest against the curve of her belly. "Then I race back here and you get to be my hero again."

"But if . . ."

"Tony, relax, we drove right past that demon this morning and it still came here first. Since I seem to have another option, I'm not going to spend the rest of the Demonic Convergence, however long it lasts, cowering behind you. Nor will I let this latest plan of Ryne Cyratane's control my life any more than I let his first plan control me. You'll deal with the demons; I'll get on with living."

"And my life?"

"Do you have a life that doesn't involve your job?" Her wave gathered in the studio beyond CB's office. "And, hey, here you are."

The door closed behind her. Tony stared at it a moment longer. He felt like he should have argued harder. If Leah stayed at the studio, then the demons would head here guaranteed, and he had a feeling there weren't many guarantees in demonology. But even on short acquaintance it was obvious that Leah was all about having things happen for her, her way. It'd likely become habit after the first couple of millennia—right about the time she'd got out of the habit of relying on other people who inconveniently died just when they were needed.

Still, at least she wasn't cowering behind him. That was a good thing, right?

The four sketches he'd made in the car were spread out on CB's blotter. His weight on the edge of the desk, Tony picked up the least complicated and stared at it for a long moment, his thumb leaving a vegetable-soup-colored print on the paper. He raised his other hand. He focused. He picked his spot. He drew the pattern.

Or not.

The blue lines sputtered and broke apart, tumbling out of the air like fireworks.

Tony braced himself and somehow managed to neither slide to the floor nor end up sprawling and drooling across CB's desk.

Afterimages floated across his vision. Blue sparks tumbling and falling. Tumbling and falling. Tumbling and . . .

He swallowed hard, belched vegetable soup, and didn't throw up.

"Go me," he muttered, staggering forward to stomp out a bit of smoldering carpet. Going actually sounded like a good idea. He needed food. Lots and lots of food.

Who the hell had moved CB's door so far from his desk?

Since Amy'd never let him live down a little heavy breathing, he clutched at the door handle and tried to stop panting before he went out into the office. It was quiet. Too quiet. The hair lifted off the back of Tony's neck . . .

. . . and settled down again as he realized that Amy wasn't at her desk. That always lowered the noise level. She'd probably sent Krista out to the sound-stage to find someone and then, with the office PA still gone, had to deliver the next urgent message herself. Given the belt of red lights blinking across the bottom of her phone, she'd been gone for a while.

Even though there seemed to be a perfectly mundane reason for the un-natural calm, Tony walked carefully out into the middle of the room, his heels barely touching the floor. Caution, yes, but also he had a suspicion that the wrong step would cause his head to fall off his shoulders. After the year he'd had, rhetorical statements became frighteningly possible, and he much preferred his head where it was.

He could hear voices raised in the bull pen as the writers bashed the last rough edges off the season's final script. It didn't take much concentration to make out the actual words.

"Because we need a little physical action here! It's a classic bit and it always gets laughs. We can't lose!"

It sounded like Mason was going to get nailed in the nuts again. The writers never got tired of slipping physical humor into the script. So far, Peter and the other directors had managed to keep this particular piece of physical humor from actually happening to their temperamental star, mollifying the writers with guest stars and bit players curled around their crotches and moaning. The writers had some issues.

He could hear Rachel Chou, the office manager, talking quietly to someone in the small kitchen.

"And just what, exactly, do you mean by that?"

Mason's voice boomed out of his small office on the other side of the main doors. Was he still with the press? And, if so, shouldn't he be back on set by now? Tony tried to remember Raymond Dark's call sheet for the day and drew a blank.

He shuffled a couple of steps forward but still missed the reporter's reply.

Mason, however, had done Bard on the Beach and knew how to project above the sound of flapping canvas and not so distant traffic crossing the Burrard Bridge. One hollow-core door was nothing to him. "How dare you insinuate that about my fans!"

Mason's fans were predominantly middle-aged women with Web sites and frighteningly explicit imaginations. Less common were those who believed that vampires truly lurked in the darkness—beyond that, they couldn't seem to agree on the particulars. Tony was fairly certain he'd never seen Henry actually lurk. Rarest of all were the fans who admired Mason's acting.

"My fans are the salt of the earth!"

Who really talked like that? Tony wondered, moving closer still. Although, in all fairness, some of those Web sites had some pretty salty language, not to mention an interesting concept of male anatomy. Or at least of Mason's anatomy. And, while he was hardly one to complain about hot man-on-man action, he was a little confused by all the Raymond Dark/James Taylor Grant stuff out there. Leaving the actors' preferences out of it entirely, Raymond Dark was a tomcat with a new conquest every week and half a hundred tragic love affairs in his past. Even James Taylor Grant had buried one true love and staked another. Lee'd dated the second actress for a while until a chance to star in a remake of *Time Tunnel* had drawn her to Toronto.

The door of Mason's office flew open, snapping Tony's attention back to the matter at hand. He barely had enough time to look like he hadn't been eavesdropping when the star of *Darkest Night* made a dramatic exit—or entrance, depending on point of view—announcing, "This interview is over!"

"Mr. Reed, you have to be aware that this show has been attracting an unhealthy amount of paranormal attention."

Tony knew that voice.

"I don't have to be aware of anything," Mason snapped as Kevin Groves followed him out of the office. "And I very much dislike what you're implying!"

"Which is?"

Lip curled, Mason turned on his heel and headed for the exit. "My assistant will deal with any further questions."

Groves blanched—which wasn't surprising given his last encounter with Jennifer—and allowed Mason to leave unimpeded. Physically unimpeded. "I will discover the truth, Mr. Reed!"

Even from across the room, Tony could tell Mason was considering whether or not he should respond.

Please, not the Nicholson!

After a long moment, Mason snorted and walked out of the production office.

Tony released a breath he didn't remember holding, then looked up to see Kevin Groves heading his way.

"We need to talk."

About to suggest a biological impossibility, Tony suddenly remembered just what exactly it was about the reporter he'd wanted to pass on to Leah. Kevin Groves knew about the Demonic Convergence. Tony had to find out how much. "Okay."

Groves opened his mouth and then closed it again, looking confused. "Okay?"

"But not here." He had to work here and the last thing he needed was for someone to see them together. Where *someone* meant Amy. He'd never live it down, especially since his breathing was decidedly still on the heavy side. "I need to eat. We'll go across the road."

Still clearly taken aback, Groves shrugged. "Sure."

"So let's move!" Before Amy got back. Tony led the way out to the street and almost didn't make it. Had that outside door always been so heavy? Groves reached past him, laid a surprisingly large hand against the glass, and shoved. "Thanks."

"Are you all right?"

"I'm fine." If anyone saw them, he could just say he was doing a bit of follow-up damage control. It never hurt to know what Mason had told the press before the headlines made it onto CB's desk.

The green light barely lasted long enough for him to shuffle across Boundary.

"We're not heading to the Duke's?" Groves asked as Tony turned and walked past the damp and deserted patio.

"Man, you really *are* an investigative reporter, aren't you? You don't miss a thing."

"I thought all you guys always went to the Duke's."

"Thought wrong."

The Duke's was a gathering place for the various actors who made the Burnaby area their home, or at least their place of employment—actors, directors, producers, but seldom crew. Crew had their own place cut from the front of an old warehouse, three quarters of the building still used by one of the bigger studios for storage.

"Okay, here's the deal." If he concentrated, he could talk without panting. "You only talk to me, and you keep your voice down."

"Or?"

"Or you'll never know what's going on."

"You don't look so good."

"Who asked you?"

"I'm just saying," Groves muttered as Tony led the way into the Window Shot, adding as they paused to allow their eyes to adjust to the gloom, "You'd think there'd be more windows."

"That's not what it means." He could feel Groves waiting for an explanation. Why not give him a freebie? "Crews used to get paid daily. They'd get what they were owed in cash from a payroll window after shooting ended, so the last shot of the day was called the window shot."

"And now you come here after the last shot of the day for the first shot of the day."

"You're smarter than you look." Bigger, too, Tony realized as they made their way across the scuffed tile floor to the empty booths under the single window. Tony was five ten; Groves was a couple of inches taller and broader through the shoulders. Not much meat on him, though, and the cheap gray suit did a lot to hide what size he had, as did the way he curled in on himself as though he expected to be hit. All things considered, not an unreasonable expectation.

The booth smelled like beer and fries and damp clothes, but Tony felt a lot more secure with the dark wood supporting him. If he craned his head just right, and the traffic on Boundary cooperated, he could see the main entrance to the studio parking lot through the streaked glass. Leah seemed pretty sure that nothing would happen for a while, but he felt better being able to keep an eye on things. Even a minimal eye.

"Tony!" The owner of the bar approached, drying her hands on a green apron. "What can I get for you?"

"Large poutine and a glass of milk, please, Brenda." Milk was like food. He'd seen a PBS program about it.

"Oh, yeah, that's healthy. And your friend."

"He's not my friend," Tony put in quickly before Groves could speak. "He's a reporter for the *Western Star.*"

"Ah." One steel-gray brow rose as she turned and gave the reporter the once over. "That cover picture last week, the creature of the night? It looked like a raccoon in a Dumpster. You guys aren't even trying."

Groves' lip curled. "I have nothing to do with the cover photos."

"Yeah, I bet I'd have a little trouble finding someone who admits they do. What do you want?"

"Coffee's fine."

"My coffee's better than fine," she snorted and headed toward the kitchen.

"Why did you tell her who I was like that?" Lacing long fingers together, Groves braced his forearms on the table and leaned forward.

"So she'll watch what she says around you."

"You think she knows things?"

Tony shrugged and sucked air in through his teeth as the claw holes in his shoulder pulled with the motion.

"What is it?"

Pointless to lie about the obvious. Lies should be held against need when they could be camouflaged by bits of the truth. "I hurt my shoulder."

Behind the glasses, dark eyes narrowed at the straight answer. "How?"

Tony's turn to snort. "You were talking to Mason, how do you think?"

"I can say you were hurt in the attack?"

"Go ahead. I'm a TAD . . ." He remembered pain in time to cut off the shrug. ". . . no one will give a shit."

"You *saw* this deranged fan?"

"Duh. You know it's funny. You believe in all sorts of paranormal crap, yet you don't believe that one of Mason's fans could go bugfuck."

"It's not that I don't believe . . ." He paused and leaned closer still. Tony got a whiff of mint and wondered, since there seemed to be no gum chewing going on, if it was a default odor. "I've met some of Mason Reed's fans," he said, "and it's a short trip to bugfuck. But there's more going on."

"More?"

"Why are we here?"

"I wanted some poutine," Tony told him as the food arrived.

Groves waited until they were alone again, until he'd emptied three creamers into his coffee, and said, "Why are we here together?"

"You said we needed to talk."

"You agreed with me."

"You've been stalking us since August."

"Because I know when I'm being lied to."

"About what?"

"Anything."

"Like creatures of the night?" Tony asked. His tone implied he couldn't believe they were talking about stuff no one in their right mind believed in.

"Yes."

Tony nearly choked on his mouthful of fries and gravy and cheese curd. "You're serious?"

"It's a . . ." Groves stared into his coffee as though he could find the missing word. Finally, he raised his head and met Tony's eyes. ". . . curse."

"You know when you're being lied to?"

"I do."

He did. And more, he expected Tony to believe him.

"What are you doing?" he asked as Tony frowned at the scuffed wood beside his bowl.

"I'm trying to decide if beating my head against the table will be worth it."

"Why?"

Because like drew to like. The Demonic Convergence was in Vancouver because Leah was there and the gate was there and he was there and—oh, yeah—Henry was there. Since he'd first met Henry, there'd been ghosts and werewolves and walking mummies . . . .

It was like murders always happening around Jessica Fletcher. Who the hell would want to live in the same town as a little old lady who solved crimes?

Or never noticing a white van until you owned one and then they were all over the goddamned place.

There was a gate to another world in the studio where he worked.

The house they used for a location shoot just happened to be haunted.

When *Darkest Night* needed a stuntwoman, they hired an immortal Demongate.

It was like eight o'clock on the WB.

And Kevin Groves, who knew when he was being lied to, was still waiting for an answer. Tony sighed. "I'm having one of those days." Absolutely not a lie. "So let me guess . . ." He took a swallow of the milk. ". . . you went to work for the tabs because they're the only ones who dare to print the truth?"

"That's right." After a long moment, Groves rolled his eyes. "Now what?"

"Sorry." Tony blinked and started eating again. "Just having an MiB moment. You'd like the regular papers to print the truth?"

"Who wouldn't?"

Good point. "Under your byline."

"I don't do what I do for the good of my health, Mr. Foster. I'm a journalist."

Or he wanted to be seen as one, which, for all intents and purposes, amounted to the same thing. "So, are you saying Mason lied to you?"

"Mason Reed believes everything he says."

"That's not an answer."

Groves only shrugged and took a long drink of his coffee. Waiting.

He knows I have something to say or we wouldn't be here together.

He believes that I have metaphysical powers, that weird metaphysical shit is happening around the studio, and he's looking for proof.

Let's not be too impressed by him sharing his lie detecting ability since I'm guessing he tells everyone. Of course he probably doesn't expect everyone to believe him.

Probably.

"Yesterday, you said the words 'Demonic Convergence' like you expected me to know what they meant. Why?"

Groves smiled. "Because I expected you to know what they meant."

"Why?"

"Nope. You asked a question, now I ask a question. That's how these things work."

Maybe it was. Almost able to feel the calories in the poutine winging off to various body parts, Tony pushed his empty bowl aside, laid his forearms on the table, and leaned forward, deliberately mirroring the reporter's earlier position. "Not this time," he said quietly. "I ask the questions, you answer them, and if I'm happy with the answers, maybe I'll tell you some of what you want to know."

Groves started at him for a long moment, then he sneered and stood. "I don't have to . . ."

"Yeah, you do. This is your only chance, Kevin. Screw it up and you spend the rest of your life on the outside looking in. Knowing things are happening but never being a part of it."

Groves' lips drew back off coffee-stained teeth. "Idiot. I want to expose it, not be a part of it."

Tony locked their gazes and refused to let the other man look away. "Bullshit."

"Everything okay here, gentlemen?"

"Fine, Brenda. I could use a coffee now if you wouldn't mind. And Mr. Groves could use a refill."

"He's not leaving?"

"No." He sat down, hands shoved under the edge of the table a little too late to hide the trembling. "I'm not leaving. Refill would be good. Please."

Tony sat back feeling powerful. Feeling like a wizard in control. Feeling like he'd just kicked a puppy. A mangy, annoying, nippy puppy that no one liked but a puppy nevertheless. He shot what he hoped was a reassuring smile at Brenda, who frowned at them both as she set a clean mug on the table and then filled it before refilling Kevin's. She frowned once more, just at him, before she walked away.

"You thought I'd know about the Demonic Convergence because of what you believe I did last summer at that location shoot, right?"

"Witnesses said you spoke with the dead. Witnesses agree you . . ."

"Yeah." Tony raised his hand. His right hand. No point in flashing the rune burned into his left at this point in the game. "I don't need to know what you believe I did. Just answer the question."

"That's what I thought." Sullen but cooperating. Wanting desperately to be on the inside. With the cool kids.

"How do you know about it?"

"I was researching you, what you might be involved in . . ." Black masses and deals with the devil were strongly implied by his tone. ". . . and I found an old book in a used bookstore. It was written in German. I could read just enough to recognize that it was about talking to the dead, so I bought it figuring I could get it translated." The sullen started falling away. Tony had a feeling that being taken seriously was a new and exciting sensation for Kevin Groves. "There was a piece of folded paper in it . . . except it wasn't paper. It was vellum. You know what that is?"

"I have no idea."

"It's a piece of calf hide tanned really fine for writing on. Point is, it's old. Really old. On the vellum was a chart drawn up by some astrologer. He wrote that the powers would align to create a Demonic Convergence and the walls between the world and hell would thin. I took his calculations to the astrologer at the paper and she worked out the dates."

"Is she the real thing?"

Groves snorted. "Not hardly. She's got a Ph.D. in math, but she hates teaching."

Damn. Tony scrapped his idea of a metaphysical Justice League.

"It's happening now, isn't it? The Demonic Convergence?"

Why not? He'd already done the math. Or had the math done for him. Mouth open to admit that yes, the Demonic Convergence was in fact happening now, Tony got distracted by the sight of his own car driving by and turning into the studio lot. Then he realized that if Leah had gone back to her place for his laundry, of course she had to take his car.

Then he noticed that there was a spot by the entrance to the parking lot where the rain wasn't quite falling.

⌇ SEVEN

"What the hell is up with you?"

Tony ignored Kevin Groves yelling behind him, concentrating on getting through the traffic on Boundary without being killed. Wizardry wouldn't keep him from dying under the oversized wheels of some guy's SUV—or under the wheels of one of the new hybrids for that matter. He might be more environmentally dead, but he'd be just as dead. Horns blared, tires skidded sideways on the wet pavement, creative profanity blasted out of half a dozen open windows, but he made it to the other side alive. From the continuing sound of horns, tires, and profanity, Kevin was right behind him.

Great.

In about thirty seconds, deciding how much to tell him would no longer be a problem.

Tony could see the headlines now: IMMORTAL STUNTWOMAN SLAUGHTERED IN BURNABY; DEMONGATE OPENS AND THE WORLD ENDS! Bright side—he'd be dead and someone else would be cleaning up the mess.

He could see his car at the far end of the lot and thought he could see Leah twisted around, rummaging in the back seat. Then the driver's side door opened and an enormous white-and-red umbrella emerged, tipped down to keep the rain from blowing up under the outer edge. Unfortunately, tipped down, it was also keeping Leah from spotting the anomaly moving across the parking lot toward her.

Lifting his left hand, Tony called the umbrella. The demon appeared as nylon and wire and wood passed through the same space it was occupying, and Leah, mouth open to demand answers, had just enough time to fling herself back inside the car as claws struck sparks off the closing door. For a heartbeat the car filled with a translucent, naked, and very pissed-off Demon-lord; then it was only Leah.

Yeah, well, I'd be pissed, too, if my way back into the world kept ducking at the last minute.

"That's a . . ."

"No shit." Tony thrust Leah's umbrella into Kevin's arms. "You might want to get behind something solid."

"I don't . . ."

"Or not. Just stay out of my way."

Fortunately, the demon was intent on peeling his quarry out of her strange new shell. Where *fortunately* didn't refer to the damage being done to his car. As he started focusing energy, Tony realized he'd pretty much run out of options. Another Powershot would use all the energy he'd regained and then some—the "and then some" was the worrying bit. He'd done a little gaming in his day and he knew what happened when stats fell into negative numbers. Leah's runes were his best chance. He was pretty sure he could remember the first one and then, with any luck, the others would fall into line behind it.

Except he couldn't quite remember the first rune.

Curves here. Crosses back. And there's sort of a circle thing . . .

Crap!

The demon shot him a disdainful sneer over one shoulder—given the excessive teeth and the glowing yellow eyes, it was a pretty damned effective sneer—and then slammed its palm down on the window. The window cracked.

He could hear Leah screaming.

Fuck!

No time to get this wrong!

He wiped out half the glowing symbol, realized it now looked sort of like the word *go* . . .

Palm against glass. A louder crack. More screaming. . . . and went with plan B. The rune on his left hand grabbed ghosts. Ghosts were energy left over when flesh rotted. Therefore, the rune should allow him to grab this energy.

Grab it and throw it.

The glowing blue *go* hit the demon between the shoulder blades and sucked into the scaled skin with a disconcerting sizzle.

The demon spun around . . .

H . . . shifted its weight onto two different legs . . .

O . . . and charged.

M

Tony didn't have to keep throwing the letters. The demon charged through them, no longer sneering, clearly intent on ripping apart this puny mortal who dared to interfere.

Puny mortal? Where the hell had that come from?

Sizzle.

Sizzle.

Sizzle.

Too close!

The world had not gone into slow motion. Too bad because he could have used a bit more time. Eyes locked on the charging demon, his breath coming fast and shallow; he was only going to get one chance. Panic lending speed, more focused than he'd ever been in his life, he scrawled the last letter in the air.

E

Not so much a *sizzle* as a *ZAP*. Like the world's biggest bug hitting the world's biggest bug zapper.

The impact threw Tony backward as the demon flared a brilliant lime green and disappeared, leaving nothing behind him but a piece of smoking pavement and the smell of charred fish. It was over before his ass hit the parking lot, a large, deep puddle absorbing most of the impact.

"What was that all about?"

He could feel power racing over his skin as he peered up through the afterimages at Leah. "You're welcome."

"It was kind of hard to see what you were doing . . ." Her voice grew shriller with every word. ". . . but those weren't the right runes!"

"They worked."

"They shouldn't have!"

Tony would have shrugged, but his shoulder hurt way too much and, from the line of warmth dribbling down his chest, he had a feeling the bandage had come loose. He should have felt like crap, but he didn't. He felt invincible. It was like the way he knew where things were when he reached for them except . . . more. He knew where the whole world was. He knew where he was in the world. No. More still. He *was* the world. Just him, no backup singers.

It was the most incredible feeling. There was nothing he couldn't do, and no one could stop him. Without really thinking about what he was doing, he healed the puncture wounds in his shoulder.

And was amazed by the new and exciting levels of pain.

"SonofafuckingBITCH!"

Then world was a big ball of rock again, and his place in it involved a puddle and a parking lot.

"Tony!" Leah was right in his face. "What did you *do* to the demon?"

"I told it to go home."

Her mouth opened and closed a couple of times. She took a step away. "Go home?"

"Yeah." Even on the lower mainland, October rain was *cold*. As the water soaked through the cheap polyester, his balls tried to climb up and sit on his lap. "You said it yourself, the demons don't belong here. I sent it back where it belonged."

"It's not that easy!"

"It is if I want it to be." Teeth clenched, he checked to make sure his arm still worked, then he got to his feet. "This is my world, not *his*." No need to define the pronoun. "*He* may need to slaughter whole villages and draw complicated esoteric symbols, I don't." Rain ran under his collar and down his back. "Intent is nine tenths of the law."

"No, it isn't!"

"It is," he repeated slowly and deliberately, "if I want it to be." He could feel the world waiting for him. What was it Leah had said earlier? He was the round peg in the round hole and, here and now, it was a perfect fit.

She shook her head, rain flinging from the ends of dripping curls. "It isn't . . ."

"Is."

"No."

"He's telling the truth."

"Who the hell are you?" Leah snarled as Kevin Groves and her umbrella emerged from behind a parked van and joined them.

Tony smiled. This might be fun. "Leah Burnett, Kevin Groves. Kevin is a reporter for the *Western Star*."

"The press? You brought in the press?" She grabbed a double handful of white and red and yanked the umbrella out of the reporter's hands. "This is mine! Why does he have it?"

"So my hands were free and I could save your ass. Again."

"Save my ass?" Her eyes widened and her posture changed subtly, her focus shifting from him to Kevin. "From a special effect? Don't be silly."

"It wasn't a . . . a special effect." Kevin scrubbed his palms against his suit. Kind of pointless given that the suit was soaking wet, but Tony had to admire the fact that he was still thinking for himself. No other straight boy had managed as much when Leah turned it on.

"Of course it was." She moved a little closer. Tony amused himself by watching Kevin's Adam's apple bob up and down as he reacted to Leah's proximity. "What else could it have been?"

"D . . . demon."

Speaking of demons, Leah's Demonlord seemed more present than usual. He noticed Kevin, frowned, and dismissed him—although Tony wasn't sure how he knew that since Ryne Cyratane hadn't actually focused on anything in this world. There was just something in the way he stared through the space Kevin was occupying that said, *I know you and you mean nothing.* Then the antlered head went up and his nostrils flared as he searched for . . .

Me.

He's searching for the power that sent his demon home.

But the Demonlord's—attention?—slid right past him.

Like I'm not even here . . .

And he wasn't, Tony realized suddenly, not according to the Leah-filter Ryne Cyratane experienced the world through. He wasn't reacting to Leah's *I'm an enormous metaphysical slut* performance, so to the Demonlord he didn't exist. Except that he obviously did since there was a demon back home blubbering about the big mean wizard who'd kicked demon butt. The Demonlord had come looking for the wizard but wasn't finding him.

Two possibilities.

Straight woman. Gay man. In the far end of both options where there was no attraction at all to what Leah was offering.

A kind of strangled moan jerked his attention back to the here and now. Offer accepted; lip lock commencing.

"For crying out loud, get a room, you two!" Rolling his eyes at such blatant and public heterosexuality, Tony took four steps back and yanked open the side door of the van Kevin had been hiding behind. Peter never locked it. He was hoping some lowlife would jack it so that he could replace it with wheels a little less suburban.

It wouldn't be comfortable, but it would be private. Privater. More private?

Leah, in spite of being quite clearly in the midst of giving a fairly thorough tonsillectomy with her tongue, acknowledged the open door, gave Kevin a shove, steered him through half a dozen stumbling steps, pushed him into the van, climbed in after him, and pulled the door closed.

Let's hear it for centuries of practice.

Kevin yelped once, the muffled sound verging on desperate.

All that adrenaline had to go somewhere, Tony figured, walking away. Leah probably just wanted to forget she'd been attacked by yet another demon and, more importantly, she wanted Kevin to forget the demon entirely. It was a more physical solution than Arra's memory erase spell, but both parties involved had to be enjoying it more.

He hadn't even reached the back door of the soundstage when a shout stopped him in his tracks and he turned to see Leah emerging, adjusting her clothes.

"That was fast," he observed when she joined him. Not that he'd been moving particularly quickly or anything since every step sent reminders of extraordinary pain up from his feet to his skull, but still . . .

"Tell me about it." But she looked happier. Grounded. The familiarity of sex erasing the terror evoked by the possibility of death and dismemberment.

Jesus, that's profound.

"He still knows what happened," he said, nodding past her to Kevin who was hoisting his backpack up over one shoulder and looking a little happier himself.

Leah glanced over her shoulder and looked smug. "He knows what I told him."

"And you told him it was special effects." Tony waited until Kevin had crossed the parking lot, anticipating what was about to happen with a certain amount of petty glee. "So, Kevin, what did you think about those special effects? Not Leah's special effects," he clarified hurriedly, "before that, in the parking lot."

The reporter shrugged and, at Tony's gesture, blushed and zipped up. "It was a demon."

Tony leaned against the building where he was out of the rain and less likely to fall over. "He has a power," he explained before the astounded immortal Demongate found her voice. "He knows the truth."

Leah frowned at him. "Seriously?"

"Yeah."

Turned and frowned at Kevin. "Seriously?"

"Yes."

Back to Tony; still frowning. "So, what? You got yourself a sidekick?"

Wizardman and Reporterboy!

That was wrong on so many levels.

The glee evaporated as he looked up and realized the shooting light was on and they were stuck outside. Only a few meters to the back door and warmth and coffee and it might as well be in Alberta. "No," he told her flatly, "I got myself someone who may know how long the Demonic Convergence is going to last."

"Wait a minute, the *Western Star*." Leah's fingers closed around Kevin's wrist and she hauled him around to face her. "You know someone's lying and you still print crap like 'I was impregnated by a Sasquatch'?"

He chewed on a corner of his lower lip. "Who says that was a lie?"

"And you're going to report on all this?"

"I don't . . ." More chewing. Tony thought he seemed torn. He was inside the story now, he'd had a look at what Tony could do, and had to believe Tony's threat about stuffing him back outside with his nose pressed against the glass. But demons, actual demons and wizards, that was a byline on the front page. "I mean, if someone noticed . . ."

"No one noticed," Tony assured him. "And if anyone did, they'll think it was a special effect. Even without Leah's . . . reinforcement."

Kevin stared at him like he had oatmeal coming out his ears. "They'd think a charging demon disappearing in a flash of lime-green light was a special effect?"

"You should see what the guys at Bridge get up to in their parking lot," Tony snorted as he pushed off the wall. The demon had obviously rattled him more than he'd thought. The craft services truck was parked no more than three meters from the back door—he didn't have to go inside for sustenance, he could go to the source. He paused on the metal stairs that led into the back of the truck and glanced down at the other two who were watching him like he might do something interesting. Like blow something up. Or fall over. Or fall over while blowing something up.

"You guys want a coffee?"

"Are you sure you should be touching stimulants?" Leah asked.

"Yes."

"Okay, then. Double cream, no sugar."

"Kevin?"

"I'm good."

Tony didn't quite hear what Leah muttered as he went inside and he was just as happy not to given that, when he came out holding the two coffees with a muffin in his pocket, Kevin was still blushing.

"All right," he said, pushing back in under the scant overhang. "When we go in, you guys go straight through to CB's office. Leah, tell him what happened. Kevin." He held up a hand for emphasis. "Don't talk to anyone in the soundsta . . . What?"

Kevin pointed to the rune on his palm with a shaking finger. "The demon had one of those. I saw it when it was charging at you!"

"Like this one?" Tony demanded, turning his hand so he could see the rune. "How should I know?"

"Right. Sorry." He pointed the rune at Kevin again, who ducked. "Relax, it's for making energies solid enough to hold."

"Yeah, well, she has them, too. All over her . . . um . . . her . . ."

"Stomach? Jesus, Kevin, you just had sex with her in the back of a van. You ought to be able to name body parts."

"I don't do that." The reporter looked seriously freaked, like reality had finally caught up and smacked him on the back of the head. "I don't have sex with women I don't know. My God! We didn't use protection! Do you know what the STD statistics are in this city? I could have caught somethi . . . OW!"

"You were hysterical," Leah explained, picking her coffee up again.

He rubbed his cheek. "I was not! I was reacting in a perfectly . . . A cult!"

Tony blinked at him over the edge of his cup. "A what?"

"You belong to a cult! You and her, and that's why you've got those things and that's why the demon did, too. You're both mixed up in something that's out of your control!"

"It's not a cult." Tony waited for Kevin to realize the truth of that and carefully said nothing about things being out of his control. Although, technically, they'd never been *in* his control. "The Demonic Convergence brought us together, and now, with or without your help, we have to save the world."

Kevin straightened, grabbing his backpack just before it hit the ground. "You don't scare me."

"He should," Leah snorted. "He doesn't know what he's doing. Making it up as he goes along. Wild cannon. Could go off at any moment. And speaking of going off at any moment . . ."

"Don't," Tony told her. This was not the time to hit back at the reporter for that STD comment. To his surprise, she didn't. "Was this the rune on the demon's hand?" he asked Kevin again.

He shook his head. "No. It was more . . . squiggly. And fresher."

"Fresher?"

"Not a scar, a wound. And not burned, cut."

Tony finished his coffee and started on his muffin while staring down at his palm. If the demons were coming from Ryne Cyratane, why would he be marking them? "He's marking them so they can hurt you," he said at last. "Slipping them between the runes in the existing spell."

"Yeah." Leah brushed crumbs off her sleeve. "I got that." She grabbed a double handful of the track top and the shirt under it and pulled them up. Her track pants were riding low on her hips and most of the tattoo was exposed. "Did it look like one of these?"

Kevin stared. And blinked a couple of times, overcome by memory. "I . . . uh . . . I . . . that's not . . . I don't . . ."

"Would you concentrate?"

"No."

"No you won't concentrate, or no it wasn't one of these runes?"

"Forget that for now," Tony sighed as the red light over the door finally went out. *What had they been shooting in there? Raymond Dark meets* The Fellowship of the Ring? "Show him again in CB's office when you've got a chaperone. Right now, let's move before we're stuck out here for *The Two Towers.*"

"What?"

"Just move."

He got them most of the way across the soundstage before anyone noticed, and by then they were close enough to the other exit that he gave them a shove and turned to face the approaching first assistant director.

"Was that who I think it was?" Adam demanded as Tony moved to block his line of sight.

"The stuntwoman we used the other night? Yeah. That was her."

"Not her. The guy. That was that reporter that's been hanging around. Graves."

"Groves."

"Right."

"Mason called him in to brag about the deranged fan." As the star of the show, Mason was pretty much untouchable. Made him handy to blame things on. "I saw him hanging around out back and had Leah take him in to see CB."

Adam had no special lie detecting powers, but he was responsible for seeing that actors and crew managed to get their collective shit together long enough to produce a weekly show. He didn't need to know the truth as much as he needed to know what would get the job done. "Mason needs his goddamned ego examined. Why is the stuntie hanging around?"

"She's with me."

Dark brows rose. Adam had been on the haunted location shoot and on the soundstage when the demon attacked—even if he hadn't been part of the battle or its aftermath. He knew . . . things. Maybe not specifics but definitely *things.* Arms folded across a barrel chest, he frowned at Tony for a long moment, but all he said was, "Good enough." Then his eyes unfocused.

Recognizing the expression, Tony reached for the volume on his radio, remembered he wasn't wearing one, and waited, growing increasingly twitchy. It was one thing to be momentarily aware of his place in the universe and another entirely to be on the soundstage unplugged. He hated not knowing what was happening.

"It's the same goddamned coffin lining we've used since the beginning, Sorge," Adam barked into his microphone. "Why is it making Mason look ruddy now? No, I don't know. Hey! Don't be calling me names in French; you want to call me names, you do it in English. Or Greek. Fine. I'll be right there." He pivoted on one heel, paused, and turned back. "Get your ass back to work as soon as humanly possible."

"I'll do what I can."

The set under the gate had been cleaned. The broken wall had been cleared away and, from the rhythmic spit of nail guns in the distance, was being repaired. The painted plywood floor had been swept. Tony dropped to one knee and dragged a damp fingertip over the floor where the demon's ashes had been. Nothing.

Crap.

"You look disappointed."

He looked up. Lee wore a pale khaki golf shirt tucked into darker khaki Dockers under a black leather jacket, over black ankle boots. James Taylor Grant was supposed to look preppie-tough; today, they'd gotten it right. Other days . . . well, no one looked tough in tennis whites. Except maybe Serena Williams. "I wanted to look at the ash." No need to lie to Lee; he knew as much as any of them. Besides, there were enough lies between them already. *And cue the world's smallest violin . . .*

"The demon ash? Why?"

"I don't know. I guess I thought maybe it could tell me something."

"Because you're working for *CSI: Second Circle of Hell*?"

Tony snickered and stood. "You want to bet they pitched that?"

"No bet. Tony, you . . ." Lee frowned, his gaze tracking up from the damp spot Tony's knee had left on the floor. "You're wet."

"Yeah." Reaching back, he yanked the cheap polyester pants away from his body. "I'm just glad I'm not wearing underwear."

Green eyes gleamed.

Had he said that out loud? Crap again. "Sorry. TMI."

"A little. Maybe." The actor shifted his weight as Tony wondered what he meant by *maybe*. "So, uh, your friend is . . . attractive."

"My friend?" He ran over the friends he had that Lee knew. "Jack? For the last fucking time, man, he's straight."

"I meant Leah." The *asshole* was silent but understood.

"Oh. Right." Duh. Attractive to Lee.

"She's got a certain . . . I mean, you can't help but react to her."

That almost sounded like an apology. Tony rubbed his temples and tried to figure out what Lee was apologizing for. Demons were fairly straightforward compared to most conversations he and Lee had these days.

"And I saw you with Kevin Groves."

Half a smile. "He's straight, too."

Half a smile back. "You sure?"

"Well, he's never had his tongue down my throat."

Unlike you.

The actor's expression suggested the subtext came through a bit louder than Tony intended.

"I didn't mean . . . Look, I wasn't . . ."

"It's okay. It's not like I thought you were hitting on me or something." Lee tried to make it a joke, but neither tone nor grin matched the way he shoved his hands in his pockets, looking suddenly young and unsure.

Which was weird because Lee wasn't young, he was—Tony frowned as he did the math, Lee's birth date being all over the Internet. Only a year older? It was just he was always so self-assured and Tony always seemed to be scrambling to survive that the gap seemed a lot larger most of the time.

Not this time.

In fact, there wasn't much of a gap at all.

Between them.

No gap.

Which one of them had moved? Tony didn't remember moving.

"Jesus, Tony. You're bleeding again."

"I was." He could feel the heat of Lee's fingers through the shirt. "It stopped."

"Hey!"

Lee jumped back, his ears crimson. It was the most awkward movement Tony had ever seen him make.

Adam scowled at them both from the edge of the set. "You," he said, pointing at Raymond Dark's mortal sidekick, "are needed, and you . . ." His finger moved to Tony. "Peter wants to know if you'll ever be doing any actual work again any day soon."

"I have to talk to CB."

"Whatever. By the coffin, Lee."

"Yeah, I'll be right there." When Adam was gone, he said, "Someday, you're going to tell me what's going on, right?"

"You know . . ."

"I meant all of it. Details."

"What, you didn't like Leah's explanation? Kind of looked like you did."

Long pause. Probably not as long as it seemed. Time slows when you have both feet in your mouth.

"Just let me know if I can help, okay?"

Been there. Done that. Got the T-shirt. And since Tony knew from sad experience how the conversation would go if he said no, he decided to take the path of not having yet another argument with Lee. "Sure," he lied.

Lee looked surprised. "With the . . ." He gestured at the floor. "You know."

"Yeah."

Wizardman and Actorboy.

Nope. Not going there either.

"Tony! Why is Kevin Groves in CB's office?"

Tony glanced down at the hand holding his arm. Specifically at the large black spider that covered the back of it. "New tat?"

"Don't be ridiculous," Amy sneered. "A new tat would still be all red and puffy and gross. Now, answer the question; has CB agreed to give that creep an interview?"

"No."

Her grip tightened. "Stop being coy."

"He . . . Kevin . . . saw something, in the parking lot."

Brown eyes rolled between the double fringe of thickly mascaraed lashes. "Saw what?"

Tony jerked his head toward the door to the bull pen, currently open a suspicious six inches. "The walls have ears."

"Yeah? Well, they also have the coffeemaker from the office kitchen." Amy's voice rose to *don't fuck with me* levels. "So unless they want me to take it back . . ."

The door slammed closed with near panicked speed.

"Start talking," she continued, "before my phone . . ." Her phone rang. "Bugger. Talk fast."

"Amy . . ." She'd filed points onto her fingernails and those points were now dimpling the sleeve of his borrowed shirt. Considering how much his amazing new healing ability hurt, it didn't seem smart to just jerk his arm free.

"Faster than that."

Talking seemed to be his only route to freedom. "Groves saw me vanquish a demon in our parking lot. I thought CB'd be the best guy to deal with it."

"Vanquish?"

"Amy!" Rachel Chou stuck her head out of the finance office. "Are you going to get that?"

Not really a question.

She let go of Tony and snatched up the phone. "CB Productions! Our mailing address? Okay, but I'm warning you right now that we use unsolicited scripts in the porta john on location shoots. Yeah, exactly for what you think.

Hello? Ha!" The receiver went back into the cradle with a triumphant clatter. "Tony!"

He'd have been safely inside CB's office if he hadn't stopped to knock. Knocking seemed like a good idea given that Leah was behind closed doors with two men. Although the thought of CB and Kevin Groves as two parts of a threesome made him want to scrub his brain out with bleach. Since no one had commanded/invited him in, he turned to see Amy standing by her desk, hands on her hips. Even the PowerPuff Girls on her T-shirt looked annoyed.

"Vanquish?" she repeated, pointedly.

"I sent it home."

"Leah's way or *BOOM! SIZZLE!* ASH!" Her hands flicked open on each of the last three words.

"Sort of Leah's way." He shrugged. "Sort of not."

"Can it come back?"

"It's not dead, so I guess it can." Just in time he remembered Amy knew the *Reader's Digest* version and stopped himself from saying, *It'll come back if Ryne Cyratane sends it back.*

"I want to help."

Thanks to Lee, he knew how to cut this off. "Sure."

"Don't bullshit me," she snorted. "I mean it."

"I know." Tony tried to sound like he'd meant it, too, even though they both knew he hadn't.

Her eyes narrowed. "Well?"

Odds were good she wasn't going to take *I'll get back to you on that* for an answer. What did it mean that he could lie to Lee but not to Amy? Was it some sort of weird psychological thing or was it just because Amy was scarier? A memory poked at him. Jack had shot the red demon, at least twice. "Bullets can hurt them. Can you find us a gun?"

"Are you insane?"

A good question and one he'd been considering himself lately. "Just for backup. In case I fall over again."

"Are you likely to?" she demanded as the door opened behind him.

Odds were good. Whatever he'd done in the parking lot had healed his physical injuries but had left him feeling weirdly fragile. Not tired, exactly. He reached out with his round peg, looking for the round hole in the universe . . . .

"Tony?"

Okay. Definitely way past time to ditch that analogy.

"Tony!"

Leah this time, not Amy. She grabbed his arm, dragged him into the office, and closed the door while he tried to decide if she looked any more disheveled than she had. He decided she didn't but only because the alternative was too disturbing.

Kevin was sitting on CB's couch poking unhappily at his handheld. "I can't get an uplink."

"I told you," CB growled from behind his desk as the reporter set the PDA on top of his open backpack. "We're in a dead zone."

"Your phone won't work either." Tony crossed the room and dropped onto the other end of the couch. His trousers squished, and he realized a little too late he should have stayed standing. But since there was *already* a damp imprint of his ass on the cushion, he remained where he was.

"You seem confident, Mr. Foster."

"Phones haven't worked since . . . Wait. Not confident about the phone thing?"

"No."

Confident. As in filled with confidence. Hey, why not? He'd just sent a demon home by force of will alone. His will. His will alone. He had been the world. He had the power! *Although it might be best to play that down a bit in front of the boss.* He shrugged.

"Ow!" The lines of blood on the shirt had dried, sticking the fabric to his skin. Specifically to his right nipple. Shrugging had ripped it free.

"I'm pleased to see that this new confidence hasn't changed you," CB growled as Tony clutched at his chest.

Weirdly, in spite of the sarcasm, CB actually did seem pleased. What had he expected? What had Leah told him? Tony repeated the latter question out loud as Leah perched on the far edge of CB's desk.

"Ms. Burnett told me what happened in the parking lot. That you returned a demon to its hell without using the proper runes. That wizards who feel they can ignore the rules are dangerous."

"I saved her ass." It seemed so obvious and yet he kept having to bring it up.

"She doesn't dispute that, Mr. Foster, but she considers it a matter of luck that you've injured no one but yourself to this point."

Tony frowned at Leah who was looking . . . smug. Not overtly, but it was there. "She doesn't like that she can't control me."

To Tony's surprise, CB smiled. "No, I don't imagine that she does."

"That's not—" Leah began, but CB raised a hand.

"Mr. Foster," he said, "has always been able to see what is in front of him. It's a rare skill. Mr. Groves . . ."

Kevin jumped.

". . . has identified the rune cut into the demon's hand as this." The sheet of paper he lifted held a new swoop and squiggle. "It is on the third circle of Ms. Burnett's interesting tattoo . . ."

Interesting? That was a bit of an understatement. Tony glanced at Kevin, who was blushing again. He'd have heard a lie even with his ears that interesting color of puce, so if Leah hadn't told them what the tattoo actually was, what had she told them?

". . . and it seems to indicate," CB continued, "that she was its primary target."

"Why?" Tony prodded.

"Because it's on my tattoo," Leah told him, smiling. Ryne Cyratane flickered behind her.

Rune-to-rune attraction was apparently true enough for Kevin's gift and banal enough to give nothing away. Looked like Leah still hadn't given up her backstory, using her demonically-fueled sex appeal to keep CB and Kevin Groves from asking inconvenient questions. It seemed only vampires and Demongates got to have secret identities while wizards were left flapping in the breeze. Tony frowned at the rune. "Did the demon in the soundstage have one?"

"There was something," CB acknowledged. "But it moved too fast for me to get a good look at it."

"I knew it wasn't a fan," Kevin muttered.

"Actually, Mr. Groves, there is nothing that says the demon isn't also a fan."

The reporter snorted. "You think they watch syndicated TV in hell? Never mind," he continued before anyone could answer. "I withdraw the question."

"Mr. Groves was attempting to access the electronic copy of the page he found." CB set the rune to one side and laced his fingers together. "His astrologer friend was only able to work out the time of the Demonic Convergence in a general way, so I suggest he retrieve the original and bring it here for our demonic consultant to study it. Perhaps, with her experience, she'll have more luck." The look he shot Leah said he figured she could do anything she put her pretty little head to.

Eww. Tony felt slightly sick.

The look Leah shot CB in turn sat just to one side of *Are you nuts?* "You're going to let him walk out of here?"

"Why not?"

"With this story?"

"Your story is safe with me," Kevin told her.

Tony snorted. The ringing tones and the hand over the heart detracted somewhat from the believability. Seemed that twenty minutes or so removed from the demon, being inside the story was no longer enough to suppress old habits. "Safe doesn't mean out of the paper, does it?"

Kevin's betrayed expression was slightly less believable than his sincere expression. After a few moments of reorganizing his face, he ended up in the general vicinity of resigned. "Okay, fine. But we're a weekly. I've got until next Tuesday at 3:00 to file, so you've got until then to change my mind, right?"

"Yeah, that sounds fair except that you've been digitally recording on that handheld, so you've got blackmail material if nothing else."

"Kevin!"

As Leah's shocked exclamation—heavy on the second syllable—caught his attention, Tony grabbed the PDA from the backpack. When Kevin lunged for it, Tony held up his left hand. "We can't trust you."

Back in the corner of the couch, as far as he could get from Tony's hand and still be on the couch, Kevin glared over the barrier of his backpack. "I'm a journalist!"

"Essentially." Still working the rune, Tony stared down at the screen and double-tapped the record icon with his right thumb. "If he'd got the uplink, he'd probably have shot the sound file back to his office."

"No, I . . ." The weight of disbelief cut him off. "Yes. Fine. I would have. But you don't understand." He lowered the backpack onto his lap and fiddled with a strap. "This is a complete validation of my entire life. Demons and wizards and sex!"

"Sex?" CB asked. One eyebrow rose.

Tony suppressed a shudder. "Don't ask." Sounded like CB's virtue was intact at least. Back to Kevin. "So you've been validated, big whoop; you've still got questions. You want to know why the demons are attacking Leah. You want to know where they come from." Tony took a moment to study the rune on his palm, then he grinned at the reporter. "You want to know how I sent something capable of smashing its way into a car out of this world using only the finger of my right hand. Hell, that's not even my good hand." He waved his left, feeling power ripple with the movement. "Not even my wizard hand. You've got to be wondering *exactly* what I'm capable of."

Not *exactly* a threat.

"Are you threatening me?"

Okay, maybe it was.

"I don't even know you guys," he continued. "Why should I do what you want?"

"Because we're trying to save the world here, Kevin."

"By suppressing the truth?"

"If that's what it takes."

"And what kind of a world will that give us?"

"One not strewn with dismembered bodies, you shortsighted jackass."

"You want that page I found." His chin lifted. "I think I've got bargaining power."

"Yeah? I think you've got . . ."

"Mr. Foster."

Tony sighed. At this rate the Demonic Convergence would be over before the conversation. "Here's a thought: you let us look at that page, you don't talk about this to anyone, and I don't erase your memory."

"No one is erasing anyone's memory!" CB's protest added a certain verisimilitude to the bluff.

Tossing her hair back over her shoulders, Leah crossed to kneel gracefully by Kevin's feet. Reaching out, she took both his hands—and his backpack straps—in hers. No sign of Ryne Cyratane and no sign CB was reacting.

She's playing the long shot. Appealing to Kevin's better nature. Given what he did for a living, wondering if he even had one seemed redundant.

"Kevin, please. Work with us. Don't just report the truth, become a part of it. Make a stand against the darkness you *know* exists. Be one of the heroes."

He rolled his eyes. "Heroes die young."

Yeah. Redundant.

"Mr. Groves, if you don't want to help, we cannot . . . will not force you." CB sat back in his chair and laced his fingers together. "Mr. Foster, return his equipment and show him out."

"Just like that?" Ragged unison from everyone in the room who wasn't Chester Bane.

"Yes."

Kevin pulled free of Leah's hands and stood. "You're just going to let me go and tell the world what I've seen?"

"Mr. Groves, I have spent my entire career ignoring what the tabloids print about me. I think I can manage to ignore this as well."

"You don't think anyone will believe me."

"Have they ever?" As the reporter sputtered, Tony caught Leah's eye and shook his head. Kevin could spot a lie and, so far, he hadn't accused the boss of lying. She closed her mouth as CB sighed. "People have no interest in the truth, Mr. Groves. They'll enjoy the story while it's being told and forget it the instant the next story comes along. It's why television is so successful."

"Reality TV . . ."

"Isn't. Now, if you don't mind, in spite of delays . . ." Somehow he made the delays seem like they were Tony's fault. ". . . I have a show to produce."

"No. You need the page I found!"

"I expect we'll continue to manage without it."

"It could have important information!"

"Mr. Foster, tell Ms. Chou to arrange to have my couch cleaned. Ms. Burnett . . ." He frowned at her. "If you intend to continue hanging about my studio, find something to do."

Kevin didn't quite stamp his foot. "You need the information I have!"

"And you haven't convinced me of that. Good afternoon, Mr. Groves."

"Then I will convince you!"

"Fine."

"I'll prove it to you!"

"Very well."

"I'll be back with that page. It has important information!"

"I look forward to you proving it to me. You will, however, have some difficulty returning if you don't actually leave." The final word carried enough volume to lift Tony and Leah to their feet as well and move all three of them across the office and out the door.

Kevin pointed a finger at the two of them. "Don't go anywhere." Then he turned and ran for the street.

"Don't let the door hit you on the way out, asshat!" One hand covering the phone, Amy flipped him off with the other. "Thank you for holding, Father Thomas; we really need to use that graveyard . . ."

Leah smoothed down her clothes; not because they needed it, more because she needed something to do with her hands. "Your boss is an impressive man."

"Yeah." Tony carefully detached the rest of the shirt from his chest. "All his ex-wives think so."

"I meant he's a manipulative s.o.b."

"They'll probably agree with that, too."

Amy hung up and grinned at them as they drew even with her desk. "I got you the g . . . u . . . n."

"I can spell," Leah sighed.

"I'm not spelling it out for you." She jerked her head toward the bull pen. "I don't want that lot to get excited. It's never pretty. Anyway, the guy's bringing it over later."

"Tonight?" Tony asked incredulously.

"This very."

"That was fast."

"I'm the best."

"You're kind of scary."

"Just part of my charm." Head cocked, she examined him through narrowed eyes. "So what are you going to do now?"

"I don't know what she's going to do." He nodded at Leah as he pulled polyester away from his body. He might have the whole world in his hand, but he also had wet fabric in the crack of his ass. "But *I'm* going to talk to Rachel and then I'm going to get my laundry out of my car and change my pants."

⤳ EIGHT

"All right, that one works for me." Peter tossed his headphones onto his chair and walked out into Raymond Dark's office, one fist pressed against the small of his back to knuckle out the stiffness of a fourteen-hour day. "Mason, you happy with it?"

"I'm happy with anything that lets me get rid of these damned teeth," Mason muttered around the fingers shoved into his mouth. "I bit my lip again."

"Bad?"

"Nothing that'll show on camera; thanks for the sympathy."

"You're welcome. Lee?"

Lee, sprawled on the red velvet sofa, waved a weary hand. "It was art. Emmys all around. Are we done?"

"We're done. That's it, people . . ." Peter raised his voice as he turned to face the crew. ". . . good work, thanks for staying late, and make sure you have tomorrow's sides before you leave."

That wasn't it, of course, but with the last shot in the can the mood lifted as everyone found enough energy to get them through wrap-up and out the door. With no demons currently ripping either place or people apart, Tony did what he always did. He made sure the radios were back where they belonged, put the batteries in the charger, ran an errand for Peter, helped Tina close the trunk she locked her computer gear into, had a short meeting with Adam about an error in the advance schedule—where meeting would be defined as Adam pointing it out and telling him to see that it got fixed—and then he was done and the rest of the crew were heading for cars and home and the sound-stage was empty.

Nearly empty.

Leah was somewhere around.

And Lee was standing just inside the door, watching him, his face expressionless enough that it was kind of creepy.

"What?" Tony demanded. He'd stopped just a little too close, almost inside the other man's personal space, but if he backed up now, he'd look like a dork.

"You're staying in case another demon shows up."

"That was the plan."

"It's not a great plan."

"Yeah? So far it's wizard three, demons big fat zero—nada, zilch, and three asses kicked. I think it's a workable plan."

"Workable," Lee snorted, rolling his eyes. Expressions were catching up to him—concern, disdain, and exasperation chased themselves across his face. "You're just going to live in the soundstage until this Demonic Convergence is over?"

"It won't last forever."

"You don't know that."

Shrugging, Tony tried to look like a wizard on top of things. "When it happened before, it ended. Precedent suggests it'll end this time."

"Precedent suggests? Precedent?" A twisted smile appeared to punctuate the silent but obvious *give me a fucking break*. "What? You've been watching Court TV?"

Tony chose to answer the actual question. "Nah, CITY's had *Ironside* running Mondays at midnight. Raymond Burr," he added at Lee's blank stare. "Wheelchair lawyer? Black-and-white lawyer show ran from '61 to '68? Dude, it's classic television."

"I'm not big on the classics." Lee sketched air quotes around the word classics, body language relaxing as they moved away from demons and wizards. "I don't watch anything older than I am."

"Your loss. You're missing your own history."

"My history?"

"As an actor."

"Ah. Well, maybe someday you can expose me." Challenging eyes. Flirty smile. Tony took an involuntary step back, not caring how it made him look. *Never a demon around when you need one . . .*

Hang on. Flirty smile?

Was Lee possessed again?

Tony cleared his throat. "Expose you?"

"To my history."

"Ah."

The pause stretched toward uncomfortably long, and Tony frowned as the expression left Lee's face. And how am I supposed to respond? We don't do that joking around with sexuality thing anymore, remember? Not since you took that one step too far—and may I point out that it was you and not me. But, hey, you responded to Leah this afternoon, so now you're comfortable in your sexuality again and I'm fair game. His brain just wouldn't shut up about it. "Look, some guys like black and white, some guys don't. Some guys try it but end up holding on to the whole Technicolor thing." Great. Now his mouth was in on it.

Any chance the anvil missed?

"Tony . . ."

No chance in hell. In any of the hells.

The coyote wouldn't have missed with that anvil.

And now it's his turn to pause—except his pauses seem to be meaningful instead of empty. I wonder if I hurt his feelings by reminding him of how he gets indiscriminating under stress? Now that's an idea; he should hang around, and if the next demon's big enough, I could do him up against the wall after the fight.

Shut up, brain!

". . . I just want you to be careful. Okay? Since there's seems to be nothing I can do to help—even if I thought you meant it . . ."

Martyr much?

". . . I just, well, be careful."

Without waiting for an answer, he was gone.

Tony stared at the door for a moment, wondered what he'd been reaching out for, and let his hand drop to his side.

"He wants you."

"Bite me."

"And you have some unresolved aggression toward him." Leah fell into step beside him as he turned and headed for the area under the gate. "You want to talk about it?"

"No."

"There's not a lot I don't know about the psychology of sex."

"There is no sex."

"Why not?"

"Because he's straight."

"Please."

"Why are you even still here?" he demanded, moving into her path and stopping suddenly, forcing her to stop as well. "I thought you were off to live your life, to take a chance, refusing to be held hostage by your Demonlord's expectations."

"That sounds like bad country music."

"You said you weren't going to cower behind me."

"I'm not cowering," she snapped. "But given what happened this afternoon, I think staying behind you might be my best option. You're here, so I'm here."

"The demons . . ."

"The demons won't be sneaking up on me if I'm sitting here waiting for them, will they?" Something in Leah's face told Tony not to press it. Told him she'd been a lot more freaked by the demon in the parking lot than she'd let on, and what she didn't want to be was alone. "Besides," she added, pushing past him, "I've got nothing that pressing to do until Tuesday anyway. What on earth makes you think that Lee is straight?"

Tony scrambled to catch up. "He sleeps with women."

"Oh, yes, that's conclusive. Moron."

"He got stupid over you."

"Ninety percent of the male population does. Means nothing. Didn't you see *Kinsey*?"

"Sure. Liam Neeson totally got screwed by the Oscars that year."

"Granted, but my point is that if most of the world's population is neither completely gay nor completely straight, then even the odds are in your favor. I'm not sure why he'd choose you to break cover with; I mean, you're just passably attractive, reasonably intelligent, excitingly powerful, remarkably pleasant, appealingly broad-minded, definitely loyal, and appallingly self-sacrificing."

Reeling under the torrent of adjectives, Tony opened his mouth to respond, but nothing came out.

"Next to a man like, say, Liam Neeson," she continued before he could find his voice, "you're practically invisible. He's someone I'd do in a minute."

"Right," Tony snorted, finding his voice. "You'd do ninety percent of the male population in a minute."

She shrugged. "Eighty max."

"Kevin Groves."

"Fine. Eighty-one." She dropped down onto the end of the chaise lounge. "It's always amazed me," she sighed, "that two men can ever manage to get together at all, given the whole lack of being articulate. Maybe he's scared."

"Lee? Scared? Of me?"

"Don't be dumber than you have to, okay?"

Tony dragged his jeans back up over his hips—they were a little big and shoving his hands in his pockets dragged them low—and sat down beside her. "You sounded like Amy."

"You discuss your sex life with Amy?"

"Okay, first, Lee has nothing to do with my sex life, and two, are you insane? Give Amy an inch and she'll take a kilometer."

A dark brow rose and one hand patted his thigh. "Mixed metaphors, that's what's wrong with the world." Leah glanced around the empty soundstage as though she'd lost something. "Where *is* Amy? Based on our very short acquaintance, I would have thought she'd be here."

"She left with the rest of the office staff. She had a date."

"On a Thursday? Good for her. I'm all for a sister getting some."

"Big surprise. Not. But it's just for coffee at Ginger Joe's—it's a Goth coffee place she likes. She's meeting a guy she knows from the net."

"You told her to be careful because she didn't know this guy, right?"

"Yeah."

"And she told you that you were the one waiting for a demon, so you should be the one being careful, right?"

"Not in so many words, but yeah."

Leah nodded, smug. "After a few thousand years, people get predictable."

"So where's your partner?"

Jack jumped and only just resisted spinning around and answering the question physically. He put most of the energy into slamming the door of his truck and managed to turn with something approaching calm. "She's home with her kids. Tony call you?"

Henry Fitzroy nodded and Jack wanted to wipe the smug, superior look right off his face. Which wasn't fair because all the guy had done was nod, but there was something about him, something that made Jack want to fall in behind him and charge the shield wall. He wasn't even sure what a shield wall was, but he fucking hated the feeling.

"Tony tell you what's going on?"

"Yes."

Yes? That's it? Fine, you want to be mister one word answer, we don't need to talk. But the dark eyes were strangely compelling, and Jack's mouth kept moving without any apparent prodding from his brain. "He thinks the demons are attracted to the soundstage, to his accumulated power at the soundstage."

"But you don't believe that."

"He's not telling me everything."

"Why would he?"

"Because . . ." Jack had a feeling that *because I told him to* wouldn't fly. "Because it's my job to protect the public!"

"I think we've moved some distance away from your actual job description, Constable."

"No, we haven't. Look . . ." He folded his arms, unable to look away but unwilling to appear compliant. ". . . I catch the bad guys; that's what I do. These are bad guys. In order to catch them—all right, deal with them," he added as a red-gold brow rose, "I need to have all the facts. Which I don't."

"Perhaps he doesn't think you can cope with all the facts."

"Well, he should try me."

"Yes. Perhaps he should."

Distracted by Fitzroy's too-charming smile, it took Jack a moment to realize that the other man's eyes weren't dark at all but hazel. Frowning, he matched his shorter stride as they headed toward the studio's back door.

"I assume you're here as backup muscle? He sent me out to buy cherry-flavored cough medicine," Fitzroy continued before Jack could answer. "A specific brand that's, unfortunately, not particularly popular." He hefted a bulging canvas bag. "I had to visit nearly every drugstore on the lower mainland before I found the volume he asked for."

"What's Tony going to do with that much cherry-flavored cough medicine?"

"He's going to do magic, Constable Elson."

"What the hell was that?"

"I think someone's at the back door," Leah sighed.

"Right." On his feet, heart pounding, Tony could barely hear short, sharp bursts of the buzzer over the thrum of blood in his ears. "Do you think it's a demon?"

"I think demons seldom ask to be let in. And I think that your boss gave the security guard the night off, so you'd better get it."

"Right." Tony headed for the back of the soundstage, his breathing almost returned to normal.

There was no security hole in the door and since Leah hadn't actually said it *wasn't* a demon, he took a moment to find his focus and wrote "go home" as small as he could manage it an inch or so from the pitted steel. If there was a demon, and the demon charged when he opened the door, it would charge right through the command and that would hopefully be that.

Except that the door opened inward.

"Having a fish fry?" Jack asked, grimacing as he stepped over the threshold. "Because if you are, your fish are burning."

"I'm not." Given that the door was in the only home it had ever known, nothing had happened but sizzle and smell. At least he hoped it was because the door had no other home to go to because a bad smell wasn't much of a weapon against claws and teeth. "Hey, Henry." Calmly. Business as usual. *Do not touch the bite on your . . . Crap.* He forced his arm down. "Did you get the stuff?"

"Every bottle left in this part of British Columbia."

"Thanks." He took the bag and turned his attention back to Jack. "What are you doing here?"

"The nutbar who works in your front office called me."

As a general rule, that wasn't a specific enough description, but . . . "Amy?"

"She said you needed a gun."

"You brought me a gun?"

"I'm carrying a gun. My gun. You're not going anywhere near it."

"A gun?" Henry asked, in a tone that managed to squeeze *are you insane* into the two small words.

"You can shoot demons," Jack told him before Tony could answer. "It may not stop them, but it sure as shit slows them down. I shot one this morning half a dozen times. Exactly six shots. I know that because there's one fuckload of forms I have to fill out when I fire this thing, so . . ." Half a pivot and he was facing Tony. ". . . you can thank me for coming back and risking yet another three hours of paperwork—involving, let's not forget, lying. And, while we're on the subject, let's not forget the interviews with my superiors during which I will also have to lie."

"You didn't have to come."

"Yeah, and risk you actually getting your hands on a weapon? Like that's going to happen."

"I think you're taking the greater risk being here, Constable. Your career . . ."

"Bugger my career. I got a one-armed dead guy in the morgue."

Tony watched Henry study Jack for a moment and then turn and flash him a smile. "Perhaps you should just thank him, Tony. After all, you wanted to bring him in."

"You did?" Jack's brows rose but he looked pleased.

"I did. Past tense. But Henry . . ." He glanced over at Henry, who was wearing his blandest expression. Like blood wouldn't clot in his mouth. "Fine. Whatever. Thanks. Come on." He led the way back to Leah and the chaise lounge wondering if he'd actually been in control for that short time in the parking lot or if he'd been delusional.

Circumstances were pushing him strongly toward the latter belief.

"And this is supposed to do what, exactly?" Jack demanded at last. He'd been amazingly quiet until they were two thirds of the way around the soundstage, so points for patience. Or he was just too stubborn to ask until the frustration levels rose sufficiently.

Tony was betting on the latter. He finished the last ward along the side wall—or as close to the side wall as he could get, which meant, in a couple of places, two to three meters into the soundstage. "It's an early warning system," he said as he dipped the number two brush back into the bowl of cough syrup Henry was holding and bent to paint the more complex rune in the corner. "Something crosses the line with ill intent . . ." He paused, squinted up at his laptop open across Jack's hands, then added a final flourish. ". . . and we'll know it in time to brace ourselves."

"How?"

"Will we know? I have no fucking idea. I've never done this before."

"The wards on your apartment—" Leah began.

"Were meant to keep things out," Tony interrupted. "But we don't want to keep them out of here; we want them in here, so I can deal with them. This is new."

"Then aren't you moving a little fast?"

He twisted around just far enough to scowl at her. "This is the fourth wall. They're long walls. I'm getting the hang of it."

"Okay, but the end of that squiggle has always turned left before."

"Fine." A little more cough syrup turned the squiggle to the left. "Happy?"

"Who wouldn't be?"

"I'm not," Jack grunted. "What happens if demons drop in from above?"

"It's covered. Just give me a minute to finish."

"And if something with claws and teeth attacks before you're finished?"

"Then we won't know until someone gets eviscerated."

"No one gets eviscerated!"

"Not if you'll shut up and let me work."

Arra's instructions said he should visualize the complex corner runes and then mentally draw a line from corner to corner, the lines crossing overhead in the middle of the square. Okay, so the space enclosed wasn't exactly square, but it did offer the biggest bang for the buck, so Tony was still going with it. He closed his eyes. Saw the runes. Drew the lines.

"Cool." Leah sounded as though she was smiling.

When Tony opened his eyes, there was a cherry-cough-syrup-colored translucent dome over the soundstage.

And then there wasn't.

Although the scent of expectorant lingered.

"Is it gone?" Jack asked, breathing through the neck of his T-shirt pulled up over his mouth.

Tony checked. "No. It's still there. That was like a test pattern to show that it worked."

A red-gold brow rose as Henry studied his face. "Really?"

Made sense, so why not. "Yeah. Really."

The second time the buzzer went off, Tony sighed and headed for the back door as though he'd never been startled, never jumped to his feet at the sound. Not that it mattered much since he could hear Leah telling Jack and Henry about how he'd reacted the last time. Jack seemed to think it was pretty funny.

First demon that showed up, Jack was going to be out in front.

When the door opened, the pizza delivery girl handed him a plastic shopping bag containing two bomb bottles of cola and began pulling the extra large pizza out of the insulated pouch. "You Tony Foster?" she asked without looking up.

"Yeah, but I didn't order a pizza."

"Come from your boss, Chester Bane. He order. He pay." She shoved the box into his hands and grinned as his stomach growled. "He say I give you message, too. He say you should answer your damned e-mail."

"Pepperoni, sausage, olives, tomatoes, mushrooms, green pepper, and double cheese; your boss knows how to order a pizza." Jack pulled a slice from the box and bit off the tip with obvious enjoyment. "None of this good-for-you broccoli crap."

"Personally, I could have done without the olives," Leah muttered, flicking a piece off her slice.

There was always someone who bitched about the toppings, Tony reflected as he chewed. It was practically a requirement of pizza eating. Three people in the group, one person bitched. Five to seven people, two bitching. Unless there were anchovies, and then everyone but one person bitched, regardless of numbers. Of course, in this particular group, the stats were kind of skewed . . . .

"You not having any, Fitzroy?"

"No, thanks. I ate before I came."

Jack shrugged and took another piece. "Great. More for me. Where are you going?"

Barely two steps away from the chaise, Henry turned and smiled at Jack. "Why?"

"Because I think, given all the weird shit going down . . ." Jack paused to wipe a bit of grease off his chin. ". . . that if we're going to work together, we shouldn't leave each other in the dark about what's going on."

"Fair enough. I'm going out to the office."

"Why? There's no one there."

Henry's smile grew a little edged. Tony shuffled back just far enough to be out of the line of fire—just in case. Better Jack caught that look than him. "Television people," Henry explained pointedly, "don't keep the same hours as mere mortals. There's probably a few people still working on postproduction . . ."

Post? Tony stiffened.

". . . and Chester Bane never leaves his office before midnight."

"You and Mr. Bane friends?"

"We've dined together a few times."

"Son of a BITCH!" Tony tossed aside his crust and clawed at the hot cheese and pizza sauce that had slid off it and onto his crotch. By the time he finished scraping and swearing, Henry was gone.

Just as well. Not like I was going to call him on making stupid vampire double entendres in front of Jack. He took another handful of napkins from Leah—who had almost stopped laughing—and scrubbed at the denim.

"You guys have some issues," Jack snorted.

Tony snatched the last piece of pizza out from under his hand. "Do not." Great. Even straight Mounties were noticing.

"Uh-huh. So why here?"

"Why not here?" Leah wondered. "They have issues everywhere else."

"No, why are we waiting here?" Jack's gesture took in the immediate area, empty but for two folding chairs, food debris, and the chaise he shared with Leah. "There's a lot more comfortable places to wait in this soundstage, so why *specifically* here?"

"I did a spell here," Tony told him, gesturing with the pizza crust. "A big one. It left a mark."

"What kind of spell?"

"I'm not sure." Teeth slightly clenched, half a shrug—Tony was a very good liar. "I screwed it up."

"It had something to do with the ceiling?"

Had he looked up? He didn't remember looking up. "Yeah. It had something to do with the ceiling. But the rest is classified. If I told you, I'd have to turn you into a frog."

"You can do that?"

He swallowed and smiled. "I could try."

Jack shook his head, but what exactly he was denying wasn't clear. "Like I said to your friend Fitzroy, I don't think we should be keeping secrets."

"Is this a police thing, asking so many questions?" Leah leaned in. Tony figured she'd suddenly remembered she had a few secrets of her own. "Or are you naturally so curious?"

No sign of Ryne Cyratane, so at least Jack had a fighting chance, but Leah on her own, being intense and interested and brushing breasts against bicep, was enough to attract male attention.

She attracted Jack's. He probably wasn't even aware he'd straightened his shoulders. "It's what cops do, ask questions."

And spout bad cop show dialogue.

Tony cleaned up while they flirted and tried not to think about what was happening in the boss' office. *Figures. The one time I could use a little e-mail distraction from a psychotic eight-year-old, I don't get an uplink.* Even if he had a cable, there wasn't a phone jack on this side of the soundstage.

"I was thinking."

Since he'd gotten used to Henry suddenly appearing by his side years ago, Tony enjoyed Jack and Leah's reaction.

"Wasn't your original plan to find the weak points between this world and the hells . . ." Four-hundred-and-sixty-odd years of Catholicism gave Henry a little trouble with the plural. ". . . and have Tony close them before they open and expel a demon?"

"Where the hell did you come from?" Jack asked.

"The original plan?" Henry repeated pointedly to Leah, ignoring Jack's question.

"Yes, that was the original plan. So?"

"So I'm not sure we shouldn't return to it."

"Hello!" Leah's eye roll was dramatic. "What happened to hunker down, protect Leah, and save the world? I'm not going on walkabout across the lower mainland if demons are coming after me personally."

"Hang on," Jack interrupted. "Why are the demons coming after you?"

Tony reviewed various meetings in CB's office and realized that only he and Henry knew Leah was anything more than a stuntwoman who did demonology as a sideline. CB and Kevin Groves knew demons were coming after her, but Jack, his partner, Amy, Zev, and Lee knew only the basics of the Demonic Convergence. *Fuck this; I need a scorecard!*

"Maybe they want my recipe for goat cheese pizza," Leah snapped. "Duh! They're trying to kill me!"

"Why are they trying to kill you?" Jack was using his "don't even try to bullshit me" voice now. Interestingly enough, it worked.

"Because I know things and that makes me a threat."

"How do they know you know things?"

"What difference does it make?"

Jack sighed, ran a hand up through his hair, and took a moment to get comfortable on his end of the chaise. "Until you jokers listen, I'm going to keep repeating that, under the circumstances, I don't think we should keep secrets from each other."

"Oh, I see." Leah's second eye roll was more sarcastic than dramatic. "You show up with a gun and suddenly we should trust you?"

"Under the circumstances, I don't think we should keep secrets from each other."

"It's the Mountie thing, isn't it?" she sneered. "How can we not trust the stalwart in red serge?"

"Under the circumstances, I don't think we should keep secrets from each other."

She spun around to glare at him, their faces inches apart. "You have only the faintest idea of what's going on here!"

"Under the circumstances, I don't think we should keep secrets from each other."

"Stop saying that!"

"Dinner and a floor show," Tony snickered quietly, well aware that Henry could hear him even over the sound of shouting. "I'm having a lot more fun than I thought I would."

"Good." Henry flashed him an affectionate grin, then turned his attention back to the battle. "But we're not getting much accomplished." He stepped closer to the chaise.

Tony didn't need to see his eyes go dark. He could read the change in the set of Henry's shoulders. In the stillness that accompanied him. The Hunter was in the building.

"Jack Elson."

Names held power. Unable to resist the pull, Jack looked up and was caught. Safely behind Henry's left side, Tony saw his eyes widen, his cheeks pale, and his hands clutch compulsively into fists. Jack would never willingly show his throat, but Henry wasn't giving him the choice.

"Some secrets are too dangerous to be lightly shared. You know what you need to know. Accept that and move on. And," he added in a lighter voice, "I've changed my mind about the validity of the original plan. Stopping the demons before they emerge now seems to me to be the safest way to deal with them."

"He has a point," Jack acknowledged slowly, frowning as though he was searching through the conversation to discover how they'd gotten this far. Tony knew the feeling.

"No, he doesn't," Leah argued. "It's not safe putting me right up next to a hole. It could goad the demon to burst through prematurely."

"So? Tony'll be right there."

"*I'll* be right there."

"Tony?" Henry's use of his name drew all of Tony's attention. To be fair, he didn't think Henry could help it. "What do you think?"

So they were going to play that game. Pretend that Tony was making the decisions until he made one Henry didn't like. Pretend that the wizard was in charge and the vampire was *just* backup muscle. Fine. Leah and Henry had ditched the original plan when he was asleep. Unconscious. He forced himself not to touch the mark on his throat and realized he'd get absolutely nowhere if he brought any of that up now.

"Leah, how do you find the weak spots?"

She shrugged. "Gut feeling."

Considering what was on her gut, he'd let that stand. "Can you mark them on a map?"

"It's not that exact. It's more like playing hot, warm, cold; the closer I get to them, the stronger the feeling gets."

"But it should be easier now that there's not a lot of them, right? Because the convergent energy has to be slamming down on only a couple of spots in order for the holes to be going deep enough for demons to come through," he tossed to Jack before the awkward questions started.

"Not exactly easier," Leah began. Paused. Frowned. Sighed. "Okay, easier to find. But harder to close."

"Harder than facing down the actual demon? These weak spots have teeth? Claws? Other unidentifiable sharp bits?"

"They will if you screw up."

"No *if* when I'm facing an actual demon." He started pacing. He was onto something. "How many weak spots out there now?"

"I don't think . . ."

"Come on, Leah. Try, please."

"Fine." She slid a hand under her clothes and closed her eyes.

"I thought she was a demonic consultant?" Jack stage-whispered dramatically.

"She's consulting," Tony told him.

"Yeah? Who? Or should I say, what?"

"There." Leah cut off Tony's answer. "There's a strong feeling that way. Deep hole." She pointed. "And a weaker one, that way. Still nice and shallow. That's all."

"So two?"

"Deep. Shallow." She looked down at the fingers she'd raised as she spoke each word. "Yes, that's two. Your grasp of higher mathematics makes me feel so much safer."

"We'll go to the shallow one first."

"No."

Tony turned just enough to frown at Henry. "What?"

"We need to go to the deeper one first because it is closer to expelling its demon. You'll have more time to close the shallow hole."

"Except that I'm making the decisions and I say we go to the shallow hole first to see if Leah has an effect. If she does, there's no chance of a demon getting through immediately. No harm, no foul. If she doesn't, then we take her near the other one."

Henry shook his head. "Reckless."

"I think you've forgotten what reckless means," Leah told him as she stood. "Tony's playing it safe."

"Tony risks allowing a demon to break through while no one is here to protect the soundstage."

"Then you stay." He tried not to feel pleased about how startled Henry had looked, if only for an instant. "Jack, you'd better stay with him." If this worked, they wouldn't need muscle out on the street. "Leah says these things are just killing machines, there's nothing magical about them, so if one does show up, you two ought to be able to knock it on its ass and hold it until I get back."

"Us two? He's a romance writer." Jack shot Henry an incredulous look.

Tony didn't see the look Henry shot back, but it wiped the incredulous right off Jack's face. "Unnatural rope's best for holding them, and there's a whole lot of the yellow nylon shit over with the carpenter's gear. Don't worry about hurting them. Apparently, there's not much actual damage you can do. Don't get eaten. You know, by demons," he added as Henry frowned.

"Eaten." Not a question, but then Jack had seen the one-armed man.

"Welcome to the wonderful world of the weird and metaphysical," Tony told him, shrugging into his jacket. "Remember, you're the one who insisted on playing; I'd have happily kept lying to you."

"You're still lying to me."

"Yeah, but not happily. And not about anything that counts." It was important Jack believe that. Tony refused to look away until he nodded an acknowledgment. "Leah, where are you going?"

She sighed as she turned. "In the interests of not having any secrets between us—before we hit the streets, I'm off to the little stuntwoman's room where I'll pee and then wash my hands. Maybe I'll put some lip gloss on while there's a mirror handy. Or do you need a definitive answer on that?"

"Great," Tony muttered to Jack as Leah spun on one heel and strode off. "You see what you started?" He jiggled his car keys, stopped when he saw Henry wince. He'd made his point, no need to annoy sensitive ears.

He wanted to say: If something does show up, don't let Jack be a hero. He breaks easier than you do.

He wanted to say: Don't you be a hero either. Let Jack shoot it a few times before you move in.

And he wanted to say: Maybe we do have issues, but we also have history, and so we've got to work through them. Because you're not going to let go, and I don't think I am either.

He settled for saying, "Be careful."

And was pretty sure Henry heard all the rest.

"So, what do I do?"

"Go west; toward the city. Drive slowly. I'll tell you when to turn."

Tony pulled out around an ancient chartreuse minibus covered in lime-green religious slogans. More than one kind of weird ended up on the west coast. "Can I ask you a question, or do you have to concentrate?"

"After thirty-five hundred years, I've learned how to multi-task, so ask."

"Ryne Cyratane's been doing this from the beginning of the Convergence, right? Directing the energy to where he needs it? So, if you only ever felt a couple of weak spots at a time, why didn't you expect the first demon that attacked you?"

"Why didn't I expect a demon to charge out of the sunset swinging an arm on a CBC Movie of the Week location shoot?"

"Yeah."

"Who the hell would *ever* expect something like that?"

Tony glanced over to the passenger seat. Leah had her shirt up and her hand resting on the exposed tattoo. "Fair enough."

They found the shallow hole in an alley off Hastings Street between Gore and Main. The Chinese restaurant along one side was just closing, so they waited while a bored young man in kitchen whites tossed yellow plastic bags of garbage into the Dumpster. Then they waited a moment longer while a pair of Dumpster divers retrieved the edible bits.

"We're wasting time," Leah hissed as Tony grabbed her arm and yanked her back into the shadows.

"So we'll waste a little," he said quietly, watching the two women, who looked middle-aged but were probably younger, sort through the restaurant waste. "This might be the only meal they get all day. What?" he asked when she turned to glare at him. "In thirty-five hundred years, you were never hungry?"

The glare softened to impatience. "Maybe once or twice, but . . ."

"We wait until they're done. They'll want to go someplace safe and eat, so it won't take long."

It didn't.

"Why do these kinds of metaphysical things always happen in alleys?" Tony wondered as they walked past the Dumpster. "Why not in the middle of the TransCanada? Or a meter over the sock counter at Sears? Or in someone's apartment?"

"Who says they don't?" Leah asked, looking ready to bolt. "All that's necessary is that something be missing to anchor the convergent energy." She indicted a rough-edged pothole in a remarkably filthy bit of pavement. "We're just lucky this one's where we can get to it."

"So?"

"So what?"

"So are you affecting it?" The pothole didn't look like it had changed since they arrived. It didn't look like the weak spot between realities either. It smelled like rotting melon and Kung Pao shrimp.

Frowning, she prodded the air over the pothole with one foot. "I don't feel any . . . Oh, no!" Arms windmilled as her foot slammed down. "It's got me!"

"Leah!" Tony grabbed her, dragged her back, and nearly dropped her in a particularly pungent bit of rotting garbage when he realized she was laughing.

"Kidding. It's fine. I don't feel anything different." She pulled out of his grip and tucked her hair back behind her ears, still snickering. "You should close it up now."

"I don't know how," he reminded her, folding his arms.

"Oh, cranky." A raised hand stopped his step toward her. "Okay, okay. Forgive me for being relieved. Before you can close the hole—or, this early in the game, just strengthen the weak spot—you have to see it."

"I see the pothole."

"Look harder."

There wasn't a lot of light in the alley; a couple of yellowing, bug-speckled bulbs over back doors and the spill from the streetlights. "I can't see . . ."

"Yes, you can. Wizards see what's there." She sighed and folded her arms, shifting her weight onto one hip. "Look harder."

"I can see where the smell of Kung Pao shrimp is coming from," he said after a minute. "And you're scraping off your shoe before you get back in the car."

"But you don't see the weak spot?"

"No."

"Okay, don't look *as* hard. I guarantee it's there, in the pothole, a place where the absence of what should be there has left an opening."

"An absence of what should be there? Dial it back a bit, would . . ." Tony froze, half turned away from the scum-encrusted bit of pavement in question. From the corner of his eye, he saw a heat shimmer—except, of course, it wasn't actually a heat shimmer—stretched horizontally across the top of the pothole. "I see it. What now?"

"Burn the runes one at a time and push them through the weak spot."

"Through?" Even cracked, the pavement seemed pretty damned solid. "Right. Why don't I just burn *close up* or *keep out*?"

"Tony, use the runes."

He shifted his foot a little farther away from a particularly nasty bit of melon. "Why? *Go home* worked fine on that charging demon."

"I know. It shouldn't have."

"But it did." He was definitely taking his turn to be smug.

"But it shouldn't have."

"But it did."

"Yes, it did. It shouldn't have, but it did. And is this the time to be experimenting with new techniques that may or may not work? That may or may not make things worse? No. The fate of the world is at stake. You risk my life and everyone else's on a whim!"

"But it worked!" Wasn't that the important bit?

"That time. Under those circumstances!" A deep breath, both hands against the clothing over the tattoo. When she spoke again, she wasn't shouting and she sounded sincere. "I promise you that the runes will work every time. Under any circumstances."

Tony wasn't sure how to take sincere. "Swear this isn't just part of your whole control issue thing?"

"You want swearing?" Garbage squelched under her sneakers as Leah stepped toward him. "I'll give you thirty-five hundred years of swearing in a minute! Write the runes and push them through!"

"One at a time?"

"Now you're being deliberately provoking."

Yeah. He was. "If it means that much to you, I'll do it your way."

"Sometime soon!"

"What's the hurry?" The shimmer was kind of pretty in an "entrance to hell" sort of way. "You said this one was shallow."

"It was when we got here," she snorted. "Why are you standing like that?"

He'd shifted to stand angled at the pothole, facing Leah, eyeballs rolled into the lower left corner of each socket. "I can see it better if I don't look at it straight on."

"You know where it is; do you have to see it?"

"I guess not." He turned to face the pothole, rubbing his eyes. "Problem. I don't think I remember . . ."

"I know you don't," Leah interrupted, pulling four sheets of folded paper out of the back pocket of her track pants. "So I brought your cheat notes."

Considering how tight she wore the upper part of those pants, fitting four sheets of folded paper in the back pocket was one of the most impressive things Tony'd seen all day.

He ended up shoving the runes through physically with the scar on his left hand, ignoring his companion's sotto voce commentary about cheating. "Is it cheating for a basketball player to use their height?"

Okay. Maybe not so much ignoring.

"You're not a basketball player, you're a wizard."

"And I'm using what I have. It's not my fault other wizards haven't had it."

"You should be moving them with power."

"Why?"

"Because that's how it's done."

Since he was the wizard and she wasn't, he decided to ignore her. As the last line of energy vanished, there was a soft, almost soggy *pop* that lifted all the hair on the back of his neck. The skin around his eyebrow ring suddenly began to burn.

"I wouldn't touch your face with that hand," Leah cautioned.

His left hand had been pressed flat against the pavement. Or more specifically, flat against elderly grease and rat droppings and more recently deposited bits of chow mein. "Gross . . ." He wiped it on his jeans as he stood. One knee was damp and he smelled like rotting bean sprouts. By no means as wiped as he would have been after a Powershot, he still felt a little hungry. "So, on to the next one or back to the studio?" he yawned.

"Why is that my decision?"

He shrugged. "You're taking the biggest risk."

Her fingers stroked the edges of the tattoo and she smiled. The smile said *we can beat this,* and for the moment at least she completely believed it.

Tony smiled the same smile back at her.

"Let's close the second one," she said.

"Great. You're driving. And I need something to eat." As they passed the Dumpster, he swerved to miss a small pile of suspiciously moving rice. "But not Chinese."

At a quarter after midnight, they were in Richmond, driving slowly south on No. 3 Road past the old Canadian Pacific Railway lands.

"Feeling's getting stronger," Leah murmured, drumming her fingers against the steering wheel. "It feels like I have slugs writhing in my navel."

Tony hurriedly chewed and swallowed his eleventh glazed chocolate Timbit. "Thank you for that image."

"Anytime." She turned left on Alexandra, slowing further. "We're close."

They found the weak spot halfway up the side of a building, anchored on a crack in the masonry. There were a few taxis down the street by a hotel, but other than that, the street was empty. Quiet. Once they parked, nothing moved.

"Is this because of the weak spot?" Tony wondered as they crossed the street. All the empty was beginning to creep him out.

"No, it's because it's Thursday night and the bars don't let out for a couple of hours."

"Right." Head cocked to one side, eyes rolled up and over, Tony frowned and lost sight of the blazing line of energy spilling out of the crack as his face realigned.

"See, this is why you learn to do it properly." Hands on her hips, Leah glared up at the building. "Unless we break and enter and dangle you out the third-floor window—which I'm not philosophically against—you're going to have a little trouble just shoving the runes through this one."

Feeling he should protest, more on principal than because he actually had something valid to say, Tony squinted the crack back into alignment. "This one's a lot brighter than the last one."

"It's a lot deeper. Better hurry."

"I could probably throw them into it."

"Whatever. Just do it."

Her tone, bordering on panic, pulled his attention off the weak spot and that, he realized as he took Leah with him to the ground, was probably all that kept him from being blinded as light flared brilliantly purple and something big burst out of the crack.

She slapped the asphalt on impact, grunting as Tony's weight drove the air out of her lungs. "Get! Off!"

"You're welcome!" As the light show from the building dimmed, he rolled off, scrambled to one knee, and aimed his left hand down the road, blinking away afterimages and breathing heavily. He wouldn't be able to see the cheat sheets through the sparkly purple blotches, so he'd have to do this his way.

Not that sparkly purple blotches suggested imminent danger.

On the other hand, the large asymmetrical shape in the middle of the road did.

Bright side, large was easier to hit.

Eyes watering, he scrawled a very quick *go home* and threw it.

Blue sparks on impact.

Blue sparks, purple blotches. It's like demonic Lucky Charms.

A sound like wet sneaker tread dragged against tile. A giant wet sneaker tread.

"What have you done?"

"I told it to go home!" He grabbed Leah's hand and dragged her with him as he rose to his feet.

"It didn't work!"

"I know!" Rapid blinking brought the street into partial focus. The demon still looked a little blurry around the edges, but Tony had a bad feeling that wasn't his eyes.

"I told you it wouldn't work!"

"You're not helping! Just stay behind me and . . ." He squinted. "I must've done some damage, it's . . ." Running seemed as close a description as he was going to get. ". . . running away."

Leah grabbed for his sleeve as he started moving. "Where are you going?"

"After it. To stop it from killing people who aren't you," he added when she didn't seem to understand. "Come on. It's not going that fast." Mostly because bits of it seemed to be moving in opposite directions.

Her fingers tightened to the edge of pain. "What part of 'if I die the world ends' are you still missing?"

"The part where it's not after you." When attempting to jerk free only proved that Leah was stronger than she looked, he waved his free hand toward the demon. "Hello! You're here, it's there!"

She frowned. "Right." And let go. And smiled. Well, showed teeth. "Come on!"

They were no more than three meters behind it as they rounded the corner onto the section of Alexandra that curved to meet up with Alderbridge Way. The demon turned an eyestalk toward them, put on a surprising burst of speed, and crashed through a poster-covered door into the only lit building on that end of the street.

Ginger Joe's.

"Raise your hand everyone who's surprised by this," Tony grunted as they ran after it.

"According to Chekhov," Leah panted, "you should never hang a coffee shop on the wall unless you plan on using it."

"Chekhov? The navigator with the bad wig on classic *Trek?*"

Leah took a moment to sneer. "Read a book." She paused as they reached Ginger Joe's. "Didn't this used to be the Café Cats Escape?"

"How would I know?" Tony asked her. "For that matter, how do you know?"

Inside the coffee shop, cymbals crashed and someone screamed.

"Never mind."

They jumped the debris of the door together and skidded to a stop. The demon had gotten tangled in a drum kit left on the small stage when the night's live music had ended and lay half sprawled across two tables—although since it still had two legs on the floor, it wasn't exactly lying. Just past the wreckage a young man crouched, leather-kilted butt in the air, head to the floor, hands over his head, the chrome studs on his heavy leather wristbands gleaming in the dim light. Tony could just barely make out two more pale faces up against the back wall, their terror lending the whole Goth look a certain authenticity.

It took him another agonizingly long moment to find Amy because the demon's bulk blocked his view. A meaty squelch gave her position away just before she danced into sight, black-rimmed eyes locked on the enemy, the hand holding the skull-shaped candle holder raised to land another blow.

"Enough staring already!" Leah snapped, racing by him. Seemed that the relief of not being the target was making her a little reckless. "Make with the runes!"

Tony pulled the papers out of his jacket pocket as Leah went up and over the demon, planting her hands between the spikes and flipping in the air to land on her feet on the coffin-shaped bar. Possibly not just coffin-*shaped . . .*

The first rune formed as Amy smacked the demon again while Leah kicked it in the head.

It roared, lunged at Leah, got tangled in the snare drum stand, and stumbled, allowing her to leap over the clawed tentacle that had whipped around toward her.

The world rearranged itself in Leah's favor.

Amy wasn't so protected.

As Tony threw the last loop on the second rune, it wrapped a hand—or whatever the hell it was on the end of its arm—around Amy's neck and squeezed.

Screw the runes!

One more Powershot probably wouldn't kill him.

As he pulled his right arm back, Amy reached behind her, scrambled amid the debris, grabbed a full cup of coffee, and threw it in the demon's eyes.

It shrieked.

Dropped her.

And charged for the door.

One meaty appendage smacked Tony in the chest, lifting him off his feet and slamming him into the side wall. He spent a moment really, *really* hoping the crack was one of the fixtures and not a rib, then spent the moment after that trying not to scream.

He could sort of hear Amy yelling that the demon had broken into the wrong damned coffee shop as he raised his left hand and sucked the two runes he'd finished back into his body. It wasn't exactly hard to find his place in the universe now given how well pain seemed to be defining it.

This is me.

This is everything else.

Everything else doesn't hurt.

I do.

Turned out the crack hadn't come from one of the fixtures.

Breathing shallowly, he focused his attention on the broken ribs, smoothing the jagged halves. Pain exploded into a thousand razor-edged shards.

When he regained consciousness, Leah was kneeling beside him and frowning down into his face. "When you heal yourself," she said softly—not kindly, but softly, "you still experience the same amount of pain you would have had the injury healed normally."

"I do?"

"Every last bit of it. All at once."

He supposed he was glad of the explanation. "That totally sucks."

"It's why most wizards don't do it."

"Most wizards," he muttered, pushing himself up into something close to a sitting position. "Right. Why don't we get some of those fuckers to help?"

"Can you stand?"

Since there was only one way to find out, Tony let her help him to his feet.

It was a little lopsided, but it was standing. Except that Amy's date was now having hysterics on a chair instead of the floor, nothing looked like it had changed. "How long was I out?"

"Couple of minutes."

"You really . . ." It wasn't as easy to mime jumping a demon as he'd expected. "You know, went after it."

"You destroyed the rune that would have let it damage me back there on the street when you burned *go home* right across it. After that, I was safe enough. Although," she added pointedly, "it didn't go home. We need to get back to the studio."

"Hang on." He shuffled toward Amy, who left her date to meet him halfway. The hug nearly knocked him on his ass, but he appreciated the sentiment. "You okay?" he asked as they pulled apart.

"Not really, but I'm faking it well."

"This is going to need a creative explanation."

Her eyes regained a bit of sparkle. "I'm all about creative explanations."

"Good, 'cause we've gotta . . ."

"Go. I know." She waved a shaking hand in the general direction of the door. "So go! Kick ass."

The demon was nowhere in sight as they emerged onto the sidewalk. There was a taxi pulling into the hotel on the corner but no other people in sight. After what had just happened, the whole area seemed strangely quiet. Strangely normal.

Totally devoid of demon.

"We'll never catch it."

"We don't have to," Leah reminded him. "We just have to get to the soundstage." She took him by the shoulders and leaned him up against the side of the nearest building. "I'll go get the car. You wait here."

As she ran off, Tony concentrated on staying upright. He knew why the *go home* hadn't worked—it had come to him just before he healed himself. Standing out on the street, blinking away the aftereffects of the demon's entry, he hadn't been connected to the universe. Well, no more than usual anyway; not in a round peg/round hole kind of way. Back in the parking lot, panic had pushed him into place. Here, just now, it had been pain. Actually, there'd been pain in the parking lot, too. Pain seemed to be compulsory.

I bleed therefore I am.

To bleed or not to bleed, that is the question.

Ultimate cosmic power! Itty bitty bandages!

This could be the beginning of a beautiful laceration.

Man, I really need a coffee . . . .

⟿ NINE

"Closed course. Professional driver. Do not try this at home."

"What are you muttering about?" Leah demanded as, with a screech of rubber against pavement, she deftly maneuvered the car around a corner at significantly more than the posted speed.

"Nothing." The best part about the level of exhaustion Tony'd reached: he just didn't care. He didn't care when Leah ran two stop signs and a red light. He didn't care when she passed on the right using four empty parking spaces. He didn't care when she ignored a detour and took a shortcut through some road-work, fighting the car through six blocks of chewed-up pavement and scraping the undercarriage on an exposed sewer grate. Actually, he cared about the last bit, since he'd be the one paying for repairs, but not enough to do anything about it.

Licking the last of the chocolate donut crumbs off his fingers, he watched the streetlights go by so quickly they were very nearly a continuous blur. If he turned to look through the driver's side window, the cracks in the glass re-fracted them into a thousand flares of moving light. "When you said before you were a stunt driver . . . you went to stunt driving school, right?"

"Top of my class."

"Because you knew you couldn't be hurt?"

"That, and because I really like to drive fast."

For a Thursday night not long after midnight, the streets were unusually empty. Tony wondered if that was Ryne Cyratane's spell helping to keep his Demongate from dying in a fiery car crash. "So that was a wicked move you made, back in the coffee shop when you used the demon like a vault and flipped up over its head. Where'd you learn to do that?"

"I played second bull dancer in a Greek production of *The Minotaur* once. Except that I wasn't in a loincloth and the demon wasn't tranked out of its little bovine mind, it was essentially the same stunt. With less ouzo, of course."

"I thought you said the bull was tranked."

"Him, too."

That probably made sense in a world where he wasn't so tired his eyes kept crossing. "Do you think we can beat the demon to the studio?"

She snorted. "In *this* car?"

"Since it's the car we're in, yeah."

"There's a chance. After all, it's not a speed demon." Snickering, she flashed him a smile. "Speed demon. Get it?"

"Yes." The chance to fight back had put her in an interesting mood. Using the *may you live in interesting times* definition of the word. "Please watch the road."

With a cop's nose for contraband, Jack had found the deck of cards shoved in the back of a drawer over in the carpentry shop. Wiping the sawdust off them, he whistled softly.

"Now these," he said, returning to the chaise, cards in hand, "are hard core. You wouldn't be interested," he added as Henry stood, "it's all man/woman action."

"Why wouldn't I be interested?"

"I thought you and Tony were . . . You know."

"We were. That doesn't prevent me from being interested in women."

"I thought not being interested in women was the point?"

"For some men. Not for me."

"Yeah. Thanks for shar . . ." About halfway through the deck, he froze. "Holy crap. I don't think that's possible!"

Henry leaned around Jack's shoulder for a look. "It's possible, but the second woman has to be very flexible. And his back's going to ache afterward."

Jack stepped away, turned, and stared at the other man. "How the hell old are you, anyway?"

"Older than I look."

"Let's hope so." If he'd been asked an hour ago, he'd have said the guy was Tony's age, early twenties, maybe a couple of years older. Now, he wasn't so sure. There was something strange about him, something more than just being ass-deep into the weird shit that went with having a wizard for an ex. Maybe it was the whole romance writer thing—that was definitely a little creepy. Maybe he'd researched exotic positions for one of his books. More comforting a thought than the possibility he'd spent his teens as a pornographic gymnast. Jack sighed. "You play rummy?"

"Penny a point?"

Because he'd noticed that the queen of hearts was unnaturally worn—noticed and then refused to think why—Jack was up forty-two dollars when Henry stiffened and dropped his cards.

"What is it?" Damn if it didn't look like the guy was sniffing the air.

"Something's coming."

"Something?" Jack tossed his cards aside and stood, pulling his weapon from his shoulder holster. "The something we're here for?"

"Probably."

To Jack's surprise, Henry flipped the chaise up on its side and shoved it toward the wall. "Get behind that."

"Up yours."

"You'll have a place to brace your weapon as well as some small amount of protection."

"And you'll be where?"

A loop of rope dangled from one hand. "I'll be attempting to . . ."

A rain of cherries cut him off.

"What the hell?"

Henry looked up and moved just enough to avoid being hit. "It's our warning. The demon is through the wards."

Jack winced as a cherry bounced off his cheek. "You think?"

And then there was no time for thinking as all at once, tentacles and claws and spikes dangled from the light grid, filling the space between the grid and the floor. It took a moment for the parts to become a whole and when it did, Jack wished it hadn't. Monsters didn't scare him—over the years he'd seen too much of what people could do—but this one gave it the old college try.

With a shriek of rending aluminum, one of the struts tore free and Jack decided that maybe being behind the fancy sofa wasn't such a bad idea. It had seemed solid. Well made. Likely to survive. He dove over the piece of furniture, rolled, and came up on his knees, ready to fire. Suddenly a line of yellow nylon rope was around the bulk of the demon's body. And then around most of the legs, snugging them in tight.

The demon screamed.

Something snarled an answer.

Jack's hindbrain sent up flares. Fight or flee! And flee seems like the better idea!

Right at the moment, denial seemed like a much better idea, but it was way, way too late for that.

Jack popped off three quick rounds at the demon's . . . head and held back the fourth when Henry Fitzroy caught a heavily muscled arm in another loop of rope and began fighting it to the demon's side.

It seemed the not very tall man was stronger than the demon.

Stronger.

Faster.

More fucking scary.

"That's not possible." Under the circumstances, a stupid thing to say, but Jack was having just a little trouble coping. *Romance writer, my ass.*

The demon hit the floor with a noise somewhere between a crash and a squelch.

A writhing tentacle-like arm split the air where Henry had been seconds before, twisted around for another blow as a second clawed tentacle came straight up out of the demon's body. No way Henry could avoid both. No way

Jack could get off a clear shot. Trying not to think about what he was doing, Jack went over the chaise and tackled the arm.

Pinned under the length of his body, it was warmer than he'd expected.

Warmer, and a little damp.

It took him a moment to realize why it smelled so strongly of crushed cherries.

Heavy muscles bunched up to try and throw him off, and, with the right leverage, Jack was pretty sure it'd be able to toss him across the soundstage.

It shifted within the confining rope.

Suddenly the floor was farther away.

Oh, fuck . . .

Henry had faced a Demonlord and bled to keep an ancient grimoire from falling into the taloned hands of the lesser demon it commanded. In comparison, this creature seemed no more or less than it appeared. Strong. Fast. Other. But not necessarily evil.

If there are, as the Demongate supposes, a multitude of hells—he slid under a clawed tentacle that would have disemboweled him—then perhaps, in some of these—another loop of rope secured the limb—we name the inhabitants demon based on appearance, not motivations.

As the creature hissed and writhed, he spun about in time to see Jack Elson lifted into the air on the largest of what seemed essentially to be its arms.

And then the arm flipped over and Constable Elson was heading back toward the concrete floor at high speed.

There were no visible joints to act as weak spots—or rather too many joints to attack in the little time he had. Racing in toward the creature, Henry grabbed the arm just under the front set of claws and kept moving, dragging it—and the constable—around until he could brace himself against the creature's own body.

Teeth bared, he managed to stop the momentum of the limb and snarled, "Let go!"

Letting go seemed like a fine idea to Jack. He dropped and rolled and crushed a little fruit, finally turning in time to see Henry drag the tentacle down to the body of the creature and secure it with another loop of the yellow rope.

No one was that fast. Or that strong.

"What the hell *are* you?" he panted, pulling himself up onto his knees.

He knew when Henry looked up and smiled. He couldn't put it into words—hell, he didn't think he could form words right at that moment—but he knew. He knew it in the way the hair rose off the back of his neck, in the way a sudden drop of sweat ran down his side under his shirt, in the way he couldn't seem to catch his breath or hear himself think over the pounding of his heart. He knew it in his bones.

No, in his blood.

And then he fell into dark eyes and he forgot that he knew.

"Hey! You guys! There's a demon heading this . . ." Tony skidded to a stop, dragging Leah, who was half supporting him, to a stop as well. He stared at the demon—which may or may not have been staring back. The eyestalks were flipping around in a way that made it hard to tell. "Never mind."

"What's with the cherries?" Leah demanded, scraping pulp off the bottom of her high-top.

"Tony's early warning system," Jack grunted, getting to his feet.

"It made cherries?"

"Apparently."

She turned to Tony, who shrugged. They had bigger problems than fruit. He shook free of Leah's hand and shuffled carefully toward Henry. Trouble was, when a romance writer slash vampire fought a demon, it wasn't the romance writer that then had to be dealt with. He could see the Hunter in the set of Henry's shoulders. In the way he was standing, his back to them, perfectly, impossibly still.

At Henry's side, he leaned forward, careful not to touch, and murmured, "If you need . . ."

"Not from you." A quiet voice. Barely audible. A voice that stroked danger against Tony's skin. "Not after last night."

Last night. This time, he didn't stop himself from touching the mark on his neck. No wonder he was exhausted; it wasn't just the wizardry. "Then who?" The emotional kickback was as important as the blood and Jack, as he'd been insisting to all and sundry, was straight. Leah was far too dangerous.

"Give me a moment."

"Sure." Terror was as valid an emotion as any other and the shadows in Jack's eyes suggested he'd seen something more frightening than the big rubbery monster tied up on the floor. Tony tried not to wonder what would have happened had they got there a little later and had pretty much buried the question by the time Henry turned, the mask of civilization firmly back in place.

Pretty much.

A red-gold brow rose.

Tony shrugged.

"So . . ." Leah sighed loudly. ". . . if you two are finished with all the silent communing, you think we could get going on sending Maurice here home?"

"Maurice?" Jack snickered, the sound just this side of hysteria.

She pushed a handful of curls back off her face and smiled, deep dimples appearing in each cheek. "What? You don't think he looks like a Maurice?"

About to tell her to knock it off, Tony realized what she was doing as Jack's shoulders squared and he rubbed a hand back through his hair, standing it up in damp, golden spikes.

"If you're asking, I think he looks like a Barney."

"Isn't Barney a dinosaur?" Her tongue licked a glistening path along her lower lip.

Jack's eyes half closed. "Barney, Fred's neighbor."

The only thing keeping them from consummating the repartee was the demon, tied and pissed off, filling the space between them.

When Ryne Cyratane made his expected appearance, Tony frowned. The Demonlord looked . . . frustrated?

Because Leah wasn't actually getting any in the here and now?

Because his demonic minions kept failing?

Because he couldn't find the wizard who kept defeating him?

Except this demon hadn't been sent back to hell, so how would he know it had been defeated? And why did he look frustrated rather than angry? A glance down and Tony realized the Demonlord wasn't even particularly interested in the whole Jack/Leah dynamic. Interested, yes, but not, well, fully.

"Tony!"

"Sorry." He shook his head as Leah turned her attention to him and Ryne Cyratane faded. He was missing something, something important, but he was just too damned tired to make the effort and figure out what it was. "I'll start drawing the runes."

"Are you strong enough?"

"Sure." Why not lie on the side of truth, justice, and the wizardly way given there was a distinct lack of choice regardless of how he felt. The demon was fighting against the ropes, rocking back and forth and in a few other less easily defined directions. "Although . . ." His stomach growled on cue. ". . . I wouldn't say no to food."

"There's half a bomb bottle of cola left," Jack offered, clearing his throat and looking everywhere but at Leah. "And some cherries."

"Close enough." Or not. The cherries had no pits and tasted like cough syrup. Fortunately, the cola, essentially sugar and caffeine, faked nourishment.

"It's weird how it can't break the rope." Jack circled the demon slowly as Tony began to burn the first rune on the air. "We know it's strong and the rope isn't that thick."

"It's an unnatural rope," Tony reminded him, squinting through the blue lines. "What's weird is that Arra would know that it would work. She never faced demons here in this world."

Leah snorted. "Where do you think her demons came from? Walmart?"

"These are not the demons I know from the past," Henry said quietly as Tony started the second rune. "This poor creature is nothing more than an animal out of its place."

"Let's not forget these things are killers," Jack pointed out.

"They kill to eat," Henry told him. "So do you."

"Yeah, well, so far I've managed to avoid ripping any arms off while I'm having lunch."

"Good for you."

"You're not entirely wrong," Leah broke in before Jack could respond. "Neither of you. These guys are on the low end of the demonic pecking order." She waved a hand at the demon on the floor. It writhed at her. "They're all about the rending and the killing and, yes, the ripping off of arms, but they're not really very motivated by anything other than the rending and the killing. Relatively speaking, they come from fairly close by. The hell that the ancient mystics saw . . ." She turned her attention to Henry. ". . . the hell adopted by your religion, that was considerably farther away."

"Your Demonlord is no beast. If he uses these creatures, then he has moved closer without using the gate."

"There's some movement within the hells," Leah admitted. "But he can't get here without help. If you want the big guys, the demons with dialogue and motivations, then you have to call for them specifically. It takes a lot of power to punch a gate through to their level, a couple of artifacts that aren't easy to get, and, if you want to survive it, a will of iron."

"Actually, it's not that hard." Henry folded his arms. "I know a not very bright young man who brought through a creature capable of speech and independent evil with a small barbecue and a few cheap candles."

"Did he survive?"

"Not ultimately, no."

She spread her hands. "I rest my case." Before anyone could demand to know what that meant, she added, "And with that kind of power he was probably an untrained wizard."

"Not likely," Henry snorted.

"Outsider?"

"Yes, but . . ."

"It's been my experience . . ." A twitch of her sweater hem directed attention to her abdomen and the physical evidence of that experience. ". . . that potential isn't particularly rare. Actually accomplishing something with it, now that's unusual. If Tony here hadn't met Arra, he wouldn't be fighting demons today. Heroes rise when we need them."

Tony let the observation pass without responding as he finished off the third rune, going over the last curve three times before it stopped sputtering. The buzz from the cola had burned off and it was getting harder and harder to focus.

"Tony?"

A cool, familiar touch against his wrist. He blinked a couple of times in Henry's general direction. "I'm okay."

"Can you finish?"

"Do I have a choice?" The demon was writhing again, bulging around the rope. "Why doesn't it make any noise?"

"Perhaps it communicates by motion."

"No, it made a noise before. Although . . ." weak sneaker-against-tile noise could have easily been made by rubbing demon against asphalt. "So we've tied and gagged it." He snickered, but he didn't really think it was funny. It was just easier to laugh than run screaming from the room. Besides, he was starting to feel sorry for the big-squishy thing. That burned-in *go home* looked painful.

"Tony."

"I'm okay."

"Look at me."

"Henry, I'm . . ." Henry's eyes were dark and the masks were gone. Hunger. Danger. Tony felt his heart race and a sudden wave of energy flood his body. He jerked back, blinked, and Henry's eyes were hazel again.

"Can you finish now?"

"Oh, yeah. Word up for adrenaline."

The red-gold brows dipped. "I have no idea what that . . ." A silent pivot toward the soundstage door. "Someone's coming."

"Tony? You around?"

"Zev?" Damn. It was Thursday. Zev left midafternoon Fridays, so he always worked late Thursday.

"Good, you're still here. I was finishing up the score on that last episode, and I just wondered if you were on the soundstage." Rising volume suggested he was walking toward them. "You know, given the possibility of demons and all. I've got this great complicated harp piece and . . ." His eyes widened as he came around the corner of the set and he stopped so quickly he rocked back and forth. ". . . never mind. So." The pause extended almost a beat too long. "That's a demon?"

No reason to deny it. "Yeah."

"Really? Okay. It's, uh, you know, big." He frowned, opened and closed his mouth a couple of times, shoved his hands into his front pockets, and took a bravado-inspired step forward. Then glanced down at the floor. "What's with all the cherries?"

"They're part of the early warning system," Jack said dryly, picking one up and flicking it into the wall.

"They must have cost a fortune. They're out of season," he added when it became obvious no one got the point. "Apples would have been significantly more cosahhhhh!" Yanked off his feet by the tentacle around his ankle, he screamed as he slid along a path of crushed fruit toward the demon.

"Don't shoot!" Tony grabbed for Jack's arm as Henry grabbed for the tentacle.

Still screaming, Zev slapped into the demon's side.

Henry twisted a loop into the excess flesh, tightened it, and shoved the music director away with the side of his foot as the demon went after more immediate prey, driving the end of the tentacle spikelike toward Henry's head.

The possibility of the demon getting free, not to mention eating his ex, added a whole new burst of adrenaline. Tony sketched the fourth rune. "Crap!" Erased the last line. Drew it again.

There was a sudden, intense smell of sulfur and Henry hit the floor beside Zev and a tangle of yellow nylon rope as the demon disappeared. Fortunately, the runes only worked on creatures not native to this reality.

Fortunately.

Really, really fortunately. Tony wiped sweaty palms on his thighs and tried to remember if he knew that.

"I assume there's a reason for all the noise?"

Swaying, he fought to focus on CB's face. "Demon."

"Screaming?"

"That was me!" Zev scrambled to his feet and thrust his arm toward his boss. "It had a mouth in its side! In its side! Not its face! It bit a hole in my sleeve!"

"How fortunate it didn't remove your arm." As Zev absorbed the truth of that, CB stepped forward and caught Tony as his knees unlocked and he began to topple. "And the smell of sulfur?"

"Tradition?"

"Are you asking me?"

Tony sneezed. "No."

"And the cherries?"

"Long story."

"I see. Mr. Fitzroy, if you could place the chaise upright again, please. Constable Elson, there should be food of some kind in the office kitchen."

Tony managed to remain on his feet as they crossed the set, but he suspected that had more to do with the grip CB maintained on his arm rather than any macho shit on his part. Although the chaise looked hard and lumpy, it was the most comfortable piece of furniture he'd ever collapsed on. No need for anyone to worry; he was just going to take a few minutes to recover the feeling in his extremities.

A little easier to do, actually, after CB let him go and moved away.

"Ms. Burnett, I thought your technique of dealing with the demons would use less energy and leave Mr. Foster on his feet."

"It did use less energy," Leah protested indignantly. "After the day he's had, any other way—his whole mano a mano way, for instance—would have killed him."

Yeah, yeah. Déjà vu all over again.

"We'll have to take your word for that. Mr. Groves is in my office with the page of demonology he found. If you could bring him here, I'd appreciate it."

"Kevin Groves?" Tony lifted his head to check if the disapproval he could hear in Henry's voice matched his expression. It did. "The tabloid reporter who's been hanging about the show?"

"That's the one." Leah answered, walking backward toward the exit. "It turns out he knows about the Demonic Convergence and may have primary source information."

"How does someone like that get hold of primary source information?"

"The easy way," she snorted, one hand against her belly as she turned and left.

"She's an odd one," Zev muttered. He had a plastic broom in his hand, the kind with a scraper along one edge. "Even for a stuntie."

"He's right," CB murmured, stepping closer to Henry as Zev began sweeping up the cherries. Tony strained to hear him; this was not a conversation he was going to miss. "There's something about that young lady that's . . . different. Unusual."

No shit.

Fortunately for Leah, Henry had secrets of his own. "She studies demons; that's got to skew things a little."

And again, no shit.

"It seems to be time," CB said, still talking quietly to Henry, "for Mr. Foster to put some serious work into that memory erase spell of Arra's."

Henry glanced down at Tony and then up at CB. "It's like you're reading my mind."

"It wouldn't be the strangest thing that happened today."

"Word." Tony snickered at their expressions, or at as much of their expressions as he could see through eyes that kept sliding closed. "You two need to get out more."

"Mr. Foster?"

"Let him sleep."

"Are you certain he's sleeping?"

Henry laid a hand gently against Tony's chest, listened to his heart beating slow and sure. "I'm certain."

"I've never seen anyone eat that fast. I mean, that was almost a whole carton of potato salad and almost a liter of milk, gone between one blink and the next." Jack brought his hands together, crushing the empty milk carton. "I don't know why he didn't choke. Or puke. Or both. You know, choke and puke. Especially considering it was potato salad and milk, for Christ's sake."

Henry exchanged a glance with CB.

"Are you all right, Constable Elson?"

"Me?" Jack's chin lifted and his chest went out. Henry hid a smile. Although the RCMP officer wasn't a small man, there was no way he could avoid being dominated by CB's bulk. "I'm fine. Why wouldn't I be fine?"

"You have been exposed today to not one, but two demons."

"So have you."

"Yes, but I'm in television."

Jack jerked his head toward Zev who was sweeping up the last of the cherries in the immediate area and muttering quietly. "He's in television and he's freaked."

"He was nearly eaten."

"Yeah, well, I'm fine." Arms folded, he swept a scowl around the soundstage. "I'd be better if I knew how that thing got in."

"That's easy enough to answer; we left the door to the carpentry shop unlocked. I didn't want any more of my property destroyed," CB added as the constable's scowl lit on him.

"We wanted it in here," Henry reminded him, coiling the yellow nylon rope, "so it could be taken down without risking innocent lives."

"Right. We wanted it in here." A glance toward the place where the demon had lain. "Okay. Then tell me this. If we knew it was coming in a specific door, why did Tony put his warning thing around the whole place?"

"For the same reason we're ankle-deep in fake fruit," Leah snorted coming around the edge of the set, Kevin Groves following behind like a puppy. "Tony doesn't know what he's doing. He's making things up as he goes along."

Jack shifted slightly so that he was between Leah and Tony. Familiar with the protective instincts of the police, Henry decided to let it pass. It was interesting that on some instinctive level the constable thought Tony needed protecting from Leah. "He's doing *fine*."

Stopped about two meters away, Leah folded her arms, metaphysical seductress buried under indignation. "Well, according to you, everything's fine. You're fine, Tony's fine. Everything is *not* fine. We have demons . . ."

"Who don't always use doors," Henry interjected. "Leaving a door open does not guarantee they'll go through it. Tony laid out his wards wide enough to take that into account."

"And the cherries?" she asked, kicking at a piece of fruit Zev had missed.

Henry waited until it rolled to a stop. "I'm not saying he doesn't need to refine his technique."

"Perhaps it would be a good idea . . ." CB's tone had nothing of *perhaps* about it. ". . . if we move to another part of the soundstage and leave Mr. Foster to his rest."

Jack shook his head. "We shouldn't leave him alone."

"No, we shouldn't."

"I'll stay with him," Zev offered, stepping carefully over the pile of fruit he'd collected and walking to the chaise. "You guys can go make plans for dealing with demons and just leave me out of them."

"If you're sure, Mr. Sero."

"Oh, yeah." He held the broom across his body like a weapon. "I'm sure."

"If you hear or see anything, anything at all . . ."

"Trust me. I'll yell."

Henry had always liked Raymond Dark's office. It was, he thought, the kind of office a vampire should have—all dark wood and heavy velvet curtains and shelves of ancient knickknacks. It had weight. Authority. It wasn't anything like his office, which tended toward beech veneer, piles of research books, and stacks of author's copies he hadn't been able to give away, but that was the difference between artifice and reality.

The black leather desk chair creaked as CB lowered himself carefully into it. "Now then, Mr. Groves; your documentation."

But Kevin Groves was staring at Henry. He swallowed once, punctuated by his Adam's apple rising and falling in the column of his throat. "You're not . . . I mean, you're . . ."

"He's what?" Jack asked from where he leaned against the corner of the set, positioned so that he could see both the desk and a bit of Tony's head on the upper end of the distant chaise.

"Good question." Frowning, Henry caught Kevin's gaze and held it. The Hunger had been buried deep, the masks were in place disguising the Hunter, and yet this reporter knew exactly what he was—which was both disturbing and useful. He smiled and then a little more broadly as, behind his glasses, Kevin's left eye began to twitch. "I'm what?"

"Nothing." Kevin started to shake as his muscles tensed for a flight not permitted to him. He stank of fear. Fear and . . .

Henry's attention flicked for an instant to Leah, tucked up in one corner of the red velvet sofa. That explained why it had taken her those extra moments to retrieve the reporter from the office.

She blew him a one-finger kiss.

"Nothing," Kevin repeated as he staggered, released but still unable to run. "You're nothing."

"You didn't see him earlier," Jack muttered.

Before Kevin could turn, Henry shook his head and the reporter froze.

"The page, Mr. Groves."

His head jerked around toward CB. Then back to Henry.

Still smiling, Henry stepped away. "We'll talk later, you and I. Right now, I think you should get Mr. Bane that page."

"Oh, for pity's sake," Leah sighed as Kevin dropped his backpack off his shoulder and began to rummage frantically in its depths, "leave the poor guy alone."

"*I* have done nothing to him. Which is more than you can say."

"Hey, I did nothing to him. *With* him, yes. Not to."

"Are you so sure of that?" *Demongate.*

She straightened. "Don't push me." *Nightwalker.*

CB cleared his throat.

Silence fell.

"What the hell is going on?" Jack demanded.

"Mr. Groves has brought us a piece of a manuscript that seems to define the Demonic Convergence."

"From the crazy monk guy Leah mentioned this afternoon?"

"That has yet to be determined." With the page on the desk in front of him, CB leaned back and steepled his fingers. "Mr. Fitzroy and Ms. Burnett are going to have a look at it."

"What, is he a demonic consultant, too?"

"In a manner of speaking." CB shot a look at the reporter that cut off an already somewhat strangled laugh.

"Tony's the wizard," Jack said pointedly. "He should examine it."

"Later," Henry said as he moved around the desk. "Right now, he needs to regain his strength." The vellum was badly yellowed, the edges touched with water damage.

"That's not from the monk's book," Leah sighed as she joined him. "It's all numbers."

"It's astrological charts." Kevin looked up from fussing with Raymond Dark's inkwell and added defiantly. "I told you that."

"How did you know it had to do with the Demonic Convergence?"

"It says so on the other side."

Frowning, Leah carefully turned the page over. In the margin, about halfway down, someone had written *charts Demonic Convergence* in pencil.

"Not me!" Kevin protested quickly. "That was there when I found the page."

"An earlier researcher?" CB suggested.

"Probably. Hang on." One hand holding back her hair, Leah leaned forward and squinted at the bottom of the page. "There's more writing, but it's faint." She carefully flipped the page. "It's on both sides. I think it was done at the same time as the charts."

"It looks around the same age," Henry agreed, when she moved out of the way so he could examine the barely visible brown marks. "But those aren't words; that's a pattern."

"Just because you don't recognize them, junior . . ." With one finger, she spun the vellum around and bent to breathe gently on the lettering. "Damp will sometimes bring the ink up a bit."

"Or damage an irreplaceable artifact."

"I think the margin notes have already lowered the value a bit."

"Still."

She flashed Henry a smile he'd very nearly seen in his mirror. The dimples were noticeably absent. "I know what I'm doing. Breath gives life to death."

"That's a total . . ." He let his protest trail off when it became obvious the ink was growing darker.

"It's a prayer," Leah announced after a moment. "Or part of one. *Keep us safe, Guardian of the West.*" She turned the page again. "*In light and life I beg thee.*"

"Let me see the other side again."

She sighed but complied. "You're still not going to be able to read it."

"No." Frowning, he traced the largest of the letters, its loops and swirls now visible. "But I recognize it."

"How?" CB demanded.

Henry straightened. "I'm not entirely positive, but I think I own the rest of the book."

"You own an ancient book on the Demonic Convergence?" Arms folded, Leah raked him with a disbelieving stare. "You don't think you might have mentioned this earlier?"

"I didn't know it earlier. But this lettering . . ." He tapped the air above the prayer. ". . . is the same. The same shape and in the same place on the page." The document as an object was familiar. It was only the content he didn't recognize. "Unfortunately, because I couldn't read it, I didn't know what the book was about. If this is a page from it, I do now. And *you* can read it."

Slightly mollified by his acknowledgment of her ability, Leah shook her head. "Why would you own a book you can't read?"

"He owns it so others can't," CB said quietly.

"Oh, my." Her eyes widened in mock outrage. "Censorship. I need to see that book," she continued when Henry didn't bother denying it.

He looked at his watch. "It's almost three. I've time to get it and bring it back here."

"Bring back coffees, too," Jack told him, reaching for his wallet. "Hit a Timmy's. Extra-large double double and whatever anyone else wants. Oh, and grab some of those special Halloween donuts with the black and orange sprinkles."

"Way to work the stereotype," Leah snickered as Henry suggested the constable call it a night.

"No." And if Jack didn't meet his gaze, he came closer than many who'd seen what he'd seen. "I'm here until this ends."

"You don't have to work tomorrow?"

"I'll take a sick day. I'm not leaving until I know what's going on."

"You know . . ."

"And," he interrupted stubbornly, "until you can guarantee no more horror movie rejects will be out and about on my streets."

"Your streets?" Leah asked.

"It's a cop thing," Henry told her before Jack could answer. "They're all remarkably possessive."

"Well, you'd know possessive. I should go with you," she added, crossing the office as he took Jack's money and folded it into the front pocket of his jeans. "Just in case."

"In case there's an attack on you while Tony sleeps?"

She moved a little closer and tossed her hair back over her shoulder. "With Tony out, you're my best bet."

Henry stared for a long moment at the creamy flesh below the curve of her ear. "No," he said at last. "Too great a risk."

"You think *that's* a greater risk than running into a new demonic minion?"

He gave her back the smile she'd given him earlier. "I do."

"What the hell is going on between those two?" Jack muttered as Leah returned to the astrological charts on the desk and Henry headed for the back door.

"You don't know?"

He turned to see Groves standing tucked in behind his left shoulder. "No," he snapped, putting some decent distance between them. "I don't know."

The reporter shuddered. "Lucky."

"You know?" Stupid question. He obviously thought he did. "So, what's going on?"

And why is a romance writer a better choice to protect her than an armed police officer?

Groves answered the actual question instead of the subtext. "She tried for power over him. He threatened to kill her."

Jack blinked. "You're completely bugfuck; you know that, right?"

It wasn't so much a book Henry dropped on the desk as a collection of loose pages stuffed between wooden covers. The pages were paler and the writing darker, but that, Jack realized, had more to do with the way Groves' page had been stored than any actual differences.

He wasn't a big believer in inanimate objects having an aura—in the last few months new and unusual animate objects had pretty much used up all available ability to believe—but under oath on the stand he'd say this book felt unpleasant. He was just as glad he wasn't the one with his nose barely an inch above the writing.

"Do you think you could avoid dropping sprinkles on a priceless literary artifact?" Henry carefully swept a bit of orange icing off the top sheet.

Jack backed up a step. Not like he minded being farther away from that book. "So what's it say?"

"I'll let you know when I've got it in order." Leah sat back, rubbing her eyes, then bent forward again. "This page seems to be more dates. This is a description of a body, the injuries, and how it was found. Oh, this is about the woman who found it and what relationship she was to the ... well to either the dead guy, a dead guy who might not be *that* dead guy, or to the person writing. Boring stuff so far."

"It sounds like a police report."

She looked up and nodded. Jack barely resisted the effort to reach out and push her hair off her face. "It could be. Somewhere in here, there's probably information on who's writing and why. It's going to take a while before I can find anything that's going to do us any good. If there's anything in here." She yawned. "I'm beat, and my eyes hurt. I need some sleep."

"We need the information."

"Then you stay up and get it."

"He can't read it," Jack reminded her as Henry checked his watch. "And we're all tired."

Dimples flashed. "Then we should all find a bed."

"Cute." A strangled noise flicked his attention momentarily to the reporter. From the expression on Groves' face, he couldn't take a joke. "But you're right ..." Back to Leah. "... we've got to sleep sometime." And finally to Chester Bane. "If you closed the studio, we could make this our command center."

The big man shook his head. "I can't afford to lose a day's work. Make it your command center with the studio open."

"And if a demon shows up when the director yells *quiet*, we all just pause until the camera's off?"

"Yes. That should be sufficient."

Jack studied his face and realized: "You're not kidding."

"I don't kid. The studio stays open."

"We should be safe enough tomorrow," Leah told him, covering another yawn. "One way or another, we dealt with the two weak spots I could sense."

"Fine." Since no one was listening to reason and since the RCMP wasn't backing his play, giving him no official weight to throw around, he'd just have to make the best of things. "Tony's security system has been breached. Is it still functional?"

"No." Leah pulled the sleeves of her sweater down over her hands and folded her arms. "I crossed it with no reaction when I got Kevin from the office."

"Why would it respond to you?"

"Everything responds to me."

She sounded so matter-of-fact about it, Jack decided not to argue. "All right." He drained the last sweet dredges of his coffee. "If we can get some more cough syrup, Tony can resecure the perimeter when he wakes up."

"Cough syrup?"

Jack explained quickly, and Chester Bane nodded.

"Get me an empty bottle, and I'll see that he has what he needs."

"Good. And tell your people that a rain of cherries is the sign to hit the deck." He glanced around the office set. "You got a shower in this place?"

"Two." The producer held up the requisite number of fingers. "There are en suites in both of the large dressing rooms, although I'd advise you not to use Mason's. Mr. Nicholas is likely to be much more reasonable, particularly as he is aware of what's going on."

"Maybe you'd better talk to him, then." Jack tilted his head back and stared over the tops of the walls, up into the grid hanging from the ceiling. "It's a big place. When your crew shows up, we'll just stay out of each other's way. We'll send . . ." He paused, leaned back until he could see the end of the chaise and frowned. "What the hell is the name of the guy with Tony?"

"Zev Sero. The musical director. Although he and Mr. Foster are no longer . . ." A pause. "Ah. With. Currently. Never mind."

"Send him home. Whether he comes back is up to you two." If it was up to Jack, he'd send Chester Bane home as well. The last thing they needed was more civilians around. "You . . ." Groves jumped. "I'm not inclined to let you out of my sight in case this all shows up on page one next to the cow that does Elvis impersonations."

"It won't." He was facing Jack but looking at Henry, picking at the cuticle around his right thumb, two spots of color high on each cheek. "I promise."

The look was either terror or love, and in this crowd, Jack figured the odds were pretty much even. "You break that promise and . . ."

"Trust me, Constable Elson," Groves interrupted, his Adam's apple bobbing as he swallowed, "there's no need to make threats. I know what's at stake. Oh, God!" Both hands rose to cover his mouth. "I didn't mean to say *stake*!"

Clearly, Tony wasn't the only one a little brain fried. "Go home. Sleep. Come back."

This time Groves turned to face Henry as he asked, "Now?"

This time Jack wasn't going to put up with it. "Hey. *I'm* telling you to go." And then he decided not to notice that Henry nodded, an almost friggin' regal incline of the head before Groves finally got off his ass and started moving.

Pausing. "My page . . ."

"Stays."

Leah leaned forward and caught the reporter's eye. "I'll take good care of it."

How the hell did she make that sound pornographic? Jack shifted his weight to make an adjustment. And it wasn't just him. There was shifting going on all over the room.

"I'll be leaving as well." Henry came out from behind the desk. "I have commitments I cannot break."

"Hey." Jack stepped into his path. "If I can break mine, then . . . uh . . ." It was too damned dark and he couldn't find his way out. He had no backup. No weapon. He was . . . was . . . Eyes, they were just eyes. "Fuck. Okay, go."

"I'll be back as soon as I can. Mr. Groves, I'll walk you to your car."

Jack watched them leave, wondering how high Groves would jump if Henry Fitzroy reached over and tapped him on the arm. He turned to find himself under examination by Chester Bane.

"You seem to be taking this in stride, Constable."

He reached for another donut and realized there were bruises on his back that were going to hurt like hell come morning. "Well, the perps are uglier, but it's hardly the first stakeout I've been on."

"You are serving and protecting?"

"Yeah. That's what I'm telling myself."

∽ TEN

Tony hoped he was dreaming, although, given the way his life had been lately, he figured there was a fifty-fifty chance he was actually physically standing somewhere . . . white. White up above, white all around, white and solid underfoot. At least he was dressed. One of those naked and somewhere white dreams would be more than he could handle right about now.

If he *was* dreaming.

"Hello?"

No echo. No bounce at all. Not inside, then.

Unless he was under a giant white insulated dome that was sucking up the sound of his voice.

Yeah. That was likely. It'd be like *The Truman Show* only without Jim Carrey. Or a set.

The air was warm and smelled like . . .

Well, that was embarrassing. The whole place smelled like him. Still, he supposed a guy who'd had a three-demon day was entitled to stink a bit if anyone was.

He lifted his left hand to run it back through sweaty hair. Stopped it at eye level.

The rune burned into the palm of his left hand—usually a thin white line—had turned a dark blood red. The rune allowed him to hold energy. Energ*ies*. Did the color change mean that the rune was holding all the white in place or was that too much of a leap?

Okay, let's go over what we know.

White place.

Red rune.

That was about it.

As far as Tony could figure, there was only one way to find out if there was a connection. He dropped to one knee and poked at the ground. It felt like a really good kitchen countertop, that stuff where the pieces got melted together and couldn't be scratched. Henry had it in his condo.

And that was as far as he got for a while.

Hard to tell how much time had passed because nothing changed, but Tony was fairly sure he'd been kneeling there for hours. Or he'd gone somewhere else and was just getting back because that sort of thing could happen in a dream. This kind of a dream anyway. The truly weird kind.

Before it could happen again, before he could convince himself that this was a remarkably bad idea, he raised his left hand and slapped his palm down on the ground.

It gave slightly. A noticeable ripple moved out from the point of impact. He rose and fell as it passed beneath him, like riding a solid wave. He watched the shadow that followed the crest until it was too far away to see. His time in television had taught him that a shadow meant a definitive light source, but apparently that rule didn't apply in dreamland.

"That was productive. Not." Rubbing the rune against his jeans, he stood. And squinted.

A black dot marred the perfect white of the horizon. Or of the distance anyway since *horizon* might be giving the distance more credit than it deserved.

Tony waited and when the dot didn't get any bigger, he started walking toward it.

And walking.

And walking.

And not really getting anywhere.

Of course, it wasn't like he had anything else to do.

"Hey! You want to meet me halfway? And I'm an idiot," he said in a less carrying tone. "What," he asked his immediate surroundings, "is the one thing I'm good at? Yes, I am amazingly good at my job, but I'm speaking metaphysically here, here being somewhat metaphysical. I can call things into my hand. I say 'come here' and things come. Now, admittedly I don't know what this . . ." In spite of squinting until his eyes ached, the dot remained a dot. ". . . is, but it appeared after I smacked the white with the rune and so, therefore, if I call it to the hand with the rune that should make up for a lack of defining characteristics. Right?"

Nothing disagreed with him.

He waited a moment longer.

"Okay, then."

Holding up his hand, reaching, Tony could feel . . . something. Something that was either bigger than anything he'd ever moved before or something that didn't want to come to him. Since the first theory allowed for a little more peace of mind, he went with that and pulled harder.

He hadn't had to use the words that focused this particular ability since the haunted house extravaganza back in August. He used them now.

Shouted them out, one at a time. By the sixth word, he could feel movement. By the seventh the black dot was longer than it was wide, kind of person-shaped. Panting, he lowered his arm and squinted again.

Person-shaped with antlers.

Seemed like he'd been trying to call a Demonlord to his hand.

So, now he knew that, the question was: Did he keep doing it?

Was *Darkest Night* the highest rated vampire detective show on syndicated television?

Duh.

His whole arm shook as he raised it, lowered it, raised it again. Apparently his arm wasn't convinced this was a good idea, but if he wasn't dreaming, Ryne Cyratane might be his only way out. Hell, if he *was* dreaming, Ryne Cyratane still might be his only way out.

This time when he called, the Demonlord didn't move. He did. His feet skittered along the countertop surface until he could see the Demonlord's face and then stopped so suddenly he nearly pitched forward. Too far away to touch—and that was probably a good thing—close enough to see expression. The Demonlord didn't look happy, that was for sure. He looked frustrated. Like he knew the thing he was looking for was right there, right in front of him, but he couldn't find it.

Me again. Tony couldn't have explained how he knew. It was like when he was on the street and some nights when the cops cruised by they were just out and about and some nights they were actively looking to score some law-and-order points, and it got so he could tell the difference. This feeling felt like that feeling.

Although, if Ryne Cyratane was looking for the wizard who kept sending his demons back to hell with their dicks in their hands, shouldn't he be angry?

"Hey!"

No response.

"Dude! If you want to talk to me, I'm right here!"

Here and not moving any closer. He could step back but not forward. There didn't seem to be any kind of an invisible barrier, he just couldn't do it.

Tony slid his gaze down Ryne Cyratane's body, got distracted for a moment or two—*Damn!*—and realized that the Demonlord's feet were likewise held in place. Back up the long expanse of skin, another moment of distraction—*Damn, damn, damn!*—and this time he saw that the Demonlord's mouth was moving.

"Okay." He ran a hand back through his hair. The frustrated expression was beginning to seem like a good idea. "You can't hear me. I can't hear you. So what the fuck is the point?"

When no answer was forthcoming, Tony reached into his pocket and pulled his only twoonie out of a handful of change. Two bucks seemed a small price to pay if this worked.

It didn't.

The tossed coin went through the Demonlord as if he wasn't there, hit the ground behind him, and rolled for a couple of meters before toppling over to wobble into stillness.

"Heads or tails?"

No answer to that either.

"Yeah, well, from what Leah says, you'd prefer tails, wouldn't you?"

He was a big guy; powerful looking with great muscle definition and enormous hands. Tony wasn't much for gym queens, but these muscles had a purpose and that made all the difference. It looked like he could rip the heads off small animals and what was more, looked like he'd do it, too, if the mood struck him. Although thick dreads covered the base of the antlers, the curved horns didn't look glued on. They looked like weapons.

He was proportional.

Oh, come on, it's hanging out there. I'm supposed to not look at it?

Fortunately, the whole rip-the-heads-off-small-animals observation was putting a damper on his completely understandable reaction.

Or not.

The inside of his right arm was suddenly very warm. Lines of warmth trailing over the skin applied with the perfect amount of pressure. It felt really good. Had he not been stuck in a dream with a frustrated Demonlord, it would have felt like foreplay.

He closed his eyes for a moment, and when he opened them again, he had an instant's flash of Ryne Cyratane's face, onyx eyes actually focused on him; then the onyx turned to jade and the Demonlord became Lee kneeling beside the chaise, one hand wrapped around his upper arm, fingers rubbing the soft skin on the inside just under the edge of his T-shirt.

Dream, then.

Hell, maybe dream *now*. He'd had this dream before, he realized as his brain took the opportunity to repeat, *felt like foreplay* half a dozen times.

"Hey."

Tony thought about pretending to still be asleep because it felt so good to have Lee touching him. Sure, it was kind of taking advantage, but he'd had a rough day and he knew that the moment he showed any awareness Lee was back in the happy hetero land of denial. Why shouldn't he take a moment's advantage? Because, unfortunately, he was one of the good guys.

So he blinked and focused and said "Hey" back.

Weird. Lee kept up the caress. Not that it was a big deal or anything, but it was definitely a caress.

Maybe Lee didn't realize he was awake. So he added, "What time is it?"

"Almost three." Although the fingers quit moving, the hand stayed where it was, and since Lee was smiling right into his face, it seemed like he knew who he was holding.

Hang on. If it was almost three, then he'd only been asleep for about an hour and what the hell was Lee doing at the soundstage when he'd been told to stay out of danger?

"Friday afternoon," Lee added, smile broadening.

Had he said any of that out loud? Or was he really so easy to re—"It's when!"

Lee's grip on his arm kept him pinned to the chaise. "Leah says you can't do the 'with one bound he was up and away.' She says you'll fall over."

His brain kept repeating, *Friday afternoon!* but he managed to catch the last two words. "Fall over?"

"Seems like your busy day turned into a busy night," Lee explained, fingers tracing tiny circles. "Leah said you needed to recover, so we've been keeping an eye on you."

Tiny circles. Warm fingers. *Focus, damn it!* "We?"

"Me, mostly." He shrugged. "I finished up just before we broke for lunch and I was going to head home, but Jack said that as long as Leah was tied up in translations, I might as well make myself useful."

"Jack?"

"Sound asleep in CB's office with his jacket over his face."

Tony ran down the list in his head. "CB?"

"Has a meeting with his insurance people." Lee glanced at the pile of broken lumber that had been part of the set on Thursday morning. "Can't think why."

"Zev?"

"I assume he's at his board." The tiny circles stopped as dark brows drew in. "You know, it's interesting, I seem to be the only person who knows about this who wasn't here last night."

"You'd be surprised at what people who think they know don't know."

"Pardon?"

Yeah, Tony wasn't sure he understood that either. "Amy wasn't here."

"Apparently, Amy was a part of the road show." He sighed and the frown morphed from annoyance to frustration. "I just don't seem to be getting through to you. I am over what happened last summer . . ."

Then why all the touchy-feely now? Oh. Right. Over being possessed.

". . . and I don't want you to protect me. I don't need you to protect me. In case it's escaped your notice, I'm a fair bit bigger than you."

"Whip it out and prove it," Tony muttered. "Size isn't the point," he added quickly. "When you're . . ." No. "I don't . . ." Uh-uh. "This is . . ." Nope. Probably shouldn't go there either. He closed his eyes and sighed. *When you're involved, I think about you. Not about saving the world or whatever part of it's in danger this month. You. I don't think I can handle seeing you in danger again. This is hard enough without all that extra emotional baggage.* How hard could it be to say that out loud? When he opened his eyes, Lee was watching him. Still holding his arm. Waiting.

Stupid question.

It was fucking impossible to say all that out loud.

Lee's turn to sigh. "Asshole. Come on, sit up slowly. I've got you."

The world made a few interesting adjustments as, with Lee's help, he dropped his feet to the floor and managed to get at least partially vertical. The soundstage slipped sideways for a moment and, true to his word, Lee was right there, his arm around Tony's shoulders. Waking up was turning out to be even more surreal than his dream. Although one thing hadn't changed.

"I stink."

"You do. Think you can make it to a shower?" He pulled away a little, half turned to face the far side of the soundstage. "Props might still have that wheelchair. I don't think we completely destroyed it."

"We set it on fire, pushed it down the ramp at a parking garage, and it slammed into a concrete block wall."

"Still . . ."

"No." Deep breath and a surge upright. "I'm fine. I'm just a little stiff."

"Whip it out and prove it." Almost under his breath. Almost not loud enough to hear except that his mouth was close enough to the side of Tony's head for the words to brush against his ear.

If he wasn't before, he was now.

He didn't close his eyes, although he wanted to. He wished he knew what Lee was thinking. What Lee'd *been* thinking when he'd been sitting and stroking and waiting for Tony to wake up. Conscious of every point of contact, he said, "Stop screwing around, Lee. Unless you're ready to cross the line, it's not fair."

The other man flushed and suddenly there were half as many points of contact. "Can't a guy help a friend who's been fried?" he asked, his mouth twisting into an approximation of a smile.

Were they friends? They'd been friendly although they'd never been the "go out for a beer together" kind of friends. Made sense. Beer and subtext was a bad combination. For the sake of getting where he was going, he supposed he could fake friend if that was how Lee wanted to play it.

"Sure. Speaking as the friend who got fried, I'm glad for the help."

As they shuffled across the soundstage, Tony nodded toward the back wall of Raymond Dark's office. A couple of grips were opening the trap and wrestling the camera through the space where the imitation Turner had been. "What's up?"

Fortunately, Lee'd had enough of innuendo. "Mason's doing the existential moment that leads us to the final episode and all those frigging flashbacks." He wasn't in the flashbacks, which cut his time in the final episode to the teaser and the tag. There'd already been discussions about an extra feature on the DVD to make up for it. "Mason and existential," he snorted. "Those are two words I never thought I'd put together."

"Does Mason even know what *existential* means?"

"It means it's about Mason. He's happy with that. He's an uncomplicated guy, our Mason."

Uncomplicated would be nice. Tony leaned against a Gothic revival pillar as Lee reached for the door. *It'd be a nice fucking change.*

Before Lee's fingers closed around the doorknob, it moved. They shuffled back as the door opened, shuffled back a bit farther as Adam came into the soundstage carrying a huge sheet of white foam board.

"So, how's the fallen warrior?" he asked, peering around it at them.

Wizard. But it seemed pointless to protest. "I'm fine," Tony told him and when Adam snorted, expanded it to, "A little unsteady."

The 1AD craned his head until he could get a line of sight on Lee. "Don't drop him," he told the actor as if he was saying, *Don't miss your mark.* "We've got one more episode to shoot and I'd like to have a roof to do it under." Without waiting for a response, he adjusted his grip and walked away muttering, "Demons want to invade, they can bloody well time it for hiatus like everyone else."

"He knows . . ."

"CB did a little explaining when the crew arrived this morning."

"I don't think . . ."

"CB thought," Lee interrupted again, "that the known isn't half as likely to be gossiped about as the unknown. Also, given what some of us have already been through, we deserved better than bullshit."

"That explains it," Tony muttered, as they proved that it wasn't entirely impossible for two people to get through the costumes that lined the hall outside the soundstage. Best to just ignore the implication that CB had given Lee permission to be involved in the fight.

"What does?"

"Your sudden attention. We're fighting a kind of a war here, so it's a two guys in the trenches thing."

"That sounds vaguely pornographic."

"I meant like in episode fifteen."

"That *was* vaguely pornographic. Mason's fan mail jumped seventeen percent after the World War I episode." Maneuvering around the gorilla suits pressed Lee's body tight against his.

Safest to blame the gorillas. It'd keep him from punching Lee in the face. "You know what I mean. Helping a fallen comrade is very butch. Very safe."

One rack of costumes ended at the door to the women's washroom, opening up enough room for them to stand side by side—face-to-face with a little distance between them. Albeit a very little distance. Tony wanted to mutter, *Take a picture, it'll last longer,* except that would be childish and there was nothing even remotely childlike about the look on Lee's face. For a long moment, he was convinced that Lee was going to kiss him. Right there. Right in front of the women's washroom and the tattered sign about no fucking when the red light was on.

Then the moment passed.

Lee nodded toward the dressing rooms, still half a dozen meters down the hall. "Come on, you need to get cleaned up."

Maybe it came from facing demons. Maybe he was light-headed from hunger. "Chicken."

"Fuck off."

Lee really sounded pissed, but to Tony's surprise, he didn't let go—although his grip on Tony's upper arm tightened until his fingers were digging into flesh. They walked in silence to the door of his dressing room where Tony balked.

"I'm using your shower?"

"You'd rather have Mason walk in on you?"

He was a heartbeat away from saying what he'd rather have. He said nothing as Lee opened the door. Nothing as he walked inside. Nothing as Lee released his arm, stepped back, and asked, "You going to be okay?"

"I'll be fine."

Well, that was something but not exactly relevant.

He said nothing as Lee tossed him a towel. Said nothing as Lee left.

As he dropped to the end of the couch and bent to fight with his shoes, he muttered, "Who's chicken now?"

At least if they were *both* chickens that was sort of a species step in the right direction. Or possibly he'd moved beyond light-headed to completely fucking insane.

Amy was setting a tray of food on the battered coffee table as he stepped out of the tiny en suite, the towel wrapped around his waist. There was no sign of Lee.

And the repressed gay interlude seems to be over; back to business as usual.

"Just so you know, I'm not accepting a supporting role." Amy stuck a fork upright in the lasagna. "I lied my ass off to the cops last night," she continued, straightening, "and I demand a spot in the front . . . Whoa, Tony, those are some interesting scars."

It took him a moment to realize she meant the crosshatching on his left pec. Most people who saw him with his shirt off didn't mention them.

"Who did this to you?" Henry'd traced cool circles over the damaged skin.

"If I tell you, what'll you do?"

His smile had been like a knife in the dark. "Make them pay."

So Tony'd told him. Hell, he was eighteen. Revenge had seemed like a good idea. He still didn't regret it.

Zev had said nothing, merely acknowledged the evidence of old pain with a gentleness that had broken Tony apart. And then acknowledged that by putting him back together again more gently still. *I so didn't deserve him.*

"Are they tribal markings?" Amy asked as he rummaged a shirt out of the garbage bag of his clean laundry.

"Sort of." They were what happened to those who got caught on the wrong turf.

"Cool."

Not really, no. But Amy was looking at darkness from the outside where it was a lot safer and practically branded. "What the hell are you wearing?"

She pulled the front of her T-shirt out far enough to be able to look down at the picture of a nearly skeletal man climbing out of the bisected body of a rotting bear. "New movie shooting in the park. I scammed it off one of the publicity guys. Werebear!"

"Where castle?" He shimmied jeans up under the towel and let it drop.

"What?"

"Are you kidding me?" When she continued to look blank, he shook his head and dropped down onto the couch. "No one cares about the classics these days."

"Yeah, yeah, tell it to your next boyfriend. And speaking of, that cutie cop wants to see you on the soundstage when you've eaten; he's taken your spot on the chaise. Lee says you can leave your clothes in here as long as you need to. Zev says try not to get killed before tomorrow sunset because he'd like to say good-bye. Adam wants to know why you can't work since you're in the building anyway. And I'd be kind of pissed about taking messages for you except I'm sucking up in the hope you'll take me demon hunting."

He muttered a negative around a mouthful of lasagna.

"I can get my hands on some holy water."

"Wrong kind of demons."

"There's a right kind of demon?"

"Damned if I know." He smiled up at her.

"Ew. Mouth closed while eating, pig person." Wiggling her fingers at him in what may have been a sign against the evil eye although it looked more like she was trying to flick a booger free, Amy backed out the door. "Don't forget the cop on the chaise," she warned as she closed it behind her.

Sometimes, Tony acknowledged, stuffing another forkload of pasta and cheese into his mouth and this time chewing with his mouth closed, the tricks a guy learned grossing out girls at twelve ended up helping him out for the rest of his life.

*   *   *

"Your friend Fitzroy doesn't answer his phone."

Tony shrugged in Jack's general direction. It had been Henry last night. Now it was Fitzroy again. At least he hadn't shortened it to Fitz—Henry reacted badly to diminutives. "He's probably on deadline."

"Oh, yeah. Romance writer." Reclining on the chaise, fingers laced over his stomach, wearing the pale blue dress shirt with the handprint scorched onto it that Mason had worn in episode five, Jack crossed his legs at the ankles. "I don't know many romance writers who can do what he did last night."

"How many romance writers do you know? And how many of *them* have you seen deal with a demon?"

"Good point. Points."

He crossed to the chaise, fighting the urge to look up at the gate as he passed under it. Technically, he fought the urge to look up into the lighting grid at the place the gate would be if it was still opening, but that was more complicated than he was up to right now. "Amy said you wanted to see me?" His attempt at not sounding defensive failed miserably.

Jack grinned. "Thought you'd like to know what you missed after you went all Sleeping Beauty on us last night and before Prince Charming showed up this afternoon."

"Who?" So much for defensive—now, he was just trying not to sound confused.

"Leah sent that actor guy you're so hot for in to watch over you." The grin broadened in a decidedly shit-disturbing manner. "I suggested he wake you with a kiss. How'd that go? I'm curious," he added as Tony opened and closed his mouth a couple of times, "because he looked like he was considering it. Good-looking guy if I was interested in guys, which I'm not."

"Neither is he."

"Bullshit. I pointed out that the place is being overrun by demons and we could all be dead tomorrow, so he should take the chance."

"He's st . . ." Tony couldn't get the word out. Apparently his subconscious would only allow hypocrisy to take him so far. "He's not interested."

"The hell he isn't. I'm a trained observer . . ." Jack unlaced his fingers and thumped himself on the chest. ". . . your tax dollars at work. The girls are either camouflage or he's willing to switch hit."

"Spare me the lame sports analogy, Dr. Ruth."

"Shut up, I'm not done. He's decided he wants you, but he's too fucking freaked to take that final step. Can't say as I blame him, him being in the public eye and all." A thoughtful frown. "Or he would be if anyone actually watched this dumbass show."

"Hey! We've got the highest numbers of any vampire detective show in syndication."

"That and a buck seventeen will buy you a bad cup of coffee." Swinging his feet to the floor, Jack sat up. "So, the story thus far: Your reporter buddy Groves showed up with that page of his. Your romance writer buddy Fitzroy went home and got the rest of the book. Your very hot stuntwoman buddy Leah knows how to read the book, and she's working on the translation. Basically, we're all waiting to find out what the hell is going on. Oh, and your freak buddy, Amy, kind of grows on you. Is she seeing anyone?"

"Not right now." He dropped onto the end of the chaise. "And forget it."

Jack made a noise Tony couldn't identify—although he was pretty sure it wasn't agreement—and said, "So, who's Arra?"

"Arra?" He needed to find out how much Jack knew, then he could craft the lie. "How do you know about Arra?"

"You mentioned her last night."

Crap.

"We were talking about the rope, the unnatural rope, and you said it was weird that Arra'd know it would work since she'd never faced demons here in this world. Then Leah said that if you'd never met her, you wouldn't be fighting demons today."

"You remember all that?"

"It's part of my job to remember the details."

That wasn't the part of his job Tony had trouble with. It was more the parts that involved the government and arresting people. And sure he'd been willing to falsify reports and get involved on his own time, but how long before the weird built up past the point he could justify not mentioning it. Justify not bringing out the big guns to try and stop it? And would that even be a problem? People had died? Tony stared at the toes of his Doc Martens. They were in the midst of a Demonic Convergence; odds were good that more people would die.

"You want me to take a guess?" Jack leaned forward, forearms balanced on his thighs. "I'm guessing she was the wizard who fingered you as a wizard and that she was from another world, like the demons are. I figure this happened back last spring when I got fed a bullshit line about what happened to Charlie Harris and Rahal Singh."

He didn't need to be reminded of their names.

"I figure she either died then, too, or went home since she wasn't around this summer while you were talking to the dead and she isn't around now."

Tony opened his mouth and closed it again when Jack kept talking.

"At first I thought you may have made some kind of mistake when this Arra was starting you out as a wizard and that's how those two men died—and that's what you've been hiding from me."

He could feel Jack's gaze on the side of his face. He didn't turn. "It's not."

"I know. Leah said something else last night."

"Um . . . take me? Take me, I'm yours?" A weak attempt to lighten the mood but pretty much a gimme.

"She said that heroes rise when we need them."

That forced the turn. "You think I'm a hero?"

Jack shrugged. "I did a background check on you," he said matter-of-factly. "I know what battles you've already won."

"Holy after-school special, Batman," Tony muttered, cheeks flushed. He hadn't won any battles; he'd done what he'd had to in order to survive.

"So what happened last spring?" Still matter-of-fact.

Why not. "Arra and I fought off a guy called the Shadowlord invading from her world. After we won, she went home." Cole's Notes version.

"The Shadowlord was responsible for the deaths?"

"Yeah."

"What happened to him?"

"He got eaten by the light."

"Is that some kind of wizard metaphor?"

"Not really."

"Here?" His gesture took in the immediate area.

"Yeah."

"Good." Jack nodded. "Good," he said again, sounding more satisfied the second time, as though he'd taken that moment to consider things and now was able to let it go.

They sat silently for a moment, Jack staring down into his loosely clasped hands. Voices across the soundstage sounded like they were coming from another world. Tony glanced up into the lighting grid and then back down at his shoes. "An old friend of mine says there's too often a difference between law and justice."

"Would that old friend be Detective-Sergeant Mike Celluci?"

"Christ, no!"

Fortunately, any discussion that might bring up Vicki Nelson was cut off by the bell and calls of "Rolling!" from the permanent sets. It sounded like they were shooting by Mason's coffin—far enough away for quiet conversation but just as well Jack didn't know that. Tony did not want to talk about Vicki Nelson with Jack.

Talking about Vicki would only lead to more lying and basking in the warm glow of even a truncated confession. Tony didn't feel like lying. With any luck, the feeling wouldn't last, but for the moment he decided to go with it.

"Cut! Reset! We'll go again from the top."

They heard the door open almost immediately after the light went out.

"Must be nice," Constable Danvers muttered, stopping at the foot of the chaise, arms folded over her damp, brown corduroy jacket. "Sitting around, head up your butt, not actually accomplishing anything."

"We had a demon last night," Jack protested.

"Yeah? I had a six-year-old who disassembled the DVD player, an eight-year-old who wants a tattoo, and dog vomit all over the living room rug. Trade you."

When she motioned for Tony to move over, he stood. "I'll get a chair." No way he was sitting between two cops. That brought back bad memories.

". . . good news is, no bodies," she was saying as he returned. "No body parts either. We had Sammy Kline making his biweekly call about lights in the sky and, this time, he might actually be onto something since there was a slightly more credible report about a flash of light across the Arm from the airport." She turned the page of her occurrence book and squinted at her notes. "Pilot saw it when he was circling for his final approach and thought it might be an explosion. Richmond detachment sent a car over, and it turned out to be some kind of gas leak and blow in a Goth coffee shop. Goth coffee shop," she repeated with a snort. "That almost qualifies as weird shit on its own."

"A demon knocked the door down." Tony told her. He hid a grin as her head jerked up. "That flash by the airport was the weak spot opening."

Her eyes narrowed and suddenly he didn't feel much like grinning. "Weak spot?" she demanded.

"Between here and the hells."

"You were there?"

He shrugged. "I was trying to cut it off at the pass."

"Great." She smiled insincerely, the expression barely reaching her mouth, let alone her eyes. "You're a cowboy now. So there was a demon at a Goth coffee shop? They must've been thrilled."

"Not really. Not all of them," he amended, remembering Amy.

"You'd think that the sort of people who'd drink at a Goth coffee shop . . . What?" she demanded as Jack growled something under his breath. "I just like saying it. We, where *we* refers to the police in general as opposed to our detachment in particular, also received a number of calls about vandalized satellite dishes, a couple of downed power lines, a destroyed pigeon coop, and, not far from here, a balcony railing ripped right off the twelfth floor. No one saw anything, though."

"It took the high ground between the coffee shop and here," Tony realized. "That's why there were no casualties."

"Not a lot of healthy pigeons left in that coop," Constable Danvers pointed out dryly. "And when you say *it*, you're talking demon, right?"

"Right. They move really fast."

"No shit."

"Can you check for more flashes?"

She shook her head. "There was only the one reported last night."

"Not just from last night," Jack broke in. "Go back at least a week," he told his partner, then turned to Tony. "You want to compare the flashes to the demons you dusted, get a count, and find out if there's any still hanging around."

"It'll get us the timing, too. Unless the intervals are completely random, we'll know when to expect the next one."

"You're smarter than you look."

"I hate to put a damper on the mutual congratulations." Danvers sighed. "But last night's report was a fluke. Pilot just happened to be passing over at the right time. No one else called it in."

"There's not much around there." It was on the edge of an industrial park, as far as Tony could remember and, that close to the airport, what locals there were would be used to blocking out lights and sound. The guests at the hotel down the street wouldn't know what passed for normal in that part of Vancouver and the staff would be too busy to care. "If a weak spot opened where there were more people, someone probably called the cops."

Looking thoughtful, she snapped the occurrence book closed, slid it into an inside pocket, and pulled out her PDA. "Worth a try, I suppose. I can access the electronic files from here."

"Not from here, you can't. You can't get an uplink any closer than the other side of the road," he explained in answer to the questioning curl of her lip, impressed by the amount of information she could convey in a sneer.

"Fine." She stood. "I'll check and then I'm gone. Some of us can't waste precious sick days saving the world. Oh, hell, I'm going to have to come back, aren't I? I can't just call you with the info."

"Let's settle down, people!" Adam's voice, rising from around Raymond Dark's coffin, dampened the ambient noise. "Quiet on the set!"

Tony glanced over toward the door. The light was still off. "You won't get to come back if you don't go away."

"You can talk after he says quiet?"

"Yeah, but you can't leave after the red light goes on."

She took two steps toward the door and half turned, one hand rising to touch the loose knot of hair at the back of her neck. "Lee Nicholas?"

"Is in Chester Bane's office with the demonic consultant," Jack told her. "I thought you didn't have time to hang around and save the world."

"I may need to ask him a couple of questions about that deranged fan." She flashed him a "two can play at this game" look and ran for the door.

"Lee's with Leah?" Tony asked when no one yelled *rolling*. He was aiming for nonchalant. He suspected he missed.

"That's where I left him. I took over out here, remember?" Leaning on the curve of the chaise, Jack raised an eyebrow. "You think he's in there shoring up his increasingly dubious heterosexuality?" He snickered as Tony shrugged, once again missing nonchalant. "Yeah, it's all right there on your face. Except the increasingly dubious bit. I added that myself."

"So what's with the lights in the sky?"

Jack straightened, allowing the subject to be changed. "Sammy Kline's a janitor out at SFU. Every payday he goes on a bender and reports lights in the sky." Pale brows drew in. "Any chance he could be right?"

Another shrug. "Beats me. I don't do aliens."

"I can't work like this!" Mason's protest cut off whatever smart-ass response Jack was about to make. When he wanted to get his point across, the star of *Darkest Night* fell back on skills he'd learned doing summer theater unmiked in leaky tents situated by a major highway that was uphill—both ways—from his drafty and unheated garret room. No one had suffered for their art like Mason. "Look! Right there! There is a cherry in my coffin!"

"Mason . . ." Peter's voice faded just below where they could hear it.

Mason and a cherry; that was just too easy. Even across the soundstage, Tony could hear the snickers.

"I called quiet, people!" Adam had been around the business too long to allow any amusement to show in his voice. "Settle down! And rolling!"

"Rolling," Tony repeated softly.

"Mark!"

They couldn't hear the scene called, but they heard the clapper.

"Action!"

"Action . . ." He wanted to be by the camera watching Mason overact, the only demons on the set the metaphorical demons in Raymond Dark's past. He wanted bad coffee and long hours and he very much didn't want to be tucked off to one side while he dealt with the weirdness du jour. He wanted his life back. There had to be a way he could deal with this shit instead of just reacting to it. Leah's original idea of preventing the demons from crossing over was a good one, but finding them by driving around the lower mainland was stupid and inefficient.

He had to stop thinking like a TAD and start thinking like a wizard if he ever wanted a chance to be a TAD again.

Yeah. That's it. Aim high.

"So this is the infamous game of spider solitaire."

"Infamous?" Tony smacked Jack's hand away from the keyboard and winced as it returned to impact against the back of his head.

"The game that masks the wonders of wizardry."

Tony shot him a sideways look as he scrolled down the index. "You've been talking to Amy."

"No law against it." He winked over the cardboard lip of his coffee cup. "And like I said, she's cute."

"She's not your type."

"You don't know that."

"You're not her type. You're way too normal."

A pale brow arced up. "I took a sick day to hunt demons."

"Maybe *normal* isn't the right word." Tony paused and frowned at the screen. "Here it is. Finding."

"What? Nemo?"

Tony double-clicked the icon. "There're a few files in here. Finding Living Creatures . . ."

"The demons are living."

"Yeah, but we're not trying to find demons, we're trying to find where demons will be."

"Time travel?"

"Not allowed."

Jack finished his coffee and crushed the cup. "Too bad."

"Finding Inanimate Objects."

"I've lost my TV remote."

"It's in the sofa cushions."

"I am in awe of your power. Nothing on finding your way to hell?"

"Wrong reference material." Tony grinned as Jack snorted. "Here it is. Finding a Power Source."

"You need to be plugged in?"

"I don't think so." He scanned the instructions. "I need a map."

"I've got one in my truck."

The wardrobe department needed more space. Which was pretty much true of every department but finance; they had plenty of space but needed more money. Wardrobe made it obvious with a leaning tower of shoe boxes, shelves six deep in hats, and bolts of fabric piled by color and weight. Since most of the fabric had been bought as remainders, some of the colors were a little frightening. A huge chart delineating what costumes were needed and when covered one wall. Sketches had been pinned up to every nonmoving surface as well as a couple of surfaces that weren't moving now but would be later. The actual clothing hung out in the hall.

When Tony came in with Jack's map, he found Alison Larkin on her knees in front of the thinnest of the staff writers, adjusting the length of an apron over a full peasant skirt. Dana, her most recent assistant, sat bent over one of the three sewing machines.

"I need to iron a map."

"We're busy," Alison snapped without looking up.

"I don't need *you* to iron it," Tony amended, wondering if she'd ever swallowed a pin. "I need to iron it."

"Why? Never mind. Don't touch that dirndl on the ironing board! Toss the sheet of white felt down on the cutting table and do it there. And Roger . . ." She slapped a hairy calf. ". . . stop fucking moving, or I'll stick you on purpose. We've got another eight of these to get through."

Be sure the map is free of creases.

Ironing the map, not a problem. Not much of a problem anyway. Getting it back to the soundstage without folding it was a little trickier. Tony shuffled sideways through the costumes, arms outstretched, swearing softly under his breath and wondering why they had half a rack of silver lamé jumpsuits.

The door out into the production office opened as he passed and only a last-second, desperate lunge to the right kept Leah—and Lee right behind her—from slamming new creases into his map.

"Tony! Good news!"

He continued shuffling toward the soundstage. "I could use some."

"It's possible that because of the way the energy is being used this Demonic Convergence won't go on as long as it has in the past."

"According to?"

"According to the book that your friend Henry provided last night." Following close behind, she waved it in his general direction.

Tony peered at it over the upper edge of the map. It didn't look much like a book. It looked more like a lot of loose, yellowing pages crammed inside a worn, brown leather cover.

"While you were sleeping," she continued, "I was working on a translation."

With first Jack and then Lee in the office with her, Tony doubted that was all she'd been doing. A glance past her at Lee showed the actor was looking a little ruffled. And wizards saw what was there, didn't they? Hey, more power to him. Tony was all in favor of everybody getting some. A happy Demonlord was a . . . well, he was a happy Demonlord, that's what he was, and a happy Demonlord was less likely to send over demons to slaughter his favorite handmaiden. *More's the pity.*

"Are you grinding your teeth?"

"No." He stepped over a pair of old steel-toed work boots painted in patterns that might look like urban camouflage on a thirteen-inch TV. In HDTV, not so much.

"Ryne Cyratane is using the energy up."

That was enough to stop him. The ironed paper rustled. "What?"

"The Demonic Convergence produces a limited amount of energy. Usually, it's spread out more and the world is dealing with small shit for months. One or two demons show up near the end."

"Because the energy burns through the hells like acid rain," Lee expanded. "As time passes, stronger drops burn right through the upper layers and end in deeper, nastier places." From his tone, he'd been the one to come up with that bit of description.

Before or after the two of them tested the strength of CB's coffee table? They wouldn't have used the couch, or the floor, or the desk . . . it had to have been the coffee table. *Why am I thinking about this?* he asked himself as he started moving toward the soundstage again—which meant moving away from Leah and Lee. Giving them room. They, of course, followed. *So much for symbolism.*

And hang on . . .

Another look at Lee. "She told you?"

The actor nodded. "End of the world as we know it."

Was he blushing? The light in the hall was so bad Tony couldn't tell. Not that it was any of his damned business. "So all this means the Demonic Convergence is going to end . . . when?"

"Sooner. We're not talking months; a month maybe. Maybe not even that if he keeps up this pace. Which raises the question, why is he going to all this effort? If demons always show up at the end of the Convergence—which, according to this . . ." The book was waved for emphasis. ". . . they always do."

"Always?" Tony interrupted.

"According to this book."

"Didn't you tell me they *sometimes* show up at the end of the Convergence?"

"That was before I had a first-person account to read. And they happen more often than I thought, too." She smiled. It was a remarkably sarcastic expression. "So now I've proved I'm not infallible, can we move on?"

He shrugged, careful not to crinkle the map.

"Ryne Cyratane is not big on . . ." Dark brows drew in. "Why are you carrying a map of the lower mainland and why you are carrying it like such a spaz?"

"It's for a spell."

"Oh. All right, then."

He managed to hold back a bitchy *Glad you approve* long enough for Leah to continue talking.

"Ryne Cyratane," she repeated, "is not big on personal effort. It would be more like him to wait and use whatever was going to get through at the end regardless. This is bigger than we thought. He's really motivated."

"Why?"

"How the hell should I know?"

"Okay." Good to know the time frame had been shortened—a half season of Convergence instead of the full twenty-two episodes—but from where Tony stood, that didn't make a lot of difference. He flattened against the soundstage's outer wall to give them room to get past. "Can one of you get the soundstage d . . ."

The soundstage door opened.

". . . never mind."

"Hello, pretty lady!" Framed in the doorway, Mason smiled unctuously down at Leah. "If you're here to watch me tape, we're done for the day, but I'd be happy to make the trip worth your while and sign a few photos. I have some in my dressing room . . ."

"She's not a fan, Mason," Tony interrupted before Leah took him up on it. Not the signed photos but the other nonverbalized offer. "She's a stuntwoman here to talk to Peter about the last episode."

"Ah." Red-gold brows drew in as he visibly retreated back out of sexual harassment territory. Fans wanted his attention. Coworkers weren't fans. "Am I throwing you off the windmill?"

"Very likely."

Gray eyes gleamed. "I'm sure I'll enjoy having you in my arms."

Ryne Cyratane flickered as she smiled up at Mason. "You have no idea."

"Leah! The *stunt!*"

"What st . . . oh. Right." She reluctantly dialed it back and the Demonlord disappeared. "It was nice meeting you, Mr. Reed." Dimples flashed. "My mother loved you in *StreetCred!*"

Tony winced as Mason deflated. This was the first he'd ever seen Leah turn off a guy's interest as fast as she turned it on. *Nothing like a reminder you used to be a network cop and now you're a syndicated vampire,* he mused as Mason stepped into the hall and squeezed past his costar. With the soundstage open before him, he could move a little faster.

Too fast to catch just what Mason muttered to Lee that Lee denied so vehemently. Given the salacious tone to the muttering, and the source, it wasn't hard to fill in the blanks.

"I hear stuntwomen are very athletic and flexible." Wink. Wink. Nudge. Nudge.

"I would never take advantage of a coworker, you cad!"

Great. His brain seemed to be lifting dialogue from Henry's books.

"What's the spell?" Leah demanded, catching up.

Tony listened to be sure Lee's footsteps were following behind them. "I'm going to search for the power signatures of the weak spots. The spell should tell us not only where they are but how close they are to opening, so we'll know which ones to close first. It's possible . . ." Not very likely, he admitted silently to himself, but possible. ". . . that it'll also map out where the next few weak spots are going to be."

"Predictive magic? Wow. You worked that out yourself?"

"Thanks for sounding so surprised."

"No." Hand against her heart. "I'm impressed. You're taking charge."

Hey, he was a hero. "Yeah, I am."

As they crossed to the chaise, Sorge left Jack's side with a wave and instructions to have a good weekend.

"What were you two talking about?" Leah demanded as Tony carefully laid the map on the floor.

Jack snorted. "I have no idea."

Somehow, staring down at the map lying flat made Tony intensely aware of how thin most people's versions of reality were. Most people believed that this was all there was. He kind of missed believing that. Dropping to his knees, he bent carefully and began to breathe on the paper.

Leah broke off explaining demonic acid rain to Jack to ask him what he was doing.

"The instructions say that the map must know the wizard. This was the least gross option." He finished up by panting at Richmond and stood. "Jack, could you . . ." His open laptop appeared at the edge of his peripheral vision. "Thanks. Now everyone step back. I need to circle the map three times."

"Shouldn't you be naked? What?" Leah protested as he turned. "So nothing would happen; I still like to look."

Jack waved a hand. "Pass on the naked: public indecency. I'd be forced to use the cuffs."

"Don't worry about the naked," Tony snorted. "I'll just be reading some words out loud while I walk. Long, complicated words so, once I start, no interruptions."

"You don't go through this when you call things to you," Lee reminded him. "You just reach for things and they're there."

He'd reached for Lee once.

"That's a good point." Jack nodded an acknowledgment at the actor. "What makes this different?"

"Do you play an instrument?" Tony asked him, grateful for the redirect.

"Yeah."

"What?"

The RCMP Constable glanced over at Leah and Lee and dragged a hand back through his hair, fingering it up into pale spikes. "Accordion."

Much mutual blinkage.

"Okay," Tony said quickly before Leah found her voice. "You know how, when you were learning, you had to think about everything you were doing—right hand, left hand, bellows, melody, words, rhythm, and mostly, you had to wonder why you didn't learn a cool instrument? And then, after a shitload of practice, a song clicks and you could just play without thinking about the bits? Come to Me is like that. It clicked. Other spells, I'm still figuring out as I go."

Since that was as good a cue as any, he started his first circle. The words were not only long and complicated, but there were a shitload of them and he barely managed to get them all in. Third circle complete and the last few words crammed in tongue twister fast, he knelt by the edge of the map, breathed on his fingertips, and pressed them down on the edge of the ironed paper.

"What are you . . . ?"

"Shhh." Leah. Who'd worked with wizards before.

He concentrated. Nothing happened. He could feel the map waiting. Could feel the information he needed just beyond his fingertips. He concentrated harder, focusing power. He could do this. He *had* to do this. *This is what I'm* supposed *to do.* Wait. Not do. He didn't do wizardry. He *was* a wizard. Something shifted and blue light spread out from his fingers, pouring like water across the map. Then, suddenly a flare. And another.

And a burst of light.

Coughing and waving away streamers of smoke, Tony looked down at the light dusting of ash on the concrete floor. "I think I'm going to need another map."

The four of them stared down at the pattern of little burns on the second map. Bad news, there were a lot of them. Maybe he was pissed about losing so many demons, but Ryne Cyratane was definitely motivated. Good news, most of the burns were very faint. Only three were significantly darker than the rest.

"What's it mean?" Lee asked, arms folded.

"If it worked . . ." Tony rocked back off his knees, picked up the map and stood. ". . . it means there's a lot of weak spots building at the same rate, and when they break through . . ."

"Wall-to-wall demons," Jack finished grimly.

Leah shook her head. "That can't be right. Henry's book said the Convergence had a limited amount of energy."

"Atomic bombs have a limited amount of energy," Jack snorted. "You need to define *limited*."

"We know for sure that Ryne Cyratane wants you dead and his gate open," Tony reminded her over the upper edge of the map. "I'm guessing he's working the convergent energy to create a lot of weak spots, so he can send through a whole bunch of demons at once, figuring at least one will get through me to you."

"And these darker ones?" Lee tapped the back of the map where the darker burns showed through.

"Best guess: they're distractions. I figure these guys won't be after you, they'll be free agents. If even one gets through, it'll start rampaging through the lower mainland and keep me too busy to close the multiple weak points before they open."

Arms folded, Leah sighed heavily. "That's one complicated assumption there, Tony."

"He's smarter than he looks." Jack gently pushed the top edge of the map down and stared at Tony. "Now, let's fill in the blanks. Who is Ryne Cyratane?"

"He's a Demonlord."

"Tony!"

Whoa. If looks could kill. "Jack's involved in this, Leah. He has a right to know." Still holding the map, he jerked his chin toward the actor. "You told Lee, and he's less involved."

"Whose fault is that?" Lee muttered.

"You're a civilian," Jack snapped. "Tony had every right to try and keep you safe."

Lee took a step forward, chin up. "He's a civilian!"

"He's a wizard!"

"He has no secrets," Tony sighed. "Leah?" He didn't need her permission, but he didn't want a fight either.

She dropped to the end of the chaise and crossed her legs. "Fine. Whatever."

"Ryne Cyratane's a Demonlord who used Leah as a part of a gate spell more than three thousand years ago and, if he kills her, he gets to come back."

Jack turned toward the chaise. "You're three thousand years old?"

Her turn to sigh. "More or less."

"You look great!"

The dimples made a brief appearance. "Thank you."

"If he kills you, he gets to come back?"

She spread her hands. "The gate opens."

"I'm guessing it's going to take more than a yellow rope to hold this guy?"

Tony shrugged. "From what I've seen, it depends on what part you're holding."

⤳ ELEVEN

"All right, this is what we're going to do." They'd moved across the soundstage to Adam's office—three wooden stacking tables arranged in an L shape, a home for unavoidable union forms, the battery chargers, and a decapitated head from episode three that the 1AD had grown inexplicably fond of. Tony carefully moved a stack of ACTRA forms and spread out the map. "These three spots . . ." He tapped the darker burns. ". . . have to be closed fast, so I can get as many of the rest shut before the shit hits the fan. The Demonlord knows there's a wizard on this side, but he doesn't know about you lot and he doesn't know that the residue in the studio is drawing his demons. Those two things might give us an edge."

He glanced around at the world's best chance to remain demon free. CB and Amy, Lee, Jack, and Leah. And Leah was pulling double duty as probable cause. They were watching him like he knew what he was doing, and he could only hope they weren't delusional.

"We'll break up into three teams. Amy and CB, Jack and Lee. Leah stays with me because she's safest there even if it turns out this lot's not after her, just here for general, all-purpose mayhem. We'll go to this spot here . . ." He tapped the map. ". . . closest to the studio and shut it down. The rest of you, you're my eyes and ears. CB, you and Amy will go here, due south down Boundary to North Fraser Way."

"South to north," Amy snickered. When everyone turned to stare, she shrugged. "Well, I thought it was funny."

Amy had come from the office with CB and refused to leave. *Either I'm in or not, and after last night, the train to not has left the station.* Reluctantly, after he'd figured out what the hell she was talking about, Tony'd agreed.

"Jack, you and Lee are heading out almost to Simon Fraser." It was insane, completely and absolutely insane for Lee to be a part of this given that meta-physical energy looking for a home seemed to consider his body prime real estate. It really pissed Tony off that his *I don't want you involved* had been canceled by one *you should stick around* from Leah. He was trying to keep Lee safe. She just liked having attractive men around. And, okay, he liked looking up and seeing Lee on the other side of the table, too, but he'd also seen Lee on his knees screaming, tortured by the dead to force him to cooperate, and he never wanted to see that again. He'd stuff Lee into a closet and lock the door— fuck the symbolism—if it was up to him. But it wasn't.

"The burn's showing in this industrial park here off Eastlake Drive. It's late enough that there shouldn't be anyone around."

"So no one out there except us to get eaten," Jack put in.

"No one gets eaten," Tony snapped. "It's entirely possible that nothing will happen tonight, but . . ." He raised a hand and cut Amy off before she could speak. ". . . if it does, get clear and then call me, and I'll haul ass back to the studio instead of heading out to the next weak spot."

"We'll all haul ass back to the studio."

Heads nodded at Jack's statement.

"Fine." A grudging admission that he couldn't stop them. "But don't go charging in until I'm here. Jack, you know how hard it is to take one of these things down." Jack nodded reluctantly as Tony continued. "We go after them with everything we have, or we leave them alone. You go in without metaphysical backup, and these things could take you out like that!" He snapped his fingers and something large hit the floor on the far side of the soundstage with a sustained crash.

After a long moment of silence, CB folded his arms. "Mr. Foster."

"I didn't do it!" He frowned. "At least I don't think I did it."

"Well, this is filling me with confidence," Leah muttered as Jack pulled his gun and moved to check it out.

"Maybe I should . . ."

CB laid a heavy hand on Amy's shoulder. "You should let the police handle it."

"Chairs!" Jack called, heading back. "A pile of those metal folding chairs fell over."

"They were stacked pretty high," Lee recalled. "Last couple of days, Adam's been talking about restacking them before they fell."

"Coincidence," Amy snorted. "No boogeymen in the shadows?" she asked as Jack rejoined them at the map.

"Not that I saw."

"But you wouldn't see them, would you? Was I the only one who heard skittering?" She glanced around the group. "Okay, I guess I was."

"Can we just deal with the trouble we know we have instead of looking for more?" Tony sighed. "Or are three demons not enough for you?"

Lee raised his hand. "Enough for me."

"Thank you. When Leah and I finish closing the first weak spot, we'll join CB and Amy and then, when we're done there, head east. Remember, if anything happens, don't try and be a hero, just call me."

"The whole 'you shall not pass' thing always ends badly," Amy added, shrugging on a plaid plastic raincoat over a black hoodie.

"Isn't that what you're telling these things, Tony? That they shall not pass?" Lee asked.

He turned to Lee, intending to deny it, and heard himself say, "Yeah."

"And if it ends badly for you?"

"I'm hoping for weeping, wailing, and gnashing of teeth. Joke," he added when no one seemed to appreciate the humor. "If it ends badly for me, throw everything you have at keeping Leah alive. The hell with secrets, the hell with not causing mass panic. Mass panic sucks less than mass slaughter."

"Do we know there'll be mass slaughter?" CB asked.

He sounded as though he was requesting confirmation so that he could hire enough extras to make *mass* a valid description, but it was still a good question. Tony let Leah answer it.

"Demons gain power from each life they take, and there are a lot of lives crammed onto the lower mainland." Her right hand lay against the tattoo; her left pushed her hair back off her face, tucking it behind her ear. "Enough lives for a satisfactory number of worshipers with plenty left over to spend on other things. Also," she added, the words gaining emphasis, "since any mass slaughter will start with *my* slaughter, I'm all in favor of stopping it."

"Start with?" Amy was on the words like a terrier.

Right. Amy didn't know that Leah was the Demongate.

"CB."

The producer nodded. "I'll give her the new information in the car."

Jack folded his arms, leather jacket creaking as he ignored the exchange, his attention locked on Leah. "People are a lot more powerful than they used to be," he pointed out flatly.

"True," she acknowledged. "And you may have powerful enough weapons to stop him, but don't think for a moment that with this many lives to feed on, he'll be the only one coming through an open gate. The last time, he was called and the gate was destroyed behind him. This time, he'll control it."

"And we already know that Demonlords have demon minions," Amy put in, shifting her weight back and forth, heel to toe. "He could, like, throw them at the military while he feeds and gets too strong to stop. Then the only option would be a surgical nuke. Pow! Hundreds of thousands more die, radiation spreads, one of his minions escapes the blast and absorbs the radiation and mutates so that nothing . . ."

CB returned his hand to her shoulder, cutting off the flow of words. "I don't like the thought of leaving the studio unprotected," he growled.

Tony didn't much like the thought either. Even if he knew where to send the bill, it seemed ethically questionable to charge for saving the world, so he'd really like a job to come back to on Monday morning. However, if he had to choose between a building and warm bodies . . . "I don't want anyone out there alone."

"Perhaps I can help with that."

Lee, Amy, and Jack jumped; Jack's hand dropped to his gun. Leah looked like nothing much surprised her anymore. CB looked unimpressed. Tony tried not to give in to nerves and snicker.

"Where the hell did he come from?" Jack demanded as Henry walked up to the table and studied the map. "No one moves that quietly."

"Clearly, someone does," CB told him as Tony started in on the highlights of what Henry had missed.

When he finished, Henry nodded. "I'll stay here. If unnatural rope works on all demons, I can work on securing anything that might show up until Tony arrives to deal with it."

"More metaphysical backup," Jack announced almost too quietly to hear. And then he point-blank refused to explain what he meant, cheeks flushing as Henry caught his eye.

Tony could see that CB wanted to say he'd stay behind. It was his studio, and he was, in his own way, as possessive as Henry. But he was smart enough to know he couldn't do what Henry could, and so he said nothing. That pretty much proved he knew what Henry was, but Tony found he didn't much care. Sometime in the last couple of days, he'd gotten over it. Hell, if CB wasn't big enough for them to share, no one was.

"Let's go." He folded the map and stuffed it into his jacket pocket. "Those three holes were almost burned through. We don't have much time."

"I thought you said that nothing should happen tonight?" Amy reminded him.

"Yeah, well." Tony shrugged. "I was trying to raise morale. And nothing should. Maybe. But we probably still don't have much time."

"Have you *any* idea of what's going on?"

"Bite me."

Amy flipped him off and headed for the door. "Be vewy vewy quiet," she muttered as Jack fell into step beside her. "We'eh hunting demons."

Jack did a passable Elmer Fudd laugh.

"Mr. Groves will be by later," CB told Henry as he followed.

Lee opened his mouth. Closed it. Sighed and finally said, "I'd be better at this if I had a script."

Since that was pretty much a given, Tony said nothing.

"Look, I just want . . . I mean. Fuck it. Be careful, okay?"

"Yeah. You, too."

He nodded and hurried after the others.

"You know," Leah said thoughtfully as she zipped up her jacket, "I was thinking it was just you, but I was wrong. You're both pathetic."

"Leah . . ."

"Don't bother saying it. I'll meet you in the car."

Tony listened to the soft sound of her footsteps die away. He shrugged a backpack strap up onto one shoulder and looked Henry in the eye. "Vicki told me to call you. You know, back when this started."

Henry smiled. "I know."

"You're a hard man to be separate from." Tony wasn't sure he understood that, but Henry seemed to.

"I know."

"With any luck, I'll close those three spots before they open, and you'll have a quiet night." Didn't cost any more to look on the bright side.

"Good luck, then."

Cool fingers rested for a moment against his cheek and, just for a moment, Tony longed for the days when he was the sidekick. "Yeah. You, too."

"I can't believe you don't know how to pick locks," Leah muttered, one hand flat against the steel door, the other working the pair of straightened bobby pins back and forth.

"Why would I know how to pick locks?" Tony demanded quietly.

"Well, you're clearly a man with a past."

"And my entire B&E career consisted of heaving a brick through a grocery store window and then sprinting two blocks carrying a watermelon."

"Two blocks?"

"Ran into a cop. Big guy. Splat. Knocked me flat on my ass."

"Hmmm."

The noise may have been in response to his story or to the lock on the apartment door, Tony wasn't sure. He glanced down at the open laptop, silently ran over the words to the Notice Me Not one more time, and hoped he wouldn't have to use it. Not only because new magic was always an exciting crapshoot, but also because he needed to hoard as much personal energy as possible given what the immediate future was likely to hold. Although he'd topped the tank with a double bacon cheeseburger and large fries on the way to the first site, he had no idea how long that would last. He probably should have bought a second milkshake, just to be on the safe side.

Leah's dimples had gained them access to the high-rise as an elderly gentleman was leaving. Ignoring Tony entirely, he'd held the door open and waved her through, making a rather explicit suggestion that Tony very much doubted he—or any man over sixty—would have the stamina to carry out, little blue pills or no little blue pills.

Dude, if yours are lasting more than four hours, someone should check for rigor mortis.

Finding the right floor had been simple. They'd taken the elevator up one floor at a time until Leah's gut had pinged. Finding the actual weak spot had been a little trickier, but they were about 90 percent certain it was inside apartment 708. Unfortunately, it seemed the tenants weren't.

Or fortunately, given how little he'd been looking forward to explaining what was going on.

"You'd think it'd be in apartment 666, wouldn't you?"

"Like I keep telling the vampire," Leah snorted. "Wrong kind of demons."

"Hey!"

"I'm picking a lock here, Tony. If someone hears us, the words *vampire* and *demon* will be the least of our problems."

She had a point.

He could hear at least one television—maybe two—and a couple of different kinds of music, but at just after nine on a Friday night, most of the people who lived on the seventh floor seemed to still be out. Or they were sitting silently in the dark behind their locked doors. Tony had no intention of ruling out the latter.

The hall smelled like sausages and a spice that bounced around the back of his nose like a pinecone, doing multiple points of damage with every landing.

"That's it." Leah rocked back off her knees and stood, reaching for the door handle. "But if there's a chain . . ."

There was. It was dangling down inside the door, unlocked.

"Nice to see they're taking home security so seriously."

"You come home drunk and the chain's a pain in the ass to get open," Tony explained as they moved inside and closed the door behind them. "And why do *you* know how to pick locks?"

"I hang around with a bad crowd in the fifties."

"You mean hung around."

"No. I mean that every century, I hang around with a bad crowd in the fifties. I like having a schedule." She didn't sound like she was kidding. Reaching back, she flipped on the lights. "Good lord."

Tony snapped his laptop closed and raised his left hand, palm out, rune in defensive position. "What!"

"It looks like your place: beige walls, cheap furniture, and an overpriced entertainment system."

"That was it? I thought you saw something dangerous." He started breathing again and his heart rate began to slow.

"No, just bland." Walking out into the living room, she shook her head. "And if it wasn't so bland, the similarities would be frightening."

"First of all," Tony muttered, sliding his laptop into the backpack, "that's a sheet on the window, not a flag, and second, this has a separate bedroom."

"Which is probably beige."

"Hey, he has a set of RexTeck speakers—3-D sound effects and an awesome bass boost." Leah's silence pulled him around. "What? I've heard great things about them."

"Heard great things about demons taking over the city?"

Oh, sure. But she could take the time to discuss interior decorating. Half turned from examining the speakers, he paused. "The weak spot's right there." He could see the shimmer hanging just in front of the floor-to-ceiling shelves of DVDs. "But I thought there had to be something missing?"

Leah moved closer and examined the shelves. "He's missing the third *Aliens* movie."

"He's not missing much."

"And *Star Trek: The Motion Picture* although he has all the rest."

"Motionless picture," Tony grunted.

"Oh, my God, he's got a copy of *The Princess Diaries*. One and Two!"

"Maybe I should just close this up before he comes home and finds you dissing Julie Andrews." Setting the backpack on the floor, he wiped damp palms on his thighs and pointed a finger to start the first rune. A horrible groan came from the far wall. "What the hell was that?"

"The elevator."

"Is it . . . ?"

"Him?" Her gesture made it clear she meant the usual occupant of the apartment. "How should I know? Just wiz."

"Wiz?"

"Wiz!"

The first rune went through the wall of DVDs with no problem. So did the second. The third got stuck.

"Stuck?" Leah moved away from her listening post by the door and glared at him. "It can't get stuck if you've done it right."

"It's right."

"Are you sure? Check the cheat sheet."

"I didn't bring it."

"Oh, for . . ." She came farther into the apartment, and hauled up her track jacket and the shirt under it. "Check the original, then."

Tony gave the rune another ineffective shove and dropped to his knees, thumbs hooked behind the waistband of Leah's track pants to pull them low enough to see the rune. Head cocked to one side, squinting a little, he moved so close he could feel the air between them warm.

The apartment door opened.

Tony glanced up to see a young man blinking at them blearily, keys dangling from one hand. When he finally managed to take in the tableau, he grinned and flashed a double thumbs-up. "Dude!"

"Ignore him," Leah snapped, tapping the tat with one scarlet-tipped finger. "Check the rune."

"Wait a minute." He was sounding less bleary by the word. "Why are you in my . . ."

"Got it."

". . . apartment?"

Tony stood as Leah turned, dimples flashing an offer no straight boy could refuse. He tugged the center of the glowing blue line farther out from the center of the pattern then pushed. With a sizzle and a faint smell of burning plastic, the rune slipped the rest of the way through.

One more.

Half finished with the fourth rune, refusing to be distracted by what was happening on the sofa, Tony felt the hair lift off his body—his entire body, not just the back of his neck. *Man, never going to get used to that.* Turning, he got an eyeful of Ryne Cyratane and had barely made the very short trip from appreciation to apprehension when a spray of red-and-purple sparks arced out into the room.

They were coming from the shelves of DVDs.

Crap!

Tony finished off the fourth rune so fast he nearly sprained his wrist. Left hand flat against it, he shoved it after the others.

And stumbled forward, unable to lift his hand.

A heartbeat later, he was wrist-deep in the DVDs.

"Leah!"

"Busy."

"I don't care!" Yanking back only threatened to dislocate his elbow. "Le—!"

Hands closed on his shoulders, fingers digging in painfully tight. Next thing he knew he was flying. A short flight and a bad landing. Lying in a crumpled heap on the ruin of a cheap coffee table, Tony checked to make sure his arm had actually come with him.

"Time to go."

"Ow. Ow! OW!" Protests didn't seem to matter. Leah hauled him to his feet and hustled him toward the door. Seemed like everything worked. Not quite to the original specs, but he was up and moving. He snagged his laptop case as they passed. "What about . . . ?"

"He got a great memory and a broken coffee table," Leah snapped, dragging him out into the hall and shutting the door. "I think he came out even. Come on. If we get into the elevator before he gets his pants back on, he'll never know what we looked like."

"What if we have to wait for the elevator?"

They didn't.

She shoved him in, charged in after him, hit the button to close the door, hit the button for the first floor, and sagged against the stainless steel wall. "What did you do?"

"Me?"

"That spot wasn't close enough to blow like that."

"It was plenty close."

"Not close enough. I'd have felt it!"

They glared at each other for a moment.

"Okay." Tony flexed the fingers of his left hand. The scar felt hot. "Let me think about this for a minute."

"Don't strain anything," she muttered, adjusting her clothes.

"Nice. I think we hit a metaphysical overload."

"A what?"

"Between that weak spot being so close, you and your tat, me and my . . ." He waved the scar. ". . . power, then the whole distracting with sex invoking your Demonlord, I think we reached a point where things started to happen."

"That actually makes a certain logical sense."

"Yeah. Thanks." Sighing, he mirrored her position on the opposite wall. "And thanks for hauling me out."

She stopped buttoning her shirt long enough to shrug. "Even I can't get a guy to ignore you if you keep hanging around."

"Not then. When you pulled me out of the DVDs."

Dark brows rose.

"You didn't pull me out of the DVDs?"

"I didn't pull you out of the DVDs."

"Then who . . ." His gaze dropped to the tat, disappearing under white silk.

"No." Leah shook her head as the door opened and they moved quickly across the apartment building lobby. "First of all, he has no corporeal form on this plane and second, why would he help you? You're trying to stop him."

"Maybe I'm not."

"What? Stopping him?" She linked her arm through his and dropped to a sedate walk as they moved away from the apartment building and toward his car. He wanted to run, but he made himself match her pace. "Since I remain unslaughtered, I think you're stopping him fine so far."

"Not what I meant. Maybe . . ." The theme from *Darkest Night* cut him off. Sliding his cell phone out of the pocket on his backpack, Tony flipped it open and glanced at the screen. "It's Amy." Thumbing it on, he held it to his left ear.

"Tony! It's out! There were all kinds of wild lights, and then it was like a bomb went off! This tanker by Ballard Power Systems totally blew! I had to call 911 before I called you!"

Shit. Shit. Shit. "CB?"

"He's making sure everyone's out of the building. I'm heading to the Future Shop warehouse to do the same! Tony, this thing was nasty looking. It took a swipe at me as it went by."

The metaphysical taint! He'd totally fucking forgotten it when he'd sent Amy out to face a demon.

To observe a harmless little weak spot.

Yeah. Big difference.

"Are you okay?"

"It knocked me on my ass, but it was like I wasn't worth its time. I'm . . ."

Call waiting beeped out the last few words.

He checked the screen. Lee. Who'd been shadow-held twice. And possessed. If Amy had a faint taint just from acting as an anchor while he spoke with a dead housemaid, Lee must have a big red metaphysical target painted on his chest. "Amy, tell me you're fine!"

"I'm fine!"

"Stay that way!" Left hand thumbed the link. Right hand unlocked the car. Stomach twisted as he fought the urge to puke. "Lee?"

"Tony! The tear ripped just after we got to it!"

"Are you hurt?"

"What? No! Jack emptied half a clip into the demon, and it lost interest in us."

Lost interest in you. "My fault."

"What the hell are you talking about?"

"I sent you out there."

"Hey, grown man here. I knew the risks."

He didn't know all the risks because Tony hadn't thought to tell him. *How could I have forgotten about . . . Hang on.* There were alarms going off in the background. "What's happening?"

"Our demonic buddy didn't so much explode out of the building as explode the building!"

"Fire?"

"No. Rubble. I thought there was smoke, but it was steam. Jack says there must've been a boiler plant in the basement. A few of the surrounding buildings took some collateral damage. The whole place looked empty; the lights were off and all, but Jack's checking for casualties. I called it in before I called you. Tony, we're going to have to stick around here. We won't make it back to the studio before . . ."

Good, because there's going to be demons at the studio! Where it looked like it would be just him and Leah and Henry, and that was how it should be. No normal people—however tainted—getting hurt. Circumstances had stepped up to the plate.

"Don't sweat it." Phone clamped between ear and shoulder, he slammed the car into gear and roared out of his parking space and down the empty street. "You're sure you're okay?"

"Yeah, we're good!"

We? Right. Jack. "Stay good."

"Can you handle . . . ?"

"Yes." Tony took his hand off the gearshift long enough to turn off the phone and toss it toward Leah. "Both of the other weak spots blew."

"Another metaphysical overload?" She didn't seem to be making fun of him.

"Probably the same one. They were timed to go off together, remember. When ours tried to open, theirs did, too, but only ours got closed. We're heading for the studio."

"I guessed." At the edge of his vision he could see her clutching the dashboard, knuckles white. "Is everyone okay?"

"Yeah. Things blew, but no one got hurt."

"No one we know."

"Hey, if you know how I can fucking save everyone, tell me now!"

"I was just . . ." Her protest trailed off as he ran a stop sign. "Sorry."

"We know where they're going, and if they do any more damage, it'll just be en route."

"And once they arrive."

"Yeah." A light rain speckled his windshield. He flicked on the wipers. Trashing the studio meant trashing a lot of expensive equipment.

"They won't be expecting a vampire." Her tone suggested she was trying to cheer him up. It almost worked.

"Who does?"

The damp roads were greasy. Speeding around a corner, the car started to fishtail. Tony stomped on the gas and fought to straighten out, cursing under his breath. Something crunched as he passed an old blue Buick Regal, but he convinced himself it was garbage on the road and not a door panel.

"You just . . ."

"No, I didn't."

"Why are you driving? Specifically, why are you driving instead of me?"

"Good question."

"Okay." After a moment, she said, "Ballard Power Systems is a hydrogen fuel development company."

"How do you know that?"

"I did some wire work around one of their tanks."

"Big boom?"

"Then, no. Tonight, very."

"Good thing CB and Amy were right there to call it in." It made him feel a little less guilty about sending them.

"Seems strange that there were two sites that led to explosions plus a . . . Jesus, Tony!" Her fingers locked back down on the dash. "What was that for?"

"Squirrel."

"You swerved into oncoming traffic to miss a squirrel?"

"He's not protected by a Demongate."

"You don't know that."

"Very funny." Not much farther. Napier Street would take them right to Boundary. "Two explosions plus a what?"

"An apartment building." He heard her settle back in the seat and wondered about her expression, but it didn't seem smart to take his eyes off the road.

"So? You said the weak spots happen anywhere something's missing."

"Well, yes, but if these three are deliberate, aimed for maximum shit disturbing, as it were, why an apartment building?"

"Population density. Lots of people screaming." Boundary traffic was annoyingly heavy. Tony slid between a truck and a hatchback and sped south toward the studio. "Furniture thrown off balconies. A distraught mother screaming that the monster has her baby."

"You had me at population density."

"I like to be thorough."

"Tony . . ."

And sometimes, just one word was enough. South of the studio, the streetlights were blowing out all along the east side of the road. *Bam. Bam. Bam.* Heading north. Shards of glass showered down, glittering in the passing headlights. Tires screamed. Horns blared. No accidents yet.

No accidents in sight, Tony amended, barely slowing to head into the studio parking lot. There was a whole lot of road in between the Fraser and CB Productions. The lot lights blew as he parked the car, and a shadow passed between him and the building.

A big shadow.

So much for beating it back to the studio and setting a trap.

Feeding off Kevin Groves had been reflex. The reporter had walked into the soundstage, realized they were alone, and bared his throat, a desperate desire rolling off him like smoke.

Henry could have stopped himself, but the emotional need drew him as much as the blood. He expected the sharp intake of breath as his teeth met through soft skin. The look of peace as he swallowed a single mouthful of blood then drew back was less usual.

"Complete truth," Groves sighed. "No codicils, no compromises." Then his eyes snapped open, and he stared at Henry in rising panic. "It's just, you know, lies. I get so tired of them. Everyone lies. You don't. Even when you are. Lying. Please don't hurt me." He stared at the drop of blood rising from the puncture on his wrist and his eyes widened. "You really did it. Oh, God." Shaking fingers fumbled his PDA from his jacket's inside pocket. "I need to ask you some stuff."

"No."

The PDA fell from nerveless fingers, the plastic case cracking against the concrete floor. "Okay."

"Go to Raymond Dark's office and sit down. Stay there. Don't move unless you're avoiding a threat." He could hear glass shattering outside.

"What about . . ."

"Now."

Raymond Dark's office was safer, given that it was not directly under the power residue drawing the demons. Safer. Not safe.

Concrete block walls, no windows into the soundstage. The weakest point was the large door the carpenters used. It had, once again, been left unlocked.

Metal screamed.

Henry raised a speculative brow. Apparently tonight's demon would rather go through the door than open it.

Though expected, the shower of cherries was no less annoying.

"Son of a fucking bitch!"

The big sliding door had been pulled half off its track, the steel scored in three parallel lines. CB was going to be pissed.

Something howled. A cherry bounced out into the parking lot.

Tony dropped his laptop case by the wall and took a deep, steadying breath. "Get in there and see if it's marked for you. If not, help Henry."

"And if it is?"

"It won't be. Maximum mayhem, remember? There's a lot less mayhem if it heads right for the person standing beside the guy kicking demon ass back home."

"That was actually very convincing."

He glanced up to see her staring speculatively down at him. "Thank you. Now haul ass." Without waiting for a response, he turned his attention back to the laptop, clutched the pull thing on his fly—the spell needed a metal ground—and recited the words of the Notice Me Not.

This demon was no tentacled monstrosity. It walked on two legs like a man and had a caricature of a man's face—two eyes, one nose, and a mouth. Except the eyes were orange lid to lid, the nose nearly invisible under a plate of its chitinous body armor, and the mouth lipless, with more of the body armor growing up into gleaming tusks. The armor changed color to match its surroundings, and it was now fading down from night-sky black to concrete gray. Henry got a close look at one of the arm plates as it knocked him across the soundstage to slam into the outside wall. When it withdrew the arm, it dangled a length of yellow nylon rope from one thick wrist.

It was fast but no faster than Henry.

Strong, but no stronger.

Four arms, however, that's a bit of a problem. This time, at least, he managed to keep hold of the rope. He rolled back under a slash that gouged the floor and managed to get a loop of rope around one leg as it lifted to stomp him. Ducked. Whirled.

"Nightwalker!"

Threw the coil of rope over the left arms to the Demongate.

She caught it. Whipped it back along the floor.

Henry kicked at the side of the demon's knee. Heard chitin crack. Scooped up the rope as he took a blow hard enough to crack even his ribs. He crashed to the floor and thought just for a moment he heard his father's voice bellowing at him to get up. His father had never approved of him being unhorsed. Snarling, Henry caught the next descending arm and threw himself back still holding it, trapping it under another loop of the rope.

Too close!

One of the lower tusks raked his shoulder, ripping through shirt and skin and filling the room with the rich scent of his own blood. At first he thought the flash of light was based in pain, but then he saw the rune take shape.

The demon veered away from the lines of blue fire, giving the Demongate a chance to slam it in the side of the head with what looked like a microphone stand.

Closing three hands around one end of the metal pole, the demon yanked it from her hands, raising it over its head to bring it down in a killing blow. At the apex of its backswing, the microphone stand went flying from its grip to land with a clatter behind one of the false walls.

"You must hate it that your master's spell protects her even from you," Henry growled and ripped a plate of chitin from its shoulder.

It shrieked.

A second rune hung in the air.

He couldn't see Tony, although it was obvious that Tony was there. Not obvious to the demon, thank God. It continued to keep clear of the runes but made no attempt to find the wizard drawing them.

*   *   *

Henry was hurt.

Leah wasn't. The world rearranged itself so that that demon kept missing her. The resulting contortions would have tied a human spine in knots. Demons were more flexible.

Lots more flexible, Tony realized as, chitin plates creaking, the demon curled around limbs wrapped in rope and charged toward Henry from a completely unexpected angle.

Concentrate on the rune!

He'd already screwed the third rune up once tonight. He couldn't afford to do it again. More specifically, Henry couldn't afford for him to do it again.

Three runes.

His head pounded as he began the fourth, keeping it next to the third as he finished it. If he drew the final rune in its proper place, the demon might realize his intent before he finished and go after him instead of Leah and Henry. The demon wouldn't be able to see him, not if the Notice Me Not was still working, but any kind of a charge in his direction would take it out from between the runes.

With any luck, his ability to move energy around was unique enough it would be unexpected. After all, how many wizards got trapped in haunted houses redolent with the waxy buildup of evil and ended up symbolically branding themselves in order to save the day? Well, the rune on his palm was symbolic; the branding part had been agonizingly real.

Tony'd just sketched in the final swooping crosspiece when the door between the offices and the soundstage bounced off the wall of Raymond Dark's sanctuary and crashed to the floor.

The wall swayed but stayed up.

It had been a soundproof door. Big, and thick, and heavy, it used to be attached to the wall with large metal hinges. The demon that had thrown it was mostly two enormous arms and the supporting torso. No head to speak of but just under where logic insisted the lower edges of its ribs should be—had logic not decided discretion was the better part of valor and buggered off for coffee—was a huge fang-filled mouth. There were no runes or glyphs or Post-it notes allowing it to take out Leah.

Jack and Lee's demon.

It had fucking well better *be Jack and Lee's demon!* Because if it wasn't, they'd missed a hole, and if they'd missed one, then they could have missed a dozen and a dozen extra demons were twelve more than Tony wanted to deal with.

He finished the final rune but didn't move it into place, waiting until the second demon joined the first under the gate.

It stood, weight forward on its knuckles, and watched the fight. Maybe it sensed the trap—hardly surprising with three blue patterns of glowing energy suspended in the air and nothing distracting it. Maybe it was waiting until the first demon took the edge off a common enemy. Maybe demons liked to see other demons get the chitin kicked off them. Whatever the reason, the gate wasn't enough to draw it between the runes.

What could he add as enticement?

What did demons want?

Foot on knee, on elbow, on shoulder—Leah leaped for the light grid, kicking the demon hard in the face. It fell back, she dangled, and Tony called her jacket and shirt into his hand.

Fabric tore, buttons bounced off demon, vampire, and concrete.

Most of the Demongate was exposed between track pants and white lace bra.

The oldest operating spell in the world. Leah'd said it was what had drawn the Demonic Convergence, so demons were obviously interested in it even when they hadn't been marked to destroy her. Since they hadn't been marked, Leah was half dressed but still completely safe, protected by the spell.

From the look on Leah's face, if this didn't save the day, demons would be a minor problem as far as Tony, personally, was concerned.

The second demon roared and charged forward.

Tossing the handful of white silk aside, Tony shouted out the words for the clean cantrip.

Scrubbing bubbles covered the floor of the soundstage, knee-deep.

The second demon started to slide, threw out a massive hand to stop itself, overbalanced and, other arm flailing, slammed into the first demon. Chitin cracked. They both went down.

Tony threw the fourth rune into place.

Leah dropped onto a spotlessly clean circle of floor empty of demons and bubbles both, landing in a deep crouch as her knees took up the shock of the landing. Henry straightened, left arm held tightly against his side, blood soaking through the shoulder of his cream-colored sweater. The empty loops of yellow nylon rope gleamed, cleaner than they'd ever been.

Slipping and sliding through the scrubbing bubbles, picking up speed once he hit the dry concrete, Tony raced to Henry's side. This was where he'd been dragged into the story, back in Toronto after another demon attack had left Henry nearly dead. He had his jacket off before he stopped moving.

Henry's gaze slid past him. "Tony?"

Crap. The Notice Me Not.

"Where are you, you little shit! How dare you use me as bait!" Leah stomped across the soundstage toward the place the fourth rune had been, kicking bubbles out of the way.

How did he turn this thing off?

"Quit screwing around, Tony. Turn the spell off."

He waggled the tab on his fly. Nothing. "I don't know how."

Henry cocked his head.

Leah threw up her hands. "I bet you don't know how to turn it off, do you? I'm telling you, square pegs, round holes, and if I ever get my hands on this Arra person, I'm going to kick her ass."

"He's here," Henry murmured, his eyes darkening.

"No shit, Nightwalker. I think the overactive cleaning supplies are a dead giveaway."

This time when Henry called him, there was no question, no doubt that Tony would answer. He said, "Tony."

Tony heard *"Mine,"* and stepped forward to meet the darkness in Henry's eyes.

They stood for a moment, barely an arm's length apart, Tony breathing heavily, listening to the song of his blood responding to the call. When Henry made no move to close the distance between them, he swallowed and said, "You're hurt."

Henry glanced at the wound on his shoulder. "So it seems." And back at Tony. "I've been hurt worse."

"Not because of me."

"This wasn't your fault."

"You have to feed." Tony watched the Hunger rise, and offered his wrist. Ignored the way his hand was trembling.

To his surprise, Henry shook his head and his eyes lightened. Not completely, but it was clear he'd locked the Hunger down. His good arm reached for Tony, pulled him close. Cool fingers clasped the back of his neck, drew his head down onto a broad shoulder. That Tony was a good two inches taller didn't seem to matter. "We can't go back to the way we were."

"I don't want to go back." But he did. Right now, right at this moment, right after sending two very large demons back to their hell, right after stopping a third, right after sending friends out into danger, he wanted nothing more than to go back to when Henry made the decisions. When life went on around him without him having to be so damned involved. "You need blood."

"Yes."

He drew in a deep breath and let it out slowly. "But not from me."

Fingertips caressed the bite on his throat that was still only partially healed. "It's too soon. And the wrong time."

They meant the same thing. Except they didn't.

The wizard in charge didn't get to lie down and have it done to him, no matter what the current value of *it*.

"Will you Hunt?"

"No."

"Amy'll be back later tonight." Is this how Vicki had felt? Like she was pimping for Henry? "She'd be thrilled." She'd be impossible to live with, but since he only had to work with her, he thought he might survive.

"Kevin Groves is in Raymond Dark's office."

"Ah." Tony stepped back, Henry's hand falling away. "Is he . . . you know, okay with it?"

Henry smiled, his teeth very white. "He likes that I tell him the truth."

"Yeah? I kind of preferred it when you lied."

"No." Again fingertips touched the bite on his throat. "You didn't."

Tony turned before he had to watch Henry walk into the office set. He drew in a long breath, let it out slowly, and noticed Leah staring at him as she shrugged into her shirt.

"I'm fine." Tying the front tails into a knot, she yanked it tight. "Thanks for asking."

"You were protected."

"That didn't give you the right to use me as bait."

"I know. I'm sorry."

The apology seemed to take her by surprise. "Oh. Okay, then. And it worked—so good idea."

"Thank you."

"Just a thought, you might want to avoid that invisible wizard thing until you learn how to turn it off."

Had Henry not been there, how long would he have remained unnoticed? "I'm planning on it."

"Good. So, about these bubbles . . ."

The remaining bubbles, those that had been outside the runes, were continuing to clean, moving out and over the soundstage.

"Just ignore them. Eventually, they'll dry out and pop."

"Leaving a sticky magic residue?"

"How do you make that sound so smutty?"

"Practice." She grinned and shrugged back into her track jacket, ignoring the ruined zipper. "Now what?"

"Now I need a confab with Ryne Cyratane."

"A what?"

Tony squared his shoulders and looked as resolute as a man could with a clump of scrubbing bubbles halfway up his leg. "We need to talk."

TWELVE

"All right, let's assume, just for interest's sake, that you haven't completely lost your mind." Finger combing hair disheveled by the fight, Leah crossed over to the chaise lounge, waited until a wave of scrubbing bubbles finished cleaning the last bit of grimy upholstery, and sat, staring up at Tony as though his lost mind was a forgone conclusion. "Why do you want to talk to Ryne Cyratane?"

"Dealing with two demons at once almost got our collective butts kicked. I'm still finding it a little hard to believe that the slapstick defense actually worked."

"You're suggesting that we're not in a Three Stooges movie?"

He snorted, and ran a hand back up through his hair. "Look, even if I deal with most of the weak spots before they open—and that's doubtful because they're not all going to be in easy-to-access places—we're still screwed. Three demons would have won that fight, and if they win the fight, they'll open your gate."

"What about the rest of the troops?"

"We don't have troops!"

"Okay, fine. Keep them out of it." Leah rolled her eyes. "You're still missing the obvious solution."

"Okay?"

"I get on a plane as soon as possible and get the hell away from here. Ryne Cyratane has committed his power to bringing the demons through at *those* points in *this* place. He's not going to be able to follow me."

Tony frowned. That seemed so reasonable he automatically suspected it. "So he'll break off the attack?"

"Are you listening to me? I just said he's committed his power."

"So he won't break off the attack?"

Her smile was scathing. "As you kids today say: duh."

"Then that's only a solution for you. And only a temporary one. He'll know where you are because of the gate, right? Then as long as the Demonic Convergence is still going on," Tony continued when she nodded, "he'll redirect things and just shove the next demons through there. Where you'll face them alone. Without the wizard. Because I'll probably die when the studio gets swarmed. And then you'll be dead," he elaborated when she didn't look convinced, "just like you would have been with that first demon if I hadn't been there."

She crossed her legs and scowled at the toe of her shoe. "You don't know that."

"Yeah, I do. So, your obvious solution is crap. The only way we're all going to survive this is by staying together and stopping that swarm."

"By talking to the Demonlord who's sending it?"

"I don't think it's him."

Brows drawn in, she peered up at him. "Did you get hit on the head?"

"No!" He bent to pick up the rope just to give his hands something to do. The scrubbing bubbles had left it not only clean but smelling faintly of lemons and free of static cling. "Jack asked me the same question yesterday," he muttered, feeling slightly picked on.

"It's a reasonable assumption when you're saying things like you don't think the demon who created the gate is trying to reopen the gate by taking out the person he created the gate on that only he'd know about," she snapped.

"Why?"

"What?"

Holding one end of the rope in his left hand, Tony began to coil it between hand and elbow. "Why would Ryne Cyratane be the only who knows about you? There's clearly more than one demon down there. Out there. Wherever the hell their hell is. Odds are good they talk to each other. Get together Friday nights, drink a little demonic beer, play a little demonic poker, talk about gates they've got set up to get back into a world where the inhabitants are easy to rend and will worship you in order to keep from being rended."

"Demonic beer?" Leah tossed her hair back over her shoulder. "Please."

"Stop fixating on the details. The theory is sound and those other Demonlords have also had thirty-five hundred years to make plans about how they'll use the gate yours left behind. And besides . . ."

The Demonlord didn't look happy, that was for sure. He looked frustrated. Like he knew the thing he was looking for was right there, right in front of him, but he couldn't find it.

". . . he wants to talk to me."

"He wants to feast on your steaming entrails."

"Maybe."

"You're not his type. Trust me."

"Look, he's been appearing when these attacks are going on, even when you're not aroused. The first time, he looked angry, and I figured it was his motivation showing and he was angry at not getting back here to the worship and the slaughter. Or maybe it was the too-close-to-water thing. Who knew? Then, after it became obvious to anyone with half a brain that there was a wizard involved, he showed up looking for me. But I don't react to you, so he couldn't find me and that was making him frustrated. Then I had a dream about him . . ."

"Oh, that's a good reason for me to stick around. You had a dream."

Tony ignored her, both hands working the rope. "He was wearing the same expression L . . . other people do when I'm obviously not getting their message."

Leah snorted. "Good luck with that since he hasn't decided what message he's sending."

"What? Wait, you're not talking about Ryne Cyratane there, are you?" No. She wasn't. "You think we could deal with one communication problem at a time?"

"He's conflicted."

"I got that," Tony sighed, tying off the coil. "Now could we . . ."

"You should kick his feet out from under him and beat him to the floor."

"Is that what you did?"

Dimples flashed. "I never have to work that hard."

That answered that question. Lee wasn't just using the women as a blind; he liked women, or he wouldn't have fallen for the primal "do me, baby" Leah was offering. Of course, liking women didn't necessarily preclude liking men. Take Henry, for example. He was about as enthusiastically nondiscriminating as they came.

Not that Lee had ever been enthusiastic.

Except that once.

With him, anyway.

He could have been enthusiastic with any number of other men for all Tony knew and was just being carefully closeted at work. Or all the metaphysical shit Lee'd been through in the last six months combined with Tony's not so secret attraction had seriously fucked with his head.

Yeah. Let's not forget option B.

Or that a whole herd of demons on the way is more important than your pathetic lack of a love life.

He leaned the coil of rope against the far wall of the set where it would be out of the way but still convenient for immobilizing creatures from hell and turned to face the immortal Demongate. "Ryne Cyratane has something to say to me, and I need to hear it."

The immortal Demongate snorted again. "Well, unless you have a really good calling plan, you're out of luck, aren't you?"

"You said you'd been in contact with him. That you meditate . . ."

"It's a postcoital meditation, Tony, and one thing I'm sure of is that since you and I have no coital in our future, there's going to be no post. Oh, wait, I have an idea. You, me, and Lee. Might be just the thing to break the ice." Grinning, she leaned back on her hands and crossed her legs. "You're thinking about it."

He was.

But then he was a guy and he wasn't dead, so that was pretty much a gimme. Actually, the evidence suggested a growing number of guys didn't let being dead stop them.

"I'm not kidding about this." Tony tried to look like he wasn't kidding. "So unless you know another way to contact him . . ."

"You could always try switching your long distance service and then having a fast wank."

"Leah."

She stared at him for a long moment. "You're serious," she said in amazement, sitting up straight.

"Completely. We'll have to use Henry as a conduit between us."

"Henry? Well," she admittedly slowly, one hand disappearing under the knot in her shirt, "that'll definitely get his attention."

"Yeah." Tony touched his throat, the skin still puckered under his fingertips.

Leah still didn't look entirely convinced when she raised her head and locked her gaze with his. "Do you even know *how* to meditate?"

"I don't think I'll have to. I think your Demonlord wants to talk to me badly enough that as soon as he has a way to grab onto me, he'll make the connection. And with any luck, he'll want to talk to me more than he'll want to destroy Henry for messing with you."

"Do you think Henry will go along with this?"

"Along with what?" Henry asked.

Tony turned as Leah answered. "A threesome to save the world."

Red-gold brows rose briefly and dipped again when he realized that no one was kidding. "Whose idea is that?"

"Not mine," Leah smirked. "Guy rips your clothes off, and suddenly he wants to get kinky."

The hazel eyes darkened just a little as he turned a disbelieving gaze on Tony. "I can't wait for the explanation."

"Because your place is a dump, Henry doesn't trust me enough to let me into his sanctuary, and I have a king-size bed."

"No surprise," Tony grunted.

Leah leaned over CB's desk to poke him in the chest. Hard. "I can still get on that plane."

He waved her quiet as Amy finally answered her phone.

"Tony!" He could hear sirens and angry shouting in the background. "There was like this massive accident by the stadium!"

"Are you all right?"

"Yeah, we're good, but there's no way we can get by. Boundary's just this total mass of twisted metal and emergency vehicles—fire, police, ambulance.

We can't even go around 'cause we're in the middle of the block. CB's a little annoyed."

That explained the angry shouting. "Where is he?"

"Right in the thick of things. I think he's trying to get the road cleared."

"When he stops shouting, tell him that we took out the two demons and the soundstage has never looked cleaner."

"Cleaner?"

"Long story." The scrubbing bubbles had petered out just past Raymond Dark's coffin. "Downside, the big steel door got bent, the soundstage door is now lying on the floor of Raymond Dark's office, and the front door got shattered. If you guys can't make it back . . ."

"We can't friggin' move!"

"Okay, then can you call the security guy and have him come around? Henry and Leah and I have something we have to do."

"Something kinky?"

His jaw dropped. *Not a lucky guess,* he reminded himself picking it up. *Just a smart-ass Amyism.*

"Oh, my God! Is it something kinky?"

Shit. He'd paused too long. "No, it isn't! It's something demonic."

"Demonic doesn't preclude kinky."

"You're right," Tony told her, hoping that the whole best defense is a good offense thing wasn't just blowing air. "It *is* something kinky and will likely involve a pair of handcuffs and a couple of liters of maple syrup."

Her snort came through loud and clear. "What, is Jack playing, too? Fine, don't tell me, and the number for the security company is on the list by Rachel's phone. Call them yourself. I'll find a phone booth and look up twenty-four-hour glass companies. Zev's gonna be so pissed he missed this."

"In what universe?"

"You know he likes to be around when things are happening."

"So we'll try not to have things happen on the Sabbath from now on."

"It's good to have a plan. Oops, I gotta go; CB just assaulted a taxi."

"A taxi driver?" Leah asked when Tony repeated the high points of the conversation.

He shook his head as he thumbed in the number for Lee's phone. "Probably not."

Lee answered partway through the second ring. "Tony? Are you all right?"

"Henry took a couple of hits, but Leah and I are fine and the demons are gone. You?"

"We're still at the site. They're digging for a custodian buried in the rubble and so far they've only found part of him. Jack's dealing with the emergency crews, but I can get a cab back to the studio if you need me."

For sex to save the world.

"Tony?"

"Sorry. Got distracted for a minute. Um, Leah and Henry and I just have some loose ends to tie up . . ." He turned his back on Leah's obscene gesture. ". . . before I start dealing with all those other weak spots, so when you want to leave there, you guys can call it a night."

"You sure?"

Sex to save the world. The perfect excuse.

"Yeah. This is wizard work now, so unless Harry Potter and Gandalf drop by to help out, I'm on my own for this next part."

"Be careful, then."

"You, too."

"So I'll see you Monday unless the world ends or something."

"Yeah, or something."

"You'll call me if I can help?"

"Sure."

"Tony."

"I promise."

"You're lying."

"I'm not." If anything came up he thought an actor in the highest-rated vampire detective show on syndicated television could handle, he'd call Lee first.

"Well, thanks for letting me help tonight . . ."

Even if it wasn't my choice.

". . . even if it wasn't your choice."

Okay. That was a little scary. "No problem."

"I mean it."

"I know."

He listened to Lee breathing for a moment, enjoying the sound.

"I uh, think my battery's dying. I've got to go."

"Right." And thank God for dying batteries, Tony thought, hanging up. So much more believable than "there's someone at the door" or "my appendix just ruptured." He looked up to see Leah watching him, wearing a frankly speculative expression. "Life was a lot easier when I thought he was completely straight," he sighed, tossing plausible deniability into the toilet.

"If there's one thing I've learned in thirty-five hundred years," Leah told him as they crossed the office, "it's that almost no one is completely anything. We're in the minority."

"That doesn't change the fact that life was easier when I thought he was completely straight."

"Can't handle the thought of reality intruding on your fantasy life?"

"Something like that."

"Listen, if Harry Potter and Gandalf do drop by, we're going to need a bigger bed."

Tony ignored her. The moment the words had left his mouth, he figured that comment was going to come back and bite him on the ass and, all things considered, that was barely a nibble. "There's at least one dead out by Simon Fraser," he told Henry as they exited into the outer office. "And Amy says there's a shitload of injuries in a pileup on Boundary by the stadium."

"We got lucky." Henry dumped a dustpan of broken glass into the garbage and straightened. "The residual power of the gate is keeping the death toll down by drawing them directly here where they can be immediately dealt with, and your forcing both weak points to blow open tonight made sure the explosions occurred when there was almost no one at either site. Things could have been a lot worse."

"You had to feed off Kevin Groves."

"I've fed off worse."

"He's a tabloid reporter," Tony muttered as he picked up Rachel's phone to call the security company, absolutely not thinking of what else Henry did when he fed. "If there's worse, I don't want to know."

Tony put down his toothbrush and stared into the mirror in Leah's guest bathroom. Quick shower to get the higher bits the scrubbing bubbles missed. Debris from the recent half dozen soft tacos—gone. Was there anything else he should do to prepare?

"Tony! Sunrise is at 6:52—pick up the pace."

Apparently not.

Leah and Henry were in the bed when he got to the bedroom, carefully not touching, their respective powers dialed way back.

"Making sure there's no premature communication?" he asked, turning to stroke glyphs into the doorjamb with one toothpaste-covered finger.

"Practicing safe context," Leah corrected. "What are you doing?"

"Warding the room."

"With toothpaste?"

"You didn't have any cough syrup." With any luck, cavity protection plus whitening and mouthwash would work as well. "This may be dangerous."

"This? Using a vampire as a conduit to contact a Demonlord? Can't imagine why you'd think so, especially considering that the last time it almost happened you stopped it with your throat." She folded her arms under the swell of her breasts. "Tell me again why I'm going along with this?"

"Because you haven't said no to sex in thirty-five hundred years."

One dimple flickered. "Well, it's not a good reason, but it's a reason."

"And you don't want to die."

"That's a good reason."

Wiping the remains of the toothpaste on the towel wrapped around his waist, he set the tube down on the edge of the dresser and approached the bed. "Henry . . ."

A pale hand rose to cut him off. "If you hadn't convinced me, I wouldn't be here."

"Sure." He'd been hoping for some kind of reassurance that this was the right thing to do. That attempting to contact Ryne Cyratane was the right decision. It seemed like a naked vampire was as much reassurance as he was going to get.

Tony half expected commentary as he dropped the towel, but either Henry's presence or what they were about to attempt—metaphysically—kept Leah silent. He slipped into the bed on Henry's side as Henry shuffled over and Tony let out a breath he hadn't realized he was holding. "Okay. Henry has to be in contact with both Leah and me when this goes down, so I think we need to . . ."

"Relax."

"What?"

Leah rolled onto her side and up on one elbow. "You need to relax," she said, sliding her upper hand along Henry's chest. "You're not suddenly directing an X-rated episode of *Darkest Night*, so let's just forget about hitting our marks, shall we? We're taking part in an ancient sacrament. With a twist." She frowned. "And a small chance of death and dismemberment. You just lie back," she continued before he could respond, "and think about whatever you have to. Leave this up to me; I used to do it professionally."

Her superior tone brought him up to mirror her position. "You're not the only one with a past."

"In this bed? I wouldn't assume I was."

She still sounded patronizing. "Just remember, I know things you don't."

"About what?"

Tony slid his hand under the sheets. Henry gasped. "About him."

Henry had not initially gone along with the idea of contacting the Demonlord. Or rather, he'd agreed with the idea but not the method suggested. Sex with Leah, given what they were, could never be anything but a power struggle, and even the possibility of sex had resulted in a loss of control he didn't want to remember. Couldn't help but remember given that his Hunger still marked Tony's throat.

"That won't happen this time because you've just fought a demon and that has to have taken some kind of physical edge off and, besides, I'll be plugged in from the beginning. When the power starts to rise—metaphysically speaking—I'll grab it and ride it to Ryne Cyratane."

"It's a dumb idea," Leah had put in, adding, "but it might work."

Tony ignored her, concentrating on Henry. "There won't be a risk of you biting Leah and pissing her Demonlord off—wham bam feedback blows you into little pieces—because I'll be there for any tooth action, and because you've been topped up recently, there's no chance of you getting carried away."

Henry had stared at the younger man for a long moment, unable to look away from the visible part of the damage he'd already done. *"You'd trust me that much?"*

"Jesus, Henry, what kind of a question is that? I've trusted you with my life from the moment we met. I've always known what you are."

That, in the end, was what had brought Henry to this place, to this bed.

He had intended to take a more active role, but perhaps between a wizard and an immortal Demongate it was safest to lie back and be used. To not be drawn into competition. He breathed in the warm, rich scent of their arousal mixed with his own and let the Hunger rise just enough to let them know they used him at his pleasure, that he had power of his own.

Tony knew how to keep himself separate from what his body was involved in—he couldn't have survived the streets if he hadn't—but separate wouldn't get Ryne Cyratane's attention. He had to be as much a part of what was going on as Leah and Henry. This was not, as it turned out, particularly difficult. Familiar skin, familiar hands, familiar need got him over the small hurdle of girly bits doing their thing off to one side and in a very short time, he was fighting to remember that he couldn't be drawn into the maelstrom—it had to be drawn into him.

Then Leah cried out.

Henry's teeth closed through a fold of his skin.

As he arced up off the bed, he could feel a fourth presence, and, opening himself up to the surging currents of power, he raced to meet it.

It was a lot like absorbing the fire he'd set in Leah's curtains.

Except this fire burned.

His heart pounded, he couldn't catch his breath, and bits of his life were passing before his eyes. No. Wait. That wasn't his life. He wasn't double-jointed. And then he was back in the white and two very large, hot hands were wrapped around his biceps and lifting him into the air.

Someone was talking. Deep rumbling. Shades of Barry White.

Tony struggled to focus and finally managed to hear words.

"What place is this, Wizard?"

Good question. It took him a moment to figure out how his mouth worked, but he finally managed to form the words, "Neutral ground."

It was a guess, but it seemed to be enough of an answer since the hands released him and he found himself sprawling at the feet of Ryne Cyratane.

The view from down there was pretty damned amazing.

"You risked much to speak with me, Wizard."

"Did I?" That was news. Did he want to know what he'd risked? No, he decided, getting carefully to his feet. "You wanted to talk to me, big guy. I made it happen. Say what you have to so I can go put on some pants."

The Demonlord's lip curled, exposing long ivory-colored teeth. Recognizing one of Henry's expressions, Tony realized Ryne Cyratane had just hung out a sign saying *Want to be eaten? Ask me how.* "You speak bravado out of fear."

"Duh." Had he come into this cold, without all those years of Henry behind him, he'd be a gibbering wreck.

"You desire me."

That was too obvious to require a response. Tony had no idea where the energy was coming from, considering the rocket ride he'd taken to get here as well as the mentioned and admitted fear.

"You have been protecting my handmaiden from the attacks of an Arjh Lord."

"No, she's been attacked by . . . Hang on." He could feel his brain begin to sluggishly work. "What's an Arjh Lord?"

"I am an Arjh Lord. Sye Mckaseeh is another." The first statement was very nearly a roar. The second merely a comment.

"Right." They'd hardly call themselves demons. And, apparently, the new one was a Scot. Which brought up another point. "Why are you speaking English?"

Massive arms crossed over a hairless chest. "I am speaking what you are hearing."

"Sure. Okay." That made as much sense as most things in his life these days and was, at least, useful. Absently scratching at his left palm, Tony backed up a few steps, hoping a little distance would help clear his head. "Look, why don't I tell you what I think is going down, and you can yay or nay the synopsis?"

Dark brows drew in. "I am unaware of your meaning."

"Just listen." He laid it all out. An Arjh Lord directing the Demonic Convergence to create specific weak spots he could use to push through his own minions, marking them so they could kill Leah, thus opening the gate and allowing the Arjh Lord to enter their world and try to take it over.

Minions needed explaining, and Tony downplayed just how easy that takeover would be. No point in giving the big guy ideas.

When he finished talking, Ryne Cyratane nodded. "It is as you say; Sye Mckaseeh is warping what you call the Convergence to her own place."

"Sye Mckaseeh is a wo . . . is female?"

"Yes. And a mighty warrior among the Arjh Lords."

"Great. A mighty warrior." Tony cleared his throat. "Look, you wanted to talk to me, what did you want to say?"

"I wished to give you, as the wizard protecting my handmaiden, the information you already possess. Your people have grown wiser since last I walked your world." He didn't sound like he approved.

"Probably not wiser, we're just more used to processing information. But if that's all you wanted, let's move on to what I want . . . need." The Arjh Lord's expression suggested Tony's needs were so low on his list of priorities they were essentially nonexistent. Time to evoke vested self-interest. "I need your help, or your handmaiden is going to buy it—die, she'll die—and you'll lose all that energy she keeps sending you, not to mention any chance you might have of using the gate yourself sometime in the future. You know, in case she finally gets depressed enough to . . ." He drew a finger across his throat.

The gesture didn't need explaining. "Go on."

"Sye Mckaseeh is creating twenty-seven weak spots between your world and mine." He'd finally taken a moment to actually count them. "Apparently three nines are a mystic number or something, but that's not the point. Very shortly we'll be ass-deep in arjh and the odds are good one of them will get through to your handmaiden and kill her to open the gate."

"You are a wizard; you hold the eternal cosmos in your hand. Strengthen the weakness before it tears. With power drawn to so many places, it will take time before the arjh are through."

"Not enough time. My world is a complicated place, and I don't think I'll be able to get to all the weak spots before they rip open. I need you—your handmaiden needs you—to slow things down on this end. The arjh end. We need you to interfere with Sye Mckaseeh's plan."

"No. I am not one who battles with the other lords for power."

Tony blinked as that sank in. "You're kidding me. You're a lover, not a fighter?"

"As I understand your use of the language, yes. And there is disunity between Sye Mckaseeh and I."

"Disunity?"

The Arjh Lord shrugged. "Once there was unity. Now there is not."

Standing on that featureless white plane, Tony had a sudden strong desire for a wall, so he could bang his head against it. "She was your girlfriend and you guys broke up and that's how she knows about the Demongate and that's why she's trying to get it open, to screw you." Same old story, add a truck and a dog and they could set it to country music.

Ryne Cyratane shrugged again. "Her arjh watch for me. I could not get close to her should I desire it."

"Hey, you fighting your way through a few of her arjh would be a distraction, at least. We could use that."

"No."

"Yeah, we could."

"No, I will not fight."

"Yeah, but this isn't a power struggle with another lord," Tony reminded him. "You'll just be smacking around a few arjh."

"I do not fight."

"Then what the hell are those horns for?"

"They are a symbol."

Oh, that was useful. Not. "Fucking great. You're nothing but Bambi's dad."

Ryne Cyratane may not have understood the reference, but he definitely understood the tone.

Actually, Tony figured as he was once again lifted off his feet, it was probably a good thing the reference sailed right on over. "I'm sorry, okay! I'm just worried about your handmaiden!" He could see himself reflected in the onyx eyes—which was more than a little disconcerting since the hands holding him did not appear in the reflection.

"I do not wish my handmaiden to die." This close, the Arjh Lord's teeth were as out of proportion as certain other parts of his anatomy—only not in a good way.

"Bonus, because she doesn't *want* to die."

"But neither will I put myself in danger."

"Not even for her?"

This new expression was not one of Henry's. Tony'd last seen it on Mason's face when CB had set up an interview with one of the science fiction media magazines. The expression of the innately selfish forced to acknowledge they had responsibilities they didn't much like.

"If Sye Mckaseeh is indeed attempting to control so many entries to your world, she will not be able to watch all of her lesser arjh," Ryne Cyratane admitted reluctantly after a moment. "It seems her continuing defeat at your puny hands has caused her to rage against you and to overextend." He smiled but, whether at Sye Mckaseeh overextending or at her continuing defeat, Tony wasn't sure. "While she is distracted by the great effort she makes, I will mark one of her waiting arjh with my sigil so that when it breaks through to your world, it will fight at your side and rend the others of its kind." *Rend* was pronounced with enough relish to supply an infinite number of hot dog carts.

"If you could mark one of her arjh," Tony pointed out, "you could kill it. And if you could kill one . . ."

"Death of her arjh, she would most definitely notice."

"Okay, back to your original plan." Tony's lower arms were going numb, but the Arjh Lord didn't seem to be tiring. "Problem is, I'm closing as many of these things as I can before they open. What if I close the weak spot you've coopted?"

"Do not."

Yeah. That was helpful.

"If my handmaiden, my priestess, my love is with you, she will know which weakness I use as mine."

Okay, that actually *was* helpful.

"Tell the Nightwalker I will allow his interference with what is mine this one time and this one time only. If you desire to speak with me again, find another way. Now go."

Tony bounced a little as he hit the ground. Bounced a little higher. The white began to darken. Higher still. Fighting a rush of nausea, he closed his eyes.

"Tony?"

Opened them to find Henry bending over him. "Bucket," he gasped, rolling for the edge of the bed. It was a good thing the wicker garbage container had a plastic bag in it because there wasn't time to forage any farther out.

A familiar growl. "Your arms are bleeding."

"Not . . . now!" His blood was Henry's. He got that. Given that no one else had ever wanted it, that usually wasn't a problem. At the moment he was a little too busy to deal with vampire issues.

He started shaking just before he finished vomiting and barely made it to the bathroom in time to empty the rest of his digestive tract. Things got a little messy anyway, and he closed the door on the scrubbing bubbles bleaching the color out of Leah's towels.

The bedroom was empty when he got back, his clothes folded neatly on the end of the bed. Reaching for his jeans, he caught sight of his reflection in the full-length mirror and paused. Purple-and-green handprints covered most of both biceps, the soft inner skin of his arms scored by Ryne Cyratane's claws. Tony scratched at a dribble of dried blood, decided against risking the bathroom while the bubbles were still working, and reached for his jeans.

They seemed loose. Barefoot and holding his T-shirt, he staggered out into the condo, following his nose.

Leah was in the kitchen stirring what looked like a large pan of scrambled eggs.

"Where's Henry?"

"Gone. Apparently, he didn't trust my closet space. I put some cheese and some cold ham into these," she continued without turning. "You're going to need the fats as well as the protein."

Considering the fun he'd been having since he got back, the last thing Tony wanted was food. "I'm not hungry," he groaned, dropping onto a stool by the breakfast counter.

"I know. You're starving." When he snorted, she turned and glared. "Do you have any idea how much energy you used tonight?" She gestured at his arms with the spatula. "You created a physical form, you idiot. Okay, maybe that was partly because of how we made contact, but I still can't believe you were so stupid!"

"I'm fine," Tony protested as she began to scrape the eggs out onto a platter. "I just got a little bruised."

"You could have been killed. How many times do I have to remind you that demons gain power by slaughter? You're just lucky that slaughtering you didn't occur to him."

"It didn't occur to him, because I was right; it's not him sending the demons. He needs me to protect you." Tony frowned, suddenly realizing that Leah's eyes were bright with unshed tears. "You're really upset."

"Of course I'm upset!" Holding the full sleeve of her dark green dressing gown back with one hand, she slammed the platter down on the counter in front of him with the other. "If you'd gotten yourself killed, what would have prevented all those demons from coming through and killing me?"

Of course she was upset.

Strangely comforted by this indication of normalcy—within his current fluctuating definition of the word—Tony flicked a bit of scrambled egg out of his chest hair and back onto the plate. "He's going to do what he can to help."

"You're sure."

"Positive." By the time he finished repeating everything that had been said in the white, the platter was empty. He didn't remember eating, but since he was holding a dirty fork, it seemed safe to assume he had.

"Sye Mckaseeh?"

"That's what he said."

"Scottish?"

"I didn't ask."

"I can't believe I'm in danger and I could die because Ryne Cyratane broke up with his girlfriend."

"She's definitely holding a grudge. And I think he's a bit afraid of her."

"He could have been lying to you."

"I know. I don't think he was, but . . ."

"But you don't have a lot of experience judging demonic veracity."

"Uh . . ."

"You had no way of knowing if he was telling the truth."

"Right." Tony tapped the fork against the edge of the platter. "Maybe I should have taken Kevin Groves with me. You and Henry have already had him; it wouldn't have been that much of a stretch."

He'd been kidding, but Leah rolled her eyes and snatched the fork out of his hand. "Fine time to think of that now."

"Eww."

"Oh, grow up. And get dressed so we can get started on saving the world. We've got twenty-seven weak spots to find and close before my god's ex-girlfriend stomps through and tries to take over the world."

"Yeah, well, you know what they say. Hell hath no fury like a demon scorned." A broad wave at her robe. "You'll be going out in that?"

"I dress very quickly."

The obvious comment was, well, too obvious to bother with. His T-shirt seemed to have more holes than he remembered, but eventually he got it over his head and both his arms. His arms hurt, but that was hardly surprising. His shoes and socks were still in the bedroom, but when he stood up to go and get them, the floor moved.

"Or maybe you should sleep for a few hours first," Leah sighed, walking around the edge of the counter and peering down at him.

꩜ THIRTEEN

He hadn't had enough sleep, and in the last—he counted back on his fingers Saturday to Wednesday—four days he'd probably lost a good ten pounds. *That's right, folks, it's not only a Demonic Convergence, it's a workout plan. Sign up now and we'll throw in the Sye Mckaseeh Diet free! All the carbs you ever wanted, but you have to get them away from an Arjh Lord before you can eat them.*

"Tony!"

The level of pissyness suggested Leah had been calling his name for a while now. "What?"

"We're here."

Here was Richmond, in a company parking lot nearly empty except for a premillennial Buick and two Smart Cars.

"The weak spot is in the lot?" he asked hopefully. With any luck, number one of twenty-seven would be an easy fix.

"The weak spot is in the building."

So much for easy. "Of course it is."

"It's a Saturday," Leah reminded him, opening her door. "I'll distract the security guard, you close things up, slam bam, we move on."

"Isn't that supposed to rhyme?" he muttered, getting out of the car. His knees hurt and his back was stiff; he felt about seventy-five. "You know, Gandalf was probably no more than thirty and the whole gray hair and beard thing was payback for being a wizard. Explains the break dancing with Saruman," he added as they walked toward the front doors. "'Cause that'd make them the right age in the backstory."

Leah turned to stare at him in confusion. "What are you babbling about?"

"The break dancing scene in the movie. Okay, it was supposed to be a fight, but, man, the fight choreographer really fell down on the job."

She rolled her eyes. "For pity's sake, read a book."

"There was a book?"

The building containing the weak spot belonged to a company called Seanix Technology, Inc.

"Number one PC manufacturer in Canada," Tony announced as they moved out of the fine mist and into the shelter under the concrete overhang bordering the front of the single story building.

"You know that and you didn't know Peter Jackson made *Lord of the Rings* from a book?"

He shrugged. "I've never had time to watch the appendices. And we have a problem."

"Besides your appalling ignorance of anything besides television or movies?"

"The security guard is a woman."

"What? That was on the sign, too?"

Tony sighed and pointed.

The tall blonde sitting behind the desk in the main lobby was intent on one of her monitors and hadn't seen them.

"You're right. We have a problem."

"Fortunately, I have a solution."

"You know a spell to take care of her?"

"Nope. I don't need magic for this."

Leah patted him gently on the shoulder. "Tony, you're gay."

"That'll help," he said, quietly pulling open the heavy glass door, "but more importantly, I'm in television."

The door got the guard's attention. Wearing a professionally neutral expression, she watched them cross to her desk. "Can I help you?" she asked, the neutrality touched with suspicion.

Tony smiled and pulled a business card out of his wallet. "I hope so," he told her, passing it over. "My boss sent me out to find a location for our next episode and with any luck, this building will have the perfect space."

"You work on *Darkest Night*?"

"I do."

"Oh, wow. I love that show! Lee Nicholas is so hot! That episode where he got captured by the coven and they were going to sacrifice him unless Raymond Dark—who they'd been hunting for centuries—surrendered to them and he was tied out over that altar; that was just brilliant! And that scene where he was chasing that mad scientist down the street after he was exsanguinating people and blaming it on vampires, that went right past my mother's best friend's ex-husband's store!" Her enthusiasm dropped about five years off her age. "It says here you're a TAD?"

He cranked up the camp, just a little. "I'm also a location scout, the photocopier repair person, decorating consultant, and, occasionally, second dead body on the right." He leaned in. "That leg at the edge of the screen after the massacre on that container ship at VanTerm—mine." CB had been way too cheap to have a leg made when he had any number of them walking around collecting a paycheck.

"No."

"Yes."

She rose up on her toes and peered over the edge of the desk. "Oh, my God, it was your leg! I recognize the shoe!"

No she didn't, it was a different shoe entirely, but Tony wasn't going to mention that. "Look . . . Donna . . ." Her name tag, now close enough to read, said *Donna Hardle*. ". . . I know you can't leave your post, but would it be possible for us to wander very carefully around the building—not touching anything, I promise—to see if we can find the space my boss is looking for?"

"I don't know; it's Saturday, and . . ."

"And there won't be many people working, so we won't disturb them. We thought about that. And besides, we'll want to shoot on a Saturday."

"On a Saturday?"

"Uh-huh."

"I'm here on Saturdays!"

"Hey . . ." His cheeks were beginning to hurt from all the lunatic smiling. ". . . that's great. You know, Lee loves to meet his fans."

Her cheeks went pink. "He does?"

"Loves to."

Donna glanced down at the card, looked over the bank of six monitors, bit her lip, and said, "I guess it's okay if you don't touch anything, and I'll have to make sure you're not carrying cameras."

"That's fair." Because if they were intent on industrial espionage, they'd surely have their corporate spy supplies out where they could be easily found. On the other hand, as he turned out the front pockets on his jeans and patted down his jacket, he gave her points for even considering it. Leah had his car keys, so all he was carrying was his wallet.

"And you . . ." Donna frowned at Leah. "Are you with the show, too?"

"Stunts," Leah said shortly, holding out her bag. "The location needs a safe fall site. Why don't you just hold onto this."

"You do stunts? That is so cool!" Setting the bag down on her desk, she keyed in a fast run of numbers and the door at the end of the lobby buzzed. "Go on through. There's a couple of guys working today; don't disturb them, okay?"

"We'll be as quiet as the mold man in episode nine."

"That was a great episode!"

Leah snorted as the door closed behind them. "Somebody should tell Donna that womb to tomb she only gets so many exclamation points and she's wasting them."

"Be nice," Tony muttered, massaging the inside of his cheeks with his tongue.

"No."

Sye Mckaseeh's potential entrance was in a multi-desk office with windows overlooking what was probably a manufacturing area. There were long tables and individual stations of tools, and if it wasn't manufacturing, Tony had no idea what it was. "I don't see the two guys the guard mentioned."

"They're probably in R&D if they're in on the weekend," Leah told him, down on her knees running a hand over the teal blue carpet. "It's under here. There's a bit of a bump. I think there was a wall taken down and the office made bigger."

When he cocked his head, he could see the shimmer. "Back up."

"What was with all the hand waving?" Donna asked as they came back out into the lobby. "I could see you on the security monitors," she added before they could ask how she knew.

"I was setting up the shots," Tony told her, peering at her through the square of his fingers. "You know."

"Of course! So cool! Did you find what you needed?"

"I think so, but now I have to tell the boss. He makes all the final decisions."

"So you don't know what Saturday you'll be here?"

"Not yet."

"That's okay, I wrote down all my days off until after Christmas, so can you try and be here when I am?"

As Tony took the piece of paper, he laid his other hand over his heart. "I will do my best."

"That's just so great!" She was handing Leah back her bag, but her attention never left him. "Tony, can I ask you a question?"

He noted the impressive amount of information conveyed by Leah's *we have another twenty-six of these things to close and not nearly enough time so we need to haul ass* expression and then ignored it. Donna had done them an enormous favor and right now was definitely not the time to be acquiring a karmic burden. "Sure."

"It's about Raymond Dark and James Taylor Grant." She lowered her voice and glanced to both sides, as if worried about eavesdroppers. "Is there, you know, a subtext there on purpose because they always stand so close together?"

"Sorry, that's standard blocking for television," Tony told her. "Actors have to be well within each other's personal space in order to get them both in a small screen close-up. There's no subtext; they're just hitting their marks."

Donna clearly didn't entirely believe him. "But they're so perfect together."

He winked, and gave his best imitation of a lascivious screaming queen. "You don't think James Taylor Grant would prefer a younger man?"

Giggling, she waved them toward the exit. "Go on. I have work to do!"

"Subtext?" Leah demanded incredulously as they walked to the car. "What was she talking about?"

"You don't spend much time online, do you?"

"I have a life. And what was with the *Queer Eye* shtick?"

He snorted as he dropped into the passenger seat and let his head fall back. "I know our fan base. Be sure to hit a drive-through on the way to number twenty-six."

"This is looking very familiar." Tony finished his coffee and tossed the empty cup into the back seat. "Isn't this near . . . ?"

"The place the tentacled demon broke through and terrorized your friend's coffee shop? Yes. Same neighborhood. And this is where our next stop is." Leah pulled into the parking lot at the Four Points Sheraton, narrowly missing two middle-aged women dragging an impressive amount of luggage.

"It's not just a residual reading from the old place that blew?"

"No. But I'd have thought it was if you hadn't mapped it and I'd have gone right on by and we wouldn't have closed it and it might have spat out the demon ready to destroy the world as we know it. Not to mention me." The parking space she chose was some distance from the building. "Probably Sye Mckaseeh's intent. Good thing she doesn't know what you're capable of."

"Yeah. Good thing." Right at the moment, he didn't feel capable of much.

"There's a few too many men in there for me to distract them all, not to mention women."

"Not to mention."

"So how do we play this?"

He sighed and unfastened his seat belt. "We get lost in the crowd."

"And if the weak spot's in one of the rooms or one of the offices or in the middle of the lobby?"

"Why don't we just cross that bridge when we come to it? And speaking of Bridge . . ." Standing just outside the car, he stared at the hotel.

"Superficial resemblance at best," Leah snorted. "Come on. Let's do this."

Dark girders held the Four Points sign out over the main entrance. Tony stared up at them, noticed a spot where a bit of paint was missing, and closed his hand around Leah's arm. "Tell me it's not up there."

"It's not up there."

"Thank you. Just look like you're supposed to be here," he murmured as they entered the building. "There's hundreds of people in and out every day. We're just two more faces in the crowd."

"You've done this before?"

Why not? It would look better if they were talking. He kept his voice low. "Big hotels with conference rooms have bathrooms tucked away in odd unwatched corners. If you're not so filthy you get noticed right off, you can use them to clean up as long as you miss the suits having their post-conference piss. Sometimes, you can score a coffee and some food from outside the rooms."

Leah looked intrigued as she guided them past the front desk. "The hotel rooms?"

"Them, too. Half-eaten room service beats dumpster diving any day, but I meant from outside the conference rooms. Pastries and stuff. Handful of creamers if nothing else."

"For all that it's been short, you've had an interesting life."

"Yeah, and getting more interesting by the day."

The weak spot they were searching for wasn't in the lobby.

Or by the pool.

Or in the Business Center.

It was in the ballroom. Although there were round tables draped in peach tablecloths set up for later in the day, at the moment, the ballroom was empty.

"And we catch a break. Go us."

"Maybe." Frowning, Leah trailed her hand along one of the long walls until she came to a narrow wallpaper-covered door. Opening it exposed a dark, empty cubbyhole.

"It's where those folding walls go," Tony said, peering over her shoulder and squinting a little to see the familiar shimmer. "You know, the kind that divides the room into smaller rooms."

"I guess this one's missing." Motioning him forward, Leah stepped back out of his way.

"Excuse me? What are you doing?"

They turned to see a man in a navy blue suit staring at them suspiciously from just inside one set of double doors. He was wearing a Four Points Sheridan name tag and the slight bulge at the waist of his jacket was either a radio or the hotel business in Vancouver was excessively competitive.

"I've got it," Leah murmured and started across the room.

For the first couple of steps, she was just a good-looking woman walking, then even Tony could see the difference as she cranked up the metaphysical attraction. Checking on the hotel employee's reaction, Tony noticed the gleam of a gold band against a dark finger.

The guy was married.

Just fucking great.

He sketched out the first rune at full speed, shoved it through the shimmer, and glanced over his shoulder.

Leah was almost at the door, the translucent image of her Arjh Lord flickering around her. "You're the manager?" he heard her purr. "Just who I wanted."

Second rune.

She had her hand against the manager's chest and he was smiling.

Third rune. At little slower because this was the one that gave him trouble.

Tony turned in time to see the door close.

Crap.

Fourth rune and he was sprinting across the ballroom before the shimmer had entirely disappeared. Fighting off a wave of dizziness, he crashed through the door, stumbled, apologized as he bounced off a passing luggage rack, and caught sight of Leah and the manager going into a conference room.

If the door closed, he wouldn't be able to stop her.

As it swung shut, he called.

The door jerked out of Leah's grip. Brass hinges creaked but held.

The look she shot him through Ryne Cyratane's torso promised a thousand years of torment and an immediate butt kicking. Tony let his arm drop back to his side and croaked, "Come on. We're on a tight schedule."

"There's time . . ."

"No." He sounded definite. Go him. He had no idea of what he'd do if she refused to listen.

Fortunately, he didn't have to find out. Leaving the manager standing confused and unfulfilled in the conference room, Leah stomped down the corridor, right past him and out into the lobby, heading for the exit. Half expecting to see smoking footprints in the carpet, Tony followed.

Disoriented by the unexpected sunshine, he had to dance around a shuttle bus and a pair of taxis vying for the same spot. By the time he was in the clear, she was already at the car. "That manager," he said before she got a chance to speak. "He was married."

"So?"

"So he was married."

Leah settled back against the trunk and crossed her arms. "Are you telling me you never got into a car or went into an alley with a married man? Most hustlers can't afford those kinds of scruples."

He didn't remember telling her in so many words that he used to hustle. Still, took one to know one. "That was different."

"How?"

"This guy, the manager, he didn't make that choice. You didn't *give* him a choice."

Her eyes widened incredulously. "So you were saving his marriage?"

"Maybe."

"You know nothing about him. He could be putting it to half the cleaning staff."

"That has nothing to do with me. This did. If he decides to betray his wife, that's his business, but we don't get to make that choice for him." Suddenly, the pavement was a lot closer than it had been. "Ow." Why was he on his knees?

"Tony?"

He blinked up at her.

"You didn't take the time to focus properly, did you? You used your own internal power for those runes, didn't you?"

"Could have." He honestly didn't remember. "I was in a bit of a hurry," he reminded her as she helped him back onto his feet. "You don't generally demand a lot of foreplay."

He expected more argument, but she was quiet as she opened the car door and eased him down onto the seat. He couldn't read her expression and he didn't trust the silence, so just before she slid the key into the ignition, he grabbed her arm. "What?"

To his surprise, she leaned over and kissed him gently on the cheek. "You're a good man, Tony Foster. A good man with power. I'm not sure if I find that terrifyingly hopeful or just terrifying."

As she effortlessly shook free of his grip, Tony sagged back against the seat and frowned. "Yeah, well, that and five ninety-nine will get you a meal deal," he said after a moment, unable to decide if he should be flattered or insulted. "Which reminds me; you'll need to . . ."

"Hit a drive-through on the way to number twenty-five. Yeah, I figured."

"Tony, wake up!"

There was a certain, *this is the last time I'm going to say this* tone to Leah's voice that dragged his eyes open. He could see trees silhouetted against a sapphire sky. "It's almost dark."

"I know. You ate and then you fell asleep, and I couldn't wake you."

"Why am I wet?"

"I said I couldn't wake you," she snapped, tossing the empty cup into the back seat and starting the car.

Now he thought about it, it was a pretty stupid question. Although she'd reclined his seat as far as it would go, sleeping in the car had left him stiff. And not in a good way. "Oh, man, I have really got to take a piss."

"There's a gas station on the corner."

"Where are we?"

"Just down the road from number twenty-five," she told him, pulling up to the pumps. "It's on a private house. Give me your credit card. For gas!" she added when he stared at her blankly.

"What's wrong with your cards?"

"The gas is going into your car."

"Right. Fine. Whatever." It wasn't until he was getting back into the car having visited both the bathroom and the convenience store, holding a bag of beef jerky and a giant sport drink and feeling much better that he realized what she'd said. "On a private house? Not in?"

"There's a piece of soffit missing. Do you know what that is?"

"Sure. I'm a wizard. We know things."

"It's the piece that fills in the angle between the roof to the house."

"Ah." He chewed a piece of jerky as she pulled out into traffic. "Bungalow?"

"Two stories."

Two stories with a porch and a flagstone walk and some bushes clipped into tight little spheres. Dark curtains were drawn over lace sheers in the front window, but a thin line of light seemed to indicate someone was home.

Standing on the sidewalk and craning his head, he could just barely make out the shimmer. "I can get it from here."

The first rune slammed up against the eaves trough and rained down in a shower of blue sparks. Tony threw the remains of his sport drink on a smoldering spherical bush. *Good thing* neighbor *in the city means minding your own business.* "Son of a bitch. I can't get the right angle on it, the porch is in the way. I'm going to have to lean out that second-story window."

"And how," Leah snorted, peering up at the house, "are you going to get to that second-story window?"

"I guess we're hunting for another location," he said as he headed back to the car.

She caught his wrist as he was opening the trunk. "Tony, people with that kind of repressed shrubbery are not likely to be fans of *Darkest Night*."

"So we expand our demographic." Shaking free, he pulled out his show jacket and shrugged into it, dropping his jean jacket into the trunk. It was the ubiquitous black satin with a blood red logo across the back, and he didn't wear it often—there were only so many Donnas a guy could face in a day—but it made him look more official and at past seven on a Saturday evening, that could only help. "We'll get whoever's in there to take me to that room because we want to use the view out of it on the show."

"They won't care."

"And we'll offer them a great deal of money."

Leah glanced at the shrubs as they walked up the front path. "That might work. Except," she added, "I get the impression CB's not going to sanction that."

"We're not actually going to use the view," he reminded her, heading up the porch stairs.

"Fair enough. But once you're in the room, they're not just going to let you lean out the window."

"No, you're going to distract them. Or him. Or her. Or the Brady Bunch. Without forcing he, she, or them to break any vows."

"Okay, Mr. I've-got-an-answer-for-everything: if it's not a him, how?"

"We'll be on the second floor."

"So?"

Tony sighed and pressed the doorbell. "You're a stuntwoman, right? Fall down the stairs."

"I don't understand." Mrs. Chin clutched at the front of her pale blue sweater with one hand and peered anxiously from Tony's card to Tony. "There'll be a television show on our front lawn?"

"No, ma'am. We just want to shoot . . . film," he corrected when she looked startled. "We want to film the scene out the window just like it is."

"But why?"

"For the television show."

"Yes, you said that, but why?"

"It'll be what one of the characters sees when they look out *their* window, Mrs. Chin."

"Except they won't ever be in your room," Leah added quickly. "We'll put the pieces of film together back at the studio."

"I see." Either she didn't, or she was confused about something else. "And you'll pay me money for this?"

That was almost a statement and definitely not what she might be confused about.

"Yes, ma'am."

"Because you always hear about how much money there is in television." She glanced at the card again. "How much money?"

"I can't say exactly, ma'am. I need to take a look and see if it's suitable and then . . ." He pulled his cell phone from his pocket. ". . . send a couple of pictures to the boss."

Her eyes narrowed. "You're not taking pictures of the inside of my house."

"No ma'am. Just the view out the window."

"And you want to do this now?"

"The sooner the boss makes a decision, the sooner we can cut you a check."

"But it's dark out," she protested, leaning just enough to see past them and get confirmation.

"That's okay. It's a television show about a vampire. But a good vampire," he qualified as her eyes began to narrow again. "It's about a vampire detective who solves crimes and protects people."

Mrs. Chin nodded, slowly. "That sounds familiar. What's it called again?"

"*Darkest Night.*" He half turned so she could see the logo on his back. "We shoot right here in Burnaby."

"I've never heard of you," she declared, but she stepped back and let them into the house.

"Oh, good heavens! Miss? Are you all right?"

Tony hadn't seen the fall, but it had certainly sounded impressive; lots of bumping, lots of crashing, and finally some very believable moaning. As Mrs. Chin ran out of the room, he leaned out of the window—fortunately, one of the old-fashioned kinds that lifted up and had no screen—twisted around, and, using the frame, pulled himself up to sit on the ledge. He had to lean away from the building, left arm stretched right out to get the runes through the weak spot, and although all four slid through, he wasn't entirely positive that it had closed. He leaned a little farther. Squinted . . .

The world tilted in an interesting way, but there was definitely no shimmer.

No window ledge either.

Porch roof, though.

And then a bush.

A bush that turned out to be just a little sturdier than he was.

Oh, that's just fucking great, he thought, rolling out onto the lawn, breathing fast and shallow through his teeth so as not to scream. *Four days of fighting demons, and I get taken out by shrubbery.*

Lying there and bleeding seemed like his best option, but unless they wanted to deal with more questions than he was prepared to answer, he had to get away from Mrs. Chin before he fell over. More specifically, he had to stand up and then get away from Mrs. Chin before he could fall over again.

Bright side, nothing was broken.

Nothing important anyway.

Thankful he seemed to be in marginally better shape than the bush, he staggered up the porch steps and peered into the front hall. Leah was sitting on a wooden chair, head in her hands. Mrs. Chin was nowhere in sight. Opening the door, he waved Leah quiet and moved as quickly as he could to her side as Mrs. Chin came from the back of the house with a glass of water.

"Oh, there you are," she snapped, her gaze flicking to the stairs as she handed Leah the glass. She obviously thought he'd just come down them and just as obviously disapproved of his lack of concern for his companion. "This young woman should be taken to the hospital."

Hospital? Was the spell no longer protecting her? "Are you hurt?"

"She fell down the stairs," Mrs. Chin told him grimly. "There could be all sorts of internal damage and I am not responsible. Those stairs are safe. I wasn't near her when she fell. I gave her a glass of water."

"Of course not."

"If you try to sue me, that's what I'll tell the judge."

"Okay, sure."

"Maybe you're right about the hospital." Leah stood and handed back the glass. "We should go now."

Tony was all in favor of that. Left arm pressed tight against his side, he extended his right. "I'll help you out to the car."

Somehow Leah managed to support most of his weight and still make it look like he was helping her. A lot of stunties were better actors than the industry gave them credit for, he acknowledged silently as he thanked Mrs. Chin for her time and the two of them moved as quickly as possible toward the street.

Leah tipped her head toward his. "You fell out the window?"

"What was your first clue?"

"Could have been the way you were upstairs and then came in through the front door. Or it could have been the crash you made as you hit the porch roof."

"Mrs. Chin . . . ?"

"Kitchen's in the back of the house. She might not have heard it."

"Is she still watching?"

Clothing rustled as Leah half turned. "Yes."

"Then let's move a little faster before she comes outside and sees what I did to her bush."

"You damaged one of her bushes!"

"The damage was mutual."

"If I let you go, can you lean on the car until I get the door open?"

"Sure." Or not so sure. The adrenaline was wearing off, he hurt in more places than he cared to catalog, and the world was beginning to tilt again. Fuck that. Tilted world had got him into this mess. Mess. Messed. Missed. Didn't miss that damned bush. Wouldn't miss it. It could just lay there and well, rot.

"Come on, Tony. Into the car."

Leah's voice seemed to come from very far away and she seemed taller. Or he had gotten shorter. And that would suck.

"God fucking damn it!" Cracking his head on the edge of the car roof helped him focus. He collapsed into the seat and whimpered a little as Leah buckled him in. *You know what needs seat belts? Fucking window ledges, that's what.*

"This isn't good."

She was sitting beside him in the driver's seat and, since he couldn't remember her going around the car, it seemed he'd lost a few minutes somewhere. She was looking at a dark stain on the palm of her hand.

"Shit. You're bleeding!"

"No, Tony. *You're* bleeding. It's soaking into your jacket. That's why I didn't see it before. How badly are you hurt?"

"I can't feel the fingers of my left hand." When he lifted them up into the light of the streetlamp, they looked kind of like sausages. "But that's good I can't feel them," he added. "Because when I could feel them, they hurt like fuck."

"Let me see where you're bleeding."

"I'm bleeding? Oh that's just great. Henry's going to kill me. He hates it when I waste . . . Um . . ." The word just wasn't there. And then a good chunk of the world wasn't there. Then what was left started beeping.

Henry pulled up behind Tony's car and was out of his own almost before the engine stopped.

"The supplies you asked for are in the backseat," he snarled, pushing past the Demongate and yanking open the passenger side door. The blood scent, no longer confined but spilling out to almost overwhelm the night, would have been dangerous had his anger at the circumstances not been so great.

Scooping Tony up into his arms, he led the way into the apartment building.

"Hey, Henry. I was just thinking about you."

"Were you?" Henry sat on the edge of the bed, his cool fingers gently gripping Tony's jaw.

"Yeah. I was thinking you'd . . . uh . . ." Interesting that it hurt so much to frown. "I don't remember. But you were there." His gaze flicked up over Henry's shoulder to Leah and he snorted. "And you were there. And there was a wizard. Oh, wait. That was me."

Smiling, Henry released him. "Don't frighten me like that again."

"You're frightened of me misquoting *The Wizard of Oz*?"

"You've been in and out of delirium for the last two hours. We were just discussing whether or not we should take you to a hospital."

"What happened?"

"Apparently, you fell out a window."

It all came rushing painfully back. The window. The bush. The bleeding. And now?

He was in his own bed, in his own apartment. His left arm was on top of the covers, forearm wrapped in a tensor bandage, the fingers an ugly shade of grayish purple and still sausagelike. With his right hand, he explored the gauze corset wrapped around his torso. If he hadn't been to a hospital . . .

"Leah does a decent field dressing," Henry said, reading the question off his face. "We don't think the wrist is broken, but you won't be able to use the hand for a few days. What happened?"

Duh. "I fell out a window."

"He got careless," Leah muttered, stomping to the kitchen.

"I didn't." Was her bad mood because she cared, or was that just lingering delirium talking? "The world tilted."

"I thought as much."

A little surprised, Tony turned his attention back to Henry. "You expected a tilted world? What? It was part of the whole Demonic Convergence thing? Next time, warn a guy."

"I expected something *like* this to happen. Not this specifically."

"Cryptic much. I thought you'd be more pissed."

"Oh, he was." Leah reappeared holding a mug. "The anger and the yelling and the accusing me of trying to kill you went on for a while. Henry, lift him into a sitting position."

Tony wasn't given a chance to protest, and it didn't hurt as much as he expected it to.

"Now, drink this."

Henry had to help him get his working arm out from under the covers, but once he had his fingers wrapped around the mug, they seemed to be holding. His mouth filled with saliva as he breathed in the meaty scent of the soup and he had to swallow spit before he could get to the good stuff. Since he didn't think he'd survive another alphabet noodle out the nose, he drank slowly without being told.

No one said anything until he finished.

"There's more."

"Good." He passed Leah the mug. "I'm starving."

"Literally."

And back to Henry again. "What?"

"You are literally starving. Your body is not up to the demands you've been making on it. That we've *all* been making on it."

"You haven't been . . ." Cool fingers brushed the scar on his throat. "Yeah, okay, maybe a couple."

"We've been forcing a couch potato to run a marathon," Leah told him handing him the refilled mug. "For the last four days, you've been using your power almost constantly. You're not in good enough shape for this."

"Thanks."

"I'm serious. The world didn't tilt, Tony. You fainted. Well, almost fainted," she qualified, stepping back from the bed and folding her arms. "That's why you fell."

"I almost fainted?"

"Yes."

"That was remarkably unbutch of me."

"This isn't something to joke about, Tony." Henry pressed his palm against the gauze. "You need to rest, regain your strength, heal."

Tony glanced down at Henry's hand. The gentle pressure remained just this side of pain. He was either saying, *I don't want you getting hurt.* Or *I'll hurt you if you try to get up.* Tony wasn't sure which. "How long do you want me to rest?"

"For as long as it takes."

"I can't . . ."

"You don't have a choice," Leah pointed out, sounding no happier about it than Tony felt. "Your body is setting the agenda now."

"Yeah, but there's still two dozen demons coming through."

"Tomorrow," Henry told him in a tone that suggested he not bother arguing, "Leah and Jack will go out and get detailed information on as many of the weak points as they can."

"Doesn't Jack have a job?"

"He has Sunday off. Amy will be here, sitting with you. Making sure you sleep and eat and don't do anything stupid."

"*Amy* will be making sure *I* don't do anything stupid? She attacked a demon with a candle."

Henry smiled. "Which is why we assume she can handle you. As soon as you can use your left hand again, you'll be driven to the easier points. You'll leave those in more difficult positions until you're in better shape and, hopefully, by then they'll be less difficult. CB thought using a location search to gain access to private property was a good idea. When we find out where the weak spots are, exactly, he'll call in some favors if he has to. Lee's willing to use his celebrity as a distraction when there's no stairs for Leah to fall down."

"You've got everything planned." Didn't mention Kevin Groves, but Tony wasn't going to remind him. He could think of a use for a man who knew a lie when he heard it and didn't want that use to occur to Henry.

He drank his soup. He slept for a bit. He ate a plate of eggs when he woke up. And he complained just enough to keep Henry from getting suspicious.

On his way out of the bathroom some hours later, having stumbled out of bed and to the toilet without actually opening his eyes, he realized the apartment smelled like lasagna and patchouli. That gave him enough warning that he didn't embarrass himself when Amy rose up out of his single armchair like the shark from *Jaws* rising out of the sea. Except it was a great white and she was all in pink-and-black plaid and . . . Okay, it wasn't a very good metaphor, but he'd just woken up so tough.

"Hey."

One of the kitchen chairs was closest to hand, so he sat on that before he fell down. "Hey, back."

"You look like crap."

"Funny, that." His wrist ached, he had enough bruises he looked like the one hundred and second Dalmatian, and his stomach felt as if it was lying flat against his spine.

Amy handed him a bunch of bananas and dropped into the other chair. "Henry said I'm supposed to keep feeding you whenever you wake up, but the lasagna isn't ready so you'll have to eat something healthy. Should you be sitting?"

"Instead of?"

"Lying down."

"Up is good for a while." That was the best banana . . . best *two* bananas he'd ever eaten.

"You're not chewing."

"It's a banana," he protested around a third. "You made lasagna?"

"Please," she snorted. "I bought lasagna; family-sized and frozen. You fell out a window?"

By the time he finished telling her the adventures of Wizardman and Stuntwoman, the food was ready. By the time he finished eating, he could barely keep his eyes open.

"Hey, have Lee send Donna a signed picture, care of Seanix Tech, okay?"

"For the third and final time," she sighed as she lowered him onto the sofa bed, "okay."

The next time he woke up, his apartment smelled like chicken, and Amy was watching *The Princess Diaries III*. He must have made some kind of noise because without turning she said, "Yes, I enjoy movies made for teenage girls.

Before you make something of it, remember that in your weakened state I can kick your ass."

Figuring he had enough going on with two dozen demons, he staggered silently to the bathroom.

"How long was I out?" he asked, returning to his kitchen chair.

"Almost three hours. I was just going to take the chicken out of the oven. Leah said this time you'd need food more than sleep."

"You cooked a chicken?"

"Like it's hard. The oven does all the work. You didn't have a roasting pan, though, so I had to make one out of three aluminum pie plates, half a roll of aluminum foil and the lid off the jar of pickles."

He didn't really want to know.

"Jack called," she told him while he ate. "They—not him but you know, they the cops—found the leg of that guard from out on Eastlake Drive halfway to the studio."

"The whole leg?"

"Most of it." She plopped another spoonful of instant mashed potatoes onto his plate. "I guess the demon got tired of carrying it. What do you figure; snack or weapon?"

"Either. Both."

"Yeah. So you're not going to have time to close all those new weak spots, are you?"

"Not if I have to lie around here much longer." Since he couldn't walk to the can and back without holding the walls, lying around seemed like the best bet.

"If you don't take time to recover, Henry says you'll die and then where will we be? At least with you alive when they come through, we have a chance. What do you think they'll look like?"

"Who?"

She rolled her eyes. "The new demons, dipshit."

"What difference does it make?"

"I'm curious, okay?"

"Leah says the more human evil looks the more dangerous it is."

"More dangerous than that one we chased from the coffee shop? Damned thing had tentacles and claws and spikes and mouths in weird places and . . ."

He held up a hand to cut short the litany. "Maybe it works better as a metaphor in this case."

"Ooooo, metaphors." Burgundy lips pursed. "Someone doesn't want to be a TAD all his life."

"I want to direct."

"You and half the lower mainland. Come on, sleepyhead, back to bed."

Next time he woke up, he definitely felt stronger. Still punctured, bruised, and unable to use his left hand, but stronger. There was a bit of blood soaked through the dressing on his side, but he could walk without holding the walls and he remembered to chew his food—at least as much as he ever did. He was back in control of his body instead of the other way around. But what would it hurt to give Jack and Leah the day to detail the weak spots? It *would* probably speed things up when he got back out there wizarding.

While Amy spooned red Jell-O into bowls, Tony phoned Zev because he wanted to talk about something that wasn't demonic, something normal. Too soon, he found he had almost nothing to say.

Depressing?

No shit, Sherlock.

As the apartment grew dark, he realized he was running out of time.

"I know that look."

"What look?"

She cocked her head and snorted. "The 'I'm about to do something stupid' look. Henry said I'm not to give you your laptop."

It didn't matter; he could call it to his hand no matter where it was.

It didn't matter; he didn't want it.

"I'm just going to lie down again."

"And sleep."

"Sure."

He closed his eyes. Concentrated. Twenty-four soon-to-be-arriving demons had a way of focusing the mind.

He needed to find the square hole to his square peg.

Or was he a round peg in a round hole?

He couldn't remember and wasn't sure it mattered.

If pain was a compulsory part of defining his place in the universe, he had it to spare. His wrist ached. Add it to the definition. His side hurt. Add it to the definition. His nose itched. What the hell . . .

The universe began to take shape around him.

There.

No.

There!

This is pain. This is me. The part that doesn't hurt, that isn't me.

And this is how those parts fit together.

Ladies and gentlemen, we are the world.

He really didn't have much time, but a quick look around from this vantage point might pick up some useful insights. Allowing his consciousness to move out from his body, he brushed against Amy and smiled to see her spirit as a blazing tower of light. Kind of like six or seven of those big opening night searchlights all shining up at the same point.

His wards were a gleaming crimson cage around the apartment, promising safety and danger simultaneously. Tony hoped they were supposed to, but what the hell did he know? Way too many of the last few scenes were being shot on the fly.

Beyond the wards, another tower of light blazed so brilliantly he didn't need contact to see it.

Henry.

Weird that a Nightwalker's spirit would be so bright.

Not weird at all considering it was Henry's.

Henry.

Crap.

No more time to play tourist.

No more time to be an invalid.

Sinking back into his own body, he took a calming breath and forced himself to relax into his place in the universe, his square and/or round hole.

Hesitated.

Remembered.

Bad idea.

Trying not to brace against the anticipated pain, he healed his wrist and the wounds the shrubbery had gouged in his side.

And then he rode that distilled pain deeper. He could see the contradiction in using magic to heal the damage the use of magic had caused. He could also see how to get around it.

His back bowed until only his head and his heels were touching the mattress. Just before he lost consciousness, he heard Henry's voice and was glad Amy wouldn't have to explain the screaming on her own.

⌒ FOURTEEN

Tony was hearing voices. All things considered, that hardly seemed worth getting worked up about, so he lay there, drifting just below consciousness, and listened to the rhythmic rise and fall of sound. After a while, he realized there were words involved.

Loud words.

"I said he was no use to us injured; that doesn't mean I told him to heal himself, and it doesn't mean he'd listen to me if I *had* told him, so just back off."

A woman's voice. He knew that voice.

Leah.

"I don't see the downside, guys." He knew that voice, too. Knew it better. Trusted it more. Amy. "Okay, he's gonna have to pig out again and get his strength back, but then he'll be good to go, and that'll happen a lot faster than it would have taken for his arm to heal."

His point exactly.

"Thank you," Leah agreed.

"This doesn't mean I'm on your side," Amy snorted. "I'm just saying."

"And what if, in his weakened state, his heart had given out? Or a blood vessel had burst in his brain? You couldn't hear his body fighting to survive what he'd done to it. I could." A new voice. A man's voice. A really, really pissed-off voice. Tony had been thinking about maybe trying to open his eyes, but it suddenly seemed smarter to wait until Henry had calmed down a little.

Leah sighed. "The point is, Henry, he did survive. He gambled and he won."

"He had no idea of what the stakes were."

"He's trying to keep the world from being overrun by demons. He's trying to prevent a mass slaughter of innocents. He knows how high the stakes are."

"And how could he have done that if he killed himself?"

"But he didn't kill himself! Have you always been such a pessimist?"

Oh, yeah. That was going to calm him right down. Realizing that if he waited for Henry he'd be lying here all night, Tony forced his eyes open. Leah and Henry were facing off by the table. Amy stood a careful distance away, leaning on the counter.

"Hey." It came out less like a word and more like a cough, but it was enough to get the attention of everyone in the room. "I smell honey garlic . . ." He needed a second breath to finish. ". . . ribs."

Amy grinned. "Leah stopped for Chinese. You hungry?"

"Star . . ." Catching sight of Henry's expression, Tony decided that admitting he was starving might not be the best response. "I could eat . . . a horse."

"That's too bad; she stopped at the good place." Grabbing a towel off the counter, Amy opened the oven door. "I stuck it in here to keep it warm."

"How domestic."

"Oh, about this much. It's a mess in here by the way. You should clean your oven."

"I figured I'd just . . . move."

"Men are disgusting," Leah announced, stepping over to the bed. She pulled a can of nutritional supplement out of her shoulder bag, popped the tab, and held it out. "Drink this first. It'll take the edge off and keep you from choking."

Although nothing hurt, he was embarrassingly weak and just starting to wonder about sitting up when Henry's arm slid under his back and lifted him up to lean against the pile of rearranged pillows. "You're good at that."

"Too much practice."

"It was my choice, Henry."

The vampire's eyes were shadowed. "I know. But she suspected you'd try a healing when you were strong enough. She could have warned me or stopped you."

"*She* is the cat's mother," Leah muttered.

"My grandma used to say that." Amy appeared beside her holding a plate of food. "So you shouldn't. And you . . ." She switched her attention to Tony. ". . . should drink that so you can eat, so you can get your strength back, so you can get back out there and kick demon ass."

Henry watched him while he drank. The supplement was supposed to taste like chocolate. It didn't. It tasted the way people who'd never had chocolate thought chocolate might taste based on descriptions of the cheap waxy shit they sculpted into rabbits at Easter.

Henry watched him while Leah quickly unwound the bandage on his left wrist and he flexed the fingers, checking that everything worked the way it was supposed to.

Henry watched him while he forked Chinese food into his mouth. Actually, all three of them watched, but Henry's gaze was the heaviest. Leah kept her expression neutral—probably so as not to provoke Henry—and Amy made pig noises.

"Want more?" she asked when he finished. "Never mind." She took the empty plate before he could reply. "Stupid question."

Beginning to feel better, Tony sat up straight and Leah leaned in to remove the gauze wrapped around his torso. Henry's hands were there first. She backed up, her own raised in exaggerated surrender.

Tony shivered as cool fingers touched his skin, checking that the punctures had healed and the bruises were gone. They lingered last against his throat where the bite mark had been. This time it was gone. The skin was smooth.

"Your choice," Henry said softly and straightened.

"What just happened?" Amy demanded as she set another filled plate of food on Tony's lap.

"Our little boy just grew up."

Pausing just long enough to glare in Leah's direction, Tony dug in as Amy snorted.

"As if."

Just after three, Tony dropped Amy off at her apartment.

"Are you going to be okay?" he asked as she leaned back into the car.

"Me? I'm fine. Why?"

"You've got to be up in three hours for work."

"I sit on my ass most of the day, I'll be fine. Besides, I've never needed a lot of sleep. What about you?"

"Me? *I'm* fine." He'd damned well better be 'cause that whole healing thing had fucking hurt.

"Uh-huh." She looked as though she was planning to argue but thought better of it. "Just be careful, okay? And thanks for letting me help. This stuff is, you know, real."

He frowned, not sure he understood. "Real?"

"We're saving the world from demons who want to slaughter and enslave us, Tony, and it doesn't get more real than that." Straightening, she hung her *Vampire Princess Miju* backpack over one shoulder. "Keep me in the loop or it's chow mein noodles under the fingernails," she growled and quietly closed the car door.

Real demons. Two words guaranteed not to show up in the same sentence in most lives. Tony watched Amy trot into her building, waiting until he saw the light go on in her apartment before he turned the engine back on and put the car in gear. It was chivalry she wouldn't thank him for, but tough. Demons weren't the only metaphysical creatures wandering around the lower mainland, and she had a big "I believe" stamped on her forehead.

Henry pulled out right behind him.

Tony'd slept all day and hadn't wanted to waste any more time, so the moment the calories kicked in, he left Leah asleep in his apartment and headed for the one easy access weak spot of the six she'd mapped out with Jack.

Separate cars because Henry had his own inflexible timetable.

New Westminster had been replacing old water mains for some time now. According to Leah, Mckaseeh had plans to pop a demon through in the trench on Fader Street. Tony drove past and stopped at the Hume Park end of the road.

"In case an insomniac across from where I'm working glances out the window and reports something hinky going on," he explained to Henry's raised eyebrow as the vampire got out of his car.

Henry made a noncommittal noise.

"It could happen," Tony muttered as they walked back.

"Is there no security on the site?"

"Just the kind that drives by every couple of hours. If they show up while I'm wizarding, you can go talk to them." He sketched a set of air quotes around the word *talk*.

"Thank you for letting me help."

Sarcasm? Tony didn't think so. Henry sounded just as sincere as Amy had and, come to think of it, just as sincere as Lee had earlier. He frowned. Why would people be grateful for a chance to die by demon? Because no one likes to sit around with their thumb up their butt when the world is ending, feeling help*less*.

Whoa. Epiphany. In a time of crisis no one wanted to feel they were less than they were.

He wasn't just sending his friends and coworkers out into danger, he was empowering them. Okay, except for Henry who was about as empowered as it got all on his own. This didn't mean he could thoughtlessly thrust them into danger, but he could stop feeling so friggin' guilty about the danger they were in.

I wonder if I will . . .

The Arjh Lord's weak point was at the bottom of the trench, the shimmer nearly indistinguishable in the dark patterns of turned earth and old pipes.

Tony peered down into the construction site, his weight sending a small avalanche of dirt off the crumbling edge. "If I burn the rune then tip it on its side, then shove it out over the trench, and you hold me in place, I could push it down into the pit without having to climb down there."

A red-gold brow rose.

"Not going to happen, is it?"

Henry pointed along the trench. "I think you'll be safest climbing down there at the end where the new pipe has been laid. It's a gentler slope."

For not particularly large values of gentle.

Surfing the last meter on a wave of rubble, Tony hit bottom buried knee-deep in dirt. He glanced back at the new angle and sighed. Getting out was going to be fun.

But first the fun of dragging his lower legs free and then the fun of getting to the weak spot without breaking his neck.

Cocking his head, he could see the shimmer, but he couldn't see his footing.

Memo to self. Next time, bring a flashlight.

First, buy a flashlight since he didn't own one.

Because he didn't need one . . .

The first couple of weeks after the haunted house, he'd practiced the Wizard's Lamp spell obsessively, but it had been months and he wasn't 100 percent positive he remembered the wording.

Or, as it happened, how much juice to give it.

Any possibility of developing night vision was obliterated in the sudden flare of brilliant white light, which broke his concentration so completely that it shut off again almost immediately.

"That was unpleasant," Henry snarled.

Tony peered up through the afterimages at where he thought Henry might be standing. "Sorry."

"Just do what you came to do and do it quickly before someone arrives to investigate that flare."

"You think someone saw it?"

"I think they saw it in Alberta."

He didn't so much find the shimmer as trip and fall into it. He expected it to feel unpleasant, but it actually felt anticipatory. A moment spent considering who was doing the anticipating added in the unpleasant.

After burning the first rune, he realized that they shed enough light for him to find a path.

"I should've just dragged a rune along with me," he muttered, shoving it through the weak point.

"Yes, you should have." Henry had, of course, been able to hear him. He wasn't sure why he could hear Henry, whether it was a vampire thing or a wizard thing or Henry just didn't care who he woke up, figuring he could handle anything that lived in New Westminster. "There's a car coming," he continued, breaking into Tony's musing. "If it stops, I'll deal with it."

"Sure." The musing was new. He never used to muse.

The car stopped right about the time Tony was pushing through the second rune. He waited until he heard Henry's quiet, "Can I help you, Officer?" and then burned the third rune on the air.

The car pulled away as he finished and he drew a two foot W—*Because today's show is brought to you by the words* wizard *and* whatever—to light his way out of the pit.

Almost out of the pit.

The slope began to crumble. "Henry!"

Strong fingers closed around his wrist and yanked, defying gravity and slamming him into the reassuringly solid barrier of Henry's chest.

"Do you have to make even the easy ones difficult?" the vampire murmured, the words cool against the back of his neck.

"I didn't make it difficult," Tony panted. "It was in a pit! What did the cop want?" he asked, pulling far enough away to see Henry's face.

"He wanted to know about the light."

"What did you tell him?"

A flash of teeth. "That he didn't want to know about the light."

Four down, twenty-three to go.

"Okay, Jack and Leah will keep mapping out the sites, so we don't have to figure out how to deal on the fly—they get the information back to CB; he works out the plan. I use the location search cover for the shopping mall and the restaurant and the garage while Amy runs interference." Tony picked up the list off CB's desk and shoved it in his back pocket. "That's a start anyway."

"If you want, I could stay here and plan with CB while Lee runs interference," Amy offered.

"Mr. Nicholas is working this morning," CB growled. "In spite of the damage to my building, we are still attempting to shoot a television show here."

She rolled her eyes. "No point in saving the world if we can't save *Darkest Night*?"

"No point at all." He wasn't kidding.

"No, no, they'll walk through the actual mall, but the chase scene will play out here in the gritty back corridors of commerce." Amy's voice drifted around the corner to where Tony was pushing runes between the brackets that had once held some kind of storage rack. "It'll be an exotic locale with lots of atmospheric shadows and very little chance of anything expensive getting broken."

The head of mall security snorted. "That's almost exactly what your boss said when he called."

"Yeah, well, he's big on nothing expensive getting broken."

It was harder to spot the shimmers without Leah beside him playing Marco Polo with her belly, and a scrawled note directing them, "Toward the back of the restaurant," wasn't a lot of help. Tony took an embarrassingly long time to find the weak spot on the wall of the walk-in freezer.

"Is there something missing here?" he asked the restaurant manager.

"Yeah, used to be a set of shelves that bolted to the wall. We took 'em out about a month ago, why?"

"Just wondering."

"Yeah? Well, I'm wondering what a vampire's going to be detecting in my freezer."

"Aliens," Amy drew the manager back out into the kitchen. "Kept on ice by the CIA. But don't worry, no one will ever connect this freezer to your restaurant, so you won't be overrun by hordes of alien conspiracy freaks. Unless you want to be."

"No, it's like there's this car accident, see, and they bring the car back here. But Raymond Dark suspects that it wasn't an accident and that the car didn't really hit a tree. Okay, it did hit a tree, but the tree really did jump out into the road."

The way the garage owner and both mechanics were hanging on Amy's every word, not to mention her cleavage and the very, very short skirt she was wearing over the black tights and combat boots, Tony figured he could have turned the '63 Thunderbird on the rack into a pumpkin and none of them would have noticed. Not that he'd do anything so heinous to such a wicked ride, but still.

Later, he mentioned that she was disturbingly good at coming up with freaky story ideas.

"I know." She slouched lower in the seat and pulled out her phone to call the office. "It scares me a bit, too."

Seven down.

Tony had an entire barbecued chicken for lunch, a 500-gram tub of potato salad, and three organic bananas Amy made him eat for the potassium. He was hungry, sure, but he still felt great. That last healing had totally been worth it.

"Leah's marked two more construction sites I can do after dark. If I can get another three tears sealed up this afternoon, well, I'm starting to think we might actually be able to win this."

"I am uplifted by your confidence. Another banana?"

"No, thanks. Three's fine."

"For the last time, Mr. White has been called away, and I don't care what television show you're from; no one goes into his office without his permission."

"I keep trying to tell *you*," Amy sighed, "that my boss phoned and spoke to your boss, and he said it wouldn't be a problem. We'll just be in and out."

Mr. White's secretary—executive assistant? Pit bull? Tony had no idea—folded her hands into what shouldn't have even remotely resembled a threatening position. Shouldn't have. Did. "Mr. White left no such instructions with me. You'll have to come back tomorrow when Mr. White is in the building."

"But . . ."

"Tomorrow."

"Will he be in later today?"

One perfectly plucked brow rose. "What did I just say?"

"Come back tomorrow?"

She smiled, not exactly in approval. "Did you want to make an appointment?"

"We had an appointment!"

"So you say. Not that it matters as Mr. White isn't here."

"Okay. Fine. We'll make an appointment."

"I'm sorry. Mr. White has no time tomorrow. Would Thursday fit your schedule?"

"What happened to Wednesday?"

"He's in court on Wednesday."

Amy took a deep breath and let it out slowly. "Mr. Bane will call Mr. White again and set something up. We'll be back."

Mr. White's secretary seemed unimpressed.

"That was a fucking waste of time we don't have." Tony sagged against the elevator wall and glared at their reflections in the stainless steel. "I should come back with a Notice Me Not on and just boogie by."

"I thought you didn't know how to get noticed again after you did a Notice Me Not."

"Yeah, well. Flaw in a brilliant plan." Without Henry around to call him back, he'd be stuck unnoticed.

"I say we just let the demon trash Mr. White's office." Amy snorted, rocking forward and back, heel to toe.

"Works for me. This could be one of the ones I don't get to."

"Unless you get to all of them, shut Mckaseeh down cold."

"Not going to happen."

Her lip curled. "Not with that attitude."

"Not with only twenty-four hours in a day."

"Time travel!"

"No." He locked eyes with her reflection so she'd know he was serious. "No messing around with time. It's a lot more dangerous than demons."

"And you don't know how to give us more time anyway, do you?"

So much for that whole locking eyes thing. "Well, no."

She bounced, once, happy with her victory. "I wonder what's missing in Mr. White's office?"

"He's a lawyer," Tony muttered, as the elevator door opened and he pushed past a neoprene-covered bicycle messenger and out into the lobby. "Where to start . . ."

"Ms. Wong, please. If you could just wait for a couple more minutes. We're stuck in traffic. Yes, I realize you'd like to go, but . . . We're coming in on Hastings. No, that probably wasn't the best idea at this time of day. Just give us fifteen . . ." Amy glanced over at Tony who raised his right hand, fingers spread. ". . . twenty minutes. No, we won't be long once we get there. I promise. Thank you. We won't be long, will we?" she asked, closing her phone.

"Hard to say, the old Carnegie Library probably has . . . Hey!" He broke off his explanation to yell at the car ahead of them. "What are your fucking turn signals for, asshole!" And broke back on at: ". . . a shitload of nooks and crannies. It could take a while to find the exact position of the weak spot without Leah."

"I don't think we're going to have a while."

"You said the library was open until ten every day, Sunday to Monday. And this is Monday."

"The person CB spoke to is only there until five and, if you'll recall, our plans did not enjoy much success in the absence of Mr. White."

Tony sighed and geared down. "I'm clinging to the hope that librarians are more helpful than lawyers."

Wizards had the same trouble everyone else did finding a parking space in Chinatown at nearly five on a weeknight. Or any other time for that matter. He thought about parking illegally and putting a Notice Me Not on the car but was afraid he wouldn't be able to find it again later. They got to the library at 5:21. Ms. Wong was not impressed. Nor was she impressed by their desire to just wander around and "get the feel of the place."

"You are not the first people who have wanted to use our interior in their television show." She folded her arms and the toe of one sensible black pump tapped lightly on the tile. "You're not even the first people this month. Tell me the effect you're looking for, and I will take you where you need to go. This does not have to take the rest of the evening."

"Couldn't you just hand us over to the evening staff?" Amy asked.

"No. You're my responsibility, and the evening staff has work of their own to do. What do you need?"

"Well . . ."

"We need a place where something's missing." Tony stepped into Amy's pause.

The librarian frowned, stared at him for a long moment, and said, "There's a cushion missing off one of the seats in the reading room. Someone walked off with it last week."

"That's a good place to start. If you could . . ." He gestured and waited.

She stared at him for a moment longer and then shrugged, the barest lifting of one worsted shoulder. "This way."

Eight down; nineteen to go.

"Talk about a hot seat," Amy snickered. "Some guy's sitting there, reading a newspaper and pow, demon up the ass."

Tony suppressed any thought of Ryne Cyratane in that context.

"I called the office when you were closing that last one because Ms. Wong didn't need to be distracted, and CB says the next one is another private house and Lee's going to meet us there at seven."

"Why?"

"Teenage daughters."

Okay. "Why at seven?"

"Because you've got to eat. And," she added before he could suggest they hit a drive-through and eat in the car, "because CB's estimating another half hour before Peter's through with Lee for the day."

"Oh, for . . ." Tony accelerated through a yellow light. "I think saving the world from demons is more important than getting Lee's last shot."

Amy snorted. "No, you don't."

No, he didn't.

"So why'd you just tell that librarian you needed a place where something was missing?"

Good question. "Honesty is the best policy?"

"As if."

"I thought she'd understand. She looked like she'd been . . ." He searched desperately for a less PAX TV way of saying it and couldn't find one. ". . . touched by magic."

Folding her knees up by her chest, Amy propped her boots on the dashboard. "Touched by who?"

"I don't know."

But she was a good-looking woman and he knew Henry Hunted in that part of the city.

"That sounds absolutely fascinating, ladies."

Tony could hear the smile in Lee's voice and knew that Mom and both girls were basking in full-on Lee Nicholas charm. There'd been shrieking when the door had first been opened and constant babbling as the whole group of them headed upstairs. When it looked like the babbling might ease up, Lee merely had to ask a question or make a comment and they were off again.

Dad had retreated behind a copy of the *Vancouver Sun* pretty much immediately.

Tony faced the five closed doors at the top of the stairs and pointed toward the northeast corner where Leah had placed the weak spot. "That room."

"Oh, my God!" The fourteen-year-old grabbed at Lee's sleeve. "That's my room."

"May I see it?"

Tony would have shown him anything if asked in that tone. If the renewed shrieking was any indication, he wasn't the only one. Fourteen raced in to tidy up while her sixteen-year-old sister tried to convince Lee that her room was infinitely better. Mom pointed out that he'd find the master suite not only bigger but more comfortable. The wink, wink, nudge, nudge was strongly implied.

Once in fourteen's bedroom, after his vision adjusted to the Day-Glo *That '70s Show* decorating, Tony discovered that the closet door was missing, replaced by a curtain of multicolored beads. The weak spot filled the space. With any luck, it was practice making the shimmer easier to see, not the imminent arrival of a host of demons.

"I might need to look at the other bedrooms," Lee said thoughtfully, when Tony gave him the sign.

More shrieking.

It suddenly became clear why Lee was willing to face demons. Demons were quieter.

Nine down. Eighteen demons were still eighteen demons too many.

"Where to after this?" Lee asked sotto voce as they walked side by side down the porch stairs. This prime space had opened up when Mom had been forced to physically intervene before an argument over who'd walk beside Lee to the curb had come to blows.

"I'm meeting Henry at a construction site," Tony told him as, behind them, fourteen accused sixteen of having been in her face her entire life. "You're okay driving Amy home?"

"Sure. You'll get some sleep? I mean, later."

"I don't need much."

"I have to admit you look better than you did." Lee's gaze skittered across the side of Tony's face and ended up locked on the path. "Better in a medical sense. We're all worried about you."

Tony took a few seconds to examine and abandon several possible responses before sticking with tradition. "I'm fine."

"You've lost a lot of weight."

"When this is over . . ." He paused as sixteen threw in an *oh, grow up* too vehement to talk over. ". . . I'll gain it back."

"I'm not saying you're looking less studly; I'm saying you look a bit thin is all."

Studly? Tony tripped over a bit of concrete edging. Lee grabbed his arm and yanked him roughly back onto his feet.

"Guys!" Amy's voice cut through the October evening like a siren. "We've got incoming fen!"

Fourteen and sixteen buried the hatchet and began yelling at their friends to hurry.

Several voices shrieked, "Oh, my God, it's Lee Nicholas!"

Several more shrieked, "Lee, I love you!"

Tony's car was across the street and half a dozen houses down. Lee had found a spot barely twenty meters away. "Run!" Tony gave him a shove. "You can make it to your car!"

"What about you?" Lee demanded as the shrieking lost vocabulary and degenerated into a primal fannish keen.

"Don't worry about me, once you're gone, they'll calm down."

"What if they don't?"

"Damn it, Lee, run!" Just for a second, Tony was sure he heard an overwrought soundtrack, then Lee turned and sprinted for his car, digging out his keys as he ran.

A chime as the doors of the new Mercedes SUV unlocked.

"Amy!"

"Already here." She glared across the hood as Lee raced for the driver's door. "And do you have any idea how much gas one of these things uses?"

"It's bio-diesel!"

"No shit?" Half in, she leaned out for another look and nearly went flying as Lee pulled away from the curb. She dragged herself in and as the door closed, Tony heard Lee getting an earful of Spanish profanity.

At least Tony thought it was profanity. He didn't speak Spanish.

News to him that Amy did.

As the crowd realized they'd lost a chance to get up close and personal with the actor second billed in the opening credits of the highest rated vampire detective show on syndicated television, they turned their nearly hysterical, thwarted gaze on Tony. Just in case Lee hadn't been impressive on his own, Tony was wearing his show jacket to impress the homeowners.

The crowd didn't know who he was or what he did, but they knew he was with the show.

They were between him and his car.

He'd never make it.

This was not the time for discretion.

Bright side, no one would believe this lot anyway.

Tony grabbed for his focus, reached for his fly, and snapped out the Notice Me Not.

There was a security guard on duty at the first construction site. A six-foot-four ex-cop from Ghana, he was studying to be an EMT. With an exam coming up, the odds were good he'd have never noticed a quiet visit tucked in between his appointed rounds, but Henry leaned just enough to raise the odds a little more and then went out to meet Tony.

Although the last of the evening's commuters kept the traffic fairly heavy over on Norland Avenue, Ledger Avenue—where the condominium complex was being built—was nearly empty. Henry heard Tony's car before he saw it. Even knowing it was there, it was nearly impossible to keep his attention on it. He found himself distracted by the hearts beating all around him; by the scent of blood, warm and contained; by the hundreds of thousands of lives that could be his for the Hunting.

Snarling, he forced himself to watch as the car stopped and the driver's side door opened and . . .

There was a woman singing in a third-floor apartment across the road. The song was melancholy, and it told him he'd be welcomed should his Hunt take him to her door.

A touch on his shoulder.

He whirled, grabbed a fistful of fabric, and slammed someone, something to the pavement—the familiar scent registering a moment too late.

"Fucking ow, Henry! That hurt!"

"Tony." Lying at his feet. Heart racing. Glaring up at him as if this was somehow his fault. "I see. You used the Notice Me Not again."

"I didn't have a choice," Tony grunted, accepting Henry's hand and allowing himself to be lifted to his feet. "There was this horde of *Darkest Night* fans ready to tear me limb from limb."

A red-gold brow rose. "The show has enough fans to make up a horde?"

"Small horde," he admitted, checking to make sure everything worked. "More like a mob, really. Very feisty, though. And pissed. So, are you planning to apologize for dumping me on my ass?" Which felt distinctly bruised.

Henry smiled. "Your spell distracted me with thoughts of the Hunt."

"So you're saying I'm lucky I only got dumped on my ass?"

"Essentially."

"Okay, works for me." He turned to study the steel skeletons of the three towers. "Leah's notes say this one's tucked up in that first structure."

Tony knew Henry wouldn't drop him. Knew it without question. His hindbrain however, currently dangling four stories up supported only by a vampire's grip on his ankles, was having none of that. As far as his hindbrain was concerned, they were going to die.

Painfully.

Messily.

On impact.

The hysterical background babbling of *OH, MY GOD!* was annoying. And distracting.

"I don't want to rush you, Tony, but the moon has risen and we're not exactly invisible up here. If a resident living on the upper floors of any of those buildings across the way should happen to glance out their window . . ."

"Yeah. I get it. We'd be screwed. Sorry."

The orientation of the runes didn't seem to matter.

Good fucking thing, too, because I don't think I could draw them upside down.

Right side up. I'm upside down.

OHMYGODOHMYGODOHMYGOD!

Ten down. Seventeen to go.

The second weak spot of the night wasn't so much in a construction site as an excavation.

"What's with the attraction to holes in the ground?" Tony muttered as they walked down the packed dirt ramp left for the excavation equipment.

"They are creatures of hell. They would feel at home in a pit."

"It's not that kind of a hell, Henry."

"Would a man spend his time there in eternal torment?"

"I guess." Based on what they'd seen of the inhabitants, it seemed a fair assumption. Although *eternal* might be thinking a bit too long term.

"Then it's close enough for me."

Eleven to sixteen.

"Oh, no," Tony protested, backing away even though Henry had made no move in his direction. "There'll be time enough to sleep when this is over."

"If you could finish it tonight, I'd agree with you, but you can't and you're becoming visibly exhausted. When you're tired, you make mistakes. When you make mistakes, you get hurt. When you get hurt, you heal yourself and, as your body becomes progressively more worn down, there is always the chance you won't survive the process."

"There's not much room for argument when you put it like that."

Henry smiled his most irritating Prince of Man smile. "Which is why I put it like that."

Television meant early mornings and habit got Tony to the studio by seven, a mere ten minutes after sunrise even though Henry had set his alarm for eight before he left. CB and Leah and Jack were already in the office. Amy arrived minutes after Tony, and Lee minutes after that, carrying a tray of coffee.

"You may be wondering why I've called you all here," Jack muttered.

Only Amy laughed.

One hand up under the edge of her sweater, Leah stared down at the map spread out over CB's desk. "Well, that confirms it. The tears are deeper than they were."

Sixteen of the burns on the map were noticeably darker.

The good news was, Leah had recognized Ryne Cyratane's ownership of the arjh coming through in the middle of the Willingdon overpass. And the bad news involved the Telus overpass and another weak spot.

While Tony and Lee had been dodging teenagers, CB had spent a couple of hours on the phone and called in some favors.

At exactly 9:45, an RCMP patrol car, lights flashing, pulled out into the middle lane of the Kingsway and parked just out from under the Telus overpass. Morning rush hour traffic, finally having dropped from insanely busy to annoyingly crowded, began to flow around it. When the uniformed constable

stopped traffic entirely, Tony helped manhandle the rented telescoping platform out under the overpass. As the guy who'd come with the platform locked
it down, he set out orange traffic cones.

When CB had laid out the plan, Tony had stared at him in disbelief. *"What
am I supposed to do while they're setting up?"* he'd demanded.

"I suggest, Mr. Foster, that you do your job. Unless there happens to be a
spell to turn straw into gold on that laptop of yours, in which case you may do
whatever you please."

As traffic began to move again, now including the area the platform occupied in their detour, he followed the steadicam operator up the short ladder
and clutched the steel railing as the platform rose.

They were directly under the weak spot. He could burn the runes in the air
just below it and then shove them quickly up and through. The steadicam
operator had his back to Tony as he shot the traffic moving under the overpass.
The occupants of the cars, used to having to accommodate a dozen studios
plus visiting productions, didn't even look up.

He was finished in just under ten minutes.

"Okay, let's go."

"I don't think so, kid. Chester Bane is paying me for twenty minutes of
brand spanking new stock footage and that's what I'm going to shoot for him."

"But . . ."

"Do I look stupid enough to cross Chester Bane, kid?"

Fair question. And no, he didn't. "Then just let me down."

"We have this spot for half an hour, kid, no more. That's bloody close to
not enough time so, again, no."

He couldn't climb down; dangling then dropping made him think of broken legs and Henry's reaction. "I'm trying to save the fucking world here!"

"Yeah, well, I only have your word for that whereas I know what'll happen
if Chester Bane pays for twenty minutes and gets nineteen fifty-nine. The end
of the world will seem tame in comparison."

Since Tony didn't have an argument for that, he folded his arms and fumed.

With the easy places already taken care of, he only got two closed that day and
one closed after dark.

Fourteen to thirteen. They'd pulled ahead by one. Two if he put Ryne
Cyratane's marked arjh on their side of the count.

As Tony fell into a fitful sleep, he held tight to the hope that they might
have a shot at winning this after all.

Three closed the next day.

Seventeen to ten.

Only two the day after that, though, and the second was nearly a disaster.

"What the hell is he doing? Does he paint graffiti on the pool? I see him paint something! I don't believe you come from vampire television. You stay! You stay right there! I call the 911!"

The Notice Me Not kept him from getting arrested, but it also kept him from interacting with anything until long after sunset, when Henry finally found him. The longer the spell was on, the harder it was to get off.

Nineteen to eight.

Twenty to seven.

Twenty-one to six.

Those last two had gone relatively easily, but now he was stuck in traffic with Leah singing along to the latest from Radiogram. They were a local band who'd recently rocketed off local playlists and into the international music scene. Tony liked the band and their music, but Leah's smug *I followed them before they were famous* attitude was driving him up the wall. She even sang along smugly.

Like I don't have enough to do without sitting here and listening to her . . .

Hang on. Had Radiogram worked the *Darkest Night* theme into their latest release?

No. That was his phone.

"Leah."

"I'm on it." She stretched an arm behind his seat, snagged his backpack, freed his phone, and stuffed it into the dock.

"Tony, it's Kevin Groves. I just got a call from one of our regulars. She says she saw something big with horns blow apart the Willingdon overpass."

Tony eased into the curb lane while he waited for the other shoe to drop.

"She wasn't lying."

And there it was.

"Thanks, Kevin. Hang up." The phone clicked off. He needed to get to the studio. He needed to get turned around. Diagonally through a gas station, out the other side, over a median strip, and into the left turn lane to more or less catch the final seconds of the advance green.

Half a block. Picking up speed. Cutting between two SUVs.

Sliding sideways on damp pavement, Tony fought the car back onto four tires. "Keep that map down. I need to see out that window!"

"You need your fucking head—BUS!—head examined! And you need to look at this."

Another half block before he could take his eyes off the road long enough to glance her way. The way Leah was holding the map, he could see six pinholes where the light showed through. Six weak points burned through. Six demons in the city. One of them was theoretically on their side, but somehow that didn't make him feel any better.

"Call CB, tell him to empty the studio. Then call Jack and Henry."

"Sun's not down. BIKE!"

He missed the cyclist by millimeters. "Leave a message."

"I have a better idea." Her fingernails had left half-moon cuts in his dashboard. "Why don't you pull into that strip mall, then you can make the calls and I can get us to the studio alive?"

Tony hesitated just for a second then bounced up over the curb and into the strip mall parking lot. This was not the time to let machismo get in the way of a professional stunt driver. Their odds would improve with stunt drivers in the surrounding cars, but he'd take what he could get. As he dove back into the passenger side and buckled up, he glanced at the clock. 5:07. More than an hour and a half until sunset.

As Leah stomped on the gas, he reached for the phone.

They'd be starting before Henry woke for the night. Then he'd have to drive out to Burnaby. They'd be fighting multiple demons without his strength and speed, and it was entirely possible they'd be finished without him. Fucking weak spots might as well have torn open at noon. "TAXI!"

"Please. I saw it. You know, we still have time to get on a plane and haul ass out of here."

Suspicion tightened his chest. "Was that why you wanted to drive?"

"No, no, I'm doing the responsible thing."

"ONE-WAY STREET!"

Leah snorted and drove half a block on the sidewalk. "You know, Tony, if you're going to save the world tonight, you really need to pace yourself."

〜 FIFTEEN

Fighting to keep the nutritional supplement pouring into his mouth instead of spraying around the inside of the car, Tony watched in amazement as Leah forced every possible ounce of power from the elderly engine, took a few highly illegal shortcuts, and beat the demons back to the soundstage. The previous two trips they'd taken had clearly been nothing more than a rehearsal for this.

"Bonus that there's never a cop around when you need one," he ground out through clenched teeth, really hoping he wasn't going to hurl as they bounced over the back curb of the CB Productions lot.

"We weren't on a major highway this time, so I doubt anyone called us in."

"You doubt?" His voice went up embarrassingly high on the second word. "You went the wrong way down a Tim Horton's drive-through!"

"Please, in this area . . ." Leah yanked the wheel hard to the left and skidded to a stop, spraying gravel over the craft services truck. ". . . they probably thought we were filming."

She had a point. A month earlier, Vancouverites had applauded an armed bank robbery; bank security hadn't intervened, apparently waiting for someone to yell *"Cut!"*

"There're too many vehicles still in the lot," Tony grumbled, getting out of the car. Sure they'd been speedy, but he'd seen CB clear the building in less time. When the big guy said *go*, it took a stupidly reckless man to linger.

Leah grabbed his arm. "Hang on." Dragging him around to face her, she licked the edge of a tissue and scrubbed at his upper lip.

"What the . . ."

"Supplement mustache. Sets a bad example for the troops."

"We don't have any troops!"

"And the demons will laugh at you." One final swipe. "There."

"Thank you." It was as sarcastic an appreciation as he could manage. "Do I look like I should be taken seriously now?" he demanded as they raced for the rear door.

"Not so much, no."

Big surprise. Not. Maybe he should get a pointy hat. Or a big sword. Or his head examined.

Charging down the center aisle, he jumped cables, dodged around equipment, stopped dead as he emerged out into the open area by Adam's desk. "What the . . . ?" He whirled to glare at Leah. "Did you know this was going to happen?"

She spread her hands. "Hey, I'm as surprised as you are."

"You mentioned troops!"

"I was being facetious."

"They want to help," CB explained, stepping forward.

"Help?" Tony moved his attention from Leah to his boss. "What did you tell them?"

"That the battle would be joined tonight. Not as part of a general announcement, but to those who knew enough to ask."

Zev, Amy, Lee—no surprise, although Tony would rather they were all somewhere safe, like New Zealand—Mouse, Peter . . .

"Sorge and Adam and Tina have kids," Peter said, one thigh propped on Adam's desk next to a half-full box of flares last used in episode seven. "Kids who actually live with them," he amended. "We sent them home."

. . . Saleen, Pavin, and Kate.

They'd all been in the house last summer. They'd survived Creighton

Caulfield and they'd heard about what had happened in the spring with the Shadowlord. They knew what Tony was, and they thought they knew what he could do.

"Your fan club seems to be growing," Leah murmured, warm breath lifting the hair on the back of his neck.

Yeah, right. Kate had never liked him.

"Guys, there's half a dozen demons on their way. Demons. Just like in the most clichéd screenplay; all claws and horns and tentacles and bad attitude. Ask Zev, ask Amy, ask CB, they've all seen them. Well, one." He frowned. "Okay, I think CB saw a couple of them, but . . ."

"Shut up," Kate snarled. "We asked. We know." She snapped the loops of yellow nylon rope between her hands. "We need to knock them down and tie them up so you can send them back right? It's a physical fight—slam, bam, kick a little demonic ass?"

"It's not that easy . . ."

"Did I say it was going to be easy? We get that they're big and strong. What we don't get is how you thought you could take them out with only the boss and a Mountie at your side."

"Hey!" Amy protested. "Lee and I were always staying!"

"Yeah, an actor and a receptionist, that'll make a lot of difference," Saleen muttered. The grip slapped a length of steel pipe into his left hand. "These things have no special powers, right?"

"Well, they . . ."

"No," Leah interrupted. "They're just big and strong."

"And ugly," Zev snorted, fingering the sleeve of his sweater.

"Then it's time we get some of our own back."

"Some of your own back from what?" Tony demanded, wondering when he'd lost control of the situation. The words "stupidly reckless" were repeating on a background loop in his head.

"The Shadowlord. Creighton Caulfield." Mouse never said much, so the big cameraman's words carried a deliberate weight.

"They're not doing this for you, Tony." Lee crossed to stand barely an arm's length away. "They're fighting for themselves. Because this time, they can."

They're not? They? The next obvious question had to be *What about you?* or maybe *Who writes your dialogue?* But he knew the answer to the second and this wasn't the time to hear the answer to the first, and anyway, there were half a dozen demons making tracks to the studio. He took a deep breath and one step to the side so that the others could see him. Everyone accounted for but Mason, and Mason's absence was hardly sur . . .

"Goddamned thing got buried in the closet!" Clutching the double-handed broadsword from episode twelve and wearing the slightly squibbed camouflage jacket from episode sixteen, Mason rocked to a stop by CB's side. "What did I miss?"

"Tony questioning our right to be here," Kate deadpanned.

Mason snorted. "*Tony* questioning? Who's the star of this show, him or me?"

"Heads up, people!" Jack charged into the group, glanced around, and obviously decided not to ask. "I just got off the phone with Geetha. There're six kinds of hell breaking lose and heading this way."

"You've been waiting your whole career to say that, haven't you?" Amy asked, snickering.

He flashed her a broad smile. "Pretty much, yeah."

"Okay." It wouldn't be in a few minutes, but right now it was. When they all turned to look at him, Tony said it again just because he liked the sound of it. "Okay. Jack, help Leah and CB position the troops. Pavin, bring one of the Fresnos to the back. I'm going to try and stop a demon at the door." He ran for the back without waiting for an answer. If they wanted to help, they could damned well be helpful.

He'd finished burning the first two runes by the time Pavin wrestled one of the small spotlights over from the office set. "Does light hurt them?"

"No. Set up here. Aim the beam through that pattern and right out the door."

"Blinding it?" Pavin asked, remarkably blasé about bright blue squiggles just hanging in the air. He used the knob on the back of the casing to adjust the beam. "So it can't see what you wrote?"

Let's hear it for tech support. "Yeah. That's the idea." He stepped out into the parking lot and drew the third rune with his eyes nearly squinted shut. "You'd better get back with the others."

The light blazed out the open door, significantly brighter than the late afternoon sun and definitely blinding. He couldn't see the rune from any angle that would get him through the door. Hopefully, the demon didn't know how this world worked, so it wouldn't realize the light was too bright. If they were lucky, it might wonder about the sudden change in illumination and pause in the doorway, giving him time to get the final rune in place. With a little more luck, it wouldn't be Ryne Cyratane's arjh who showed up, wasting a perfectly good trap or trapping one of their best chances of surviving this.

Good idea, Tony, use up all your luck before the fight even starts.

As he burned the fourth rune, he realized there was something not quite right about the ambient noise. The familiar background sounds of the city were less familiar than they should be. He'd nearly finished when those sounds separated into squealing tires and breaking glass. Less screaming than he'd expected, but there'd likely be time for that later.

Half a Honda Civic rolled past the edge of the building. Tony slapped the

last curl on the fourth rune and dove behind the garbage can at the craft services truck, rune clutched in his left hand. The demon charged around the
corner still holding the other half of the car.

What I'm holding beats what you're holding . . .

. . . unless you decide to throw the car at me. Crap!

The twisted hunk of metal crashed into the gravel right in front of the
garbage can, covering Tony in glittering bits of safety glass and slamming
the can into his shoulder.

He didn't think he made much of a noise, but when the dust settled, the
demon stood just outside the beam of light, eyestalks turned toward him,
the bit on its face that corresponded to a nose twitching and testing the air.

Not good on a couple of levels.

The runes wouldn't hang forever and a little experimentation over the last
few days had proved that the longer they were in place, the less kickass they
became.

Also, the plan was to avoid the ultimate wizard and demon one on one for
as long as possible. A Powershot would knock him on his ass and out of the
fight, so if it turned out to be inevitable it had to happen late in the game.

From inside the soundstage, a girlie shriek. It sounded like Mason.

The demon's head went up, exposing the get-Leah rune cut into its chest.
Hard to tell, given the arrangement of its features, but it looked embarrassed.
Maybe not Mason, then. Maybe some demons were less demonic than others. Grumbling under its breath, it stepped into the light, hissed and reared
back, eyestalks withdrawing into the top of its head.

Tony had started moving as the demon moved. As it reared, he shoved the
fourth rune into position.

It had time for only a truncated howl before the runes flared and it disappeared.

"Yes! One down!" He'd just started breathing normally for what seemed
like the first time in half an hour when a clawed hand closed on his bruised
shoulder.

There were only three entrances to the soundstage.

Three entrances. Six demons. Basic math.

Crap.

And fucking OW!

"Wizard."

Talking? That was new.

Ignoring the blood dribbling down from the points of the claws, Tony
twisted as far as he could in the demon's grip. It looked sort of like a miniature
Ryne Cyratane, although more Texas longhorn than Bambi's dad, and it wore
the most obvious of the Arjh Lord's attributes sheathed up like a dog's. Unlike

the single rune on the chest of the first demon, the black runes carved into mini-Ryne's chest were oozing blood over a pattern very nearly as complex as Leah's. It seemed that slipping an arjh into another lord's plan took more than a fake mustache, but since Sye Mckaseeh seemed to recruit from further out on the horror show spectrum, that wasn't really surprising.

"Help wizard."

"Yeah. Fine. Release wizard!" The claws hurt as much on the way out as they had on the way in. "All right, if you're going to . . . never mind." The completely blank expression suggested he keep it simple. "Follow wizard!"

It's a little like live action Zork, he thought as he ran into the soundstage, the demon hard on his heels. Eat snake. Thank you, that was delicious. I can't believe Henry still has that game on his system. And not a good time for silent babbling, Tony. Pull it togeth—Fuck.

Three of the other four demons had arrived.

There wasn't room for all three of them directly under the gate, so they'd spread out within the confines of the set, turning the entire area into a seething mass of multicolored flesh and weaponry. Kate and Pavin were trying to loop a tentacled lime-green demon in rope while Saleen whaled on any bits he could get close to with his pipe. Amy, Lee, and Zev had another cornered. No, it had Zev cornered. No, they had it cornered. Jack was down on one knee, blood dribbling from the corner of his mouth. Mason was fighting sword to claw with the upper right arm of another of the chitin-covered demons yelling something that sounded like "Parry, thrust, riposte!" while Mouse silently fought the lower right, and CB dealt with the left side. Peter sagged against the wall, gasping for breath, arms wrapped around his torso. Leah was nowhere in sight. Since the point of this exercise from the invaders' perspective was to open the Demongate, CB had stashed Leah somewhere safe.

And a good thing, too, since all three demons had a single, familiar rune etched into their chests. Or the equivalent area.

Tony pointed mini-Ryne toward the battle. "Fight demons!"

Mini-Ryne seemed less than enthused. "Help wizard."

"Fight demons!"

"Guard gate."

Left palm flat against the center of his back, Tony shoved him forward. "Fight demons!" Whether the pressure of the rune convinced him or he'd run out of excuses, mini-Ryne finally charged into the fray, and Tony raced for the extension ladder. CB and Jack had been insistent that he not be in the middle of the fight; there were too many demons and if one of them realized he was the wizard, in the absence of the Demongate he'd be the center of all the demonic attention by default.

From the top of the ladder, he crawled out onto the lighting grid.

Technically, this was not someplace he should be, but the grid was built to hold hundreds of pounds of lights and sooner or later, every electrician or light tech in the business ended up with his feet off the ladder or scaffold. Since he was neither, it was a good thing CB ran a flexible studio. Had demons been attacking a CBC studio, the world would be screwed.

He burned all four runes into the air beside him before he looked down.

Lime-green-and-tentacles had moved away from the corner. Amy had danced inside the tentacles and was pounding a second, foot-long ash stake into the main bulk of its body. Lee bashed the end of a tentacle against the floor with an antique mace, ducked a second, and slammed a third away from his head at the last minute. Zev stood to one side cocking a crossbow, a length of the yellow nylon rope tied to one end of the quarrel.

They weren't bringing it down, but they were definitely holding it in place.

"Welcome to the set of *Darkest Night*," he muttered, stretching along the grid. Vampire shows inevitably acquired a lot of interesting weaponry. He dropped the first two runes into place and was ready with the third when Amy screamed, her leg caught in one of the demon's unexpected mouths. Distracted, Lee went down, lime-green coils around his torso. *You don't get to be distracted!* he reminded himself. He was already doing the best thing he could do to help. Third rune down. Placing the fourth rune got tricky until Zev got off his shot, dropped the crossbow, and tried to tangle the demon's legs with the attached rope. A glancing blow from the chitin-covered demon drove him forward into the grasp of another tentacle. Adjusting for Zev's weight, the demon jerked back against the first three runes. It shrieked as it brushed up against the power. As it charged forward, Tony threw the fourth rune into position.

"And action!"

Light flared.

Amy, Lee, Zev, and a meter of tentacle that had been reaching beyond the area the runes enclosed lay panting on the floor—although strictly speaking the tentacle wasn't panting as much as twitching. Amy had both hands clamped against her thigh, blood seeping between her fingers. Rows of tiny holes in Lee's jeans were beginning to darken. Holding the quarrel with the rope in one hand, Zev crawled toward the crossbow.

Focus on the demons!

Something grabbed his ankle.

He probably should have wrapped both arms around the grid and hung on, but that occurred to him a second late. Turning, Tony caught a glimpse of a familiar mouth with too many rows of black teeth between red scaled lips.

The sixth demon.

And then he was falling.

He curled in the air, landed on his right side, heard a bone snap. Since it wasn't his skull, he was actually okay with that. Arm maybe. No. Higher. Something in his shoulder. It hurt to breathe.

Then it really hurt as red-and-scaly flipped him over and raised a hand, trio of ten-centimeter claws extended. As the claws swung down for a disemboweling stroke, Jack caught the arm, shoved his gun in the demon's armpit, and pulled the trigger.

On a good day, which this wasn't, Tony had no idea how many bullets Jack's gun fired, but it seemed to go on for a while. Five, ten minutes. Or maybe his sense of time had gotten scrambled by the fall because there was no way the demon should have waited that long to bring its tail around and smack Jack off his feet.

On the other hand, its arm flopped uselessly, so who knew?

One arm flopped. The other was working fine. The first strike removed the front of Tony's jacket and most of the T-shirt under it. For some reason, losing a second jean jacket in the line of duty really pissed him off, and as the demon threw back its head and screamed in triumph, Tony cocked his right elbow just enough to raise his hand off the floor.

He'd spoken the first four words of the Powershot when Kate appeared holding two lit flares that she slam-dunked into the demon's gaping, tooth-lined throat.

The explosion was unexpected.

Welcome, but messy.

"Too fucking gross," Kate muttered as Jack returned, kicked aside a twitching slab of meat, and grabbed Tony's raised hand. On the way up onto his feet, Tony discovered he'd broken his collarbone.

"You okay?" Lip curled, Jack flicked a wet, lavender glob off Tony's shoulder.

Lavender?

"Hey! Tony! Are you okay?"

"Sure." He was standing. He was breathing. Everything from his eyelashes to the ends of broken bone grating in his chest hurt, but he'd deal with that later. Out of the corner of one eye, he saw something long and green whipping toward him. He ducked before he realized the tentacle was no longer attached.

Jack hauled him upright again. "Tony?"

"I'm fine."

What he first thought was a disbelieving snort turned out to be the sound of another tentacle being ripped free. Mini-Ryne, his horns dripping dark fluids, sat on top of the remaining lime-green demon, removing tentacles and deftly avoiding the many mouths trying to take a piece out of him. His victory would have been more impressive had the demon not been wrapped in so much rope it looked like it had been swept up by some kind of deep-sea fishing net.

This tuna is not demon safe. StarKist doesn't want demons with good taste, they want . . .

"Tony! Focus!"

Right. Focusing.

"Not the face! Not the face!"

Mason's shrieked protest spun Tony around in time to see the actor flung backward by the chitin demon, the sword he still held bent into a tight vee. Roaring a challenge, the demon charged after him. Mason was seconds from losing his face entirely when CB roared a challenge of his own, pounded across the soundstage, and slammed a shoulder into the demon's middle in a perfect offensive tackle.

The demon went down.

Buildings would have gone down.

Unfortunately, CB went down, too. Worse, the demon bounced back up again dangling ropes like fat yellow streamers. Zev had clearly gotten off a couple more shots with the crossbow and just as clearly no one had been able to take advantage of them. It bent enough for its upper left hand to grab one of CB's ankles, and when it straightened, CB came off the floor.

Which pretty much proved that the demon was as strong as it looked.

The demon swatted Mouse away with its right hands. It seemed obvious that CB's head was about to be slammed into the concrete.

Tony jerked out of Jack's hold, grabbed his right wrist with his left, lifted the right arm to shoulder height then whipped it back and around while screaming out the words for the Powershot. Given the broken collarbone, the screaming was nonnegotiable. As his arm started back down, his right wrist slapped into his left palm, aiming the blast of energy that burned through chitin breastplates.

CB hit the floor with a solid thud, momentarily obscured by clouds of falling ash drifting back and forth.

No, wait. That back and forth, that's me. Swaying, Tony sank to one knee. "Check CB," he panted as Jack began to bend. He needed time to recover, and if it turned out they were going to have to buy that time, they'd need CB's strength. Fortunately, Jack got the subtext.

Keeping his breathing shallow and his right arm supported by his knee, he turned just his head toward the only surviving demon. Mini-Ryne seemed to have eaten his way through to the life-sustaining bits and was now clearly sitting on nothing but meat.

For a long moment, the loudest noise on the soundstage was enthusiastic chewing and swallowing.

"Did we win?"

All eyes turned to Mason, who was crawling out from behind the upturned chaise lounge. When he looked up and realized he was the center of attention, he tried to pull the sleeve of the camouflage jacket up over his bare arm. "Well?" he demanded petulantly as he realized the sleeve wasn't going to stay. "Did we win or not?"

The only demon in the room seemed to be on their side.

"Yeah." Tony sucked in as much air as he could, hoping for enough volume to carry over the rising tide of sound. "It looks like we did." The nail on his baby finger curled up, dropped off, and wafted slowly to the floor.

Mason was limping on a wrenched knee but unbloodied. Besides innumerable small cuts, CB had broken three fingers on one hand but ordered Jack away to deal with his own injuries. Mouse's nose had been broken again. Peter, Saleen, and Jack had cracked or broken ribs. Jack also had a split lip and a broken tooth. Amy and Pavin had been bitten. Amy had also got a bit of demon in the eye when Kate had blown it up. Lee, Zev, and Kate had long lines of tiny cuts from teeth in the edge of some of the tentacles. Zev had a line across his back and Kate's went around one arm. Lee's leather jacket had protected most of his torso but his pale jeans were marked with spiral blotches of blood.

"Should've worn your motorcycle chaps," Amy noted from the floor as Zev cut away the leg of her 100 percent organic hemp cargo pants.

"Good thing he didn't," Zev snorted. "We needed Tony's mind on the job."

Tony considered protesting, but it was a fair assessment, so he saved his strength. CB was the only one not coming up in varying shades of purple and black, but that was because CB was the only one too dark for the bruising to show. They were walking wounded, all twelve of them. Emphasis on walking.

"No one died," he said. And then because it was important, he said it again. Louder. "No one died."

It was almost funny watching the various gazes tracking around the space, checking to make sure.

Jack pulled his T-shirt down over the binding Kate had just wrapped around his ribs. "Not in here," he reminded them grimly, "but Geetha told me there were at least seven dead out on the street before this started, plus a shitload of critical injuries. We didn't avoid a body count, not by a fuck of a long shot."

"No one here died." CB's tone suggested no one argue this time. "Right now, I think we deserve to celebrate that."

Tony was thinking about that lawyer, the one with the weak spot in his office and when he caught Amy's eye, he knew she was thinking the same. Nothing they could have done about it then. Nothing they could do about it now. He'd just have to keep telling himself that. He didn't remember sitting down, but since he was on the floor, his back up against the underside of the yellow chaise, he must have. Little bits of broken glass surrounded him like glittering confetti. One of the lights had fallen at some point during the battle; crashed to the floor where every part of it that could shatter, had shattered into the smallest pieces possible. They'd been lucky. If it hadn't hit so hard, they could have added shards of flying glass to the *"things trying to kill us"* list. Tony had no memory of hearing the impact.

"Now then," CB stepped over the headless body of the red-scaled demon like it was of no consequence, and swept an imperious gaze around his domain. "We can't all hit an emergency room at the same time. Ms. Anderson, you're in the best shape. I want you to drive . . ." He stared at his crew standing clumped together and came to the obvious decision to save time. ". . . Peter, Mouse, Saleen, and Pavin to Burnaby General. They're used to the strange accidents of the entertainment industry, and with all the chaos in the area, there should be no problem."

"What about . . ." Kate jerked a thumb at mini-Ryne, currently pulling a line of linked opalescent bladders from deep inside the body of his meal.

"I doubt Tony will need all of us if he has to deal with . . . him."

Tony expected a protest, but Kate merely rolled her eyes. "Okay, but I can't fit five in my car."

"We'll take my van." Peter went to pull the scraps of his shirt back on, sighed, and tossed it on the floor. He waved those mentioned toward the exit. "It seats seven."

Limping heavily, using his piece of pipe as a cane, Saleen fell into step beside the director. "Dude, why do you have a van that seats seven?"

"Garage band."

"Seriously?"

"No."

"Hey!" Tony wasn't sure they heard him—given the distance and the whole about-to-pass-out thing—but all five paused. He needed to say something but wasn't sure what. Finally, he shrugged his one usable shoulder. "Thanks."

Weirdly, Mouse spoke for the group. He moved the dripping handful of flannel shirt away from his nose and grinned, the bloodstained teeth and eyes already swelling shut making him look particularly disreputable. "Wouldn't have missed it."

The other four, even Kate, nodded.

"Hang on," Amy called out, head cocked so she could glare through her nonwatering eye. "If they leave, who's going to clean this mess up?"

They were gone before she finished asking.

Tony braced himself for her protest, but CB began a second set of instructions before she got the chance. "Zev, take Amy and Lee out to Eagle Ridge. One of the demons came through near there. That gives us a readymade explanation for the bite and the claw marks. If they ask, you were all out there because we're thinking of shooting at Heritage Mountain."

"And if they ask why we waited before coming in?"

Formal cadences returned with the raised brow. "I think Mr. Nicholas' talent extends to providing a little attitude."

"I could," Lee admitted, folding his arms. "But I'm not going anywhere until this is over."

Amy echoed his action from the floor. "Neither am I."

"Hardly seems worth going all the way to Eagle Ridge on my own," Zev pointed out with a careful shrug.

"You're all bleeding," Jack began, but Amy cut him off.

"You call this bleeding?" she scoffed, folding her good leg under her and using Zev's uninjured arm to pull herself to her feet. "I lose more monthly. Besides, you're bleeding, CB's bleeding, Tony's bleeding . . ."

He was? He glanced down at his bare chest between the shredded wings of jacket and shirt and blearily focused on the lines of red rolling down from his right shoulder. Oh, yeah.

". . . and you guys aren't leaving."

"There is still a demon to deal with," CB told her. "Not to mention, as you so helpfully pointed out, the mess."

"Wizard!"

"Whoa!" Amy's head whipped around so fast her hair separated into bicolored layers. "This one talks?"

"Yeah." Tony shifted position slightly and regretted it a lot. "He talks. What do you want?"

It was hard to tell because of the gore encrusting his face—plus Tony's vision was a bit wonky—but mini-Ryne looked worried. "Demongate?"

"Safe." Frowning hurt, too. Quel surprise. Not. "At least I think . . ." He turned to CB, who took three long strides and dropped to one knee beside him.

"If you cannot send this creature back, Mr. Foster . . ."

"I can do it." It might be the last thing he did for a while, but he figured he had enough left in him to draw four final runes. *Let's hear it for endorphins. Yay endorphins.* As long as he didn't have to hurry. Or, apparently, stand up. "Uh, Boss? Little help."

The big difference between being lifted onto his feet by Henry and CB was, well, about a foot vertically and at least that much horizontally. CB was a big guy and Henry was . . .

Henry wasn't.

That meant something. Tony frowned. Winced.

"Ms. Burnett is outside in my car." CB's voice was a low growl against his ear. "Parked up against that outside wall . . ." He nodded across the soundstage to the wall closest to the gate. ". . . she is close enough to the gate and to you that her own metaphysical signature should be masked and she'd be able to make a fast getaway should we have lost this fight. I doubt very much that any demon would have been able to catch her."

"Drove the Jag today?"

"I did."

It seemed like a plan. Actually, it seemed like a good plan, especially the masked signature part. "Have you been reading up on this shit?"

"Mr. Groves has suggested a number of very helpful publications."

"I'll bet. And she's going to stay out there . . . ?"

"Until one of us goes and gets her."

"Demongate."

"I told you, she's safe." Hang on. That wasn't a question. The first time the demon had asked. This time . . .

"Would whoever's been calling for me, please shut the fuck up? I'm not deaf, and I'm moving as fast as I can."

Most of his weight still on CB's arm, Tony turned in time to see Leah stop walking and raise a hand to her nose. The other hand was tucked under her clothes, pressed up against the skin of her stomach.

"Oh, wow. It stinks in here. Smells like offal and peppermint with the faintest hint of sulfur." She frowned over her hand at Tony. "You had to ash one?"

"Yeah. Leah . . ."

"Demongate!"

"What the hell?" She jumped back, then stopped and blushed. "Right. This is the one that's here to help and . . ."

When she stopped talking, Tony turned and stared at mini-Ryne. Standing on the partially eaten demon, he was, in turn, staring at Leah. His eyes were black, lid to lid, and even six meters away, he could see his reflection burning in them.

A heartbeat earlier, Tony would have denied any ability to move without help, but he pulled free of CB's hold before Leah's lips started to form the question and was standing in front of her before she asked it.

"Lord?"

"Boss!" Even as a physical barrier, he sucked right now, but when Leah tried to go through him instead of around, it gave CB enough time to grab her arms and hold her in place. Tony was pretty sure he was still standing, not exactly upright, not unless the studio had acquired a recent lean to the left, but standing. As he tried to straighten, he caught sight of Jack beginning to move.

Circle of yellow rope dropped around the demon's shoulders.

Jack in the air, then crumpled motionless against the base of the wall.

Lee on one knee, one of the demon's arms wrapped round his throat.

Amy's scream lingering.

And the tableau froze.

It happened just that fast.

Ryne Cyratane smiled, now clearly in control of mini-Ryne's body, his attributes no longer sheathed. "I think we should talk trade, Wizard."

"Trade?" It took a moment to sink in. Finally, he dragged his gaze away from the six inches of detached claw protruding from Jack's chest and shoved his reaction behind old familiar shields. "You want to trade Lee for Leah?"

The demon looked confused. "Who?"

"Her!" Tony jerked a thumb over his shoulder.

"Ah. That is not the name I knew her by when she was my handmaiden, my priestess, my love."

Leah leaned toward him, her arms angling back in CB's hold. "I am not your love!" she spat, tossing a curl of hair back off her face.

"Am I not?" He didn't seem too upset by her reaction. "Do you not remember . . ."

"I remember that you slaughtered my entire village!"

Hang on. "You said you were over that," Tony reminded her.

Her shrug was a bit truncated given her position. "Yeah, well, you were right. Maybe I still have some issues."

"So if CB lets you go?"

"I'd be in his arms in a heartbeat." No need to define whose arms. "Sorry. It's a built-in response, and guess who built it in."

The Arjh Lord cleared his throat. Tony turned to see Lee fighting for air, clawing at the arm around his throat. "You don't seem to be taking this seriously, Wizard."

"Stop it!"

He loosened his grip just enough for Lee to draw in a painful sounding breath. And then another. Tony breathed in with him. In. Out. Finally, clutching the demon's arm with white-knuckled fingers, Lee wheezed, "I'm so fucking tired of being the designated damsel in distress."

"Yes." Ryne Cyratane smiled down at him. "I can understand that." Even while wearing a body not his own, there was such understanding in his voice that Tony had a sudden epiphany about how he'd convinced Leah's people to worship him. Lee actually looked comforted.

"Okay." Tony cleared his throat and tried to sound a little more like he was in charge of the situation. "If we trade—Lee for your ex-handmaiden—then you'll kill Leah the moment you get her and the Demongate will open and you'll be here in the flesh, not just riding in the flesh of one of your arjh."

"Yes."

Tony fought the urge to preen under the Arjh Lord's approval. "This was your plan all along, wasn't it? You used Sye Mckaseeh as camouflage—while we were concentrating on her, you could slip in unnoticed."

"No. I took advantage of the situation when I had time enough to mark this body as a vessel rather than merely as mine."

"A spur of the moment kind of thing, then? With the added benefit of pissing off the ex?"

"As you say, an added benefit. And why should I not reclaim my hand-maiden and then this world?"

"Because I'll stop you."

"You forget." The demon's grip tightened momentarily. Lee fought for air and then sagged, gasping.

"Okay, so we trade. What's in that for me? As I see it, Lee dies either way."

"The man dies now in front of you. Or later with you."

"Dude." Leaning on Zev's arm, Amy glared from between eyelashes clumped into damp spikes. "You'll kill him the instant the gate opens just like you killed Jack! He's the only thing here that's a danger to you."

"As I said, *later*. I did not specify how much later." He swept a dark gaze over her, head to toe. "You will enjoy my new world, little one. I promise you that."

"Bite me!"

"Perhaps." This was most definitely not the same smile he'd given Lee. Lee's had been compassionate enough to be believed in spite of the choke hold. This was pure seduction. Only the choke hold hadn't changed.

To Tony's surprise, Amy brushed a strand of hair behind her ear and limped forward, eyes locked on the demon. "Maybe we can . . . OW! Zev! What the hell was that for?"

"You were walking toward that!" Zev nodded toward Ryne Cyratane.

"I was not!" Measured the distance from Zev to the demon. Noticed how close she'd come. "Oh, crap, I was." She slipped the glare back on as the two of them began limping backward to the wall. "You're very convincing."

From seduction to amusement. "It's part of my charm."

"And it would be one hell of a lot more charming if you didn't have bits of that . . ." She jabbed a disdainful finger toward the remains of his meal. ". . . between your teeth."

"We will speak later, you and I."

"The hell we . . ."

"Slaughtered a whole village," Zev reminded her urgently.

"So what?" Behind the streaks of mascara, Amy wore the expression she usually reserved for those who wore fur. Or sweater sets in a nonironic manner.

"Your friends are intriguing, Wizard." The Arjh Lord gave Lee a little shake. "But not entirely correct."

"About?" Tony demanded. And then he had it. "I'm not the only danger to you, am I?" After that, it was one small step. There weren't a lot of names in Ryne Cyratane's current address book. "It's Henry, isn't it? He could take that body out, even now." Tony'd missed the implications when Kevin called to tell him the overpass had blown. The overpass had blown *first*. "You pushed this arjh through, creating a cascade like we did the other night because you had to be sure all this happened before sunset so Henry couldn't help." He knew he had it by the way the demon's lip curled. "Humans mean less than nothing to you, but he's another power."

"Um, Tony . . ." Amy rubbed her sleeve under her nose. "Henry's a romance writer."

CB rumbled an unnecessary caution behind him. Tony didn't need to be warned; he'd been keeping this secret a lot longer than the big guy had.

It had to be past sunset. Tony glanced at his watch. Crap. Not even close. How could they have destroyed five demons and been betrayed by a sixth in so little time? Okay, fine. So he couldn't keep things from happening until Henry got here. He'd just have to keep talking, to keep the demon talking until he'd regained enough strength to blast the Arjh Lord right out of his borrowed body.

Yeah. Like that was going to happen. He had no idea how he was still standing and the soundstage kept wavering in and out of focus like they were about to go to flashback.

Still, he had to try. Hopefully, Ryne Cyratane would see slouching as a sign of disrespect instead of an inability to straighten his spine. "The sun will set after you've taken over, you know. Henry'll still be around to kick your ass."

"Once the Gate is open, I will rule with many arjh. And I will gain power from slaughter."

He'd forgotten about that bit. "Killing Mckaseeh's arjh gave that demon you're wearing power enough to activate the runes on his chest, didn't it?"

"Yes."

"But you're using up that power maintaining the link."

This was the most unpleasant smile of all. "Yes."

"Ambitious change requires help; timing is everything." The fortune in Leah's cookie from way back when they'd first met. He'd forgotten it until now. "So I'm about out of my two hundred free minutes?"

The amount of bone necessary to hold up his borrowed horns kept the Arjh Lord from frowning very deeply. "You make no sense, Wizard. But if you mean that you are out of time, then, yes." And he tightened his grip. "Choose."

Lee's face began to purple, green eyes bulging. He clawed at the demon's arm, head immobile, body twisting and thrashing.

Eyes locked on Lee, Tony almost missed Amy's charge.

"Zev!"

The music director's tackle took her to the floor, stopping her just short of the demon. Without the injured leg she might have made it.

"No! No! No! Bastard's not killing Lee like he killed Jack!"

"You're right, he's not; I'll trade!" Tony wasn't positive they'd heard him, but Amy stilled, Lee began to breathe again, and the demon beckoned with his free hand.

Tony turned just far enough to meet CB's eyes. He had to offer Leah to the demon, so this whole thing fell apart if the boss kept hanging on. Forcing his right hand high enough to close his fingers loosely around Leah's forearm, Tony saw CB's gaze flick, just for an instant, to his broken collarbone. Broken on the right side. *Come on, boss. If I'm using my right hand for this . . .*

Then, although he hoped it looked like he was jerking her away from safety, he hung on as Leah stumbled forward pushed by CB, the movement turning them both back to face the demon.

This demon was not Ryne Cyratane. The body was merely a meat puppet controlled by the Arjh Lord's energy. Back in Leah's condo he'd called energy into him. Called his own energy back. Called the fire.

These days, if he wanted something to come to him, it came. It took next to no power and it took almost no thought.

It came regardless of any solid object that might be in the way.

As Leah stepped out in front of him, Tony held his left palm against the small of her back and concentrated. Focused. Called.

The energy that was Ryne Cyratane tried to come to him through the only thing in the room designed to hold demons. He went through the Demongate.

Leah jerked once, made a noise somewhere between agony and ecstasy, and dropped to her knees, her arm pulling out of Tony's useless grip. On her knees, she curled forward, wrapped her arms around her stomach, and keened.

On the other side of the soundstage, the demon was merely a demon. Onyx eyes widened as the runes cut into his chest healed. He threw back his head and roared.

Still holding Lee.

Before Tony could figure out what to do next, Jack had the muzzle of his gun pressed into the soft tissue of the demon's throat and was emptying it up into the skull. There were no exit wounds. A skull with horns like that had to be hard. Tony half thought he could hear the ricochets as blood dribbled from the demon's eyes and ears and nose.

Ryne Cyratane's ex-puppet hit his knees much like Leah had. From his knees, he pitched forward to slam facefirst into the concrete.

Zev crawled to Lee's side while Amy threw herself at Jack.

"I thought you were dead, you son of a bitch!"

He groaned and stumbled back as she made contact, then moved her slightly to one side so he could pull out the claw. "I was wearing . . ."

"A flak jacket or Kevlar or whatever the hell you lot call those things now! I can't believe I fell for one of the oldest fucking clichés in the business."

"Actually, the claw got snagged on the bandages wrapped around my broken ribs and curved around instead of going in."

"Then why didn't you get up!"

"I thought I should reload."

"Bastard!"

"Ribs!"

As Tony hit the floor beside Leah, Jack and Amy moved into the traditional end-of-scene mind-the-broken-bones clinch. It'd never work, Amy was too out there and Jack hadn't gone out far enough but, what the hell, there was nothing like a traditional endi . . .

"So it seems you managed nicely without me."

Tony blinked up at Henry's face and then past it at the ceiling of his apartment. Two things occurred to him. The first, that he had no memory of leaving the studio. The second, that Leah had a valid point about all the beige. He'd been looking at this ceiling a lot lately and boring didn't begin to cover it. Periwinkle, however, was out of the question. What the hell was up with her and periwinkle anyway?

"Tony?"

His gaze slid back to Henry's face. The eyes were a little dark, but it was mostly Prince of Man with just enough Prince of Darkness to command attention. He looked . . . worried? Crap.

Before he could ask, Henry had an arm around the back of his neck and a cup of water at his mouth. He drained it, and then another before he got the question out. "What did I miss?"

"A day and most of two nights."

"No." Attempting to get up on his elbows, he discovered he couldn't move his right arm. And that would be because it was strapped to his body. Holding the sheet up in one hand, he stared down at the bandages and then back up at Henry. "I broke my arm?"

"Collarbone."

The memory of pain. "Right."

"I know a very discreet doctor."

Impossible not to snort. "Well, you would, wouldn't you. But that wasn't what I meant. You look like there's shit hitting the fan and I've missed being there for it."

Henry took a moment to work that through and then he smiled, wrapping his left hand gently around Tony's jaw. "I was worried about you."

"Me?" His throat was sore. He wondered if he'd forgotten some screaming.

"You were unconscious for a day and most of two nights, Tony. Leah insisted you were fine, that your body needed a time out to recover from the metaphysical strain you've been putting on it, but I suspect she was saying that just to keep me calm."

"I've seen you not calm." The coolness of the vampire's touch felt good against heated skin. "Calm is better."

"Perhaps. Fortunately, although your heart had slowed, I could hear it beating strong and sure and was willing to wait a while. About an hour ago . . ." He moved his hand from Tony's jaw to rest it lightly on his chest. ". . . it began to speed up. It reached its normal rhythm just before you opened your eyes."

"My heart had slowed? I was hibernating?"

"Essentially."

"Cool."

"You need to . . ."

"Pee, Henry. It's been a day and two nights, I really need to pee." His stomach growled. "Is there food around here I can take with me into the can?"

Tony's memory returned as he ate. Not the part where they carried him from the studio but the rest: the battle, Ryne Cyratane's betrayal, and his defeat.

Betrayal . . .

"Lee!"

"Bruised but fine."

CB and Jack had gotten rid of the bodies. Henry didn't know where and hadn't asked. "Why would I? This wasn't my fight."

"You upset about that?" Tony wondered, his hand paused in the bucket of fried chicken. "That we didn't, you know, need you?"

"Honestly?" Red-gold brows dipped down. "A little." And rose back up again. "It's a conceit of mine that I'm essential when it comes to saving the world. But mostly, I'm proud of the way you've grown into your power. Proud that you found a way to prevail against nearly unbeatable odds. Proud that you refused to quit and kept fighting long after many would have given up."

"Hey!" Tony jabbed a chicken bone indignantly in Henry's direction. "I couldn't give up; I was responsible for those people. They wouldn't have even been there if not for me."

"And, mostly, I am proud of that."

If his ears got any hotter, they were going to ignite and there was a suspiciously damp itch in his eyes. "Henry, I'm carrying some serious negative father shit, and you're creeping me out here."

"You'll have to get used to it if you're going to keep saving the world."

"Yeah, well I'm not . . ." He sighed as Henry smiled. "I am, aren't I? This kind of crap is just going to keep right on happening."

"You said it to me once; like is drawn to like."

"Yeah, yeah, and then I said it to Leah. I'm a font of freakin' wisdom." Looking into a future full of metaphysical bullshit, he sighed again and reached for the last piece of chicken. Paused, hand back in the bucket. "Leah. What happened with Leah?"

"Happened?"

"After I pulled Ryne Cyratane through the Demongate. Is she all right?"

"She's fine."

"She's really pissed, isn't she?"

"She's a little . . ." Henry visibly considered and discarded several words. ". . . annoyed."

Tony didn't see Leah until early November—her agent had called while he was recovering and she'd gotten a job doubling on a CBC Movie of the Week being shot up in Hope.

"Being immortal doesn't pay the bills; falling off a railway bridge in a corset and bloomers does. I'll see you when I get back."

His entire response had consisted of: *"Yeah, but, Leah . . ."* and then he was talking to a dial tone.

The Demonic Convergence was still going on, but without Sye Mckaseeh's manipulations, things were coming through from a lot closer to home. Tony was out for no more than a couple of hours most nights tracking down weird little odds and ends and sending them back where they belonged. With the exception of a city employee working in the old sewer tunnel under Highbury Street who ran into a rat carrying a short sword, no one got hurt. Kevin Groves became an invaluable filter—most reports came first to him, and he could tell if the weirdness was real or homemade. In spite of a few very visible incidents, there was a remarkable lack of hysteria from the general population. The people of British Columbia had always been more willing than the rest of the country to adjust reality to suit them, and the contrary attitude of Vancouverites kept them from agreeing on just what exactly they'd seen.

During the day, they were so busy getting the last episode of *Darkest Night* in the can before going on hiatus there wasn't time to replay the whole climatic battle scene in any detail. Maybe a few people strutted—as soon as they stopped limping—and maybe Mason thought a little more of himself than usual, but his ego was so enormous already it was hard to tell. Mostly they worked at getting the stains off the floor under the gate and got on with the job. Where *they* included Tony. CB'd given him as much time off as he was getting if he wanted to remain employed.

TO: tfoster@darkestnight.ca
   FROM: bestbane@darkestnight.ca
   u r teh suckhead!

TO: bestbane@darkestnight.ca
   FROM: tfoster@darkestnight.ca
   when you get back, i'll teach you what i can

TO: tfoster@darkestnight.ca
   FROM: bestbane@darkestnight.ca
   OMG! I <3 U!

A small part of Tony held out a forlorn hope that something eldritch would attack and rip him limb from limb before he had to make good on his promise. Most of him had grown resigned to the inevitable, where *the inevitable* had been defined by powers with a vicious sense of humor as his boss' youngest daughter.

"Nothing." Amy hung up the phone and looked up at Tony and Zev. "That's four days since Kevin's had anyone call about something going bump in the night. Maybe Halloween was the last."

A pair of half-meter-wide, phosphorescent-green, eight-legged visitors had made the traditional Haunted Village at the Burnaby Village Museum out on Deer Lake a little more authentic than most years. By the time Tony found them hiding under the carousel, they'd been completely terrified by the giant bat on stilts and were more than willing to go home.

"Halloween does have a certain satisfying end-of-season feel about it," Zev admitted. "And that means this whole thing lasted about a month."

"Golly, Tony." Amy batted bright orange eyelashes suggestively in his general direction. "The Demonic Convergence is over and the show's going into hiatus, so *everyone* who works on it will have some free time. What are you going to do?"

Before Tony could answer her, the door to CB's office opened. A motorcycle helmet cradled under one arm, Leah paused on the threshold and grinned. "Ah, that's so sweet. Spanky and his gang. Oh, stop looking at me like that." Eyes rolling, she crossed toward them. "I got back last night. I would have called."

Tony ignored the excuse. "Henry says your tattoo changed."

"That was a little abrupt. What's up your skirt?"

"We were still in the Demonic Convergence. You should have checked in before you left, just to be on the safe side."

"Should have?" Arms folded. Lip curled. "You're not my keeper, Tony," she snarled.

She'd had millennia to work on that whole "don't fuck with me" thing, and it was definitely definitive. Zev took a step sideways, putting more of Amy's desk between them. Amy looked like she was taking notes. Tony didn't really give a crap. All things considered, attitude from an immortal stuntwoman was pretty fucking low on his list of things to be impressed by.

"I'm the only wizard we know of," he told her flatly, "and you're walking around with the oldest working magic in the world etched into your stomach. I need to know what's going on with it."

Leah's eyes narrowed, and she stared at him for a long moment. "You used me to defeat Ryne Cyratane. You had no idea what slamming him back through the gate would do to me, and yet you did it anyway."

"I knew what Ryne Cyratane would do to this world. Reshoot the scene and I'd play it the same way."

"Would you?"

"Yeah. I would."

Unexpectedly, she smiled, set down the helmet, and unzipped her jacket. "Okay, then."

"Can you say anticlimactic?" Amy muttered.

"Anticlimactic," Zev acknowledged.

Leah grinned and pulled her fuchsia turtleneck up off the tattoo. "You were expecting a fight? I made my point when I blew town, leaving him to his own devices, and besides, he's right. He should have a look at this, just in case."

"In case of what?" Amy demanded as Tony peered at the interlocking circles.

"These are new," Tony announced before Leah could answer. He traced the inner circle, his finger about a millimeter above the skin. "And there wasn't this much color before." Not only the new runes in the inner circle but a few of the unchanged runes were now a deep crimson. The color of fresh blood instead of dried. "What does it mean?"

"I don't know. You're the wizard."

"Yeah, but . . ."

No *but*, actually.

"I guess I'll have to find out," he said, straightening.

Letting the sweater drop, Leah leaned forward and kissed his cheek. She smelled like cinnamon. "I'm not going anywhere for a while, I'll help. There's not a lot about demonology I don't know."

"You didn't know Ryne Cyratane would betray us."

"Please!" She smirked and reached for her helmet. "He's a demon, what did you expect? Ciao, Antonio!" A second kiss on the other cheek and a wave with her free hand as she headed for the door. "Bye, kids. See you around."

"You going to stop her?" Zev asked quietly.

Tony shook his head. "No, if I need her, I just have to call." He rubbed the palm of his left hand against his thigh. "You guys want to go get a beer after work?"

"As if," Zev snorted. "CB wants the score for the last episode tweaked again. He's looking for a John Williams sound on a Chet Williams budget. I'll be here all night. Probably tomorrow night, too."

Amy leaned out and dropped a stack of old sides into the recycling box. "I'd love to, Tony, but Jack and I are going to a zombie retrospective."

That was unexpected. "Jack's into zombies?"

"He's not *into* so much. He thinks they're funny." She shrugged and pulled a strand of hair out from the inner workings of her skeleton earrings. "I figure as long as we're both enjoying ourselves, no harm no foul. Say, I know . . ."

Tony had always found ingenuous a worrying look on Amy.

". . . why don't you ask Lee if he wants to go for a beer?"

"Why don't you ask Lee if he wants to go for a . . ."

"Zev!"

Not at all repentant, Zev sighed. "You're willing to go mano a mano with invading wizards, haunted houses, and enough demons for a theatrical production of *The Inferno*. What are you so afraid of when it comes to Lee?"

"I'm not afraid. Lee's . . ."

"I swear, Tony, if you say straight, I'm going to feed you Amy's stapler."

"Hey!" Clutching her stapler protectively, Amy rolled her chair over to the other desk. "Use Rachel's. She's never in the office anyway."

Tony took one step back, just to be on the safe side. "It has to be Lee's choice."

"Why?" Zev folded his arms and glowered. It was a surprisingly impressive glower.

"His career . . ."

"Why would you affect his career?" Amy snorted. "You likely to do something kinky in public?"

"Actually . . ."

"Zev!"

"Earth to Tony; no one cares but you. So Lee likes guys as well as women.

Big whoop. Most of the world has more important things to worry about than a bisexual actor in a third-rate, syndicated, vampire detective television show."

"Yeah, but . . ."

"Hey. No buts. End the freakin' suspense." She tossed Zev the stapler. He made threatening gestures with it, and Tony surrendered.

If the whole thing blew up in his face, he'd be able to blame his alleged friends. And office supplies. Which was a dubious comfort.

Lee's dressing room door sat partly open and Tony had a moment's fear, relief, fear that he'd already left. There'd been talk about an offer to do an *Amazons in Space* movie in the Australian outback during hiatus, but he had no idea if Lee'd got the gig. Between the end of the Demonic Convergence and the end of the season, they'd been so busy they'd hardly said two words to each other.

Yeah. That was the reason.

If he's not here, it's a sign and . . .

He was just taking his cell phone out of the charger. He turned. Saw Tony. Froze.

Okay. That's not exactly a welcoming expression. I should just back away slowly . . .

On the other hand, he did have a very threatening stapler waiting for him.

Oh, what the hell.

Tony stepped into the dressing room, reached back, and closed the door. One of Lee's brows went up.

"I didn't know you could do that."

Both brows dipped down. "What?"

"The single brow thing."

"Oh. Yeah. Since I was kid."

"Cool."

A long moment of silence. It wasn't a very big room. They were no more than an arm's length apart.

Tony wasn't sure which one of them sighed first. He ran a hand back through his hair. "One of us needs to stop being such a guy about this."

"Yeah, except we're both guys."

"That's not a problem for me."

"Me either."

It happened just that fast.

Where *that fast* ignored the events of the preceding six months, all leading up to this moment, with the possible exception of those events that had been leading up to world domination, mass slaughter, or actually shooting an episode of *Darkest Night*.

Now he finally knew where Lee was, Tony wanted nothing more than to make magic, to hold out his hand and call the other man to him—but the smoop levels had already risen to nauseating heights. He felt like he'd stumbled onto a Rainbow Network Movie of the Week and this was the part in the soundtrack where the female vocalist would come in with the power ballad. "So what do we do . . ."

Lee tossed his phone aside, grabbed Tony's jacket in both fists, and swallowed the last word along with the lower half of Tony's face.

Later, when they finally broke for air, Tony felt he needed to make one thing perfectly clear.

"I never once thought of you as the damsel."